FROM WEDNESDAY TO JUDGEMENT

BY

BERNARD BANNERMAN

ISBN (Print): 978-1-911124-98-6
ISBN (Ebook): 978-1-911124-99-3

CONTENTS

The Last Wednesday

Chapter One 5
Chapter Two 24
Chapter Three. 43
Chapter Four 64
Chapter Five. 84
Chapter Six. 105
Chapter Seven 126
Chapter Eight 147
Chapter Nine. 168
Chapter Ten 188
Chapter Eleven 207
Chapter Twelve. 227

Controlling Interest

Chapter One 253
Chapter Two 276
Chapter Three 296
Chapter Four 322
Chapter Five 349
Chapter Six 369
Chapter Seven 392
Chapter Eight 412
Chapter Nine 436
Chapter Ten 458
Chapter Eleven 476
Chapter Twelve 498

The Judge's Song

Chapter One 527
Chapter Two 547
Chapter Three 566
Chapter Four 585
Chapter Five 601
Chapter Six 619
Chapter Seven 639
Chapter Eight 658
Chapter Nine 678
Chapter Ten 698
Chapter Eleven 719
Chapter Twelve 747

Orbach's Judgement

Chapter One 781

Chapter Two 802

Chapter Three 822

Chapter Four 841

Chapter Five 862

Chapter Six 882

Chapter Seven 901

Chapter Eight 920

Chapter Nine 942

Chapter Ten 963

Chapter Eleven 987

Chapter Twelve 1008

THE LAST WEDNESDAY

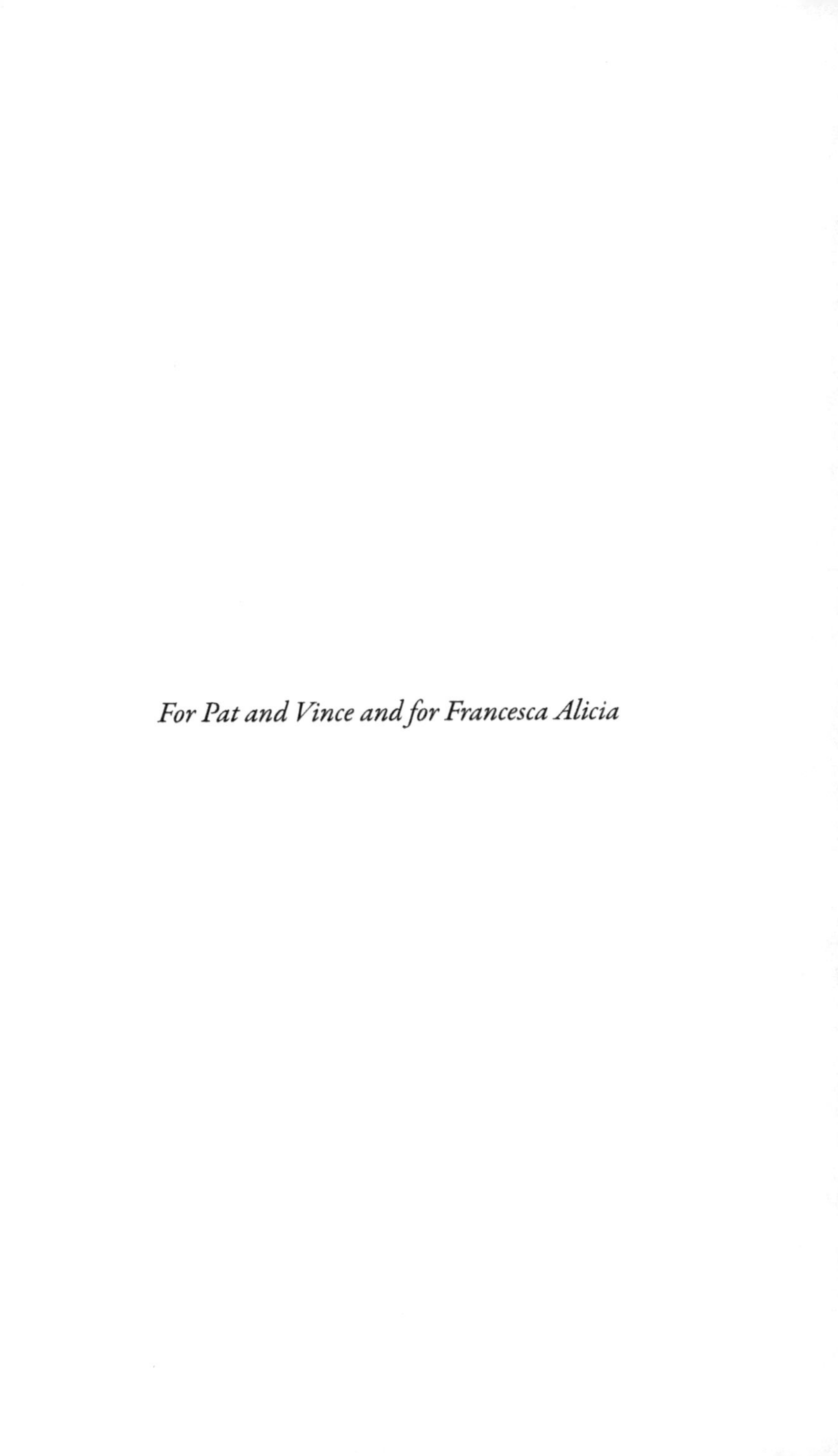

For Pat and Vince and for Francesca Alicia

I'd never been tailed before. I knew one idea was to shake him. I just didn't know how. The other thing to do is tuck yourself out of sight, jump him, grab him, throw him up against a wall, slap his face every which way but straight and beat out of him the name of his boss. There's a third thing you can do. Get home as fast as your legs can carry you, and make damned sure you double lock the door.

The 'phone was ringing as I came in, out of breath. The voice at the other end was garbled.

'Say it again,' I ordered.

'I said, Art Farquharson was killed last night.'

CHAPTER ONE

'Who's paying you?' she asked.

'How many of you people have got to die before you do something about it?' I didn't answer.

We stared at each other: she gave way first.

I could guess why. She didn't like to look at me. I wasn't a pretty picture. She didn't want to remember.

It was a long time ago that we were together. I had cut a very different figure. I was young, good-looking, bearded, radical, and going places. I weighed about three stone less.

Nowadays, I don't wear a beard, though if I forget to shave for a few days the difference is hard to tell. My politics gave up the ghost when food and drink were in short supply. I don't often have anywhere to go and when I do it takes me ten times as long.

'Are you still practising?'

'Getting near perfect,' I said jauntily but without a great deal of originality.

'Well, anyhow, yes, a bit. I haven't got an office. I do ... bits and pieces from home ...'

I figured: let her go on asking questions. When it got to my turn, she'd owe me some answers.

We were sitting in the Covent Garden Plaza. On the lower deck. Outside the wine bar and rib joint. We used to go there before. It seemed as good a place to meet as any. It wasn't too far from the Temple, where her chambers were, and though it wasn't cheap, I was on expenses.

I guess I should have said: Anne's a barrister and the way I got to know her is that I'm a solicitor. A lot of people don't really understand the difference: solicitors are the ones who rip you off in an office, while barristers sell you out in court. Solicitors work in firms; barristers work in chambers. There's a bunch more I could tell you, but I doubt you really care and I know for sure I don't.

'How's chambers going?'

It was a long time since we'd met: we'd gone in diametrically opposite directions. She'd gone up, I'd gone down.

'OK.' She shrugged:

'It doesn't feel like the same place any more, you know ...'

Anne was in Alexander Keenan's chambers. Alex Keenan when he wanted to remind you he was just one of the boys. They were, so they claimed, 'special'. Chambers which only defended criminals, never prosecuted; they acted for tenants, not landlords; employees not employers; battered women, not the violent man. They were 'political' and proud of it.

Anne could pass for working class — at a pinch. Her father had been a union official. She'd been a social worker first, later took up law. When I knew her, she was about twenty-nine, but still in the last year of her training, as a pupil barrister. Also, heavily feminist, and stridently gay.

She wasn't what you'd call conventionally attractive. As a matter of fact, she wasn't really attractive at all. She was overweight, wore glasses that couldn't have suited her less, and dressed like she was putting out the garbage. But, like everyone else, she didn't like to think of herself as unattractive. Somewhere deep inside of her, the only way she could convince herself she wasn't the next thing to a sack of potatoes was if once in a while she made it with a man.

That was why she'd got it together with me.

She hadn't changed. In the fifteen minutes and most of a bottle we'd been sitting there, she'd begun to think: well, maybe he isn't too disgusting, too fat, too bleary-eyed, too embarrassing, to remind herself she could turn men on as well.

I'd changed, though. Sometime during the last five years, as I groped feebly to find the safest gutter, I'd lost interest. I don't mean in her particularly, but in it all. It wasn't worth the effort.

'Where're you living?' she asked. This was standard. Probe a bit; find out if he or she is living alone; what part of town (after all, and just for example, you'd have to be pretty desperate to go south of the river); is the desire enough to do it in your own home, even if it means waking up with an alien being in your bed, not just having to be polite to them first thing in the morning, but having to fix them coffee, maybe even something to eat.

'Same place,' I answered.

I wasn't exactly being honest with Anne. She'd asked if I was practising, and I'd said I was practising from home. She assumed that meant: practising law, as a solicitor.

The last time I did anything as a solicitor was when I sued my former partner for twenty thousand pounds, as my share of our firm, and settled out of court for five hundred.

That was some years ago, soon after Sandy kicked me out of the office when I turned up strung out on cocaine at two o'clock in the afternoon while she'd spent the morning explaining to some handjob in a purple gown and a horse-hair wig to cover his remaining few hairs why it was we hadn't prepared the case, told the client (for which read: thieving little bastard) he was due in court to watch the scales of justice come down against him, or instructed a barrister to put up a show our villain could complain about while he spent the next five years sewing mailbags.

Yeah, I was still in the same place. In all manner of ways. Same home. Same clothes (you'd be surprised how they last when you haven't got any money). Same waiting around for my father to die and leave me enough money to take off for someplace else. Same disillusionment with law, the legal system, lawyers and — above all — so-called left-wing lawyers, getting a healthy living pretending to fight the state on behalf of the oppressed and all along taking away from the victim the one true solace he or she ever had: they never gave me a chance.

So, I'd given up law, more or less. Instead, I hung my shingle out as what the glossies call a private eye. I put my name in the yellow pages. (Let your fingers do the walking. Let your money do the talking.) I advertised in the legal press: 'confidential enquiries and process serving by qualified solicitor.'

You can guess which I got more of. In the last three years, I hung about outside more council houses than you've had bad hamburgers, waiting for some violent husband to show up, so's I could overawe, overwhelm and overpower him with the majesty of the law by hitting him on the nearest part of his anatomy with a bit of funny parchment that's got Latin written all over it and that tells him he's not allowed to beat up on his wife any more, and run like hell.

I'd like to say: I've scraped by. I'd like to say that to give you the idea I'm not the lazy, incompetent slob I'm making myself out to be, but a modest, unassuming bloke, rich in integrity, downplaying his achievements. Unfortunately, neither would be true. I haven't scraped by (anyhow, on what I've earned), and I'm sure as hell not modest, unassuming or rich in integrity.

I'd place the time at about three or four months before this meet with Anne I've left you in the middle of that I can set my hand on my heart, wait for it to calm down, and assure you that I'd definitely stopped scraping by. Meaning? Meaning I owed more money than I could dream of. Meaning that if the people I owed it to were clean, decent, down-to-earth capitalists who understood what a fine and proper and natural thing it was to go bankrupt, that's where I would've been. Meaning, the people I owed money to weren't clean, decent or down-to-earth.

One of the reasons I'm so scathing about south of the river (the other is some residual sense of good taste) is because I live so close to it. I live on Redcliffe Square, which some of the residents like to call — imaginatively — West Chelsea, an area of London no cab-driver ever heard of. The rest of London knows it as Earl's Court, otherwise Kangaroo Valley from years ago when all the Aussies used to hang out there, otherwise Fag Alley.

You don't need a lot of insider information to work out why it's called Fag Alley. That's where all the gays live. Well, maybe not all of them, but enough to seem like it. And certainly, all the gays of a particular type: leather-jacketed, slightly balding, mustachioed, the sort you wake up in the middle of the night and find pissing on your carpet — or you.

But what people don't know quite so well is that it's got its own mob. By mob I mean exactly what you think I mean. Gangsters. Hoodlums. Thugs. The only difference between them and the best the East End has to offer is that they slit your arse open before they cut your balls off. They're into all the usual rackets. Gambling. Prostitution (female, male, and who knows or cares). Drugs (soft or hard). They lend money, too.

Of course, only a fool borrows from them. Only a fool, or a down-and-out solicitor with vague expectations of a timely parental death, whose brain isn't working too good. (You are wondering: what's the difference? 'Are the two mutually exclusive?' I hear you cry. There is a difference, though. The solicitor is qualified, a professional person, he is educated. That means: he does things the same way a fool does but he gets the chance to do a whole lot more of them).

About ten months ago I borrowed five hundred quid from one of these Earl's Court community workers. Even I knew it was a pretty stupid thing to do, but, I guess, if you're born lucky you'll find your way out of any mess, and if you're born unlucky it won't make that much difference.

About five months ago, this community worker's colleagues came around to my Redcliffe Square basement in order to discuss my problems with me. Specifically: why I hadn't paid back the money.

I told them about my mother dying ten years ago. That didn't impress them. I told them my youngest sister was a drug addict. That didn't impress them either. I told them my oldest sister was a schoolteacher. One of them was a wee bit shocked, but it still didn't make a real difference. I told them my father was bound to die some day: they asked if I'd put a contract out on him. Finally, we reached an agreement: I told them I'd pay them back within the week.

Now this is where else fools and solicitors are different. A fool couldn't've done what I did. I don't say he wouldn't have thought of it. He just wouldn't have had the chance. I went to see my bank manager. He was pleased to see me. He was another community worker, concerned about my problems. I told him a different story than I'd told the other lot. I told him I was past all my difficulties. I told him I was going back to work. I told him I'd had an offer from a property company, that I could handle their portfolio if I set up in practice again. I told him that was what I was going to do.

People don't understand banks. They're frightened of asking for money from the bank manager. They think every time they're overdrawn the bank manager breathes fire and puts his commandoes on red alert. Wrong. Consider: you're a nice, sweet, respectable, responsible person. You earn your money and you pay your keep. Maybe once ten years ago you wrote out a cheque that might've bounced if the multi-national corporation or local authority you work for happened to go bust before they paid your wages. That's about the worst you ever did. How much do you pay the bank?

Right. You don't pay the bank peanuts. If you've got more than the next month's mortgage payment sitting in your account, you don't get charged for anything. No charge per transaction. No charge for cheques drawn or paid in. No charge for standing orders. No charge for having an account. They even send you those pretty little books and plastic cards with magnetic strips on them free of charge. (If you ask nicely, they give you neat little covers for them — also free of charge.) You're not worth sweet fanny adams to the bank.

Where do you think banks get their money from? They get it from lending it. They get it from overdrafts they've terrified people into thinking they have to pay back. They get it from taking risks. Not too great a risk, mind you, 'cos the bank manager who doesn't get the right rate of returns isn't gonna be lending in South Kensington for much longer. (I'm told that in Hackney you can borrow a fiver if you leave your car as security.) That's what bank managing is about. Calculating risks. If you're a good risk, there's no limit to what you can have. If you're a bad risk, well, you might still pay some of it back.

That's what I did. I borrowed money from my bank manager to re-establish myself as a solicitor. He lent it me to re-establish myself as a solicitor. Also, he lent it me because my family has been banking with his lot since before his father'd started dreaming about someone to carry on the clerking. But he lent it me.

My other community worker was impressed. It's interesting. Money gets you money. Also, it gets you respect. He said to me: 'How come you didn't pay up before?' I said: 'It was tied up.' Suddenly, I was no longer a bum he was extorting 20% per month from, but an institution he was investing in. He said: 'You and I should get together. We should get to know each other better. We should get real close.' I looked down at his pants. A thing like that could hurt. I passed up the opportunity.

There is, of course, an inconsistency in what I have chosen to reveal thus far. On the one hand, I have admitted lying to Anne Godwin about 'practising'. On the other, I'm telling you how I financially organized myself back into practice as a solicitor. There is a solution, if you read the small print. I didn't say that in fact I'd gone back into practice as a solicitor.

The solution, such as it is, poses a problem you'll have worked out for yourself. I had to come up with money, to pay the bank with (or go bankrupt. I should have mentioned: a bankrupt solicitor gets what is quaintly called 'struck off the roll'. For those of you who don't know what that spells, I get to not be a solicitor any more. In turn, I get to not borrow from the bank any more. Around and around.)

Now, funnily enough, by some sort of coincidence, how I burrowed my way out of that one and how I came to be back in Covent Garden drinking wine with Fat Annie, and wondering if my client would believe a meal on expenses, have just a little bit in common. I'll tell you about it.

It didn't happen suddenly. For about two months, I lived pretty high off the bank. My bank manager wasn't that much of a fool. He'd done one pretty dumb thing: lending me money. But he wasn't so stupid as to think it'd start pouring back in the very next day. (As a matter of fact, it would've been a disaster if it had. The whole point was — remember — to make a profit out of it, i.e. interest. Just in case, or 'cos he got the wobblies, he sent me a couple of clients. I had to lie my way out of acting for them without explaining I didn't have a current practice certificate any more, and hadn't paid the compulsory professional insurance.)

Then for another couple of months I worked really hard at process-serving. I touted for work like crazy. I rang every solicitor I'd ever acted for and hustled them for work. I slapped parchment on more bums than I care to remember. I got hit by three of them, but only one of them hurt more than my pride. One of the advantages of being fat is people aren't too sure if you're strong, or just overweight.

Process-serving was, of course, getting me nowhere. I was about ready to think in terms of an extended vacation abroad, and I wouldn't have been sending my bank manager a postcard. Maybe I'd sting the community worker for a bit of 'investment money'. Split was on my mind.

Then I got a call. Funny thing. Just before that call, I would've said I'd used up all my chances (and there weren't that many to begin with). Right after, I had this feeling I was on my feet bigger than when I'd been at the height of my (so-called) career. Funnier still: I was right.

'Can I speak with' (note, not 'to') 'Mr Woolf, please ...'

'Who's calling?' (I did my imitation of Lily Tomlin.)

'I don't think he'll know my name. It's Mrs Nicholas. Is Mr Woolf available?'

'I'll see for you, Mrs Nicholas. Can you tell me what it's in connection with?'

'Oh. I see. Perhaps ... Perhaps you would remind him he once stayed in my house. In Wiltshire.'

I thought fast. She sounded too old for someone I'd slept with. I was certain (well, as near as I could be), it wasn't someone I'd borrowed money from. Wiltshire? I hadn't ever been in Wiltshire. For a start. It's south of the river. Isn't it? I was getting about ready to tell her I wasn't available when she said:

'Is that Mr Woolf?

Wily old bitch.

'I'll put you through now,' I sneered.

'Mrs Nicholas? David Woolf here. How can I help you?' My voice dropped three octaves. 'You don't remember me, do you, Mr Woolf.' It wasn't a question.

'Well, I'm ... er ... Of course ... That is to say ...' I wasn't normally lost for words.

'There's no reason why you should,' she added quickly: 'You stayed in my house, a few years ago, with my son Jack ...'

Now that was a name that rang a bell: Jack Nicholas. I was sure I knew it. I just wasn't sure why. It wasn't 'cos it sounded like Jack Nicholson. It wasn't 'cos it sounded like Jack Nicklaus. Just in time, I remembered: he was someone I'd been at school with.

'No, I don't think you were at school with my son ...'

Wrong again.

'My son was a barrister. His chambers came to our home. A sort of, well, he-called it a chambers' outing. I think ... Your wife ... One of the members?'

My wife? I hadn't been married. Ever. Had I?

It was enough, though, to put me on the right lines: Anne Godwin; chambers; Jack Nicholas — they used to call him the Jackdaw, the way his head was shaped, and he'd talk — lecture or argue, I never heard him do anything else — his head bobbing at you like he was stealing the eyes out of your skull.

'Yes, of course,' I lied: 'I'm sorry I didn't recall. How are you, Mrs Nicholas? I cared about as much as I cared if it was raining outside.

'Thank you. Yes. I was wondering ... I gather you're not practising, as a solicitor ... Any more ... But ... I saw an advertisement ... In a magazine ... Would it be, the Law Society's Journal?'

'Law Society's Gazette. Solicitor's Journal. Yes, I advertise in both of them. Could have been either.' She wanted me for one of two things: confidential enquiries, or process-serving. The odds were stacked in favour of the latter.

'Yes. Thank you.' What a grateful lady, I thought. 'You read about my son? You weren't at the funeral, I think. Of course,' she added quickly: 'There was no reason why you should have been. You weren't that close. But your wife was there ...'

There are times when even I am impressed by my intellect. I worked out the Jackdaw was dead.

'I, er, well, she wasn't my wife ...' Was all I said. It wouldn't've caused me convulsions to say I was sorry the jerk was dead. I just never thought of it.

'Oh. Yes. Thank you.'

Stop with the thank-yous, I screamed silently.

'I was wondering ... Would it be possible ... To see you, Mr Woolf? On a ... Well, confidential matter ...'

Like: confidential as in confidential enquiries? Hell, yes, no one wanted to see me on one of them before. I didn't even know what they looked like.

We arranged to meet in exactly a week's time. She would, she said, be in town in any event, and she would rather see me while she was already up. She didn't say: it would be more convenient to see you while I'm in town anyway. More like: when I have another excuse to be in town.

We were going to meet in Harrods tea-room. That was good for me for two reasons. First of all, it was near enough for me to walk, which saved the bus-fare. Secondly, I could tell her it was near where I 'was' (she wasn't to know if she was talking to my office or my home). If I was near Harrods, I might well be (for all she knew) in an office in South Kensington, or Knightsbridge, or — even! — Belgravia.

'How will I know you?' I remembered to ask.

'I'll remember you, Mr Woolf. I never forget a face.'

I thought: this may be it. Five years ago, there was only one face to remember. Now, there were at least two faces, and a handful of chins.

Part of me expected her to no-show. It could be a gag, from the one or two people I'd stayed in touch with who had followed my decline with cathartic attention to detail. Or, she might have chickened out. Most likely of all, no one went to Harrods for tea any more; the store worked their way through the telephone directory to book dates with suckers like me who'd've ordered something they had to pay for before they worked out it was a con.

'Mr Woolf?' A lady of about fifty-five, greying hair, and wearing an extremely large hat, hovered over me. Her hair was what they called blue-rinsed. She was wearing a dark grey suit. She looked so smart she could've been one of my mother's friends.

'Right. Mrs Nicholas?' I remembered something I'd been taught at school between Latin and cricket and bending over for the house bully: I stood up.

'I did have difficulty remembering you,' she admitted: 'You've changed.'

I was fat. My suit was worn and had forgotten the name of my neighbourhood cleaner. My shoes would've fainted at the sight of boot-black. But I had shaved. With a blunt razor, admittedly, but no one could say I had more than a six o'clock shadow.

It was three o'clock.

'Can I get you some tea?' I offered. I hadn't used all the bank's money yet, though tea at Harrods might well take care of what was left.

'I think that must be for me to do, thank you,' she said quietly.

We weren't meeting socially, I wasn't, eh wot, a gentleman taking a lady to tea — but professionally, and she was the client, for which read she was about to buy me.

I inclined my head with what I hope looked like graciousness but was thinking how many days can I survive on cream cakes.

After the waiter in the waistcoat had dumped the silver salver, and Mrs Nicholas had played mother (she'd just lost a child, it was the least I could let her do), we got down to business with a directness that would've made my community worker look like he was dissembling.

'Did you know my son Jack had died? Before I telephoned, I mean?'

'Well, no, to tell the truth.' (Buy me tea at Harrods and I'll tell you no lies.)

'I, uh, don't move in the same circles any more ...'

'I gathered.' She was no dufus. (Dufus = jerk = dumbo = idiot = someone who lives south of the river = etc.)

'He died five weeks ago.'

She paused. For a second there, I thought she was waiting for me to say something. Then I realized it was deliberate. She was weighing things up in her mind. Once she said what came next, a secret idea had turned real.

'I want you to investigate his death, Mr Woolf. I want you to find out … how it happened …' Then, in a whisper, she added:

'I want you to find out who did it, Mr Woolf …'

I swallowed hard. The back of my throat was dry. My hand was trembling too much to hold a cup. This sort of thing didn't happen. Not to me.

'You. Want. Me. To. Find. Out. How. Your. Son. Died? OK?'

'Yes. That's correct, Mr Woolf. I'll pay, of course,' she added quickly, as if my hesitation might be on account of I thought she was asking me to do it as a favour. For staying in her house maybe?

To myself I repeated the words over. She wants me to find out how her son died.

I was caught between two conflicting impulses. I oughta put as much distance between myself and this fruitcake as I could. But there could be a lotta loot in it.

I needed time to think:

'Uh, maybe you should tell me what happened?'

She nodded slowly. Picked up her cup. Sipped her tea. Quietly. Not a slurp, not a gulp. The way if other people ate or drank I might just have found them a bit more tolerable to have around. Then she told me.

'He died in an accident. He was on his bicycle. It was on a Wednesday, the twenty-fifth of last month. It happened at a quarter to eleven. He was on his way home from his chambers.'

The big deal wasn't exactly crystal clear.

'He had carried his bicycle on to the train and only had a short distance to go to reach home.'

At least she was giving me plenty of time to think. It was about as interesting as an advert for Kellogg's cornflakes.

'I think I ought to say, the police said he was intoxicated.'

For the first time, she was talking a language I understood.

'The driver did not stop. He hasn't been found. There was an inquest. His head of chambers represented us. Alexander Keenan. You know him, of course,' she added flatly.

It depends what you mean by know. I wouldn't exactly say kissing cousins.

Another pause. She was getting to the real point.

'My son ... Jack ... He was ... He was a very careful man, Mr Woolf. Even as a child. He was well-behaved, never in trouble, always cautious. It may ... It may even be that he carried it to a fault.'

'What was the verdict?' I wanted to get her back on the track. I needed a eulogy to Jackdaw like a hole in the head.

'Thank you. Accidental death. But ... But it was really that he had died ... as a result of drink. I do not dispute that he had been drinking. I am in no position to do so. There was a blood sample. Some of his colleagues had been drinking with him. But it seemed to be all that the coroner paid any attention to. He kept saying how dangerous it could be on a bicycle, because people only think about the dangers of driving a car in drink.'

I nodded sombrely, suppressing a smile at the quaint old expression 'in drink'.

'I ... I felt he was using my son's death, Mr Woolf. Using it to make his point.'

I shrugged: 'Coroners like to see their names in the newspapers ...'

'Yes. Thank you. I understand that. But he wasn't really interested ... in how Jack died. I felt ... I felt none of them were, Mr Woolf. None of them,' she repeated, and for once I was ahead of her: none of them, including Jackdaw's colleagues.

'You see ... What I said about being careful: he had been drinking, so he took the train home most of the way. That was Jack. If he had been too drunk to travel on his bike, he would have walked from the station.'

'Maybe.'

It wasn't enough to mount a state trial on. The police said he was too drunk to be riding his hike. There were independent witnesses who said he'd been drinking. To me it added up like the guy was simply too drunk to be out on a bike, and here was a mother who didn't want to have to carve on a gravestone: 'A loving son — dead, drunk and incapable.'

She read my thoughts. Like an open book. I was really bad at this private eye game.

'Is ... Is there a Mr Nicholas?' I was playing for more time to think. I remembered the 'phone call: she'd wanted an excuse to be in town, other than me.

'Yes. My husband, Jack's father, is the Reverend Nicholas of St Thomas'. He does not know I am seeing you,' she answered my barely concealed question. She went on to answer the next one without being asked, too:

'My husband is a highly-regarded figure in the church, Mr Woolf. You are not a church-goer, I think?'

'No, I'm Jewish.'

'Ah, yes, thank you. We are a very tolerant family, Mr Woolf. I think — I hope — that's where Jack got his own tolerance from ...'

It's always the first thing they tell you: they don't mind.

'He has ... He has a philosophical bent ...' She was back on the Very Rev:

'It has been a considerable strength in our lives. He believes — a lot of people find it difficult to accept that this is a sufficient explanation for the vicissitudes of life — that what happens is truly God's will ...'

I wanted to ask: what does vy-sissy-tunes mean? Fag music?

'No more than I does my husband believe that Jack was drunk when he ... When he had his accident ... But ... But he believes it was God's will, and it does not disconcert him not to know more about what happened ...'

'But it disconcerts you, right?' I thought I might as well show I'd been listening. As well as eating.

She nodded slowly:

'Yes. It does disconcert me.'

Vengeance is mine, saith the mother.

For the second time, she read my thoughts:

'I don't know, Mr Woolf. I don't know why I'm doing this. I don't know why I'm seeing you. I may ... I am not stupid, Mr Woolf. I know I am a mother who has lost her son. I know I am in grief. But something ... Just a feeling ... A mother's intuition if you will ... I have to know exactly what happened ... He had ... He had so much to live for. He was brilliant. I know one should not lightly use the word. He was married: he had a charming wife, a beautiful son ...'

'Mrs Nicholas ... Forgive me ... A lot of people with a whole lot to live for got drunk and died in a crash ... Others too ...' Those without so much to live for.

I don't know what made me speak my mind like that. I certainly wasn't acting like I needed her money. Maybe I was getting a little frightened. If I took her money, if I took the case,

I'd have to start working on it. I didn't like the idea of poking around someone's grave. You never knew where the body'd been.

She wasn't even remotely thrown by what I'd said. She even smiled a little, for the first time since she'd arrived:

'Yes. Thank you. I'm glad you said that. I told you that I have had those thoughts for myself. If you hadn't said that, I should have had somewhat less confidence in you ... I should have thought you were just ... Is "taking the case" the right expression? For the money ...'

'Don't let yourself be bought for a one-liner, lady,' I said. I'd meant to say it to myself but I said it out loud. There was a long silence. My riposte had hardened her resolve. I was her man and she was certain of it. To fill the gap between the waistcoat asking if we wanted another pot and bringing it, I asked:

'Why'd you choose me?'

'I saw your advertisement. In a magazine in my son's house. It seemed ... like a sign,' she added quietly.

'How'd you recognize my name? It's been a long time.'

'I thought I recognized it. When I got home I looked it up.'

'You looked it up?'

'In the visitors' book,' she added, as if it was obvious.

'Ah, right.' And I truly did remember. Theirs was the only house I was ever in which had a visitors' book.

After she'd poured more tea I asked:

'If your husband doesn't know ... How're you going to pay me?'

'I have private money, Mr Woolf. It's not my husband's. He knows about it, of course, but he has always insisted I keep it to myself. I would ... I would have left it to Jack ... Now I shall leave it to Phillip ...' She caught my question again:

'His son … But … It doesn't matter. I don't need to explain, do I? You need to know I can afford your services. That's all, isn't it?'

'Well, I guess I need to know you didn't rob a bank …'

For the very first time, she laughed:

'I didn't rob a bank, Mr Woolf. What are your charges?'

I didn't answer for a moment. She probably thought I was deciding what was fair. Truth was, it was the first time I'd ever had the choice. Process-serving was all fixed-rate. I tried to think.

'It's one hundred a day … Plus expenses.' I only just remembered to add the bit about expenses.

She didn't bat an eyelid. I should've said a hundred fifty.

CHAPTER TWO

Remember how that programme used to begin? 'There are ten million people in the naked city ...' (I think it was ten.) Well, there's eight million in London.

Looking for someone who'd knocked someone else off a bicycle was like looking for the proverbial needle in a haystack.

There are only two ways to do it. One is to keep the pressure on, and hope the needle pops out like a squirt of pus from a pimple. The other is to set fire to the hay-stack and sift the cinders. If the needle still no-shows, there's only two explanations. It wasn't there to begin with. Or you're not that good at looking.

I got a bunch more information from the holy man's lady wife before we split. Basic stuff. Like where Jack had lived. What he'd been working at. History. His course in life from public school to the Bar. Did he leave any money?

I found out his money went to his wife in trust for the kid. I remembered his wife. She was a lawyer too, a solicitor and very rich in her own right. As for the kid, even the son of two lawyers was unlikely to have wacked out his daddy before he reached the age of four.

Everything she told me spelled out just how good the Jackdaw had been. He was close to his family, didn't cheat on his wife, and he had devoted his life to those less fortunate than himself. His father wasn't the only one on talking terms with God: Jack and his wife were active Christians — socialist Christians, but Christians nonetheless.

Of course, he'd had the breaks. He had come from a wealthy family, strictly top drawer. He had gone to one of the best public schools, where he had been a prefect and then either head of his house or head of the school; I never did catch which. He'd gone to Oxford. After Oxford, the Council of Legal Education to read for his bar finals. Then pupilage in a commercial set a relative arranged for him. He had every reason to be confident that he would move on and up at the Bar at his usual pace.

What I learned from his mother told me his confidence had not been misplaced. He had appeared as a barrister in the House of Lords, in the Court of Appeal, some of his cases had been reported in The Times. The chambers had continued to grow. He had been, until his death, a senior member of the group, one of Keenan's closest confidantes. The younger members, in pupilage or just out, came to him for advice and guidance. He loved to help them. I can bet he left them in no doubt just how much he loved to help them.

He'd even been big enough for his death to get a mention in some of the legal press. 'The name will be familiar to many of our readers. He had the rare skill of making what is for many an obscure subject interesting ...' The writer didn't have the same skill and I didn't finish the piece.

It wasn't a whole lot to go on. I tried another tack. Retraced his steps the night he died, from Blackfriars to Dalston Junction on the train, then along the Balls Pond Road, which became St Paul's Road, to where he and his family lived in a four-storey house overlooking Highbury Fields. I stood outside the house and thought for a long time: finally I figured — maybe three hundred grand.

I didn't go in. I might have been able to get away with 'just passing — offer condolences' to Penny Nicholas, but I wanted to keep the shot for later. I still wasn't clear enough in my own head where I was going, and what I was after.

I was, as they say, getting nowhere fast. I didn't really have a clue what I was doing. I was trained as a lawyer. That meant applying the lawbooks to my client's case. There were no textbooks for this one. I wasted the best part of a week after my visit to the Nicholas' house in Highbury pondering and analysing — like I had a case to present in court — what was the best way to go about it.

I set out on a sheet of paper all I knew about Jackdaw. It didn't cover a single side. I set out on another sheet of paper all the people we knew in common, and who I was still in touch with. That didn't cover a single side either. I set out on yet another sheet of paper all the different approaches I might adopt. I gave up wasting paper.

Another line was as fruitless as the visit to his house. I rang the cops:

'I'm afraid you'll have to make a formal request for information, sir.'

There was no: my local's the Red Lion, my poison's a large scotch and my mouth can be opened for a fiver slipped across the table under a newspaper open at the racing form. A formal request meant a letter to the Commissioner. I wondered what the Commissioner drank.

There was, however, one mouth that opened easily the moment I gave it an ear. That was the coroner. People in England don't understand the coroner system. They think coroners operate like judges. Detached, distant, inaccessible, addressed only by lawyers, thoroughly biased. I'd found out years ago they function in a different way: investigative, they'll talk and listen to anyone who's got anything to say about a case they're handling, and then they'll decide it the way they'd already made up their minds in the first place.

I knew the coroner for the area where Jack Nicholas died. I had met him years before on a case. A house of bedsitting rooms burned down. I represented the kin of a Kentucky Fried Special: three limbs, deep fried. They seemed to think the landlord was to blame. Something to do with too many people, lousy wiring, cardboard walls, no fire escapes and the last time the extinguishers were inspected was when the owner'd bought the job lot second-hand. It had been a big enough case (meaning: the coroner'd got enough headlines) for him to remember me, and to agree to see me.

'Come along in Woolf ... How can I help you?'

I'd forgotten what a pretentious prick he was. 'Woolf.' That sort of handle had gone out a hundred years ago. He was — as many coroners are — both a doctor and a barrister. This one was young, black-haired, wearing a dress jacket and grey-striped trousers, a gold watch-chain across his slender belly. He placed his glasses carefully on the leather blotter. Locked his fingers as if in prayer. Waited.

'You handled the inquest on a friend of mine. Jack Nicholas. A barrister. Got killed on his bicycle. Do you remember?'

'Yes, of course. It was only a few weeks ago. I didn't know he was a friend of yours …'

The sentence trailed off as he realized how ridiculous it sounded: why or how the hell could he have known. Even if it had been true.

'You, uh, found the accident had happened because he'd been drinking?'

'Good lord no. The verdict was accidental death. If I'd been certain it was caused by drunkenness, I might even have directed a verdict of death by misadventure.' He looked perplexed, as if he genuinely did not recall that drink had figured in the case.

'I was told … You had a lot to say about …'

'My dear Woolf. That's entirely different. Of course I did. The fellow had been drinking, you know. Quite a lot as I recall. But … No, drinking had nothing to do with the verdict. One must … After all … How shall I put it? Well,' he smiled and held out his hands, not so much in supplication as if welcoming me to the club:

'Use one's opportunities. Bit less of a wasted life, eh, if one can say something to save others …'

She had said Jack's father was a vicar, hadn't she? Not a coroner.

'Had he … Well, how drunk was he?'

The coroner shrugged:

'Enough. I don't remember. I say, Woolf, you are just here because he was a friend, aren't you?'

Gentlemen and lawyers have one thing in common. They don't lie to one another. Not so's anyone can find out.

'Of course, of course. I know the family. It caused … Some distress, shall we say?'

'The remarks about alcohol. I see. I did ... I did think of that, of course. I could tell that the mother was upset, but that was only natural. The father ... A churchman, I believe?'

He was checking to see if I really did know the family.

'Yeah. St Thomas.'

'He seemed ... Very stoical ... You don't encounter that much these days,' he added wistfully.

After a second, he went on:

'But the principal reason I believed it was fair to say what I did was Alexander Keenan. You know him of course.'

Everyone so took it for granted I knew him he was beginning to feel like an old friend, instead of someone I'd only met a few times, a number of years ago.

'What about him?' He'd had his one bite at checking me out.

He frowned. The lines on his brow furrowed. It created a splendid impression. Profound thought. Weighty consideration.

'You know what a trial is like, even in my little court ...' For 'little court' read the place he ruled like it was the turnstile at the Pearly Gate.

'There's a certain amount of ... exchange between bench and bar ...' He was likening himself to a judge, sitting 'on the bench'.

'One indicates what one is thinking ... The direction one might take ... It's all, how shall I put it, understood. The public don't follow, of course, but one says one thing, and counsel knows how to react, to tell you whether or not he's going to go on and fight the point, or whether he can live with it ...'

It wasn't a foreign language. Quite. It was long enough ago I'd last done it I had to remind myself how it worked. The judge might say:

'One could interpret the position in this way, Mr Woolf ... Your client ...' Did/did not mean to do this or that = is/is not guilty of the offence.'

In reply you say:

'With respect, sir, I would have thought ...' Meaning you won't buy it. Or:

'Quite, sir. That's something that's clearly open to you. In law, that would mean that my client would be not guilty as charged, although guilty, perhaps, of the lesser offence of ...'

It's all very proper. Nor is it confined to a final finding. It's: 'why don't we tackle this bit of it like this or that ...' A highly skilled judge knows exactly when to start extracting agreements from counsel, a little bit at a time, until, like a chess game, he can get the result he wants:

'Given what you accepted an hour ago must have happened on the 5th, Mr Woolf, and given the provisions of section thirty-eight, wouldn't you think I'd be bound to find against you?'

Uh. Er. Um.

(People think lawyers fight each other. Bullshit. One or other of them is fighting the judge, who has already decided which side he's on.)

What the coroner was telling me was that he'd early on decided to dress the Jackdaw's death up as death by drunken biking, and Keenan had acquiesced. The question was:

'Why did you want to take it that way?'

'It seemed to me ... That was what it was about. There was an oddity. After all, the fellow had put his bike on the train. The journey must have sobered him up. The rest of the route was well-known to him. It isn't that busy a road at that time of the night. It wasn't that far to go.'

Right. That was what his mother thought. But my question stood.

'He was ... Have you seen the photographs?'

I shook my head. I remember seeing a seven-by-eight glossy of my client in the bedsit case. It didn't turn me on.

'He was very badly damaged ...'

Maybe after all he wasn't dead. Just returned to manufacturer for repair.

'The collision was clearly head-on. Very hard. Very fast, I would have said.'

'Is that what the police said?'

'Er, not in court ...'

He meant: yes, in his own room, where I was talking to him. It was all, of course, off the record; what the papers call 'unattributable'.

'So why? You haven't answered my question ...'

'No more I have,' he said softly, reminding me he wasn't obliged to see me, let alone to tell me any of this. It could also have been read as: I haven't told you anything.

He brought the tips of his fingers together in a spire. He was thinking. He was wondering whether to go on talking to me. Eventually, he must have decided. He'd gone this far. If he clammed up now, it'd look as if he had something to hide.

'The alternative ... Unlawful killing. Death by person or persons unknown? Would that have helped the family? Would it have helped anyone? What would we have been talking about? Manslaughter,' meaning death by reckless driving:

'Not murder, to be sure ...'

'To be sure?'

For the very first time he began to think he maybe ought to be listening to me, instead of the other way round:

'Do you know something, Woolf? Are you holding something back?'

'Is it impossible?'

'Have you got any evidence? Anything? Even a motive?'

I shook my head:

'No. I just want to know.'

His eyebrows furrowed. Irreverently I thought: those are fine eyebrows; they belong on an actor. Or a politician.

He was thinking: I was behaving like more than a friend, curious about an accidental death. But he was locked in to the conversation and too stupid to find a way out of it.

'There was no reason ... I accept it was an odd accident. But odd accidents do happen. There was nothing else to go on. The police wanted to shut the file. Keenan was content. For me to have held out would have been ... Arrogant?'

I was going to get nothing more out of him. For all his pomp and circumstance, he was just one more cog in the machine, helping the wheels turn smoothly.

He did two things for me, though. First, he had confirmed the information I'd been given by Mrs Reverend: there were peculiarities about the accepted version of Jack's death; and, Keenan himself had been happy to go along with it.

I knew now where I was heading. The chambers. I rang as soon as I got home:

'Can I speak to Anne Godwin, please?'

'She's not here.'

I always love the friendly. helpful attitude adopted by left-wingers. It's part of the spirit of collectivism. It's not my job to be nice. It's his. Or hers.

'Can I leave a message?'

Silence.

'Can you tell her Dave Woolf rang?'

Something clicked with whoever was at the other end.

Dave Woolf. A distant name. But a solicitor. Solicitors bring barristers work. That made me important.

'I'm terribly sorry, she's on holiday. Can I help you at all? Did you want to instruct her?' Meaning: brief her, meaning bring her some work, and them some loot.

'No. I'm an old friend. When will she be back?'

'Hold on a minute. There's another call.'

I might as well have said I was the tax inspector.

A mere ten or fifteen minutes later, the mongoloid got back to me.

'Who was it you wanted to speak to?' she asked.

'Lev Bronstein, if he's around.'

'Who?'

'Anne Godwin. You said she was on holiday. When will she be back?

'Oh. She's only just gone ...' I heard her call out to one of her fellow clerks:

'How long's Anne gone away for, Jo?'

I spent another five telephone units establishing it would be at least two more weeks before Anne would get back.

If I'd still been in practice as a solicitor, trying to brief her, it would have been a good excuse to do nothing about the case for a while. If I was genuinely only calling up as a friend, it wouldn't've mattered. But I had a lot of money to make in a hurry. I needed to keep the clock ticking.

After I hung up, I wondered what one of the great American detectives would've done in my situation. I didn't have a gun. Or a fast car. Or a leggy blonde girlfriend.

Me? I opened a bottle of wine. Then I put a tape in the cassette player. Listened to Beethoven. The Fifth. I'd drunk half a bottle by the time he reached the glorious second movement. It was my favourite sound in the whole wide world, heard that way.

Next stop was better. I skimmed the evening paper and found a treat. I'd been so hyped up on seeing the coroner I'd forgotten what day it was. Hill Street Blues. Even better, there was no technicians' strike. The programme wasn't just listed in the paper. It would actually be broadcast.

I took my 'phone off the hook and settled in for an hour's visit to my spiritual home. Maybe I'd get some help from Captain Furillo, Howard Hunter ('Now we've got a problem here. Jack Nicholas is of the dead persuasion') or Mick Belker, with whom I identified most of all, except he seemed to like his parents.

I wasn't far out either. Mick gave me my clue. He was setting up some hoods who were trying to milk the owner of a fish-market. Put his mike in the mouth of a salmon trout. The point was, as he always did, he went undercover, took up the role of a fish-salesman himself. By the time I switched off, wishing I was rich enough to buy a video so's I could watch it all over again and any evening I liked, I knew which way I was going.

It was strange walking back in through the swing doors of Keenan's chambers. He had the whole top floor of a building in the Middle Temple. Middle Temple? It's one of the four Inns of Court where almost all the barristers practising in London work.

Inns of Court? Well, hell, I don't know how to describe them. This isn't an introduction to the English legal system: I just know all barristers have to belong to an Inn. They're like freemasons and elks and other clubs who wouldn't have me as a member even if I could afford the subscription.

Anyhow, the four Inns own these tracts of property. Oceans of calm in and around the City of London. Fine old buildings. Like an Oxford or Cambridge college. Ample lawns. A croquet hoop here and there. A garden party, a big white tent and a brass band. They weren't exactly the sort of place most of Keenan's clients would feel right at home in. Not quite Notting Hill, Brixton or Hackney. More the sort of place the good lady Nick would expect her son to work from. If he wasn't dead.

Keenan was expecting me. I wasn't kept waiting one minute. He even came out to greet me, shake hands, offer me coffee before we settled down. I said yes. I needed time to shake off that cloying sense of climbing back down into a cesspit I thought I'd drowned in years ago.

'So tell me about this book,' he invited as soon as he was settled safely behind his desk.

He wasn't a fool. You can carry consorting with people too far. If you didn't keep the barriers up, they might forget you were something special.

I haven't told you much about Keenan, except he was a socialist. (Whatever that meant. Time was, I thought I was. A few others did too.)

Despite the Irish name, he was from older English stock than Jack Nicholas. He could trace his ancestry back to the seventeenth century, when his great-great-great-great-etc. had been foreign secretary or something like. For several years, Keenan had been dignified with the title QC. That is to say: a senior barrister.

For all his wealth, family standing and personal confidence — born with a psychological silver spoon in his mouth — Keenan was actually a most charming man. He was difficult to fault, except for an odd, lingering impression that his interest in the working class wasn't that different from the interest his ancestors might've expressed in the family retainers.

Physically, he was unprepossessing. Short, stout, with thin metal-rimmed glasses, and a shock of hair that was already turning white. The most distinctive feature about him was: in contrast to my several, he didn't have a chin. I mean, like, no chin at all. But a colleague who'd seen him cut himself swore it ran red, so the other thing you'd've expected wasn't true at all.

'Well, it's a book about the British left ... Particularly, the legal left. Obviously, you can't write about the legal left in isolation from the left as a whole, but that's the focus ...'

It sounded good. Convincing. Meaningless garbage, of course, but convincing meaningless garbage of the sort, if my memory didn't fail me, the left loved to spout at one another during long nights in the pub or all day Saturday arguing for control of a pathetic voluntary agency or an unknown splinter faction of a rarified political party.

He nodded wisely:

'I can see that. Why the legal left?'

'Don't you think ... Sometimes ... We ...' I threw the 'we' in casually, hoping he'd ignore the rumours he was bound to have heard about my own activities over the last few years:

'We epitomize the contradictions. Working against the establishment, but within it. Dependent on it for a living, but seeking to destroy it. Fighting to protect people from its excesses, but legitimizing them.'

The words rolled off my tongue like it was only yesterday. I wished I could remember what they meant.

I noticed that the way he held his hands while listening wasn't that different from the coroner I'd seen before the weekend. As if to spite me, he unravelled his fingers and picked up his mug of coffee, slurping from it the way I hated. I guess the guy had somehow to show he wasn't pure aristocrat.

'Who's commissioned it?'

I smiled secretively:

'I'm sorry. I've been asked not to say for the time being.'

He didn't seem to know enough about publishing to recognize the answer as pure bullshit. Nor did I.

I felt inspired. My cover was sheer brilliance. Mick Belker couldn't've done it. He wouldn't've known, as I knew from years in the business, that lawyers love to talk about themselves, and that left-wingers love to talk about themselves, and that in consequence there was nothing so irresistible to a left-wing lawyer than an opportunity to talk about himself.

I leaned back in my chair. I almost didn't have to do any more. Just sit there. It would all flow. He asked me:

'I heard you'd left practice. Have you been writing since?'

'Thinking, let's say.'

I grinned openly. He was positively eating out of my hand. Making a show of interest in me. I was going to put him on paper. I was going to bring him publicity. It didn't matter how famous they already were: they always wanted more.

'Who else have you seen?'

He made it seem like an incidental.

It was the perfect question. After my answer, I would own him:

'No one. Yet. I thought I'd start with you ...'

It really cost him. To keep the smirk off his face.

'And where do you want to start?'

'With your chambers, I should think. After all, it was a pretty major thing to do, to set up a group the way you did ...'

He knew what I was referring to. You probably won't. I'll explain.

Theoretically, any barrister is obliged to take any case which he is competent to do, meaning professionally competent to do. He is not supposed to reject work because he is, for example, pro-landlord or pro-employer. The idea is that his expertise should be available to anyone, no matter how mighty or how humble.

But it's a funny thing. If you're a solicitor acting for a landlord or an employer looking for a famous name to do your dirty work at a very high level of pay — maybe five figures for a day's work — you find that any barrister you want is easily available. Whereas if you're acting for a tenant or some other jerk on fixed-rate, legal aid scales of pay, suddenly the same guy's awfully busy, terribly sorry, would love to do the case, but ...

It isn't exactly news that lawyers haven't got a hard-earned reputation for working for the oppressed. Given the financial background, and the class lawyers have come from, you'd be a fool to expect anything else.

What Keenan did that was different from most of the rest of the bar was to set up a group, a chambers, which specialized in the problems of the poor, the victims, the disenfranchised and the dispossessed, operating — contrary to the rules — on behalf of them and them alone.

'Well, you know, it wasn't something that just happened ...'

He meant: I spent years thinking my way into it, organizing it, before anyone else got involved, or has to be mentioned.

I nodded sombrely, as if this was exactly what I wanted to hear. I took out my notebook. Made like I was writing notes. He wouldn't need prompting for a while.

It took the best part of an hour to get on to the history of the group itself. There were very few of them when they started. Keenan. Four other men, one woman.

I remembered some of those early people. Wishart. Red faced to the point where it looked like he was going to catch fire. Spoke like he was about to burst: staccato, rapid gunfire, too quick to keep up with. Fat Harry Matheson. The best company of all. He couldn't find clothes to cover the whole of his body all of the time. His belly flopped outside of trousers he could barely keep up.

Carrie — Caroline — Creemer. Slim. Attractive, if ice is nice. When she wore trousers, they were tight enough to count the pubic hairs. Soon after they started, they had been joined by Sue Cannon. Thorough. Hard-working. A little soul who drank a bit too much to cover up the strain of practising as a barrister. It didn't come as any great shock to me when she decided to switch over to being a solicitor.

'And Orbach?' I could afford a certain amount of shall we say less than friendly questioning. It was consistent with my cover.

'Russel Orbach. Yes. He was with me at the beginning ...'

He didn't want to talk about Orbach. He was torn. He wanted to co-operate with me, he wanted to be invited to talk, to be written about. But he didn't want to talk about Orbach.

I had no real reason to press him on the subject, save authenticity, and perhaps a chance to persuade him into wanting all the more to talk about something or someone else.

Orbach was, apart from Keenan, the best known of the founders. Aggressive, arrogant, argumentative. He was like a whole bunch of other Jewish professionals I'd known, especially lawyers.

There had been problems. Orbach had split from the group a few years after it began. Every kind of rumour flew around the movement. Not just the movement: the profession as a whole had their eyes on Keenan's chambers, and it loved to gossip.

Mostly, the rumours were, Orbach was doing too well. By the time he split, he was highly successful. Not too long after, he, too, had become a QC. What the anti-Orbach faction said was: he wanted to get out there and earn some real money. The anti-Keenans summed it up pithily: 'the politics of envy'.

'It wasn't just the founders,' Keenan bit: 'There were others.'

He reminded me that they'd been joined after a couple of years by a relatively well-known barrister. Jeffrey Jones hadn't stayed either. He had taken up politics full-time, and was one of that new breed of left-wing councillors who live on their allowances and spend their days in meetings.

After Jeff Jones, there had been a gradual influx of new people. Over the next couple of years while I was still in touch, four or five new barristers and a new clerk. Until recently, I'd never thought any them to be of much consequence. One of these, though, was Jack Nicholas.

'Didn't I hear he'd died recently?' I asked, as disingenuously as I could manage.

'Yes. He was in an accident, on his bicycle. We miss him a great deal.'

'I'm sure. I met him a few times. I think ... Well,' I laughed, as if mildly embarrassed:

'You probably won't remember. But I and Anne ... Godwin ... We had a short, er, relationship ... I think during that time, I went on a chambers' outing ... To his house. Would that be right?'

'His parents' house. Yes. We went too.' The 'we' wasn't royal: he meant himself and his wife.

Now he mentioned her, I remembered his wife. How could I forget? She was one of the biggest bitches I ever encountered.

Rich as Croesus. And titled. The Lady Helen: she was so neurotic, if Freud had to cure her, she'd've become his life's work.

'He was still young ...' I had a bit of leeway before I was showing excessive interest.

'Yes.'

Funny that. I got the impression he was no keener to talk about Jackdaw than he was to talk about Orbach. I said, as pleasantly as the substance allowed:

You see, I can't take an uncritical approach ...'

'Of course.' He waved a hand as if he welcomed close scrutiny.

'I just wondered how you thought you had done, in terms of ... Shall we say cohesion?' The spectre of the left.

He shrugged:

'Orbach is the only one who left us, but continued at the Bar. Doesn't that say something.'

'I don't know. It just seemed to me ... Well, that you'd lost more than just Orbach ...'

'What do you mean?'

I reached up to see if my head was still in place, or whether he'd snapped it off completely.

'Well, there was Sue Cannon. Jeffrey Jones. Orbach. Unless I'm mistaken, you had a couple of pupils who didn't stay ...'

'Mary ffoulkes? She's on television now.' Presenter on a consumer rights show. I caught it once in a while.

'No. There was another. At the beginning?'

'Bob Carter.'

'Yes.'

Keenan nodded:

'But not a good barrister ... That was all ... We were unlucky.'

And he was bristling. He hadn't come down off of my question: you've lost a lot of people. I couldn't quite make the connection.

'Then Jack Nicholas ... That was different, of course ...'

Keenan nodded, like he was miles away:

'You know about the others, of course?'

'Meaning?' I had the upper hand for the moment, and didn't mind showing it.

'Peter Wishart ... and Carrie ... Caroline Creemer.'

I shook my head:

'I hadn't heard they'd left.'

'No. They didn't. They died too. I thought you'd know that. Most of the group are in their thirties. Three deaths,' he scowled, bitter, as if it was personal between him and God:

'Three deaths in the last eighteen months ... It's hard, David, I tell you it's hard ...'

He looked straight at me, genuinely grief-stricken, though whether for the loss of personal friends, or of soldiers in his small, private army it was hard to tell.

Me? I said nothing. I was thinking. I was thinking: he's right. It is hard. And not a little bit odd.

CHAPTER THREE

I remember a line from one of the early James Bond books. It went something like this:

'Once is happenstance. Twice is coincidence. Three times is enemy action.'

What do you call four?

About seven thirty, he suggested we call it a night, and go for a 'quick one.' I knew about lawyers' 'quick ones'. They were the ones that hit you hardest. You weren't expecting to get smashed. They sort of crept up on you and by the time you knew it, you were well away. I'd spent the best part of the last several years perfecting the art.

The pub he took me to was just outside the Inner Temple. 'The Witness Box'. There were a couple of tables on the street, but the bar was downstairs. Like a dungeon. It was crowded at the time we arrived, mostly with barristers. The sound of plum hitting roof of mouth bounced off the cellar walls.

Several of his colleagues were in the pub. Mainly the younger ones, people who'd come in even after Nicholas. But Jane Daws was there, who'd joined at about that time and whom I'd known before.

I never did quite understand what tagged her a socialist: she spent more time dressing and making up than reading the Collected Works. When she opened her mouth she sounded like a fishwife: high-pitched shriek, everything she said was either plain stupid, or just superfluous. She wasn't bad looking, I guess, in a superficial sort of way: curly, mouse-brown hair, light eye make-up, skinny.

When we came in, Keenan was quick to explain what I was up to, and that I was interested in how come so many people had left his group. They were on their best behaviour. I don't mean actually good. The best they knew how in the circumstances. They wanted me to see them as one big happy family.

I was introduced to the others. Errol Cornell was mid-twenties, black; hanging from his shoulder was a 'personal stereo'. The things that drive you crazy on the underground. Not loud enough to listen to, but making a monotonous, tinny scratching sound that prevents you concentrating on anything else.

Then there was Gerry Gilligan. He was a tall, thin bloke, with a biker's helmet and a tarnished leather jacket at his feet. I didn't figure him for gay. Quite the opposite. You could smell what the women were thinking about him.

I'm talking about Jane Daws. And Marguerita Bradkinson. If anyone could've made me want to bother again, she was it. In stark contrast to Jane, she was dressed down — sloppily, chaplinesque in baggy trousers, scuffed shoes, a jacket that was too big for her by several sizes. Also: messy long blonde hair. Nor slim. Indeed, distinctly chubby. But impish. The sort of face you could think it was worth the effort just to wake up next to. When she went to the toilet, my eyeballs went with.

The other woman was, like Cornell, black. As I recollect, when I last knew those chambers there hadn't been a black face amongst them. I guess they were in fashion, because, suddenly, there were two. I must be racist or something because I couldn't get all the way round her name. She didn't have much to say for herself. Just sat watching Gilligan, and Keenan. Not me.

It wasn't only the women who had the hots for Gilligan. I'd met Arthur Farquharson before. He joined the group, I guess, a year or two earlier than Anne Godwin. In those days, he was extremely suave, women rang up for him all the time; in the pub after a conference there was always one lying around in his pocket. His prematurely balding fair hair gave him a distinguished look, his face was all kindness, and he dressed like daddy's allowance was more than the rest of them had to live on.

He'd come out pretty soon after joining. His clothes had gone butch: leather jackets, designer dungarees (with a wee red loop on one side that couldn't hold a toothbrush, let alone a hammer,) thick, hob-nailed shoes. Also, a bushy moustache. If I hadn't seen him on the streets of Earl's Court just after closing time, I'd seen a thousand like him.

Keenan left us soon after he'd bought a round. It took me a little while, but wasn't difficult, to bring the subject back to Nicholas. They were willing to talk about anything I wanted. So long as it had to do with them.

Marguerita asked, all innocent eyes and joggling boobs:

'Do you really think a lot of people have left? I mean, for the size of the group, and the time it's been going?'

I hadn't until Keenan gave me the full break-down.

'Perhaps not. Not for the straight bar, anyway.' I had the key to answering all their questions. Implying they ought to be viewed somehow differently from other lawyers was enough to show I knew they were 'special'.

'But if you add the three who died,' I dropped in casually.

Gilligan was watching me closely. I had to be careful.

'Yeah. You've certainly been kind of unlucky ...'

'Unlucky? Dropping like flies,' a voice boomed from above and behind me.

I grinned. I'd know that voice anywhere:

'Fat Harry ...'

'To the last pound...' He grabbed a stool from a neighbouring table and stuck it halfway up his back-side:

'How are you? We haven't seen you around here for a long time. I thought you'd quit practice? Did you bring me a brief?'

I laughed. He had that effect on me. Anything he said could make me laugh.

The conversation came back to the less voluntary deserters. I was interested in them all, and had to remind myself that it was Jack Nicholas for whom I was being paid to find a palatable epitaph.

'I heard he'd been drinking a lot the night it happened ...'

I spoke offhandedly. It was like throwing a dart straight into someone's eye. You could hear a corpse fart.

'We don't talk about it much,' Harry said firmly. He was the most senior member present, and not afraid to remind them:

'We miss him a lot. We were all very fond of him ...'

I don't like it when people lie to me. This was a group of fifteen to twenty barristers. And socialists. There wasn't a cat's chance in hell that they were 'all' fond, let alone 'very fond', of him.

Gilligan got me out of Harry's corner.

'He hadn't had that much to drink ... None of us had.'

Harry frowned at him. The others looked embarrassed.

For a moment, it looked as if the party was going to break up. Fat Harry got up to leave, which took care of half the bodyweight in the pub. Art Farquharson, too, after one, last, lingering, eyeball caress of Gilligan's lanky limbs, headed for the wilds of my part of town. The black woman had children to attend to. Errol followed her out.

That left Gilligan, Marguerita Bradkinson and Jane Daws. And me.

I had to get things moving. Desperate, I went to an extreme: 'Anyone want another drink?'

That's another thing about lawyers. They're all mean. They never say no. The round cost me the best part of three quid. I wrote down a fiver for expenses.

'How did you get on with Alex?' Jane asked, bright green.

'He has a lot to say ...' I grinned, to let them know I was an ally.

You'd never hear a word against him, though. Their relationship with him was positively umbilical. It was all between the lines. He had such a great reputation, he had been around so long, they could never hope to catch up. It gave them security. At a price. Forever the shadows.

'He represented the Nicholas family at the inquest, didn't he?'

Gilligan's eyes narrowed. He was beginning to wonder what time I was keeping.

'It was a gesture. For the family. We were genuinely upset, you know.' Like I said, every word she spoke was superfluous.

'I'm not surprised,' I said mildly:

'If you take the people who've gone off somewhere else, and the people who've died, that's quite a chunk of the group you've managed to lose ...'

Gilligan to Bradkinson: quick look. I took a shot in the dark:
'Why did Orbach leave?'

It was a fair question for my cover. But my interest was about as genuine as their grief over Jackdaw.

'Before our time,' Marguerita said, sucking Gilligan up into her answer.

All eyes were on the Daws.

She flushed:

'You know we don't talk about it,' she told the others.

'Hey, what's the big deal?' Somehow I managed to convey: if we don't talk about what I want to talk about, we don't talk.

Gilligan said:

'"Twas in a foreign country and besides the wench is dead ...'

'But who was the wench?'

I told you there'd been a lot of rumours at the time Orbach left. I also said most of them had been about money and professional jealousy. I should've added, the song of sex could also be heard in the not too distant background.

Jane Daws got up to go to the toilet. My eyes stayed behind.

'Tell me about the others ... Wishart and Creemer.'

'Pete died ... Oh, about eighteen months ago. It was in Germany. He was there for a conference. You know he was very involved in Germany?'

I had a vague recollection. From years before. Soon after they started up as a chambers. He'd been peripherally involved, providing support — theoretical, moral, political, maybe legal, not actual or practical — to one of those German revolutionary groups which followed Baader-Meinhof. They had a name like: Red September, February 29th, White Christmas.

'Wasn't Orbach involved in that too?'

'The first I heard,' Gilligan answered.

My information was all out of date, from before they were born as barristers.

'What happened?'

'There was a fire. In the house where he was staying. It was pretty grisly.'

'We do seem ... We do seem to meet violent ends ...' Marguerita was genuinely frightened.

Gilligan reassured her:

'If people are going to die, at our ages, the odds are it won't be peacefully in bed.'

If that was his idea of comfort, I'd like to hear how he put the frighteners on. Marguerita had gone completely white. As Daws returned from the lavatory, she got up for them to leave together. Without Gilligan.

He watched me watch Marguerita leave.

'I thought you'd be going with her ...' I said.

'Nah. I've been. There's some places you don't want to go back to. You know?'

I knew. But I wouldn't mind finding out for myself.

We were the only two left.

'And Carrie? Did she meet a ... violent end too?'

'Yup.'

I waited.

He didn't tell.

I could've asked.

I could've bought him a drink.

I did neither:

'I guess I'll see you again. I'll be around for a bit.'

He grinned:

'Maybe.'

'Meaning?'

'Meaning like you've said, people don't seem to last long around here. I might not still be here.'

He didn't give a damn.

I decided I liked him. He was a real A1 shit stirrer: and, stirred shit was what the doctor had ordered.

I'd picked up enough to think about. The question was: where now? I knew what Captain Furillo would do. He'd leave it over for a week 'till the next episode. I couldn't give it a week. But I would give myself a night to sleep on it.

Sleep's a good sorter. You burn up what doesn't matter and wash off the rest to see it good and clear. When I woke, Jack Nicholas was light years away. The things that mattered were: the split with Orbach; and, all those advocates appearing before the highest court of them all

I had no in to Orbach except the same cover I'd used on Keenan. From what I remembered, Orbach was about ten times as smart and therefore ten times as likely to see through it. I did have another in that seemed worth a try.

One of the people who'd left the group was Sue Cannon. To become a solicitor. Remember? She was part of that small minority I'd kept in touch with from the old days. She'd always been kind to me. Given me as much work as I wanted. As a matter of fact, though I hate to admit it of any lawyer, she was one of the kinder people I ever knew.

Of course, she had her faults. They used to call her the drain. Because she could pour it away. Or the mouth for obvious reasons. (I mean: she talked a lot. Not the other. So far as I knew.)

I got my interview with her by shock tactics. Rang up and offered to buy her a meal. I even took her somewhere good: M'sieur Frog on the Essex Road. Her end of town. A lot of people seemed to have moved up that way. Only I was still stuck in bedsit bogland.

It was quite a few days before we met. I hadn't seen her for two or more years. Our transactions were always on the 'phone. She was there before me. So much for the joys of public transport. She waved at me from behind our table and her spectacles. She looked good.

'Hey. You lost weight.'

Her size of person (midget) couldn't carry spare.

'Yup.'

I glinted down at the ashtray:

'Ah ...'

I remembered when she'd quit. She'd undergone hypnosis to walk away from forty a day. That was when she started to put on weight. Switched from jeans to loose dresses.

'Nothing I like to see so much as someone fallen off the wagon ...'

She held a pack out to me. I shook my head:

'Uhuh. Smoke my own.'

Camel. And Southern Comfort to drink. When I could afford them. Which was now.

The owner came over:

'Hallo. Haven't seen you for a long time. Shall I explain the blackboard?'

We both ordered. Sue took a special: a fancy baked salmon. I was into as many steaks as I could put down to expenses. While it lasted.

'Wine?'

'Sue? Still drinking?' As if it could be in doubt.

She stuck her tongue out at me.

'Well? You're eating fish ...' I hesitated.

This was why I like Sue. Straight to the point:

'A bottle of house white for me. And a bottle of house red for him.'

It took to when we were considering whether to order another bottle each, or just the one more between us, to get the conversation around to Keenan's chambers.

'D'you ever regret quitting?'

'No. Certainly not.' She wasn't lying.

'D'you see much of them?'

'I brief one or two of them. That's all.'

'I guess … You wouldn't really have any close friends left there … Not since Carrie …'

She frowned:

'We weren't that close, you know. Not after I left.'

'I always thought …' It wasn't feigned surprise but genuine.

'You know how it is when you belong to these groups … When you leave, suddenly it's gone, you've become a non-person. With us or agin' us.'

'I never belonged to one …' Or anything else. But I had a faint idea what she was talking about.

'Why'd'you leave, Sue? You never really told me …'

'Oh, I don't know. It all seems so long ago now.'

We settled for a further bottle each.

'Things changed. As people joined. It wasn't the same as when it started. It was exciting at the beginning. New … Adventurous. We were like a family, or a team. It was personal, and the theory was that bit less important. We trusted each other, and each other's instincts. Later, it became all theory, no feeling, for each other or anyone else. I began to get sick of it …

'It's not very easy to explain. I'm a socialist, a believer,' she laughed, 'But I'm a realist. When we had a lot of people, a lot of theoretical chatter, everyone was trying to be leftier than thou ... Left-wing one-upmanship. There's always a yet more radical posture. It made me feel, well, there was lot of hypocrisy ... People, some of them with private money — actual or in anticipation — or good practices, making a living off the backs of the poor, and translating themselves into their saviours ... You must know the sort of thing I mean?

'Me. I got out.' But what she was saying put into words many of the reasons I'd quit.

'It's difficult to remember the examples now. Ireland. That's always a good one. Justifying the violence; oh, not supporting it, of course,' she ladled sarcasm all over the last two words, 'but explaining it. But, you know, they didn't have to live with it, and, well, some of the violence has been pretty extreme, pretty inhumane, unjustifiable on any terms ...

'But that's just an example. You got the same sort of attitude towards anywhere else in the world ... Anywhere except England, of course. Like India and Pakistan, Germany, the Middle East ...'

'How'd Orbach feel about that?' The Middle East. Israel. As a Jew, I knew I had mixed feelings.

She shrugged:

'I don't suppose any of them stopped to ask themselves. You weren't supposed to have feelings, just theories ...'

'Was that why he left?'

She shook her head:

'I don't think so. It may have been part of it ... Alienation ... I certainly felt that ...'

'Orbach,' I prompted:

'What actually happened? I never found out ...'

'Me either. They were pretty close-mouthed about it ... I know there was talk of legal action, by him ... Against them ... But I don't know for what ... I caught some of the rumours ... I should think you did too ...'

'It was all about money, wasn't it?' Meaning it wasn't.

'There was a rumour ... Nothing more than that ... That he'd been having a scene with Helen ... Helen Keenan ...'

I laughed out loud:

'She was ten years older than him!'

'So?'

I had displeased her.

She was getting to an age when there were people she fancied who were ten years younger than her.

I shrugged:

'I remember Orbach. And her. I went on a weekend in Wiltshire, chambers' outing, where she was. That was after he'd left, of course. But I wouldn't have thought ...'

She shrugged too.

'I don't know. That was what I heard. I couldn't find out more ...'

She was admitting she'd tried.

The owner hovered over us.

We discussed dessert and more wine for a few minutes. We used the break to visit, in turn, the toilets. I worked at a couple of French cartoons on the wall to make sure I'd forgotten everything I'd learned in school.

Once we were both sitting again, and the hardest part of breaking up meringue chantilly was over, I asked her what I really wanted to know.

'Tell me about Caroline? What did happen to her?'

She shuddered.

'I don't know all the details. I got it all second-hand. From the papers or from the group. But ... What I heard was that she was with this guy ... A black man ... Not quite living with him ... But seeing him a lot ... They had a row ...'

She really didn't want to describe it. She wasn't putting on a show. I wanted to hear. I had to ask:

'Go on ...'

'There were a lot of people ... Who said ... It was a heavy relationship ... I mean ... Very emotional ... Maybe violent ... He ... Well, I don't know ... I mean ... Didn't you read about it? It was all over the papers at the time!'

'I ... Well, I haven't been reading the papers for a while ...' Anyhow, not the stories with a lot of words in them.

'Oh, hell. He killed her. That's what they said and that's what it looked like. He had gone, gotten out, out of the country, back to Ghana, by the time she was found ... In her flat ... Did you ever go there? I did. Lots of times. That made it worse. I could see it. In her living-room. That's where they found her. Stabbed.'

She looked down at her wine. They'd already cleared away the dessert plates. I couldn't figure why she wouldn't look at me for a while. Then I saw the tears. Dropping slowly from her eyes. Two by two. At a steadily increasing pace. Who'd've thought it?

Eventually she looked up. She didn't bother to hide her tears. There wasn't much point. She finished off the story:

'She'd been stabbed eighteen times. I heard ... Her parents had her cremated ...'

She meant: she wasn't something to have stuffed and mounted over the mantelpiece.

She offered to drive me home. The amount she'd drunk, I figured the odds in favour of the tube.

I got on at the Angel, changed at King's Cross and walked home from Gloucester Road, instead of Earl's Court.

If I hadn't, I doubt I would've noticed I was being followed. Guys walking behind you down the Earl's Court Road late at night aren't news. When they don't bother, you might as well start hiding the mirror.

I played the usual games. Down Bina Gardens, turned left instead of right on the Old Brompton, back up Gloucester, right at Stanhope, all the way down through Harrington Gardens 'till I came out opposite the South Kensington station and cut through the arcade. He was waiting for me across the road, on the other side.

It was still possible I was a damned sight prettier than I was used to thinking. I crossed over, passed real close, gave him the bold eye of invitation, walked on and turned ostentatiously back to show I wanted him to follow. I was close enough when I looked around to see the sneer on his lips that told me it wasn't my arse he was after.

I'd never been tailed before. I knew one idea was to shake him. I just didn't know how. The other thing to do is tuck yourself out of sight, jump him, grab him, throw him up against a wall, slap his face every which way but straight and beat out of him the name of his boss. Oh, yeah. There's a third thing you can do. Get home as fast as your legs can carry you; and make damned sure you double lock the door.

The 'phone was ringing as I came in, out of breath.

The voice at the other end was garbled.

'Say it again,' I ordered.

'I said, Art Farquharson was killed last night.'

My caller was Gilligan. He was drunk. Dead drunk.

'How? When? Where? Tell me what you know.'

I hadn't missed the point: killed, not died.

'I don't know much. I only heard this afternoon. Was in court. When I got back ... Everyone knew ...'

'Tell me.'

'Not much to tell. He was found in the street. In Earl's Court. That's where you live, isn't it?'

I didn't rise to the innuendo.

'Do you know exactly where?'

'Coleherne Road. I remember the name. He used to mention a pub called the Coleherne. Where his cottaging clients hung out.'

Cottaging = public lavatory pick-ups = police set-ups = criminal charges.

I knew both. The pub, and the road. They were gay centres. Coleherne Road and the streets off it were where those who hadn't scored some company before closing time hung about to try their luck later.

They were about a minute away from where I stood, listening to what Gilligan had to tell me.

I began to sweat. The combination was claustrophobic. The physical nearness of the death. My involvement with those chambers.

Gilligan told me a bit more. I could have guessed some of it. Farquharson's body was a mess. Either he didn't have the details, or he couldn't bring himself to tell me. I didn't particularly want to hear. I'd got the general picture.

He had died in the early hours of the morning. The body hadn't been found 'till seven o'clock. The possibilities were wide open. Killed on the street. But no one who hung around Coleherne Road in the wee hours of the morning would have wanted anyone else to know that was where they street-walked.

Or, killed somewhere else and dropped where maybe the killer figured Farquharson'd feel most at home.

Neither of us spoke for a while.

Eventually, I asked the question I should've asked at the beginning:

'Why're you telling me?'

He laughed loudly:

'Didn't you want to know, Mr Woolf?'

'That's a Jewish habit, answering a question with a question. Gilligan doesn't sound Jewish to me?'

'Doesn't it?' He answered a question with a question. And hung up.

It took me the full minute to walk there. My tail took about six seconds longer. The spot was marked in two inanimate ways. It was roped off, between portable uprights. And, a uniformed policeman stood guard. I'd never seen Coleherne Road so deserted at that time of the night. Maybe the copper wasn't cute enough.

I walked past on the other side of the street. Crossed over at the top, opposite the Coleherne pub, and turned right. My tail would be getting giddy: we were going back the way I'd galloped home before the call.

I wasn't in a hurry this time. It was just before half past twelve. Still early. It took me a few minutes to find exactly where I wanted. A dim light in a smoked-glass shop window, with no markings outside. The door looked equally uninviting.

I rapped hard enough to hurt my knuckles. The door opened about a millimetre. One of the gorillas Lewis keeps around like barristers have clerks glowered out at me. Fortunately, he recognized me. He oughta. He'd been a most welcome visitor in my home. Discussing my family. And my welfare. And my debts.

He swung the door back silently. I always figured he had a hard time with words. I checked he wasn't planning to communicate with me the way he was most at ease. He kept his arms at his side. But his fists were clenched.

'Lewis here?' I asked chirpily, as if he might just be hanging around on the off-chance I dropped in. A bit of bone in the middle of his jaw disappeared inside his chins. I think it was his idea of affirmative.

I tripped up the stairs. I wasn't afraid any more. Light-headed. Like I was stoned.

'Sit down, David. It's nice to see you. Very nice.'

He spoke softly. Like he'd heard the Corleones do in the Godfather movies. Like someone had maybe told him refined gentlemen do.

He was dressed cute, too. A light, pale blue suit, of a hue that had not become modish until recently but cut like a thirties gangster. If I was into tie-knots, I'd wonder where he found the one that brought it out, high and firm, before it fell back in to his waistcoat. It had the same effect of making him look slender that a woman's boobs can have on her waistline.

'Would you like a drink, David? What would you like to drink?' He could not have been more solicitous. That was community work for you.

He held up his glass in suggestion.

'What is it?'

'Kir royale.'

I knew what that was. Champagne I couldn't afford with French alcoholic Ribena I couldn't stand. Besides, though light-headed, I wasn't exactly celebratory.

'S'Comfort?'

'Sure, David, whatever.'

He was the first person ever to recognize my personal abbreviation for the peach-based liquor which was one of the few original American alcoholic beverages to have gotten beyond the stills.

He snapped his fingers.

I sighed. I'd spent half three-score-and-ten years trying to learn how to do that. All I got was sore finger tips, and a tiny, brushing sound like I was trying to mimic a personal stereo at a distance.

'Large?'

'Leave the bottle ...'

The bunny reject suppressed a grin, and did as she was bid. She must have thought I was one of Lewis' closest. I got to him though: in just a fraction of second, a frown crossed his face.

'Ice?' She asked.

I shook my head, poured my own, and threw it down my throat like I hoped it would be the last job I ever had to finish.

'There's something on your mind, David ...'

'Yup. There's something on my mind.'

'You want to tell me about it?'

He coulda made it as a psychoanalyst if he hadn't got so many fuck-ups of his own.

'Last night. A queer got killed on Coleherne.'

'A lot of young men ... Of this persuasion ... Die ... Their games can tend to get a little rough ...'

Then he waited for me to go on.

'This one ... was a barrister ...'

He nodded. He knew.

'That makes it sort of news, don't you think?'

He shrugged:

'Perhaps. Is he ... Was he a matter of concern to you?'

That was delicate. 'A matter of concern.' It could mean what I let it mean. Lewis knew I was legal by qualification. And para-legal by so-called employment. His question could mean: professional relations. He'd never worked me out sexually. It could've meant something else.

I dignified his discretion:

'Yeah. Professionally. I've known him a few years. We had a bit to do with one another recently. As a matter of fact, I saw him about ten days ago.'

'A friend, then?'

If he was going to help me, he was entitled to know why:

'No. I was ... Interested in him.'

I helped myself to another wine-size shot of Southern Comfort.

He might've spent years practising to sound like a gentleman, but he couldn't help himself:

'Did you say ... You were paying for that?'

I grinned:

'Nope.'

I felt cocky:

'Some day, Lewis, you'll call it in ...' The favour.

He sighed, as if I might single-handedly bankrupt him:

'I always liked you, David. Even when we ... had our little difference ... That was business ... Just business ... I couldn't, you understand, I couldn't handle it any other way ... But ... That is why I like you ... Because I knew, I could feel,' he lowered his voice, and yet somehow managed to emphasize the last word:

'I could feel you understood ... That it wasn't ...' He thrashed around for another word, but that which is born of cliché must die as cliché:

'Personal ..'

'Sure, Lewis ...'

God only knew where I'd found my confidence. I felt like I was twenty-five. and had just won my first big case as a qualified solicitor.

He thought for a moment. Decided I was right. He didn't mind being into me for a favour.

'I can't tell you much. His name was Farquharson, but of course you know that,' he corrected himself. It took him time to recall he was dealing with someone who wasn't a complete ape.

'It didn't happen where he was found. He was brought there. No number. No make. The boy who saw isn't too fond of the butch pastimes …' Like cars.

'Will you give me his name?'

Lewis shook his head. His boys belonged to him. Body and name.

'Anything else?'

'You know what sort of state he was in?'

'No. I didn't cop the news.'

He laughed. To make up for his earlier ill-grace, he reached over and refreshed my glass.

'They're not telling it on the news …'

I waited. My stomach didn't. It was already churning as if it already knew.

He leaned towards me, and dropped his voice, to a whisper. Not, I should say, out of secrecy. Nor another bout of delicacy. More like a treat too good to share:

'Double-barrelled, up his …' He didn't need to finish. I was already there. So was a third of a bottle of Southern Comfort. In my mouth.

When I got back from the bog, Lewis had been joined by a face I didn't know. He grinned when he saw me. Held out a hand in welcome.

'Meet my solicitor, Mr Woolf. This is Detective Sergeant Dowell. An old friend. An old friend indeed.'

'I've got to go, Lewis. Nice to meet you, Sergeant. Speak to you again?' I shot at Lewis as I raced myself to the door.

'I'm sure. I'm sure.' I heard him answer me.

I stopped running about two and half inches from the steps to my flat, leaned against the railings to gather my breath. That, I thought, was stupid.

CHAPTER FOUR

I got through what was left of the night without an invasion by armed police. Nor were they waiting for me outside my door when I emerged shortly after midday.

Nor, so far as I could tell, was anyone following me when I made my way up to the corner shop to buy the papers.

Lewis wasn't right about everything. The papers had got it, in full. They were happy to use it. I was spoiled for choice.

The Times. 'Police are still investigating the death in Earl's Court on Wednesday night or Thursday morning of Mr Arthur Farquharson, a barrister …'

The Sun. 'Barrister Art Farquharson's death in a sleazy street haunted by homosexuals is still puzzling police …'

The Guardian. 'Thir hav ben know furth devments in th allegedly French Prime Minister insisted that his homolexusal murdr. ..'

The Star. 'ADVOCATE'S ANAL ENDING.'

The moment of light-headedness which had carried me to my community worker's command centre had vanished. It was replaced with another, much more familiar, feeling. Not to put too fine a point on it, I was scared shitless. Someone out there was into death in a heavy way. I was supposed to be finding out who. You know what killers do to people who find out what they're up to. Before you can talk to anyone else. Ugh.

With mixed intentions, I rang the Nicholas residence. His holiness answered.

'Is Mrs Nicholas available?' I asked in my snottiest tone of voice.

'Who is this, please?'

'This is the furniture department at Harrods ...'

'Oh, just a moment, please.'

I figured them for the perfect couple. Her with her thank-yous; him all pleases.

'Mrs Nicholas? Mr Woolf, furniture department at Harrods ...'

'Yes, Mr Woolf ...' she dropped her voice:

'The Reverend Nicholas has gone into his study. Did you want to see me?'

We had arranged this 'call-sign' at our initial interview.

'Yes ... Please.' The word didn't taste as bad as I had expected.

'Can you tell me ... Do you have some news?'

Did I have some news? Sure. Me and every newspaper in the country. I figured she hadn't hit them yet.

I got out of telling her. With a bit of luck, she'd've heard for herself, before I met her. We made a date for the next day, Friday. Same place, same time. It was acquiring the air of an affair.

I had twenty-four hours to make up my mind. There was quite a lot of me inclined to — if you'll forgive the pun — jack it in then and there, tell Mrs Reverend I wasn't her man, even give her the money back if she asked politely.

On the other hand, I'd be lying through my eye-teeth if I denied I was excited. There was another feeling. Obscure. One that took me most of the day to dig out of the recesses of my underused conscience. Something about an obligation to see it through.

There'd been about a year between the first two deaths. Approximately six months again to the next. Farquharson had followed after only two more. It was too much like the sort of coincidence I didn't believe in to think it had nothing to do with the fact I was around and asking questions. Like I said, put the pressure on and hope the needle pops out of the haystack. It wasn't way outside the realms of possibility it was me that had pooped the pimple that was Art.

I spent the rest of the day doing a little research. I wanted to know more about the Creemer killing. As with Farquharson, the papers said a great deal, but told me nothing I didn't know. Wishart was harder work: He hadn't attracted a lot of attention in life; likewise in death. I finally found a paragraph in the Guardian, which, once the print had been unscrambled, suggested he had probably died twenty-four or forty-eight hours before the story appeared. Good times must've flown. It was closer to two years than the eighteen months I'd been told.

It seemed to me obvious that I was now investigating the methodical despatch of a barrister's chambers.

There are two aspects of this I found faintly confusing. First, albeit of lesser importance, was the fact that anyone could conceivably consider barristers worth killing. Secondly, the fact that the investigator was I. I brushed these irrelevancies aside, and settled down to study.

The difficulty with the thesis was the way Carrie Creemer had died. With the others, what was known was nothing. That left me free to believe what I wanted. Anything could be true. But from the newspaper accounts, and the little Sue Cannon had added before we separated at M'sieur Frog's, there was nothing at all to connect Creemer's man to her chambers.

Of course, we didn't actually know he had done it. It didn't need him to have fled the country for it to have looked that way. Given cops' attitudes to blacks — especially those with the nerve to sleep with a paleface — he was like as not to have been charged even if he'd made the call that brought them in. If he had come back, and found her the way the papers described, he would have every reason to fear the consequences, and might just lack that unshakeable faith in British justice that could have led someone else to the nearest 999.

If I put Creemer's death on one side of the line, and her colleagues — sorry, comrades — on the other, the way it weighed up didn't balance. Ignore Creemer. Consider Wishart. Nicholas. Farquharson. They added up — in James Bond's terms — to enemy action. Look across the line at Creemer. Without the possibility that her boyfriend was innocent, it would still hardly change the dip of the scales. With that possibility, I was amply justified in what I believed.

My only job the next morning was to get hold of Anne Godwin. She was in court first thing and I didn't catch her until just before I had to go and see my client.

Somehow, I got the idea I wasn't exactly the burning desire she'd returned from holiday dying to fulfil.

'Dave?'

'Yeah. Dave Woolf ...'

'I know.'

She wasn't questioning who I was. Just why.

I figured they'd had enough to talk about in chambers, since she'd been back, that no one had told her about my arrival on the scene.

Wrong again.

'Alex mentioned you'd been in to see him ... Why do you want to see me?'

'Well, isn't that a warm welcome,' I muttered, mildly mortified.

'Well, OK, I suppose so, if you really want to ...'

Gee, thanks.

It wouldn't be until after the weekend that she could fit me in, though.

Beggars can't be choosers.

I was so late, I not only took a taxi, but even forgot to write down the fare.

Mrs Nick took her usual time getting down to business:

'What have you found out, Mr Woolf?'

'Hadn't you better sit down first?' I helped her off with her coat, placed her hat on the vacant chair, and showed her how it was done.

I had already ordered tea. I wouldn't answer until she had drunk half a cup. After all, it was her money.

'Now. Tell me.'

I don't know why. You can't explain this sort of thing. She wasn't just a client any more. But a frail, middle-aged woman, whom I liked and wanted to help. I felt ... I don't know. Filial?

'I've ... You've read the papers?'

I had hoped that between yesterday's call, and today's meeting, she would've got halfway there.

I could remember a similar sort of sensation when I was in practice. I'd be really tied up in someone's case. Writing letters. Making calls. Negotiating a good deal. Then they'd come to see me. I'd be bubbling with success. They couldn't understand. They thought I was selling them out. They hadn't been into the dark corners of their own cases like I had. Nor heard what the other side had to say. They hadn't gone through the tunnel I was being paid to find an end of for them. They couldn't appreciate the light when they saw it.

She shook her head slowly:

'My husband sees the papers. He's usually a day or two behind. I don't read them until he's finished. We don't ... He doesn't ... We don't,' I was relieved she'd decided who she was talking about:

'We don't pay a lot of attention to worldly matters.'

She meant: he doesn't.

'I'm sorry. There's been ... Another death ...'

She understood immediately what I meant. She went as ghoulishly white as her hair was blue-rinsed. I pushed her cup and saucer towards her.

I almost pushed her the tray of cream cakes too, but I guessed it wasn't that good an idea and stopped myself in time.

I told her what I knew. I edited it. I told her there had been four deaths. Until the day before yesterday, there were only three. I admitted I might have been ready to ascribe three to a lousy run of luck. Wishart and her son seemed accidental. Creemer had certainly been murdered, and the finger pointed at an untraceable African.

'Three deaths ...' She had managed to forget the fourth.

'But they're so young ...'

She was going is the direction I'd followed.

I told her what, after all, were the only two solid points of information about her own son:

'The accident was suspicious, or ought to have caused suspicion. That is correct. Your impression that no one cared, including his colleagues, would also seem to be correct. But ... Well, I have no idea yet why Keenan wasn't anxious to turn the inquest into a search for something more ...'

'Thank you.' She had heard nothing new, unless that she was right came as a surprise.

There was a cupful of silence.

'You ... You don't believe my son's death was an accident, then?' She returned to my company.

I shrugged:

'I don't know, Mrs Nicholas. I don't know,' I emphasized the last word:

'But, no, to use your word, I don't believe it. Wishart? Well, accidents do happen. Creemer? People get killed ...'

'You haven't told me,' she reminded me softly I still hadn't filled her in on Farquharson.

'And I'm not going to.'

The sun must've burst into the room, because my face felt hot and flushed.

'But ... It wasn't an accident?'

'No, ma'am. It wasn't an accident. I'd say. Closer to the Creemer killing.'

She was taut with tension. Her first instinct was predictable:

'You must go to the police, Mr Woolf. You must tell them what you know.'

'What do I know, Mrs Nicholas? Nothing. Precisely nothing. Two accidents. Two murders. They must know that much for themselves, already.'

'But it's a matter for them. Wouldn't you agree?'

It's a funny thing. I could swear she was playing devil's advocate. Manoeuvring me into saying:

'I'm not sure.'

'Why?'

Not: of course you must go to the police, Mr Woolf; how could you think of doing anything else; you must leave it to the experts; they'll know what to do. Why? It was my job to give voice to her instincts.

I didn't answer her at once. I hailed the waiter. Tea, hot, lots of it. There's an idea about to be born. I waited 'till after it had arrived, and even until after it had been allowed time to mash. She poured.

'Just suppose ... Suppose I'm right that what we're looking at is ... Well, some sort of vendetta against your son's chambers ...

'And go to the other thing. I said Keenan wasn't pushing the coroner into a corner. Now maybe that's innocent. Maybe, just maybe, he was trying to minimize publicity, pain, and so on ...'

She waved her hand impatiently: that wasn't it.

'All right. If that wasn't it, then why? Then whatever it's about is something known, at least to Keenan, possibly others in the chambers ...'

I should have paused at, instead of brushing aside, the question: why would anyone think barristers worth killing?

She digested my reasoning with as much struggle as if I'd tried to get her to eat a hearty meal laid out on her son's coffin. But she was no slouch. It didn't take her too long to get there:

'Whatever that would be ... Would be something Jack knew about?'

'Maybe. Or was involved in.'

'I don't think, Mr Woolf, you knew my son very well. He would never ... He was never ... He could never be involved in anything ... Anything ...'

She couldn't finish the sentence, so I did it for her:

'Anything shameful? I don't know, Mrs Nicholas. I'm not saying he was. But you hung in there while I spelled it out for you. And we both got to the same place. Maybe ... Maybe what you or I might not consider shameful, he would. Who knows? Do you think ... Are you sure you knew him that well?'

I was taking the risk of upsetting her. You don't make omelettes.

I stopped thinking.

Time stood still.

I don't think I have ever in my entire life met anyone as stupid as me.

'Mr Woolf? Mr Woolf? Are you all right?'

I nodded slowly. All right. But not all there.

'Have you got a diary, Mrs Nicholas?'

'Yes. Of course ...'

She fished her Protestant Page-A-Day from her handbag:

'Here ...'

It was my turn. I tried the other words:

'Thank you.'

From the inside jacket of my pocket, I took the notes I'd made the night before. I didn't really need to bother. I knew what I would find anyway.

'They had a meeting ... A chambers' meeting ... Once a month ... On the last ...'

'The last Wednesday. I know. Whenever we were arranging to see them, it was the one permanent commitment ...'

I pointed to the dates on my notes. And then to the dates on the page of her diary which had last year, this year and next set out at a glance.

'No. I don't understand ... Oh, wait a minute. Oh ... Oh ...'

For a second, I thought she was going to faint. Until that moment, we were talking suspicion. Perhaps strong suspicion. Perhaps probability. From then on we were talking proof positive. Each of the deaths had taken place on the last Wednesday of a month.

'Don't you think ... That ... That's enough to go to the police with?'

I shrugged:

'Maybe. Yes. Sure. I can go to the police. I can tell them what I know. Then. They take over. OK? Is that enough for you?'

Logically, she ought to say: yes, do that. That was what her life's experience should have dictated. This was not about her life. It was about her son's death:

'What would Jack have done?' I asked softly, gently, as only someone with an unbeatable hand can do.

She nodded slowly. Her son was a socialist. In a barristers' chambers. He trusted the police about as far as Lewis did. Or me. I was gambling some of it might have rubbed off on his mother.

'I ... I don't agree with him ... I don't think he was right ... But ...'

Jackdaw's politically assumed hatred of the police coincided with what she wanted. She couldn't have spelled out why. A dash of faith in Jack. A gut feeling that if the police got their hands on it, it would turn out wrong, or not turn out at all. A light seasoning of wanting to keep control of it.

We talked money before we split. I'd long run over the payment on account. She didn't flinch when I asked for the same again. Wrote a cheque out. And paid for the tea. As she rose, she smiled:

'That's not all you've cost me today, Mr Woolf…'

I raised my eyebrows in question.

'Couldn't you have thought of a department other than furniture? Where I could have bought something small?'

I laughed as she left.

I was still laughing as I noticed a familiar face rise from a table by the door, and follow her out.

Then I stopped laughing.

We wove our way through the store, like a New Year's Eve dancing snake by relatives who couldn't bear to touch one another. Mrs Nicholas. My unfruitful fan from the night before. Me.

In furniture, he and I hesitated. He wanted a good position to watch from and catch her exit. I couldn't locate myself until he had.

The lady didn't linger long. I grinned as she gazed at a group of dining-room chairs. She was checking prices, observing details, preparing her explanation of why she had changed her mind about a purchase.

Outside, the doorman hailed a cab for her. Gimbo hovered nearby, to catch her destination. Then, nonchalantly, uninterested, he walked down to Hans Place, where he was parked. As he crumpled and threw into the gutter the ticket stuck on his windscreen, he turned and saw me watching. He made no attempt to hide from me; stared straight at me; grinned. As I approached him, he climbed into his car and drove away without another glance.

I wandered slowly back towards my flat. Stopped for a drink at the Drayton Arms. Settled into a corner from where I could see both entries to the bar. Waited as long as it took me to read the London Standard from cover to cover — ten minutes, including the stock market prices. Then, home.

The light was on in my flat. The safety lock wasn't. I'd been burgled 'till there wasn't anything left worth stealing. I was more scared there'd still be someone inside.

'I hope you don't mind,' the Detective Sergeant held up a glass.

'If you've finished it, I will ...'

'Not at all. I brought a bottle.' He gestured to the mantelpiece. He had too.

'I was right, wasn't I?'

'S'Comfort? Sure. Shall I help myself?'

'It's your flat ...'

'Uh. Right. Which sort of reminds me ...'

He shook his head:

'Warrant? Nah. Never believed in them. You don't need them if you've got grounds to suspect a crime in progress.'

'And you've always got those?'

He laughed and finished off what was in his glass:

'If I haven't when I go in, I usually have by the time I leave.'

He looked a bit like a weasel. I felt I ought to get out a tape-measure. Check he was regulation minimum height. But it was his head that was small, and sharp, not his body. I decided maybe not to get too fresh.

I sat down opposite him, and pushed his bottle over. He poured himself another shot. If it'd been full when he arrived, one thing he did well was to hold his liquor.

'I've been checking up on you, Mr Woolf ...'

'Surprise, surprise.'

'You don't have a practice certificate, do you?'

'Uh. Practising certificate? Right. I've heard of them ... They're, well, sort of expensive ...' Checking up on people was something else he obviously did well.

'But illegal to practise without ... So if our mutual friend ...' Lewis.

' ... Calls you his solicitor, I've got to draw one of two conclusions. He's a liar or you are practising illegally. Which one would you go for, Mr Woolf?'

'Well, I guess that would depend ...'

'On?' When his eyes narrowed, you wouldn't've thought he could see the camel, let alone the needle.

'On who you want to hurt more?'

'Wrong, Mr Woolf. Your premise is wrong. I don't learn anything when I find out Lewis is telling me lies ...'

'OK, it's a fair cop, guv, you got me bang to rights ... Except ... You can't prove that I'm actually practising ...'

'No. But your bank manager thinks you are.'

'Ah'

DS Dowell — I had just remembered his name — had been working overtime. I'd change banks if I could find another one to take over the debt.

'He says ... Of course, he could be a liar too ... We could always pit your word against his ... He says he loaned you money on an assurance that you were going back to work as a solicitor ... And, indeed ...' He reached into his Marks & Sparks jacket and pulled out his notebook:

'That you told him you had the promise of work from a property company ... Called ... Drakus Barkell? Is that right?'

"So?'

'So obtaining a bank loan by deception is obtaining a pecuniary advantage by deception and is an offence under the Theft Act as ... I think ... You ... Must ... Know ...' After a long, melodramatic pause, he added:

'Sir.'

It makes me very unhappy when people call me sir. I know it can't be genuine respect, so it's gotta be a put-down.

'You ... Uh ... You've discussed ... This ... Er ... Aspect with my bank manager, have you?'

'Certainly not, Mr Woolf.' He looked shocked as he flatly contradicted what he'd told me ten seconds before:

'Discussing a man's private financial affairs with his bank. Whatever next? Is nothing sacred, etcetera, etcetera ... No. I merely made some discreet enquiries. He happened to pop out for a moment, while I was in his office. Left the file on his desk, you know ... Careless ...'

'Christ, he's got all that written down?'

Dowell nodded dourly:

'Contemporaneous note, I shouldn't wonder ...'

Contemporaneous notes were admissible evidence in court. The odds in favour of twelve good men and true believing a word I said were lengthening as quick as we were getting through the S'Comfort.

'There is ... no such company as Drakus Barkell, is there, sir?'

I grinned:

'Name came from an old legal magazine. But ... You haven't come here to arrest me, have you ... ?'

It might've been a question, but I was pretty sure of my ground. No detective buys a bottle of a guy's favourite hooch, breaks into his house and waits half the evening for him to arrive home just to bust him for a little bit of pecuniary advantage.

'No, Mr Woolf ... Or may I call you Dave? No, Dave, I haven't ... Nor've I come to put the bite on you.'

He was way ahead of me. I hadn't had time to think it.

'So?'

'So I've come to have a drink with you ... That's all. OK?'

'Lewis. You want something on Lewis? I'd better tell you I don't know him that well ...'

'Wrong again, Dave. I can have Lewis any time I want. I don't want. He's ... He's useful where he is ...'

He was, of course, a much bigger cake to take a slice out of than me.

My confidence had returned. He could've had me, hut didn't want to. He didn't want money. That meant he wanted something else.

'You enjoying this?' Tap-dancing.

He tossed his little head lightly, rhythmically, from side to side:

'I don't mind. You?'

I laughed:

'I haven't eaten. I'm going to scramble some eggs, toast. Got a bit of bacon, too ... You want?'

'Yup. Go down nicely on top of this.'

He followed me into the kitchen. Carrying this with him.

While I cooked, we talked about the usual things: the three Ws — weather, women, and wallies we knew in common.

We ate in silence.

Then we got down to business.

'Art Farquharson. I understand you knew him?'

Dear Lewis. Such a nice, trustworthy chap.

'Wrong again, Davy ...'

'I don't mind Dave ... But Davy? Do you have to?' My father called me Davy. With his money he could call me anything he chose.

He chuckled:

'My name's Tim. The last person called me Timmy needed plastic surgery.'

'Well, Tim, give ... *Genug mit der guessing ...*'

'You've been hanging around Disraeli Chambers ...'

'Ah. I don't suppose you'd believe I was briefing them on a case? No. I didn't think so.'

'Question. Why? Question. What do you know? Question. Where are you going?'

'Answer. Privileged. Answer. There's a lot of second-hand wigs for sale. Answer. If I knew, I probably wouldn't be here.'

'Let's talk wigs. Wishart was first. Then Creemer. Then Nicholas. Then Farquharson. Four deaths. Right?

'Right. What else do you know?'

He sighed:

'Not enough. They don't seem to trust me; As far as they're concerned, it's a lot of coincidence. They spend so long in court telling juries we're stupid or liars, they've begun to believe it. What do you think?'

'I think maybe you ain't necessarily stupid ...' I passed on the other.

'A guy in the station ... Few years back ... In his locker ... Had this cartoon pinned up ... Showed two hippy types returning home and finding they'd be burgled ... The guy's saying: "We've been robbed — call the pigs ..." Geddit?'

'They're not ...'

'No. That makes me suspicious. Doesn't it?'

'What do you say?'

'I used to say: Wishart was a well-roasted accident. The coon cooled Creemer. Nicholas? Well, all right, let's say I was getting suspicious. But ... He wasn't too drunk to ride his bike. And whoever fucked the faggot's got a funny sense of humour.'

He'd told me nothing.

'Why did the police go along with a coroner's cover- up?'

'To help me. Even if you've got an accident verdict, you can still prosecute for murder. It has no real effect. Except to make whoever it is feel a little safer ...'

'Equals careless?'

'That's the usual scenario. Who're you working for?'

'Mrs Nicholas ...' What the hell. He'd find out sooner or later.

'What do you figure?'

'I figure on giving up the case. It's way out of my league. One thought ... A some-time member of the group? There's a few who've left ... in a not-so-happy atmosphere ...'

He shrugged:

'Would any barrister have the bottle?'

'You're the copper ... You tell me.'

He poured us both another drink:

'What else do you think?'

'What do you want from me?'

'You've got contacts ... You're one of them ... They'll talk to you ...'

For the first time it occurred to me. He was a little jealous. I was a solicitor, a professional. He was, after all, just a pig.

'Which means?'

'Which means we work in two ways. I stay outside ...'

'And I work inside?'

'Clever boy ...'

I thought this over for a long time. Say, ten seconds?

Tell me, officer, Detective Sergeant, Timothy dearest, or whatever you want me to call you. What happens if I decline to assist you in your enquiries?

Well, sir, you remember that business about the bank manager ...

'I said,' he reminded me:

'What else do you think?'

I couldn't see the harm in telling him:

'A grudge against those chambers ... Yeah?'

'Probably. Why?'

I gave him the last Wednesday. He hadn't known about the regular chambers' meetings, although he had put the dates together.

'Let's narrow the field down a bit ...'

'Give ...'

'Take the four who are dead. Wishart and Creemer were in at the start, right?'

'Right.'

'But Nicholas came later, and so did Farquharson.'

'Right.'

That gave us a date to start from. Whatever we were talking about was no earlier than when Farquharson — last of the four to join the group — had done so. As an end-date, we could take when the deaths started, when Wishart died, the first to go. Six years: 1976-1982.'

'It's a lot of time ...' My lack of enthusiasm was ill-concealed.

He shared out the remains of the bottle:

'You scared of hard work, Dave?'

I shook my head:

'Not hard work ...' I paused, then asked:

'You been following me?'

'Me?'

'Your people …'

'It's a funny thing, Dave. If everyone who was being watched by the police really was being, and everyone who thought their 'phones were tapped was right, and everyone who swears the police open their post … You know? Nothing else'd ever get done.'

'I didn't ask about anyone else …'

'Sorry, counsellor. No. Are you sure you're being followed? It's easy enough to think … If, maybe,' he grinned:

'You're a little nervy …' Spelled scared.

I threw what was left of my drink into the back of my throat:

'Yes. I'm sure I'm being followed. And by someone who knows my movements before I get there …'

It was a fair guess. Gimbo might've followed my taxi from home to Harrods. But I hadn't found one 'till I was already on the Old Brompton Road. Where would he have been parked? Could he have gone back for his car and caught up with my cab? He hadn't even tried that game with Mrs Nicholas.

For the first time, I had a feeling I'd caught Dowell off balance. His face was pale enough for the difference to be hardly discernible. But I could've sworn he blanched.

All he said though was:

'I'm not having you followed. I've not tapped your telephone. All right?'

I shrugged:

'Then who is?'

He didn't even bother to deny knowing. Picked up his glass, drained it, got up and walked out of the flat. He hadn't given me a number to reach him. He'd be in touch with me.

It was late. I went to bed so's the hangover didn't start before I had a chance to sleep some of it off.

I've told all I knew by the time I saw Anne. Nothing else happened. I learned no more. Before I met her, I'd made up my mind to tell her what I was really up to. What I didn't expect was her reaction:

'Who's paying you?'

'How many of you people have got to die before you do something about it?'

A lot of silence. A little meaningless chatter. Then she said, softly, going straight hack to the question and counter-question that counted:

'Alex already is.'

CHAPTER FIVE

At the end of the week after I saw Anne Godwin, Russel Orbach was in Oslo.

I know, because I was there too.

When I saw him, he was with an elderly lady.

I wasn't. I was with a young one: Marguie Bradkinson.

I wasn't too sure what I was doing there until I saw him. Then I began to have an idea.

Also, I began to feel not so very different from how I felt immediately after Anne Godwin told me:

'Alex already is.'

Stupid.

I'd been set up.

And it felt like: not for the first time.

'Alex already is.'

I repeated the words after her like an incantation. Like she was teaching me the language. I had this image of a massive concert hall, filled with people, all chanting:

'Stupid. Stupid. Stupid.'

The whole world was ahead of me. Only I had taken so much time to work it out I thought it was the biggest mystery since Peter asked Paul:

'Who shopped the boss?'

If I'd been given the case, you'd still be wondering.

I contemplated my shoes.

They were big, to fit big feet.

They could do a lot of walking.

South of the river?

I put this suicidal thought aside and comforted myself with the thought that if I'd realized sooner just what a secret it wasn't, I'd be down more than a thousand pounds.

'Tell.' I spat the command at her from behind gritted teeth.

She'd been watching me think. It was that obvious. The wheels grinding.

She shrugged:

'What's to tell?'

She was evading the question.

The penny dropped. She hadn't sensed how stupid I felt. The penny climbed back into my pocket. The whole world wasn't ahead of the game. Only them. And me.

'Forgive me, sweetheart ...'

I paused to give her time to tell me to lose the language.

She didn't.

Then I knew for sure she was on the defensive.

'There's someone out there,' I waved a hand expansively as if to take in the skies, 'till I remembered abashedly we were in the confined well of an enclosed market: 'who doesn't just want you dead, but is getting on with the job like he was being paid piece-rate? Diggit? You know about it. Right? Well, there's one tiny question; not, perhaps, the most important in the world, but just one wee curiosity that's niggling away in the back of my mind. Who?'

She shrugged again. Maybe it was some new kind of esoteric exercise: I-shrug. Like I-sometric.

I tried again:

'Let's start at the beginning. What do you know?'

'We know ... We know some one's ... Got it in for us ...

She had the grace to blush at how lame it sounded. Like some solicitor wasn't sending them work any more. Or a friend was badmouthing her behind her back.

Spreading foul rumours — like she'd once had a scene with me.

The conversation didn't pick up. I squeezed out of her that: after Jack died, someone spotted the dates; their suspicion turned to certainty the night Art Farquharson took a shit the wrong way round; and, they hadn't told the police.

'Why not?'

She bit her lower lip.

I-bite?

'Anne,' I said gently:

'I'm asking you why not. If you don't answer me, I'm going to ask you again, now, here, and real loud — how come you haven't told the police there's been four murders? You want me to repeat the question? How come you haven't told the police there's been four murders?'

The second time I raised my voice just a bit. Just enough to make the point. She didn't give me the chance to try-out for cheer-leader.

'People ... People are afraid ...'

'I should think they are ...'

She shook her head:

'No. That's not what I mean. Yes. They're afraid that way too. But ... They're afraid of what will happen if it gets out ...' She was almost whispering by the time she finished.

I still didn't get it.

'You know. Can you imagine? If this gets into the papers! Even if it just gets around the profession! We'll never get another brief!'

I was about to tell her she ought to practise advocacy at the funny farm. Trying to get in. But there was something in it.

The law's a strange business. It's a small world. Very small. There's maybe thirty, forty thousand solicitors, but most of them are out of London or south of the river and don't count. And there's only three or four thousand barristers. Most of them in London, in chambers in the Inns of Court. If one of them farts in open court, the others've heard about it before the stink's gone.

It'd take no time for this to reach the ears of every solicitor, every barrister and every judge that matters. What'd happen then? Well, you might think it'd earn them a lot of sympathy. It doesn't work like that. Lawyers are human beings. They'll react normally. They'll figure: one, the chambers must've done something pretty bad to someone; two, we don't want to get caught up in any scandal; three, maybe whoever's doing it'll turn on anyone who's associated with them — like a solicitor who sends them work; four, who wants to waste time instructing someone who may be dead by the time the trial starts?

Of course, it wouldn't be a hundred per cent. There'd be the ghouls. The nutters. The peepshow artists. The vicarious thrill merchants. They'd still bring them work. Just to be able to hang around. Just to get in on the act. You can imagine for yourself the sort of work they'd be doing, and the sort of creeps that'd he bringing it to them.

I could see their point of view. But:

'Does it really add up to enough not to report it to the police?'

'I don't think so. But ... Well ... The others ...'

'Does everyone know?

I meant: everyone in chambers.

She shook her head:

'No. There hasn't been a chambers' meeting since ...'

For the first time, she laughed, though not what you'd call wholeheartedly:

'If everybody knew, I don't suppose there'd be another chambers' meeting ever again.'

I ignored the competition. Making jokes was my job.

'Who does know?'

'Alex.' Obviously. And obviously she'd name him first.

'Gerry Gilligan.' That figured.

'Harry. Mick.' Barron. One of Jack Nicholas' contemporaries and, as such, one of the longer-serving goons.

'Jane Daws. Do you know her?'

'I saw her in the pub.'

'Marguie Bradkinson?'

'Yup. Her too.'

Leaving aside the last couple of names, she'd listed all the weight in chambers. The older, more senior members. Those with influence. That is to say, those who were left. It made a point:

'They're being taken off the top ...'

'Yes. It seems that way.'

'Gilligan? He's with you. Thinks you ought to tell the police?' Gilligan wasn't senior, but it was clear to me that he wielded influence. As did Anne. They got in to the club through ability, not age.

'You can never tell what Gerry's really thinking. I think he agrees. We usually do.'

'Then the negs are Keenan, Harry and Barron, right?' I didn't bother with Daws or Bradkinson: we were concerned with the thinking members of chambers.

'Yes.'

'Are you going to take it to the full group?'

'It's difficult. If we do ... People talk ... You know how it is, Dave. Everyone tells someone else. Confidentially, of course. We might as well report it or publish it as tell the whole group.'

'But I know now ...'

'Yes,' she sighed: that was a problem.

'You haven't told me ...'

Who was paying me.

'No. I haven't.'

'What happens now?'

'About?'

'About everything. What do we do? What do I do? About me knowing.'

'What do you want to do?'

'Tell Alex ...' Run to daddy.

'I want ... I want a little more time, Anne. I want to think things through.' I shifted gear:

'What's your best guess?'

'Someone who's got a hell of a grudge against the group ...'

I admired the understatement.

'I don't know.' She emphasized 'know' the way I had with Mrs Nick — a lawyer's trick. It stank of false humility. I, a lawyer, wish to make clear that I am not talking about what I know. Ergo, you cannot hold me responsible for having said it. But I am a lawyer. The fact that I am saying it at all is a very strong indication that there's something in it. Whether based on unrepeatable or unusable information, or merely an educated guess, isn't something you can ask. Because I'll only answer:

'I don't know ...'

'But?'

'Maybe ... A former member?'

That was what I'd thought, too; 'till Dowell had damned it with faint praise — not enough bottle. Because I knew I'd never have the courage to cream anyone, I'd accepted his answer with alacrity.

'Is that possible? Can you think of anyone?' In particular.

'No,' she said, after a split second's hesitation.

She asked:

'Are you going to the police?'

'Not for the time being.'

I didn't need to lie. The police, after all, were coming to me:

'I'm not instructed to ...'

'Yeah. You always do what you're instructed.. .'

I sometimes didn't used to.

She picked up her glass. It was empty. Held it up to me to ask: another bottle?

'Sure ... Why not.'

She was not a happy lady.

We stayed until closing time. We walked up to the station together. Bought our two-zone tickets. At the foot of the stairs, where we took separate trains, from opposite platforms, she hesitated. Then asked:

'Wouldn't you ... Couldn't I ...'

I didn't help her out.

'Oh, hell, Dave, I don't want to go home, alone ... I'm frightened.'

'It's OK,' I comforted her:

'It isn't a Wednesday ...'

She scowled, and turned away without another word. It might've been what she said. It wasn't what she meant.

I got a rare full night's sleep before the 'phone started. In quick succession I had two calls; I still wouldn't like to guess by which I was more taken aback.

The first was from the cutie, Marguerita Bradkinson. She was about to leave for court and wanted to catch me before she left home. Sorry she didn't have much of a chance to talk to me in the pub the other night. Very interested in what I was doing. Would I, by any chance, be free that evening to come to dinner at her house.

The second was a blast from the past that caught me just as I was going hack to sleep again:

'Dave?'

'Ugh.'

'Dave, this is Sandy ...'

Sandy? Sandra? Sandra Nicholl? My former partner? The woman who had personally, single-handedly, totally and utterly destroyed my career without hardly a helping hand from me? That Sandy?

'Come again?'

'C'mon, Dave. I still recognize your voice ...'

'I don't know ...'

'What don't you know?'

'Whatever it is you want. Where the files are? What barrister I instructed? Whether we won or lost?'

She laughed:

'I don't want to know anything, Dave ...'

'Then give. What do you want?'

'You're not being, well, very friendly, dear ...'

People don't realize how like spouses business partners are. They know everything about you. What clothes you've got. What you like to eat or drink. What makes you tick. How you'll react. What sort of mood you're in. Even why.

'As I recall, we weren't on very friendly terms when last we spoke ... Dear ...' I threw back to see how it bounced.

'No. Well, that's past ...'

'Maybe for you.. .'

This's another of my great, unique wisdoms. When people put the boot into you, it's a one-off action. They forget they ever did it. But if you're on the receiving end, the sting settles in for a long stay. You gotta live with the consequences. Maybe forever.

I didn't bear Sandy any grudges. She was right in what she did. I wasn't doing the firm any good. More important than that, I wasn't doing the clients any good. Most important of all, I wasn't doing me any good either.

'How are you, Sandy?'

'OK. I guess. I'd like to see you. Are you free for lunch? I'll buy ...'

Two meals in one day. I'd burst.

We met in High Street Kensington. A new restaurant. Posh. Expensive. I'd never been inside before.

She was there before me. She looked good. She was in a dark suit which meant she'd been to court. Her hair was permed, which she didn't used to do. But she still didn't need any makeup and hadn't put on a pound.

We'd never made it. There were times when I wanted to, and maybe when we came close. There were times when I suspected she wanted to, and perhaps not even just casually. In the days when I thought I was the next best thing to Paul Newman (actually, it was Kris Kristofferson), I used even to wonder whether setting up in practice together wasn't some form of sublimation, on her part of course.

She got up as I fumbled my way to her table. Came around it. Took my hands like we were long-lost buddies (which I guess we were — only we got lost a long time before the partnership broke up). Kissed me on the cheek.

She was making me nervous. We'd been together five minutes, plus five on the 'phone made ten. She hadn't torn my head off once yet.

While we chose, we chattered. I asked about her headaches: she'd always suffered from them, still did. I asked about the firm. It was just called 'Nicholl & Co.' We'd been going to call it 'Nicholl & Woolf,' but we could hear it coming, nickel and dime.

'It's doing well ... There's a lot of work ... There're five full-time solicitors, two articled clerks ... Seven reception and secretarial ...'

'That's big ... How many partners?'

'Just me, Dave ...'

She looked me straight in the eye:

'My first partnership experience didn't work out too well. Made me a little chary ...'

I grinned:

'You got out cheap. Look at you now ...'

There was something about her I couldn't place until the waiter was taking our orders and I had a chance to sit back and watch. She was more confident than ever I'd known her. In the early days, when we'd started up together, just about everything she did cost her a high dose of nervous tension. She was wound up like a clock. Me? I was so laid back I didn't know if it was Wednesday or Saturday.

'How's Bernie?' I asked after the waiter'd gone. Bernie had been her bloke for six years when I met her; a decade of loving service by the time we broke up. I couldn't stand him. He was an accountant and, by all ... whoops, some said he was the best fiction writer in the world of figures.

'We split up,' she said defiantly:

'Soon after you ... Left.'

'Ha. Left. Got kicked out!' I scowled, but gently, so's she'd know I meant her no malice.

'You look good, Dave ... Better than I expected ...'

'Meaning?'

'Meaning I heard you ... Er ... Had a bit of a rough time?'

I wanted to get the subject off me:

'And the other one?'

All the time she'd been with Bernie, she'd been having a scene on the side. On her side and on his too. I never knew who it was. Someone outside our world, she'd always said. Those times I didn't figure I was her one true love, I guessed this other guy was. The only thing I knew for sure was: it couldn't be Bernie. She had far too much good taste.

'That ... That didn't work out either. I still see him, but ... We don't ... You know,' she laughed lightly:

'I thought we were supposed to be talking about what a rough time you've been having — not me.'

'Ain't no supposed to be ...'

The waiter brought our starters. She was on weight-watcher's avocado. I was into herring and sour cream. She'd ordered wine.

She held up her glass:

'It wasn't all bad, Dave ...'

'Not quite. Cheerio.' I gulped at my drink, to hide the fact she'd managed to touch me.

'What prompted this, then?'

Turbot to follow. I'd forgotten how much I liked poached turbot. I was branching out. Losing my fear that the next meal would be the last and it had better be steak.

'I heard … I heard you'd been seen around … I've wanted … For a long time … I didn't know how to, what to say to you, you know? It wasn't an easy time for me either, Dave. Either before, or during it, or after. I've …' She grabbed my hand:

'I've missed you. Missed working with you, I mean.'

I could've been flattered. Instead, I was suspicious. I didn't believe in coincidence. Remember?

'What is this, Sandy?'

She looked quite maudlin:

'We were very close, Dave. You were my best friend.'

'C'mon, c'mon. Give, give …'

She laughed again:

'You don't change, do you? Straight to the point.'

'The way I was brought up.'

She knew what I meant. Nicholl had been Nichstein when her grandfather landed in the East End.

'Where'd'you hear I was back?'

'Three places,' she said:

'Disraeli Chambers. Sue Cannon. And a funny little detective sergeant from Scotland Yard.'

Like I said: small world.

While we were still in the restaurant, she told me more about herself, the way she was living and working, and why she wanted to see me.

She was a single woman, mid-thirties, the sole proprietor of a successful firm, with five young lawyers working for her. Two of them had done their apprenticeship with her and had only recently qualified. They were no problem. One of the others was temporary. But the two who had been with her a while were pressing to get into partnership, wanted a slice of the profits.

It wasn't, she said, meanness, though I got the feeling she'd hardened up since I left. Maybe to do with breaking up with Bernie. Or the other guy. No one else around. Had to look out for number one. It was, rather, that I'd been her only professional partner, and look at how we'd been. She was, she said, simply scared to take on two new people alone, both of them men, to find herself maybe the minority partner.

It rang true enough. No one falls out as viciously, as painfully or indeed legally as messily as lawyers. There's an old saying: the lawyer who acts for himself has a fool for a client. At the moment of break-up, that's what's happening, people are acting for themselves, and they do some pretty damned stupid things.

'Me? You want me back? After what we went through?

She smiled wanly:

'Sucker for punishment, eh?'

'Sectionable, I would've said.'

Compulsory incarceration under the Mental Health Act.

It was the part of her story I trusted least. She couldn't really want me back. Could she?

She grabbed my hand again:

'You went crazy, Dave. You'd had enough. You were screwing more women, popping more pills, than a rock star. You wanted out, dammit, Dave. It wasn't me that made you go. You did it. You forced me to do it. But don't tell me I wanted it to happen.'

'That wasn't how you acted outside court ...' When she gave me five hundred and wrung out of me an absolute waiver of any further claims.

'Come on, Dave. The firm had more debts than assets. Goodwill and the last four months of a lease were all we were arguing about. Your outstanding bills amounted to zilch. Hell, you hadn't done anything for a year!'

'Yeah, yeah. That's old music. It doesn't play why you should even begin to think of bringing me back ...'

'Maybe I like you,' she said softly.

I snorted.

'Anyhow, what makes you think it'd be any different now? Huh?'

'I didn't say it would be. I'm only saying ... What about giving it another try?'

'Jesus. You make it sound like we were married!'

'A firm's a sort of child, isn't it? Didn't you used to say that to me?'

'Yeah, sure, when I was trying to get you out of one of those damned moods of yours. You know? The "I just wanna be a little woman and bring up children" number. If you'd had kids with Bernie, they'd be long-firm frauding with the pocket money by now ...'

After we'd eaten, we went for a walk. It was a warm, still slightly bright day. Only a bit overcast. Muggy. But in England you grab it when you can. We walked along to Kensington Palace Gardens, through to Hyde Park.

We sat and watched the ducks. They were cute. There were a lot of people in rowing boats. They weren't so cute.

'Gimme the bottom line, kid,' I put on my best Bogey. As in: Bogey goes to Wall Street.

'Come back. See how it works out. Give it, say, a year, two years ... Then we'll look at it ...'

I finally sussed it out. I could be used to stall her insistent but would-be erstwhile employees. Dave may be coming back. After all, it was his firm too. He started it with me. We're going to give it a while, and work something out. We'll have to postpone any decisions on other new partners 'till that's been sorted. She couldn't play that sort of game with a stranger, an outsider: only with someone who had a claim prior to theirs.

I put my arm around her shoulders, and hugged her close to me:

'I just remembered why I liked working with you,' I whispered in her ear as if I was about to ask her to marry me:

'You're the most conniving, scheming, manipulative bitch I ever did meet ...'

No offence was intended, and none was taken:

'That's the nicest thing you ever said,' she fluttered her eyelashes sarcastically.

I didn't take my arm away. Nor did she pull free. We looked each other in the eyes. Like they do in the movies for a couple of frames before cut to pink flesh and that delicious tension: will they/won't they (show her boobs)? Something was stirring. It took me a while to recognize what it was.

She didn't resist. I'm not even that sure who it was finally took the plunge. Me or her. It was just happening.

'This is crazy,' I murmured after:

'I've known you ten years ... We've had some of the worst times of my life together!'

She laughed:

'Such nice things you tell a girl.'

I shook my head violently to clear it. Got up. Walked round behind the bench. She didn't move. After a while, I went and stood behind her, laid my hands on her shoulders. She reached up with her arms crossed over her body and placed her hands on top of mine. That was when I thought I saw a familiar shape across the pond. Gimbo. I cleared my throat:

'I've got an appointment ...'

All the same, I went round and sat beside her again.

She was frowning.

'What is it, Sandy?'

She shrugged:

'I don't know. I thought I had it all worked out. That it was just ... business.' She laughed tightly.

'Look at me! Thirty-six years old and acting like I've never been kissed before! That's all it was, wasn't it, Dave? Just the wine and the sun and should auld acquaintance, eh?'

'I dunno, Sandy. These days, people always seem to be asking me questions I can't answer. It's worse than being back in practice. Nah. It didn't mean anything. Just like you didn't ...' mean the offer to come back to work.

We both stood up at the same time. Looked at each other for a while. Then she said:

'Which way're you going?'

I gestured vaguely in the direction of Hyde Park Corner, the underground station.

'Fine. I'll go that way.' She turned up the Park, north towards Marble Arch. I was too far away to tell which one of us Gimbo followed.

Three hours later I was dining with Bradkinson.

I'd shown up late. Couldn't find the damned house. Hackney's a maze if you weren't born there. If you were, you probably never found your way out. I didn't know what happened to Gimbo either: he was getting better at tailing me; or I was getting worse at spotting him.

I'd guessed it would just be the two of us. Dinner á *deux*. I hadn't guessed, though, she'd have such a fancy pad. Or, from the way she dressed, that she'd keep it so well. I was so obviously impressed she took me on the grand tour. It was a big house, plenty of plain wood, floors, doors, cupboards, window-frames. The wall-paper matched the blinds and in the kitchen, the crockery; in the bedroom, the sheets. Habitat or Liberty's. Off the main living room was a sun and plant room: glass, with creepers up and across the ceiling.

That was where she'd laid it out for us to eat. Formally informal. Studiedly casual. I stretched out on an old stuffed sofa like I'd lived there all my life. The room had that effect.

For a while, she made a half-hearted effort at talking about the politics of their chambers, my ostensible interest. We managed to keep the conversation on this tedious plateau until she'd cleared the main course away. Then she rolled a joint, to help us through dessert.

I'm no literary genius; even if I was, I couldn't get next to a stoned conversation. Almost every time I've been good stoned (which is a lot less than all the times I've been stoned at all), I've wished I'd had a tape recording to play back later. The only time I ever did it, though, I couldn't listen past the first five minutes.

All I've got now is snatches of talk, a recollection of a rolling sea, floating fantasies, watching as if from another room as they turned into reality.

Her asking:

'How old are you?'

'How old d'you think?'

'Oh, really old. Like. More than thirty?'

I chuckled:

'Closer to forty. How old're you?'

There was a gap before she answered:

'Twenty-four ...'

She was thirteen years younger than me. It seemed like a lifetime.

'What d'you want with me?'

She'd put out a bowl of nuts, a cheeseboard, and a packet of After Eights. Our first physical contact was as our hands brushed, grabbing for more. We'd got the munchies.

'You aren't a very happy man, are you Dave?'

It reminded me of a scene in a movie. I played it over.

Then I tried to describe it.

'Did you see The Big Chill?

She hadn't even heard of it.

It didn't have music by people with names like Desmond Desmond, Foul Foreskin or Carved Carcass.

'These sixties people ...'

'Like you?'

'Sure.'

Another long break while I scanned the faces.

'One of their friends is dead. Suicide. His girl- friend ... Your sort of age ... I guess ... And they ask her: "Was he happy?" She says: "I don't know. I haven't seen that many happy people. How do they act?"'

'No, then,' she answered for me.

'You didn't answer my question either ...'

'I'm scared, that's all, I'm scared.'

Without either of us having admitted that was what I was really interested in, we both knew what she was talking about.

'Who told you?'

'I guessed ...'

Maybe yes. Maybe no. Maybe it didn't really matter.

I went to the lavatory.

When I came back, she'd moved to the sofa.

It didn't call for a lot of imagination to stretch out beside her.

I stopped asking why.

At least for a time.

I woke up again, in her bed, in the middle of the night. The digital radio clock was shining in my eyes.

I couldn't find the dimmer.

I slipped out of the bed and padded to the door. Paused in the half-light thrown in through an un-curtained stairwell window. There was a full length mirror just inside the door. I've created world speed records zipping past mirrors. Tonight, I hesitated, glanced back, there was something different from the last time I looked.

I crouched back inside the sofa where it had all begun. I could've been cold if I'd chosen to take it that way. Instead, it was the edge that kept me awake to think.

Things were changing all around me like a kaleidoscope on acid. Even I was changing. I was so used to thinking of myself as a drunken bum, a fat slob, a lump of camel turd a desperate doe wouldn't piss on., I hadn't noticed myself tightening up, losing weight, getting physically sharper the same way I now spent the major part of each day using my brain constructively instead of trying to forget I had one.

Maybe, after all, it wasn't so weird Anne Godwin had been prepared to give it another whirl. Maybe what'd happened in Hyde Park that afternoon either. Maybe this evening too. Maybe these things happened all at once or not at all: something to do with being turned in on oneself. Maybe it never rains but it pours.

Lot of maybes.

They didn't answer all the questions, though.

Like: why had Marguerita gone this far out of her way to pull me.

Like: why had Sandy been prepared to bait her line with an offer to return to work.

Like: why didn't Dowell reel me in, instead of turning me looser even than before.

Like: why was Disraeli Chambers every which way I looked.

Like: why did someone hate them enough to ...

She didn't speak. Curled up opposite me in the chair she'd started out from. She'd put on a nightdress, to protect herself against the night, or against me.

I watched her. I didn't feel anything. Unless, perhaps, a little grateful because it'd been a long time since I'd managed to get it together with any woman. Otherwise, zilch.

If she'd said then:

'D'you want to go home?'

I would've said:

'Yup.'

If she'd said then:

'I'm sorry. It was a mistake.'

I would've said:

'Yup.'

Instead, she asked:

'You ever been to Norway?'

'Where?'

'Norway,' she repeated.

Well, of course, Norway. Where else should we be talking about?

'Why?

'I'm going there next week ... Just for a week ... I'm attending a conference, for a couple of days, and I thought I'd turn it into a holiday ... You want to come?'

She said it casually, like to a movie or to the shops.

I guess my look asked wasn't this what was known as a little bit sudden. We hadn't even woken up next to each other yet, than which there is no more acid test.

She shrugged.

She looked sort of defenceless and cute and sweet tucked into the chair.

'I was going on my own anyhow ...'

'Where're you staying?

'In Oslo. Some people Alex knows are involved with the conference ...'

That at least would be true. Alex had friends everywhere.

I didn't even remember to ask what the conference was. Instead, just:

'How'd we get there?'

CHAPTER SIX

'Where's Keenan?' I demanded as I stormed into the clerk's room.

They looked at me like I was mad.

I was. Not crazy: angry.

'Where's Keenan?' I repeated.

I wished I was an American detective. I'd've flashed 'em with eight inches of grey steel. Very hard.

One of them shook her head:

'He's away ...'

That much didn't surprise me.

'Where?' I snarled.

They shook their heads in unison, like they'd been practising for vaudeville.

I wasn't going to get anything out of them. I turned and slammed back out of the door, yelling over my shoulder:

'You'd sell your mothers.'

Downstairs, I walked through Gilligan, returning from court carrying his helmet in one hand, and a blue wig-and-gown bag in the other.

'Will you tell me?' I demanded, marginally but undiscernibly less aggressively.

'What?'

I repeated my question:

'Where's Keenan?'

To my extreme annoyance, he laughed:

'I told them it wouldn't work ...'

I knew exactly what he meant. Norway. Bradkinson. Me.

Before I went, I'd made a date with Mrs Nicholas. Partly, it was out of a residual sense of honour: even if she could not listen, I ought at least to tell her what tune I was playing. Also, I needed her authority for the unexpected expenditure.

We met in the usual place. I arrived early. The ponce in the pin-striped outfit gave me a knowing look. He figured he knew how I was making bread out of her dough. I scowled back, to let him know there were other things I could knead. Like his face.

'Thank you.' She sat in the chair I held out for her:

'Have there been any developments?' She was as quick off the mark as ever. This time, though, she explained, conspiratorially:

'The Reverend Nicholas has an appointment in town. I said I would come with him, to do some shopping. I have to meet him at four o'clock.' It didn't leave long.

As fast as I could, I brought her up to date: the conversation with Anne Godwin, and, somewhat more pertinently, that with DS Dowell.

'Did you tell him? I mean ... That I ...'

'I didn't have a lot of choice,' I answered, without elaborating. Like most civilians, she was under the impression that orders from the police superseded those of the holy ghost.

'Thank you. Yes. What happens now?'

'That's the other reason I wanted to see you. I want ...' I hesitated, unsure how to put this with delicacy:

'I want to follow a hunch. Someone ... A member of the group ... Has invited me to go away with her.' I dropped my voice for the last word:

'A lot of this ... Detection ... You have to follow your nose, follow the breaks ... I saw her recently, the other day ... Out of the blue, well, not completely, but anyhow, she asked me to go with her to Oslo for a week. I don't know ...'

It was a lawyer's know.

'I don't know what it's got to do with everything that's happening ... I don't know that it does. It could be, well, genuine, personal, but ... Even if it simply strengthens my ties, gets me more information, I think it's the sort of fluke I can't afford to ignore ...'

After a bit, rather sheepishly, I added:

'Or afford to pay for myself ...'

It sounded lame. She could spot it too. I felt like I was under a microscope. She wasn't stupid: I was talking about a week away, with a woman, on her money.

I wasn't lying. I wasn't doing it for that. That might be how it was wrapped, and I'm not talking old newspaper. Inside was a sliver of truth. It all seemed too much, too coincidental, too happening not to take part in it.

'Do you know ... what it will cost?'

'The fare'll be the best part of two hundred,' I admitted:

'I don't know, 'till after, how much of it will be your time ...'

'Do I know her?'

'Marguerita Bradkinson?'

'Yes. She was at Jack's funeral. It's an unusual name. She's ... a most attractive young woman, Mr Woolf.'

I swear she was about to call me by my first name. I'd also swear there was a smile between her lips.

'Would I be ... doing something wrong, do you think?'

I knew exactly what she meant.

I laughed out loud:

'I'm no Lord Peter Wimsey ...' He was the only investigator I could think of who was also supposed to be the perfect gentleman.

'Go.' She had made her decision.

'Thank you for telling me. You'd like another cheque, I expect ...' She wrote it out on the spot and pushed it across the table to me.

I hesitated before picking it up. Covered it with my hand and looked her in the eyes:

'Why? Why do you trust me?'

'Shouldn't I, Mr Woolf?'

I shrugged.

She got up to leave:

'But you can pay for tea today,' she smiled.

She got as far as the door before she turned and walked back to our table. She said quietly:

'When I came to see you ... Only a little more than a month ago ... I told you I didn't believe how they said Jack died. I was right. You found that out. It isn't easy ... It isn't easy to go on with it now ... I don't mean the money ... But ... We have to finish what we started, don't we?'

All the time she was talking, I was looking down at the table, not at her. I didn't look up when I answered:

'I wish you'd go away. I'm beginning to like you.'

'Is that really such a hardship, Mr Woolf?'

I raised my eyes, to meet hers:

'You think I'm doing this work instead of law because I like people, Mrs Nicholas? You must know ... You must have worked out what sort of life I've been living ... I don't exactly claim I was happy, but I slept nights ...'

'And before, when you practised law?'

'I didn't. That's all. I didn't sleep, anyhow not naturally, not without a little help, and I don't mean what the doctor prescribed.'

'Because you cared?'

'Something like that I guess.'

After a bit, when she still didn't go away, I added:

'It doesn't matter. I'm not being paid to tell you what makes me tick.'

'Thank you.'

She left.

We were flying from Gatwick. It was an early morning flight, and we stayed together the night before, at my flat.

I didn't know what she was about. Between the first night and the night before our departure we'd spent one more evening together. She'd come to my place that time also. I'd even cleaned it up. She had a case in court the next day. She wouldn't stay over. We just talked about this projected trip. I'd got no more out of her about why she wanted me to tag along.

This time, we went to bed early, and fucked ourselves to sleep, which in my case didn't take much. Just like the last time I slept beside her, I woke in the middle of the night and got out of bed. I sat at the table where I'd talked with DS Dowell, smoking Camels, sipping S'Comfort.

Like that first night too, she was woken by my absence and came to join me.

'Tell me?'

'What?'

'Why are we going to Norway together?'

'I like you. Just that. Really. I've ... Been alone for a while. It gets lonely in the house. I used to share it ...'

I interrupted:

'How long've you had it? How'd you afford it?'

The part of London she lived in didn't cost peanuts. A few people had bought there before gentrification, when it had still been dirt cheap, but she wasn't old enough.

'Inheritance. I've been there about five years.'

'Go on.'

'I stopped sharing it about two years ago. Before that, there was me, the bloke I was with, another guy and a girl ... Not together ... It was all such a big effort. I had to spend half my time making up for the fact I was the owner, it was my house ... Compensating, you know ... The other half of the time was rows. I can't remember much good about when I shared it ...'

'But it does get lonely?'

'Yes. I don't find ... Relationships ... Easy ...'

'That's supposed to make you special?'

It sounded crueller than I meant.

'Sure. I know. But ... I'm me.'

I'm the only one I know about.

'And?'

'And you seemed lonely too ... Oh, that wasn't all of it. The chambers' thing. Of course. Gerry told me. About you. I'd guessed you were lying about the book. I didn't want to go away alone. I wanted ... It's difficult to explain. You're connected, but not connected, if you see what I mean?'

It made sense. I was part of it, because I knew about it. But I wasn't involved. I wasn't one of the group. I wasn't subject to it. I wasn't vulnerable. Like her.

'Now you tell me ...'

'Why I agreed to go?'

She nodded.

I poured us both a shot. Drank mine. I needed time to decide, not to work out why but what to tell.

'Mixed reasons. I've been in a lot of weird places, the last few years. I mean, in my head mostly. These last weeks, months, I've been coming out. That's a ... Well, all right, lonely fits. Where I've been has been just me. Now I'm finding my way back in. I mean ...'

I laughed:

'I didn't even know that was what I was doing, to begin with, and I still don't know if it's what I want ... But ... It is what I'm doing. So, I guess, I'm fumbling for how to be with people again. And ... And you wanted to be with me. So, what the hell ...'

'I'd do as well as anyone? To try it out again?'

She didn't seem to mind.

'Our ... Intentions? They fitted. That's enough, isn't it?'

'You're being paid? To investigate? To go with me?'

Ruefully, I nodded my head:

'I wouldn't've had the money otherwise ...'

'I would have paid,' she hissed, angry for the first time.

'Didn't like to ask,' I mumbled.

I got away with it. She touched my hand in apology.

Gatwick's the most unglamorous airport in the world. Especially at seven in the morning. When you go to Heathrow, you feel like you're really travelling. International. Cosmopolitan. Gatwick's a glorified bus-station. Package tours. Loud English, many of them drunk despite the hour; if they weren't football hooligans on their way to Hamburg they might just as well have been.

I'd never been in Norway before. Or any other part of Scandinavia. I always figured it as somewhere worth visiting. Fantasies about liberated blondes. It felt much more abroad than, say, France or Italy or even Greece; countries I'd been to on holiday often since I was a child.

The people we were to stay with met us at the airport. They drove us back to their apartment, slap in the centre of the city, in a ten-year-old VW that looked like we might have to get out and push. They were full of questions about Keenan. I sat in the back, staring out, a bit dopey from want of sleep, still wondering what the hell I was doing there.

The conference started two days after we arrived. I was invited to attend, but declined. It was a disarmament conference. I'm not a believer. Not, I hasten to add, on grounds of defence policy. I look around me and all I see is scum. Different levels of scum, maybe, but scum just the same. My policy is: nuke 'em all, start over, maybe we'll make a better job of it next time around. We could hardly do worse.

It was the second day on my own that I saw Orbach. It was at the Munch Museum. Norway's artist, the way Grieg — I had learned since my arrival — was the nation's composer, and Ibsen their playwright. I wasn't there because I love art. I was there because it was raining and cold and I couldn't find anything else to do except drink myself into a stupor at prices so creative

Sandy's ex- might've thought them up as a way of increasing tax-deductibles.

It took me a while to place him. If Disraeli Chambers hadn't been uppermost in my mind. I might not even have recognized him. I hadn't seen him for maybe five, six years. He'd aged in that time almost as much as I had. Put on weight, a lot of it. Was almost completely grey. He wore a Norwegian cardigan, an anorak over his arm, he was holding the elbow of a lady old enough to be his mother.

I crept up close. For the first couple of minutes, I thought I must be mistaken. They were speaking in Norwegian. Don't ask me what they were saying. But just as I was about to quit, he stumbled on a sentence and broke into an unaccented English that killed my doubt. His companion replied in English, though, as with many Norwegians I'd heard in these last two days, with very little trace of direct accent at all. Just a slightly musical intonation.

I stayed behind them throughout the exhibition. The rain had stopped and I yearned for the uncluttered, uncultured outdoors. They were doing every last painting, every etching, every last lithograph. They strolled out and wandered back towards the town centre. I felt less self-conscious about following them than I might have done in London, where I'd be wondering what everyone else on the street was thinking. Even if I could've read the minds of these people, it would've been in foreign.

At Oslo's Central Station, they didn't go directly to buy a ticket. Glanced at their watches. Hovered by the newsagent. They were waiting for someone. He ran up, obviously late, and kissed the woman. I'd put money on he was her son. He touched Orbach's shoulder: old friends.

I was right behind in the line and still didn't hear where they bought tickets to. I stepped up to the window and mumbled:

'The same ...'

'*Hva?*'

'The same ...'

I could afford to speak a little louder now they were out of earshot. The gamble on his English paid off:

'You want the same place?'

'Sure ...'

'Four kroner ...' Not much. Therefore, not far.

'What platform?'

'Number five ...'

As I hurried to platform five, I glanced at the ticket. Damn. It didn't tell me where I was going. Just where I'd come from. I had to sit in their compartment, make sure I saw them dismount. I'd've rather put some distance. If he paid me any attention, he knew me well enough to remember. The same way Disraeli Chambers was on my mind, maybe I was on his.

It was a small, local, commuter train. We weren't on it for ten minutes. They got off at a place called Ljan. They walked slowly, idly, happily, up the road, away from the station, down another road, without a pavement: Ljabruvn is what it said. I had learned 'vn' was an abbreviation. Therefore, Ljabruveien.

I hovered outside, a way down the street, freezing cold. What the hell was I supposed to do now? It was well past the time I ought to have been back at the flat where we were staying. We were going to a party.

Orbach came out of the house. He wasn't wearing his anorak or a coat; just the cardigan. He walked straight at me. As he approached, I kneeled down, as if to retie my shoelaces. I was wearing boots.

'Would you like to come in, Dave? It's cold out here ...'

Ugh.

Er, well, hello, fancy meeting you here, in an Oslo suburb of all places, what a coincidence, haven't seen you for years, how're you keeping, sorry I have to rush, let's stay in touch, shall we?

I followed him into the house. He introduced me to his companions, explaining:

'They're very old friends of mine. Of course, in a way, so is Dave ...'

'Would you like some tea, Mr Woolf?'

'A drink, I should think,' Orbach suggested:

'To warm you up.'

He was the one needed warming up. I never met so much *sang froid* in one place before.

He nodded at them as if to say: I'm all right, you can leave me with him.

'Perhaps we shall see you again ...' The mother said as they left.

I had a feeling: not very likely.

'You're right at home here?'

He smiled:

'Of course. They are my oldest friends. I visit them each year. I have known them ... Oh, for close on twenty years. Since ... Since I was over here.'

Then I remembered. Orbach had not followed the conventional path of, say, Jack Nicholas. (Remember Jack Nicholas? No? Well, it doesn't matter. He wasn't very memorable.) He'd left school young, went abroad, come back and gone to university three or four years later than normal. His time abroad had included time in Norway.

'Every year. You come here every year? At the same time?'

'As long as I can remember. Originally, the older son of the family was my friend. Christen. He's in Bergen now. That's on the west coast, a long way. So I don't see him these days. But Mor ... She was, well, something of a mother to me, and I grew very fond of the family as a whole. So I come back. Each year. And Mor and I visit the Munch Museum. You see, they change the works around. He left so many, they can't exhibit them all at one time. And we go to the opera. This is the opera season, you see,' he added, in explanation of the timing of his annual visit:

'And we walk in the hills behind Ljan. And I breathe fresh air. And walk clean streets. And perhaps we spend a couple of days in their mountain hut.'

He smiled, like a man describing his own vision of heaven. Perhaps more aptly, a soldier home from the front. He was at peace.

'Now. I've given you some answers. Perhaps you'd be so kind?'

'Well, I feel pretty stupid ...'

'You followed us from the Museum. Why? What are you doing here?'

'I think ... Well, I know, now at any rate ... I was duped into coming here. To see you, I think.'

He nodded calmly, as if he knew all along:

'Perhaps. Also, I think, to get you away from Keenan? What do you think? That too?'

'I think ... I think maybe what I think isn't that well-informed ... Not as well-informed as you, anyway ...'

'No. Well. I've had longer at it than you. I know them a little better.'

I remembered something else about Orbach. The reason everyone hated his guts, at Disraeli Chambers and elsewhere. Because he always did know. Everything. And he wasn't ashamed to show it. I never figured it, myself, as showing-off, in itself, or for its own sake. More like: this is what I know, correct me, improve on it, add to it. A man in constant quest for knowledge, who did not suffer fools gladly, or at all.

'What do you know?'

'I know that you have been investigating the deaths of four members of the group. I know, today, now, just this minute, that they want you to think I'm responsible. I say they,' he laughed:

'I mean him, of course. Alex. None of the others could tell the time of day if he didn't show them what the numbers meant.'

'And?'

'And what?'

'And are you?'

He chuckled:

'I wish I had had the guts to kill them. I hate the bastards. Every one of them. Except, perhaps, Alex. We were very close once. I don't think you ever lose that sort of closeness. And, well, I understand him, understand the way he's behaved, towards me, he had his reasons and they weren't all bad. But the others? I wouldn't piss on them if their brains were on fire ...'

'But you didn't?'

'No, Dave, I didn't kill them ...'

The young man poked his head around the door and asked something in Norwegian to which Orbach replied:

'*Nei*,' which I just about worked out meant 'no'.

He explained to me:

'He wanted to know if you were going to eat with us. They are a phenomenally polite people, the Norwegians. I love them. If I didn't have such a damned parochial job, I'd live here. Come, I'll walk you back to the station, put you on the train ...'

On the road down, he pointed out the sights, identified trees and plants, paused for me to look at a particularly fine house. We passed a man on his way back from work, who called out to him in Norwegian. He replied, relaxed, at home. I don't know how much of what he told me was true, but he wasn't lying when he said he'd like to live there.

'We'll talk again. In London. Not here. This is not the place, for me.'

'Do you know where Keenan is?'

He shook his head:

'No. Find out. Come and see me when you can tell me.'

Marguie was waiting for me at the flat. The others had gone to a party, leaving her directions how to find it. I went into our bedroom and started to pack.

'What are you doing?'

'What does it look like?'

'Why? If I hadn't know better, I could've sworn she was genuinely hurt.

'I saw him. I've done what I was brought here for ...'

'What? What are you talking about?' She took one last crack at conning me.

'How was it, Marguie? How was I supposed to see him? With you? Were you to take me out to Ljan, for a nature ramble no doubt, spot him by accident, leave me no chance to talk to him, something like that?'

She blushed but said nothing.

'Do you people really think I'm so stupid? So what if I saw Orbach here? What was it supposed to mean? Tell me. I'd really like to know.'

'I don't know. I don't know so much. Geir,' the man whose apartment we were staying in:

'Geir knows him. They used to be friends. Through Alex. When Alex and Orbach fell out, Geir took Alex's side. It was Alex's idea. If you saw Orbach, Geir talked to you about him, you'd think, well, it would all come from you.'

'Where is Alex?'

'I don't know. That's the truth. It was all his idea.' She shrugged, she didn't need to spell it out.

At the door, she took my arm:

'I wish you wouldn't. Couldn't you stay anyway? I do like you, Dave, honestly, it wasn't all ...'

I snorted.

'You don't even know if there'll be a plane tonight ...'

'I'd rather sleep on an airport bench. You know? You understand what I mean?'

I was glad I said that. It made it better when that was how I had to sleep. It gave it a sense of purpose.

I couldn't get on a flight until late the next day. There were only two to Gatwick and the first one was full. I was ready to flake by the time I got back to the flat. I sank into the bath, grateful I'd forgotten to turn the boiler off. Though it was only mid-evening, I was planning on straight to bed.

I should've known better.

'You didn't send me a card,' was his opening accusation.

'I didn't know you cared,' I mumbled.

I was already half asleep at the time. If the bell hadn't woken me, I'd've been all the way.

'I thought,' he picked up the empty bottle of S'Comfort I'd bought in the duty-free at Oslo and been drinking from all day while I waited, on the 'plane, on the train, and finished in the bath:

'We might go for a little drink ...'

I knew exactly where he meant. I also knew he would brook no argument:

'Who's paying?'

Drinks at Lewis' were as costly as Oslo.

'He is.'

'In that case … Would it trespass unduly upon your tolerance if I took a little time to attire myself?'

'You what?'

'I wanna get dressed …'

He muttered beneath his breath. Something that rhymed with banker.

It was, after all, the only thing I had on him. Professional superiority. I was, by profession, a lawyer. Ergo, a gentleman and a scholar (*pace* the odd marguie-doll that managed to scrape through). On the other hand he was professionally a sub-moronic get. Though I did not doubt some native, perhaps even nurtured, nouse, he was duty bound to by-pass it as often as occasion allowed.

Lewis was not amused at our double-act. It would seem that the good sergeant had omitted to inform him of the acquaintance we had fostered since first introduced.

'Tim … Dave …'

'Lewis …' I said.

'S'Comfort …' said Dowell.

'S'coming,' he flicked his fingers at the waitress who'd served me the last time I was there.

'No thanks, Lewis,' Dowell calmly disinvited him.

Lewis shrugged his shoulders:

'Suit yourselves.' I would've sworn he swallowed a 'darlings' as he turned away.

'It's leave the bottle, isn't it?' She grinned at me.

'You got it.'

'Fancy her?' asked Dowell.

I shrugged:

'She's about my mark ...'

He knew exactly what I meant:

'No more lady lawyers ... For a while?'

'Something like that.'

One of the reasons I tried to keep as much distance between myself and Dowell was an unfortunate characteristic that cropped up whenever I was obliged to keep him company. I had a tendency — terrifying enough in theory, regardless of the reality — to tell the truth.

'Holiday. Bradkinson. Marguerita.' He prompted.

'Ah. Pity about that.'

'Tell time ...'

'Not much to. Met a very nice gentleman. Lawyer. Orbach. Name ring a bell?'

'And?'

'And Keenan set Bradkinson up.'

'Why?'

'I figured, so's I'd be staying with a charmer called Geir I couldn't pronounce his last name, who was once a friend of Orbach's and still a friend of Keenan's and he'd fill my head with a lot of nasty tales about Orbach and lo and behold Bradkinson'd make sure I just happened to spot him lurking behind a clump of pine and I'd put two and two together and make four.'

Dead bodies.

'And?'

'And, Orbach figures, so's Keenan can play naughty games behind my back. So? What do you know?'

He frowned:

'Not enough. Not enough by half.'

'But you know things you're not telling me.'

'Maybe. Maybe there's others know things they aren't telling me either.'

'How'd'you manage to meet up with Sandra Nicholl?'

He sighed:

'Good looking lady.'

'Look, sunshine, you leave your fantasies out of mine.'

'They're not exactly alike,' he said. He didn't mean our fantasies either. Nicholl And Bradkinson.

'Tell you what ... You met Lady H?' Keenan's wife.

He shook his head.

'Well. I have. You can have her. All to yourself. OK?'

'Not from what I've heard,' he muttered. He did not mean he could not have her; just not to himself.

'What now? I asked.

'Another drink?' He poured.

Lewis passed by. Dowell grabbed his sleeve. It reassured me to see him so friendly with others.

'Come and join us ...'

Lewis arched his eyebrows:

'Bored with one another already, dears?'

He'd had a few in between.

'And I thought I'd made the match of the moment ...'

'Ere, guv, alliteration's my lark, innit?

The girl brought him a drink.

'What in the name of god is that?' Dowell asked.

'It's called a White Russian. Vodka. Kahlua. Cream.'

Dowell and I exchanged a glance, held our unadulterated glasses up to one another: down the hatch.

'Your fancy fairy,' Dowell began:

'Didn't dance ...'

Everyone was elbowing in. Unfair.

'I told you all he knew,' Lewis answered:

'What made you think you'd get more out of him anyway?'

'You can't give someone ten years ...'

'You can't take ten years away from them ...'

I thought: charming, charming couple.

'Would anyone care to fill me in?' I began. Quickly, I remembered Lewis was present:

'Let me put that another way. Would anyone care to brief me on this?'

'You ain't got a practising certificate, remember?'

'Ugh.'

Lewis was confused. He knew less about practising certificates than I did.

Dowell relented:

'The little faggot who saw the car drive off ... Had a chat with ...'

'Ah. What's he got that I haven't?' I asked Lewis, pained. I'd wanted the same favour.

Lewis said:

'You really need telling, you already got the answer ...'

'I want it straight, Lewis ...' Dowell began.

I couldn't help myself:

'Hardly the right person to ask, I would've said ...'

Dowell scowled.

'Was it a fag did it or not?'

'Nope. That's my first and my last.'

To make the point, he got up and left the table. Leaving his White Russian behind.

'You knew that,' I remarked after he was out of earshot.

'Sure,' Dowell admitted.

'So? Why'd'you ask?'

'I just wanted to make him tell me.'

'You're a cynical bastard, Dowell. You know that?'

'Yes. I do. It's part of the job. You ever think about it? My job. All I ever deal with is scum. Murderers. Rapists. Heavy villains who wouldn't hesitate to blow someone's head off for half a thou. That's now. Before. When I was a wee baby suckling, as you'd no doubt call me, I spent my days and nights chasing after bag-snatchers, baby-snatchers, cop-a-feel and run merchants, people who'd break into your home and crap on the sheets ... Don't you people ever think why we get like this?'

'Nice speech,' I answered:

'I suppose you think it's a doddle defending them against bent coppers, biased judges, and bloody juries? Or that it's all fun-and-games dealing with battered women, beggars, booted out workers or plain batty tenants? Don't give it me, Tim, I've already got it.'

We sipped in silence. And something I could've sworn was kissing cousins with mutual respect.

'You didn't answer my question about Sandy Nicholl ...'

'It's no sweat. To "bump into" a solicitor. At court. They're the easiest coincidences. OK?'

'I guess. But why? Why did you want to?'

He looked at me like it was obvious:

'Because of Keenan, of course.'

I shook my head:

'You're going too fast for me.'

'You were her partner. You know.'

'It's late. I'm tired. I slept on an Oslo airport bench last night. I've been slurping S'Comfort all day. Don't play games, Tim. Just, you know, tell me, OK?'

He shrugged:

'I thought you knew. She's been Keenan's piece on the side for years; if anyone knows what this is all about, she will ...'

CHAPTER SEVEN

Gimbo was back.

'Who is he?' I asked Sandy, as we peeped out from opposite ends of her curtained bay.

'Police ... We've seen him before ...'

I snarled: 'we' meant her and Keenan.

I wanted to say: he isn't police. How was I to know? Tim Dowell could be playing me for a patsy the way everyone else was. It was fast becoming a national sport, one at which crippled geriatric mental patients could excel.

I rang her the morning after my return. At the office. She sounded surprised:

'I thought you were abroad ...'

'Well, uh, you know, maybe I couldn't wait to see you again ...'

She got my point. After a pause, she said:

'Do you want to come over this evening?'

She lived in Kentish Town.

I kissed her on the cheek. Which she let me. Deliberately, I kissed her on the lips. She could taste how little I meant it and pulled away.

Behind her back, as she led the way into the living room, I grinned.

Finding I knew things I wasn't supposed to was some consolation for realizing I hadn't awoken from a three-year slumber the man most likely to make it in multiple marriage since Henry Eight. But not much.

'You want a drink?'

She hovered at the sideboard.

'Want? No. Need more like.'

I didn't really mind about Marguie. She was cute and sweet and young. God, she was so young. But I'd always known. Even when I'd admitted to Mrs Nick she was paying for kicks she wouldn't read about in my final report. It had never been nothing but hors d'oeuvres.

Sandy was different. I already knew I liked her. I could get along with her, at least when I wasn't obsessed with not getting along with anyone: self included. Finding out I could also fancy her put her into a class I'd never believed existed. What I'm trying to say is: I minded.

'You wanted to talk ...'

'Whose idea was it?'

'What?'

'Everything ... Everything from day one you rang me up ... None of it ... was you ... Was it?'

She smiled ruefully:

'Some of it, Dave ... You're not going to believe me ... But ... Some of it ...'

'No, you're wrong.'

I had a flash of insight.

'I do believe some of it was you. The bit about coming back to work. So's you could put off your other people. That smells like you.'

She winced.

'You wanna tell me. Or you want I should tell you?'

'I'll ... I'll tell you.' It saved a small slice of dignity. Not enough. But where she was at, even a small slice counted.

'I've been seeing Alex for ... years ... It was him ... All the time we were working together. I wouldn't ... I wouldn't've done anything ... Anything that might've ... Hurt you? Misled you? For anyone else.'

I was supposed to he grateful.

'Was it true? When you said that you weren't sleeping with him any more?'

'Yes. That was true.'

She was the one who was grateful, that I'd asked the question. She must've thought it indicated interest. All I wanted was the truth.

Keenan had seen through my spiel about the book: between one and three minutes after we'd started talking. If that long.

Keenan had set Sandy up to jump on my tail:

'Why? What did he want?'

'I don't know. He was very vague. He said he'd seen you again. Suggested maybe I ought to find out what you were really up to. He knew ... I'd told him before ... I sometimes regretted, well, the way the firm had gone ... He said maybe I ought to do something about it ... See you ...'

She laughed, nervously, lightly:

'So, you see, you're wrong. The idea we might work together again, that did really come from him, at least just at this moment.

But, and this is the truth, Dave, there was no more to it than that. I only did it because it prompted me to do something I'd wanted to do for a long time. I didn't, you know, promise to report back to him or anything like that. I wasn't spying. Maybe he wanted me to, but I hadn't agreed. OK?'

I got up to refill my glass. The price ticket was still on the cap. I smiled:

'This's from before?'

She nodded:

'How'd you know?'

'There's nowhere you can buy S'Comfort for seven pounds nowadays!'

She bit her lower lip nervously:

'Make me another drink, Dave.'

G-and-T, like the good English lady she wasn't. When I took it to her, she grabbed my wrist:

'He ... He never suggested ... What happened in the park ... That's the truth, Dave ... I swear it ...'

'That's supposed to be some big deal?'

'That's supposed to tell you ... Oh, shit, I don't know.. .'

I pulled my hand away. But gently.

We sat opposite each other in silence for a while.

'I wish ... I wish I had got in touch with you before ...'

I shrugged:

'I don't suppose I'd've been interested anyhow ...'

Neither of us had said which we were talking about: working together again; or ...

'It's a funny old world, isn't it, Dave? You can know someone so well, and not at all. Or, different sides of them.'

She smiled wryly:

'It isn't news to me that I ... liked you ...'

That wasn't news to me either. The news was that I liked her too.

'Do you want to eat here?'

I almost said yes. It was the wrong thing for her to say. Trying to take us in one direction reminded me of the other. The one I was there to follow.

'You still haven't said why ...'

'I've known, for a long time, about the killings ...'

'How long?'

She hesitated for the last time. Goodbye and hello.

'Since Peter Wishart died.'

I absorbed the information slowly. It meant a great deal. Since the very beginning, Keenan at least had known it was some kind of vendetta against the group. It didn't necessarily follow that Anne Godwin had lied to me. It could also be that Keenan had kept it from her, perhaps from everyone else in the group, until they, with their usual slow wit, had finally managed to work out the obvious.

'And?'

'And what?'

'And what have you known?'

She wasn't enjoying the transfer of loyalty. Despite myself, I was glad it upset her to tell me the secrets she had secured during the affair with Alex. I wouldn't have liked to think of her as betraying anyone — even Keenan — easily.

'Shortly after Pete died, Alex saw someone ... A woman they'd known before ... A German woman who used to live in London ...'

'Who?'

'Her name was Helga. She'd been, you know, around ...'

I did know what she meant. Around lawyers, probably around all professionals, a scene, a circle, grows up; comprised partly of professional supporters — assistants, secretaries, clerks, students, even clients — it also has its social purpose. It's a mutually satisfying arrangement. Those whose activities aren't sufficient in their own eyes to sustain an adequate sense of participation latch on to the lawyers; the lawyers surround themselves with people, dependants, to massage their egos and reassure them how important they are.

In left-wing legal circles, that scene takes in a much wider range of hangers-on. There are those in related fields — law centres, legal advisers, lobbyists, journalists, political activists, for example.

Because politics (unlike law) crosses frontiers — and it is of the essence of left-wing politics that it ought to be a world-wide struggle — around left-wing lawyers has grown up a sort of forum, an international, socialist jet-set — again, part professional (only, now, the profession of politics) and part social. It wasn't difficult to imagine a German woman called Helga fitting in, or just hanging around.

'Back in ... Well, the early days of Disraeli Chambers ... 1974. 1975. 1976 ... You remember ... Didn't we even go to a couple of meetings there? Some of them were heavily involved in Baader-Meinhof, and the things that were happening in Germany. Particularly Alex, Wishart, Creemer and Russel Orbach ...'

'Yes. I do remember. Orbach wrote an article?'

'Yes ... Helga was involved ...'

I shrugged. I didn't remember any German women. I would have. For all my innate bias against Germans, I had a weakness for lean and fit cropped blondes. Helga would have registered. Either because she was. Or, disappointed, because she wasn't.

Sandy continued her story as she made us another drink. After she set mine down beside me, she went and drew the curtains, to shut out the sound of the rain. She carried on talking, standing behind me, her hands on my shoulders, needing physical reassurance. Not because of what she was telling me but because she was telling me at all.

'Helga went back to Germany.'

'Where?'

'I don't know. She met Alex on a visit, here, a few weeks after Pete died. Naturally, he brought it up. She told him she'd heard about it. And ... That it wasn't an accident ...'

'How did she know?'

'I only know what Alex told me, Dave. She told him Pete had had enemies. In Germany. At first, Alex said, he assumed she meant right-wing enemies, possibly the police, but not necessarily. It wasn't what she meant at all. She told him: on the left ...'

'But why?'

I got up, accidentally knocking her hands off my shoulders, and paced about. I was excited because I felt I was getting somewhere at last. But confused. I didn't begin to understand the whys and the wherefores.

'No. I've never fully understood it either. The story is ...'

'Alex's story?'

'Yes, in effect. Some of the German underground ... The people who came after Baader-Meinhof ... Believe they were betrayed ...'

'By Disraeli Chambers? How? That's ridiculous! How could a band of English barristers betray them? They weren't defending them! They couldn't have had privileged information! What then?'

She slumped down in the chair where I'd been sitting:

'It's no good asking me ... I just don't know ... You see ... Alex ... Well, you've met him. The English upper classes are different from you or me,' she parodied Scott Fitzgerald's famous line about the very rich:

'I had an affair with Alex for, oh, the best part of six years ... On and off ... He'd come and see me late at night ... Or, he'd tell his wife he had a case out of town and pretend to go off the night before, and instead come here and get an early train ... We never went out together ... Or away ... And ... I don't want to say he was secretive about what he told me as well ... That's not really what I mean ... It wasn't that deliberate ... But for all the time I knew him, he never completely opened up with me ... As if, well, he never could, perhaps never would, with a woman ... Even a lover ... It wasn't on, do you see? It wasn't done to tell your woman everything ...'

'I don't want to hear about it ...' I meant: their affair.

I was thinking about the idea of a betrayal from Disraeli Chambers. It wasn't as implausible as I'd first reacted. One of the consequences of the social set surrounding socialist lawyers was an incidental channel of communication. It acted as an information catalyst. It is part of the status, the chic, within such groupings to be better informed than others, to be the possessor of secrets. That is a contradiction because people — someone — have to know how trusted you are, on the left, and the only way of proving it is by at least occasionally revealing what it is you know.

I was standing at the sideboard, doing what came most naturally within reach of a bottle. She got up and stood beside me, again placing her hand on my shoulder:

'Just let me say this, then.'

Her voice was choking. I glanced round. She had tears in her eyes. I turned away. I didn't need it.

'We haven't slept together for years ... He's gone on coming to see me... Turning up late ... Like he did the night he talked to me about you ... A bit drunk ... Wanting ... Trying to ... You know. I just want you to understand it's me that's said no ...'

'So what, Sandy? So fucking what?'

'You're hurt, aren't you, Dave?'

'Who? Me? Forget it. I don't get close, and I don't get hurt.'

We were both more than a little pissed. Otherwise, she might have let it go then. Instead, she whispered:

'Are you sure?'

'What do you want from me, Sandy?'

She grinned:

'You know ...'

I did know.

I glanced at my watch. It was nearly ten o'clock. She followed the movement of my eyes.

'What's that for?'

Was I going somewhere else?

I shrugged:

'I wanted to know what time to put down that I stopped work ...'

She laughed:

'Bastard ...'

'Do you still know what you want?'

She nodded. She was shivering. I would have left.

Only, I was too.

After, I lay on the bed, my arms folded back above my head. She got up to go to the bathroom. Pee. Wash. I watched her come back towards me. I was aware of the differences with Marguie.

Sandy's body was no way as firm; when I ran my hand across her sallow skin, it felt like crinkled cotton, not taut satin. When Sandy walked, her breasts, though as big as Marguie's, swung heavily from side to side, instead of wobbling precariously but lightly up high.

She was real. In bed, she knew what her body wanted rather than merely surrendering it to my pleasure. I felt: where she is now, what her body has become, is an arrival. In comparison, Marguie was at the beginning of a journey. Where she ended up would be somewhere so different she would have become someone else. Maybe that someone else would be an improvement; maybe not. The point is: the end was uncertain.

It was woman versus girl.

She lay down beside me again. Rolled over, and placed her breast on my chest, crossed her leg over to let it lie between mine. To both our astonishment, I began to respond. She lifted her head to look at me, laughing:

'You're not so old after all ...'

'It's in a state of shock ... Like a chicken twitching after its head's been cut off ...'

'God, you've got such a nice line in sweet-talk ...'

'You've said that before ...' In the park.

'I'm sorry ...' About the circumstances in which we'd re-encountered one another.

'It doesn't matter ...'

'It does. I wanted this to happen. Oh, years ago I used to want it. But, since we met the other day ... And now I feel, well, nothing can come of it ... Because you won't trust me.'

I didn't answer. If I'd said, sure, forget it, of course I trust you, I'd've been lying, and she'd've known it. On the other hand, I wanted to trust her. You could've knocked me over with a feather: I wanted this to be happening; I wanted something to come of it.

She did things then that were her way of telling me what she felt, what she wanted, what was possible, without using words. I can't explain what was happening as she did so. I wasn't overwhelmed by pleasure, lost in lust, riding waves of passion or anything like that. It was a far calmer, more rewarding, more peaceful sensation. While it was going on, it was washing away the years between. Not just the last few years since I'd left the firm. But years before while I'd looked in every place but the obvious, that which was closest to home, for substitutes which had never come close to satisfying.

It was midnight before she asked:

'Are you going to stay?'

Her voice said please do.

I wanted to.

I had a job to do. Something like this didn't figure in how I was going to finish it off.

I got dressed again. She just put on a dressing-gown.

That was when I glanced out of the side of the living-room window, to see how the weather was doing. I called her over:

'Who is he?'

She came over to look out.

'Police. We've seen him before.'

I snarled at the 'we'.

But, after all, I couldn't remain angry about Keenan and Sandy.

He was standing underneath a tree, about fifty feet down the road, beside a car that might or might not have been the one I'd seen him drive off in after our encounter at Harrods.

I thought about leaving out the back. It would have meant burglarizing my way through someone else's house. Sandy's garden was surrounded by other gardens and houses as far as the eye could see. There was no access to the open streets.

Well, hell, I thought, it was time to resume the relationship. He hadn't been around since before I'd left for Oslo with Marguie Bradkinson. I waltzed out of the house, as if oblivious to his presence.

Where Sandy lived wasn't the sort of street cabs crawled down in the middle of the night. She'd offered to drive me home, or to somewhere I'd catch one, or to call for one to collect me, but I'd refused. The air would clear what was left of the Southern Comfort, and the confusion.

I was halfway down the next street before I looked around. I couldn't hear a car following me, so I figured he must be on foot. To my surprise, he still wasn't in sight. I crossed over, before walking slowly back up to where the roads met, in case he was just a bit further behind me than I had expected.

It wasn't so much astonishment when I realised he wasn't following me at all — at least, tonight — as chagrin. He was still in the same place. Watching Sandy's house.

That meant one of two things.

Either he was watching Sandy. Or else he was waiting for someone else.

If it was the latter, I had a fair idea of who that would be — Keenan.

If it was Keenan he was waiting for, that also meant two things.

Either Sandy hadn't told me the truth about the current state of their relationship. Or else Gimbo was way out of date.

The reasons I didn't want to believe Sandy had been lying to me don't need spelling out. I had one line, which was fixed in my memory, and which helped me decide not only that Gimbo was waiting for Keenan, and that he was doing so because his information was archaic, but that also said Sandy was right when she identified him as police. Last night, Dowell had said to me:

'She's been Keenan's piece on the side for years ...'

Gimbo and Dowell were sticking their snouts in the same trough.

It told me something else, too. That afternoon I'd been to Disraeli Chambers to try and find out where Keenan was. They'd professed not to know. Downstairs, Gilligan had claimed he didn't know either. It looked like: nor did the police.

It took me half an hour to find a cab. I was about to tell him the story about West Chelsea when I changed my mind. I wasn't that far from where Gilligan lived.

The lights were on throughout the house. I glanced at my watch. Only one o'clock. That's a time when sophisticates are still trying to select sleeping partners for the night.

I knew the woman who answered the door, though I couldn't put a name on it. She didn't recognize me either.

'Gerry here?'

She held the door back and stepped aside to allow me to enter.

Banged at the nearest inside room:

'Gerry. Visitor.'

It took him a minute to open up. Kept his body in the gap so's I couldn't see in. All he was wearing was trousers. I grinned:

'Sorry ...'

'I'll be right out, OK? You want to wait in the kitchen?'

The lady of the house led me down. By now, she was also thinking she'd met me before. I remembered her. Journalist. Left wing journal. We resumed acquaintance.

'Ah,' she said when I'd identified myself:

'You're the one that's writing about them ...'

'That's right.' Gerry entered door right:

'You want some coffee? Good night, Cynthia.'

She laughed:

'So subtle. Good night.'

'Not a confidante, huh?'

'Who is? Who do you trust?'

'Try me ...' I mimicked the airplane commercials.

'Why?'

"Cos you rang me that night ...'Cos — according to what you said this afternoon — you didn't figure me for a fool ...'Cos I'm insane enough to give up a week away with your colleague's tender young flesh to get on with the job ... Any of them reasons do?'

He shrugged:

'You'd go stir crazy hanging out with Marguie for a week ... She only knows one thing and doesn't even do that well ...'

'Maybe her training wasn't that great,' I said softly. I had no brief for Bradkinson, but the evening had made me mellow.

For a second he dithered between anger and amusement, and, undecided, acknowledged:

'Fair enough ...'

'Did it surprise you I came back?'

'No.'

'Why not?'

'Nothing does any more ...'

'What's your game, Gerry? What do you know? For certain?'

'Too little. Like everyone else. Just that it's going on. And that someone'd better bring it to a halt before we're looking for smaller chambers to work from.'

'Is' that why you rang me that night? 'Cos you think I can sort it?'

His brow furrowed:

'I don't know. Do you know the reason you do everything?'

He was pretty close to why I'd taken up doing nothing for a profession.

'I know it's a grudge thing, against the group, but you don't need an elementary pass in detection to work that out. I know Keenan thinks its political. And ...'

'German?'

He was impressed:

'Yes.'

'And?'

'And what?'

'Do you believe him?'

'Yes and no.'

Lawyer's answer. Covered all the available options.

'What has Keenan told you?'

'That Peter Wishart — and others — were mixed up in things German. One of their gestures of political solidarity. That some people got killed. By police. Members of a German gang. There were one or two survivors. Or the group had comrades. Anyway, apparently someone out there believes the way things happened was Disraeli Chambers' fault ...'

'How so?' I'd got a bit more out of him than I already knew. Sandy's word 'betrayal' had been coloured red. I don't mean political red. Blood red.

'A date. A time. A place. Don't you remember it? I do: I was still at University. The police hit a house, claimed to have killed eight terrorists ... It was big news at the time ...'

I had a vague recollection:

'1978? 1979?'

'1978. After Ulrike Meinhof was murdered in prison. Before the others were too.'

I wasn't about to quibble with 'murdered'. As I recalled, even the straight British Press never bought the deaths of Ulrike Meinhof and, later, Andreas Baader and the remaining gaoled members of their gang, as anything other than a final senterce, passed and executed not by the courts, but by the German police and their associates.

'And? Was there anything in it? Did Wishart know anything? Could he have leaked?'

'I don't know. I'd say ... It's possible he knew ... I don't know about the other ...'

He went back to the kettle:

'You want another coffee?'

'Sure. If you are ... I sort of had the impression you were being waited for? Anyone I know?'

'No.'

He glanced around:

'You want to check?'

I shook my head. I couldn't think it mattered.

'You said: yes and no. What did you mean?'

'I meant ... I can't really explain. I get an uneasy feeling ... That we're still not being told the whole truth ...'

'By Keenan?'

'Yes.'

'Tell me where Orbach fits into this?'

I'd put my finger on it.

'That's what I meant. You have to remember, I wasn't around when the split with Orbach happened. He's very bad news in chambers. All the ones who were around at the time hate him. They won't talk about it. If you ask, you get a different story each time. As if they weren't even totally certain how it happened themselves. Just that ... Well, it was bound to have been his fault. Everything was. Everything bad before he left and ... This is where he connects: everything since. He's like the chambers' bogey man, the devil incarnate: whatever goes wrong, some people believe he must be at the back of it.'

'Paranoia?'

'Maybe. But you know what we used to say. "Just because I'm paranoid doesn't mean they don't hate me".'

Nor did it. I remembered Orbach's venom in Oslo.

'Who is it ...' I paused, to try and form the question before I asked it:

'Who is it in chambers believes Orbach's involved? I mean specifically, not just because of what you said,' about the assumption of intervention.

'You want me to say Keenan, don't you?'

'I don't want anything, Gerry. Except to get to the bottom of this,' and get it behind me.

'All right. No, not Keenan. At least, he's never said so. You see, there's no hatred between Keenan and Orbach. There never was so far as I can tell ...'

'I heard, Orbach and Lady Helen?'

'Sure, I heard that too. But, well, Keenan isn't like that. I doubt he'd care, and he certainly wouldn't let that turn into hatred. Keenan ... Well,' he laughed, and said something not so dissimilar to a remark Sandy had made earlier:

'I don't think he feels deeply at all. About anything. I mean, the upper classes don't, do they?'

'If Keenan didn't believe Orbach was involved, why'd he send me to Oslo?'

'From his point of view, just to get you out the way. Also, with Orbach there, it fitted with what others would like to believe ... Keenan's a master of expediency ...'

'Do you know where he's gone?'

'No. I wasn't lying. None of us know where. But I know why.'

'Ah.'

'He's gone to meet someone ... I don't know a name ... I don't know a place ... but you might call them an intermediary ... He's trying to get through ... To bring it to an end ...'

'Brave man,' I commented.

After a bit, I asked him:

'Why not the police? Or do you also subscribe to the proposition that the practice is worth any price?'

I did, however, now understand what Anne Godwin had meant, even if they weren't the words she had used.

It was not the reaction of the profession at large that she was worried about. Just their bit of it. Their particular clientele. Much worse than some vague possibility of scandal, apparently worse even than a rather novel tax on membership, was the prospect of being held up as traitors to the left. Their practices were those of quote unquote radical lawyers. From what I had already managed to gather, those practices didn't amount to much at the best of times; since Orbach had left, they were based on Keenan's reputation alone. If something like this came out, what little there was would disappear altogether.

'What do I know?'

'You could have told them ... Before they had to work it out for themselves ... You might have one more member ... Or maybe you didn't care that much for Art Farquharson?'

He didn't bat an eyelid at the accusation:

'You can investigate me as long as you like. I'm not a murderer. And I don't know any more than I've told you.'

'You don't think much of them do you, Gerry? Why are you still there?'

He shrugged:

'It's not as easy as all that. All my life ... As long as I can remember ... I was a socialist ... And all I wanted to be was a barrister ... Crazy ambition ... Crazier than you know ... It wasn't exactly the sort of thing members of my family went in for ... My dad was a tailor ... And I don't mean John Collier ...' He named a major clothing chain store.

'I went to Oxford ... On a scholarship ... Got a grant through the Council of Legal Education ... All the time thinking: I wanted to get in to Disraeli Chambers ... I was going to get in there ... And: I did ...'

'And?'

It wasn't all it was cracked up to be.

He shrugged:

'It's a joke, really ... They're no worse than other left-wing lawyers ... Especially at the Bar ... Poncing around playing politics ... Patronizing their clients ... Sitting around in meetings ... Endless bloody meetings ... Discussing Ireland and Palestine and all points East ... Going to the pub feeling smart ... Clever ...'Cos they're different ... For half of them it's an excuse for not bothering to try: they lose because the court's're against them — or the client — never because they didn't work hard enough or because they just blew it ...'

'Are they wrong?' About the courts.

'No. That isn't the point. The thing is ... About being a left-wing lawyer ... It's all in the way you fight the case ... Above all, it's in the way you lose ... You've got to win on the facts and law and force them ... The courts ... To show their true colours ... That's when you're winning politically ...'

'What about the client?'

'If it's winnable, what I said gives them the best chance too ... The best professional chance ... No?'

'Maybe. What's it got to do with the price of eggs?'

'The ones that got cracked?'

'Yup.'

'It's all mixed up together. It's an unreal world. Look at the left-wing lawyer ... We've staked our claim to being special, different, because we're left-wing ... We're the ones who both know the law, and poke two fingers at it ... That's our point of pride ... But, all the time, disregarding the rhetoric, in fact we are barristers, lawyers, just like all the others, and that's all we know how to do. So we're frightened to go too far, frightened to jeopardize that status, to lose it. But politically, that's the one thing we can't admit to ... It would undermine our claim to being more political than lawyer ... It's a latent force ... And it's a fear ...

'I think things get very confused. The lines are completely unclear. Not between what's legal and illegal ... We know that, just about ... But between what lines a political lawyer, a left-wing lawyer, ought to respect. On the one hand, you're being driven to show you're not a servant of the law, politically that you're just using it; and on the other is that fear ... So who or what is there to tell you what to do, when to stop, how far to go ... Across the line ... In either direction ...'

'What are you saying?'

'Just ... That all things are possible ... Maybe Wishart did know things he ought'n't to ... Maybe he, or someone, did leak ...'

'Which doesn't explain how Keenan thinks he can bring it to a stop, or what Russel Orbach's got to do with it if anything, or why you don't believe Keenan's telling you the whole truth, or, for that matter, assuming it all hangs together the way it's been spelled out, what we're going to do about it ...'

He smiled:

'Meaning you don't like speeches that don't give you answers.'

'Meaning I've had an awful lot of them recently ...'

'Where do you go from here?'

'Apart from home?'

It was pushing three.

He nodded.

'Keenan, I guess, when he gets back. When will that be?'

'I'm not sure. But before the next chambers' meeting ...'

'Ah, yes. I'd forgotten about that ... Maybe it ain't so brave to go, provided he gets back by Wednesday ...'

We had the same thought at the same moment:

'How does that fit in?'

It was the feature that had made me think, earlier on: chambers' member.

We also had the same answer:

'Russel Orbach?'

'It does seem ... Every time I turn around ... He's standing there ... Watching over my shoulder ...'

'You're catching chambers' paranoia, Dave ...'

'Yup. And every time I see him. He's laughing.'

CHAPTER EIGHT

The night of the next chambers' meeting, I had two invitations. I was growing popular. It was a pleasant sensation.

The first invitation — in time — was the one I did not finally turn up to. It came from the man who sometimes qualified as 'the good', but more often as something slightly more selective, such as 'that bastard'. By whom I mean to refer, as you will doubtless have worked out for yourself, to Timothy Dowell.

'How would you like …'

I held my breath.

This was usually the point in the conversation when routes violently diverged.

Thus, the next phrase might well be: 'To spend a week in the slammer picking your schnozzle …'

Or else, it could be:

'To get pissed at Lewis' …'

Or, with a little stretch of the imagination:

'A reward for all the good work you've done so far ... From the informants' fund ...'

As it was:

'To go camping with me ...'

I paused for reflection. There were several available explanations. He had found in me the son and/or best boyhood friend he'd longed for but never had. He was as faggy as Farquharson and liked it best in the open air. The murderer was a member of the boy scouts. He had finally flipped.

'You wouldn't ... Er ... Like to elaborate on your intentions, would you?'

'There's a four syllable word in that sentence, Woolf. I've warned you ...'

'Sorry. How about: whaddayamean?'

'I mean this. Tomorrow is what? OK. You got it.'

'And?'

'And I'm proposing we take certain precautions ...'

'Like?'

'Would you believe I'm going to camp out in Disraeli Court? Me, plus two of mine to each of them?'

'Nah. You need a contract on the Queen for that sort of man-power.'

'One on one?'

'I'd believe you if you said thirteen of you to fourteen of them and you need me to make the numbers ...'

He snorted:

'You think I'd trust you to follow one of them? I wouldn't give you to the first dark corner.'

'You could give me one of the men. I don't lose them quite so fast ...'

He grinned wickedly:

'You only said that before I did ...'

'Tell me about it ...'

'You know Disraeli Chambers ...'

I did indeed. These days: better than I could recall the layout of my home.

Disraeli Chambers was in one of the buildings in a courtyard — Disraeli Court — in the Middle Temple. There were about ten buildings in Disraeli Court, each containing between two and five sets of barristers' chambers, one or two with solicitors' offices, and on the top floor of most of them lived the odd geriatric judge or senior barrister.

At one end of the courtyard was the back of a big hall, where barristers dined and ceremonial occasions took place. The main door of the hall was, however, outside Disraeli Court. There were only two exits from the courtyard, and from the buildings within it.

Dowell proposed to site his men in the basements of the buildings. They would be able to see anyone who left any of them, and follow whichever exit they took. His allowance was somewhat lower than I had estimated — a mere eight souls plus himself (who had no soul), but he banked, on experience, on them leaving in groups, and several of them passing what was left of the evening after their meeting ended getting plastered in the pub. Once his men had escorted safely home the loners who went off in other directions, they would be able to return to duty before closing time. It was a gamble, but calculated.

I neither accepted, nor refused. I asked:

'Is Gimbo one of your men?'

'Who he?'

I described the man whose fidelity to me had proven so fickle, and that was now transferred to Sandy Nicholl.

Dowell wasn't dumb:

'You asked me before if I was having you followed? Same?'

'Sure.'

He shook his head. Not guilty. But, just as on the previous occasion, not without a shadow fleeing across his face.

This conversation took place on the Tuesday afternoon in a café near New Scotland Yard. It ended with my provisional acceptance of the invite.

That was before a telephone call the next afternoon. From Lady Helen Keenan.

'Yes,' I confirmed it was indeed I.

'You don't know me ...'

That was her first mistake. I had met her. She had forgotten. I sometimes forget people myself, anyone can. But to forget me?

I didn't remind her. After all, 'twas in another county, and besides, our host was dead.

'But my name's Helen Keenan ...'

That was the second mistake. She was the Lady Helen. And no one was supposed ever to forget it.

'I was wondering whether we could meet, this evening ...'

'It's Wednesday ...'

'Yes. Alex will be at the chambers' meeting ...'

She was not concealing that she wanted to see me without him there.

'OK. Where?'

'Could you come to the house? The children ...'

'All right. What time?'

'The earlier the better. Six-ish?'

That would give us plenty of time to talk before Keenan got back.

Tim Dowell was out:

'Could you tell him his friend Dave rang and can't make our date tonight?' I left a message seasoned with a touch of pay-back.

Lady H led me quickly into the living room. It was five past six and the bottle of red wine on the coffee table was getting low. By it lay a corkscrew, and the cork, which suggested it wasn't exactly a long time since it lost its virginity.

'Shall I get you a glass?'

'Fine ...'

While she was out of the room, I took a quick look around. The furniture was a studiedly casual mix. Some of it was probably antique; the sofa was perspex and plastic; on the walls, there were revolutionary prints, and framed pictures of the ancestors — Keenan's and hers; the dining table was stainless steel, but the chairs tucked beneath it covered in velvet.

On the open bureau lay an airline ticket. I was just about to read it when I heard Lady H's heavy-breathed return. Instead, I swept it beneath my jacket, and thence into my wallet pocket. Too bad if it was unused: there was enough mess about the room to lose the Crown Jewels, let alone a thin folder of paper. If it couldn't be found, doubtless it could be re-issued.

'You wanted to see me.'

It was her job to open.

I sipped the wine carefully. Cheap red wine. I placed it gingerly on the table. Just looking at it made my stomach churn.

Lady H was a startling woman. She attracted without being attractive. Like a blazing fire attracts a child. She had a mess of auburn hair tumbling about her hawk-like head, perched on top of a body that resembled a dumpling more than an hour-glass or a pear. When she walked — as when she had re-entered the room — it was as if she was fighting the air-space to get through. She spoke much the same: ill-concealed but possibly impersonal hostility; habitual aggression; defiance.

'You're investigating the chambers' murders,' she stated matter of factly.

These days it was about as much of a secret as the location of Buckingham Palace.

'OK.'

'I want to tell you about Russel Orbach,' she continued, ignoring me, and as if the connection was obvious.

I didn't say anything.

'Russel Orbach is a vicious, cruel man, who hates my husband, and who hates me.'

The last person who'd remarked on Orbach's hatred was Gilligan. He said Orbach hated chambers. He was correct. I know, because that was what Orbach had told me. Orbach had also said: he didn't hate Keenan.

She waited.

I waited.

I gave in first:

'Why?'

'Orbach is a maniac. He's very clever. I'll grant him that. Brilliant if you like. But inhuman. He's conceited. He thinks he's the cleverest and most important man in the world. For years, he conned all of us: particularly Alex and me. He made us believe in him politically, professionally and even personally. All his difficulties — and he's a difficult man, God knows — had to be forgiven, overlooked, he had to he helped through them ... Personal problems, emotional, psychological, professional ... It was everybody else's duty to comfort and protect him ... Especially ours ...

'You must have met people like that. It's never easy to know if they are worth helping, because they really are gifted people — the awkward genius! — or if they're simply egocentrics demanding attention for no greater end than itself ... Or plain mad, bad or selfish ...'

I wasn't very comfortable with this part of her statement. It was a little too close to home. I could recall, in my professionally successful days, more than one girl-friend making similar observations about me, usually in the middle of a terminal row.

'Sometimes, you never find out. Sometimes, you can only find out by looking back on what they've actually done with their lives, in their work. Most great men have been difficult. But, sometimes, they make a mistake, reveal their true personalities, show themselves for what they really are ...'

'And Orbach? That was what he did?' Left to herself, she might continue to develop her thesis for longer than we had left. I wasn't convinced she didn't like the sound of her own voice as much as, by implication, she was saying Orbach did.

'Yes.'

'How?'

It was, at least in one sense, the sixty-four thousand dollar question. The answer was worth about two bits.

'He raped me. Here. In this house. In front of the children.'

I had to say something.

I thought quickly.

'Ah.'

It wasn't, perhaps, profound. But it came closest to expressing my reaction.

'Here? In front of the children?'

You read about this sort of thing. It does happen. It can happen when a child is tiny. Or if the rapist ties the children up first. Or if he's got a gun or another weapon. Somehow it would not focus with Orbach's face in the frame.

'Well, they were upstairs, in bed ...'

Edit one.

'Didn't ... Didn't you cry out? Didn't they hear?'

'It wasn't ... Well ... It wasn't a physically violent rape ...'

Edit two.

I was beginning to enjoy this. Your starter for ten points: what is rape without physical violence, in front of the children who are in another room?

'A woman can be raped in ways other than with physical violence, you know, Mr Woolf. There are other ways of overriding what the woman wants. Negating consent. Conning someone. Persuading them they want something, when they don't.'

I nodded. I'd heard. I'll go further. I even accept it. But Lady Helen? By Orbach? It simply wasn't credible. She was — on present performance and past recollection — one very tough lady, who knew her mind and didn't allow anyone — including Keenan himself — to tell her what was in it.

She filled in some local colour. Orbach had been involved in a long inquiry. Earning a lot of money. Attracting a lot of media coverage. He had been working hard. Drinking. Hyped up. Full of himself. Came around one evening. Keenan had been away for the weekend. She'd not wanted to let him in, she said. He was already drunk. He'd insisted on coming in.

She'd gone on drinking with him to keep him company. He'd been angry with Keenan: some petty dispute over chambers' politics. He'd started attacking Keenan, abusing him, in front of the children. She'd sent them upstairs. Still he wouldn't go. In the end, she left him. Went up to see one of the kids. When she came back down, he was in their bedroom; in the bed, waiting for her.

'I felt sorry for him. He obviously couldn't cope with all the responsibility of the inquiry. He'd told me he could hardly get it up any more, because he was so tired from the strain. I didn't know what to do. It was a habit to want to help him, to let him have whatever he wanted, so I did ...'

Her son had heard them. Stood outside the door. Called out. They'd stopped. He'd left.

'I couldn't explain ... To John ... My son ... I couldn't explain to him how Orbach could have behaved like that. He couldn't understand. How could he understand? It was because of that, because of John, that I couldn't go on covering up for Orbach any more ...'

She'd told Keenan. He had been reluctant to accept how it had happened. He didn't want to believe ill of his professionally blue-eyed boy. Orbach had been his pupil, then his favourite son. He had been his most successful trainee. He had become his closest ally in chambers, confidante, supporter, even, on occasion, someone whose lead he could himself follow.

She had gone to the group. She had talked with Carrie Creemer. Carrie had been horrified. They were socialists, feminists; the oppressive behaviour of someone who purported to understand how women could be dominated by men was so much less forgivable than that of someone who was ignorant. She had started to talk with others in the group. They had asked Orbach to leave.

'It's true. They didn't handle it well. They relied on Alex to deal with Orbach. But Alex couldn't. He never could. He still didn't want to believe bad of him. Orbach could convince him of anything. He was ... He still is I suppose ... Brilliant with words ... Articulate ... The perfect advocate ... He could convince you your name was something else, it's a different day, to stand on your head ...

'Orbach wasn't in chambers much, hardly at all, he was into this inquiry full-time ... Alex used to go and see him, for lunch, to help him with his work ... All the time Alex was seeing him, the rest of chambers thought he was talking it through with Orbach, but actually he was talking about anything but ... It's one of his weaknesses, burying his head in the sand ... None of the others wanted to see him ... I think they were frightened he'd use that incredible mind to win them over ... None of them could stand up to him individually ...'

So they'd done it collectively instead.

'You're saying, no one asked his side of the story?'

'What side was there? There was nothing to hear. It would all have been lies.'

'Forgive me, Lady Helen ... I'm a lawyer ... They're lawyers ... We're trained to know there are two sides, to hear the other side!'

She shrugged. That was our problem. We were the lawyers. Not her.

'That was why ... Someone mentioned an action, legal proceedings ... Because of the way they did it?'

She nodded.

A key in the door.

I only had one more question.

Why had she wanted to tell me all this without Alex being present? When I saw the look on his face as he walked in and saw me, I had my answer.

He swung on her, livid.

It took all his training as a gentleman not to start shouting at her in front of me.

Alex Keenan still didn't believe his wife's account of how she came to be found, by their son, in bed with his best friend.

To put it at its simplest, like any good Victorian, caught in the act, she screamed rape.

Keenan helped himself to what was left of the wine and slumped into the sofa.

He still hadn't even said hello.

Then he said:

'Bitterness ... A sense of injustice ... Perhaps a feeling of betrayal ... He built that group with me, more than anyone else ... They ... No, we ... We kicked him out of it, behind his back, when he was bogged down in that damned, damned inquiry and could do nothing about it ... He was already exhausted from it, we were already concerned he wouldn't make it through without a breakdown ...

'It was cruel. I didn't want it to happen. They were jealous of him, resentful because he contributed so much more to the group than any of them ... Perhaps they were jealous because he and I were so close too ... It was, I suppose, their one chance to separate us, separate him and me ... We were too powerful together ... They thought he had too much influence over me ... They could do it, through Helen ... They used it ... But ... I let it happen ... I was the one person who could have stopped it, told them it was not their business ... I didn't. That made me responsible for it. For it all.'

'For four deaths?'

He shook his head fervently:

'I don't believe ... Not with all of that ... I don't believe he would do this. It wouldn't be Russel. It just wouldn't be him.'

She laughed and got up, turning on him in scorn:

'You still can't hear a word against him! God, you're so stupid!'

She swung out of the room, slamming the door behind her. Keenan jumped up and followed her out, motioning me to wait where I was. I used the time to examine the airline ticket. It had been used. Keenan had been in Paris while I had been in Oslo.

I held the ticket in my hand, tapping it against the arm of the chair. As I intended, he saw it as soon as he came back in.

I held it out to him without comment.

He shrugged and took it from me.

'Who did you go to see?'

'Someone ... A friend ...'

'Helga?'

He winced. That told him Sandy had talked to me.

It also must have told him where her loyalties now lay.

'I'm not going to tell you, Dave. I won't ... I won't involve anyone who isn't already involved ...'

I thought about that last sentence for a moment. It sounded good. Responsible. Serious. It was entirely circular and, as such, utterly without meaning.

'And?'

'And what?'

He had not sat down again. Paced nervously up and down in front of me.

'And did you get what you went for?'

'I think so, Dave, I think so,' he almost whispered:

'God, I hope so!'

The doorbell rang. He went to answer it. A voice most familiar asked:

'Is Mr Woolf here, Mr Keenan?'

I got up to greet my friend.

We stood, the three of us, in the hall.

'Good evening, Mr Woolf ...'

He was telling me to keep it formal.

'Sergeant ...'

'I wonder if you'd mind accompanying me, sir ...'

'Not at all, sergeant. Where are we going?'

'Down to Disraeli Chambers, sir. You see,' he turned to Keenan:

'I'm afraid there's been another death, sir.'

Keenan went as white as the ghost someone as yet unidentified had just become.

He could hardly get out the word:

'Who?'

'Mr Matheson, sir, Mr Henry Matheson.'

Fat Harry.

'Oh, God no ...'

Then:

'If you're going back to chambers, should I come with you? Can I come with you?'

'I'd rather not, sir, if you don't mind, not at the present, it's not a pleasant sight, sir ...' Dowell really didn't like Keenan.

'What do you want me for?' I barked.

'I think you could help us with our enquiries, sir ...'

He was building up police suspicion on the premise that it could only increase Keenan's confidence in me.

'I've been here, all evening ...'

'If you don't mind, sir, accompanying me ...'

I shrugged and followed him. At the door, as he strode away, I glanced back at Keenan, leaning still against the wall:

'Do you still think you got what you wanted in Paris, Alex?'

I waited until we had driven away before I grinned:

'How'd'you know I was here?'

He didn't answer.

There were other, more pressing questions that took priority.

He wasn't happy.

I knew why.

He told me without asking:

'No, we didn't catch the fucker.'

I simply couldn't help myself:

'I thought I was supposed to be the one ...' That couldn't be trusted.

'Can it, Dave ... I don't feel funny ...'

'How?'

'Would you believe? Inside. Down the stairs. Broken neck.'

'Fat Harry ... You know ... If he did fall ... He probably would break his neck ... I mean ... D'you know what that guy weighed?'

'To the last ounce. It's already in the preliminary report.'

'They got scales that big?'

'Nah, you dummy. They cut him into sections and weighed them one at a time.'

He pulled in to the side of the road.

We weren't anywhere near the Temple.

From the glove compartment, he withdrew a hip-flask, and offered it to me first. I wasn't disappointed. Drank deep enough for him to say:

'Don't forget me ...'

I passed it over.

A tramp hovered outside, looking in the window. He leaned down. Please.

Dowell lowered the screen.

The tramp reached in eagerly.

Dowell grabbed his wrist, ripped it inside the car 'till I heard the old man's head bang on the roof. Then he twisted his arm straight and shoved hard out again. The man fell back against railings, slid to the ground.

I'd been in a similar posture myself, not that long ago.

Dowell heard my thoughts.

As he wound up the window, he said:

'No. I didn't have to. I'm sorry.'

'Tell him ...'

'He won't notice ...'

The sick thing was: he was probably right.

He started the car again.

'You normally get this het up?' Over a death.

'Nope. Just this one. I don't like to be taken for a sucker ...'

Join the club.

We drove on to the Embankment, and turned illegally right at the bottom of Middle Temple Lane. Like they were ramps, up and over the speed-humps at a speed that shook what was left of my stomach into White Russian.

Inside was littered with policemen, and other officials. For all his lowly rank, they treated Dowell with respect. Even the uniformed inspector spoke as if to a superior.

One of what I guessed was his own men took Dowell aside. Dowell frowned. A quick, heated exchange. His man nodded earnestly. Dowell looked like he could kill.

'I've got to make a 'phone call. I'll be back. Wait here.'

So's I wouldn't get bored, he left me on the landing where Matheson had fallen. It was marked out in chalk. Just like in the movies. Only bigger.

Dowell was gone ten minutes. Once he got back, he told me the tale.

The chambers' meeting had started at about six thirty. Dowell and his men and women had searched the building.

No one else was left in it. The other chambers and doors were all locked. His army had been — as planned — discreetly placed in the basement areas of the other buildings.

Nor had Dowell's calculations disappointed when the members started to leave. Several had — as expected — gone off in a crowd to the pub. A couple — he didn't tell me which, or even of which sex — left arm-in-arm, which was novel gossip but nothing more. Keenan had bounced determinedly out, on his loyal way to the Lady Helen: he alone of them had — as head of chambers — a parking permit and therefore a car to go home in. That was when Dowell had himself left the site.

Eventually, they were all gone, save Harry Matheson. The remaining two officers were sure they had not missed him. They hardly could. Instead, however, an unknown figure had emerged. It was too dark to get a full description, but they had been sure it was not another, unaccounted member of chambers. They took radio instructions from Dowell; one of them followed quickly after the stranger while the other went inside the building.

'He didn't get far ... The guy went out the right hand alley. My man was behind him. At the corner, someone tripped him up, whacked him pretty hard, left him on the ground, and followed after our target. My man got a good look. There were definitely two ...'

By that time, the last of Tim's tin-soldiers had found the body.

Dowell led me back out of the building. We walked towards the hall which took up the whole of the end of the courtyard.

'Dinner in progress?'

'Yes.'

The unusual directness of his replies told me I was getting warm. To be on the safe side, I checked:

'The other buildings?'

'Mostly unoccupied. One or two working late. They check out. Nothing.'

'Access?'

He shrugged:

'It seems so ...'

'How?'

'Come on, I'll show you ...'

He had the freedom of the Temple that night.

We walked in through the huge oak doors of the dining hall. I had been in such halls before, although not this one. In the entrance, there was a noticeboard, to which were pinned announcements, including one for the dinner that evening.

The dining hall itself was lined with portraits of the good and dead. Pardon me: the good and the dead. Great judges of yesteryear. A few who still sat on the bench.

'Tasty bunch,' I muttered.

'I'd rather have them with me than agin' ...' Dowell admitted.

'You have,' I reminded him.

The barristers ate at long, school dining-tables, ten or a dozen each side, seated on benches. There were twelve tables in all.

The top of the dining-hall was to the rear of the building. There was a raised platform, on which stood a table longer and wider than those at which mere barristers ate. Around it was arrayed a set of fine, carved, high-backed chairs, with deep red leather seating. That was where the Benchers — masters — of the Inn ate.

There was a door in the wall behind them. Dowell took me through. Immediately the other side, steps led down, I guessed to the kitchen. The Benchers' food would be brought up this way, instead of by the entrance-hall through which came the fodder for the fools at their feet.

Past the steps down, another door led into a lounge of sorts. We were now at the absolute end of the building. The other side of the wall was the courtyard. At the right, I spotted the private facilities. I grinned at Dowell:

'Always wanted to do it somewhere like this.'

I was disappointed. It felt no different.

When I came out, he was slouched tiredly in a deep leather armchair.

I was tired too. I stretched out on a sofa opposite, without taking off my shoes.

'Careful, ducky, you'll scuff the leather ...' he said.

'You hate them as much as I do, don't you ... ?'

He didn't answer. I checked out:

'The kitchen ... Way through the basements ... Into Disraeli Chambers?'

'Yup. And no lock on this side. Just a solid, iron bar to lift ...'

No wonder he was glum.

'They got a guest list?'

Of people who had dined.

'Yes. And no.'

Yes, they had a list.

No, Russel Orbach's name wasn't on it.

'Could ... Could the man who came through the door have fitted Orbach?'

'Nope ...'

Could he have been the outside man, who'd helped the murderer get away?

'Nope,' he repeated firmly.

'Have you checked him out yet?'

He shook his head and answered distractedly:

'No grounds ...'

'That didn't bother you when you decided to come visiting me ...'

'You ain't a QC ...'

His heart wasn't in it, though. He was on automatic answerback.

I laid my head against the sofa:

'Who'd ever think a bunch of loony-tune lefty lawyers were worth the effort! God knows! Even the physical effort ...'

'That's easy,' he muttered:

'Another loony-tune lefty ... You're on the left, Dave ... Isn't it true? You lot save your real hatred for each other ...'

There was something in it: when the right are in control, the left only have each other to exercise any power over.

There was something else in the air. He wanted to tell me but wanted me to guess. I played back the record of the conversation thus far. I came to a gap. Which I wasn't supposed to hear.

'Gimbo ...'

Bingo.

'I'm not telling you this ... You understand?'

I waved aside the unnecessary qualification.

'Special Branch ...'

Political. Strictly political.

I wasn't surprised. I'd almost been there on my own.

An idea was racing round my head so fast I almost couldn't keep up with it, pin it down long enough to say it:

'He was the man outside. He stopped your copper. That's it, isn't it?'

My voice was rising, as if I was afraid of it.

He didn't answer.

He didn't deny it, though.

'But why? For God's sake, why?'

He laughed bitterly:

'Why not, after all? What does he care if someone croaks a lot of commie creeps? They're doing him a favour, really. Him and his mob. Less to keep an eye on, eh?'

'Come on, Tim ... I can buy that. But why'd he want the one who did it to get away?'

'You have to understand these people, Dave. They're not really part of the police, in the way the public'd understand. They're an institution all on their own. With their own purposes to fulfil.'

I didn't interrupt him to point out he'd used a four-syllable word.

'What they deal in is international. Favours for their opposite numbers. Trading information. Raising debts. It's more important to do a favour for someone, to get them to owe you, than to get a result. Murder ... They're just not interested. It's a local problem, for local bods like us ...'

'Yeah, OK, I can dig that. But why actually stop you doing your job?'

'Because ... Because he wanted to follow him, of course. He's not interested in Disraeli Chambers. He's not even interested in one crazy Kraut ...'

It was the first time he had hinted at the hun-factor in my hearing.

'How'd you know about that?'

I was getting put out by how little I could learn that everybody else didn't seem already to know.

'I only learned about it today. I did your drum just before I came over here earlier ... That was how I knew where you'd gone ...'

'Go on.' I wasn't offended.

'He wants to trace the gang … That's all, really … all there is to say. He'll do anything, screw anyone, to get it.'

'And that was the 'phone call you went off to make? To him?'

He laughed out loud:

'Christ, no. I don't get to speak to him. I spoke to my boss. He suggested we weren't interested in the number two man. What he told me, which wasn't much, tied up with what you've told me.'

'You're guessing, then? What you're telling me is a guess?'

It's funny. I really didn't want to believe it. I'd enough corny sucker faith left in the honour and integrity of the British police not to relinquish the last of it without regret.

'Me? I ain't telling you nothing. I don't know what you're talking about.'

That made two of us.

CHAPTER NINE

The newspapers had more of it.

A barristers' chambers was the subject of a murder campaign. Five barristers were dead. While two were thought initially to have been accidents, it was now considered virtually certain that they had all been murders. The police were making no comment. Nor was Alexander Keenan, QC, head of the chambers and well-known left-wing lawyer, other than by way of expressions of regret and respect for his dead colleagues.

For once, I felt ahead of the game. Not far. But I knew more than they did. There was no mention in the papers of the German connection. Or of the last Wednesday curiosity. Nor, of course, of Special Branch interest. Dowell's boss was identified as the officer in charge, which was another obvious error. There was no mention of Russel Orbach. That was not so obviously an error. I was still a long way from proving it was an error at all.

I had his offer to see me. Once I could tell him where Keenan had been while we were in Oslo. I now could.

We met at his home. he lived m Highgate, in a ground floor flat. He lived relatively simply, and alone.

'How long have you been here?'

'Four or five years ...'

'You used to live with Margot McAllister?' The MP.

'Yes.'

The back room was a kitchen-diner, with French windows out to a long garden. There were few other houses in view. A lot of trees; a lot of space. It reminded me of his affection for the Norwegian countryside.

'Nice flat ... Is the garden shared?'

'No. It's all mine. Nowadays, when houses are converted into flats, the local planning authorities tend to require sharing, so everybody gets a little and no one gets enough. This was an earlier conversion. Come. I'll show you the garden ...'

From the other end, we looked back at the house:

'Ugly, isn't it?'

He meant the back extension which had made the house large enough to hold three flats, all, he said, as spacious as his own. 'They wouldn't allow that either, nowadays ... But they'd be right ...'

Housing, planning, environment — these were his subjects.

'If you don't mind me asking, why did you and Margot McAllister separate?'

He smiled thinly:

'It's not your business. It's not relevant. But since you ask, it was to do with her going into Parliament. ..'

'Because she's Labour?'

'No. Because she's in Parliament. I ... I like to be left alone, at home ... I like my space uninvaded ... An MP is on constant call ... The telephone doesn't stop, nor the doorbell ...'

'But ... You were still together ... When you broke up with Disraeli Chambers?'

'Ah, I see where you're leading. Yes, we were. But it wasn't because of that. She knew Helen Keenan. We were all very close. To say she was angry, at both of them, would be understatement. Did Helen tell you: that she had long been trying to sleep with me? That she had said so, in front of Margot — and Alex? That I had refused, had not wanted to?'

I shook my head. He knew damn well Helen Keenan would have told me nothing of the sort.

'I don't want you to misunderstand. I'm not particularly proud of what happened. But she was at least as responsible for it as I. She had her first chance — Alex was away, I was drunk, and very, very depressed. I'd already been contemplating either chucking up the inquiry, or getting medical help to finish it, before it all ... happened ...

'Did she also tell you: when the kid came down. I was the one who went up and talked to him, not her? I spent half an hour or longer with him. We were talking well. I don't want to say it wasn't traumatic, but he was fifteen years old, sleeping with girls, highly intelligent if a little neurotic — with parents like that, who wouldn't be? He understood, he was responsive, it was a dialogue ...'

'Why, then?'

'A lot of pat phrases come to mind. Some friends of mine afterwards called her Lady *Nolle Tangere* ... Lady Thou Shalt Not Touch ... The Untouchable Princess ... I wasn't actually supposed to call her bluff.

'Also ... Over the weekend ... It happened on a Friday ... Before Alex got back, she was calling me up ... Calling Margot, too, but

Margot had gone away on the Saturday morning ... After I had told her, I hasten to add ... And I got angry with her ...'

'Because she was calling you?'

'No. Not at all. Because of what she was saying. It was all about Alex, and her, and me too if you like. What a big deal it was. How heavy it might be. As if ... It's not easy to explain at this distance ... But as if she was trying to turn it into something significant in their personal lives ...'

'And was it?'

'On its own, certainly not. Alex and she hardly ever slept together. She slept around a lot. He didn't care. He never cared about it. Though the opposite wasn't true ... He wasn't allowed to sleep with anyone else ... Though he did ... But, of course, you know that. She was your partner ...

'That was one of the things that made it so absurd. She actually said I did it to get back at him, you know, to hurt him. But he never was hurt by her screwing around.. . That's part of the point, I suppose ... She wanted him to mind ... So she made it something he had to mind ... Maybe she thought he'd mind if it was me, because I was one of his best friends. When that didn't work, she claimed rape, because that was something he had to mind ... If he believed it ...

'During our few conversations afterwards he was quite emphatic that he didn't care about my having slept with her ... I wouldn't have let it happen if I'd thought for a minute he would have minded ...'

'I still don't see why you got angry with her?'

'Because we were grown up, we knew what we were doing, more or less ... We'd chosen our ways of life, our morals or lack of them ... We were responsible, and responsible for the consequences, such as they were ... I was worried about John

... Though I'd talked to him ... I knew a reaction was possible, probable even ... I was worried that we'd hurt him ... But he was the last consideration on her mind ... during those calls.

'I didn't express myself very well. I was trying to say that he was the one we should be thinking about, talking about. I put too strongly that I didn't care about ourselves, you know, her, me, Alex ...'

I saw. Hell hath no fury.

By the time Keenan got back, she had her story ready. She couldn't make a big thing out of an affair with Orbach, because he patently didn't want to know, had made obvious he regretted it had happened at all, not merely or even primarily on account of John, but because he wasn't interested in her.

It doesn't need a degree in psychology to watch it evolve. It had been a misconception. The unthinkable had happened: he had touched her without adoring her. She had to give an account of it to Alex. Either, it had been her mistake — at least in part — or, she had no responsibility for any of it. He had done it. Against her will. Rape.

'It's ... Forgive me ... But it all seems so petty!'

'Oh, it is. It ought to have fizzled out. But so long as Keenan wasn't buying her story, she had to find someone else who would. So she went to chambers. She had to make it true in her own mind, by making others believe it. I'd go further than that. I was the only person in the whole world who could positively know she was lying. She had to wipe me out, out of their lives, which meant out of chambers. She knew the jealousy and the hatred of me there ... She's a clever, manipulative, scheming woman ... She used them; they used her... An unholy alliance.'

He laughed:

'They were so frightened of me … I've never really understood why. But, I was in chambers, the evening they were meeting … It was a regular, scheduled meeting, we had them the last Wednesday of every month …'

I knew. Oh, I did know that.

'Anyway, because of the inquiry I wasn't normally attending, but I happened to be there for half an hour or so at the beginning, to check my post. They knew I was in the building. So, they shut the doors, and whispered behind them. Even when they were all assembled, all together, they didn't dare invite me in to hear what I said … They wrote me I was to be asked to leave …'

We were sitting by the French windows, inside. He sat with his back to the wall, staring out where none of the nearby houses could be seen. From where I sat, a handful of other properties were in sight — lights on, people in occupation.

His account of the break-up was — if somewhat more full — almost identical with that which Keenan had given me.

'So they got Harry Matheson?'

He turned our talk the way it had to go.

'Who's they?'

'Don't you know yet?'

'Maybe. Do you?'

'In a general sense … Yes, of course.'

Of course. Orbach the omniscient.

'And why?'

'Yes, that too. You?'

'I know what I've been told. Betrayal. Vengeance. Things like that.'

He smiled. He knew the way I put it could fit the German theme. Or his own feelings.

'Would you like another drink?'

Throughout our conversation, he had been polite, and mildly spoken. Even when he recounted the tale of the break-up. He lived — of choice — quietly, and alone. He spent his holidays walking or going to museums with an elderly Norwegian lady who he called 'Mor', meaning Mother. He was a distinguished civil lawyer, who spent his time not shouting down judges or cajoling juries, but calmly advising on fine points of law well out of the limelight.

It should have led me to like, even to trust him.

I had to take one direction or the other.

'Are they right?'

'Meaning?'

'Were they betrayed from Disraeli Chambers?'

'I would say ...' He chose his words carefully:

'They have reason for what they believe.'

'Are you in touch with them?'

'I have friends. As does Alex. We still have some friends in common ...'

'Which is why you haven't asked me where he was while we were in Oslo?'

'Correct. Did you find out?'

'Yes. Paris.'

'Not bad. But not good. He went to Paris first. But he didn't stay there.'

'Where?'

He thought for a moment. Whether there was a reason not to tell me. Whether he had a reason for doing so.

'Lyons. His meeting was in Lyons.'

'What did he go for? What did he think he could achieve?'

'He's an advocate. He went to advocate.'

After a minute, perceiving that I had not followed his point, he continued:

'He went to advocate a cessation of hostilities. He went to talk about the left, the need for harmony, to stop tearing each other apart ... In this case, quite literally. He went to try and convince them Disraeli Chambers had nothing to do with what happened. He could not prove it. It is impossible to prove a negative. He could only urge, and argue and advocate ...'

'And he failed ...'

'Yes. He failed. You see, Dave, you know this, you were a lawyer once ...'

I wasn't sure I liked that. I was still a lawyer. Technically.

'The hardest job for an advocate is when his own case is weak, and he's trying to disguise that weakness, structure his argument around it, hope no one notices ... It's been my experience you can almost never do it. Perhaps the court or the other side won't be able to identify just what the weakness is, but they can sense that it's there ...'

Which brought us back to his earlier answer: they had reason for what they believed.

'Where do we go from here?'

He laughed:

'We? I'm going nowhere ... You seem to have forgotten: I have no objections to what is happening at all ...'

He spoke as if his attitude was the most natural, or the only reasonable one that someone in his position could adopt.

'Really? You really approve of this, because of what happened? You hate them that much?'

'Yes. Unequivocally yes. They're scum. Hypocritical scum. There's nothing worse than false godheads. They attract a lot of people with the prospect that change is possible, they are different, they can find a way through. Actually, they're the same as those who don't try and change things ... But the fact that they profess to be different makes them far worse ...'

'You ... You were part of them ... You helped build those chambers ... Keenan says that, still ... You were responsible, for what happened with Helen Keenan ... However much she was responsible, you had your part in it ...'

He wasn't angered.

'All true. There's a difference. I meant it. I meant what I said and what I did. Whether we're talking now about politics, law or, if you like, morality. I had my views, my theories, and I said them and acted on them and lived by them and was prepared to take the consequences of them. My mistake was, I thought that was true of the others ... Actually, it was pure cant, and their behaviour, and her behaviour, was just the same as if we had none of us spent our lives subscribing to particular beliefs ... You know, Dave, scratch an English socialist and what you find is pure English, the socialism's skin-deep ...

'There's an old story. A group of Englishmen decide to have a revolution. They form up and march on Buckingham Palace, which they plan to take by force. As they approach, the traffic lights turn red. So, of course, they stop.'

'I don't know ... I don't know which is more right. A lot of words but restrained action, or carrying the words through into action, regardless of the consequences, in the name of integrity ...'

'It depends, I think, on values. Human life. Pain and violence. It's painful and violent to kill someone, but it's short and sharp and cathartic in the sense that it often diverts the need to kill others. Or, the other way, involves a lesser pain, less violence, not lethal, spread thin but lasting long.'

I got up to leave:

'Don't you think ... that it's a good thing we don't have to make those decisions ... Because ... gods and governments do it for us ...'

He didn't answer. He did not like to lie. He did not consider himself bound by the decisions of either.

I had planned to visit Sandy after Orbach. Instead, I went home. I sat on the tube back to Earl's Court profoundly depressed. I was certain of two things: Russel Orbach had not committed the killings; and, the incident with Helen Keenan had much more to do with it than met the eye.

Ten days had passed since that last chambers' meeting. Getting on for a month since I had seen Mrs Nicholas. I was not surprised to receive a letter from her. I was surprised, however, when she asked me to come to her home.

I spent the night before at Sandy's. She drove me to the station. It had been a good evening and a better night. On the train, I gave myself a break from Disraeli Chambers. I didn't even prepare what I was going to say when I arrived.

'Mr Woolf?'

The dog-collar would have told me who he was even if I'd never seen him before.

He was such a caricature of the country clergy I expected a beat-up, twenty-year-old Austin for transport. I'd forgotten: the family had money, and plenty of it. I sat instead in the spacious front seat of a Swedish Saab. He drove it like Le Mans.

'I told my wife I wanted to meet you from the train, Mr Woolf ... She has, of course, told me everything ... I wanted to form an opinion of you, as it were on my own ... Do you mind?'

'That depends on what your opinion is ...'

He liked the answer.

'And what news do you bring us, Mr Woolf?'

I wasn't sure he'd like the next:

'I don't bring us any news, Reverend. I bring it to my client. If she wants to share it with you, that's her decision.' The 'my wife has told me everything' could've been a blind.

'Fair enough ...'

I'd forgotten. He wasn't the argumentative sort. The lord giveth, the lord taketh away and if the lord don't choose to tell you why you don't holler and scream and bitch about it.

Mrs Nick greeted us at the front door. It was, of course, a big house, for it could not otherwise have accommodated all those barristers, all those years ago. Given recent developments, you would've thought they might've moved somewhere smaller.

We shook hands. Now she was on home ground, she was all mother. None of the hello, how are you and what have you got to say that marked our Harrods tea room sessions. More: make yourself comfortable, you must be tired from the journey, would you like to wash up, we'll have something to eat first.

There were limits on what I could tell them. The Russel Orbach involvement was out of order — I had neither evidence of its relevance nor indeed a rationalization. Just a dash of old-fashioned intuition. I merely mentioned him as someone I had talked with.

Nor, of course, could I so much as hint that the reason Fat Harry's hitman got away was an police demarcation dispute. I could say, without lying, that the man had got away: Gimbo had lost him within quarter of an hour.

I did give them more than they could get from the newspapers, though. After all, they were paying me a ton a day, plus expenses, and even The Times only cost thirty pence. I gave them, then, the accredited insider version. The group had got mixed up with revolutionary Germans. Those Germans had been wiped out. Someone connected with them, or possibly a surviving member, was convinced they'd only been caught because of a leak that started at Disraeli Chambers.

I was not surprised that her first question was:

'Was it true?'

'I don't know. It … It's generally agreed … It may have been. People who … get involved with activities of this sort … Well, they can learn things … They didn't … wouldn't have the caution that those actually participating would have … One of them might have been careless. Or … have talked …'

'Not Jack, Mr Woolf,' his mother insisted.

The Reverend Nicholas looked more shocked by what he now understood was his wife's prime concern than by the story I had told.

'I said, I don't know. I don't know that they did have information, I don't know if they did leak it, if they did I still don't know who or who to, and I certainly don't know if it was accidental or deliberate. The chances are we'll never know any of those things. All or most of those who would ever have known for sure are dead.'

'Which suggests …' The Rev asserted himself:

'That there would not seem to be much more you can do for us, is there?'

That, of course, was what I had been afraid of.

Mrs Nicholas was disappointed when I didn't come straight back at him with fifty different reasons to carry on. Instead, she did.

'No one has been caught yet …'

'The police are involved now …'

'What about the other members of chambers?'

'That's not our business, dear.'

'It's still so vague, so uncertain.'

'We know Jack's death wasn't what they said.'

'There are other lines of enquiry, which you could follow up, aren't there, Mr Woolf?' She called for help.

I told you several chapters back, I liked this lady.

'Certainly. For one thing, I am absolutely sure that there are still lines of contact ... Between them, and people in this country.'

'People who are ... responsible?'

'No. That's not what I'm saying. But people who are around. I've mentioned a couple of them. Keenan believed he could get through to them. He didn't, of course, as we know. I mean, he didn't succeed in stopping it. But he saw someone ... Possibly just an intermediary ... A woman, I think ...'.

'Do the police know about that?'

That was a difficult question. Certainly they knew Keenan had wanted me out of the way, which meant he was up to something. On the other hand, I had not told Dowell where Keenan had gone, nor had the scribbled notes he would have read in my flat have given him enough to work it out, nor had 'they' — in the shape of Gimbo — managed to keep up with him. Dowell might, of course, already have asked Keenan. He would have been told the same as me. Nothing.

'Why haven't you told them?' he asked.

'I didn't have instructions to do so ... From your wife.'

She concealed her smile. She knew me better than that.

'You must tell them, Mr Woolf. Mustn't he, dear?'

'I don't know. What do you think, Mr Woolf?'

It was the first time I had been forced to ask myself why I hadn't told Tim Dowell that part of the conversation with

Keenan. Or, indeed, when Sandy had told me the day after I got back from Oslo.

'You have to follow through the consequences. If I tell that to the police, they will be bound to do something about it. They'll have Keenan in. The papers may get hold of it. Let's suppose, and it's a fair guess, he won't tell them who he saw, and where. Then the issue becomes barrister withholding information in murder hunt. Keenan's under a different pressure, outside pressure, pressure that's got little or nothing to do with what happened in the past, but is all about his present conduct. It seems to me, well, that that would be less productive ...'

'Than what, Mr Woolf?'

'Than leaving him where he is ... Sweating ... About what he knows, and what he hasn't told anyone ...'

The Reverend Nicholas took one last shot:

'But he might tell them ... He might tell them even though he wouldn't tell you. After all, they are the police.'

She answered for me:

'Exactly, dear. Think of Jack ... Think of what Jack would have done ...'

I swear he muttered something unsaintly underneath his breath. All he said out loud though was, resignedly:

'It's your decision ... Dear.'

The way he said 'dear' wasn't that different from the way I'd said it to Sandy a couple of times in the not too distant past.

Sandy was at the station. It hadn't been arranged.

'You waited here all this time?'

'You flatter yourself ... get in.'

I waited to be told.

She waited to be asked.

I'd played this game before.

With someone I didn't like.

Lady H.

The comparison didn't help and I was glad this time it was she who broke first.

'In the back of my mind ... You remember talking about Helga?'

I was hardly likely to forget.

'I had an old file, of miscellaneous papers, from those days ... Minutes, and the odd letter, and leaflets ... That sort of thing. It was in our dead-file room ...'

All solicitors have a store for their closed cases. You never know, for sure, if something might go live again.

'Filed under what?'

'A pile of other junk,' she answered, knowing that wasn't what I meant.

'What have you got?'

'Her name. Helga Schroeder. It's stupid. Because I should have remembered. The psychologist's daughter.'

Sandy had done a degree in psychology, at University College in London, before she had studied to become a solicitor.

'This Schroeder. You know where to reach him?'

She laughed:

'He was dead before I ever met her.'

'How come you didn't remember the other night?'

'It wasn't a big thing, meeting her. Just at the end of a meeting. I caught her name. I said: any relation? she said yes, and was fairly embarrassed. He was very right wing. I mean, bordering on the Nazi. After the war, he was imprisoned in France. And for some years after, he had worked at a hospital in Lyons. It was when you mentioned Lyons last night that the penny began to drop ... So I went looking for the file. I didn't say anything, in case it didn't turn out,' she added, anxious to allay any residual mistrust.

'Not bad,' I conceded.

We went back to her house. I was beginning to spend more time there than at home. The food was better. I didn't have to clean up.

I had a name. I also had a place. I made one 'phone call — to clear the expenditure — and another — to book the ticket. The next afternoon, I was on a plane for France.

Only once I got there did I begin to wonder where to start looking. Another needle in another haystack. But Lyons — unlike some of the parts of London where I had been scavenging — was too pretty to burn down.

I wasted three days asking questions to which I got no useful answers.

'Are there many Germans here?'

'Where do they go to?'

'Did an Englishman called Keenan stay in your hotel?'

'Are there many left-wing groups in this town?'

'Where do they gather?'

'Has a German woman called Schroeder stayed in your hotel?'

'Did you serve dinner to an Englishman accompanied by a German woman?'

I even followed a few lithe, blonde women, on the somewhat less than sophisticated grounds that the French were Latins and ought accordingly to be dark-haired and darker skinned.

I was contemplating two unpleasant courses of conduct. I could call up Dowell, tell him where I was, and get him to OK co-operation from the frog pigs. Or, I could go home with less to show for it than I brought back from Norway.

Then I had a brainwave. The sort of idea that made me worth every penny of the hundred pounds a day I was being paid.

Sandy had said Helga's father used to live in Lyons. I looked in the telephone directory. All good things come to those who waste their time and their client's money.

I took a taxi straight there.

No one at home.

I sat inside a café across the road, sipping café noir and pastis alternately until my palate couldn't tell the difference between them.

I tried again when it was dark and good Germans should be honouring the curfew. Still no answer.

I couldn't drink any more so I settled down to *stek-frites*. The meat was, though thin, tender, and the chips fried crisp. I had moved on to *vin rouge*, because I didn't know how to ask for anything else, but watered down with Perrier. I was well into my second glass when a woman entered the café, and came and sat down at my table without a moment's hesitation.

She snapped at me in French.

'*Nicht sprechen französisch*,' I utilized what was left of a one-year course in German during my childhood, liberally seasoned with Yiddish.

'You don't speak German very well either, do you?' She observed in perfect English.

'I came to France once, with a few friends. On one of those day trips, shopping expeditions, you know? The boat was French. One of them went up to the bar and ordered for us. When he came back, he said to his girl-friend how pleased he was to find he hadn't forgotten the language. She said: "You'd break into Swahili if the alternative was silence".'

'I don't understand,' she frowned.

I'd forgotten. Krauts ain't got no sense of humour.

'It doesn't matter. I'm the opposite. I can't speak any language but English, and even that's not my own ...'

'Where are you from?'

I always do this, whenever I meet a German:

'I'm a Jew ...'

'With a hatred of Germans. Yes. That is all right. Now. What do you want?'

'I want to talk to you.'

'We are talking.'

I glanced around, to indicate that there were people at nearby tables.

'The French consider it beneath their dignity to hear anything but their own language, too ...'

'It's ... confidential,' I still wasn't comfortable:

'And you're the one who didn't open your door when I came up ...'

That was a guess. That she had been inside at least at my second try and watched me cross back over to the café. She didn't contradict me.

'I do not know you. What is your name?' She was obviously a well brought up lady. You don't take someone into your home at least until you know his name. Even if killing them's a possible way to pass the evening.

'Dave. Dave Woolf. We haven't met. But we might have. We used to go to the same places, we have some shared acquaintances ...'

'In London?'

'Yes. We used to go to the same type of meetings ... At places like Disraeli Chambers ... And our acquaintances include Alex Keenan ...'

She didn't bat an eyelid. By this time, I figured, she had worked that much out for herself.

'Perhaps I do not know who is this man?'

She had also figured out: I wasn't police, I had no clout, she didn't need to be afraid of me.

'I didn't say he was a man ...'

It might've been short for Alexandra.

She threw her face up in a classic — if adoptive — French gesture of dismissal. If that was the best I could do.

'Still you have not told me what you want.'

She was hard. She was not going to budge.

'I would like to meet someone. I think you know how I can do that. I want to meet them and talk to them. I am not police, I promise to tell nothing to the police, there's things I need to know from this person. He can say where, when, in what country and what conditions. I must meet him.'

She thought for a moment.

Then she asked:

'What is his name?'

I shook my head from side to side, slowly:

'I do not have a name. Please. Get him my message. Ask him.'

'Where are you staying?'

I gave her the name of the hotel.

She rose.

'Perhaps,' she paused.

Then she added, but clearly in a different sentence:

'I might want to know where you are staying so that I can complain to the police that you are pestering to me.'

I shrugged.

What the hell; everybody else did. Why shouldn't I?

'You will see.'

I had to wait forty-eight hours. She would take her time. Make sure neither I nor anyone else was following her. I did not know if she would be making contact with him in person, or by telephone. But *les flics* didn't come calling on me.

I spent a lot of the time walking, anywhere but near her apartment. I even took in a couple of movies I'd wanted to see in London but not had the time for. One of them was, as I had assumed, subtitled. The other was dubbed into French. I only stayed five minutes. I ate and drank a lot. I'd say: Lyons is one of the towns I now know my way about best of all.

She caught up with me as I was out walking, on the bridge, beginning to think the shot hadn't paid off.

'Do you have an answer for me?'

'Yes.'

'And?' I almost grabbed her in my eagerness.

'Go home, Mr Woolf. Just go home.'

'What is that? No? Or ... Wait there?'

She shrugged: it was an infectious habit.

'You sent a message. I bring an answer. It is: go home. That is all.'

I looked at her.

She stared right back.

She was hard as nails.

She said:

'I hope you have a pleasant flight ...'

CHAPTER TEN

We passed into a new phase of killing. Killing time.

It was mid-month. The inner circle, those in the know, anticipated no activity for another couple of weeks.

The police, however, could not afford to take chances. Each and every surviving member of the group, willing or not, was accompanied at all times of day and night by an officer of the law. It was, of course, a guarantee that no German would come near them and, as such, an assurance that we stood not a chance of catching anyone actually in the act.

Anne Godwin's spectre of a fast disappearing practice had become a reality, though not quite for the reasons she had expected. While the officers were prepared to wait outside rooms in which conferences were being held, the sight of six feet of silver and blue politely holding open the door was enough to deter most of their criminal clientele.

This period marked, and this activity reflected, a decline in the fortunes of the only member of Her Majesty's Constabulary I had ever, albeit only fleetingly, termed friend.

It would be fair to say that he had not exactly covered himself with glory the night of the Matheson massacre. (Bodyweight made it an appropriate term.)

In addition, as Dowell had so carefully not told me before he disappeared from the scene, there were those on high who did not share his sense of priorities.

He was not taken off the case altogether. Insultingly, he was given the task of co-ordinating the duty roster of bodyguards.

'Do I detect the kindly hand of the gormless Gimbo behind this move?' I asked on one of our outings to the all-night café with so many differences.

'Gimbo ... As you choose to call him ... And, of course, were I to admit he existed ... Is a four-eyed get with wrinkled walnuts for bollocks ...'

There was one major drawback to the increased frequency of these occasions. Lewis had implied that if we didn't start at least occasionally paying for our liquor, he'd show us a variation on water into wine. To wit. Southern Comfort into cold soda.

Tim Dowell could hardly put in for expenses.

Which left me.

We were keeping company for the same sort of reason that Marguie Bradkinson had claimed she wanted me to go with her to Oslo. We were participants in the same performance, although the curtain had got stuck and the show couldn't yet go on.

He tossed his — Mrs Nick's — drink to the back of his throat.

'You're a greedy pig, Dowell,' I remarked boredly, for want of anything even vaguely interesting to say.

'Probably ... I told you before. It's a pig job. Pig world. Pig people ...'

'You sound like Orbach ...'

'You're obsessed by him ... There's not a jot of evidence he's got anything to do with it ...'

'Agreed. Not evidence. But I know he is.'

'I'll tell you why you think that, if you like,' as casually as if inviting me to buy another round.

'Go on ...'

'You think you're him. Or he's you ...'

'Wha ... ?'

'The way I see it. You're both lawyers. You've both got pissed off with ... What did you call them the other night? Loony-tune lefties ... You're both Jews, too ...'

'What's that got to do with it?'

'Quite a lot. You're both outsiders. You don't feel you really belong. It's hard work for you to go on belonging.'

'Belonging to what?'

'It doesn't matter really. Whatever you want to belong to. In this case, groups, your profession ... He quit Disraeli Chambers ... You quit your job ... It's easier for you to do that. Get out. Become the outsider you think you are anyway. That's what you've got in common. But that's all ...'

'He didn't quit ... He was pushed ...'

'You can make it happen ... To yourself ...'

'They teach you psychology at police college nowadays?'

'As a matter of fact, yes. But not that.'

'Where'd'you get it from?'

'From a book ...'

'I didn't know you could read,' I bantered for time to absorb what he'd said. There was more than nothing in it.

He hadn't spelled out why this alleged identity crisis should lead me to suspect Orbach of an involvement beyond that of merely keeping himself informed. It was implicit. If I had been in Orbach's position, I feared I might have wanted to do something similar.

'Oh, yes, I read comics, and pin-up magazines ... And a book called Resistance to Conforming ... You ever read it?'

I shook my head.

'It's by a man called Schroeder. A professor of psychology. A German.'

I shut my eyes to give me time to think.

It had not come from anything I had written down. Since his last confessed unscheduled visit to my home, I had been taking precautions. I had written notes because I needed to write things down to clear my head. At the end of the day, I was either going to write a damned full report for Mrs Nicholas or a novel about the whole incident or both.

So I did not and could not burn them eat them swallow them chew them tear them into tiny pieces and flush them down the loo. Instead I posted them to their eventual owner, the aforementioned Mrs Nick. Not to read but to keep safely for me.

'Gimbo?'

'I told you before. He and I aren't on talking terms. No. So far as I'm aware, he knows nothing.'

'Why?'

'Why what?'

'Why haven't you told him anything?'

'Because the only people who know are you and me. And, I would have thought that was already one too many ...'

'You still haven't told me how you found out ...'

'No more I have.' He sighed:

'I suppose I ought?'

'You suppose right.'

'I opened up your girlfriend's office last night. My, she's thorough, notes of everything ...'

'Do you even begin to understand that the way you keep pilfering people's premises without a warrant is unlawful unconstitutional *ultra vires* unethical un-palatable and unpleasant?'

'What was the Latin bit in the middle?'

If he recognized it as Latin, he didn't need an answer.

'Oh, fuck it, Tim ... Why're you telling me?'

'You're wrong, you know ...'

'What's wrong?'

'All those fancy words you used. All the law says is you can't use what you find in evidence. That's different. Isn't it? It doesn't mean I can't know about them ... I suppose, thinking about it, it might be a little bit of trespass ... But I never harm anything, or anyone, and I never take anything so it isn't criminal damage or burglary. Right, Mr Woolf? So sue me in a civil court ...'

I sighed. I didn't even bother to ask what would happen if I reported him. He knew I wouldn't. Nor, if she gave a damn about me, would Sandy.

'What are you going to do with the information?'

'Not much more than I have already.'

'Which is?'

'Reading the collected works of the aforesaid father ... That's what Sandy's note says: Helga, Schroeder's daughter ... Then the name of this book sort of not written on the note, more like a doodle around it.'

'She studied psychology ... At college ...'

'Oh. I wanted to do that. I did law instead.'

'You did law at university,' I repeated.

By the end of the sentence, though, my voice had ceased to show surprise. It explained a lot.

'How come you're only a sergeant?'

'Oh, I've got my inspector's exams. Had them for years. But, well, it's a sort of positive discrimination in the force. In favour of idiots. They make a lot of fuss about wanting it to be more of a graduate profession, and they send a dozen or more inspectors or chief inspectors to university each year, to get a degree, usually law, sometimes sociology ... But they're the only ones that really do well out of being educated ... They've already shown they can stomach the mass stupidity ... Anyone like me — and there are few, very few — who've got an education beforehand, we have to prove ourselves, work really hard to show it won't get in the way ...'

While he was talking, I was thinking. All he'd got was a name. Helga Schroeder. He would, of course, have to be even more crass than the average copper he'd now admitted he wasn't not to connect her with the German gremlin in our game. But he'd said he was going to do nothing with the information. Which meant he had appreciated for himself that she was not the person we were actually after.

'Let me think out loud. Just to show I didn't waste my expensive education either ... You know she isn't the one we want ... Right?'

'I'd a fair idea ... She's what? A contact? Who Keenan went to see?'

'Agreed. And abroad.'

'Yes ...' He'd worked that out too.

'So if you do anything with it, you have to work abroad ... Which means giving it to Gimbo?'

'Not necessarily. But the effect would be the same. Once it goes on to the circuit, outside the country, his type will be involved. If not him immediately, it'll filter back to him.'

'Which means action maybe gets taken abroad ... Which means not here ... Which means maybe not for these murders but ... But what?'

'I don't honestly know. But I'd think, with some idea of what sort of people we're talking about, terrorists, international networks, you've read it all in the papers ... We'll clock in somewhere about ninety-ninth in the list of people wanting a piece of him ...'

'Why does it matter to you, Tim? You can't bring them back ... It brings it to an end ... So?'

He laughed:

'Buy me a drink ...'

'Another?'

'I'm an outsider too, Dave ... In my own way ... In my own scene ... In the police. Educated copper. What a joke. What a lot of jealousies. What a lot of obstacles placed in my way. I've often thought, it must be like what being black or Jewish is like ... Oh, not so difficult, and I can always change, by getting out ... There were Jews at my school. We used to give them a hard time. That was before the blacks came, of course. It was the best break your lot ever had ...'

'Thanks for nothing, I'd left school by then ...'

'It's not important. I just wanted you to know I do have some idea of what prejudice is ... In my own little way, in my own little world ... God, the amount of times I've walked into a new station, ready to be one of the lads ... Only to be greeted by the station sergeant: "So you're the college boy, eh, well we'll soon knock that out of you ..." Or some similar such shit ... I could understand it if I was throwing myself about a bit, you know, putting them down, showing off ... But I learned not to do that early on; and I'm not bad at hiding it now ...'

'Jesus. She's paying me a ton a day for some copper to cry on my shoulder?'

'Right,' he grinned, brought back to the point:

'Because if I follow it up that far ...' He held up his thumb and forefinger as if indicating — a drink this size:

'There's no way I could bring it back home. Even if we find him on English soil, with what we've currently got, he'll be out of the country before you can whistle the Red Flag ... And ... And I want the bastard here. Not there. Here.'

'Which is the bit that matters: here, or that you want to be the one to get him?'

'Maybe both ... Maybe, just maybe ... I make no admissions, you see ... But maybe I don't want to read he tripped down the cell stairs in some German gaol, or committed suicide like the rest of that mob were supposed to have done ...' Another unbeliever:

'And maybe I don't really care about international terrorists and the like. Maybe that's all over my head, there's too many ifs and buts and pros and cons and all the rest of it ... So I'm better off out of it ... I don't want to be in Special Branch, I don't want to get involved in that. Just policing the community ... That's the phrase nowadays, isn't it? That's for me ...'

'Don't you care, if all he'll do is twenty, thirty years, for what ... five lives now?'

'Do you believe in topping?'

'No. I thought you would. I thought all policemen did.'

I realized what I'd said, and laughed out loud:

'What was that word you used? Prejudice?'

'Something like that. No, I don't really care ... He's what, thirty? He's got to be thirty, now or not far short, if he's paying off a debt that old ... He goes to prison for twenty years. Comes out he's fifty, maybe more: the court'll probably stick a minimum recommendation on him. What do the new rules say?'

'I don't know. But twenty years sounds likely ...'

'So, he's fifty and he's too old to get a job, start again, he won't even know anyone or have anywhere to go ... Everyone will have forgotten him ... All your radicals who'll think he's some kind of hero or martyr ... And will they? If what he's done for is murdering this mob?'

'What I said the other night ... You don't really like them, do you?'

'Nah ...'

'Why?'

He shrugged:

'Who needs a reason? Would you buy a used wig from one of them? No, I don't like them. It's not 'cos they're left-wing or help the poor ... The whole idea of lawyers professing to be on the side of the oppressed ... It's a contradiction, isn't it? The only people they've liberated is themselves, financially, intellectually ... Making sure there's always an oppressed class is essential to them ... It's what they get their living from ...'

'What about the clients? Don't they matter? Does it matter if people pretend they're doing something special, something political, if they're also making a positive difference to individual lives? If they didn't have the politics, they'd probably end up in commercial work or city firms screwing every last penny they could out of the system, and to hell with the wee people's problems. It's just their way of convincing themselves to do that particular job ...'

I don't know why I was defending them. Maybe because what he said was also true of many years of my own life.

'There's a lot of good, sympathetic lawyers, who do a good job, like that, without making all the noise about it ...'

'I think that'd probably qualify as another Orbach line ...'

'The difference is, between me and friend Orbach, and assuming there's something in what you believe ... All I've said is, I don't like them. I don't go around wanting to see their heads chopped off ...'

'I thought it was me was supposed to be like Orbach?'

'I said that's what you think. I didn't say you were. I told you what you've got in common. I said that was all ...'

'Maybe ... Maybe not ...'

'Maybe, friend Woolf,' he said quietly: 'Maybe that's what you've got to decide ... Which you do want to be: him or me ...' He grinned: 'What a terrible choice in life ...'

I'd been back from Lyons four days when I got the first call. It was from a coin box. It was seven thirty in the evening.

'Mr Woolf?'

'Yes ...'

The voice was accented.

So I wanted to believe.

I was so keyed up I couldn't be sure.

Even after his next sentence:

'Take the M4. Drive to Newbury. Find a street. It is called Wendon Way. Park outside number 100. Wait there. Do it now. Be alone.'

He hung up before I could tell him. I don't have a car.

I rang Sandy at home. She wasn't in. Just her damned answering machine. I got as far as her cheerful but unoriginal 'hi' before I put the receiver down. Then I called her office.

There was no reply, of course, from the switchboard. I dug her private number out of my book. No reply. I cursed, replaced the receiver again and was wondering how the hun would feel if I turned up in a minicab when my own 'phone rang.

'Did you try to get me just now?'

'Oh, Sandy, oh yes I did! Why didn't you answer?'

'I was on the loo ... I picked it up on your last ring ... Are you coming over?'

I'd forgotten a tentative date.

'Oh, no. Listen. You have to do something for me. Can you come here. Right now. In the car. Lend it me. It's urgent, Sandy, I wouldn't ask, but ...'

She hesitated for about five seconds. Then, she said yes.

I spent the time I had to wait on bended knee. Praying. First, in thanks for Sandy's existence. Secondly, that she wouldn't have an accident on the way over. Thirdly, that I'd be safe in Newbury.

I'd double locked the door and was standing upstairs on the pavement by the time she arrived. Held the door of her car open for her. She said:

'I'll come with you ...'

I think she expected the answer, because she didn't put up much of a fight. She got out, leaving the keys in the ignition, and stood to one side while I slid into the driver's seat and adjusted my distance from the pedals, the rear-mirror, the wing-mirror.

'How's this work?' I pointed.

'Push the tape in first. That switches it on. Then adjust the volume. It ejects itself at the end. You don't have to switch it off. There's an automatic cut-out.'

'Right ...'

I turned the key. The petrol indicator rose jerkily to the top. She had filled it on the way over. I glanced at her and she nodded in confirmation. I took the hand-brake off and started to pull out.

'Hey,' she called:

'Don't you have anything to say to me?'

'Like?'

'Like thank you? Like where you're going? Like when you'll bring it back? Like do I want to wait for you and would I like the keys to your flat? Like have I got the cab fare home?'

I thought about it. Lot of questions. I muttered my answer:

'I'm beginning to think you're all right, kid ...' and drove off with her yelling after me:

'What? what did you say?'

That was a close call. She'd nearly heard me. I had to get a grip on myself. Within a hundred yards, I was beginning to make sense again.

Have you ever driven into a strange town, in the middle of the evening, with nothing more than a street name to tell you where to go? It isn't easy. As a matter of fact, Newbury isn't that easy to find at all, once you get off the motorway. But I made it to the town centre, before I stopped the car, got out and — like I was taught when I was a child — asked a copper where Wendon Road was. He had to radio in to find out. That took another five minutes.

Inevitably, it was outside the town centre, back the way I'd just come.

It was after ten by the time I had Wendon Way, and the right number house. They're pretty houses. Detached. Lot of distance between each driveway. There were no lights on in the front of number 100.

I sneaked in and peered through what turned out to be the kitchen window. There were lights at the back of the house.

After a couple of minutes, a tall, slender, gracefully grey-haired, bespectacled woman came in, and started to make a hot drink. She looked about as German or gangster-like as Captain Furillo's lady-lawyer-wife on Hill Street Blues.

I settled down to wait in the car. Sandy didn't have Wagner, so I put some Mahler on the tape-deck, to make him feel right at home. After half an hour, I switched to Beethoven, my fifth. He was German too. We might as well both be happy.

Still no show. The lights started to go off, one by one, in the house. I walked straight round to the side where the front door was and rang. I heard the lady call out in a strong northern accent:

'Hugh. There's someone at the door.'

A bespectacled man of about seventy, with white hair and a sharp white beard, wearing an artist's smock, opened up, wielding a paintbrush like a weapon.

'Yes?' He asked, curious but polite:

'Can I help you?'

'My name's Dave Woolf ...' I answered.

He thought about this for a moment.

'Yes,' he said again:

'Is that with an e or without?'

'Without. And two os.'

He nodded wisely:

'That's the second most common spelling. I knew a family who spelled it with one o, and no e on the end. That's most unusual. I don't suppose ... Well, no, hardly, you wouldn't, would you ...'

I saw his point. I might as well be called Smith as be related to his friends the Wolfs.

From upstairs his wife called:

'Hugh?'

'Coming, dear ... It's a mistake, I think ...' He turned to me:

'It must be, really, if you spell it with two os. Don't you think? We can't stand here chatting all night. Good night. It has been most pleasant.'

He didn't wait for my answer, but shut the door firmly in my face. I had to agree. It did seem to be a mistake. I waited until one o'clock before I gave up and drove back to town.

I had three choices. I could drive straight home and get the car back to Sandy the next day. That was the most convenient course of action for me. Or I could drive to Sandy's and post the keys through her letterbox. That would certainly be the most convenient for her.

I compromised. I drove to Sandy's, and rang the bell long and hard enough for her to come and let me in.

'Have a nice drive, dear?' she asked sarcastically.

'Certainly. I met a charming man who once knew some people called Wolf who spelled their name with only one o, but no e on the end ...'

She absorbed this slowly. It was quite a lot to take in at nearly three o'clock in the morning.

Obviously, it was more than she could cope with. She trotted back to bed, leaving the door open so I could see her climb into bed. She sat up, and pulled her nightdress off, adjusting her position so she was clearly only taking up half the bed, leaving the other half pointedly vacant.

I sighed. I was tired. Dog tired. Like I couldn't hardly walk. She wasn't inviting me to go for a walk. That was how we were engaged when her 'phone rang.

'I don't believe this,' she murmured as she padded off to the living room to take the call.

She stood in the doorway:

'It's for you ... dear,' the last word was wearing a little thin.

'Didn't happen to say who, by any chance?'

I'd've put money on Dowell. Roster organizer or not.

'Mr Woolf,' the same voice as before:

'It would seem ... You were not accompanied to Newbury ...'

He hung up having communicated to me that the purpose of the exercise was to see if I did go on my own. He had been following me. He had another message: he knew where I now was.

We both sat up in bed, clutching our knees.

'How did he know my number?'

'I was about to ask that ...'

'So? Answer already. You're the detective ...'

'I'll give seven possibilities. One, he took the number of the car and told a policeman it had scraped his. They're not supposed to help out this way, but if they don't you'll pretend you want to prosecute, just to find out who it is. So they have to go through a lot of paperwork that's wasted. Instead, they'll usually get you what you want over the radio ... Which is: name and address, enough to look the number up in the telephone book. There's a problem with it. It takes a hell of a lot of familiarity with the system here ...'

'It's not bad, though ... How'd'you know about it?'

'I used to do it for our clients. Pretend I'd been in an accident myself, you know, ask the nearest copper I could find ...'

'Maybe coming back to work isn't that good an idea ...'

With ethics like mine, I could get us both struck off.

'It got results,' I protested. I still hadn't told her, and didn't like to tell her, it wasn't a patch on some of the methods adopted by Sergeant Dowell.

'What are the others?'

'Orbach told him. Keenan told him. You told him. Dowell told him. Gimbo told him. How many's that?'

'Five — six in all — and one of them I didn't like ...'

She waited for an apology.

I climbed from the bed and stared out the back. It looked on to her garden. For all I knew he could be waiting there.

'Sorry,' I mumbled.

'What was the seventh?'

'Oh, easy ... Someone we haven't thought of yet ... You know: the surprise answer at the end of the show ...'

I got back into bed and put my arm around her.

She pushed it away, roughly.

'Hey, I said I'm sorry ...'

'Listen, Dave. I heard what you said in the car ...'

The trouble Disraeli Chambers were in was as nothing.

'And, you know, you're behaving like a complete arsehole ... Just like you used to ... I don't want that. If you want to be with me you trust me and that's fine and you're right to and let's lie down and cuddle up and maybe more ...

'If you don't trust me, don't give me any crap. Just get your clothes on, get the hell out and don't bother coming back. You know? I haven't done everything smart in my life either ... But I'm not going to make the same mistakes twice over ...'

What could I say to a speech like that?

'But ... Sandy ... It's four o'clock in the fucking morning and it's freezing out there!'

She swung on me like she was about to tear my eyes out. Then she saw the way I was looking at her and burst out laughing, and hugged me instead.

Yeah, I trusted her. After all, I didn't seem to have a lot of choice. I'd gone too far with her already for it to make any difference. It'd just be cutting off my nose to spite myself.

For want of anything better to do while I awaited my next call, I rang Dowell with the number of Sandy's car and asked him to check if it'd been the subject of a radio accident enquiry the night before. Negative. That narrowed the options down. To six. Or rather, five. Of which one was anyone's guess.

I didn't like this marking time. I wasn't good at it. I felt like a prize race-horse, or a football player, when rain cancels game at the very last moment. Chomping at the bit. I was so jumpy, I even hung out at Sandy's office, drawing up formal bills for clients from the notes on case-files. It was always one of the jobs I was better at. Gave me a chance for some creative writing.

He played me for a sucker again. This time it was Brighton. I nearly refused to go at all. My father came from Brighton. I had to wait at the end of the West Pier, in the freezing cold, with next to no one else about, and all of the arcades shut up for the season. All I got out of it was a stick of rock Sandy chipped a tooth on and didn't thank me for.

I wondered. How come you never read about this part of it in thrillers? How come you never see it on Hill Street Blues? I knew the answer, because it was exactly what I felt like doing: putting the book down, or switching off.

The third time he rang, also from a call box, right after he opened with his unvarying introduction:

'Mr Woolf.'

I butted in.

'This time had better be for real 'cos I ain't playing any more. Geddit?'

It sounded good, I thought, as I listened to the dialling tone. The sucker had hung up on me.

Thirty seconds later, there was a rap at my door. He was standing there, carrying a holdall. He must have called from the 'phone box in the square. I was more surprised it was working than to see him.

He pushed past me, slamming the door shut behind him, and poking his head into room after room until, satisfied, he settled down, still clutching the handle of his bag.

He was not as I had imagined him. He was thicker set and darker haired. His face was heavily pock-marked. He wore glasses. But at least they were rimlessly revolutionary. I put him at about my own age. Nearer forty than thirty.

'I suppose it'd be idle to ask your name?'

He smiled.

Ye gods. A hun with a humour.

'Don't you think ... Well ... It's a little risky here? I mean, it's a basement, there's no way out, you know.'

'Should I not trust you, Mr Woolf?'

'Trust, shmust ...' There I went again.

'I don't know, man. I don't know what that means. I haven't told anyone. You've followed me to Newbury and Brighton and my girlfriend's and God knows where ...'

'Everywhere, Mr Woolf. For the last few days, everywhere ...'

'Well, you're better at it than Special Branch. I spotted their man the first day I was tailed ...'

As I said it, I realized I didn't know if it was true, how long Gimbo had been up my backside before I picked him up on the tube home from the Angel.

'They are not so good, the British police ... I think ... Perhaps ... They do not have the experience of those in my country ... Perhaps ... They do not take it so seriously ...'

Christ. Another damned philosopher. Next thing he'd be telling me it was all because Britain had never been invaded by a foreign power.

'Some of them are good ... Perhaps better than you think. I had Dowell in mind, not Gimbo.

'It is possible.' He placed his holdall on the table. From it he extracted what looked to my television-trained eye suspiciously like a sub-machine gun.

I glugged silently.

When I was at public school, we had cadet training. We went on a camp once, to somewhere on Dartmoor. It was the miserablest two weeks of a pretty miserable childhood. The only good moment was when we got to play with sub-machine guns. Only they didn't look anything like the one he had placed in front of him on my table. The difference was between the Wright Brothers' Flying Machine and Concorde.

'You wanted to talk with me, Mr Woolf ...'

Now I'd got what I wanted, I couldn't remember half the questions I'd started off with.

What I really wanted to do was just gaze. I'd never been involved in a murder case — even as a solicitor. I'd never seen a murderer before. Not in real life. Flesh and blood. Also, this guy had whacked off five barristers whom I knew. He had run rings round me and Dowell and the British Special Branch and presumably the German police and just about everybody else you could think of. He'd earned me my first real bread for what seemed like many years. He'd got me out of a gutter in which I looked like drowning. He'd incidentally set me up in my first affair for longer that I cared to recall. And, he was sitting in my flat as calm as you please, resting his hand on a sub-machine gun.

Just how kitsch can you get?

CHAPTER ELEVEN

I sat in the waiting-room of Malcolm Harryngton's chambers, with only two thoughts to keep me company. One was I was spending a hell of a lot of time buzzing around barristers these days. It was a pain in the butt. As Sandy said, if that was what I was going to do, I might just as well be back in practice. (No. She had not given up that most crazy of all her ideas.)

The second was marginally more particular. Of all the barristers I had recently been to call on, only Harryngton had kept me waiting. Keenan hadn't. Orbach hadn't. It did not endear Harrygton to me.

I had met him before, years and years before. In the earliest days of practice, in my enthusiasm, I had joined an organization which went by the less than catchy title of the Progressive Lawyers Campaign, inevitably and invariably abbreviated to PLC. They didn't quite march through the Inns of Court waving banners, but it was seen as that sort of thing.

Malcolm Harryngton had also been a member of PLC. He was, even then, something of an odd man out. With his pinstripes, waistcoat and fob-chain, in contrast to the off-duty jeans the rest of us wore, and the y in the middle of his name. None of us ever quite understood his interest or his involvement. In the event, we had never been close and had lost contact completely by the end of the decade. We were now to resume acquaintance.

My heavy heinie and I had hung in there 'till the light was beginning to creep in to my cave-like abode.

We talked in the darkness. I did not think it would be tactful if, say, Tim Dowell popped into join us. Nor could I afford the risk of his ringing at the bell, and wondering why I refused to open up to him. He was smart enough to work it out for himself.

There were, one could say, three interests at play. Disraeli Chambers' interest in maintaining what was left of their present range of questionable talent. Dowell's in an arrest. Mine in finding some final answers.

We had, therefore, quite a lot to talk about. He was far more forthcoming than one might have anticipated. Early on, I asked whether he wasn't taking a few more chances on me than I might merit. He didn't answer for a second, then touched with his finger the trigger of his favourite toy.

'You might, well, perhaps, maybe, not have it with you at the time when it mattered ...'

He smiled. He had such a pleasant smile. It gave me the shits.

'Do you mean in a court?'

'It's not beyond the realms of possibility ...'

'No, it is not impossible. But I do not think it is likely, do you? That they will keep me alive?'

'I would have thought ... I don't want to sound naive ... But ... Here, in this country, you know ...'

'It is not here I am wanted …'

He was right. Not by Special Branch. Not by the police hierarchy. Only by the drum-busting Sergeant Dowell, who was now organizing fuzz-rosters to keep the dufuses of Disraeli Chambers alive.

'Still you have not told me what it is you wish to know.'

'I suppose … I suppose I'm curious why you agreed to see me, without knowing what I want …'

He shrugged. They even did it in Germany. *Ich*-shrug.

'The game is … How shall I say? Drawing to a close, is it not? For a time at least I think we must call it stalemate …'

'That didn't stop you at the last meeting …'

'Yes. I had my plans. I saw the police, of course. My plan was still working. Why should I stop? Now. I think it is different. They are guarding the bodies, not the office …'

He was a realist.

I felt strangely disappointed in him.

I hadn't thought he'd let anything get in his way.

'So you came to see me … to break the stalemate?'

'Perhaps. Also. I was curious. You found your way to me. I do not think that was from Keenan … Am I correct?'

I nodded. Then asked:

'Mightn't it've been Orbach?'

His face was impassive. I figured he was trying to decide whether or not to let on that he knew him. It was the first time he acted simply as if I had not spoken. He was to repeat it later.

I started back at square one.

'Why have you been murdering members of Disraeli Chambers?'

'Because they betrayed my comrades …'

'What happened?'

He told me about the night they were taken. First he explained some background.

What the press called gangs, revolutionary organizations, fractions or whatever, rarely existed the way they were perceived. A name might be taken: Baader-Meinhof/Red Army Faction was the best known; a date was a common designation. They did not operate, or subsist, in permanent groups. Rather, individuals, or perhaps a couple, who went their own ways the rest of the time, utilized one such name for a particular action.

It was for this reason that so many managed to evade the law for so long. The police looked for gangs. They knew, of course, the names of individuals and would, as it were, settle for one or two at a time as available. But their operations were oriented towards organizations. When they caught one or two members, they could claim to have done no more than limited damage. Only when they caught several at once — enough of whom they could identify with a known group — could they claim destruction.

This was only possible for very short periods. When the people who were to use a gang name for a specific, single purpose first came together, then planned and trained together. It ended when they had struck.

The options for the police were, accordingly, restricted. They could aim to capture a small number, who could be convicted of an equally small number of incidents, or they had to hit a larger group at a much earlier stage, before they had actually committed any offence together. This meant that there was little chance of conviction — and translated in practice into the alternative of elimination. Once dead, they could be accused of, and in absentia called to account for, as many charges as the police wanted to claim.

The night it happened was the first night a new grouping — albeit to fly under an existing flag — had gathered.

'How was contact maintained? How did you find each other?'

'There is a network, in Germany, and elsewhere, through which this can happen. These are people who are sympathizers, but not participants. They help us escape, they help us survive, they help us make contact with one another.'

'Lawyers? Are there lawyers amongst these people?'

'I would say, no. Not knowing who we are. Lawyers have their uses, when one is captured. Then, also, they have their job and they understand their position. Before, they are a risk. They do not understand their position. They are frightened. It is harder ... How shall I say this? It is hard to play a strange part in a familiar performance, more hard than when you are completely from outside. Do you understand me?'

'I think so.' He meant, I think, that a complete outsider would find everything utterly unreal. He would be compelled to play out the fantasy in itself, without reference to any criteria. It is not a fantasy for a lawyer to have dealings with the wanted. But the way they would be called upon to act, in this contact network, would be too different from their normal role.

They had gone to sleep. There were nine of them. He had heard a noise. He had awoken. He believed it was nerves. He could not get back to sleep. He was lying in the attic. He had gone up on to the roof. Perhaps in order to reassure himself. Perhaps for some fresh air. Perhaps some sixth sense told him to get out. He did not know now which it was. He had saved himself by less than two minutes.

'I did not see anything. I could only hear. They did not shout a warning. They were military. Faces darkened. They came in and the shooting started.'

'Where were you?'

He smiled:

'It is corny. I hid in the chimney.'

'Didn't they look up it?'

'Possibly. It was blocked up at the bottom. At the top there was a cover. I took it off. I climbed in. I pulled the cover back on. It was possible to go across the other roofs. That is what they did. They looked for me, I am sure. They must have seen my sleeping-bag. Empty. But they never looked in the chimney. I was lucky.'

'How long were you there?'

'Nearly two days. I did not dare to come out before. It was cold. I was not properly clothed. I was frightened. Also, I was ashamed. Because I should have warned my comrades, or I should have died with them. Do you not think?'

He was asking me.

I didn't answer. It was way beyond the experiences I had had.

'You haven't told me ... Why Disraeli Chambers?'

'Ah, yes. Yes. That is your question.'

He paused to collect his thoughts.

'In the evening, when we were eating, Klaus Friske talked of England. He had been in England. In London. He had met some lawyers. Barristers they are called. Keenan. We knew Keenan's name, of course. He had met some colleagues of this Keenan. The woman Creemer. He did not say. But I think he was slept with her.'

Damn me if I wasn't close to correcting his grammar.

'We were amused. They did not know what he was — not a lot. They were like children. They wanted to get close to the fire. But not too close. This is not uncommon. Also in Germany. They can be excited. They think it is dangerous. Glamorous.'

He was bitter:

'They see it for a few minutes or a day. Like the television. They do not live it.'

'Is Helga ... like that?'

'No. She is clear. She knows what she will do. She knows what she is believing. Her father ... Schroeder ... Perhaps a little bit to make amends ...'

'Why do you do it?'

I wasn't talking Disraeli Chambers any more. He thought for a moment, then shrugged again:

'*Ich kann nicht anders ...*'

To my surprise as much as to his, I remembered. Luther. I can do no other.

'You know Luther?' I asked.

'I was three years in the seminary ...'

Holy shit.

I shook my head:

'No, I don't understand ...'

'Are you a socialist, Mr Woolf?'

'I don't know any more. I used to think so.'

'What do you do?'

'I was a lawyer, too.'

It was all right for me to put it in the past tense. After all, it was my life. I just didn't like it when others did it.

'Now? You are not a lawyer?'

'Nope. I'm nothing really. I'm doing this job ... For a relative of someone you killed ...' I pre-empted his question:

'But in between acts, I tend to do a lot of nothing ...'

'Yes, I understand. But it is not an easy choice. To do nothing.'

'Is what you do an easy choice?'

'No. But some people — I — cannot do nothing.'

'Was this all you could think of to do?'

I didn't really need to ask. That was what he was saying. His frustration was no different from mine. It was just that he couldn't sit still.

'And now? Why so much time, for such ... God, they're such petty, pathetic people ... They can't be worth it!'

He laughed:

'Again. *Ich kann nicht anders.*'

'And, again, I don't understand ...'

'You see ... After that night ... It has not been easy for me ... To make contacts ... It has not been possible for me ... To be involved. Do you see?'

'I think so. You're too badly wanted by the police?'

'No, not at all. This is not a problem. But I am not trusted ... Now do you see?'

I saw.

'What you said ... That your friend ... Klaus? Was that his name ...'

'Klaus Friske. Yes.'

'Because Klaus had been around Disraeli Chambers just beforehand ... That's the whole basis for thinking they betrayed you?'

'No. It was a suspicion. Also. I knew ... We knew ... There were very few people who could have done this. Who knew where we were, and when. Klaus ... He did not admit ... But when he drank ... In a foreign country one is less careful, yes? With a woman perhaps ... I think it is likely ... After, I have had plenty of time to think ... I think it must have been from there ... Not direct, not deliberate, because they did not know so much, but originally from there or from somewhere close to them ... This is what I think for myself ...'

'Have you been told it, by anyone else?'

This was another occasion when he acted as if I had not spoken.

'What happened when you saw Keenan? Why did you see him?'

'Helga asked it of me. There was no reason why not.'

'It might have been a set-up?'

'So also you. I take care. With Keenan, also, I take care ...'

'Did Helga ask you to see me, or just pass my message on?'

'She passed it on. But I did that for her also. Because you might have come back. Or to give her name to the police.'

'Perhaps ... But Helga asked you to see Keenan?'

'Yes.'

'And you agreed?'

'Yes. She has been a friend, for many years ... A good friend ... Perhaps now the only friend ...'

'But also a friend of Keenan's?'

'She has many friends ...'

Not only Keenan.

'What happened at the meeting?'

'You know, I think, what happened.'

'Did he ... He denied it was them?'

'He said so. He said it was not them.'

'But you didn't believe him?'

'No. This is correct. He was ... How shall I say? He was hiding something ...'

'Did Helga ever ask you to see Russel Orbach?'

I thought for a moment he was going to do his mental disappearing act again. Instead:

'You have asked me before about him. Why?'

'I don't know. It's a feeling. A hunch. He knows a lot. He was one of them. He split up with them. Badly. He hates them ...'

'It is powerful, hatred. I think, perhaps, the most powerful emotion.'

Before I could stop myself, I said:

'You should know ...'

'No. This is wrong. I do not hate. I ... I just do.'

Actions. Not words.

'You didn't answer my question ...'

'No. She did not ask me.'

'But have you see him? Since?'

I hadn't asked the question. Or so it seemed from his reaction. I tried a different one.

'Why the last Wednesday? Why always then, their meeting day?'

'This is easy. The first time. This was chance. Coincidence. The man Wishart. After. I can always know, one of them will be there. Yes?'

I had to admit. It is hard to have a meeting with no one present.

'I can be here. Before. I can watch. Choose. Perhaps one, perhaps two, perhaps more. I have the time to understand where they live, how they travel, their movements, their habits. For a little. But enough. Then. On the Wednesday. I have my choice.'

'You ... I don't believe you could have done it all without some inside information,' I said bluntly.

'Why is this?'

He was a calm bugger all right. About as cold as I felt and as Orbach had acted in Oslo.

'How'd'you know who is who? How'd'you know who was a member at the time? It was Klaus who was here, not you ...'

'Before it was Klaus. After. I have been here after. They are going a lot to meetings, to conferences, to the drinking afterwards ... Me also.'

'Is it so easy? You can't have used your own name, you must have had to avoid people who knew you. You would have had to come in as a stranger. Is the left that easy to infiltrate?'

He laughed bitterly:

'Yes. It is that easy. Consider. It lacks organization, just because it is on the left, it is out of power. It does not have uniform or rank or system. No cards for entry. No security police. When the left gather they might as well do it in the public park ...

'Also. The left ... The people are perhaps not so suspicious. In themselves, do you not think, left people are of a nicer ...' He got lost looking for a word:

'Inclination. Is that the word?'

'Maybe. It'll do. Disposition?'

'Yes, this is the word I am looking for.'

'Your English is pretty damned good.' A lot of it was better than mine.

'I am studying English at university. Then, also, after, in the seminary,'

'OK ...'

'Perhaps also we can say, because the left always wants more people, they are less careful about who they take ... Do you think?'

'Maybe.'

He was right, though. How many left-wing gatherings had I gone to, where we had behaved as if we were co-conspirators in some secret scheme, and yet I had not known the names of half the people present, let alone what it was that qualified them for admission? Put it the other way round. Who the hell knew who I was half the time, or what I was doing there?

That was how we spent the night. Batting between politics and philosophy, personalities and picking up the details of how he had waged his war. He drank me out of coffee, and I drank me out of all the booze there was left in the flat. I didn't feel even remotely pissed.

'You said ... You wanted to break the stalemate?'

'Yes ...'

'Do you think we have?'

'No. Of course not.'

'How did you think it would? Or could?'

'I do not know. Perhaps. Do you think it was from them?' For a second, he was like a little boy, needing to be told he'd done his homework or the washing-up right.

'I don't know. I don't think ... Well, I don't think you're doing any good ... I think, maybe, you've made your point ... You won't get anywhere else with it ... Who's left to wipe out? Jane Daws? Mike Barron? They're about the only two still around from that time. They're not worth the effort. They're people of absolutely no consequence ...'

I felt incredibly alone. Here was I. Sitting with a man who was a murderer. A lot of people would have liked to be in on the interview. I knew now more about what had happened than anyone else — my present companion apart — in the whole world. Yet I felt nothing. I was numb. Positively anaesthetized. Not just, or perhaps at all, by tiredness. That had come and gone and come and gone it didn't matter any more. But a whole different kind of weariness. I felt, despite myself, utterly indifferent. He could kill Daws, or Barron, and I didn't give a damn. He could get away. It didn't matter. I had discharged my duty to my client.

I couldn't let it go like that. I couldn't just say: later, alligator; thank you and have a nice day; take care on your journey home. The one thing neither he nor I knew was whether his comrades actually been betrayed by Disraeli Chambers, or by someone else. For some reason which I can't explain and I'm not sure I can justify, that alone of all of it seemed to matter the most.

He left as suddenly as he had arrived. I was not to tell anyone I had seen him. He promised: he would be in touch again. I had an idea: next time it wouldn't be from across the square. Also, I was by no means sure that our next encounter would be as amicable. Just as I would undoubtedly spend a long time thinking about him, he would be thinking about me. If I had made the slightest slip, or if I now did anything he viewed with suspicion, I knew, from what he had described, how he liked best to express his disapproval.

I slept about three hours. An uneasy sleep riven with images. Everybody was at the party. The living and the dead. No one made any sense. No one seemed to think they needed — or even ought — to try to do so.

Two things he had said stuck in my mind. How it had to be them, or else someone close to them. And, how easy it is to infiltrate the left.

That was when first a body — in a pin-stripe suit — then a face then finally a name forced their way out of the faculty mockingly known as my memory. Malcolm Harryngton.

I'd caught the story long after I'd left PLC. It had first been run in one of the London weekly listings magazines, which incorporated a few pages of hard news. It had been taken up by the Guardian newspaper, in the context of a larger piece on infiltration. It must have been back in 1979 or 1980, and my only interest was because I recognized Harryngton's name.

He was alleged to have been an establishment informer against left-wing legal activism. PLC wasn't mentioned. It could not itself have been the subject of his attention. Rather, a way of meeting those on its left who, in turn, might wearing other hats be involved in the sort of adventure his masters wanted to know about. For example, members of Disraeli Chambers. I even had a vague idea Keenan had figured in one or other of the articles, offering — as usual — his opinion.

I couldn't get to the Guardian in time to use their library that day. I rang Sandy. She didn't remember him at all well, could add nothing to what I had already recalled for myself. Anne Godwin and Gerry Gilligan had never known him. I wasn't ready to try the name out on the two people at the centre who would certainly have been around at the same time, and whose memories, in sharp contrast to my own, were elephantine, Keenan and Orbach.

After my weekly fix of Hill Street Blues, I mooched round to Lewis's. I wasn't looking for Tim Dowell, especially, though I wouldn't have minded if he'd been there to keep me company. I was beginning to miss him. It felt like it had been a long time.

What I wanted was a word with the man himself.

'All alone tonight, then, Dave?' Lewis leered.

'Looks that way ...'

'I'll buy you a drink if you don't tell Dowell ...'

We were served by a male waiter. Young. Slicked back black hair. Tight trousers. After he left us, Lewis said:

'Teaching him the business, you might say ...' I was intended to spot the double meaning.

'The first time you came in here looking for me ... I mean, recently ..." Not when I had borrowed money from him. "You said I might want a favour from you some day. Do you remember?'

I grunted non-committally. Not until I knew what the favour was.

'What is Tim Dowell up to?'

'Why are you asking?'

'He's been coming here a great deal. Not just with you,' he added archly, as if it might make me jealous:

'In the past, whenever he came, he had a purpose in mind. He wanted something. Now, he sits and drinks, and watches. Me. The waitresses. The other customers.'

It was quite an admission. He was spooked.

'Maybe he fancies you, Lewis,' I was feeling bold.

He looked pained:

'I am trusting you, Dave. Do you understand what that means? Do you understand how rarely I do that? Do you understand?'

I was not to joke.

'Sorry.'

I did actually feel it. He was showing his age. There were at least ten wrinkles now where there'd only been nine and three-quarters before.

'Maybe he's just unhappy. He's ... Well ...'

I didn't want to be disloyal to Dowell either.

'He hasn't exactly got the confidence of his superiors any more ...'

'It's this business with the barristers, isn't it? Are you involved in it, Dave? How much do you know?'

'Not a whole bunch. You helped us out. You knew before anyone else anyway ...' When he'd told us Art Farquharson wasn't a fag-killing.

He shivered at the memory.

'I don't like it, Dave. It isn't natural. Murdering lawyers, I mean. They could get scared. Then where would we be? Who'd we go to?'

I laughed:

'I don't think this lot would've been your scene anyway, Lewis ... Strictly political.'

He tutted. He didn't approve of politics. They weren't natural, either.

'Is that it? Is it political?'

It wasn't so much that I wanted to pay off the old favour, as that I had another in mind: 'Yes. Heavily.'

He breathed out. It was nothing that would interfere with his business.

He enjoyed being informed.

'Lewis ...'

Despite myself, I dropped my voice. It was not so much caution, as nerves.

'Would you ... How would I ... Lewis ... I'm not a little scared myself ... I want ... I need ... Oh, shit ...'

He tutted again. I guess he thought bad language wasn't natural too.

'I want a gun ...'

There. I'd said it.

The ceiling didn't fall.

The only thing I was frightened of was that he'd say yes.

'You want a gun? You, Dave? Want a gun?'

He was like a stuck record.

I knew what he was thinking. I was a sometime lawyer, turned highly qualified process-server, whose most dangerous activity hitherto had been the quantities I could consume of Southern Comfort.

'That's what I said ... I want a gun.' I felt stronger about it now I knew a bolt of lightning wouldn't strike me dead for saying it.

He thought some more about it.

'Do you know how to use a gun, Dave?'

'Sure. I watch Hill Street Blues every week. You sort of, well, crouch down behind something, or someone, and point it, don't you?'

'It isn't a laughing matter, my friend ...'

I declare, he was genuinely concerned about me.

'No, I know. But ... There's people around ... There's been a lot of killing.'

'Has anyone been threatening you, Dave? Why don't you let me take care of them for you ...'

I couldn't dream what I'd owe him if I did.

'They're not your scene, Lewis. Like I said. Political.'

He knew what I meant. He'd seen The Long Good Friday. The one where the gangsters get into a war with the IRA. The gangsters lose.

'They're crazy ...'

Politicals. Terrorists. He didn't say it but we were both talking about the same thing.

'Got no respect ... Just crazy.'

'Now'd'you see why?'

'You ought to keep out of it, Dave. It's not your scene either ...' What he meant was, I couldn't handle it.

'I ... Uh ... I don't think, you know, in a shoot out or something like that, sure ... But, well, I'd just feel better, you know? A sort of comforter ...'

'Try sucking your thumb ... Or ...' He grinned.

Which told me I could have what I wanted.

'And ammunition?'

'I'll tell you what I'll do. I'll load it for you, Just the once. I'll show you how it works. Just the once. But that's it ...'

'How much is it going to cost me?'

He held up the fingers and thumb of one hand. I blanched. It was five days' work. Still. I might be able to claim it on expenses. Or use it in trade when I'd finished the job and started to spend the loot I'd earned. If, that is, I was around to do so.

I didn't see Harryngton until after the next weekend. On the Monday. Which put us two days away from the next chambers' meeting. I saw him at four-thirty, traditionally the barristers' conference time, when they've finished for the day in court.

He hadn't changed much. A bit plumper. More prosperous. I didn't like to ask but wasn't the gold chain silver the last time I saw him.

'I haven't seen you for a long time ... Are you still practising?'

I didn't bore him with my usual rejoinder.

'You're obviously doing well. Still enjoying it?'

'The old cut and thrust, eh ...'

He'd make a good coroner. They had the same sort of style.

'Are you still a member of PLC?'

He frowned:

'No. I left.'

'Why?'

'I think you know,' he pursed his lips:

'What do you want to see me about?' He'd frozen over.

I thought of saying: I think you know.

'That, I guess. You've ... Uh ... Read about Disraeli Chambers?'

'Of course.' Who hadn't, in and around the profession. If they could've got cover like this for being alive, they'd've earned enough to retire by now.

'I've been interested in it.'

'Interested?'

'Investigating ... around it. For a client. A relative of one of the members. Late members.'

He inclined his head graciously, as if to say: I am prepared to respect your reasons for asking questions.

'How can I help you, then? I am, as you know, not on friendly terms with them ...'

'You were around, with some of them a few years ago. Keenan. Orbach.'

He shook his head:

'I didn't know Orbach. I might have seen him once or twice. He wasn't as active as Keenan. Keenan was at PLC a lot. And ... at other meetings. But Orbach's no longer there, didn't you know that?'

'Yes, I knew. So you haven't seen him, recently?'

'At court once or twice, possibly. Not to speak to. I suppose, we nod when we pass ...'

'And Keenan? Do you nod at him?'

He chuckled:

'I would say, no, we are not even on nodding terms ...'

'Why not?'

'Again, you know that. You know what was said about me.'

'You didn't sue ...'

'What for? Being accused of being in some sort of relationship with the authorities is hardly libellous. Libel has to lower you in the eyes of right-thinking members of society, you know ... I was only lowered in the eyes of the left,' he smiled thinly at the jocular way he had put what was not a joke.

What I wanted to know was: how much truth was there in what they had written? It was likely to be the last question I'd be able to put. I wasn't banking on an answer. I slipped another in first.

'How close were you to Keenan'

'For a short time, we were friendly. He came to my house for dinner, with his wife. Some people ... People like yourself I would say ... Found me an unusual type to have an interest in PLC and the movement ... I could say: that was your prejudice. He didn't have that sort of prejudice. After all, we weren't so dissimilar although he was and is of course much better known and much more successful than I ... Professionally as well as politically ...'

'Did you go there?'

'Where? To his house? Yes. There were a few meetings ... I dropped in on a couple of occasions ...' He chuckled again:

'Lady Helen ... As they say, quite a lady ...'

And he was no gentleman.

CHAPTER TWELVE

He caught up with me as I left Kentish Town station, on my way to Sandy's.

'You will see your friend ...' He sounded jealous. Wistful. It's no fun giving up all aspects of a normal life. Staking everything on one type of action, with the probability of just one way for it all to end. Knowing that must happen. Waiting for it. For that time when he'd be able to do what he couldn't do now. Nothing.

'I will see my friend ...'

'Have you told her you have seen me?'

'No.'

I wasn't lying.

Automatically, we had cut down an alley.

He checked behind us.

'I'm not being followed ...'

'I have followed you ...'

'Since when?'

'Since yesterday morning ...'

I shivered.

'Who was this you are seeing?'

'A barrister. Not a member of Disraeli Chambers.'

'And which is his name?'

He produced from his pocket a sheet of paper on to which — presumably while he had waited for me to come out again — he had copied the names from the boards which all barristers maintain outside their chambers.

I picked one at random.

Not Malcolm Harryngton.

A woman's name.

I hoped she didn't have two young children and a dog.

Quickly, I added:

'She is nothing to do with this. An old friend,' I laughed nervously:

'Because of Sandy ... I had to see her. Do you understand?'

He didn't believe me. I didn't blame him. It wasn't a good story.

He said:

'It is tomorrow ...'

Wednesday. The last in the month.

'And?'

We understood one another. He wanted an end to the stalemate. I wanted an end to this job. We both got what we wanted when we finally knew for sure who had betrayed his comrades. I said:

'I have to see Keenan ... He's the only one who can help ...'

Then he surprised me:

'Are you sure?'

The name he'd ignored the other night.

I glanced down at his holdall.

He followed my eyes.

So long as he was carrying it, I could not give him the chance.

'Where?' he asked.

I looked long and pointedly at the bag again.

'No bag.'

'Do you promise?'

It was kind of pathetic. I had no other way. Though he might be a killer, he had shown no evidence of being dishonest.

'I promise.'

'Both of them ... That's what you want, isn't it?'

He nodded slowly.

I felt an almost sexual excitement. It was what I wanted too. It had become what I needed.

I could hardly get the word out:

'Sandy's ...'

'Tonight. It must be tonight. After nine o clock. Perhaps much later. You understand me. Perhaps you must wait all the night.'

'I understand ...'

'Do you promise, also?'

He meant: no set-up.

'I promise.'

'Go ...'

I went.

Sandy wasn't home, I let myself in.

I had a lot to do.

I had to get Keenan there.

And Orbach.

And keep Sandy out.

She was still at the office. I caught her on the private number.

'I want you to do something for me ... Two things, really ...'

'What?'

'Will you ring Keenan? Find him ... Wherever ... Get him to come here ... Before nine o'clock ... Can you do that?'

I didn't like the reasons why I knew she could.

'You said two things ...'

'I'd like it ... if you didn't come back tonight.'

She whistled through her teeth. It scratched in my ear.

'You'n'Alex, huhn? Who'd've thunk it?' She was playing for time.

'Well, you know, I guess I need a little variety ...'

'Dave ... Are you in ... Well, are you in danger?'

Who? Me? Ha! What a joke! Danger? What was danger to a man of my calibre and experience? What did I care if a gang of German gunmen burst into her house and ventilated it with sub-machine guns? I could handle that shit. Wasn't I Captain Furillo and Clint Eastwood and Mick Belker rolled into one? Had she never heard of Krypton?

'I think ... No, there's no danger,' I lied:

'I wouldn't ask, otherwise, you know, for you to get Keenan here ...'

I figure she was weighing up: just how much of a bastard was I capable of?

'Why can't I be there, Dave?'

So, already, she wasn't stupid.

'I just think ... You know ... The things that are going to be said ... It'll be pretty heavy ...'

She was silent for a moment.

Then:

'If I can find him, I'll get him there ...'

On the other, she had no comment.

I waited for her to ring back and confirm she'd clicked with Keenan. Immediately after, I rang Orbach.

I'd been much more concerned about finding Keenan. He had a thousand and fifty things to do every day. Meetings. Speeches. Wife and children. Chambers. Somewhere in between, I knew it was also his habit to wangle a woman if he could. Orbach was very different. He left work as early as he was able. Sped home. Shut the world out behind him. And sat, looking at the empty space behind the trees.

'I want to see you,' I sounded as terse as I felt.

After a pause, he said:

'I'm at home …'

'I want to see you here …'

'Where's here?'

I told him. Adding:

'It's not far …'

'Yes, I know that. Why do you want me there?'

'I don't know what time, but I'm going to get a call, here, tonight. A foreign call. To be precise, from Germany.' I meant it to sound like 'phone call. Otherwise, it was near enough to be true. These other guys. They'd all been running around, making an ass out of me, telling me half-truths, or omitting essential information, but always reserving to themselves the gentleman's privilege of saying that they had not lied.

He hesitated longer than the time before but he couldn't resist.

Sandy had told Keenan to be there at eight thirty. I asked Orbach to arrive at nine. It was cutting it fine, but I didn't doubt we were in for a long wait. He would probably be watching the premises even now, perhaps he had followed me straight back, so as to ensure I didn't pack the house with police before his arrival. He would want to be as sure as the circumstances permitted prior to his entry.

I didn't actually care who came first. I only didn't want them bumping into each other on the doorstep. If either of them saw the other before coming in, there was a real risk he'd walk away. Once I had them inside, I was going to keep them together. If necessary, with a little help from my new friend.

I had an hour to kill. Pardon. To waste. You think I'm going to tell you I took a belt or two to bolster my courage. You'd be wrong. More like a tumbler-full.

By quarter to nine, Keenan was still no-show. I was beginning to sweat. When the doorbell rang, I ran to open up, grab whoever was out there — I swear I didn't care which one — and pull him inside.

It was Keenan. He was, of course, more than a little surprised, and not a little disconcerted, to see me:

'Sandy ...'

'Yes, I know. I asked her to.'

It wasn't, I suppose, tactful. I couldn't help reminding him.

He didn't like being conned. Maybe he would've walked. I told him it was no more than slight redress:

'I liked Oslo ...'

He shrugged. That was over.

'Would you like a drink?'

'You still haven't said what you want ...'

'No more I have. I wanted to talk with you. Away from your chambers. Away from your home.' It was the second place I mentioned that caused his face muscles to tighten up.

'OK ... Scotch and water ...'

I was in the kitchen fetching the water when the doorbell rang again. I cut straight out into the hall, which left him in the living-room, to let in the next contestant.

'This way, please,' I said, before he had a chance to speak, and Keenan to hear his voice.

The way they stared at each other wasn't the way Livingstone must've stared at Stanley. More like the way Hitler might've felt if Churchill had walked into the Berlin bunker shortly after he'd swallowed his cyanide brew.

Orbach spoke first:

'Alex. It's been a long time.'

I held my breath. And, inside my jacket, my gun.

You could see Keenan mentally tossing a coin. Deep inside he had wanted this confrontation for a long time.

'Russel ...'

They were stalking around each other like prize cocks.

Then Keenan grinned, and held out a hand.

Orbach accepted.

'Now what?' he asked me.

'Now we talk ... But ... A drink?'

I still hadn't brought Keenan his.

Orbach shook his head.

He wanted it clear.

Keenan was still wearing a suit. He had, presumably, been in court earlier that day. Had no chance to change. Orbach, on the other hand, had been at home when I caught him. He was wearing a Norwegian knitted cardigan, with silver-plated buckles down the front.

'I've had an interesting couple of discussions recently, with a pair of Germans,' I opened once we were all settled down.

Neither batted an eyelid.

I had to remember. I was dealing with two highly experienced barristers. Not just barristers, but Queen's Counsel, the alleged cream of the cream. They were, probably, amongst the cleverest people I had ever known. Perhaps the cleverest of all. It was more likely true of Orbach than Keenan. But with Orbach present, Keenan was on his mettle too. I was not going to score by trick questions or shock tactics.

I still wasn't near expecting my visitor. To my surprise, though less to theirs who knew it wasn't my place, I heard a key slide into the lock. I was so stunned it took me a minute to get up and go for the door. Sandy came straight in. She looked at me defiantly. Her home.

'Alex,' she acknowledged:

'Russel. We haven't met for a long time ...'

'True,' he said:

'I seem to recall you stopped briefing me several years ago ...'

Sandy flushed.

My face asked what was this about. Orbach explained, matter-of-factly:

'After the split, a lot of people lined up behind Disraeli Chambers. They'd heard the rumours. Decided I must be in the wrong. None of them came to ask me of course. Suddenly, I was no longer the lawyer I'd been the day before.'

'Russel ... It's long ago ... You've done well ...' Alex said.

I'd forgotten. Keenan had once been Orbach's pupil-master. He had a history of authority to dip into when it suited.

Orbach wasn't impressed:

'Everything I did, I worked for, Alex. Nothing was handed me on a platter ...'

Sandy had gone out to the kitchen. She could still hear. She came back in, shaking her head:

'Russel, Russel. You don't need to be jealous of him any more ...'

She was right. On both counts. He was jealous. He didn't need to be.

Alex tried once more to take command:

'Dave, you asked us both here. What for? For this? You said ... You had seen some Germans ...'

I wasn't sorry to see the set swivel in my direction. Like Sandy, I did not find the sight of two middle-aged men bickering like school-children exactly edifying.

'Yes. Helga Schroeder was one of them ...'

Orbach and Keenan exchanged a glance.

'Who was the other?' Keenan asked.

'I don't know his name ...' I grinned:

'But we all know who I mean ...'

'I'm glad if they do, but ...' Sandy said pointedly.

'Sandy. I said you shouldn't be here ...'

'I'm here. It's my home. You're my lover. You're my friend,' she told Keenan, consolingly rather than rubbing salt in that particular wound:

'I'm entitled ...'

Orbach explained:

'He's seen the man who committed the murders. That's right, isn't it, Dave?'

'Yes.'

'You said you were expecting a 'phone call tonight, from Germany, was that true or was that just to get me here?'

'It wasn't what I said. I said a call. Not a 'phone call ...'

'Ah ... I see ...'

Orbach was the only one to do so. He relaxed. He, at least, planned to enjoy himself.

It was exactly then that he arrived. He banged hard on the door, instead of ringing the bell. I shot up to let him in. He brushed past me, immediately flinging open other doors. Not just doors to rooms — the kitchen, the bathroom, the bedrooms — but also to cupboards within.

As promised, he was not carrying his holdall.

It took him several minutes to complete his search, satisfy himself the house was clean.

Then he smiled at Keenan, and held out a hand which, with obvious reluctance, Alex shook:

'We meet again,' the German said.

Alex didn't answer.

'Hello, Rainer.' Russel, too, held out a hand, which the man whose first name I now had for the first time, took.

Rainer bowed slightly, politely, to Sandy:

'We have not met. But, I think, we have spoken ...'

She was the most ill-at-ease. The least involved. Accordingly, the one with the greatest amount of spare attention to concentrate on the least salubrious aspect of the encounter. To wit, that the man she was now entertaining in her home was a murderer.

'Can I ... Would anyone like a drink, or a coffee? Something to eat ...' Heredity told. At a time like this, she could resort only to the as yet unfulfilled role of Jewish momma.

'Sit,' Rainer ordered.

Heredity told again. She sat.

'Now?' He looked at me.

It was my show.

I'd just begun to wonder whether it was that good a play after all. Which was, now I'd finally got the curtain unstuck, a little late in the day.

'I would say ... You want to know who betrayed your comrades ...'

'I know who ...'

'I don't think so ... You thought you knew who ... You had some reason for what you thought ... That was the way you put it, wasn't it, Russel?'

Orbach smiled pleasantly.

He didn't care what happened. He just didn't care. He'd got his confrontation with Keenan. All the bitterness and the pain accumulated over those years since he was ousted from the group would find some sort of resolution tonight.

'I think ... I'd say it was not a bad guess ... But it wasn't quite right. You were encouraged to think it ... By Orbach ... Correct?'

Rainer didn't answer so Orbach did it for him:

'He presented me with a theory of how it had happened. It would be correct to say ... I never disabused him of it ...'

'Why not?' I snapped.

'I think ... I think that is not for me to say. I was, of course, and am under no duty — legally — to tell Rainer anything ...' He was pointing out, accurately so far as I could tell, that he had committed no crime by failing to correct the German.

'Would you not say ... A duty to tell the police what you knew? Of meeting Rainer ...'

'This is the first time we have met in this country, Dave ...'

'Ah, Oslo.' I hadn't thought of that.

I remembered what Helen Keenan had said about Orbach. The great manipulator. Whether or not it had been true prior to his fall from grace at Disraeli Chambers, he had made it true since. This was his revenge. Gilligan said he was viewed as a devil. Already condemned as such, he had nothing left to lose by acting like one. He was probably telling the truth when he claimed not to have told Rainer it was them; but it was just as true that it was his responsibility that Rainer went on thinking it.

'What you do not tell me, Mr Woolf, is if I am right ... If Russel is right,' he looked straight at Orbach, without anger, but also without his customary smile. He was confirming Orbach's role in leading him on.

'If I can adopt what Russel just said, I don't think that's for me to say ...'

Which left Keenan.

He was white as a sheet.

'Shall I help you, Alex?' I asked gently.

He shook his head:

'Don't. Please.'

From his coat pocket, Rainer produced a pistol. I cursed:

'You promised ...'

'I promised only the other gun. This ...' He held it up for all to see. I was already aware it was in a different class from that with which Lewis had provided me. Like the difference between a three-legged race and the Olympic marathon.

He placed it gingerly on his lap.

'Now ... Alex ... Please,' he prompted.

'Cat got your tongue, Alex,' Orbach hissed:

'Or a bitch?'

'You bastard ...' Keenan spat back at his oldest friend:

'You would have told him, wouldn't you ... In the end, after the others had been ... finished ... Wouldn't you?' He shouted, half-rising in his chair until Rainer motioned with the weapon for him to resume his seat.

Orbach shook his head slowly:

'I don't know, Alex. I really don't know. I didn't tell him. Did I? I could have told him, anyway ...'

'Oh, no, you couldn't. He wouldn't've bothered, with the others ...' He was shaking:

'Wishart. Carrie. Jackdaw. Art. Harry. You killed them, you did …' He was almost weeping.

'No, Alex,' Orbach remained calm:

'You. You far more than me. We both knew. All along. But it was your responsibility to tell him. Not mine. All you did was remain silent. Like you always did. Like you did … over me.'

'How could I?' Keenan was openly crying now:

'How could I?' I. I. I. It echoed round the room.

Rainer spoke softly:

'Now you will tell me …'

He was asking me.

I told him the story of the left-wing infiltrator called Harryngton with a y. Who'd gotten close to Keenan. Closer still to the Lady H. Close enough that one night, chatting as even the most ill-suited and casual of lovers will do, she told him what she'd heard from Keenan, who'd himself heard it from Creemer, about a clandestine left-wing gathering in Germany.

She had not noticed at the time when he pressed for further details. What city? Really, how courageous, he must have replied. What sort of house, what sort of locality? She didn't know what it was like. I know the town. Do you know an address? She mentions the area. Perhaps he says: that's clever; middle-class area; the police'll never find them.

She'd known afterwards, of course, when the two stories about Harryngton hit the papers. That was when she would have told Keenan. How badly they'd been taken in, how far she'd let him in. What they'd talked about that last night they'd slept together.

And Keenan, in turn, had told the only friend in whom he confided just about everything. The only member — as he then still was — of his chambers who might just possibly be as strong as Keenan himself, on occasion perhaps stronger. Even father-figures need someone to turn to once in a while.

'I told you she was poison, Alex ... I said she'd bring us both down in the end ...'

Keenan covered his face with his hands. He'd been trapped. Orbach was right. Once his comrades had started catching the consequences, it was his responsibility to let the Germans know how it had happened. He had had the means. Through Helga Schroeder. But he had spent his whole life protecting Lady Helen against her own follies. It was a habit he didn't know how to stop.

The smile had gone — I had the premonition for the last time — from Rainer's face. He lifted the gun. Not as if he was about to use it. To remind us all. Not even that he had it. But that this was his way.

'You ... All of you ...'

I didn't have the courage to invite him to exclude Sandy. Or me.

I scratched my stomach, inside my jacket, until the back of my nail struck against the butt of Lewis' gun.

'You have played with me ...'

Keenan shook his head:

'It wasn't ... That wasn't my intention ...'

Orbach smiled thinly. He wasn't about to deny it. He'd played with all of them. He still didn't give a damn what happened.

I glanced at Sandy. She was biting her lower lip. Scared. I mouthed:

'I m sorry ...'

She smiled back, though a little sadly, as if to say: I don't blame you.

'What happens now?' Orbach asked cheerfully.

I glanced at my watch. It was half past eleven. I said:

'Nothing ... For half an hour ...'

No one got it except Rainer. It still didn't reinstate his smile. He explained:

'Wednesday. It is Wednesday in half an hour. Yes. I think Mr Woolf is right ...'

We had some sort of reprieve.

Not a long one.

It felt like a year we sat in silence. It was no more than ten minutes. Everybody was thinking. None of us believed Rainer would simply walk away from it. He had gone too far to leave the job unfinished. Logic gave him Keenan. He was the only one still in the chambers, and of everyone present the man with the greatest responsibility for the betrayal with which it had all started.

Yet it was Orbach who had led him astray, who had let him waste his efforts on a bunch of people who had been as innocuously inactive in this matter as in any other. In so doing, he had diverted him from his true target.

Orbach said, to Keenan, as if Rainer was not there:

'No, Alex, I would never have told him. I couldn't have done that ...'

Keenan nodded. He knew it was true.

'Do you remember ... When everything was happening at chambers ... There was a letter, I'd written you and Helen ... A personal letter ... You handed round for them to read?'

'Yes. I'm sorry. That was wrong.'

'It doesn't matter now. The point is. Afterwards, when everyone around us was working up a lather about how terrible I was and what I'd done, you wrote me a letter. Also a personal letter. What you wrote meant you never believed what Helen said. You signed it with love. I never used that, on you ...'

A letter like that would have upset everybody's apple cart. Maybe, after all, Tim Dowell had a point. That Orbach had wanted it to happen. Had perhaps engineered it.

Keenan nodded again. They had fought their war, like opposing generals who had studied together at the same military academy, and who had for each other not merely respect but affection. They had done anything they could to destroy the enemy army, but always seeking to protect from harm those feelings of friendship for each other.

'I do not want to hear of this,' Rainer hissed:

'This is not for your quarrel ... It is for mine ...'

'I don't know, Rainer,' Orbach spoke as if they were discussing which film to go to, rather than arguing for their — our — lives:

'It's all about betrayal ...'

'How can you ... What they did to you ... How can you consider that with what they did to us?'

Orbach shrugged:

'Sure, it wasn't at the same level. But the point's the same, isn't it? Betrayal by those you have every reason to trust. Betrayal by those who have claimed and received your respect and your confidence because of what they say they stand for. Betrayal by your own side is so much more embittering than betrayal by your known enemies. Betrayal by hypocrites sheltering behind false masks ... What does it matter for which betrayal they were destroyed? The point is ... that they had to be destroyed ... Isn't it?'

He asked the last question not of the German but of Keenan.

'God, no, Russel ... God, no, they didn't have to be destroyed ... They never did anyone any harm ...'

'Or good ...'

'So what? So what if that's true … That they never did anyone any good … Did they deserve to die for that?'

'That's not what I'm saying. For claiming to do good … For the lie of the claim … For that …'

'You, Rainer, you do not agree with him! You cannot agree with him! What you have done, with your life, what your comrades did, before they died … It had nothing to do with this! That is the betrayal … You, too, have been betrayed …' He started to laugh, close to hysteria:

'Now we're all equal. We've all been betrayed. By each other.'

'Oh, God, please,' Sandy spoke:

'Please … Please Rainer … I'm going to be … I have to …' She was clutching her side, like she was having a seizure.

I went to her, put my arm around her.

'I have to go …'

'Let her go to the toilet, Rainer, please …' I begged.

He hesitated.

Then nodded.

She ran off into the kitchen.

I got there a split second before he did.

After all. I had been half-living in the house for several weeks, while he'd only been around the once, and layout wasn't what had concerned him. The way to the toilet was through the hall. The kitchen led only to the back door.

He rose from his seat waving the gun.

There was Keenan.

And Orbach.

And me.

Had I betrayed him too?

He was spoiled rotten for choice.

It was like a tableau.

We were all frozen in position.

I was still crouched by the chair Sandy had been occupying.

Keenan had half-risen at the same time as Rainer.

Orbach sat unmoved and unmoving, exactly as he had throughout.

I grabbed for my gun.

A familiar voice screamed:

'Armed police ...'

Everything was happening at once.

I never heard so much noise.

Suddenly, it was like someone switched the television off.

My last thought before I lost consciousness was: damn; now I'll have to wait 'till next week to see what happens.

It was only until the next day.

I woke in hospital.

I was in a private room.

I couldn't feel my right arm.

I wasn't too sure how much of the rest of me was still there either.

After a couple of minutes, I started to hurt.

I figured out what had happened.

I'd got shot.

I was relieved at least my keen intellect was still alive.

The door opened.

Sandy came in, carrying flowers.

'Shit ... I must be dying ...'

She laughed:

'I thought it'd be nice to have something pretty to look at while I waited ...'

'Other than me, huh?'

She put the flowers down, sat on the side of the bed and, cautiously, kissed me gently on the lips:

'I'm sorry,' she said.

She was sorry?

'It was my fault, really,' came a voice from the door:

'My persuasive skills, you know ...'

'How you doing, Tim?'

'Fine ... You?'

'I don't know. You tell me.'

'Nothing serious. Grazed a bone. Maybe took a bit out of it. You won't notice.'

'Great ... Make sure they keep it ... I'll send it to Mrs Nicholas.'

'I spoke to her,' Sandy said:

'She was very upset. I got the impression she sort of liked you ...'

'Yeah. Some people do. I'm an acquired taste.'

After a bit, I asked:

'Someone going to tell me what happened?'

Sandy explained:

'He came to see me. He said you were in a lot of trouble. He told me you'd gone and got a gun. I was frightened, Dave. When you rang me, at the office, asking to get Alex there, I called him ...'

'Not bad for a roster organizer?' I addressed the graduate officer.

'Well, maybe I wasn't exactly completely confined to that job ...'

'I knew you were lying when Lewis said how much you'd been hanging around. Why?'

'Give the Kraut a chance to get next to you ...'

'And all that guff about Gimbo?'

'No, that was true. He's pissing himself …'

'And?'

'I was in Sandy's garden … Came through a house in the street behind … With, er, well, a couple of colleagues … We had more in the streets around … As soon as Sandy opened the door, we moved … They were coming in the front at the same time …'

'You still haven't told me yet …'

Who got who.

Dowell breathed on his knuckles and rubbed his lapels, although without a lot of enthusiasm. He'd got Rainer. It was just the way Tim hadn't wanted it to end.

'Poor bastard … Still, I suppose it was what he wanted … The others?'

'Nope. You were the only other one got hurt …'

They would have to live with it. It would get out. One way or another. These things always did.

'He made a terrible mess of the house,' Sandy commented:

'Before they got him …'

'I thought … I shot …'

'Yeah. We pulled your bullet out of the ceiling plaster …'

Oh. Uh. Not exactly marksman-like.

Sandy asked:

'I was right, Dave, wasn't I? You couldn't've handled it …'

I looked at her, my mouth agape:

'Me? Not handle it? Huh! No sweat. If you'd left well alone, I wouldn't be in this mess now …'

'You'd be in a fucking coffin,' Dowell said.

'Exactly. What's this room cost? Who's going to pay for it?'

'I'll advance it, out of your salary,' Sandy smiled:

'How about it, Dave? You're no detective.'

I scowled:

'The hell I'm not ... Where's my next case?'

Dowell laughed:

'I'd wait a bit, if I were you. Think about it. I mean. Just for the first time. Ever. Think about it before you do it.'

He got up and, glancing covertly at the door, slipped something out from beneath his jacket:

'I don't know what this'll do to you ...'

He'd brought in a half of the only true comfort I ever knew.

'But since you didn't get killed in her house, I thought you'd like another chance here ...'

Sandy snatched it from him.

I held out my only working hand, pleading.

'Uhuh,' she shook her head:

'Me first. I'm finally going to find out what this stuff tastes like ...'

CONTROLLING INTEREST

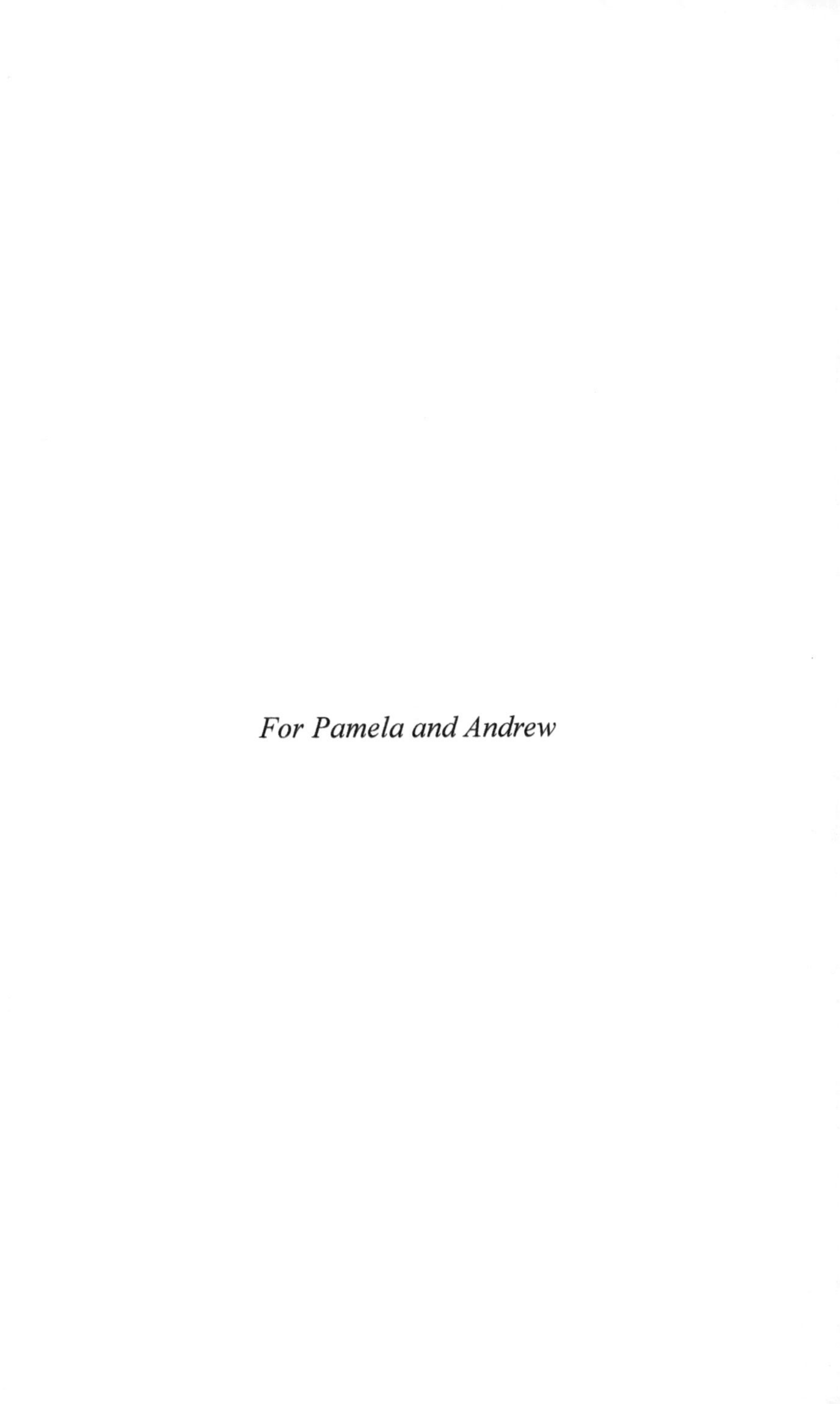

For Pamela and Andrew

I went back down the stairs to Kat's office with Tim. It was sealed, but he broke it off and ushered me in. It still had the faint, acrid, chemical smell that follows forensics. In the pub, he'd shown me the photos, so I knew exactly how she'd been found. Sitting at her desk, slumped over it, most of her head missing. The window-frame was still stained, but someone had cleaned the glass. The top of the desk was ingrained with copper-coloured blood. I ran my finger over it, morbidly: 'I liked her, Tim. I liked her a lot.'

CHAPTER ONE

'Jabulon,' he said.

'Jabu-who?' I asked.

'Jabulon,' Russel Orbach repeated like he was telling me the time of day.

'And who, when he's at home, is Jabulon?'

'You asked me — or would have done so if you knew anything about grammar: of whom is Andrew Mather more frightened than his father, and I am telling you - Jabulon.'

We were at Frederick's Restaurant on Camden Passage in Islington, in the downstairs, glassed-in garden room, and I was paying.

Two questions spring immediately to mind. The first is why we were in Frederick's, rather than my usual eatery in North London, M'sieur Frog's. The food at Fred's is twice as expensive, and because the cuisine is nouvelle you only get half as much. The answer is that I was foolish enough to invite Orbach to name the place for our meet and he had the sense to make it cost.

Which leads to the second question. Why was I dining with my arch-bogeyman — if not enemy — Russel Orbach? The answer is somewhat more complicated than to the first question. I have to go a little way back in time to explain. At least as far back as the morning I attended on Ian Mather — Iron Ian as he is known throughout the legal profession in which his stature is about as near to the top as mine is to the bottom — at his office off High Holborn.

I could see why they called him Iron Ian. His manner was as flexible as a rigid steel girder. He sat across a desk bigger than the bed platform in my Earl's Court basement apartment, where between jobs I spend the greater part of my life. It took me several minutes to cross the office after I was ushered in by his secretary's legs. But apart from the leather desk set, the desk was entirely empty of files or documents; only that morning's *Times* lay on it, at an angle so true it must have been set in place with a T-square.

'Did you know?' He asked by way of opening greeting, turning *The Times* around so that I didn't need to read it upside down, and pointing to a two inch column towards the bottom of the front page.

'I heard,' I said.

I'd heard the night before, when Sandy rang to tell me. Once upon a time, Sandy Nicholl and I were partners in a law firm in north London. Nicholl & Co, not Nicholl & Woolf. Once upon another time, she kicked my butt out of the office so hard it took me several years to pick myself up out of the gutter I landed in. I bore no grudges. She was right. I was doing myself more harm than the firm. My specialism was defending drug dealers; I liked to get paid in kind.

In the middle of the Disraeli Chambers' case, we'd re-encountered, not entirely coincidentally, and she'd jolted me with an altogether different kind of shock: we became lovers and so had remained, on and off, since. At the time of her call, we were off, and its subject-matter had quite a lot to do with why.

The article began:

'The body of a woman solicitor was discovered by staff arriving yesterday morning at the Holborn offices of the prestigious London solicitors, Mather's. Katrina Pankhurst, 32, had been shot. Police are investigating.' The article was accompanied by a photograph, ten years old, probably the formal picture taken at the admission ceremony. I'd read another paper already that morning, *The Times'* sister-paper, *The Sun*. They had somehow obtained a more recent, holiday snapshot, and published a picture of Katrina Pankhurst in a bikini.

Katrina. Kat, I used to call her, sometimes to her annoyance. Hanky Pankhurst on other, less public occasions, when she wasn't in a position to deny it. For a few months, now about seven or eight years ago, Katrina had been employed by Nicholl & Co as a locum for an assistant solicitor on maternity leave. She had done her training at Mather's; in short order married, quit work and separated; after she left us she went back to Mather's. During her stay with us we had, in a desultory fashion, been lovers. Our affair ended the day she returned to Mather's.

I waited for Mather to continue. I had been summonsed the previous afternoon, with a letter hand delivered by a uniformed flunky carrying a bright red leather bag. He stood at my basement door, hesitating at the vision of me unshaven, bleary-eyed, hangover and still not dressed:

'Mr Woolf?' he asked doubtfully.

I mumbled ambiguously. He might have been a debt collector, though most of those from whom I borrow money don't employ uniforms to get it back. More like animals.

'Mr David Woolf?' he repeated.

I shrugged:

'I guess. Whaddayawant?'

'I have a letter for you, sir, from Mr Mather, from Mr Ian Mather.'

I got the point. God wanted my attention. I held out a hand and, reluctantly, he passed it over. I started to shut the door in his face, but he shook his head:

'I'm to take an answer back, sir.'

I felt like telling him to bottle my bad breath and take that back to his lord and master. But most of the reason my breath was bad was booze, and most of the reason I was drinking was because I didn't have money to eat. I ripped open the envelope to see what Mather wanted. I read that he required to see me, on a professional matter, the following morning at nine o'clock. I was invited to confirm to the bearer that this would be convenient.

Convenient it wasn't. At nine in the morning, I am largely incapable of coherence. Like Tallulah Bankhead, I hardly knew there were two nine o'clocks in the day. The most I can normally manage is to roll off my bed, hang onto the railing to stop myself falling off the balcony, slide down the ship's-pitch steps and try to stay upright until I reach the lavatory. I re-read the letter. I hadn't imagined it. There was definitely a reference to a professional matter. As reluctantly as the messenger had handed me the letter, I conceded that I could keep the appointment.

I promptly went back to bed. It wasn't that I needed more sleep, even in anticipation of an early start the next day. More that I had nothing else to do. My last case had ended abruptly when I'd informed my client that the man his wife was sleeping with was a considerable improvement. I hate sex-snooping almost as much as I hate serving summonses. With divorce available from mail-order catalogues, you'd think no one would care anymore: but they still want to know who. That was a month before, and I hadn't worked since.

I lay in bed with my arms folded behind my head on the pillow. What could Ian Mather want with me? A firm like Mather's has a couple of the larger investigative outfits on retainer, and its pick of all the rest. Its clients were rich enough to afford the biggest and best. Mather himself was believed to be so powerful he could use the police as an alternative, even if no crime was involved. He was a sometime freemason, a member of the governing board of the United Grand Lodge of England and Wales, the central body of freemasonry throughout the English-speaking world.

If that wasn't enough, the firm's principal client was Sterling Latimer: Latimer International, Latimer Communications, Latimer Chemicals and Pharmaceuticals, Latimer Computers, Latimer this, that and anything that people can be seduced to spend money on. Most Latimer subsidiaries were so powerful that they constituted a significant economic influence in their individual areas of operation. When Latimer called, so they said, the marshals of democracy, the captains of industry and the colonels of military juntae alike came running. Though an American, Latimer had made his first millions in this country, before returning in triumph to buy up most of his native land. What could Ian Mather want with me?

While I waited for him to explain, I withdrew a pack of Camels from the pocket of my cracked leather jacket. Even I knew a leather jacket wasn't conventional wear for a visit to a man like Mather, but it was the only one I had apart from my suit, and that was still waiting to be cleaned after I fell into a puddle outside Lewis' night club on the Old Brompton Road after an otherwise spectacularly uneventful evening a couple of weeks before.

I'm not sure if I really enjoy Camels, but did you ever hear of a private eye smoking Silk Cut or Number Six?

'I'd rather you didn't smoke,' Mather said flatly, expecting to be obeyed.

I shrugged:

'That's OK. It's been nice meeting you. We could do this more often, whaddayathink?' I got up and started the long, slow trek back out of his office, picking my feet one at a time out of the deep pile carpet. Between the cows that produced the leather furniture, and the sheep that grew the wool, Mather was keeping the animal kingdom pretty well occupied, if shorn.

I'd almost reached the door, believing my bluff had been called and silently cursing my stupid pride, when he snapped:

'Wait.'

I didn't turn around. There was a word missing: please.

Instead, he used his intercom to tell his secretary to bring in an ashtray. I didn't tell him I didn't mind using the floor but waited for her to come in, so I could follow her across the room again, watching the way she moved and wondering if it was still possible to get it up at Ian's age. Though he didn't look it, I knew he was in his early seventies. Money's a great way to keep your health: I'd like to look that good at his age. As a matter of fact, I'd like to look that good now.

I sat down again. He was a clever man. He'd let me win the first round so that I wouldn't be so willing to gamble on the second. He brought his hands together in a spire and asked:

'What is it with your sort, Woolf?'

'What sort's that, Mather?'

'What is it you want, Mr Woolf?'

'You asked me to come to see you. I want you should tell me why. I want you should stop talking to me like I was a junior articled clerk. And I want you should tell me how much you're going to pay me.'

'I take it that last is the most important?'

Now I knew what sort I was. Whenever I meet anyone new, I have an irrational impulse to tell them I'm a Jew. An old Jew I once talked with about it explained that it wasn't pride, but self-defence. If you don't tell them straight out, they're bound to come out with something racist, and that's embarrassing because either you have to put up with it, which makes you feel like a coward, or provoke a hostile scene, which reinforces the image as excitable and aggressive. I should have listened to him and told Mather before we'd even begun.

We glowered at one another for a full minute. I hoped he had someone to charge for it because I was certainly going to make him pay me.

'I know about you, Mr Woolf. When this happened, yesterday, I called for Miss Pankhurst's personal file, and saw your name. She worked for you for a brief period. Your name was familiar, and I remembered it from the Disraeli Chambers' business.'

I remembered it from then too. I'd like to describe it as my biggest case, but the truth is it's the only big one I ever handled. A bunch of left-wing barristers were being offed, one by one and it took me from number three to number five to make the connections needed to bring it to an end. In my moments of fantasy — which means whenever I'm not asleep — I like to think of myself as the lawyers' investigator, the way some surgeons can be described as who doctors would choose to be operated on by.

'What happened?' he asked, apparently idly. Most of the true story never came out. Too many people would have been embarrassed: Russel Orbach, for example.

'What happened is what you read. The rest is privileged.'

He didn't argue. By accident, I'd given the answer that allowed him to open up:

'It's about Miss Pankhurst ...'

That much I'd worked out for myself. But all I said was:

'It was Mrs, actually. Pankhurst was the name of her first husband, while she was at university.' For that reason, she used to say, it didn't count. 'She got a great deal of mileage out of the name, but the big secret was, it wasn't her own to start with.'

He looked at me blankly. I don't think he got the point. I'm not even sure the name Pankhurst meant anything special to him at all. Women's suffrage was still a bit progressive for his taste. Apart from his own daughter — one of his four children in the firm — there were no women partners, nor of course Jews or blacks.

He cleared his throat:

'I want you, uh, to investigate, Mr Woolf. I want you to investigate her death.'

I paused to take it in. He was a pillar of the establishment, a believer through and through in all things English and Tory-blue. Granted, a member of his staff had died, and not of the heart-failure which comes with the pay-packet in a place as pressurized as Mather's. All the same, his only instinct ought to have been to leave the matter in the hands of the police.

'Why?'

'Why what, Mr Woolf? That is what you do, isn't it? Investigate?'

'Yeah, I guess. Sometimes. But why do you want me to investigate her death? That's what I'm asking.'

He swivelled around in his chair, so that his back was to me, and I heard him sighing as he stared out the bay window. When he turned round again, he looked like he'd aged a decade. The silver hair, each one laid in place by Prince Philip's barber, was now white, and maybe there weren't that many of them after all. He was slumped back in his chair. You could no longer line up the Coldstream Guards by the cut of his suit.

He coughed to clear his throat again:

'My sons, Mr Woolf. My sons are partners in this firm.'

'I know.' All the same, the name of the firm had remained Mather's, the apostrophe before the 's', not after it. It had never been Mather & Co, nor certainly Mather & anyone else. To write it as Mathers was near heresy.

He was having a hard time telling me. I decided to help him out:

'Your sons are partners in this firm, and two of them had affairs with Katrina Pankhurst, right. You're worried how an investigation will impact on them. You're worried what comes out. You don't want me to investigate; you want me to shadow the police investigation, and protect your image.'

The blood had drained from his face when I told him I knew his sons had both, at different times I hasten to add, had affairs with Kat, and I don't think he heard the rest of what I said because all he asked was:

'How did you know?'

I shrugged:

'It's my job, knowing things. That's why I don't think you really want to hire me, Mr Mather. Because I'm not into saving faces; I want to know who killed Kat, far worse than you do; I'd like to see them swing for it, but since we don't have the death penalty anymore, I'll settle for a minimum stretch of a quarter ton. If I start working for you, that's what I'm going to be trying to do, and if one of your sons is involved, that's what's going to happen to them.'

My speech contained a lot of bravado. But I meant some of it. At least the bit about wanting to see whoever killed Kat swing for it. I don't generally believe in the death penalty; people are pretty shitty anyhow, and most of us don't hang for it. But there's a small number of offences in which I have no doubt it's still essential: stealing from me, getting in my way and hurting my friends. I don't have much to steal, I don't go nowhere much, and I don't have so many friends I can afford to lose.

He began to catch up with me:

'I said I knew about you, Mr Woolf, and I do.' He opened a drawer in the desk and withdrew a folder: 'This is your file,' he extracted a computer print-sheet.

'My file? I got a file at Mather's?' I was genuinely astonished.

'We keep files on everyone we can, Mr Woolf,' his lips twitched in what I'm fairly sure was an attempt to smile.

I'd never really understood before what they mean by advanced information technology. I thought maybe it just meant you got information at the touch of a button rather than a touch of a secretary; I'd rather remain old-fashioned, especially when they look like Ian Mather's.

Solicitors keep files, of course; case-files. The only reason a firm would retain a file on another solicitor would be if the solicitor in question was one of the parties to an action, not merely the opponent's representative. But I could see the value of storing information about how lawyers conducted themselves, their procedural weak points, their sharp tactics, their resources and contacts, their strengths and their Achilles' heels.

'What does it tell you, Mr Mather?'

He closed the file before he answered, to emphasize that he'd pre-read and absorbed it.

'It tells me you're a fighter. It tells me you never let go. It tells me you don't settle unless you never even had a case to begin with.' That was the good news. 'It tells me you did better by your clients than you did by yourself. It tells me your respect for the law was hardly greater than theirs. It tells me that if you hadn't left practice, you probably would have been thrown out of the profession.'

'I was,' I said: 'I didn't leave my practice, I was thrown out of it by my partner.'

'Sandra Nicholl.'

'Yup. Sandy. We're good friends now, though. And Kat was a good friend. I saw her about a month ago.'

He nodded, understanding I had now told him how I knew about her and his sons.

'And what else did she tell you, Mr Woolf?'

'Most of what else is worrying you. In particular, she told me about the leaks.'

'Ah,' he expelled air. The worst was over. The thing he found most difficult of all to tell me was something I already knew.

A murder on the premises is bad news for a law-firm. It discourages clients. It's natural. After all, as the barristers at Disraeli Chambers had discovered, clients aren't keen to start off a case with a lawyer who is not expected to live to see it through. It also discourages recruits, which is damaging to a firm like Mather's with a large reputation, a lot of clients, but very few partners. They need new, young, salaried blood to put in the hours, charging for which keeps the profit-sharing partners in new carpets, cars and caviar.

But a thorough professional would prefer a murder to a leak any day of the week Even a client on legal aid — than whom there is no lower — doesn't want a solicitor who can't keep a secret. And Mather's clients' secrets are worth a lot more than those of a tenant confronting eviction or even a drug dealer confronting cold turkey and turnkey. Aside from Latimer — and that's a fairly hefty aside; Kat reckoned more than a million chargeable pounds a year — their clients included major banks, share-issuing public corporations, patent-owning engineering companies, every branch of the media, and on occasion the government itself.

The idea of Mather's as untrustworthy was about as absurd as suggesting that Prince Charles is a KGB agent. (I think I'm not allowed to say the Queen, even in jest. Mind you, if most of MIs 5 and 6 and the Queen's art adviser have at one time or another been in the pay of the alleged enemy, maybe the idea isn't that absurd after all).

But that was precisely what Katrina was suggesting when we met. It isn't what I'd been expecting to hear when she rang. Then, I thought maybe after all these years she'd finally realized what she'd been passing up, though that isn't what I said when I returned her call.

'Looking for work, huh?'

'Yes, sure,' she laughed: 'I'm really likely to give up a job at Mather's to come scavenge in the gutter with you.'

'What, then?' I waited optimistically, and wasn't too disappointed in her reply.

'Are you free to meet sometime soon?'

'I could make time. Any day between now and next year any good to you?'

'Gee, I don't know, Dave. What about the year after? Next week? Monday evening?'

'Not re-married, I gather.' Only the unpartnered, and the very long married, volunteer an evening, and I've already explained that I knew she couldn't be the latter.

'Right. Nor looking to,' she put a damper on my hopes.

She wasn't a great looking woman. A bit overweight. Her hair was a mess and her dress sense was markedly inferior to her ability at law. But she was warm, and good company. We used to get stoned, go out to the late night supermarkets, stock up on sweet goodies to feed the munchies, and come back, usually to her place rather than mine, to settle in front of the fire and gradually undress the night away. I'd always thought, she knew what she. liked and she knew how to get it.

We met in the Freemason's Arms on Longacre. Despite the name, they let women in. She was late and I was already a large Southern Comfort -no ice, no soda -ahead. She dumped her bag beside me and apologized:

'Sorry. Conference with counsel.'

A lot of people don't understand the English legal profession, and that includes a lot of lawyers. The profession is split into two. There are solicitors, who the client has to see first; but if a matter involves some extremely difficult legal task like looking up a bit of law, or has to go to court, the solicitor instructs a barrister to advise or represent. They're the ones with the fancy wigs and funny collars. It's a very cosy relationship, which means the punter has to pay for two lawyers when he probably doesn't even need one: the solicitor who rips him off in the office, and the barrister who sells him out in court.

Conferences with counsel happen at the end of the day. The client and the solicitor trek down to the Temple, where most of the barristers in London work; so that the barrister can find out what a case is about before he actually stands up to present or defend it in court, usually the next morning. With two lawyers in attendance, both paid by the hour, conferences invariably take twice as long as they ought.

Kat gestured at my drink:

'Another?'

'When did I ever say no? Besides, you've already told me there's no point staying sober.'

She pulled a face:

'Still as obvious as ever, Woolf.'

'I wouldn't like to disappoint.' I swallowed the last of my drink and handed her the glass, watching her disappear into the after-work throng and re-emerge efficiently, with a refill for me and a gin and tonic for herself.

She had changed. She looked good. She'd lost weight, her hair was expensively coiffed, and I guess she spent more of that Mather money on clothes than she used to spend of Sandy's and mine. But, then, there was much more of it to spend. Mather's — for all the Scots influence in the firm — paid well: that's how they managed to keep their salaried solicitors without offering too many of them partnerships.

We bantered good-naturedly while she unwound, swapping names and gossip. She asked about Disraeli Chambers and I told her a whole lot more than later I was to tell her boss. I asked if she ever briefed them:

'No way. They're far too left-wing for Mather's.'

'What about. Orbach?' He was already an ex-member when I was involved. Indeed, his efforts had been directed towards making many more of them ex-: ex-members and ex-humans. Orbach was a Queen's Counsel, which is a senior barrister and a mark of considerable success, professional and financial. She shook her head:

'You have to be a card-carrying Tory or a freemason — preferably both — to screw a brief out of Mather's.'

'But not to be employed there?' I doubted she would have joined the Tory party: it already had one female star and she didn't like competition. And the freemasons don't have women members.

She shrugged:

'To get to be partner. Anyway, I'm friendly with most of the children so I guess I'm protected.'

'How many are there?' At that time, I knew only that Mather's was, above all else, a family fiefdom, but I didn't know any of the details.

'Four,' she told me, listing them briefly. The oldest was Randolph, then came Martin, then — in age but, on account of her sex, not next in the pecking order of the firm's hierarchy — Allison Mather Hoyt, and finally the spoiled brat of the family, Andrew.

'Are they all in London?' Mather's had three provincial offices: Manchester, Birmingham and Bristol, serving the north, the midlands and the west of England. I'd read an article about the way they had linked the offices up to share resources, using computers and other technological innovations I didn't begin to understand.

The article was in the *Law Society's Gazette,* the journal of the profession's governing organization, on the principal committee of which Ian Mather had also served, and on sub-committees of which some of his children still sat. I read it not because I was interested in technology, but because — like everyone else — I'm fascinated by power and by how the rich spend their money.

She confirmed that all the children were in London:

'So's John Gauldie. He's the second partner. He and Ian have been together for ever.' The firm had been founded by Mather shortly after the Second World War. He had had, as they used to say, a good war; he had served his country proud, and his country was going to serve him proudly back. His father was a Scots industrialist and that for which Mather's was earliest known was the way Ian had put his father's money into resources and facilities long before the rest of the profession reluctantly shrugged off the habits of the last century and caught up with this. In this respect, Mather had learned from the Americans.

Kat had booked a table at the Cafe Pelican on St Martin's Lane. It's a French theme cafe. The waiters wear long-tailed tuxedoes, carry trays of pungent French pastries high above their shoulders, call out to one another with heavy, guttural accents, sport six o'clock shadows and reek of Gauloise. At least one of them had probably once taken a day-trip to Calais.

I wasn't complaining. Kat was paying.

'I figure I can afford it better than you.'

'I ain't arguing, Kat.'

'Don't call me that,' she hissed: 'I've told you before.'

She wasn't the only one who thought it sexist to call women by a diminutive. Sandy used to get angry with me about some of my pet abbreviations. Once, for a whole week, I insisted on calling her Sandra Jane, which is her full name. We reached a sort of truce when she sent a postcard to my home listing all my male friends I call by an abbreviation. The list didn't cover the card, but that's only because I don't have many friends.

'What do you want me to call you? Ms Pankhurst?' Am I the only one who finds Ms completely unpronounceable?

'Try calling me by my name,' she snapped.

'You're beginning to sound like a wife,' I protested mildly: 'I thought you said ...' I let the sentence drift back into the nowhere it had begun. She caught my meaning:

'I know about you and Sandy,' she said.

It wasn't exactly a state secret, but we'd been out of touch for a long time and, so far as I knew, she and Sandy had never been close. I wasn't pleased she knew; I've never been able to think of an answer to female solidarity as an excuse not to hop into my bed. Since the revised Katrina had arrived in the pub, I was less willing to accept the limits she had set for the evening than I had been on the 'phone.

'How?'

'I heard. I can't remember who from. It doesn't matter. It didn't surprise me. I always expected it.'

'You did?' I was truly shocked. It had been the last thing I expected when Sandy and I had reencountered, and we'd never got it on when we'd been in partnership.

'Sure. Anyone could've guessed you'd end up together. You were made for each other, like a couple of old trees planted next to one another in a clearing in the forest.'

Kat had a feel for metaphors. I'd forgotten that too, as well as not to call her Kat.

We were into the second bottle, and main course (steak: if I'm not working, I grab it when I can; it might be my last meal for a week) before she began to talk about what was worrying her. It took me more probing than I get from the dentist on my once every five years visit, and that's saying something.

'You gonna tell me why you called, or do I got to drag it out of you like pine needles from a carpet after Christmas.'

'Hey, that's not bad. Can I have it?'

'Be my guest. I'm yours. So? Tell. If it's not my body you're after, what's on your mind?'

'Couldn't it be I just wanted to see an old friend?'

'After these years, you suddenly can't wait to see me? Really.'

But she wasn't listening to my answer. People often do that, like they aren't expecting me to say anything worthwhile.

'You are a friend, aren't you, Dave? I mean, I know it was never that big a deal between us, and I know we haven't been in touch forever, but whenever I think about you, you know, I always think of you like a friend, I'm very fond of you.'

Her eyes were watery. I took her hand:

'I'm your friend, Kat. I'm not saying I wouldn't mind being more, but I'm at least your friend. O.K.?'

She laughed:

'You never give up, do you?'

'What's the line that reminds me of?' I asked.

She knew exactly what I must be thinking of. The reason she and I could communicate so easily, even after such a long break, is because we both believed that few of life's truths couldn't be found somewhere in Hill Street Blues. The show had finished in the States by this time. They kill everything good in America: the Kennedys, Martin Luther King, John Lennon, the Cavett interviews and now Hill Street.

But England was — as England is — years behind, and we were still only half-way through the penultimate series. To help locate it, Robin was at this time still pregnant with Mick's Kid.

'It's in the pilot. La Rue's chatting up Joyce Davenport who he doesn't know is having an affair with Furillo. She says: "Have you quite finished, detective?" And he says, meaningfully: "No, ma'am, I don't finish for a very long time. I just go on and on."'

She was right. It was the line I'd been reminded of:

'And she pours a cup of coffee on his crotch, right?'

Thus did we fully re-establish communication between us.

The story came, when it came, in bits and bobs, like she had upended a jigsaw box and a few pieces were already stuck together to make tiny, but identifiable, parts of the whole. She didn't present it like the skilled lawyer she certainly was. But, then, she wasn't consulting me as a lawyer, only as a friend.

'Did you read, a while ago, oh, maybe a month ago, about the L.C.P. business?'

I shook my head. Unless someone's paying me to do so, I don't read much. Not even the papers. Anyhow, not the ones with a lot of words in. That's why later I didn't turn to *The Times* for an account of her death, but to *The Sun.*

'You must've,' she insisted: 'It was the largest single personal injuries settlement ever in English legal history.'

It struck a faint chord in the back of my befuddled mind. I'd probably heard it on the TV. news.

'Babies with bits missing?'

'Yuk, but yes.'

I also managed to remember, or work out, that LCP meant Latimer Chemicals and Pharmaceuticals.

'Your case?'

'Not mine personally, but the firm's of course.' Of course. It was hardly likely to be Nicholl & Co. On either side. Way out of our league.

'What about it?'

She hesitated one last time, but since she'd booked the evening to tell me, and had to pay for the meal anyway, she went ahead:

'We should have been able to fight it and win. All the evidence was on our side. God knows it ought to have been:

most of the expert witnesses worked at some time or another in an institution funded by Latimer, and even if they didn't would want to tap him for research money eventually.'

'I love scientists. They've got the same sort of integrity we lawyers have.'

'I thought you called yourself a private eye these days?'

'Mostly I don't call myself anything. Go on,' I wasn't going to let her back off now. It wasn't that I gave a damn about the subject — personally, I think babies are a pretty bad idea anyhow: they shit and piss and vomit all over the place, and they can't make decent conversation. But I like to know things that others don't, just for its own sake.

'There was just one report which was damning. It was very damning, too. We had it, of course, but the other side got their hands on it and that was it. We had to settle.' I swallowed the impulse to point out that hands was what the other side were missing.

'Wouldn't it have to have been discovered anyway?'

Her eyes shone: this was the bit of the job she loved best. Out-manoeuvring the opposition:

'Hell, no. Discovery's for the birds.'

Discovery is the process by which one party to civil litigation has to disclose to the other the documents pertaining to the case which are in his possession. He also has to list those which have been in his possession, even if they no longer are. The only things not discoverable are documents which were prepared with the litigation in mind, such as witness statements, instructions to counsel and correspondence with the client.

In England, discovery is done by lists prepared by lawyers. That way, so the theory goes, the other side can rely on its integrity. The implication of what Kat was saying was that their disclosure in the case would have been less than complete.

She explained how it worked. You only have to discover what is or has been in the possession of a party to the action. In English law, every company is a separate legal person. Latimer had so many subsidiaries, affiliates, even spare companies kept for just such an eventuality as this, that he could show his lawyers a document — for them to evaluate and advise on — in the name of one company, even though what it affected was the affairs of another.

I sniffed:

'It's about as sharp a practice as any of mine.' I didn't like it, either. It was a practice only available to the wealthy. It is procedures like discovery which are intended to place everyone on an equal footing before the law. I didn't need telling the law wasn't equal, but I didn't enjoy being reminded.

'Why're you so surprised, Dave? Didn't you teach me that lawyers are about beating law not upholding it? Mather's aren't different; just better at it. Anyway,' she continued: 'The scientist who did this particular piece of research was no schmuk. He took it to Latimer in the States. I don't know who. One of the Latimer's companies. Coincidentally — I'm sure you're going to find this difficult to believe — he came to the conclusion that his research method may have been unsound just about the same time he was offered some very heavy funding, by Latimer of course.'

'So recanting in open court wouldn't be particularly convincing, right?'

'Right. Meanwhile, and just in case the other side did get hold of it, a copy was sent over here. And that's where the leak came from.'

'Ah, come on, Kat ... uh ... rina. How'd'you know it came from Mather's? It could've come from anywhere. It's a classic case for a bleeding heart leak.'

'I agree, which rules out Mather's. But Latimer — in another incarnation — has developed some heavily sophisticated copying equipment, which means you can trace exactly where a copy came from, even several copies down the line. Part of the settlement was, they got back the leaked copy. And Latimer says: it came from Mather's.'

I still wasn't impressed. One leak don't a flood make. Why had Katrina called me out of my cellar to tell me about it?

'Because it's not the first. It's not even the second. I don't know how many leaks there have been from Mather's, but I do know quite a few.'

She told me about them. The first had been a libel action, where the defendant newspaper's principal witness had some long-spent form under another name which nobody knew about — or was supposed not to. Next had been a society divorce, where the husband had a half-million pound estate in the Bahamas his wife hadn't been told about in an admittedly extremely brief marriage but which, again, she found out about just in time to cash it in. The client, and his wife, had both been friends of Randolph and Andrew: Martin and an assistant had to handle the case; the other brothers were too close.

Last of the ones she told me about was a commercial landlord-tenant dispute, which hinged on for how long the landlords could be proved to have known about a construction defect. At the last moment, a discreet connection was made which fixed them with liability dating back several more years than admitted and qualified the damages for inclusion in the telephone directory. In other cases, there were files not in the right place at the right time, and that reappeared shortly before the position of a Mather's client took a sharp downward plunge. And, she assured me, I didn't want to. know about stocks and shares: insider dealing.

I heard her out, but something was missing. She wasn't implicated in any of the incidents. She wasn't a partner. She didn't stand to lose financially, nor even if the unthinkable occurred and the matter became public knowledge, would it be her reputation that suffered. I reminded her of an elementary proposition:

'Lawyers are human. They all talk. Granted, they don't usually to the other side, but who knows who's connected to who. They have to talk, you know that. They have to show off to people just how important they are, how privy to privileged information, how trusted. And to do that, once in a while, they have to, well, spill the colour of their beans.'

She pulled a face:

'That's one of the worst mixed metaphors I've ever heard, Dave.' Then she paused for thought: 'Isn't it?'

'I don't know, Katrina. That isn't the point, anyway. The point is: it isn't really enough to be worth a first-class stamp on a letter home, let alone to spend an evening with me. Is it?' There had to be more.

CHAPTER TWO

Without answering, she got up and went to the lavatory. On her way back, she stopped to talk to our waiter and ask for her bill.

'I'd like to go home now. You can come with me if you want.'

I have had more romantic propositions. But beggars can't be choosers. Meekly, I rose and went for a piss while she settled up, just in case I'd misunderstood her offer to pay.

We took a cab back to her flat in Maida Vale. I hate taxis. Not only are they expensive, but the drivers are unbelievably boring. They insist on expressing opinions about everything, and their views are mostly somewhere to the right of Attila the Hun, sometimes even as far to the right as Margaret Thatcher or Ronald Reagan. They're so stupid, they believe they're worth listening to.

There is, however, one time when it is safe to grab a cab. That is late at night, when you're with a person of the opposite sex. Sub-moronic as the average cabbie undoubtedly is, he (and it always is he) can just about make the connection between being left to your own devices and the size of his tip. We sat in the back, a safe distance apart, in silence. I had been idly window-shopping for about ten minutes before I identified the snuffling sound beside me. Kat, gently and effortlessly, was crying.

'Hey, hey,' I slid along the seat and put my arms around her shoulders, drawing her head down onto my shoulder, stroking her hair: 'It's OK, Kat. Whatever it is, it'll be OK.'

She sniffed back her tears and pulled away:

'Careful. You wanna know what that hair cost?' She covered up with humour.

'Funny. They gave it away free the day I was born.'

'Looks like it,' she said. But she took my hand and held onto it so long I decided she might have begun to change her mind about the evening's end-game, though not firmly enough to make me give the driver a tip any larger than I thought I could manage without physical retaliation.

I remembered the very first time I had seen her apartment. She had been working for us for about four weeks, and we had been flirting — the way the single, at a loose end, do — for three weeks and seven days. Popping a head round the door at the end of the day, asking about 'a quick one' (drink). Those quick ones are the worst: they creep up on you unprepared, and the next thing you're too drunk to do anything with it. I think I'll use it as the title of my autobiography: 'Just A Quick One'.

That day, I had been appearing in West London Magistrate's Court, which was too near home for me to contemplate trekking all the way back to the office at the end of the day. But I needed a file for my next case. Kat's home in Maida Vale was about half-way to mine. She agreed to take the file with her, and I would call up for it later. After a couple of solitary joints,

I floated over around nine o'clock, and twelve hours later that was the time I left.

We almost always made it at her flat. It was the sole possession with which she had emerged from her second marriage. It was a millstone: it cost more to run than she could afford. Her husband was some kind of City whiz-kid. Ostensibly, his company was engaged in corporate publicity and promotion, like when someone's stock needed a boost before it made a takeover bid, or in order to avoid one. But their fees were often paid in kind, and Tony Galucci had a finger in so many pies I always wondered how he could tell what each one tasted like. (I wish I'd thought of that while she was alive: Kat would have liked the metaphor. It wasn't mixed. Was it?)

They weren't married long: less than a year. Which was — she told me — why she had no claim on him even for sufficient support with which to pay for the apartment. But it was a nice apartment, especially compared to my own. It had lights that came on and went off, a lavatory that flushed, hot water, a refrigerator with food in it, at least some of which wasn't mouldy, and I was fairly sure it had been dusted since she moved in.

Also, it had furniture. This, too, was an improvement on my place. In 1974, they changed the laws so that furnished tenants got the same sort of security as unfurnished tenants. My landlord took this defeat gracefully, and when I pointed out that I could feed myself for a month boiling the bugs in the furniture he provided to keep me out of legal protection, he allowed me to junk it, a mere twenty or thirty years after the end of its useful life. Unwilling to risk a change of what passed for his heart, I did so within days: years later, I was still trying to decide what to replace it with. It hasn't changed much since.

I was surprised now to see that she had let her apartment deteriorate, given how much care she had taken to prevent her own deterioration showing. The furniture was the same as when I had last seen it, and the years between had taken their toll. I wasn't convinced she'd dusted it since either. Some of the wallpaper was peeling and the light-bulb had gone in the lavatory, which was bad luck for her when she had a male visitor as drunk as by then was I. It was the apartment of someone who was living on the verge of leaving it.

I found her in the kitchen, sniffing a half-empty bottle of red wine. She passed it to me:

'What do you think?'

I waved it under my nose and hesitated:

'It depends.'

'On what?'

'On whether there's anything else.'

'Depends what you mean by anything.'

My puzzled frown told her I didn't understand. She said excitedly: 'We could do some dope or coke.'

I shook my head:

'I stay away these days, Katrina. It reminds me of too many bad times, and it's dangerous to shop for.'

She smiled a superior smile:

'Depends where you get it.'

I didn't ask her to elaborate. I had the impression that though she enjoyed boasting about access to privileged supplies, she wouldn't've told me anyway. I asked:

'Anything else to drink?'

She shook her head sadly. I shrugged — also sad — and took a couple of glasses off the shelf, leading the way into the living-room. I settled on the sofa; she secured herself in an armchair a couple of miles across the room and began talking almost at once.

'Why am I always someone's bit on the side, Dave? Why can't I find someone to stay with?'

'Hey, Kat.' She didn't tell me to lose the language, so I knew she was genuinely depressed, not just making what we sixties' people like to think of as casual, everyday conversation: 'It ain't that bad. You couldn't wait to pass up my offer to settle down with you for the night.'

She stuck her tongue out at me in a last attempt to keep the conversation at a level that didn't require a qualified psychotherapist in attendance.

'It's Martin,' she announced: 'It always has been.'

I worked out the code without difficulty. Martin Mather.

'Even while we were, you know ... ?' I asked curiously.

She nodded.

Why did I mind?

She said:

'And while I was married. Before, during, after. That's why I had to hold onto the flat. We were supposed to be a secret so he was never keen on my being at his house, but it's not far from here.' She laughed nervously: 'That's why I told Tony I wanted to live in this part of London.'

It takes style to persuade a husband to buy a home for the convenience of a lover.

'Is Martin married?'

She shook her head:

'He never has been; I doubt he ever will be.'

'I'm surprised then. I would have expected a Mather to enjoy something a little less ...' I was going to say tacky, but the word tact intervened: 'Well, a bit more classy.'

Now you know my idea of tact, you understand why I'm a private eye, not a diplomat.

'Oh,' she brushed aside the reference to the state of her apartment: 'It's been years now, it was in much better condition then — you remember. And Randolph doesn't care ... I think maybe he even likes it. He likes the idea he can move in every kind of circle.'

My comprehension took a nosedive. I asked for a translation into single-speak.

She explained. She'd been involved with Martin since she went to Mather's as an articled clerk, straight out of college. It had always been a clandestine relationship: upright Ian would not approve his boys having it off with the hired help. Martin had his own house, even then:

'Martin has his own money. Ian kept them on a tight purse until they became partners, and he made them wait to become partners until they turned thirty, one by one. But Martin had — has — an investment company on the side. Cross Course, it's called. It's not a big thing, but it turns over a lot of money, and he's made a bundle out of it, though he doesn't really do much anymore. Tony's involved in it, too: that's how I met him. They're partners. And ...' She changed her mind and didn't add whatever she had been about to say. I didn't push. At that point, no one was paying me to probe parts of her story she didn't want to disclose.

'You said "during",' I said cautiously.

She nodded. Martin, her lover, had introduced her to Tony, his partner, and even while she was married to him, she hadn't given Martin up. Like I said: style.

'He left you, didn't he? I always thought it was the other way round, that he was carrying on ...'

'I let you think that. He was very good about it, though. One day, he just came back and sat in here, drinking, for hours, without talking. Then he said: "It's not working, is it?" And I said: "No." Then he said: "You're seeing someone else, aren't you?" And I said: "Yes." And he went inside and packed a bag and came back in and said: "You can keep the apartment," and that was it. No hysterics. No Latin macho screaming and shouting. I don't know how it would have been if he knew it was Martin at the time ...'

'Does he know now?'

'Yes. We've stayed in touch, stayed friendly.' She stopped talking for a moment and I understood why. Her marriage hadn't meant much more than our affair. Nothing did. Her emotions were wrapped up in Martin and everything else was just a way of passing the time. 'One night, he told me he'd worked out it was Martin and I couldn't lie to him so I said it was.'

'What happened between him and Martin?'

She laughed uneasily, again like she was only telling half of it:

'Tony told me he could live with it. He said: "Martin's twice my size, twice as strong and I make twice as much money because of him." I don't know about the money, but otherwise he's right. Martin is very tough. He works out at Cannons three times a week. You don't want to get into a fight with him.'

Me, I don't want to get into a fight with anyone. After Disraeli Chambers — maybe when I was still in the hospital — Sandy said to me, during one of our incessant arguments about whether practising law or detection was worse for my health — that I was as about as violent as a teddy bear, and half as threatening. She wasn't far out. I may be the only private eye in recorded history who is positively a physical coward.

'Did you know he qualified the long way?' They'd changed the rules recently, to limit the profession to university graduates, presumably to justify the levels of its fees. But until then it used to be possible to qualify by means of five years' articles and day-release study. That was 'the long way'. 'He had to. He was thrown out of school when he was sixteen. He lost his temper and there was some kind of fight and someone else ended up in hospital. Ian Mather had to go and collect him and take him away immediately. He drove him straight down to the office, took him upstairs, and told him he could either knuckle down and qualify — the long way —or he could walk out of his life then and there.'

'And Martin qualified,' I prompted.

'Martin can do anything he sets his mind to.'

'So Tony let it go?'

'Yes.' Her eyes shone. I'd discovered something else that turned her on as much as sneaky legal manoeuvres: Martin getting away with it.

'How does Randolph get into this?'

I'd said the wrong thing. She shuddered. She wasn't ready to talk about Randolph yet. She tried to keep on talking about Martin for a while. She told me how they used to slip out of the office during an afternoon, or they'd wrangle an out-of-town conference. Then, when she got married, he'd come see her at the flat while Tony was at work:

'Once, he even made an appointment to meet Tony the other side of town and showed up here instead.' Again, her eyes glistened, and not with tears, though I suspected they weren't far behind. I thought: charming, charming company she kept; but despite myself, I envied the man's nerve.

After Tony left, it was easier: he could come around whenever he felt like it and, so long as she was working for Nicholl & Co (which meant, save the first month, as long as she was sleeping with me), he did so often, though they were still secret lovers and never went out in public together, which was why she still had time and room for yours truly.

'I'm sorry, I just realized how horrible this must all be for you to listen to.'

I shook my head. Initial reaction aside, I didn't mind:

'I learned a long time ago, no one's going to write a book about my sexual prowess.'

I've always believed there's no such thing as the great lover, in isolation. Not unless we're talking style of spilling seed into a tissue. There's two of you together, or nothing. I'm not saying this is right; it's just what I believe that makes me feel better than believing anything else. Now you also know why I'm not a philosopher any more than a diplomat.

'So what happened when you went back to Mather's?'

'Ah,' her eyes clouded over. This was the painful part. She resorted to the easiest, clearest way to tell me: 'I figured I'd got it all worked out. I knew Martin through and through, you know. I'd never have anything more than a little bit of him. I was like that scene where Robin and Mick have split up, and he's living in Howard Hunter's trailer. It's in the fourth series, I think. It's his birthday, and he's lonely, and he comes back and she's let herself in and is sitting in the dark, with a tiny birthday cake with a solitary candle on it. Mick says; "I haven't changed". Robin says: "I know I'll never have all of you, but I'd rather have a little bit than none at all".'

'And that's how it was with you and Martin?'

'No. That's how I thought it would be. But I forgot something about Martin: the way he always has to be in control, ahead of the game. For all his toughness, he's frightened to let go with other people, to be vulnerable to them. In my case, that meant he always had to want me less that I wanted him. Once I'd lowered my sights, he had to lower his too: from where they started out, that meant he didn't want me at all.'

I shook my head:

'Kat, Kat. You're a lovely lady. Why do you do this to yourself?'

Without realising it, I'd struck the chord marked Randolph. She burst into tears, this time not the quiet, flowing tears that I had heard in the taxicab, but great sobs that wracked her body as she covered her face, like she was clinging onto it to keep it one piece:

'He hurts me, Dave, he hurts me.' I got up from the sofa and went and knelt down in front of her, pushing her legs apart so as to be able to hug her tightest:

'It's OK, it's OK, Kat.' I'm not that original when it comes to reassurance. I've only got the one lie.

She hugged me back so hard I thought I'd break. I could feel her breasts against my face and the next thing I knew she had grabbed the back of my head and was kissing me hard on the lips, hard so it hurt. For a moment, I kissed her back, but if it was what turned her on, it was doing nothing for me and I pushed her away as gently as I could; withdrawing from between her legs and then settling down on one side of them, so I could keep one arm around her and not pull completely away.

She was still crying.

'You don't know, you don't know the things he does.'

She wanted to tell me, but it was the last thing I wanted to hear. I didn't mind knowing that she had been in love with an erstwhile lover, throughout our time together, or even that she had been sleeping with someone else; I did mind hearing that what turned her on was something so alien to my own idea of loving fun it seemed to mean she can't have been turned on with me at all.

'But why, Kat? Why go along with it?' It was the same question I'd asked before, but this time at least I knew what I was asking.

She had calmed down enough for me to return to the sofa, and what was left of the gut-rot wine. I finished it: I figured it was doing a kindness.

'I don't know,' she said dully: 'Maybe it's how I feel about myself.'

'How did it start?' 'It' could mean her and Randolph, or what Randolph did with her.

'I'm not sure. He's not a particularly handsome man. Quite cruel looking, really, which is appropriate. He's been married three times already. More than me even. We started between numbers two and three.' She caught the look of horror as it flickered across my face. 'Oh, yeah, sure, I'm that dumb. I let him go off and marry someone else and come back. Maybe I was punishing myself for Tony; letting him do the same thing to me I'd done. Once, I went down into the dead-file basement and read his divorce papers. It was easy, no one ever goes down there.'

'I thought lawyers always used another firm?'

'The Mathers didn't get rich giving their money to anyone else. Andrew acted for him: Martin wouldn't, and I suspect Randolph didn't dare ask Allison. She doesn't do divorce. She didn't enjoy her own, and she doesn't enjoy anyone else's. Except she did mine: as a friend. But there was nothing in it. Anyway, I was trying to tell you,' she scolded me for an interruption she had seized on with alacrity: 'I read the file. And his wife — this was his second wife — he married a Mary and two Megs: Meg One and Meg Two. The second one went off to live in Purley afterwards. I mean: Purley.'

I understood what she meant. I shuddered sympathetically. Purley was the last gas station before hell.

'She complained in the petition that he'd opened a bottle of champagne between her legs. And he'd scribbled on the photocopy, by way of reply, "but it was a good vintage." The awful thing is, at the time I laughed. Imagine how it must have hurt, but I laughed.'

She paused for breath. I stayed silent: I didn't want to be told off again.

'Sometimes I think Martin set it up. It was soon enough after I came back. Well, it was long enough after that I'd got the message that Martin wasn't going to play with me anymore. And Randolph just came into my room and said, taking for granted I'd agree, "drink after work?" So I did say yes. And you know what was the biggest turn on? He took me to his home. I thought: wow, here's a Mather who's not afraid to have me in his house. Did I tell you about Andrew?' She went on apparently disjunctively.

I shook my head, hoping I wasn't going to hear she had had a full house. I wasn't. She said:

'He's the youngest. He's the prettiest, too. A bit pudgy and pouting but gorgeous, like you just want to curl up to. I've forgotten his name — there's a council leader who was on the television the other night — he looks a lot like him. Not

Livingstone,' She hastened to add, lest I got the wrong idea, forgetting Livingstone was no longer the leader of the Greater London Council but a Member of Parliament instead. They'd abolished the GLC to get rid of him; maybe next they'd abolish Parliament. But though commonly called Cuddly Ken in the papers, he was about as pretty as a piranha on the prowl.

She said: 'Another of the left-wingers.' It didn't do anything for me: the idea of a fanciable politician is also alien. 'Everyone spoils him, even Ian. Mr Goody Two Shoes. Stayed at home through university and college of law until he got married. Beautiful wife, ex-model; two beautiful children. They're still married. They have a flat in town, and a house somewhere in South Oxfordshire where he plays the young country squire every weekend. House parties filled with the beautiful people.'

'D'you ever go?' She hesitated, then shook her head: 'Even though, you know, even though Martin and Randolph go there quite often, I'm not allowed.'

I understood what she meant. The outsider. The child who doesn't get asked to the party so often it becomes a yearning. Not a question of not being asked, but not being allowed. It was the story of my childhood, too.

'And the rest of it: how did that start?' She hadn't answered the second part of my question. 'One night, it was really just playing around at first. He was tickling me, only it was getting rough and I told him to stop and instead he turned me over and started to spank me, like it was a joke and then he'd pulled down my tights and it wasn't a joke and, you know, I could feel how turned on he was, more than he'd ever been before, and .. .' She blushed: 'I was too. That's not such a big thing, I suppose, you read about it. But it's different when it's you. And he put me on the floor ...'

She shuddered: 'Oh, Dave, he hurt me so much,' she didn't want to say the words, so she gestured to let me know what she meant: 'And none of it was a joke anymore or a turn-on,' and she couldn't finish her sentence for sobbing, so I got back up and knelt beside her again, stroking her expensive hair to say it's OK, I don't think any the worse of you for it, but I didn't say it out loud, because I wasn't sure if I meant it and maybe she would sense the uncertainty or insincerity.

She told me a bit more before I left. Other things he'd done with and to her. He, too, had not allowed marriage to interfere with his fun. She felt, she said, like a rubber ball bounced back and forth between the two brothers:

'Only, that was it,' she concluded bitterly: 'I never did get to bounce back, to Martin I mean. Maybe that was why I went along with it, because that was what I expected, but it never happened.'

And, unless it had happened in the last month of her life, it never would. I was suddenly tired. Selfishly, I told her so. I told her I didn't mind going, or staying, but I think she knew I didn't really want to stay. She shook her head:

'At the moment, you know, I want you to stay and keep me comfort, maybe play bodies together. But when I wake up, I'll be embarrassed and ashamed and I won't want you to be there. So just go, Dave. Please go.'

I got up and she got up too. At the door, she hugged me and whispered:

'I wish we'd meant more to each other, Dave.'

'We mean plenty,' I answered loyally: 'Speak to me.'

I felt her nod against my chest, and then she turned and went back into the living-room as I let myself out. That was it.

I left her alone for a few days, then rang her at work. They said she was tied up with clients and would ring me back, which she didn't. So I tried calling her at home, but I only ever got her machine. Finally, I wrote her a postcard — with a first class stamp on even — and she didn't answer that either. Now she's where they don't deliver mail so it's too late to write and tell her it didn't matter, after all, I didn't think any the worse of her.

Which is why I wanted to find her killer and see off the bastard who'd left me on the hook of my guilty conscience.

I said; 'Which is it you're really worried about getting into the papers, Mr Mather? The involvement of your sons, or the possibility of leaks?'

'Do you think there's a connection?' He asked hollowly.

I shrugged: 'I don't know what's connected. But things usually are.' Katrina had asked to see me, and what she'd told me was everything. So everything was where I had to begin: 'What do you think?'

He sighed to say he didn't know, more expressively than words would have done. I was enjoying — if that was the word — a rare view of Ian Mather. A tired old man, resorting to an unsuccessful, underworked, underpaid, unethical and possibly unhygienic unemployed solicitor to solve his problems for him. I asked:

'Why me? There's a hundred different people you could ask to handle your problems, Mr Mather. Why come to me?'

'Are there, Mr Woolf? Consider the type of investigator we use here. They work for other City firms. They are well connected. How long do you think it would remain a secret that I had commissioned an investigation into Mather's ... my own firm? That information alone would do untold damage.'

'The police?' I said half-heartedly.

He snorted contemptuously: the problems would be even worse.

'Put one of your own staff onto it, then. A partner?'

'And who should that be, Mr Woolf? To whom should I show greater trust than I am prepared to show to everyone else? There are only ten London partners, and four of them are my children.'

He didn't need to repeat: with two of whom the deceased had at some time or another been having an affair and who were, for that reason, excluded.

'With the exception of John Gauldie, who started this firm with me, all the partners have been with me since they qualified. I could not possibly show one of them so much greater confidence that the others would be bound to feel that I suspected them.' I had a feeling he was overstating the problem: solicitors aren't the sort of people who come quickly to the conclusion that they might be the subject of suspicion.

'Gauldie, then?'

He shook his head:

'Like me, he's no longer a young man, Mr Woolf. He is extremely busy. He supervises all the Latimer work and is in charge of all our litigation. You cannot imagine what that involves.'

I formed a perfect picture of one million beautiful, mint-fresh pound coins neatly stacked up in my Earl's Court basement. I could imagine it alright; easily.

'John ...' He hesitated in order to look for the right words: 'John gives a great deal to this firm. But he has other interests, and he also commits a great deal of his time to them. If I asked him to take this on, it would interfere with his other activities, and I couldn't do that.'

I read a lot into the 'I'. I remembered something else Katrina had mentioned. I, too, hesitated. Notwithstanding my earlier fit of calculated pique, I wanted to investigate her death. Regardless of remuneration — it would be a lot easier doing it for Ian Mather than for the only other available client: myself. I knew that what I was about to ask might also be my last question on the case. But there was no point starting it any way other than how I intended to continue:

'Those other interests of Mr Gauldie. Would that be freemasonry?'

He bristled visibly. Freemasons are a closed society. They used to be called a secret society, but recently, in a vain attempt to diminish popular suspicion, they started referring to themselves instead as a 'society with secrets'. For myself, I couldn't see the difference. Actually, there have only ever been two secrets associated with freemasonry: who is a freemason, and what it does. They even employ secret handshakes and other signs to identify each other.

'Mr Mather,' I said hastily, reassuringly, remembering the answer I had given about Disraeli Chambers that had pleased him: 'Nothing you or anyone else tells me goes any further than you as my client.' I was lying through my eye-teeth: it would go wherever helped me solve the case. I went on: 'I know you want to say that what I asked is none of my business, and perhaps you're right, but I can't do this job unless I'm allowed to decide what's relevant and what's not.'

For the second time since the interview had begun, he swivelled around in his chair so that I could not see him while he thought about it. Clearly, the question I had asked struck another chord that no one was supposed to be able to discern beneath the deafening drumbeat of death. (I'll go anywhere for an alliteration). When he turned round again, his face was ashen:

'You don't understand what it means to me to have to talk about these things to a ... stranger.'

I didn't say out loud what I could have reminded him: he'd invited me in. It wasn't necessary, because I also understood that he had made his decision.

'John Gauldie is a mason, yes. So am I. So are two of my sons. So are most of the partners. So are several of the assistants. That is in no wise suspicious. The craft, Mr Woolf, is designed to make better men of us; it is hardly surprising if we keep this firm in the hands of those we know and have such substantial reason to trust. I take it from your interest,' he added dryly, recovering a little of his composure: 'That you are, another of those who consider freemasonry to be the root of all evil in this society. We tend to get blamed for almost everything that happens.'

I chuckled:

'Know the feeling. No, to tell you the truth, I know very little about it and care less. I, well, I've read the odd article and seen the odd picture, you know, of your ceremonies ...'

He didn't blush. If you've ever seen a picture of a masonic ceremony, you'll understand why I consider that something to his credit. During initiation, for example, a candidate has to cover his head with a hood, put a noose around his neck, expose a nipple, roll up one trouser leg and wear an apron and a slipper on one foot instead of a shoe. And I'm not talking about school-boys: freemasons include some of the most powerful men in the country — in the City, the armed forces, the church, the police, industry and commerce, politics, the judiciary and the rest of the legal profession, the media, even the world of entertainment.

Something like one in six or seven adult males — for which read, white males — in England is supposed to be a freemason. But that doesn't make it a cross-section of society, even if you ignore the casual omission of persons of the female persuasion and a different colour skin. Although they are said to come from all walks of life — and do: one of the principal objections to freemasonry in the police force is its membership from the criminal fraternity — what they have in common is that they are well-established materially, and plan to get better.

Freemasonry brags about its charitable objects, but only those with something to spare can afford to be charitable. I've always viewed it as a faintly ridiculous, institutionalized version of the establishment — the old boy network — of which I'm no part anyhow, so it doesn't tread on my toes and I don't need to tread on its. All its alleged combinations and conspiracies would happen even without the aprons. You don't need to persuade or corrupt someone who already wants the same things you want.

I didn't spell any of this out to Ian Mather. I'd made my point, and now that he'd conceded it, I didn't know what to do with it. Instead, I reminded him there was one other matter left outstanding:

'We still haven't talked about money.'

.'What are your usual fees, Mr Woolf?'

I'd already decided how much to lie:

'Four hundred a day, Mr Mather.'

That, as nothing else had managed to do, brought the colour back into his cheeks:

'I doubt you've ever earned half that, Mr Woolf.'

I grinned what I hoped was disarmingly:

'Fine, my usual fees are what I can get away with, and I figure that's what you're good for.'

For the first time, he allowed himself a full smile:

'We charge on the same basis, Mr Woolf.'

Lawyers didn't need Freud to tell them people only listen to what costs enough to hurt.

I took his answer as agreement and had started to rise when his 'phone rang. I waited as he listened to his secretary, and as he hung up he waved me back into my seat.

'The officer in charge of the case has arrived to see me, Mr Woolf. I think it would be a good idea if you were to remain.'

I was doubtful. Policemen like private eyes the way Hitler had a soft spot for Churchill. I suggested:

'Just say I'm working for you. Don't spell it out.'

He didn't look too happy at the idea of starting our professional relationship by lying about it, but the door had already opened and there was not time to argue. I didn't turn around. Not even another review of his secretary was worth having to watch a member of Her Majesty's Constabulary for a moment longer than absolutely necessary.

It was a mistake. Mather was already introducing us before I could stop him:

'This is Mr Woolf, Inspector. He's working for me.'

That all too familiar weasel-shaped head broke in half in a ripe guffaw:

'Don't be bloody stupid, sir. Mr Woolf doesn't work for you. Mr Woolf doesn't work period. He doesn't know the meaning of the word.'

CHAPTER THREE

It was a long day, so long I could charge twice.

We didn't stay with Mather. Just long enough for Dowell to dictate the terms on which I could remain on the case. I told him everything; he told me nothing. Promising confidentiality as glibly and as insincerely as I had done, he extracted the underlying cause of Mather's concern: not so much his sons the lovers, but his lawyers who leaked. Dowell was quick to consent to my keeping this part of the case.

We withdrew from Mather's office and resumed our conversation in the nearest hostelry. I don't know why, but pubs in the City of London open earlier than elsewhere in the capital: it was only a few hundred yards to the city-line.

He bought the first round, finishing his before the barman brought change. He smacked his lips:

'Ah, God, that's good. I'd forgotten.'

One of his few redeeming features was an affection for Southern Comfort — no ice, no soda. I had introduced them;

they made a handsome couple. He explained now that his wife wouldn't let him keep it in the house; one night, he'd worked his way from the top and he and it had ended up empty at about the same time. Nor was it a drink to be found in the average police club.

Tim Dowell had a distinct drawback for one of his professional persuasion. Not only had he once picked up a book, he had read it, all the way through. In fact, though he is understandably deeply ashamed of it, he has a law degree. The British police hierarchy prefers its subordinates to be uneducated and incapable of thinking for themselves. They probably do a lot of recruiting amongst cab drivers.

As the barman brought our refills, I spotted a pair of city slickers leaving a table and told Dowell to grab it, soon enough for me to be able to ask the barman, behind his back, for a receipt to claim the round on expenses. Have you ever asked a barman for a receipt? It's only marginally safer than failing to tip a cabbie.

'What do you know about freemasons, Tim?' I asked as I joined him.

'Enough to steer well away from the subject. Why?'

I shrugged:

'I thought a lot of your people were.'

The outgoing Metropolitan Police Commissioner had been so worried by the extent of freemasonry on the force that he had issued a Code of Guidance politely suggesting policemen reconsider compatibility of the craft with the job. Newman commanded enormous respect in the force: so much so that, within months, a number of masonic policemen, rather than resign membership, had formed a new Lodge all of their own, the Manor of St James.

'I thought you had to belong if you wanted promotion?' I pursued lackadaisically.

Dowell was uncomfortable enough to get up and go to the bar for, our third round in not so many more minutes.

When he returned, he was shaking his head, as if puzzled:

'Odd thing, that. Barman asked if I want a receipt as well. Christ, you're a mean sod, Woolf.'

He had also bought a plate of sandwiches, which he placed in the centre of the table.

'You're just jealous you can't claim,' I stretched out my hand for a half-round of processed ham and processed cheese on processed white: Sandy would have a fit.

So did Dowell. He caught my wrist, the sandwich half-way to my mouth, and brought it firmly back to the plate where I released my grip.

'Buy your own,' he snarled.

'I made you bacon and eggs once,' I complained.

'And I saved your life, sunshine,' he reminded me: 'So that makes us even.'

My life was worth to him approximately the cost of the two fried eggs and three rashers of bacon he had greedily gobbled on his first — unsolicited, uninvited, and literally unwarranted — visit to my home.

'You don't want to talk about freemasons, do you, Tim?'

He shook his head, then, reluctantly, explained:

'My old man was one. I joined for his sake. It wasn't a big deal in those days. I stopped going as soon as he died. I don't suppose I went to a half-dozen lodge meetings. But you're right, you know, it helped. At a time when I was under a lot of flack because of my degree, it was the one thing that worked in my favour.'

'How could you go through with it?' I asked disgustedly: 'All that crap with a hood over your head?'

He smiled wearily:

'You know what it's for? To cover up your laughter. No, you're right, it was bloody rubbish. We all make mistakes, Woolf,' he reminded me.

'Most of them at Mather's are masons, right?'

'I don't know about that,' he lied. 'I don't think the Pankhurst woman could be anything to do with it: remember, no women.'

'They fuck, don't they?'

'Do they? I suppose so; to have children, you know. But I don't think they're allowed to enjoy it.'

It was my round again. When I returned, I changed the subject:

'You gonna tell me what happened, or what?'

He didn't put up a protest, just as I hadn't objected in front of Mather when he claimed it would have to be a one-way street. Those were the rules. You said one thing and did another. Put like that, it ain't so different from everything else.

Katrina had been killed between nine and eleven in the evening. She had been shot, through the mouth. There were no traces on her hand: suicide was not suspected. I grimaced:

'Gangland stuff?' It was the traditional way to leave a note on the corpse warning others not to talk so much.

'Wants to look that way. In my experience, gangsters couldn't give a damn how they get it done nowadays, so long as they get away with it.'

'Since when did you know anything about gangsters?' His role when last I'd known him was somewhat specialized: he co-ordinated — or shadow-boxed — with Special Branch, the political police. One way or another, the crimes he handled always enjoyed an extra dimension. When he didn't rise to my question, I asked: 'What about the weapon.'

'Thirty-two. That's about as useful as knowing the get-away car had four wheels. They give them away free in boxes of cereal.'

'And?'

He told me what little more they yet had. The firm kept a late-book, for fire-safety purposes. Anyone in the building after eight, when the night watchman came on duty, was supposed to ring down, and anyone who came in had to sign. There was a back exit, but no evidence of forced entry. The watchman on duty swore no one could have come in or left without his knowledge.

'They always say that. It's paid sleep.'

Dowell shook his head:

'I believe him. He's fifty-four, not in the best of health, laid off from his last job and he won't get another if he loses this. Besides, he used to be a special.'

Few people realized that the British police still use what are known as Specials, part-time amateurs to supplement the full-time amateurs.

'Right, right, can't possibly have been asleep.'

'You don't believe in anything, do you, Woolf,' he sneered.

'Not true,' I held up my glass and studied the lonely residue of the one holy spirit I religiously worship.

'You get it,' he said: 'You're charging it.'

I didn't like to admit he had so embarrassed me with his earlier observation I hadn't asked for a receipt on the last round. But we'd still only be even.

According to the book, there had been five other staff in the building, and one outsider. A solicitor had been in conference with his client until late, and they backed each other up. His wife was an office-administrator and had waited for him: they were going out to dinner. Another solicitor and his secretary had been working:

'They can prove it. They were incorporating some faxed material into a contract, and faxing it out again overnight.'

I'd heard of fax, but didn't understand why it could prove the point.

'Don't tell me you haven't got all the modern technology in your basement. And you such a highly paid private detective. Ask Sandy.'

'We're not speaking just now.'

I said earlier Kat had something to do with why Sandy and I were in off mode. I hadn't told Sandy where I was going the night I saw Kat. When I did tell her, after the non-event, it was with the casualness of the complete innocent. Sandy, however, wasn't convinced. She accused me of not telling her beforehand so as to keep my options open. Even my most voluble protests could not conceal that she was right.

When she'd rung me on the evening after Kat had been killed, knowing I probably wouldn't have read an afternoon paper nor watched the local news on television, she had been apologetic, guilty about her earlier outburst. I had been too shocked by the news to take the opportunity to bring us back together, and now I was engaged on the case, I doubted I would see her until it was over. She doesn't like my detecting at the best of times; looking for the killer of a lost lover would be even less endearing.

Dowell explained how a fax worked. Each page was time-stamped as it was transmitted. That meant that when the solicitor and his secretary claimed to have received the material during the afternoon, they could prove it; when they said they'd sent it out again overnight, that could be proved too. I still didn't see why they couldn't slip in a killing between Clauses Seven and Eight of the contract, but unless it was chargeable, there'd be no reason.

I took out my calculator and totted up the score:

'One more.'

'Wainwright, Christopher, greaseball. Says he was working late before going out. Reading a file. Everything I hear says he needs the brownie points. He's thirty-four, by which time he ought to be a salaried partner, but I've yet to hear a good word about his work, and I can't imagine anyone saying anything good about his personality.'

'I gather he impressed you. Why's he still there, then?'

'I'm not sure. It's curious. His older brother is a friend of Randolph Mather, and it seems Randolph got him articles with the firm. Maybe he's just managed to hang on.'

'Do the Mathers have to sign in?'

'Theoretically, everyone does. Ian's not usually there that late, and Gauldie — the other senior partner — leaves on the dot of seven every day, even if he's in the middle of an interview. All the partners have an administrative brief: Martin's the one who instituted the late book. But the watchman says the others aren't as regular as Martin would like to believe.'

'Tell me about the Mathers.'

'Three brothers, and the tastiest solicitor you ever saw outside of L.A. Law.' I was glad he'd kept up with Bochco, the man who made Hill Street and moved on to L.A. Law before he blew it with the half-hour and half-hearted Hooperman. It's probably top of the ratings in the States.

'You're a happily married man, Dowell; leave her to me.'

'I love my wife; I love Southern Comfort; I even quite like my job at times. I'd throw them all up for a weekend on a desert island with Allison Mather Hoyt.'

'Can they all account for their movements?'

'More or less. The mother — Ian's wife — has got Alzheimer's Disease.' I raised a quizzical eyebrow and he explained: 'Premature senility. Progressive deterioration of the brain. What they say Reagan's got. Said to be prevalent amongst Jews. As a matter of fact,' he grinned.

I knew what was coming and waved away the inevitable insult.

'Hoyt goes to the nursing home every evening. Stays until about nine o'clock. That night she went home to Highgate and called a couple of friends, long-distance: she's on the test circuit and it checks.' England was moving in the same direction as the States: soon we would all receive itemised accounts to help us decide whether the people we telephone are really worth the cost.

'Ian was at home in Hampstead and the servant can vouch for him. Martin was at his gym: Cannons in the City. He's playing in a local squash tourney. Went on 'till late with drinks after. Randolph was with some woman. Andrew was at dinner, with his wife, and then went on to the Clairmount.'

'Gambler?'

'Apparently. The owner says he's got quite a tab. Didn't want to tell me to the last pound, but he hinted eight to nine thou.'

Over a final drink he asked:

'How're you going to tackle this one, Dave? This lot ain't Disraeli Chambers.' Something else we had in common was contempt for the comrades of the left-wing bar. The clients they had to content didn't have either the choices or the experience to spot when they were being short-changed.

Where we differed was, I've never thought lawyers generally were anything special. I suppose the reason for the difference is, Dowell never practised.

'It's a big myth, Tim, They're not so sophisticated; they just wear smarter suits than the rest of us.'

'They've got to have something: they're Mather's.'

I shrugged:

'Maybe. But whatever it is, I don't have it anyhow. If I try and play their game, they'll run rings round me; it's brute Woolf or nothing. It's all I know.'

We wandered back to the office off High Holborn at about half the pace we'd left it. Along the way, I swept up some dust:

'Randolph was with some woman: Kat was supposed to be his woman.' I briefed him on Randolph's idea of loving tenderness: 'And, uh, you ought to know my own relationship with her wasn't exclusively professional.'

'That much I assumed; I never knew you to spend ten minutes around a woman without at least trying.'

'Unfair,' I protested: 'I never made a pass at Mrs Nicholas,' my client on Disraeli Chambers. She was in her sixties and married to a vicar.

As we went up the main stairs towards the office where Katrina had been found, the man himself came down. I didn't know it was Randolph to begin with, of course, but as he passed us, he swivelled and turned his eye on me.

'You must be Woolf,' he thrust a hand out at me: 'Randolph Mather.'

Kat's description had been apt. There was something cruel about him, though I couldn't tell if it was in the eyes or his mouth. He was tall and beginning to bald, and a roll of paunch poked over the top of his waist-band, but he was, like his father, impeccably and expensively besuited, and if the shirt and tie weren't silk they were an impressive imitation.

I was pissed enough to remember my manners; I ignored his hand. I didn't say anything. If I said anything, I'd lose my cool. There was just too much hatred waiting to get out. Instead, I just shrugged and brushed past him as if he didn't exist. The look on his face suggested my gesture was more effective than if I'd taken a swing at him.

Sobered by the encounter, we carried on up to the first floor landing where, to my surprise, I found that the incident had been witnessed. A man — who I guessed immediately was Martin Mather — leaned against the wall, his hands in his pockets, grinning cheerfully:

'I trust you know how to make friends as quickly as you do enemies, Mr Woolf ... Dave?'

'Dave, sure. You're Martin Mather, right?'

I was predisposed to like him: Kat had loved him for most of her adult life. He couldn't be all bad: she'd loved me a little bit, too.

While Randolph's face showed traces of Ian's, Martin could have been the child left in swaddling clothes on the door-step. He neither looked nor dressed like either of them. He was much shorter, greying, and beefy like the muscle-hungry work-out fanatic I already knew him to be. He was wearing slacks, a tweed jacket and a striped shirt; the tie around his neck looked like it had been knotted by a sodden sailor in a force seven storm.

'My father asked me to find you an office and what my father asks, I do.'

'Always?'

He frowned:

'What's that mean?'

'It means I wouldn't like you to think calling me Dave put you above suspicion, is all.'

'Or: maybe you know how to make friends, but why bother?'

'Something like that.'

'Katrina told me you were a screwball.'

Behind me, Dowell coughed.

'We're keeping the Inspector waiting while we play, Dave ...'

'Not at all, sir, I was merely agreeing with your description of Mr Woolf.'

Mather chuckled:

'Do you think it's worth settling into your office, Dave?'

'What do you think, Martin?'

'I think ... I can't see Randolph running to Daddy to explain why you were rude to him, can you?'

'So you're aware of, uh, your brother's predilections, then?'

'I'm aware of everything, Dave. That's what I'm good at.'

'But you never did anything to stop it?'

'I wasn't her keeper. What did you do?'

I couldn't think of an answer so I gestured for him to lead on to my office.

Main man Mather's office was on the ground floor, so this was my first venture on high. I saw immediately why they needed a 24-hour security service: walking around the wide first floor corridor was like strolling through the halls of a museum. One entire length was given over to pictures, one or two of which seemed familiar, but different than I remembered them from prints or posters I had owned at various times in my life. It took me a while to work it out: they were the originals.

Another stretch contained a display of medieval armour and weaponry. Martin, turning round, caught my scared scowl at a sword sharp enough to shave with. He said:

'Yes, it is real. Late fifteenth century. That too,' he pointed to a spear that looked as if it still had a powerful point to make: 'John Gauldie is the buff.'

It wasn't the sort of bric-a-brac Nicholl & Co could have kept around the office, but few of Mather's clients came from the same criminal inclination,. and if they didn't like the size of the bill, they had an accountant call up to query it instead of, as ours, reaching out for the nearest lethal instrument.

'How about law reports?' I asked naively. They were what most solicitors used to hide the peeling wallpaper.

'There's a library on the second floor. Why? Did you think you might want to look something up?' He added sarcastically.

The value of the wall-furniture diminished as we rose. Obviously, he had decided to please me: I'd been placed in an attic room so small I could sit behind the desk at one end and shut the door at the other without getting up. I nodded:

'It'll do. Key?'

He took it out of his jacket pocket.

'Only one?'

He smiled smugly:

'Sure. Apart from the security desk. And my master.' I didn't mind; I'd keep most of my material in my head, and the rest of it at home.

'Drop down and see me when you're ready to talk,' he said as he left.

I went back down the stairs to Kat's office with Tim. It was sealed, but he broke it off and ushered me in. It still had the faint, acrid, chemical smell that follows forensics. In the pub, he'd shown me the photos, so I knew exactly how she'd been found. Sitting at her desk, slumped over it, most of her head missing. The window-frame was still stained, but someone had cleaned the glass. The top of the desk was ingrained with copper-coloured blood. I ran my finger over it, morbidly:

'I liked her, Tim. I liked her a lot.'

He shrugged:

'If I say I'm sorry, does it make it any better?'

'You're a hard shit, Dowell.'

'And you're too fucking soft by half. That's why we work out together. We do, don't we, Dave?'

It was oddly reminiscent of Kat asking me: We are friends, aren't we?

I nodded hesitantly:

'Tim, are you telling me everything?'

He held up a hand:

'Scout's honour.'

'You weren't a Scout, too, were you?'

After he left, I wandered back to my room to work out a plan of action (for which read to sleep off the Southern Comfort). Half-way up the stairs, a frowsy, grey-haired, bespectacled, middle-aged woman clutching a folder attached herself to me:

'Mr Woolf? I'm Marion Mortimer. Mr Martin has assigned me to assist you.'

I stopped to study her. I was beginning to go off Mr Martin. I had plans to use Mr Ian's secretary for my humble needs. She swept past me and — a couple of hundred feet higher up, where the air was thin — waited patiently for me at my door.

'I brought you this,' she said, handing me the folder.

I opened it. It was a directory of all the partners and qualified staff, office numbers and locations, home addresses and 'phones, how to access the central computer, Lexis, fax, and a bunch of other gadgets I'd never heard of.

'I'll attend to all your correspondence Mr Woolf,' she added: 'That is, if you're going to be writing any letters. I shouldn't imagine you will be writing any letters, will you, Mr Woolf?' She asked conspiratorially: 'I mean, private detectives don't, do they?' She said, her eyes sparkling.

'No, I don't suppose I'll be writing any letters. But, uh, I'll probably need help making out my expenses' claim.'

She had begun to hop nervously from one foot to another: 'You are going to find out who killed Katrina, aren't you, Mr Woolf?'

'Well, that's really a job for the police, Miss ... is it Miss?'

'Mrs, Mr Woolf. Arthur ... That's my husband ... Arthur and I have been married for nearly twenty-five years, you see.' There was something else she wanted to tell me, and, eventually, she came out with it: 'I don't trust that Inspector Dowell, Mr Woolf. He has a small head.'

This, I have to concede, was clinically correct. At first sight, I'd wondered how he had achieved minimum height requirements, but it was only his head that was small, not the rest of him. I wasn't entirely sure that the size of his head reflected on his trustworthiness, but I couldn't fault her instinct so I didn't pursue the point.

'Arthur and I, we like jazz, Mr Woolf. Every Monday evening, we go to jazz.' I tried to keep the boggle inside my eyes. The sight of her and my image of Arthur bebopping in some smoky room above a pub was a little more than my booze-befuddled brain could cope with.

'Sometimes, well just the twice, Katrina came with us, you see, Mr Woolf. I was so fond of her.' Suddenly she was blubbing and I had to get up to offer her my chair, the only one in the room.

'It's OK,' I said lamely, and in conformity with custom: 'It's OK, you know. I was fond of her, too.'

She sniffled back the last of the tears, and got up, suddenly all office-efficiency again:

'Well, that's alright then. Now, I've written my number on the outside of the folder; you only need to dial the last three; press nine for an outside line. And if you press down that button marked exchange, followed by my number, it means your incoming calls will be diverted to me.'

It was clear as mud, but I decided it would be easier to work out for myself, by trial and error, than risk another teach-in. Before she went, I asked if she could obtain another chair, an upright: there wasn't room for anything else. At the door, she turned:

'Oh, and Mr Woolf, would you like to tell me what you drink?'

I did a double-take:

'What makes you think I drink, Mrs Mortimer?' It came out closer to 'tink I dink'; you try it after half a dozen large Southern Comforts.

'Why, Mr Woolf, all private eyes drink. I've read them all.'

Great. Wonderful. Now I was going to have to live up to her fantasies. I decided not to ask who was her favourite, in case she said Spenser. All that food would be the death of me.

'Right. I drink. Whaddayawannaknow for?'

'So that I can arrange for the hospitality room to send up a bottle, Mr Woolf, of course.'

After all, she hadn't been Martin's idea of a joke. I told her, and promised to introduce her at the end of the day, if she stayed around as late as four o'clock when my evening session usually began.

I was spoiled for choice where to begin. Gauldie, three male Mathers or. Recalling Dowell's description, I picked her number out of the internal directory. To my disappointment, her secretary said she was unavailable at present, but promised to get back to me as soon as Ms Hoyt had a spare moment. I tried to convey to her that my time was the firm's money, not that of a mere client, but I was left with the distinct impression that I would not rate top ranking on Allison's message pad.

I still wasn't ready to talk to Randolph. Martin had positively invited an interview, which meant it would be wholly uninformative unless I first acquired a little bit of material to barter with. Andrew was in conference with counsel, and no one knew when he'd be back. Reluctantly, I decided to start at the top.

Gauldie's secretary told me he would be happy to see me in a half-hour's time. I don't know how long she had worked for him, but happy and Gauldie were mutually exclusive. He must once have been exceptionally tall because now, even slightly stooped, he still towered over me as he ushered me into his room. He didn't offer to shake hands, so I guess he already knew I wasn't a mason. He was gaunt, with high cheek-bones, and his hair was prematurely thinning.

'Mr Mather told me you handle all the Latimer, litigation, Mr Gauldie?'

'That is correct. I am the senior litigation partner, so all litigation is my final responsibility.'

'Which also means all the leaks there have been,' I pointed out.

He said:

'I am of course finally responsible for that, too, Mr Woolf. But in practice, there is a large. volume of litigation and I cannot of course oversee it all.'

'Of course, of course,' I reassured him: 'But it does mean you have access to everything. What I'm wondering is, who. else does?'

He pursed his lips:

'Almost all of the partners, Mr Woolf. You see, we take our corporate responsibilities very seriously here. Randolph works closest with me. Then Martin, for example, is in charge of office administration, and training. That gives him access to all the firm's files. Young Andrew is in charge of bills on account. Many of our clients are far too large and well established for us to seek an initial payment on account: it would cause offence. But people do not object to interim accounts for work already undertaken. So it is young Andrew's duty to make sure that all of us — but, of course, especially the assistants and the salaried partners — are up to date in that respect.'

When I was in practice, our main concern was to win the case: at Mather's, that was secondary to keeping the cash coming in. He listed other 'corporate' duties, identifying partners by name. He attributed no special obligations to Allison Mather Hoyt. I asked. He pursed his lips again: perhaps he was practising kissing.

'Mrs Hoyt,' not, note, Ms: 'Mrs Hoyt is a partner, of course. Let us say she has a roving brief to assist others in their responsibilities.'

In his view, she was a partner in — and because of — name only. Aware he'd displayed more animosity than might be considered diplomatic, he hastened to add: 'Of course, you could say that Randolph does no more than assist me.' He couldn't let it go at that: 'That would be a considerable understatement of his contribution to this firm, Mr Woolf. He is a very fine young man, and a fine solicitor.' Now I knew what Gauldie thought of Randolph, I knew what to think of Gauldie.

'And Martin? How do you get along with Martin?'

He sniffed, like the name stank. Ian had told me that two of his sons were freemasons: I knew which one wasn't. As if he could read my mind, Gauldie said:

'Mr Mather said you asked about the craft.'

By now, I knew enough of the lingo to understand he wasn't talking about carpentry or creative accounting.

'It would be a grave error, Mr Woolf, and of course a grave waste of resources, to pursue that line of enquiry. I hope I make myself clear.'

Dowell's immediate response had been: 'enough to steer well away from the subject'.

'Mr Mather has already — shall we say extended? — the bounds of necessity on the subject. You would not, I am sure, wish to embarrass him further.'

Me? Embarrass anyone? May my throat be cut across, my tongue torn out by the root and buried in the sand of the sea at low water mark, or a cable's length from the shore, where the tide regularly ebbs and flows twice in twenty-four hours, as the freemasons say (in the initiation ceremony).

'Mr Gauldie, I don't want to offend you.' May my throat be cut across, etcetera. 'There's only two things I want to find out about: who killed Katrina Pankhurst, and who's been leaking the firm's secrets. I take it you've already told the police everything you know on the first subject ...' I paused for him to nod: if I'd paused until he nodded, I'd be pausing yet. 'How do you think — for example — the LCP report got out?' Remember the LCP report? Babies with bits ... Right, you remember.

'I don't know, Mr Woolf.'

'Who worked on that case? Katrina didn't.'

He smiled spookily:

'People do not only talk at the office.'

I was surprised: I would not have excepted him to know she and Randolph were a number.

He didn't. He went on:

'She and Martin were very close friends.'

'But you do all Latimer's work. You and Randolph, right?'

He laughed with warmth enough to freeze-dry:

'We are in charge of it, Mr Woolf. Two people could not do all of it. Both Martin, and Mrs Hoyt, assisted at different times on that issue, although so did many others: it was a massive action. You are aware of the other leaks: Westmoreland House — Martin's case; the de Peyer divorce — Martin and Wainwright; the News libel action — Martin and young Andrew.'

'I think I'm beginning to get your drift,' I said dryly: 'Martin Mather is the common factor.'

Yet again his lips pursed:

'I should hate to think it. I'm only stating what your examination of the files will disclose. The obvious, you might say.'

'But Katrina was clean: she wasn't involved in any of those actions. And for the record, she and Martin weren't "close" as you put it, ever since she returned to work here.'

He shrugged indifferently:

'That would simply suggest that one thing had nothing to do with the other, would it not, Mr Woolf?'

I got up:

'Yeah, sure. I guess I ought to thank you for your help.'

'Mr Woolf, I ought to tell you: I do not agree with Mr Mather's decision to employ you.' I'd never have guessed.

'I will be loyal to it, of course, but I do not agree with it. These are matters for the proper authorities. Only.'

I was being pointed at Martin, so that was where I'd go. I found the office Marion Mortimer shared. She told me he was interviewing prospective staff in a room on the ground floor. Before I left her, I gave her a list of files I wanted to find in my room when I got back up. She promised they would be there: along with the something else she had promised me.

I waited while Martin finished his interview in progress. I could see in: the door was half glass. The candidate was a young, black man. As I shut the door behind us after he left, I said:

'I take it he won't be getting the job.'

Martin chuckled.

'I wondered when you'd get around to that,' meaning he knew I was Jewish: 'But you're wrong, you know. We have black employees, and Jews, and our quota of women. I always thought it was a good idea employing a Pankhurst; kept the women's lobby at bay. We'll have to think of something else now.'

I ignored the sick humour: he was trespassing on my territory. 'But not in positions of prominence or power. That's what matters.'

'Oh, come on, Dave. We don't get the applicants. People go to their own. Look at the black and Asian firms, or for that matter the Jewish firms. Sandy Nicholl was Jewish, wasn't she?'

'She still is, so far as I know. So?'

'So, you were a pair of Jews. We're a family of Scots. We employ our own kind, too.'

His father had said something similar, but he was referring to freemasons,

'Wainwright? Is that a Scottish name.'

'Ah, well, we all make mistakes.'

'How's he survived?'

'Andrew claims he's useful to him. I don't know why: he's only worked with me once, and that was enough.'

'That's enough? Andrew's say-so?'

'His productivity is acceptable.'

'Measured how? Billing time?'

'Yes, of course, how else? The ones who do the least are always the hardest to fault.'

'And Andrew is in charge of billing, right?'

His eyes narrowed as he took my point, but he nodded. I shrugged: I didn't have anywhere else to take it. I decided to order up some stirred shit instead:

'Gauldie says all the leaks are in your dyke. Care to comment?'

It didn't faze him:

'I can add up. What it means, though, is all the leaks we know about. Doesn't it?'

I inclined my head to one side in acknowledgement: it was a defence sufficient to create a reasonable doubt.

He glanced at his watch.

'You're going to have to forgive me now. I have another interview.' He picked up the file: 'This one's one of yours. Who do you think I should give the job to — him or the black?'

Suddenly, his complacency drew blood. I snapped:

'I'd take the job and shove it up your arse, Mather, 'f I was you.' I slammed out of the room so hard I thought the half-glass would shatter. Typically of my bad luck, it held.

Marion had fulfilled my every whim. For some reason that was beyond me, there were two glasses, but otherwise everything was as ordered. I rang down to the desk and told them I'd be staying late: past eight o'clock, if they cared to tell the night-man when he came on duty. And if Andrew Mather came back after his conference, I'd like to see him.

I filled a glass and settled down to the part of this Job that I like the least: reading and making notes. I read the de Peyer file first, remembering what Kat had said: it was a juicy divorce. It made me wonder what I was doing wrong. The man was upper class, desperately rich and, from the photographs snapped by his wife's snoop, fit, extremely well-hung and attractive to women (plural) so perfect I'd only ever dreamed they existed. Mind you, his wife was no slouch. He, too, had been snooping on her. The barristers in the case must have enjoyed receiving the briefs: uplifting material.

On its own, the leak didn't count for much. Through their short marriage, he had never disclosed a half-million pound estate in the Bahamas. He claimed there was no way she could find out about it: it had hardly been declared on his tax returns. At the last moment, what would have been a successful settlement from his point of view took a nosedive when her solicitor wrote notifying Mather's they intended to inform the court that financial disclosure was incomplete — and that the Inland Revenue were bound also to be interested.

Similarly, the leakage of a witness' past record in the News libel action wouldn't make a headline in its own right. As I started to read the file, I remembered the case. One Maurice Francis, Viscount Stonefrost, had sued for a gossip item which implied he had been dealing dope to a close coterie of nobs, sods and assorted snobs. The witness' name was Ron Fitzpatrick, an allegedly reformed character who had once played a minor part in long-firm fraud under a different first name — John — for which he had suffered a fine and a suspended sentence, both of which were time-expired.

Technically, the conviction would not be admissible, but once Stonefrost knew about it, the balance tilted in favour of a substantial settlement. Stonefrost had taken the money and run: to the Bahamas, I noted under the heading of unnatural coincidences. Within a year, he had worked. his way through his bonus, and was found floating in a swimming-pool, with more cocaine than blood in his veins.

It was nearly midnight by the time I reached Westmoreland House, and my mind was in no condition to tackle the technicalities of landlord-tenant law. I'd done a few cases years before, when I was in practice, but there would be little in common between defending the tenant of a rent-controlled leaking apartment against a claim for arrears of rent, and the sort of war waged at the expensive end of the commercial market. I was so bad at that sort of work, I never even claimed against my own landlord for the condition of my damp basement.

Andrew Mather was no show, nor likely to at the witching hour. I put the file aside, and let myself out without waking the watchman: it was the same one Dowell swore would never sleep on the job. I was too late for the tube, so I had no choice but to take a taxi. Though tired, I was too hyped up for sleep: there was only one place to go: there only ever is.

Lewis greeted me as if it was a month since he'd seen me, not a mere couple of days. I felt pretty much the same way. Lewis is: fat, old, a friend, a faggot, a villain and a club-owner, in that order. Since the AIDS' scare, he's slowed down. and now lives with Malcolm, who manages the club for him, and who he keeps hold of by a judicious blend of threats and a promise to remember him in his will. If I knew Lewis, the promise would be discharged with the age-old vaudeville line: 'Hi, Malcolm'.

I'd once made the mistake of borrowing money from Lewis, and only just survived the collection call from his gorillas. Later, during Disraeli Chambers, he had endeared himself to me when he had looked for a way to explain that their threats of violence didn't mean he didn't like me, and had been forced back on the immortal cliché: 'It was only business'.

Lewis is something else I forgot to mention. He is extremely canny. As the Disraeli Chambers case drifted towards its demise, I'd badgered him into selling me a gun. Then, in time enough to save my life, he told Dowell what I'd done, only omitting the name of my supplier. In fact I had first met Dowell at his club. Since the case, I'd continued to come round whenever I had nothing else to do, which is most nights. We have an agreement: when I'm out of work, I drink for free; when I'm not, I pay double. He thinks he wins; I think I do; we're both happy.

I didn't have to order. One of the waitresses brought the bottle. Oh, yes, he employs women too: some of the clientele is straight; he's not proud; he'll rip anyone off, regardless of sexual persuasion.

'Lewis,' I asked: 'Are you a freemason?'

He guffawed:

'Me, Dave? Hardly. Not my type of dressing up. Know what I mean?'

'What do you know about them, Lewis?'

He shuddered:

'They're wicked, Dave. You don't want to get involved with them. Remember that eytie?'

I knew who he meant: Calvi, the man they called God's banker, found hanging beneath — significantly — Blackfriars

Bridge, a so-called suicide no one believed. Lewis' warning to stay clear of them was the third of the day.

'You working again?' he asked as I helped myself to another drink, trying to sound casual instead of concerned about the cost.

I'm like George Washington. I cannot tell a lie. I equivocated:

'I might have something coming up.'

'What sort of line?' Lewis doesn't pass up any information, no matter how insignificant.

'Law. Mather's. Do you know them?'

'Not going to take you on, are they?' He cackled so hard I thought Malcolm might be about to inherit.

'What's so funny?' I asked indignantly.

'You, at Mather's, know what I mean?' He chortled.

I gathered he had heard of the firm.

'They might, you never know,' I sulked.

'They might appoint me a judge of the Old Bailey, know what I mean?'

'What do you know about them, Lewis?'

'Not a lot. Not exactly my type of brief, are they, know what I mean?' Mather's knew less about criminal law than Lewis.

He frowned. He was thinking. He had to come up with something about Mather's that no one else knew, to save face:

'Once upon a time, long ago, probably before you were born, there was a nasty piece of work called James Mather. Never Jim, mind you: James. He was a Scottie, from Glasgow. Things were different then: a couple of villains fell out, they broke a few bones, swung a bit of lead, know what I mean? Not like today someone ends up supporting a motorway or fish-food for sharks. But him, he was heavy ahead of his times. Shooters, knives, he was greedy and if anyone got in the way it was the last time, know what I mean?'

I pulled a face:

'What's the connection? It doesn't sound like he was a partner in Mather's.'

'I once heard, someone said, I can't even remember who or where, he was related. Anyway, he disappeared about the end of the forties, maybe the early fifties. For a while, it was thought he'd tasted his own medicine, but then I heard he was in America, and starting over. That's all. Sound like anything to do with what you're interested in?'

I shook my head:

'No. I'm interested in things ...' I hesitated to look for the right phrase: 'Well, commercial.'

Lewis persisted:

'He was commercial, too, you know. He got his start in the black-market. During the war, know what I mean.'

I shook my head again:

'Too old, too distant. This's tied up in the girl who got shot the night before last. Even if I was, she wasn't born then.'

'I read about it. Very nasty. It's unnatural, killing lawyers, know what I mean?'

'You never used to, Lewis.'

'Never used to what?' I'd confused him.

'Use that appalling expression, "know what I mean?". I liked it better when you got your lines off American movies instead of British television.'

He could take it. He rocked in his chair with laughter again and squeezed my knee hard enough to hurt me and catch himself a cheap thrill:

'You don't change, Dave, you don't change. Know what I mean?'

CHAPTER FOUR

There were two calls on the answering machine when I got home. The first was from Martin Mather:

'I'm sorry about what I said earlier. It was inexcusable. Let me make it up to you. Come to my gym tomorrow night; work out a little, then we can have dinner. What do you say? Tell me in the morning.'

The second was from Sandy:

'Dave, it's me. I was wondering how you were feeling. I really am sorry about Katrina, Dave, I liked her too. Oh, shit I hate these machines. I need to talk to you, Dave, it's time we talked. We can't keep carrying on like this, Dave. We're off more than we're on. Oh, I shouldn't have started. Look, just ring me, please.'

Like I said: it was a long day.

I didn't ring Sandy; it was too late, and I was too tired. Oh, shit, as she would say: I didn't ring Sandy because I couldn't face talking to her. I have a real problem with Sandy. A bit like the old Groucho Marx line, how can I stay with anyone who'd stay with me? I love Sandy, just about as much as Katrina had always assumed, long before I knew it; but it's easier to list the things that are wrong with our relationship than to remember what's right.

My idea of first thing the next day, when I got in around eleven, I again tried to pin down Allison Mather Hoyt, without success: she was at a client's, and there would remain for the rest of the working day. I also rang Martin's secretary to confirm the date for that evening. I spent half an hour following a whim in the firm's dead-file basement: I didn't stay longer; it was dank, damp and unpleasant; I could see why — as Kat had said — no one ever went down there. Then, reluctantly, I put my head down to complete the task I'd left over: reading the files on Westmoreland House.

It was less complicated than I had expected. A block of offices was in a condition so bad the tenants all had to relocate elsewhere for almost two years while remedial works were carried out. The landlord company's liability ran only from when it first had notice of the problem. There was a long period when notice could not be proved, until a link was disclosed between one of the directors and a previous owner of the block, who had certainly known about the defect. The argument was over the compensation for this period. Given the size of the block, the number of tenants affected, commercial rents and their temporary relocation costs, the difference ran into real money.

What I also discerned from the file was that the barrister acting for the tenants was Russel Orbach, Queen's Counsel. Contrary to what is believed across the Atlantic Ocean, Queen's Counsel do not advise Her Majesty. The title reflects rather the majesty of their fees. A QC, or silk as they are called because of the special robes they wear in court, can command several thousand pounds for a single day's work: some of them can command that much for an hour's conference.

I'd known Russel since we were both young, progressive lawyers, undertaking work for the poor and seedy usually for no fee. He was one of the founding members of Disraeli Chambers, which was one of the groups of barristers, specializing in poverty, welfare and criminal defence work, established in the 1970s. His specialism was civil law: planning, housing, building, local government. He was very good at it indeed.

That was one reason why he was unpopular with his colleagues. Another was that he had refined arrogance to an art form: a martial art. Argumentative, four steps ahead of a discussion, also a Jew, and intolerant of the intellectually idle or deceitful. What he did best was make enemies. Eventually, his colleagues — whoops, sorry, comrades — summoned up sufficient courage to oust him from the group, at a meeting he was not invited to attend, on the basis of allegations he was not invited to answer. They handled themselves so badly, he successfully sued them for a substantial sum of money.

This is where he and I differed. I didn't mind that he would never forget or forgive their cruelty, or their cowardice. I would also like to be able to remember all those who have done me harm, but the list is too long. But I would have settled for the money and for the undoubted professional benefits that accrued — including his appointment as silk — after he left. Instead, years after the event, he still allowed his bitterness to eat him up, and his desire for revenge to dominate his life.

I knew, of course, that he no longer worked only — if at all — for the impoverished: but I had thought he had left landlord and tenant behind to concentrate on local government to the exclusion of all else. Given the number of tenants claiming at

Westmoreland House, and the size of the damages, my first question was whether he would still be living in his compact, one-bedroom apartment in Highgate, or whether he'd invested some of the loot in something larger. I decided not to wait until the evening to find out, but rang him at work instead.

'Is Mr Orbach in chambers?'

'Who's calling him?'

'Mr Woolf …' I hesitated then, suspecting he might not otherwise take the call, added: 'From Mather's.'

There are few barristers — QCs or mere mortals — who will refuse a call from Mather's.

'Just a minute, sir,' the clerk sounded like he'd suddenly been doused in ego-massaging balm.

'Russel Orbach,' said a voice I was once sure I never wanted to hear again: 'Can I help you, Mr … er … ?'

'Woolf. With two "os", I added dryly.

Silence told me he'd got the point.

'What do you want, Dave?' He asked quietly: 'Why did you say you were calling from Mather's?'

'Would you have taken the call otherwise?'

'We'll never know now, will we?' He had recovered his composure: 'Well?'

'Yes, thanks, you?'

'That's not very original. What do you want, Dave?'

'I am working at Mather's, actually.'

'Not as a solicitor?' He was more outraged at the idea than Lewis had been. It isn't fair. Just because I think I'm a rotten lawyer doesn't entitle others to the same opinion.

I let the insult pass.

'I was wondering … I'd like to see you. Would you be willing to see me?'

'That would depend on why.'

'What would you say ... if I invited you to dinner?'

Orbach lived alone. He sat in a chair overlooking his garden, at an angle from which no other properties were visible, a rare luxury in London. He slept, ate and listened to classical music: all on his own.

On his own, once a year, he went to Oslo, to stay with a family, and tour the Munch Museum where they changed the exhibits annually, with a woman old enough to be his mother, who indeed he called 'Mor', Norwegian for mother. I didn't know for sure that he had no friends, but that was the impression he gave and it's difficult to imagine whose choice of a relaxed evening might be to spend it with Russel, Josef Stalin excepted. This was the flimsy basis for my belief that I might be able to tempt him to meet me. I was taken aback when he replied:

'Where?'

'I don't know. I hadn't thought about it.'

'Frederick's. Camden Passage. Tomorrow night at eight o'clock. You book.' He hung up without waiting to see whether the time or place were convenient to me.

I asked Marion to make the booking and had just hung up on her when the door burst open and Randolph Mather presented himself, without appointment, warning or even a bouquet of flowers. He glowered:

'I want to talk to you, Woolf.'

I tilted my chair backwards. The hell with the job. This was personal.

'The thing is, Mather, I'm not sure I want to listen.'

'Now, look, Woolf ...'

'I doubt that'd be much better than listening. You look. Kat was a friend of mine. She told me about you two. I didn't like it. I didn't like her going along with it, but I guess it wasn't really my business anyway. But that does not mean I have like you or tolerate you the same way. I read your divorce files, too.'

I watched his mouth fall open as he digested the import of the world 'too', wondering if it'd stop before it hit the floor: 'Oh, yeah, she'd read them. She told me. It doesn't do her any harm now for you to know that. But I decided I'd have a look for myself, to see what kind of scum you are.'

'You had no right.' He'd recovered his voice.

'Wrong. I had every right. I look at whatever I want. I look at whatever I think might give me an answer. Any time you want to stop me, your firm can start looking for a lot of new business,' I spelled out the risk to their reputation.

Stupid he wasn't. He swallowed and nodded.

'Now we've got that out the way, whyn't you tell me what you came in here for?'

He nodded again, the bald-patch at the top of his forehead glistening in the strip-lighting:

'I know ... I understand ... I know ...' Was he ever going to make up his mind? 'I know what Katrina must have told you. But ...' He was changing his story about once a word. 'I didn't see her that night. Well, I did see her that night, but we weren't together. That's not quite what I mean.'

This guy was an allegedly articulate partner in one of the most reputable firms of lawyers in the country: there was hope for me yet. 'We were both here that night. Late, I mean. We ... Well, we didn't ring down. I know we're all supposed. to, but people don't always. If you're going to stay for just a few minutes after eight — well, I mean, most of us work late most nights of the week. You know the job. You were a lawyer too.'

I hate people using the past tense of my profession. It's my prerogative.

'I still am,' I reminded him dryly.

'Yes, yes, I'm sorry.' His attempt to ingratiate himself by treating us as members of the same club had backfired.

'You weren't going to stay for just a few minutes, were you?'

'No. It wasn't the first time. We went out for a drink about six, and came back just before eight. We had a couple of cases to talk about.'

'Which?'

'What?'

'Which cases?'

'Well, it was just one case actually.' He'd made love to her in the office. As he said, not for the first time. Under pressure, he admitted he got his kicks fucking her in Iron Ian's office, along the spacious sofa, across the king-bed-sized desk or sprawled out on the pure wool pile carpet.

He insisted there'd been nothing about it that was — he paused to look for the right word and descended pathetically on 'special' by way of euphemism for violent. Afterwards, they had separated while still in the building, both returning to their respective rooms, he to collect his things, she to catch up on some work. He hadn't seen her again. Ever.

He was a very worried man. Though all of them were civil lawyers, they watched enough television to appreciate there must have been an autopsy, and sperm would have been discovered. There was no doubt the police would want to know where it had come from. Well, whose. What wasn't clear was of what he was more frightened: the inference that might be drawn by the police, or that his father might find out.

I could have let him down gently. I could have told him the police already knew about him and Katrina. I could have told him that his father also knew. There was no need for his father to find out exactly where they had been accustomed to perpetrate their penetration. I could have reminded him she'd had her mouth blown off, and the police were looking for a gangster, not a sex-slayer.

I thought for a while about all these things I could say to reassure him, then said:

'I can see why you're worried, Mather. I wish there was something I could say.'

During my silence, I think he began to appreciate some of the answers for himself. My reply told him one of two things. Either I was stupid, or I still wanted him to hurt. His eyes narrowed, his lips pursed just like Gauldie's, I recollected the meanness I had observed when I was first saw him. He had recollected it too.

'You think you're pretty clever, don't you, Woolf? You ought to be careful. My father isn't the be-all and end-all of influence.'

I studied his expression. He was already regretting what he'd said. I asked:

'Would that, by any chance, have something to do with other kinds of brothers?' Freemasons call themselves 'brother', like in a union.

'I don't know what you mean,' he threw his head back and rose and left the room in one, flowing movement. I watched him go, curious: What had he really wanted to tell me?

Martin shrugged, after I'd told him the tale: 'Who knows? Randolph moves in a mysterious manner.'

We were in the restaurant at Cannons, some hours later. I'd arrived late and found him pacing impatiently in the lobby. He had to sign me in, and pay for a visitor's card which I could use to enter the different facilities, like the pool, the sauna, the gymnasium itself or the bar. He steered me away from the stairs that would have taken me up to the women's changing room, and led me down to the men's.

I hate locker-rooms. All those male bodies, arses smaller and pricks bigger than mine, people walking nakedly, with assumed casualness, calling out to one another so fast and lah-di-dah I automatically scoured the floor for plum-stones. I picked a relatively discreet locker: Martin had his own regular spot.

Then he was standing in front of me, telling me to hurry up, in swimming trunks that revealed more than I had to conceal. There wasn't an ounce of fat on him. He rippled like in the movies. He shifted weight from one foot to another, a workout in its own right.

'I thought you could use the exercise,' he remarked: 'Swimming's good, but it wouldn't be enough. You ought to join, work out properly. And cut down on the alcohol.'

'I tried, but I never did get hooked on the good god body beautiful,' I admitted, somewhat unnecessarily: 'And I'm not likely to now.'

'Well,' he said cheerfully: 'If you don't now, there's not likely to be a lot of then in which to change your mind.'

'Thanks,' I muttered, clinging on to the banister of the wet steps to the pool, terrified of slipping and making a fool of myself.

I paddled around the shallow end while he dived straight into the roped-off section for lap-swimmers. When he'd finished, he pointed to a separate hall:

'Jacuzzi?'

'Does it hurt?'

He shoved my shoulder lightly, and told me he'd catch up with me in the bar in forty-five minutes' time. I got the message: it would be exactly forty-five minutes. I spent ten in the jacuzzi, one in the sauna — how can people can do that to themselves? — three minutes in the shower, and half an hour getting a head start.

He arrived in company with a man with a nose so large, in America he'd have to register it as a lethal weapon.

'Dave, Tony,' he introduced us casually.

I rose to shake hands. Martin asked:

'What you would like to drink, Tony?'

'I'll have a small whisky.'

'Dave?'

'Southern Comfort. No ice. No soda.'

I knew I liked the man. He read 'small' for his friend to mean 'large' for me. As we lawyers like to say all the time: *inclusio unius, exclusio alterius.*(I can't translate it because I don't speak Latin, but it means that if you qualify one thing, the qualification does not apply to another. What it really meant was: I got a larger drink.)

'I gather you work with Martin,' Tony said as we sipped our drinks.

'Sort of. What do you do?'

'Finance. A bit of this, a bit of that.'

'You have a mutual acquaintance,' Martin chipped in: 'Katrina Pankhurst. Tony is the former Mr Pankhurst, if you see what I mean.'

'Tony Galucci,' I muttered. It just hadn't occurred. 'Out of curiosity, Martin: do you ever do anything that isn't designed to shock?'

'Not if he can help it,' Galucci said gloomily: he hadn't found it funny either. 'I don't really want to talk about her,' he said, lifting himself out of his chair: 'I'm going to be late. I'm meeting Beat.' Unusual name, I thought: as in Beet Hoven?

'Squash tomorrow?' Martin asked.

'I'll ring you. Nice to meet you, Dave.'

I watched him leave until he stopped to chat with a couple of people still undressed for sport. He was an odd man; weaker that I would have expected Martin to be in partnership with, if Kat hadn't in effect forewarned me. Weaker, too, than I would have expected her to marry, without knowing she wanted a man she could run rings round. I asked:

'Who's Beat?'

'Beatrix Kelly, Beat for short. A splendid, and beautiful, accountant.' I was shocked: I didn't know there were women accountants.

He went on:

'She runs Cross Course for us. You do know about Cross Course, don't you.' It wasn't a question. I nodded.

'Well, you see,' he leaned over towards me, speaking confidentially: 'Beat was Katrina's sister.'

'And Tony's not meeting her on business, is he?' Now I knew what Kat had been holding back. 'Tell me about Cross Course. What's it do? How'd's it work?'

'Like any other any similar enterprise. People bring us money. We turn it into more. It started as a sort of hobby; I went through a period when I thought I wouldn't want to stay in law. Tony brought in the contacts. That's what he's best at: meeting people. It's not big: just a handful of staff, and Beat. I don't have that much to do with it anymore; Tony and Beat run it between them and like a good capitalist, I sit back and draw my dividends.'

The club restaurant was the other side of the arches under the railway into which the gymnasium had been built. Martin ate fast; unhealthily so; faster even than me. It was a contradiction. He talked fast, too, with his mouth sometimes still full, before he swallowed whole chunks of steak each one of which would in my most desperate days have fed me for a week. He was amusing, talking about people I now knew at the office, dribbling bits of gossip, most of it irrelevant to my work but all of it thoroughly enjoyable.

'Do you know Russel Orbach?'

'The silk?'

'Yes.'

He shook his head, and neatly sprayed the apron of a passing waitress with red wine: 'I never met him. He's still a bit left-wing for our taste. Why do you ask?'

'I just thought you'd get along. He likes things which hurt people, too.'

'Come on, Dave. Everyone loves gossip. It's half your living.'

'Right. So I can afford to be pious about it: I only deal in it 'cos I have to. What you'n'Orbach've got in common is, you don't bother to conceal how much you like it.'

'How do you know him? Ah, yes, I forgot: he was involved in that Disraeli Chambers' business.' He'd no more forgotten than had I.

'What would you say,' I asked hesitantly: 'If I told you it's been suggested to me that Andrew might be financially — uh — over-extended?'

He knew what I was suggesting:

'No way. I'm sure he and Marilyn don't confine themselves to their income, but there's no reason why they should. You've got to remember, when you're a profit-sharing partner in Mather's, your income can vary a hell of a lot in a year, and you don't know exactly how much you'll get 'till the end. So really people live against estimate, rather than actual income.'

'But you wouldn't think Andrew was actually in difficulty?'

'No. If you haven't already realized, my father doesn't approve of things like debt. If he found out, Andrew might as well change his name. But it still wouldn't convince him that Andrew could betray him.'

'What if I proved it to you?'

'The same. There's no chance. If he was a million pounds in debt.'

'Tell me about Randolph.'

He shrugged:

'Randy? What's to tell? He's aptly named. He's been through three wives: and through may just about be the operative word. They spoke not well of him 'when they left,' he added dryly.

'What or who's he up to now?' Katrina had not been the only string he played his bow on.

'Most of the female staff. He says baldness is a sign of virility, and he's trying to prove the point, I think. I'd feel sorry for him, if he wasn't enjoying himself quite so much.'

'And do they?'

'The staff? God knows. Who cares?'

It was difficult to discern how much was affectation; and how much he really meant.

'He wasn't that easy to follow, when we were young. He was clever at everything: school, sports, drama, art, music. Oxford. Mr Perfect. Mr "I'm in charge". That's what Randolph likes, you know: it doesn't matter what it is; if something's going on — and where Randy's concerned, something always is going on — he can't stand to be left out of it, and he has to be in charge of it. Andrew idolized him; he still does a bit. But he was much younger; it's different when you're nearly the same age. It's a general truth, isn't it? He joined the brotherhood young,' he added, assuming — correctly — I would know what he meant: freemasonry. 'By the time Randolph was at Oxford, I'd gone sour.'

'Which means?'

I had an idea, from my conversation with Kat, but I wanted to hear it from him. He shrugged with false modesty:

'I had to leave school in a hurry. There was a fight. And some broken ribs. And a broken jaw, too, as a matter of fact.'

'Remind me not to invite you outside,' was all I said.

He laughed away his disappointment that I had not asked for the gory details:

'It's a thing of the past. I had a violent temper, and the skills to go with it. I still have the skills, but no longer the temper.'

'Great. So when you hit me, I'll know it was a perfectly controlled act?'

'When I hit you,' he said softly: 'You won't know anything. Not for a while anyway.'

I shook my head disgustedly:

'You really do have a problem, Martin. You don't know who you are from one minute to another: macho bully, sophisticated seducer, skilful solicitor or maybe all three. You'll have to be suspect number one.'

'True, absolutely true.' He was not at all disconcerted: 'All you need is a motive.'

'Money? Family revenge? They're usually somewhere on the list.'

'I don't need the money, and revenge implies an extent of emotion that doesn't fit our family. We're a cold-blooded lot, like our father, I suppose. Do you know, my father has a half-brother, in America, who he hasn't spoken to for more than thirty years?'

Sometimes you want them to know how much you know, and sometimes you don't. I shook my head.

'They hated each other. My uncle had to emigrate, oh, about nineteen fifty. I'm not supposed to know anything about it, but he was something of a naughty boy and managed somehow to embroil my father in his affairs, professionally. Affairs I might add in which the police became involved. He fled the country and couldn't even come back for my grandfather's funeral. My father threatened to tell the police he was here if he did.' Lewis had been right.

'You obviously do know a bit about it.'

'A bit.' He didn't elaborate.

'Tell me more about Andrew,' I suggested instead.

'Andrew? Dear, sweet, precious, unimaginative, conservative young Andrew. Law at university, College of Law, Lodge member, straight to Mather's, lived at home until he got married.' He told me, as Katrina had done, about his apartment in town, the country house, the house-parties.

'D'you go?'

'A couple of times. It's fun. A lot of young women, a lot to drink, and otherwise. Maybe he's not so conservative in some respects now. The mind and much else boggles. Mind you, with Marilyn in charge it could hardly be otherwise. She was a deb and a model and she's still a gorgeous lady. I wouldn't mind,' he added, surprisingly crudely.

'Do you?'

'No. Somehow, I don't think father would approve. But the thought's crossed my mind, and I know for certain that it's crossed hers too.'

He was confident about his sexuality in a way I envied. I could see the attraction. He might have mastered his temper, but there remained a distinct energy that I imagined would be appealing to the sort of woman who wanted a man much more powerful than herself. Despite myself, I could see why Katrina had put up with him.

I waited to see whether he would volunteer information about Allison, and when he didn't I asked.

His brow furrowed as he looked for the right thing to say about his sister:

'I think she's probably the reason I could never settle down with anyone. I'm half in love with her. I mean, I would be if she wasn't my sister,' he corrected himself before I picked him up on a Freudian slip so classic I couldn't believe of him that it had been accidental: 'Kat came closest. Does that surprise you?'

He was fishing to see how much I knew about them.

'That's a trick question, Martin. You're trying to make "closest" sound like "close". It could mean anything; like, you went two nights with her, instead of just the one.'

'What are you? A solicitor, a private detective or a shrink?'

'There isn't that much difference. They're all people that people talk to. It's just that shrinks earn more.'

He smiled, but he'd lost interest in the conversation.

He snapped his fingers at the manager for the check. I hate people who can snap their fingers: it's one of those macho things I can't do, like using fingers to whistle for a cab.

'Answer a question, Martin,' I asked while we waited:

'Has any of this got to do with freemasons? Your father and Gauldie are; Randolph and Andrew are. Are there others? Why aren't you?'

'That was several questions. I'm not because I think it's a load of rubbish. I don't like the way people become members: word of mouth, who knows who is a good chap. It's just not my style. Have you ever seen their regalia? As for your other questions: yes, there are several other freemasons in the firm. A lot of people joined — I suppose like Randolph and Andrew — because their parents were. Father was on the Board of General Purposes, that's the governing board. But Gauldie is much more powerful: he belongs to Royal Arch Freemasonry as well. That's supposed to be the spiritual side of it. It all brings in a great deal of work. As for your first question, no, I can't see what it's got to do with anything. I doubt someone's passing out secrets with Lodge Lists.'

'Why do you say you only suppose Randolph and Andrew joined because of your father?'

He hesitated for a long time before he answered. Then he smiled thinly:

'Let's say it attributes a degree of disinterestedness to Randolph that's somewhat out of character.'

'You really don't like him, do you?'

He hesitated again, then admitted disarmingly:

'No, I don't. So you should take everything I say with a pinch of salt. The truth is, I don't really understand Randolph: I never have. I don't understand what makes him tick.' Suddenly, sharply, a bit nervously, he laughed: 'That doesn't say much. I don't understand what makes me tick either.'

'Last question. Given the number of leaks on cases you've been involved with, how come you haven't tried to do something about it before? Why'd it take a killing to call me in — or someone?'

He frowned; thinking seriously — probably for the first time that evening — about his answer.

'I suppose, when something as serious as a possible leak happens, you think up a thousand other explanations, and put the idea out of your mind. D'you understand?'

I understood alright; it was how I'd spent half my life — avoiding reality. I said:

'And a killing can't be avoided quite so easily.'

The manager brought his bill, and he avoided a reply.

Unlike his oldest brother, Andrew gave me plenty of warning of his visit: he knocked at the door before he blew it open. 'You're spreading rumours I'm in debt,' he accused instead of introducing himself.

Kat's description of him as pretty was apt. I could also see why people prefixed him as 'young'. He was callow, pink-cheeked, a bright and beautiful blond, and as he stood in front of my desk, his mouth was turned up in a sneer that did his lips so proud if I swung both ways I'd want to lick it off.

I liked the way he'd leaped to the conclusion that what he'd heard was what I'd said: it was typical of a lawyer to ignore the possibility there might be another side of the account. As, however, he happened not to be wrong, I decided it would be unfruitful to point this out to him. I also lacked the incentive I enjoyed with Randolph to put the boot in. I said:

'It's a problem when you investigate in a closed environment. Everyone gets to hear every question you've asked, and starts reading a lot more into it than may be accurate.'

He wasn't very smart; he read my answer as a denial. I gestured to the uncomfortable upright and he sat down on it careful not to cut across the crease in his trousers.

'Coffee?' He nodded, and I buzzed Marion. I lit a cigarette before it arrived. He asked:

'Can I have one of those?'

He managed to get it alight with difficulty, laughing nervously:

'I don't usually smoke. Just occasionally.' I thought for a moment he was going to add I shouldn't tell daddy.

'Is it true, though?' I asked after Marion had been and gone.

'What?'

'That you're in debt?'

He flushed:

'Why have you been asking?'

I shrugged:

'Things I hear. Like, maybe, gambling?'

The colour drained from his face. I was sorry: he was much nicer to look at before.

'You don't like me, do you?' He said suddenly: 'You're trying to find something.'

I waited, without comment. It was news to me, but when people give me a headline, I like to hear the whole story.

'It's because of Katrina at the house, isn't it?'

I groaned inwardly: I'd asked her, and she denied it. Outwardly, I shrugged lightly as if it — whatever it was — didn't much matter to me.

'Look,' he said heatedly: 'I know things got out of hand. It was all a bit crazy. It wasn't my fault, honestly, you have to believe that. She didn't blame me. I talked to her about it, did she tell you that too?'

A lot of detection is like this. People think you already know something, so they tell you about it anyway. I held up a hand: if she hadn't wanted me to know, I didn't want to listen to the details. She had said she had never been to his house. He'd said enough for me to get the general idea why it was something she wanted to forget.

'I asked you about money. Specifically, gambling.'

He shifted so awkwardly in the seat, I wanted to reach over and re-arrange his trousers. Maybe I should introduce Lewis to him, as a reward for getting it right about the absent Mather.

'I gamble a little. I can afford it,' he said without conviction.

'Andrew,' I said gently: 'I'll level with you.' Why should I be different? Everyone else was lying to me. 'I don't think it's got anything to do with Kat's killing, But you've got to understand, I'm under a duty to your father to find out what's going on in this. firm, his firm. Money is a motive for leaking information. You understand me?'

He licked his lower lip:

'I'm not stupid. I understand. There's nothing I can tell you. Just, you're right, it's got nothing to do with Katrina's death ... Or the leaks,' he added hastily.

I shrugged:

'Fine. There's something you don't want to tell me, so bad you don't mind your father finding out you've got a gambling debt bordering five figures,' I wanted him to be certain I really did know and wasn't just guessing: 'That's OK with me. You sure it's OK with you?'

He shut his eyes for a moment, as if I'd hit him. When he opened them again, he nodded slowly, like someone unsure what he wanted, but who didn't really have a choice. Which left me wondering: what or who could scare him more than his father?

Russel Orbach was waiting for me at Frederick's. There was one advantage to staying with Sandy; sometimes, she'd let me borrow her car. Tonight, I had to take the tube. I was, of course, late.

He was already at the table, and deep in conversation with a small, dapper Jew he introduced to me as the owner. It wasn't the sort of establishment I imagined belonging to a Jew: the table was in the lower room, glass-encased, with trees growing up the middle. The wine waiter wore a medallion and poured like he was on-stage at the opera. The waiters were the real M'sieur Coy they were only imitating at Cafe Pelican. The menu contained more sea-food than the Chief Rabbi had banned, and the special of the fortnight was tongue, which I also recalled from my distant past was the wrong side of *frum* (orthodox).

We made what passed with Orbach as small talk during starters. He asked:

'What sewers are you scouring at present, Dave?'

I asked: 'D'you see much of Lady Keenan?' The eye of the Disraeli Chambers' storm.

He asked:

'What are you doing at Mather's?'

I asked:

'Get much work from them, do you?'

Suddenly, without forewarning, he said:

'A woman was killed at Mather's. You're investigating. Why would they call in a private detective of their own? Whatever happened isn't the first thing they're worried about. There haven't been any earlier deaths, at least that I know about. They're worried about something else. What worries a solicitor? Leaks. You want to talk to me about Westmoreland House. You want to know how we found out about the connection.'

I couldn't help myself: I stared at him in frank admiration. I was supposed to be the detective. My duty of confidentiality to my client prevented me confirming this accurate assessment, so I merely said:

'Not bad,' which did as well as 'yes'.

The waiter brought our main course. It gave me a breather during which to think of what to ask next. I needn't have bothered. He was in complete control.

'What makes you think I'd know?'

'Because you like to know everything.'

He cut into his pork and shook his head with equal energy: 'Wrong. Sometimes, if you know where information comes from, you can't use it, or you may owe a duty of disclosure to the court. So it may be positively necessary not to know.'

I'd forgotten: he might not have minded seeing a few of his colleagues wacked off, but he was riddled with professional integrity. I'd spent the evening before with Martin Mather, though, which wasn't a bad way to warm up for a round with Russel Orbach:

'You're not saying you don't know.'

He smiled: Orbach enjoyed the game much more than the outcome. His hair was darker than I remembered. And the beard which distinguished him from so many of his smooth-cheeked colleagues at the bar, where facial hair is frowned on. I asked about it.

'I had an operation, hiatus hernia. Do you know what that is?' I shook my head and he told me. It sounded appropriately vile. He went on: 'Anyway, as a side-effect, my hair started to grow darker. It was astonishing: I had dark roots and grey ends, as if I'd hitherto been dyeing my hair grey to look older. The consultant was delighted. He cut off some of it, so as to prove it hadn't been dyed.'

I hadn't noticed, but the owner was standing behind us, about to ask whether the meal was satisfactory.

Instead, he laughed merrily:

'That old story,' he said.

Orbach explained:

'That's how we know each other. We share a consultant. The best in the business.'

I thought: it's a long way for a radical lawyer to travel.

I meant him, not me: Frederick's; swopping medical stories with the owner and I didn't need to ask if it'd been on the National Health. He was inhabiting a different world than he used to, or than I was familiar with. But I dare say the Mathers would be totally at home here.

The owner sat down, invited by a movement of Orbach's left eye. I'm not sure what instinct made me ask, while he was still there:

'Are either of you a freemason?'

'Is,' Orbach corrected.

I scowled; Mather wasn't paying for Orbach to give me a lesson in grammar; no one was that rich.

The owner said:

'I used to be. Why?'

I shrugged and Orbach explained:

'My ... uh ... acquaintance is investigating a firm of solicitors with strong masonic links.'

'Oh, Mather's,' he said nonchalantly.

I was beginning to wonder why we bother to advertise ourselves as 'confidential'.

'What's Royal Arch freemasonry?' I asked.

I don't know if he would have told me or not, because at that precise moment the manager approached and whispered something in his ear which caused him to rise and apologize for leaving us. Unlike my question, it was probably something really important, like whether someone's beef was rare or not.

But Orbach answered:

'Freemasonry has two sides. There's the freemasonry everyone knows about, which is craft freemasonry and meets in Lodges, and there's Royal Arch freemasonry, which meets in

Chapters. About one in three craft freemasons is Royal Arch. Craft freemasonry has a lot of ritual, but it's nothing compared to Royal Arch, some of which borders on the black magic.'

'I take it the answer is "yes", you are a freemason?' I confess I was surprised, though I'm not sure more that he'd join or that they'd have him. He reassured me:

'No, I'm not.'

'You know a lot about it,' I accused, before I remembered that I was talking to someone to whom an allegation of knowing something he wasn't supposed to anything was a compliment. He explained:

'One of the London Borough Councils — Hackney conducted an inquiry into freemasonry. I did a job for them afterwards, and I had to read the report. Not because of freemasonry,' he added: 'I think. the man who conducted the inquiry concluded that if there was organized freemasonry in the Council, it had to be a good thing, because nothing else was organized. So he spent most of his time writing about their management: that was what I was concerned with. But I read the stuff about freemasonry, too. It interested me, and I read some other books about it later.'

I tried to focus on what he was saying, but accidentally he'd managed to extract a splinter from the conversation with Katrina. She had said that Andrew Mather reminded her of one of the left-wing Council leaders. Russel talking about Hackney told me which: its leader was the chubby-cheeked would-be chilling challenge to Thatcherism she'd had in mind. Another unnatural coincidence?

'You still haven't told me about Westmoreland House,' I reminded him.

'No more I have. And you still haven't told me why you think I might be willing to help you — this pleasant occasion aside, which will hardly equal the bill you'd get if you approached me formally.'

I said:

'Well, Russel, I know how interested you are in truth and fairness and things like that.'

He grinned disarmingly.

'For auld acquaintance?' I tried again.

He shuddered: old acquaintances, in his framework of reference, usually meant old enemies.

'Katrina was a friend of mind,' I said suddenly, thinking honesty might be the best policy. Even if it wasn't accurately an answer to his question, it was both true and the sort of information that might well lead even a cynic like Orbach to help.

I should have known better. He laughed:

'I haven't yet paid everyone off for all my own friends who got hurt; why should I bother with yours?'

There was no alternative but to level with him:

'I figured, you still wouldn't be too keen on the whole history of Disraeli Chambers making headlines.' If in doubt, blackmail; everyone's got something to hide.

'That's better,' he said huskily: 'I just wanted to hear you say it. I don't like hypocrisy, Dave, you know how much I don't like hypocrisy.' His view of his erstwhile colleagues at Disraeli Chambers as hypocrites — not, it must be said, a view without firm foundation — had led him, in substance if not in any form susceptible to a criminal charge, to orchestrate the demise of some of their number.

I knew now why he was willing to meet with me. Disraeli Chambers had been his most painful experience: while he was a member; and, later, when he took his revenge. He still couldn't let go of the experience. I was a part of it. It was still the time or the event during which he had felt most alive. He used to live — I recollected — with a woman who was now a Member of Parliament, Margot McAllister. He told me once they had separated because he didn't want all the interference in his private life that went with a public profile. I wondered how she felt: to have to take second place to a wound in all probability he had inflicted on himself.

I knew why he was a skilful lawyer, though. The way other people found themselves talking to me about things they — erroneously — believed I already knew, I found myself talking to him. I told him about the leaks — not in any detail, but enough for him to feel gratified that his analysis of what I was doing at Mather's was correct. I told him about the firm's freemasonry connections, about which he already knew. I told him about Randolph's way of demonstrating desire, and about Andrew's apparent addiction to the gaming table.

He told me, which I already knew from the files, that neither Andrew nor Randolph had anything to do with Westmoreland House. He told me, as was from the files also quite obvious, that the leak had to have come from Mather's. In other words, he told me nothing new. Then I asked him:

'Everything I hear says Ian Mather ain't a man to take kindly to a gambling habit. And there's more to it than a gambling debt, I'd swear. So what I want to know is, who is Andrew more frightened of than his father, so much so that he won't give me enough explanation to stop me running to Ian with the story?'

'Jabulon,' he said.

'Jabu-who?' I asked.

'Jabulon,' Russel Orbach repeated like he was telling me the time of day.

'And who, when he's at home, is Jabulon?'

'You asked me — or would have done so if you knew anything about grammar: of whom is Andrew Mather more frightened than his father, and I am telling you — Jabulon.'

'Fine. That tells me a whole bunch. So who is this Jabulon guy?'

'Jabulon,' he explained: 'Is the god of Royal Arch freemasonry ... Of course,' he added, as if it ought all along to have been obvious.

CHAPTER FIVE

'I'll wait in the car, shall I?'

I was hoping she'd agree. I don't like hospitals, hospices, homes or anything which suggests death, disease or decline.

I also had reason to expect to be told to stay in the car. A visit to meet one's ageing and unwell mother is an unconventional opening gambit between a man and a woman, whatever the basis of their encounter.

I was the man. The woman was Allison Mather Hoyt. For the last week, I had been trying to fix a time when we could meet. She was a busy lady, but finally, this very afternoon, she had said:

'I can see you this evening. I have to go to see my mother in the home.'

She said 'the home' as if I ought already to know about her mother's condition, which as a matter of fact I did.

'You can come with me, and we can talk afterwards. I'll buy you dinner. Alright?'

The words came out staccato: she was used to laying down the law, and to having her commands obeyed. I was tempted to tell her to piss off, but a number of things stopped me.

One was that it was becoming increasingly irritating that I hadn't yet managed to talk with her. Another was the nervous undertone I sensed beneath the assurance, which softened its blow to my pride. The third was: Allison Hoyt was — as Dowell had foreshadowed — a spectacularly gorgeous woman, and, surprising as this may sound, it is not often that a spectacularly gorgeous woman offers to buy me a meal.

We didn't talk much when we left High Holborn. She wove her sports Mercedes through the rush-hour traffic as if she was at Le Mans or maybe like Kojak after he reaches out to put the detachable siren on the lid of his car. The difference was: no one else was giving way. I spent most of the journey in a state of abject terror, tightening and re-tightening my seat belt, praying to a God I'd long since ceased to believe in. If the car-'phone rang, I decided I'd jump out: it would have to be safer.

The home was in North London, Whetstone or Finchley — somewhere out beyond the realms of good taste, in the Prime Minister's very own constituency. But for the sign which announced it as a 'medical nursing home', it could have been just one more of the generous houses set back from the road which reminded me of the sort of property I'd been brought up in: wealthy suburbia, leafy, clean, two cars to a drive and a nanny for every other child.

'No. Come up with me.'

'But ... I don't know your mother.'

She smiled grimly:

'She won't know you either.'

Her tone brooked no argument. I followed her in through the automatic, glass doors. As soon as we were inside the hallway, a glance to my right confirmed the Thatcher connection: a framed display of newspaper cuttings and correspondence recorded a visit the Prime Minister had paid to the home, a half dozen years before. My keen investigator's intelligence told me: this was a private home, not state-run.

Allison acted as if she owned the establishment. Maybe she did. Her mother's room was behind the first-floor nurses' station. I went in after her. The room was bright but boring: an iron-framed hospital bed sticking out from one wall, fitted utility wardrobe, plain painted wallpaper, there was a card-table in a corner on which had been set out portrait photographs of the family; by her bed, just a jug of water.

Her mother was white-haired and gaunt. Even covered by a sheet and blanket, she was evidently wasting away. She stared at the ceiling, and did not turn to greet her daughter, or move as Allison bent to kiss her taut forehead. Allison held a finger to her lips, to warn me not to speak. She pointed to a stool against the wall beside the window, opposite the foot of the bed. For herself, she selected a chair at the side of the bed.

We sat in a silence so loud I could hear my trepidation ticking over. Allison's mother was completely still; I could not see her breathe. Occasionally, she moved a muscle, or closed her eyes for a few moments. Once, she twitched, as if to throw off a fly I also could not see. After a while, Allison said:

'It's me.'

There was a long pause before her mother replied:

'It's no good. It's no good. What do you think?'

'I think it's no good, too.'

'You have to do it right.'

'There's no choice, mother,' Allison seemed to understand, even though I couldn't.

The hardest thing to take about her mother's nonsense was the physical strength and clarity of her speech. If she had spoken feebly, or perhaps with long pauses between individual words, it might have been less contradictory; it would have helped me keep in mind that she was past all recognizably rational life.

I watched Allison, rather than her mother. There was no mistake. She really was as good-looking as I'd thought. Tall, flaxen-haired, wide-mouthed, bright-eyed, dressed in a striped blouse and a light grey suit with high heels to match that looked fit to burst in the right places, and disappeared temptingly in others.

Though calm, there were tears in her eyes. I thought of my mother, long dead, taken by cancer many years before, comparatively young: I had cried then, and now I couldn't remember crying for her since.

'You've got ... The ... Numbers. What do you think?'

'I don't know what you mean, mother.'

'Well, you ought to know. It's your job to know.'

'Tell me again.'

'It doesn't matter. Go now. It's no good.'

'I've just arrived. I want to sit here for a while. I've brought someone to see you. He's a friend of Daddy's. He's a friend of the boys.'

'Go away. You're stupid. You ought to know.'

The thing that struck me most was: she was astonishingly beautiful. Her facial features were so clear, distinct, as fine as ever I had seen or studied. I was in the presence of death, but a slow and painful death, borne with a dignity I doubted I could achieve in full possession of my faculties, let alone, as she was, in possession of next to none. I knew Allison's mother was only in her late sixties or early seventies. She looked the way I'd always imagined those in their eighties or nineties would look.

We didn't stay long. It seemed like just a few minutes, though afterwards, when I glanced at my watch, I realized we'd sat there for more than half an hour. Her mother had little recognition of who Allison was, and I wondered why she came here — as I'd heard, most nights of the week — to suffer the torment of fundamental alienation, an uncrossable abyss. But as she leaned over her mother to kiss her good night, her mother smiled and it was easy to imagine how this alone made the visit worthwhile.

Then, when she whispered to her mother:

'I love you,' her mother replied:

'Me too.'

I didn't wait for Allison. I bolted down the stairs two at a bound, and rushed out into the car-park, gasping for air, fighting back tears, leaning finally against the car, my head resting on my sleeve. It brought everything back: my sister's 'phone call — 'come now, not much longer'; the three of us in the hospital ward; after, they'd cried, and I, to my ever-lasting shame, had walked away, not to let go until I reached home and could weep and weep and weep in private until the sobs came out dry. It had been as if there was nothing left between myself and infinity.

I think my tears made Allison's superfluous. She looked at me curiously, but didn't say anything while she unlocked the car, and slid behind the wheel, waiting for me to join her. I felt a fraud: I was supposed to be mister hard-boiled, and I'd just disclosed I was barely cooked.

We drove, as we'd started out from High Holborn, in silence, towards Highgate, where she lived. After I'd calmed down, I said, by way of explanation:

'My mother died.'

'Yes. I guessed. I'm sorry.'

'I'm sorry about yours, too. How long has it been?'

'A year like this, but two or three years in all. I keep thinking it can't be much longer. But her heart's as strong as an ox.'

'Is it always this bad?'

She laughed:

'Bad? That was good. She didn't hit me tonight. Sometimes, she's so violent they have to restrain her.'

'She's ... I hope you don't mind me saying this: but she's incredibly beautiful.'

'Yes,' she sighed: 'She was always a beautiful woman, but never so beautiful as now. It's so damn, damn unfair. Sometimes, I just can't cope with how unfair it is.'

She drove no less adventurously than before, though there was now little traffic on the roads. When we stopped at lights, she said:

'The hardest thing is: she knows. I mean, she knows she's alive, She knows she's in a bad way, she knows it's all gone — her life until now — and all she wants is to die. When it started, after we put her in the home, when she was more lucid than now, she told me so, she begged me to make it happen, there were two months when she simply wouldn't eat. They put her on an intravenous drip — I didn't want them to, I wanted them to let her go. But by the time I won the argument, and they took the drip out, her mind had deteriorated further, and with it her will — her will to die. Now I think she blames me, because I haven't helped her die, because I can't do anything to release her from ... It ... This.'

We pulled up at the Highgate Village Wheelers fish restaurant. Like magic, there was space outside, which she seemed to take for granted — a lady for whom magic happened all the time. She'd booked a table: they knew who she was, no one asked her name, the manager greeted her warmly. He led us to our table and asked whether we wanted a drink before our meal.

Allison shook her head:

'Wine with it.'

It was time for self-assertion:

'I'll have a large Southern Comfort. No ice. No soda.'

'I've heard you're a drinker,' she was polite enough to wait until the manager had departed to investigate my peculiar order before she made her comment.

'I've heard you ain't,' was my less than witty riposte.

'What else have you heard?'

'That you're an extremely hard-working solicitor, very clever, so clever that you might have made partner even if you weren't who you are. And I've heard it said there are people who've been with the firm long enough to remember you once smiled, though nobody's putting money on it.'

She had to fight not to lose the bet:

'I don't see a lot to smile about, do you?'

'Yes, sure. You're a lovely woman, you're rich, you drive a Mercedes, you're having dinner with me — hell, what've you got to complain about?'

The waiter hovered; we ordered fish; she ordered wine.

'Does it make you feel nervous. Mr Woolf? Being taken out by a woman, I mean?'

'Nope. It makes me nervous being called mister, though.'

'What do people call you normally? Hey, you?'

'On a good day. Waddayawant the rest of the time. Try Dave. I promise it won't bite.'

She examined me curiously, much as she had outside the nursing home.

'I've heard a lot about you, too, Dave.'

I waited. We were on my favourite subject. She made me beg. 'So, tell.'

'Let's see now. I've heard you were kicked out of your previous practice by your partner — Sandra Nicholl — because you were too stoned to know what time of day it was. I've heard you've been scratching a living as a private detective and but for the debacle at Disraeli Chambers would probably be waiting outside someone's home right now trying to serve them with a divorce summons.'

She paused to take stock, then continued:

'I've heard you're supposed to be some sort of left-winger, but can't decide which. I've heard you're now having a scene with your ex-partner, but can't resist hopping into bed with anything in skirts.'

I winced at that, but could guess the source: the late and momentarily less lamented Katrina Pankhurst. She continued blithely:

'I've heard Randolph was so pissed off about your appoint-ment he actually came in on time, to try and talk my father out of it, and Andrew dared contradict Iron Ian for the first time since he stopped wetting his pants. Martin says he quite likes you and doesn't give a damn, but if the other two care that much about it and the money's right, he wouldn't mind handling a contract on your life.'

As she spoke and gathered pace, she finally gave way and grinned:

'It must be nice to be so popular, Dave.'

'I dunno. I never had occasion to find out,' I sighed: 'How come Martin'd take the contract? He need the money?'

'No. But he's awfully into that sort of butch pastime, haven't you noticed?'

'I gather he doesn't hang out in seedy, Earl's Court gay-bars. But that doesn't say much.'

'I feel closest to Martin, though that doesn't mean much. Andrew's the one who comes to talk to me most: cry on big sister's shoulder. But I don't see much of any of them — socially, I mean, we work together a lot. You've probably realized by now that feelings aren't high on the Mather family agenda. We don't talk much other than work. And I don't know if Martin realizes he's the only one I actually care about. Did you know he goes to a gym three nights a week?'

'Yup. He thinks I ought to do the same,' I added wryly: 'Seems to think I ain't fit,' I patted the Sahara of my stomach.

She examined me critically:

'He may have a point.'

I shrugged:

'It's hard enough work just staying drunk, y'know?'

For only the second time, she smiled:

'Yes, I'm finding out.'

Contrary to what I'd said I'd heard, or perhaps for that reason alone, she'd drunk more of the first bottle of wine than me. Reading my thoughts, she signalled the waiter to bring us another.

We'd finished the main course, and I slouched back in my seat:

'Why've you been giving me the run-around at work?'

'Why not? I hadn't made up my mind what use you were to me.'

'Lady, you got balls. You're supposed to be use to me, not the other way around. Anyhow, how come you found out all that shit about me?'

She shrugged:

'Second nature. D'you ever think of this: I'm a Mather; I'm his child as much as they are; and Randolph's been married, and Andrew's still married, and I've been married, but I'm the only one who gets to change her name, and now nobody even knows I'm a Mather anymore. You know, the old Avis line: we try harder.'

'What happened to Hoyt?'

'He was a bastard. I still spend at least ten minutes every day wondering why I married him, and then the same again wondering how come so many of my friends married shits just like him. I figured finally: there's a lot of truth in Freud; we're all looking for our fathers; and our fathers were all shits. Maybe fatherhood is just a shitty idea: it's a pretty fundamentally oppressive relationship — parent and child, 'specially a father and his children, don't you think?'

She'd poured and drunk the first glass out of the new bottle as soon as it was set down on the table. I didn't mind being asked and taken out by a woman, but I minded one who could drink more than me. My bladder was full but I was scared that if I got up to empty it, I might miss the best part of the programme.

'I try not to think about it. I know I wouldn't want children ...'

'Why not?'

'Hell, I don't know. They might grow up to be like me. That's a good enough reason, isn't it? You didn't have any children with Hoyt, did you?'

'No and for the same reason. They might've grown up to be like him. Or me. Ah, shit, I'm drunk, you know that don't you, Woolf? Is that what you're waiting for? To get me pissed so I'll spill all the family secrets — or the firm's — which is the same thing. Or are you trying to get me into bed?'

'You didn't tell me what happened to Hoyt,' I avoided her questions, mostly because I still didn't know which was true.

She sneered at my cowardice, and got up:

'Back in a minute', she slurred.

I'll tell you — in the interval — what I sometimes think is the true reason I can't settle down with Sandy. It's embarrassing, because it's so shallow. But. I love legs. I don't mean Sandy hasn't got good legs: she has excellent legs. But she's short, and they're short, and when I mean I love legs what I mean is I love long legs. Legs like Mather's secretary's legs. Legs like someone you're sitting opposite on the train and you start at the high heels and your eyes climb up her tights until they disappear and all you want to do is follow.

Legs like Allison Hoyt's, as I watched her weave her way across the restaurant, wishing I could go with. I was thinking about this so hard, I forgot to take the opportunity to go to the toilet myself.

The waiter hovered:

'Will you be requiring dessert, sir?'

I didn't require dessert, but I wanted dessert. On the other hand, I didn't know if Allison wanted dessert. At this particular moment, I figured our relationship was decidedly rocky. Was it worth risking what might be left of it by making the wrong decision? I ordered profiteroles, for both of us.

'Give me a cigarette and I'll tell you what happened to Hoyt,' she said as she sat down again.'

'I didn't know you smoked,' I pushed over to her the pack of Camels I'd left out on the table.

'I don't. Just once in a while,' she said, just like her kid brother.

'Tell me about Hoyt, then,' I said when she'd finally — and with difficulty — got the cigarette properly alight.

'He was a salaried solicitor at Mather's, and if we'd stayed together then he'd probably've become a partner. When things started to fall apart, my father saw him and told him it wouldn't make any difference in the firm. Then Randy saw him, and told him he might as well start looking for a job. Then Martin saw him, and suggested he make a will before it was too late. Then Andrew saw him, and offered to find the money for him to set up in practice somewhere else.'

'And he did which?'

'Well, the only real choices were trust my father, or trust Andrew. He trusted Andrew. So Andrew helped him just like he said he would. He found someone else looking for a partner and Hoyt went quiet as a mouse to his firm.'

'And?'

'And then they all set to work. Hoyt and his partner started the firm with a thirty thousand pound injection of capital, Hoyt's share of which was borrowed, and an overdraft limit of twenty thousand pounds. A year later, they needed an overdraft of fifty thousand. A year after that, they needed an overdraft of a hundred thousand. Every time they got a new client, they lost two others.'

She paused to savour the story, then continued:

'By the time it was over, Alex personally owed the bank a hundred and eighteen thousand. Then — and only then — did we start to discuss the divorce. He's working at the Law Society now, earning maybe sixteen-eighteen thousand, and living in a one-bedroom flat in would you believe it Finsbury Park.'

Her eyes shone, not with pleasure but excitement:

'We Mathers, we have our own special little way, y'know?'

'And what's your own special way mean for me, then?'

She took her time selecting a reply. I watched her swirl them round like a selection of the finest dresses on a rotating rack in a store.

The waiter gave her time to think. He delivered the profiteroles pompously, with a performance so riveting it wasn't until after he left that she asked:

'What are these for?'

'I ordered what I wanted. I'll have yours.'

If I'd been asked to guess beforehand what her answer was going to be to my question, it wouldn't've come out as it did:

'You wanna sleep with me, Woolf?'

This time, she left no room for me to avoid the proposition. I stuffed the last of my profiteroles into my mouth, and pulled her plate towards me.

I don't think my hesitation pleased her. She expected the same. obedience in her personal life as professionally.

I chose my words exactly, with the sort of attention to caring detail that only committed self-interest could secure:

'Yes. And. No. I think you're extremely good-looking, very sexy, and physically there's not much more I'd rather do than go to bed and play with you. On the other hand, you're a pain in the arse, ruder than I am, and care even less how much damage you do to a person's feelings. For a relationship, I'd probably take the chance; for a screw, I'd rather jerk off.'

As I spoke, the blood drained out of her face, and the resemblance to her mother became more marked. There were no smiles left at the dinner table. She bit her lower lip, to stop herself showing hurt. Inside, I screamed out to apologize, touch her, comfort, explain I'd had to say all that to get clear of the clutter and confusion by which our evening had been marred. Instead, I grit my teeth, rose, bowed mockingly, and said:

'I'm pig enough already not to hang out with other pigs. We might suit each other, but we don't need each other.'

I left, proud of my resolve, calculating that as and when Sandy and I got back together, I could turn it into something she'd be proud of me for, and regretting I hadn't had the time to finish my second dessert.

I was still waiting for a taxi when she came out. At first, she ignored me, and unlocked her car as if I was no more than a passing member of the dirty raincoat brigade. She couldn't carry it off, though, and instead of getting in behind the wheel, she turned and dangled the keys:

'I'm too drunk to drive. Will you take me home?'

I shook my head, not to say 'no', but meaning it wasn't a good enough apology.

'You're right, Woolf, you are a pig. I'm sorry I'm one too. Will you please take me home?'

She reached inside the car and inserted the key into the ignition. Then she walked around it as stilted and careful as a drunk, and settled herself into the passenger seat.

She lived in a characterless, but modern and probably expensive apartment development near enough she could have walked if she was really worried about her ability to drive. There were half a dozen low-rise blocks, surrounded by a low wall, flat-roofed, insipid red-bricked, aluminium windows, entry-phones, pallid plants, turfed plots, a handful of lock-up garages and signs which said 5 m.p.h. and which I ignored. I parked at the back, contradicting an instruction to 'Leave Garage Doors Clear.'

At first, she headed for a door, then she swung around and pointed up a grass bank:

'Go on, lead the way.'

I did as bid, though not without stumbling badly enough to stain the trousers of the new suit I'd bought in anticipation of Mather's money. She took off her heels before she clambered up after me.

'Where are we going?' I whispered.

It was an adventure. A trespass. Children exploring an abandoned house.

'This way.'

Beyond the apartments, in the middle of the gardens, was a fenced-off section. She held a finger to her lip, as she had done in her mother's room, but in entirely different vein. At the gate, she fiddled for the right key, unlocked it and held it open for me, before pushing it gently back behind us, reaching through the bars to close the padlock.

It was a swimming pool. She took me to the end furthest from the apartments, and sat down on the grass, pulling me down beside her.

'It didn't used to be fenced,' she said quietly: 'But a couple of years ago, some people went for a midnight dip — and a bit more. The older residents didn't like it, so they fenced it off a few days later.'

'Local kids?' I asked idly, wondering when and if she was going to let go of my hand.

She giggled:

'They thought.'

She stood up, still holding my hand so I had to do the same. She pulled me up and pressed herself against me snaking her free hand around the back of my neck until, all arguments aside, my lips met hers and we kissed open-mouthed and wet, like guzzling ice-cold water on a boiling hot day. She stepped back as suddenly as it had begun, letting go my hand, pushing my head away so she could see into my eyes, as puzzled and as curious and as wounded as if I had grabbed her.

Before I could protest my innocence, though, she had stripped off the jacket of her suit and let it fall on the ground. I was still wondering what her game was as she unbuttoned her blouse and peeled it off proudly revealing full breasts held up by a half-bra. Then the bra came off.

'Come on,' she hissed: 'You too.'

She didn't wait to see if I did as I was told, but lowered herself into the water, drawing in her breath sharply at the cold.

It brought back a memory, so old and in parts so revealing, that I'd conveniently managed not to think about it for several years.

In my early twenties, keen and unfulfilled, I'd met a woman in a Mayfair coffee bar and we'd talked and talked until the early hours of the morning. Gawky and unsure, I'd said to her as we left:

'Let's walk through the Park.'

There were no barriers to prevent access to Hyde Park; just a low fence a midget could've stepped over. We walked, occasionally hand in hand, down to the Serpentine Boating Lake. When we reached the hut from which boats were hired out I invited her:

'Let's go round,' thinking maybe I'd score a kiss or cop a feel. As soon as we were standing on the wooden jetty she cried: 'Come on,' pulling her dress over her head and diving into the water before I realized my luck.

I followed. We swam out first towards one of the tiny islands, but were scared off by cackling geese. Instead, we swam to the middle of the lake where the rental boats were moored for the night. I climbed into one and it was her turn to follow me. Scared, I said to her — little realizing how commanding I must have sounded:

'Lie down,' so we shouldn't be seen.

She obeyed; I did the same; I slipped a hand under her head, to protect it from the hard and wet deck. After that, I couldn't have cared less any longer whether or not we were seen from the shore.

It is the postscript to this tale that embarrasses. A few weeks later, I was in the same coffee lounge, chatting to — or up — another woman. I can't remember the first one's name, but this second one was Lindsay. When we left at closing time, I said:

'Let's walk through the Park.'

With markedly less enthusiasm than I or my previous night-walking companion, she agreed. I wasn't worried. I knew the magic formula.

'Let's go round,' I said when we reached the boathouse.

This time, I had to take the lead:

'Come on in, it's fine,' I called from the water.

Hesitantly, Lindsay did so. I didn't bother with the island, but swam direct to the cluster of boats in the centre and, equally single-minded and determinedly, clambered in to one.

She swam around the boats, hung onto mine with one hand, but refused to climb in with me. Eventually, I gave up my desperate design and, frustrated, jumped out. The oarlock went straight into my armpit, so fast and so hard I hardly felt it. Clutching my arm to my side instinctively, the way a chicken without its head carries on twitching for several minutes more, I doggie-paddled single-pawed to the shore.

Back on the jetty, Lindsay helped me dress, and took me to St George's Hospital. I was dazed and still unsure just what had happened. They cleaned me up, and gave me a shot of SPentothal. My only recollection of the hospital is of the doctor saying:

'If it had gone an inch deeper, you would have lost the use of your arm for life. But that wouldn't have been long, because you would have bled to death by the time you got to shore.'

Lindsay walked me home — to the same rented, basement apartment I still occupy — and assisted me into bed, bringing me a hot milk drink to see me off to sleep. I have no memory of her leaving, only that as I lay there, still under the drug, and she sat at my side, I said:

'It's too late for you to go home. Why don't you stay the night?'

There were no boats in the swimming pool at Allison Hoyt's estate. No boats, but Allison floating, teasing, encouraging me to sink my overweight body into the uninviting cold, night water.

I shook my head:

'Uh-huh. You can catch a cold if you want, I've money to make in the next few days.'

Eventually, she realized I was not going to give in. Sulkily, she climbed out and slipped on her blouse and skirt without bothering to try and dry herself off. Without a word, she let us out of the enclosure and we slid back down the grass bank, landing close to where I'd left her car. We stood there for a moment, each hesitating for different reasons.

I didn't want to go inside. I knew what might happen, and how difficult it would be to put up any resistance. She was as appetizing stripped for service as the description in the menu. But it still felt wrong.

On the other hand, I'd hardly endeared myself to her so far and willing though I'd been to walk out when she gave me the excuse in the restaurant, she had apologized. If I now left her in this ambiguous position, I'd be the one at fault.

I can only guess at her reasons. Torn between persisting with the play she had initiated in Wheelers and pushed further at the poolside, or accepting — with whatever ill-grace she could muster — the apparent rejection. But after all, I'd only refused to join her in the water, so I wasn't that surprised when she tossed her head towards a back door into the block.

'Come on,' she hissed: 'I'm freezing.'

Her apartment was locked up like a New Yorker's, with three different bolts before we could get in. It was a surprisingly small flat: the entry lobby was the dining area off which led doors to the kitchen, the living-room and a short inner lobby which gave onto two further rooms and bathroom. She told me to go into the living-room and pour myself a drink:

'Me too. Brandy.'

There was no Southern Comfort. I had to make do with Drambuie. I could hear the shower running in the other half of the apartment. I wondered if she was waiting for me to bring her drink through: I'd already seen all she had to offer, but inside would be that much more intimate.

She didn't bother dressing. She curled up in her bathrobe on the sofa. I was safely ensconced in a matching armchair. She was the first to break the long silence:

'You gay?' she slurred.

I grinned:

'Not that I'm aware of. It's like a man saying a woman who won't sleep with him is frigid, isn't it?'

She inclined her head graciously:

'Fair enough. But you were turned on downstairs,' when we'd kissed: 'Is it Sandy Nicholl? Or scared of AIDS?'

I lit a Camel:

'If the Big C don't get you, the Big A will.'

'We could use something,' she made her final offer. She — correctly — read my silence on Sandy to mean I'd brushed her first question aside as not worth answering. 'No. It's not that. I'm not really scared of AIDS' I laughed nervously: 'More like scared of you.'

She savoured this admission for a while:

'That's the damn problem. You all are. I'm surrounded by men who're afraid of me, sexually. It's sexist. Like, if I'm a successful lawyer, I can't possibly have enough left to be a successful woman too.'

'Maybe,' I shrugged: 'But you already told me what happened to the last guy that got involved with the boss' daughter.'

'You're not going to stay, are you.' It wasn't a question; more like an accusation.

I shook my head again:

'Nope. Sorry. You must know part of me wants to.' I was finding it increasingly difficult to hold hard to my resolve: 'I've got to go. I'll pick up a cab on the street. Really, I'm sorry. Maybe, some other time,' I tailed off lamely.

She followed me to the door, biting her lower lip, holding her bathrobe tightly together. At the door, she took my hand:

'We wouldn't have to do anything,' she seemed on the verge of tears: 'Can't you see? I'm lonely. I'm scared.'

It still felt too close to a command for comfort.'

'I know. We all are,' I said as I opened the door.

CHAPTER SIX

I was an inch out the door when she accused:
'Just like you walked out on Kat.'

I froze. I said, without turning:

'I didn't walk out. I wanted to stay. She made me leave.'

But I was not telling the whole truth and she had made her point so I pushed the door shut with me on the inside.

'You have to level with me. If I'm going to help, you have to tell me what you know. Do you understand?'

She bit her lower lip and nodded. She crossed the room and put her arms right around me and hugged me and said:

'Later. Please.'

After all the come-ons and turn-downs of the evening, I was in no condition any longer to refuse. I let her lead me by the hand to the bedroom, where she turned down the cover of the bed and climbed in quickly, like a little girl waiting for daddy to kiss her goodnight.

At the time, it seemed like it went on for ever, far longer than I knew it or I could. When finally we had finished, we lay there, drenched in sweat, gasping for breath and holding on tight, relieved we hadn't drowned.

After a while, she let go and sat up beside me. I was drifting off to sleep. When I awoke, an hour or so later, I was alone. I could hear her taking another shower. She didn't return to bed. Instead, she made us each a cup of tea, and we sat in the living-room, she in her bathrobe, me with a towel wrapped around my waist, talking the way we should have spent the evening talking but I was glad we hadn't.

'Tell me who else knows.'

'Knows what?' She asked dully.

'Knows you leaked the report.'

'How did you know?'

'I figured it out. That's my job. There were precious few people who qualified for plumber of the year award. You were one. The money motive didn't hold: the plaintiffs were relatively poor people, represented by solicitors on legal aid who wouldn't ethically be able to pass on a bribe even if the parents collectively had the cash. The odds against finding one parent, with enough money for a bribe, prepared to shell out and share rather than make a private deal, are infinite.

'For a long time, I concentrated on the freemasons: they're supposed to be into sharing secrets, aren't they? But it wouldn't add up: you'd have to find two good freemasons — one either side — and that was hardly likely.

'Then there was the notion of some sort of grudge motive, but that had to mean whoever it was wanted to see Latimer walk out on Mather's which wouldn't tie up with who had the opportunity. None of you would want that: it's a lot of regular money on account to say good-bye to. Besides, I said to Kat, it's a classic case for a bleeding heart leak. Once I started thinking that way, it narrowed down the field: I'm not sure any of your brothers have got a heart, and John Gauldie's belongs to freemasonry alone. I was looking for a connection to a deformed child.'

I swallowed my tea: 'But it's all the same, isn't it? Deformed child needing constant care and attention. Mother beyond all reason in hospital. They're just different forms of disability, which make life hell both for those who suffer from it, and for those who have to look after them ...'

'We had the money,' she interrupted: 'Most of those parents didn't. Imagine what it's been like for them. Especially the women, the ones who have to do the day-to-day caring.'

'I'm not criticizing you did it, Ali. I might've done it. But I need to know who knows.' I'd already guessed the answer by the time she said, flatly:

'Only Katrina knew.'

'And that's why you're scared?'

She shrugged but didn't reply.

'What you haven't told me, why do you think there's a connection?'

'I don't know there is. But Katrina was scared. She told me she was; she told you so.'

'Now you tell me,' I insisted gently.

And so she did. She told me the bits and pieces she had picked up not merely over the last two or three years, but back in the family and the firm history. It was the account of a child, still trying to work out why grown-up life wasn't as much fun as she'd been brought up to expect.

She told me about her Uncle James, who she had never met and of whom her father would not speak. From her mother she drew a picture of a man who scorned the rules by which everyone else had to live, and who viewed his younger half-brother with a mixture of amused contempt and patronizing protection. A man who might one day turn up at dinner-time, uninvited, and remain for the evening, eating and drinking everything that was available, but that had been laid out for everyone else. On another, he would take them out to expensive restaurants, insisting that even the young child Randolph eat the very best.

She knew from her mother, too, that her father had mixed feelings about James. James was older. He had known a time when their own father was not so wealthy, when they had still been living in Glasgow, until after Ian's father's second marriage, to Ian's mother. When they moved south, Ian was still living at home, but James took off on his own, in and out of one venture after another.

Ian had served in the war, with distinction; James had secured a medical deferment on unknown grounds that were probably corrupt. Afterwards, when Ian and John Gauldie set up the firm, James was their first, and for a while best, client: it was the time when the brothers saw the most of each other. They were very close, and Ian would not hear a word against James.

One day, Ian had come home, silent and brooding. Ali's mother had known beforehand that there were problems concerning James, but in those days, and given the sort of relationship she had with Ian, she had been told nothing about them. Shortly after, James disappeared and when Ali's mother brought up his name, she was told to forget him, to forget he had ever existed.

Naturally, to the children as they were born and grew up enough to acquire a scent of the story, it was exciting, rich terrain for the imagination: a spy, lost in foreign parts, imprisoned for service to his country or at the other extreme for crimes too unpleasant to mention. Randolph affected the superiority of the only one who 'knew' his uncle, but it was a pose: James had gone when Randolph was four or five years old.

'I've heard,' I offered: 'That he maybe wasn't honest.'

'I know.'

'How?'

'Martin. Martin went to the States when finally he qualified. It was his treat, his reward.' After the long route to qualification.

'How did they meet?'

'I don't know much. I know my father made him promise not to look for James, and I know Martin met him. He'd never tell me, except he insisted he hadn't broken his promise, so it must have been an accident or a coincidence.' She no more believed it than I was supposed to. 'He only said he's very rich and that he — Martin — realized it wasn't all honest. But he said James was beginning to put his money into legitimate activities.'

I pushed a little further:

'I've also heard ... Perhaps, violent?'

She frowned:

'Where did you hear that? Martin's never ...'

'No, not Martin. Someone else. Don't forget,' I said: 'I'm supposed to be a detective.'

'Was it Dowell?'

'Why'd'you ask that?'

'I don't know. I just get a feeling about him. Like he knows more than he lets on.' She was probing me.

My turn to shrug:

'Maybe. He's no fool. A long way from. D'you know he has a law degree?' She shook her head, uninterested. 'He shouldn't be underestimated. I've made that mistake.' A mistake that saved my life. 'Anyway, what's to hide?'

She wasn't really listening. She was starting a whole new train of thought. She said:

'I don't trust John Gauldie.' She said, and stopped, needing a prompt.

'Why?'

'There's something devious about him. Sometimes I think he hates my father.'

'I thought freemasons are supposed to be about brotherly love?'

'Sometimes I think he's trying actively to undermine my father. Randolph looks up to him more than he looks up to father: he's influenced Randolph more than father has, and much more than father realizes. That makes it true of Andrew as well. My father is much, much the better lawyer, intellectually, but John has always conducted the greater share of the litigation. He's tactical: they admire that more than they admire father's type of law. But it goes beyond that: there's a loyalty to Gauldie that transcends even their loyalty to my father.'

'They've been partners for ever. Surely ...'

'No, no, you're wrong.' When she shook her head to emphasize her point, she was even more beautiful. It was hard to continue the conversation instead of bringing her back to bed. 'Of course he never says anything. But I've seen the way he looks at my father sometimes. He's a thousand miles away and he's not listening but he's thinking and what he's thinking is how much he wants to be the senior partner, how he doesn't want to have to account for himself to anyone else, how he wants it to be his firm.'

'He must own a major slice?'

'Not that big. It was always my father's money, from his father — maybe from James, too. Probably not actual cash; probably just from his work. He brought all his 'business associates'. I've looked in some of those old files, right back to the fifties, and they're fascinating. Hundreds have a file note: referred by James Mather. If you include them, he was our biggest client before Latimer. But Gauldie handled almost all of them, while my father chased the better class of client, the old masonic families, the banks in the city, established companies.'

'How well do you know Latimer?'

'Not very. He's a remote figure. I've met him, of course; he's very charming. He got his start in this country, did you know that?' I nodded. It was all I did know about him. 'We did all his early work, and it just grew and grew. One of our solicitors went to work full-time for him.'

'A partner?'

'No. Initially, there were only four partners. One died young, and the other retired a couple of years ago. That's why Randolph's third in line — which is a big gap from John Gauldie.'

'What about Latimer?'

'John Gauldie's always handled his work, like he did my uncle's; well, for years now with Randolph. But if there's any issue — oh, I don't know, like over money, fees, the way a case has been conducted, a really major decision — Latimer won't talk to anyone except my father. That's who he really trusts, even though it's John who's done all the work. I think that's what John resents. He's nearly sixty, but so far as the firm's principal client is concerned, he might as well be Ian's articled clerk.' I knew the feeling.

'So why doesn't your father allow him a greater share, or a greater say?'

'He relies on people, but he doesn't really trust anyone, father, not anyone.'

'Not Martin?' I could understand him not trusting Randolph. But Martin was supposed to be the favourite.

'He's never approved of Martin's investment company and even now Martin's not especially involved in it, he resents it.'

'What do you know about it?'

It kept cropping up, in the background and sometimes in the main frame too. I'd sensed its relevance when Kat had talked to me; then. Dowell had referred to it; and Martin had produced Tony Galucci like a heavy hint.

She smiled:

'Do you know the origin of the name?'

'No.'

'It's Katrina. It was a childhood nickname of Katrina's.. The person who runs Cross Course Beatrix Kelly — well, she's Katrina's sister.'

I said:

'I don't get the name.'

'I don't know how it started. Beat is Katrina's older sister and it was something silly she called Katrina when she was tiny but that stuck. Maybe because she was always cross or always chose the difficult path or something like that. Originally, the company was Martin's, and it was called something else — I don't remember what. Beat had been in America, then she came back and went to work with Martin, which is how Martin met Katrina and how when she finished her finals she got offered articles with us.'

'Did Martin know Beat in America?'

'I don't think so.'

'And Galucci?'

'He was a business contact of Martin's, which is how Katrina met him.'

I shook my head:

'You people certainly believe blood's thicker than water.'

She didn't reply. Just stared at me as tears welled up and began to flow down her cheeks. It wasn't, perhaps, the most tactful way of putting my point. I went over and sat beside her, putting my arm around her shoulder, stroking her hair.

'Ali,' I said gently, anticipating that the end of the conversation was approaching: 'Are you telling me all you know?'

'I don't know anymore; I don't know what's relevant.'

'What about Andrew. How much is he involved in everything?'

'Everything. what?' She sniffed, pulling away. She got up and walked to the cabinet, from which she extracted the Drambuie bottle I'd damaged earlier. She held it up. I'd never refused before and could see no reason to start now.

Her question wasn't looking for an answer. She was saying I had no better idea what 'everything' was than she said she had.

I tried on her the same as on Martin:

'Maybe he's got money troubles.'

'Why? What makes you say that? What do you know?' She asked all in a bundle.

'I hear he gambles.'

She snorted:

'Tuppence halfpenny.'

'You sure?'

'Sure I'm sure. He likes the glamour — or she does; they like the late nights and the bright lights and the beautiful people with money to burn; but he's as Scot as the rest of us.'

Next morning, she dropped me off at home so I could change before I came into the office; neither of us wanted to be seen arriving together. My home was full of surprises: post that wasn't all bills, and a flashing answering machine. The machine hadn't seen so much activity since six debt collectors tried to contact me on the same day.

One of the calls was from Dowell: he'd be in to see me at Mather's at eleven. He sounded terse, less than friendly. The hour was odd: the pubs still wouldn't be open, even in the city. Another call was from Sandy, repeating that she wanted to talk with me: it was important. The letter that had attracted my attention as soon as I came through the door was addressed in a small, neat hand, in an embossed envelope. I extracted a single sheet, only a small part of which had been written on, in the same economical hand:

'The settlement allowed the landlords six months to find the money. We had to agree because they would otherwise have gone into liquidation; it wasn't certain we would get the money at all. They did pay, but a few weeks later someone bought the company — very cheaply, I hear. The question is: who? R.O.'

Signing himself with his initials was not an affectation: while an ordinary barrister signs his full name to a written opinion, a QC signs only initials.

I was not especially surprised to hear from him: I had not expected him to let it end with our dinner. Like Lewis, he had still to prove that he knew something others didn't know. I had a good idea what I would find out when I looked into who bought the landlord company: the same name that kept cropping up, Cross Course, was, I figured, bound to feature somewhere in the transaction. Later on, Dowell willing, I'd go down to Companies House and read me some records.

I made it into the office just in time for Dowell. I passed Allison on the stairs. Out of anyone else's hearing, she said:

'Are we going to meet tonight?'

'Sure, if you'd like to.'

'Maybe it would be a good idea for me to come to your place.'

'Why? It's really not very nice.'

'I just thought, well, I've got the car, and … You get a better idea about someone from where they live.'

I wasn't sure she'd like the ideas she'd get about me from my basement. But she had a point when she mentioned the car. I compromised:

'Whyn't we say you'll pick me up, and then we'll stay where seems best?' We agreed she'd come over after the nursing home, which meant around half past nine.

The brief exchange reminded me I had yet to return Sandy's call: I couldn't go on avoiding her forever. The trouble was, I still didn't know how I wanted a conversation to turn out; Ali wasn't making it easier to decide.

Marion buzzed me Dowell was on his way up: I asked for coffee for two. She said she'd already offered, but he had refused. She took it I still wanted mine. I told her she took it correct and I'd take it — and his — black. As I hung up, he came in. He had one of his men with him. I didn't know him: they all look alike to me.

"Morning, Tim,' I said, cheerful with cause: 'I gather you don't want any coffee. Sure?'

'Certain, thank you, sir,' he said more formal than since the first time we ever met. I hate it when people call me 'sir'; I know it can't be real respect, so it has to be sarcasm.

'This is Detective Constable Pratt. He'll be taking a note of our discussion.' He looked at me defiantly, daring me to make a joke about the officer's name. If my coffee had arrived to wake me up, I probably would have.

'The trouble is, Tim,' I said, incapable of calling him 'officer' or 'Inspector': 'There's only room for one extra chair.'

'So I see,' he said slowly and mournfully: 'Pratt will have to stand, then.'

I thought I saw a twinkle buried deep in one eye. He had seen the office at the same time I had; he knew as well as I did it couldn't take two spare chairs. He didn't mind Pratt having to stand. It made it a little easier for me to pretend to behave seriously.

'What can I do for you?'

'I was wondering if you have spent any time down in the basement, sir?'

I frowned: how did he know that?

I nodded.

'When?'

I told him.

'And how long were you there?'

'Maybe half an hour; maybe a bit more and then again maybe a bit, less. Why?'

'If you'd just answer my questions, sir. Are you quite sure that you might not have been there for somewhat longer?'

'Sure I'm sure,' I'd picked up the expression from Ali.

'Did you smoke while you were down there?'

'There's a no smoking sign.'

'Yes, sir. And did you obey it, sir?' I winced: he was laying on the 'sirs' with a trowel.

'Of course I didn't bloody obey it, Tim. What's all this about?'

The no-smoking school is vicious, unfair and utterly sadistic. In the good old days, it was much more democratic: we all got a little bit ill every day, those of us who smoked only marginally more so than those who enjoyed, free of charge, the second-hand benefits. Now, there are no smoking signs every place you go. The effect on an inveterate smoker is inevitable: it is a constant reminder of an addiction which makes you want to light up another, long before you would otherwise have done so.

Dowell opened his briefcase and — at precisely the moment Marion Mortimer brought in my coffees — extracted a polythene evidence bag, containing a large number of half-smoked butts. He swung it distastefully across the desk at me and asked:

'You recognize the brand, I take it, sir.' Camels.

Marion put my coffees down, wrinkling her nose:

'Disgusting habit, I say.'

She removed my ashtray from the desk and waved it dramatically in front of my face before dumping the contents unceremoniously into the metal trash-can behind my seat, sending up a cloud of ash. I sighed; it was going to be one of those days. There was only one plausible reaction: I lit a Camel and blew smoke at them.

After she had left, Dowell asked:

'Do you think these might be yours sir?'

'You gotta be kidding. I can't afford to smoke that many in a half hour. Nor can I afford to waste half of them.'

He sighed:

'Very well, sir. That's all I have to ask you at the moment.'

He turned to his assistant:

'That will be all, Pratt. Wait for me downstairs, will you?'

'Right, guv.'

I pulled a face behind his back as he left:

'Do people really do that?'

'What?'

'Call you "guv"? Like on The Sweeney.' The Sweeney = Sweeney Todd = Flying Squad; back in the seventies, when the occasional British television production was still worth watching.

'That one studied The Sweeney instead of going to school. He's perfectly named,' he scowled.

'So what was all that about?'

'Just what it seemed. You're the only one here smokes Camel. We found about ten, twelve butts. I had to establish if they were yours.'

'What if I'd said they were?'

'Then it wouldn't have suggested that someone hid out down there for quite a long time, would it, arsehole?' I relaxed: we were back to normal. Whoever had hit Kat had entered during the day, and waited in the basement until the time had come to go upstairs. What that led to was:

'How did he know no one ever went down there, and how did he know she'd be here late?' The second question was more interesting than the first, which was a matter of general knowledge and general good taste.

'I'd say, yes, it's interesting.'

I muttered:

'Randolph.'

I'd already told Tim about Randolph's visit to see me and the information he had wanted to seem reluctant to disgorge.

'Seems that way.'

'What about day visitors? Are they all checked in?'

'Mostly, but not if they're just in and out: like messengers, for example.'

'So who got messengers that day?'

'It's not recorded. The doorman remembers a couple specifically, and he says there isn't a day when something or other doesn't arrive from one of Latimer's companies — often more than once. Usually, things are left off at reception, but sometimes something has to be signed for by a solicitor or a secretary. Then they'll send them up rather than ask whoever it is to come down. Time is money, remember?'

'Yes, thank God,' I was being paid for my time for a change.

'What's new, Dave?'

I leaned back in my chair, wondering what to tell him: 'You ever heard of James Mather?'

'Another legal luminary?'

'More like illegal. Would you be able to look back at files in the late forties and early fifties?'

'If it's worth my while. Why?' I outlined what I had learned. I also asked: 'What about enquiries in America?'

'They're not easy to pin down. Too many jurisdictions. You end up going from pillar to post. Local police, state police, immigration, customs, Organized Crime Task Force, Attorney-General's office, FBI, IRS, DEA, HAND.' I raised an eyebrow to query the last: I'd heard of all the others, even the Internal Revenue Service and the Drug Enforcement Administration.

He smiled wryly:

'HAND. Have A Nice Day. It's the one they always mention last. Just before they hang up.'

'Will you try?'

He shrugged:

'What do you want to know?'

'What he's up to, 'I suppose.'

'What are you saying?'

I shook my head:

'Nothing, really nothing. Just, well, if you know there's a villain somewhere in the shrubbery, don't you like to have some idea what part he might be playing?' Another mixed metaphor to scatter with Kat's ashes.

'What else?'

'What time do gambling clubs open?'

'The Clairmount? Around the middle of the day. Why?'

'Again, I don't know. But would you have any serious objections if I paid a visit? I'm curious about this debt of Andrew's. He's hiding something; his sister says no way would he gamble that high.'

Again, he shrugged: why not? As he left, I thought it was all most suspicious: he was being too co-operative by half; it was entirely out of character to let me follow up my leads myself. He preferred to claim them for himself. I sighed: I had enough mysteries to worry about without that too; it would have to wait its turn.

I was just about to leave for Companies House when the outside line rang:

'Dave Woolf.'

'Sandra Nicholl,' she said dryly.

'Sandy. Hi. I was going to ring you. How'd'you know I was here?' The last sentence would have earned me a ten minute reprimand from Russel Orbach.

'A good guess. Once I realized you were working again, it wasn't that hard to work out what on.' I never said she was stupid.

'We ought to meet,' I said.

'What a good idea. I wish I'd thought of it.' Ouch.

She said:

'I'm ringing from the Law Society. What about lunch?' Double ouch. I couldn't lie my way out of it: my lies last in her presence like ice in a blast-furnace. We arranged to meet in the only place either of us could think of on the spot: the Freemason's Arms, where I'd met Katrina.

'I, uh, was figuring maybe you wouldn't want us to be seeing each other if I was working on it,' I said lamely, once we'd settled into a corner with our respective refreshments: white wine spritzer for her.

'And for the month before? Maybe you were waiting for the case to begin?' Sandy has a tongue you could circumcise with.

'Fine, you wanna row,' I downed my drink: 'Let's have a row already.' I got up to fetch another. I can't fight with Sandy when I'm sober: it's an unequal contest; I'm not saying I win when I'm drunk, but at least it don't hurt so much.

She looked at me curiously when I returned, like she was trying to figure out what she'd ever seen in me. I wondered if she'd tell me. I reached out and took her hand:

'I do love you, you know.'

'Yes, I do know. It's not about that, is it? I'm getting too old for all of this, Dave; I don't want to spend my fortieth birthday wondering whose bed I'll be sleeping in, or sleeping in my own alone.' It was hard to think of her as beginning the approach to forty: she looked ten years younger.

'What do you want to do, Sandy?' I didn't want her to say it, but I could neither say what it was she wanted to hear nor else could I bring it to an end myself.

'I don't want to give you an ultimatum, Dave, but I can't keep on like this. If you can't — oh, shit, I don't know — I want to say "grow up" but it seems such a trite thing to say. Just that, though: grow up; we're both getting older; we've both got to start settling down or we'll wear ourselves out. Think about it, Dave, think about what I'm saying. And remember, if you don't want me, someone else just might, y'know.'

She jumped up, grabbed her handbag and left the table so fast I didn't have time to ask if she was going to the lavatory and coming back, or leaving altogether. After another quarter of an hour, I got the message, finished my third and somewhat belatedly followed her out of the pub, vaguely thinking — hoping? — she might still be in the street, waiting for me. It was lunch-time crowded: everyone else in the world was on the street, except Sandy.

I could no longer face the idea of reading fiches — microfilmed records. My alternative for the afternoon appeared a lot more attractive. (I try to avoid the word alternative in case I misuse it. Years ago, I was at a meeting with Russel Orbach. Someone launched into a tirade in which she claimed there were only three alternatives. Russel brought her to a standstill by insisting emphatically that she was wrong. Once he had everyone's attention, waiting to see how he would flaw his opponent's argument, he said: 'There can only be two alternatives.' I'd looked it up when I got home and — as usual — he was right. Now you know why people — uh — love him.)

The Clairmount was a bright, white modern building not far from Knightsbridge, which also meant I was half-way home. The main door was open, but there was so little activity inside I wasn't sure the gaming rooms were. I was glad I was wearing my suit: the place was plush enough that even Ian Mather — if I could picture him with a gambler's green eye-shade drawn down on his forehead — would be comfortable. I told the man at Reception I'd like to see the boss.

'What would that be in connection with, sir?' Another smart-arse.

'It's private. Perhaps you could give him my card?'

He studied it disdainfully, but handed it nonetheless to a uniformed messenger and jerked his head towards a door. In a few minutes, the messenger returned and led me in.

"Mr Woolf?'

'Right. Dave. Mister makes me nervous.'

'Private detectives make me nervous,' he smiled disarmingly and gestured. to a seat. He looked vaguely familiar, but I couldn't place him, and when I asked he denied that we'd ever met.

'Would you like something to drink?'

'Depends what's on offer.'

He waited. I asked. He didn't even raise an eyebrow. He took a bottle from the bar and poured me one, pouring his own from another bottle I couldn't see the label of.

'This is very civilized. People don't usually offer me a drink when they don't know what I want.'

He shrugged:

'Private detectives don't come to a club like this threatening trouble. I have — uh — too many good friends just outside the door, ready to come to my assistance.'

I held my hands up:

'I'm strictly non-violent. I'm sorry: I don't even know your name.'

'Michael Matheson. Mike. How can I help you?'

'I'm working for Mather's, the solicitors. I think you know one of them.'

He didn't say anything. Who owes gambling money is supposed to be as privileged as any information held by a lawyer: more so than much of that held by Mather's. Until someone welches on a debt: then the clubs like to go very public indeed.

'I think he owes you a lot of money: let's say eight to nine thousand pounds.'

'If you already think you know that, why are you asking me?'

'It's a funny thing, Mike, but a couple of the people who are closest to him insist there's no way he'd be that heavily into a gambling debt. How does it tally with your experience of him?'

'As you say, I know who he is. If he owed me that much money, he'd be good for it, wouldn't he?'

'What is that you're drinking? Cold tea?'

He chuckled:

'Apple juice. Do you want a refill?'

'Sure. D'you never drink?'

'I have one at about eight o'clock, and then a couple again between ten and midnight. That's the maximum on an ordinary, working day. It's a lot easier to pour myself something than to explain.'

'How long have you been in this racket?'

'A few years.'

'And you own the club?'

'My name's on the licence.' Another barrack-room witness.

'I don't know a lot about it. How'd's that work?'

'You have to declare any financial backers to the Commission; they can refuse your licence, or revoke it, if they're considered undesirable.'

'And yours is the only name on the licence?'

'Correct. And as it's a matter of public record, no, I have no declared backers.'

'You must be a very successful man, Mike. It's a lot of club, a lot of expensive central London property, for a solo operator.'

He didn't rise to being called a liar.

I said: 'I got a friend owns a club, maybe you know him? Lewis.'

'I know him. He comes here once in a while. Why?'

'I dunno. I was thinking, maybe, you might like to give him a call, check me out, y'know?'

He tilted back his chair much as I like to do behind my desk, only he had lot more space. I saw his eyes dart downwards. He invited me:

'Come and have a look.'

The desk — from my side — was solid oak. From his, it was solid screen. There were twelve small screens, on which he could see, I presumed, every part of the club.

'Let's say for the sake of argument that I ring Lewis, and he says you are a good chap and I ought to help you. Is he going to give me some special reason? Like I'll get my kneecaps shot off if I don't, or you're the Commissioner's son and I'm in trouble come licence time?'

'I wish. No. But he'd probably say I was a friend of his and any help you could put my way would be something he'd view as a personal favour.'

He laughed out loud:

'You know Lewis. The godfather. He's a character: he gets away with it, too. You still haven't told me what you want to know. Or why.'

'Why's not so difficult: you've already been interviewed by the police about young Andrew's whereabouts.' Even I was doing it now: young Andrew.

'That's what you're investigating?'

'Right. For Ian Mather. So we can say I ain't investigating to get Andrew into trouble.'

'I've already talked with the police. He was here that night. I'm quite certain of that: in fact, I could prove it to you.'

'How?'

He smiled.

'These,' he gestured below his desk: 'Are all on video. We video each evening's play, in full. Of course we only keep a selection.'

He explained the circumstances when they might wish to keep a video: where there was contention over a game; where a large cheque had been paid and not yet cleared; on occasion, violence could break out, notwithstanding the genteel atmosphere he sought to maintain; and, of course, when the police came around to check an alibi.

'Alright. Show me.'

He hesitated for a moment, then nodded: he hadn't expected me to call the boast, but if he refused it'd look like he had something to hide. He crossed the room to a large, locked cupboard, where I could see several racks of videos, neatly labelled presumably with dates and by gaming room. He picked one out and slotted it into a video machine next to the cupboard, switching on a television set that was independent of the screens hidden in his desk. I remarked that the set-up as a whole must be costly:

'Tax deductible,' was all he said.

He had to play with the fast forward and reverse for a while before he found Andrew.

'Who's the woman? His wife?'

'Which one?' I pointed to the one I'd meant, but as I did so glanced at the other, at the same table but not necessarily with them. She also looked familiar, though again I couldn't place her. Matheson confirmed my first choice as the former model, now Marilyn Mather. She and Andrew made the perfect pretty pair.

'And the other one?'

'Anabelle de Peyer,' he hopped from one foot to another, uncomfortable where I was leading him. Last picture of her I'd seen, she was wearing a lot less. As I turned away, I saw yet another familiar face: to my surprise, Anabelle de Peyer's companion of the moment was none other than her sometime assistant legal adversary, Christopher Wainwright. I remembered what Katrina had said: Martin only took the case on because Andrew and Randolph had claimed to be too close to it. I began to wonder just what that meant.

I think Matheson was hoping I'd got enough, because he started to say:

'If that's all ... ?'

I sat down again:

'I don't think Andrew ran up that debt. I'm thinking of telling Ian Mather about it. My guess is, he won't let Andrew pay and he'll put you to proof.' What I meant was: he wouldn't get paid without establishing exactly how the debt arose.

He understood. He tossed his options around like a salad. He could call my bluff, in case that's all it was, but he was likely to be out of his money for a while at best, and perhaps for as long as a law suit. He could ring Andrew, and find out just how much influence I really did wield, but that meant admitting how much he'd already told — or, rather, shown — me. He could consult with whoever really owned the club, which I didn't think meant talking to himself, but that wasn't what I was supposed to think. One way or another, I was trouble, and all I wanted to go away wasn't a lot more than he'd already given me.

'No source. Not even to Ian Mather. Right?' I nodded. My fingers weren't crossed, but my toes were. It never occurred to him I might want to tell the police. What everybody knows about private eyes comes from movies, TV., or books, when we're always at war with the law.

'The debt was Wainwright's. Andrew guaranteed it. Not that night, but a few weeks ago. I had to call it in. I'm not going to tell you anything else. That's it.'

It was enough.

CHAPTER SEVEN

As we planned to eat near my house, we had parked on the Square where I live. Walking back from the restaurant, Ali wanted to stay, rather than drive us both up to Highgate. I could think of no good reason why not. Though still tired from the previous night, we had energy enough to practise doctor-and-nurse for an hour or two before, this time, she drifted off to sleep ahead of me.

I was still lying awake, enjoying the notion and occasional touch of the bright and beautiful brand new body beside me in my bed, when the good reason we shouldn't have stayed rang. It was nearly three o'clock in the morning. I grabbed the 'phone quick enough to stop it waking her. I greeted the caller with the warmth he or she deserved:

'What?'

'I think you'd better come in to Mather's, sunshine,' said the voice of the only policeman I've ever even been tempted to refer to as friend, and that while I was still suffering the post-operative effects of the removal from my shoulder of a bullet.

I repeated:

'What?' But I was already beginning to guess.

'More a question of who,' he said, his sarcasm designed to soften the news. I waited. He told me. I repeated in an altogether different tone:

'What?' And hung up. I thought: this is no fun any more; no fun at all.

I debated waking Ali, but she seemed so comfortable there was no point depriving her of a little while longer in innocent slumber. She had made me sleep on the side of the bed nearest the edge of the platform, in case she fell off: a new dimension to fear of flying. Carefully, I crawled around the bed and stepped cautiously and backwards down the stairs. The bed-platform, which I had built myself, was as solid as a rock: creak-free it was not.

I dressed, set the answering machine so that if the 'phone rang again it wouldn't disturb her, and scribbled a note, telling her I had to go out; if I didn't come back she should make herself coffee and simply slam the door behind her: I'd been robbed so many times there was nothing left to steal. I was about to tape it to the top of the bed-platform steps where she was bound to see it when I realized it was a bit curt. I added: 'love'. But I didn't sign my name nor even an initial, so it couldn't be used in evidence.

After I left the Clairmount, I'd had time to kill before she caught up with me, so I had decided to pay a visit on speculation to a house I was never otherwise going to be invited to. I was professionally pleased with my discovery, but personally uncomfortable: Andrew was the weakest of the brothers, the apple on the lowest branch, and Wainwright hardly counted at all. It was going to cause a lot of grief, to no obvious advance or achievement.

Martin's address proved to be a huge town-house in Maida Vale. As Kat had said, not so far from where she lived that he couldn't keep in condition while he ran around. From the solitary bell outside the front door, it was clear he occupied the whole house. I rang it long and hard, only a quarter-expecting him to be in, and so only a quarter-prepared with an opening line when he opened the door.

He scowled.

'That's a nice way to greet an old friend.'

'I took you to my gym, not my club. What do you want, Dave?'

'Not going to ask me in? Kat said you were choosy about who you let in; not even her. What's the big mystery: you keep gerbils?'

I once knew a lady WHO kept gerbils: in her bedroom. It was not a turn on.

He sighed:

'I suppose you'd better come in.'

I didn't say anything: for once, I'd run out of flip remarks.

It was a handsome house. I don't think I've ever thought a house was handsome before. It's a word I like to keep for when I look in the mirror extremely drunk. The hall was wide and though, like mine, it had no carpet, it wasn't because he couldn't afford one, but because the wooden slats were a prize feature, polished to a gleam, setting off a Persian rug the price of which would probably merit at. least an honourable mention in despatches, and a couple of paintings that would not have looked out of place in the corridor at Mather's.

He led me into his study. It reminded me of somewhere else: Ian's office. There were a lot more wooden features, and paintings, but it was richly carpeted wall to-wall, and the alcoves each side of the fireplace were lined with old-looking volumes, some of which he'd probably even read. He hesitated whether to sit behind his desk, or relax in front of the lit fire, in the winged, leather armchairs. To be helpful, I lowered myself into one of the armchairs without being asked.

'I suppose you want a drink, too,' he didn't wait for my answer either. He opened the bar of a redwood cabinet and reached inside almost without looking, to extract a fresh, friendly and familiar bottle.

'I thought you weren't expecting me?'

'I could say, I knew you'd be around at some point, but the truth is, I thought I'd see if I could find out what makes you tick. This seemed to be your major preoccupation, and therefore a good place to start. We haven't long, have we: you're meeting my sister shortly.'

'She told you?' I was surprised: I thought we were in agreement it wasn't something we wanted to advertise.

'It's hardly likely Sandra Nicholl rang to tell me.' That was another reason he reminded me of Orbach: two out of every three remarks were calculated to wound. 'I told you I know everything that goes on.'

'Yeah. You never got around to telling me how you find out, though.'

'A man I once knew, who caught me by surprise, he said: "Never ask how someone found something out; it shows them you couldn't have done it; work out for yourself how it was done, and next time you'll be able to do it to them".' He settled down opposite me, true to his word trying out my sin for size.

'It's a nice line, but I don't know, Martin. I have a theory that people who claim to be able to find things out are really just very good at finding a use for everything they hear. Waddayathink?'

He chuckled:

'Very good. Can I use it?'

'Sure. I probably stole it from someone else anyhow.'

'You still haven't told me why you're here.'

'This is true. You still haven't told me why you don't like visitors.'

'I'm not sure the one equals the other.'

'Will you, though?'

'Tell you? Why? Why do you want to know? What part does it play in your investigation, Dave?'

'You know, just because I ask a question doesn't mean I know the answer. People got guilty consciences. They figure, a detective, he asks something, he already knows. So then they talk more than they need to. If I really did know, I'd've solved all my cases before I began. A lot of it's just, you know, poking around.'

'Great. I can tell my father he's paying you four hundred a day to poke around.' He paused, but couldn't resist: 'A lot of places.'

'That's vulgar of your own sister. I thought she was the reason no one else was good enough for you?'

'She's a grown up; she can do what she likes, with whom.'

'Yeah, I see. You've gone off her now she's slumming.'

'I really can't work out how much of your self-abasement is an act, and how much of it is an astute, accurate, objective self-assessment.'

'I have the same problem. Listen, I'll tell you. I only ever knew two ways to find a needle in a haystack. One way, you keep the pressure on until it pops out like pus from a pimple; the other way, you burn it down and rake over the ashes. Waddayathink?'

He grimaced:

'I think it's pretty disgusting either way. One way you get a face full of someone else's poison; the other way, you risk setting fire to the whole field. Aren't you worried about the damage you can do?'

'I didn't ask myself into thy father's house. That's another way of looking at it. It's a house of cards. Somewhere inside, the joker's been used, only the rules say you can't. Maybe the joker's the top card, you just lift it off and you ain't done too much harm; maybe it's only a little way down, and the harm's still repairable; maybe it's right in the bottom layer, and you've got to pull the whole house down. The point is: the rule got broken, and everything that's built on top of it deserves to come down with it.'

'Like the American legal adage: the fruits of the poisoned tree?'

'Yeah, I watch L.A. Law too.' If the starting-point of an investigation is unconstitutional, everything that results from it is inadmissible evidence. We're much more civilized and tolerant in England: the police perhaps get a rap across the knuckles, but it's up to the judge how much he lets the jury listen to, which is usually everything.

'It's an easy thing to say when it's not your own house.'

'Is that why you won't let anyone in here? In case they poison it?'

'Something like that,' he admitted. Suddenly, he seemed lonely. Why did a man like that live all alone? He was not bad looking, he was fit, he was wealthy, he had a beautiful house, he was witty. I had none of those things, and yet I now had Allison.

'Like I think I said, my upbringing wasn't a tale of mixed emotions — more like none at all. At least this is mine, only mine. Now you tell me why you came here.'

I paused to think about it first. I had come as much to work things out for myself as to lay my news on him.

'It's your father's house of cards I'm dismantling. He's my client. I owe him a duty of care. If I find any of you had anything to do with Kat's death, I wouldn't hesitate to turn you over to the police, if I couldn't push you out of a high window first. But unless and until that's what I find, I've got to be careful, haven't I — not to do any of you more harm than you deserve. For your father's sake. Right?' He didn't say anything, so I repeated: 'Right? That's right, isn't it?'

He nodded slowly, and cautiously. As if he half-suspected what was coming. I expelled air, then held up my glass for another. He went to fetch the bottle: it'd be less distracting than repeatedly having to rise for a refill. He said:

'Only don't blame me if you're pissed by the time you meet Allison. Or is that why you've come here, to get pissed first?'

'I didn't think it was, but it's as good an excuse as any. Yes, I don't want to talk about work with her tonight.'

'You getting serious about her? Kind of quick, isn't it?'

'She's a special lady, like you said. Yes, I could get serious about Ali.'

'Then don't call her that to her face, or you'll be out on your ear.'

'God, not another one. Katrina ...'

'I know.' Of course he knew: I'd almost managed to forget.

I studied the fire. I had only just appreciated it wasn't real. The flames were real, but the logs and coals weren't. When I was a kid, they had electric artificial fires that couldn't even fool me: bits of wire-mesh coloured charcoal, and a fan inside to give a light-bulb a mild, flickering effect. This was a century ahead. Now I'd noticed, I could see the gas pipe leading into the fireplace.

Martin waited impatiently, refilling his own glass. I said:

'You like it, then? Is Wainwright a freemason?' He didn't quibble with my sudden change of direction, or answer about the Southern Comfort; I was finally and belatedly getting down to it.

'Wainwright? I believe so. Why?'

'Freemasons are supposed to help each other, aren't they? They call it "fellow-mason in distress" or something like that. It's part of their obligations.' The 'obligations' were what they called their membership oaths.

He laughed, and recited:

'"'All these points I solemnly swear to observe, without evasion, equivocation, or mental reservation ... under no less a penalty ... than of being severed in two, my bowels burned to ashes, and ... scattered over the face of the earth and wafted by the four cardinal-winds of heaven, that no trace or remembrance of so vile a wretch may longer be found among men ..." That the sort of thing you mean?'

'I thought you weren't one.'

'I'm not. Shall I do another?' He went on without waiting: '"These several points I solemnly swear to observe ... under no less a penalty, on the violation of any of them, than that of having my throat cut across, my tongue torn out by the root, and buried in the sand of the sea at low water mark, or a cable's length from the shore, where the tide regularly ebbs and flows twice in twenty-four hours, or the more effective punishment of being branded as a wilfully perjured individual, void of all moral worth, and totally unfit to be received into this worshipful Lodge ..." One more?'

I nodded, fascinated.

'"All these points I solemnly swear to observe ... under the no less penalty ... than that of suffering loss of life by having my head struck off". When we were young, I used to sneak into my father's study and look at his books: it was most emphatically, strictly forbidden under threats just about as dire. So, naturally, I couldn't resist. But the others did. Maybe that's why I was never interested: you're not supposed to read all that rubbish until you're a long way in, by which time you've already swallowed so much of it, what does a bit more matter?'

'What have medieval weapons got to do with it?' I had just that day discovered a dead-end half corridor off which an alcove concealed a full suit of armour. I stopped to say hallo and introduce myself before I realized it wasn't going to answer back.

'Nothing so far as I'm aware. What made you think they did?'

'What you said, about Gauldie being the buff.'

He laughed:

'Gauldie's a buff about anything that looks good and makes money. He's profoundly acquisitive. He's the original poor boy made good good good. You should see his house. He didn't have money behind him,' like Ian: 'I think there's a sort of coincidental connection, an overlap perhaps: freemasonry and heraldry, insignia, coats of arms, symbols of authority, that sort of thing. English craft freemasonry started at the beginning of the eighteenth century, but the spiritual roots go back into the Bible: King Solomon's Temple. The real fanatics trace it step by step through the ages.'

He gave me another recital:

'"Father of All!

"In every age,

"In every clime adored

"By saint, by savage and by sage,

"Jehovah, Jove or Lord."

'I daresay Gauldie's interests overlap; that's all. The women in the firm tend to hate it, but no one else cares: if it makes Gauldie happy ... It's worth a fortune, and it makes an impression on some clients: the old families, you know. Don't forget, though we're well-established now, we're a young firm, only post-war; between my father and John Gauldie, they used every trick in the book to grow so big so fast. You haven't told me why you asked if Wainwright is a freemason.'

'Would Andrew help him out, as a fellow-freemason, like to maybe eight, nine grand?'

'Your gambling debt?'

'Wainwright's gambling debt.'

'I see. No. Andrew has his good side, but that sort of generosity with money isn't it. The lady Marilyn likes the lolly too much.'

'In that case, I think perhaps Andrew's in a lot of trouble. Wainwright's blackmailing him. I don't know what for. Do you?'

His expression remained impassive. Instead of answering, he asked me:

'Why are you telling me about it?' Then he remembered to add: 'If it's true.'

'It's true. You just said it couldn't be friendship.'

'It's consistent with what I already told you: Andrew covers for him. He was originally Randolph's friend. Well his brother was. And I've never understood how Andrew got so close to him: they've nothing in common. So what you're saying fits.'

'You didn't tell me if you know what he was blackmailing him for.'

'No more I did,' he said softly.

'Tell me the truth, Martin. Do you know, or is this part of the "all-knowing, all-seeing" act?'

'I could say the same to you: do you know, or are you pretending to know in the hope I'll talk about it?'

I poured myself a fresh drink and glanced at my watch: we could sit sparring all evening and I doubted either one would come out much ahead. I said:

'No, I don't know. But I'll tell you what I think. Wainwright's been going with Anabelle de Peyer. Did you know that?'

'I heard.'

.'He worked with you on the divorce case. I looked at the file. It was fun. You had P.I.S on her tail, and a very lovely tail it is too. Let's just suppose out loud that Wainwright got very turned on by her: hell, I did. Let's also suppose that after he's been to the lavatory and made love to a loo-roll, he decides he wants a taste of the real thing. OK so far?'

'It's plausible. You think he went to her offering information in exchange for a chance to get between her legs — and, as you'd say, very lovely legs they are too. Is that your theory? It hardly implicates Andrew.'

'No, it doesn't. That's why I don't think it's right. Wainwright's a conceited son of a bitch; I don't think he'd expect to have to pay for it.' I'd never spoken with Wainwright, but I'd seen him around the office, and I recollected Dowell's opening critique. Wainwright was another of these modern lawyers who look fit enough to give legal advice while running in the marathon. In my day, lawyering was a sedentary occupation, with occasional bursts of horizontal activity that were never enough to compensate for all the chain-smoking, continuous-drinking and waiting around to visit a client in the clink.

'Go on,' Martin prompted without contradicting me. I already knew he had no greater love for Wainwright. Then he interrupted: 'Wait. You're going to be late. Let's ring Allison and tell her you're here. Alright?'

'She'll already be on the way. Ah, right,' I had forgotten about the car 'phone. Back in the days when I still owned a car, they didn't have mobile 'phones, or if they did, no one wanted me to find out about them. I'm a lousy driver at the best of times, and distracted by a call I doubt I'd've survived five minutes.

He punched about ten digits, like long distance. She must have answered on the first ring. He said: 'I think I've got your date here. Do you want to come and pick it up? It's going to be late otherwise.'

He chuckled, and disconnected.

'What's the joke?' I wasn't enjoying being tossed around between the Mathers, anymore than Kat had.

'She asked me to keep you sober enough to stay upright.' It wasn't quite the tender loving message I'd've liked him to have to relay. 'You've reached the point where Wainwright wants la de Peyer — an excusable impulse — and you don't think he'd expect to have to pay for it. You were going to try and relate this to my baby brother.' He did know. I was tempted to tell him to carry on the tale, but maybe I wanted to show off a little to my new girlfriend's big brother:

'I think he found something out about Andrew almost by accident, anyway by accident in his terms and blackmail came later, maybe once he realized he wasn't going to cut it at Mather's any other way. My guess is it was her idea. She probably let him, have the first taste or two for free, to get him hooked — and I doubt that'd be difficult — and then she suggested he start to pay. Maybe she sung him a song about how she wanted the divorce over, she was only stringing it along because she didn't really believe her husband's declaration of assets: that's consistent with some of the previous correspondence. If she could only find out the truth for sure, the sooner she could be free for her new toy-boy. How'm I doing?'

'It's an interesting account. I wouldn't place it beyond the bounds of possibility.'

'So leaking was her idea. I imagine his first reaction would probably have been to refuse. Don't forget, he hadn't been that long qualified. It needs a sort of nasty, cynical confidence that only comes with experience; he'd still've been a learner, full of the high-sounding ideals they pump out at college. I think … I'll admit I'm guessing now: I think she had a way to persuade him that leaking wasn't that bad, that everyone did it some time or another, even … Andrew.'

I waited. He closed his eyes for what seemed like a long time, then' started to speak, choosing his words carefully:

'Stonefrost and de Peyer were friends. Friends of Randolph, too.'

'Stonefrost was guilty, wasn't he? I mean, of what was written about him?'

'Yes. Beyond any shadow of a doubt. He'd been dealing to his society friends for many years. Everyone, even Randolph, did some of his dope, back when they were students or just out of college. Remember, this was the sixties or just after. No one thought it was a bad thing. It was admirable, appealingly piratical: we were stealing the world away from under our parents' noses. Most of us gave it up, gradually, and went on with our lives and our careers; I had less to do with it than others, because I didn't go to university, which was the hotbed.'

He took a sip of his drink, calculating his words carefully before continuing: 'But people like Stonefrost and de Peyer had nothing to go on to. They didn't have or want careers: they had family money, and expectations and all that was required of them in return was to marry and raise children — more sons — to inherit the family estates in due course. Boredom, greed, looking for excitement, hooked on sex, drink, drugs, travel, money. I should think in time they needed much more money than ever they were allowed by their parents. We've all known lots of types like that.'

'Speak for yourself. My druggies had plenty of things to escape from, not impatience to inherit.'

He dismissed my objection with a wave:

'Really? That go for you, too? You were qualified, a partner in a practice — not a bad practice — what made you choose drugs, Dave?' I winced: I'd forgotten he had access to the firm's file on me. He went on: 'Randolph quit doing drugs early on, but not before our baby brother had been attracted to the glamour and the glitter: the night-clubs, coming-out balls, pictures in *The Tatler, Queen,* other magazines no one with a jot of intelligence would even open and that you only ever find in the waiting-rooms of Harley Street surgeons.' Me, I wouldn't know how to find Harley Street. 'Oh, yes, and then there were the gorgeous debutantes and models — like Anabelle, or Marilyn. It doesn't matter: it's a lot of stupidity, but no great sin.'

'Isn't it?'

'What do you mean?' He asked sharply.

'I asked Katrina if she'd ever been down to Andrew's house in the country. She said she hadn't. But Andrew told me she had. Andrew thought I had it in for him, because of that visit. Wonder what he meant, eh?'

He shook his head:

'I don't know. I never knew she'd been. With Randolph?'

'I don't know that. I wouldn't let Andrew tell me; if she didn't want me to know, then unless I have to, I don't want to hear. But I got the general picture: "things got out of hand", he said.'

He nodded unhappily, reading the same into it that I had.

'Andrew got into that scene, you're saying? He bought his drugs from Stonefrost, didn't he?'

'Yes.'

We were both lawyers; we both understood the implications. On the one hand, he was the perfect lawyer to represent the newspaper: he knew for sure that the libel suit should be lost. On the other, the implications of the action were serious — for him as well as for a lot of others. If Stonefrost lost, like Oscar Wilde, the police would have to investigate: who could say who might be caught up in it.

'Why did he take the case?'

'The News was bought out a few weeks before the action began. The new owners were old clients of my father. It was a big case, a lot of money; of course we took the case. Then Gauldie assigned it to Andrew. He tried to wriggle out of it — pressure. of work and all that. But he wasn't under nearly as much pressure as others, and he could hardly tell Gauldie the real reason he didn't want to do it.'

'What happened?' I could guess, but I might as well have him tell me.

'Andrew tried to get it to settle. God, he was so unlucky: nine out of ten libel actions settle. But they were using some barrister who hadn't been in court for a while, a publicity junkie, who got all gung-ho about it. You know what the libel bar's like: they prefer to sit in chambers raking in their consultation fees and carving up the case with their opponent over a bottle of fine wine in El Vino's. He had the bad luck to get one who was looking for a scrap.'

'Is that the best you can say — unlucky? It stinks, and you know it. If Andrew had an interest, he had no right acting.'

'Oh, grow up, Dave. We all make compromises with ethics every day of the week.'

'Some compromise: he leaked John equals Ron Fitzpatrick's record?'

'Yes.'

'How long have you known?'

'Known? Known for sure: about ten minutes. Suspected? Since the leak. But I'd never made the connection to the de Peyer case. There's something else you ought to know.'

He hesitated, but he'd started and there was no turning back.

'I don't think Andrew did it entirely out of fear for the personal consequences: after all, it might never have rebounded on him. It might: put Stonefrost on the spot, he was pretty much of a sneak, he may well have started trading names to the police. But it might never have happened. You got close to the rest of it earlier when you asked about freemasons in distress: Stonefrost and Andrew were in the same Lodge. I think Francis Stonefrost put a lot of pressure on him to find a way to help.'

'Ah.' It explained Andrew's fear of his father ever finding out. As well as whatever fury it unleashed over the breach of confidence, he would also be guilty of an abuse of freemasonry. I asked: 'And de Peyer?'

'I don't know that. But I wouldn't be surprised. We've acted for his family for a long time, and they certainly were. That's how father got their business, you see.'

'I thought people weren't supposed to join for reasons of self-advancement?'

'I don't think my father did. His father — my grandfather — was a prominent mason, master of his Lodge for many years, and a district grand master for a while. My father was a late child, my grandmother was my grandfather's second wife. I don't think they were very close; it was more a case of father wanting to emulate him.' Like Martin was emulating his father the way he'd set up the study where we sat.

He went on: 'But once you've joined, you're bound to get a lot of business out of it. People turn to their own; I've said that before, haven't I? If you actually believe all that crap, then you trust someone else who does. So, yes, he got the business of a number of old, masonic families, including the de Peyers. It was de Peyer who Stonefrost went out to stay with when he died.'

'I logged the location. It gives us game, set and match against Wainwright, doesn't it? And of course against Andrew.' I remembered something from our first evening together: 'You lied to me. You told me Andrew would never leak.'

'No. I didn't. I said he wouldn't leak if he was a million pounds in debt. He'd never leak for money, Dave, however much he likes the stuff. But he leaked out of some stupid, misguided sense of masonic loyalty, of fear for the implications, or both. And how far does any of it get you? It gives you two leaks, but there's two more to go, and what has any of it got to do with Katrina's death?' He didn't know I had now traced three, rather than two, leaks, and I wasn't about to tell him. Instead, I said:

'That's the connection I don't see, which is why I said I don't really want to use any of this, unless I'm sure it's necessary.'

'Does that mean you won't tell father?'

'I can't say that for sure. We've still got the problem of Wainwright. I can't just do nothing about him, can I?'

'Would you ... Would you let me take care of it? It's really not your business, Dave; it's not what you're here to find out about. It's a family problem. I'll handle it.'

The doorbell rang before I got a chance to answer him, and Martin got up to answer it. Before he left the room, he turned and said:

'It's not necessary to tell Allison either, is it?'

'Necessary? No, I shouldn't think so. Why?'

He smiled winningly:

'She tries to sound a lot tougher than she is. She's fond of her baby brother. Please.'

It tied in with what she'd told me about Andrew crying on her shoulder, so I shrugged mine and gestured for him to go let her in. I felt stale, and she'd be the welcome fresh air.

'Looking glum,' she said, leaning over to kiss me boldly, to show she wasn't inhibited by being in her brother's house: 'Maybe you'd rather I left the two of you to go on playing together?'

He hadn't followed her into the room, so I stood up, put my arms right around her and held her close, to feel the whole of her body next to mine and remember just how good it felt.

Martin returned and coughed discreetly:

'Your drink, ma'am.'

He had made her a white wine spritzer: the same as Sandy drank. He had a couple of cubes of ice in one hand, which he dropped into his own glass before topping up his drink. I pulled a face:

'Do you have to?'

'Try not to cry. We can't all be big tough he-men who swallow it neat. Besides,' he sipped: 'Have you ever tried it? It's better. Go on,' he held out his glass.

I shook my head:

'There's precious little to cling onto in this life. Leave me what I've got.' It was our last exchange on the subject that had occupied the evening until then.

We stayed only half an hour. Politely, Ali invited Martin to join us, and he dithered, drawing out his refusal while he watched how much I didn't want him to come with. Eventually, he declined:

'No, I've got things to do. Go on, children.'

That was how it felt. Let out to play. Away from all the adult, serious talk. We held hands as we walked to her car, and once inside, kissed again, hands finding other parts of each other to cling onto. She broke away:

'I'm hungry, and after all you've drunk, you need to eat. Come on.'

We dropped the car off outside my house, and walked down to the Fulham Road, where there are more restaurants than residents. You don't need to book, but you do need to be fast on your feet if you don't want to get hustled inside some real dumps. I had intended to take Ali to an American restaurant, but it had changed nations and now was Armenian. Only the sawdust on the floor looked the same. We ended up in a French pancake house, dutifully eating one savoury and one sweet pancake each, washed down with delicious, sparkling French cider, as unlike its English colleague as Perrier and seven-times re-used London tapwater.

'You were talking about Andrew, weren't you?' She said once we were settled.

'What makes you say that?'

Either she had sixth sense, or she wasn't telling all she knew. She shifted uncomfortably in her seat, but she still looked good enough to eat.

'I overheard the end of a conversation between Martin and Andrew the other day. It was more like a fight, and. they don't often fight, those two. I was coming to see Andrew, and they stopped when I came in and Martin went off to the gym. Andrew wouldn't tell me what it was about and, well,' she laughed: 'It was only the day before yesterday, and I've been a bit preoccupied since.'

She reached out a hand to take mine: 'Happily so. I was going to try to talk to Martin about it today, but as soon as I went in to see him he wanted to know why I looked like the cat that'd had the cream. So I told him, I had.'

I shivered: I was getting horny listening to her; it felt unreal — like it was happening to someone else; I wanted it to be real.

'Tell me what you heard,' I said when we finally let go of each other before our pancakes froze.

'Martin said "it's got to stop" and Andrew said "it's not up to me". It might've been nothing: they could've been talking about a case.'

I frowned:

'You didn't think so, or you wouldn't be telling me about it.'

'So,' she pressed: 'Am I right? Was it what you were talking to Martin about.'

I gave her the only honest answer I could:

'I don't know. I thought I knew what I was talking to him about, but I'm not so sure now.'

CHAPTER EIGHT

The Lord, it is said, moves in a mysterious manner. (Martin said the same thing about Randolph.) All I say is, he or she isn't in Dowell's class. Throughout the case I had been disconcerted by his apparent anxiety to assist me in any direction I wanted to take; I knew it had to be a blind; nothing he ever does is that simple; if he was being helpful at one level, he was hindering me at another; he doesn't know any other way to operate.

By the time I arrived at Mather's, I had decided that, even if the case wasn't real fun anymore, I could still pretend. I reached this conclusion during a brief, but for the most part thankfully silent, cab-ride in to the city. I had no choice but to take a taxi: the London underground doesn't yet run all-night, though it's likely to do so as soon as the unions have been beaten into sufficient submission to make of it a profitable undertaking.

Because it was so late, and I had enjoyed no sleep at all, I wasn't quick enough as I climbed into the cab to close the window before the driver started to mouth off:

'Odd time to go into the city, isn't it? You one of these city-types like to get in ahead of everyone else? I had one in the back the other night, went into the office at four o'clock every morning, regular as clockwork. Only needed three hours sleep, he said. Know how he did it? I asked how he did it. He told me how he did it. I'll tell you how he did it. What he did ...'

'Friend,' I leaned into the opening: 'I am going into the city to look at a body. It's dead. It'll do without sleep forever.'

I slid the window shut before he could say another word. I could see his expression in the rear-view mirror. He was thinking. It was an effort. He was thinking: maybe I'm a doctor; maybe I'm a policeman; but maybe, just maybe, I'm the killer going back to make sure I really got the job done.

He still hadn't recovered either his composure or his conversation by the time he pulled up outside Mather's office, at the arse-end of one of a proliferation of police cars parked at excited angles. Two ambulance men stood by their vehicle, smoking while waiting to collect the package. A lot of ambulance men smoke. Why not? They're familiar with more effective means of population control.

The door was half-open but a uniformed bobby about half my age barred my way:

'Can I help you, sir?'

I shrugged:

'No, I don't think so.'

'Funny. Very funny. I can hardly keep from laughing ... sir.' His face didn't change expression.

I sighed

'That's what all the girls say. I'm from the cadaver collection corporation; I came for the corpse.'

'You sick shit,' said a familiar voice from within, pulling the door wide open: 'You've never. actually seen one, have you? Come on; come in and lose your virginity.'

He was right: for all the deaths at Disraeli Chambers, I had not seen any of the bodies. The only one to have died in my presence had the courtesy to do so after I was shot and had passed out. Like everyone else, I've seen a million actors die, but only the occasional news-picture of a real person. On screen, the difference doesn't tell.

Unlike Katrina, he had not been shot. Whoever had killed him had twisted his head until it sat on his shoulders exactly the wrong way round. He was lying on his stomach on the floor, staring straight up at me

'Take a good look, Dave; smell it.'

I wrinkled my nose, hoping he wouldn't notice I was also scrunching up my eyes. It smelled like a public toilet that hadn't been cleaned for a month.

'Lots of them let go at the last moment of a slow death. They lose all control. It all adds to the fun; you'll be able to make jokes about it tomorrow, I expect.'

I swivelled on my heel and headed for the real toilet. I thought I was going to throw up, but I didn't. I stood a long time over the basin, leaning my head against the cold mirror above. I was a little short of breath, but that was all. When I raised my head, I saw Dowell standing in the doorway, watching to see how I'd handle it.

'Let it go if you can. It helps.' He wasn't angry anymore.

I shook my head:

'I don't think I need to. What do you know?'

'Quite a lot, actually. He came in very late; around midnight. Signed in. Wasn't trying to avoid anyone. He looked happy the watchman said, like he'd had good news. He was dressed casually, not for the office, so he probably wasn't intending to stay 'till morning; it wasn't some kind of all-night work-jag. Anyway, that was hardly his style. He asked if anyone else was in and seemed a little surprised at first when told no, but then chuckled, like a private joke.'

'What about downstairs?' The dead-file basement. 'File' might have been superfluous.

'Nothing.'

'Earlier? Who was here?'

'Randolph. With a typist for a while.' He sneered: 'I suppose he was doing some dictating.'

His brother had said he was working his way through the female staff.

His man Pratt poked a head into the lavatory:

'Coffee, guv?'

'Yeah.'

'Me too,' I added; I would have waited forever if I'd waited to be asked.

Pratt glanced at guv who nodded wearily:

'Yes, yes, get him a coffee too. It might get a confession quicker than beating him up.'

'Guv?' Pratt was puzzled. I think he lived in a state of permanent puzzlement; Dowell was trying to drive him further into it and out of his life.

'Coffee. Two. Mr Woolf's room upstairs. Can you remember where that is?'

'Alright, guv, you know, alright,' he objected to the insult with all the articulation he could assemble.

As if we hadn't been interrupted, Tim continued:

'And Martin. Martin came in around ten. He and his brother were talking for a while. When the watchman went around, neither of them were here: he says. That's why he told Wainwright there was no one in. But.'

'But he didn't see them leave,' I finished off for him gloomily: I wouldn't mind if Randolph Mather had murdered Wainwright; I'd like to think of him having to spend the remaining years of his active life getting it where he'd hurt Katrina putting it. But I like Martin; enough that when I remembered his last words to me — that he'd handle the Wainwright problem — I knew I wasn't going to enjoy repeating them.

I stood at the window, staring out over unlit roofs, watching the moon awaiting the arrival of the soul of Christopher Wainwright, if he had one. I don't think I like death much, even when I don't like the dead person. It's a bit too final, too decisive, too unequivocal for my taste.

'Come and fetch me when they're done, OK?' he said when Pratt brought our coffees.

'Right, guv,' Pratt stopped sulking;' he finally had a task that would stimulate and stretch him. He had to remember where to find Dowell for however long it took forensics to finish their work.

We sipped in silence. I saw what he meant: it was disgusting, far worse than a beating. Finally, he said:

'Waddayaknow, sunshine?'

Gloomily, I placed first one then another of my client's sons into the main-frame:

'He was blackmailing Andrew; I told, Martin; Martin said he'd handle it.'

'Martin,' he mused: 'He's the one spends three nights a week in the gym, bit of a tough guy, right?'

'I heard.'

'And Martin was here this evening. Tidy, isn't it?'

'Look, Tim, you need a lot more than that. You said Wainwright didn't arrive until after midnight. Maybe Martin was shacked up with someone by then?' I was clutching at straws: no one had suggested Martin was currently seeing a woman, or for that matter a man; he lived alone, and that was how he liked it.

'Anyway, if the night-man didn't see them leave, he wasn't on the door all the time; which means either of them or someone else could have let someone in.' I reminded him: 'He's alibi'd for the night of Kat's death.'

'So? Different method, different motives.' At first, I thought he was simply playing with Martin; now, I began to think he was serious.

'What do you want him for? What about Randolph? Were any calls made out of here this evening?' Had someone rung Wainwright? Who?

'No and yes. Not through the switchboard, because though it's automatic, it lights up if a call goes out, and the watchman says not. But they've both got private lines.'

'I don't suppose,' I suggested without a lot of optimism: 'They're not on the test circuit, are they?'

He hooted derisively.

'They have places like Highgate on the test circuit 'cos they only make ten calls a day. Full of your lot,' he snarled unhappily. I winced: if he was resorting to racist cracks that low, he was really hurting over tonight's incident. I knew why: he always got angry when people dropped dead in the middle of a case; it offended his sense of professional pride; sometimes, it even interfered with his method. 'To put the City on circuit would cost next year's national debt. There's no way to tell if either of the private lines were used, by whom or to whom.'

'Watcha going to do?'

'Already done it. I've sent cars for them both.' I read 'both' as the older boys, not Andrew, whose potential involvement was unknown until I disclosed it.

'Great. You send one for Iron Ian?'

'Nah. I don't want him cluttering up the scene until forensics're finished. Besides, why shouldn't he get a few more hours' sleep? They say it's hard enough getting any sleep at all at his age.' It was unmentionably uncharacteristic for Dowell to show so much consideration. I decided not to mention it.

'What else do you know, Dave?'

I sighed: it was unfair; just because he had a badge, I had to go first.

'Remember the name Stonefrost?'

'Vaguely.' It was a lie. Tim Dowell either remembered things in excruciating, intimate detail, or not at all. The only thing he didn't remember was when it was his turn to buy a drink.

'Libel action. Drugs. Settled well for him, especially since he was bang-to-rights.' Guilty.

'Yes?' He stifled a yawn; I was boring him; he wasn't hearing anything he didn't already know.

'That was what Wainwright was blackmailing Andrew about. Andrew probably bought some dope from Stonefrost; also, they were members of the same Lodge; Andrew helped him win. Wainwright found out indirectly through a mutual friend, possibly another mason, called de Peyer. He was bonking Anabelle de Peyer.'

'Like you're bonking Allison Hoyt?'

'How'd'you know that?' I was genuinely shocked, wondering if he had a tail on me, or her.

'I didn't 'till now.' I'd fallen for the oldest trick in the book; the one I told Martin about; asking a question, banking on the accused giving you the answer.

'Pig. You want I should go on?' I sipped some more coffee: it didn't improve with cold.

'Go on. So far you've given me society, drugs and sex: does it get interesting?'

'Funny. She knew from her husband that Andrew Mather had done a no-no to help Maurice Francis, Vice-count Stonefrost off the hook, so she persuaded Wainwright to do the same for her.'

'I seem to remember, when I studied law, there was something called "privileged information". Do they still have it?'

'We're living in different times than when you and I learned our law, friend. Today's lawyer is as involved in the market-place as his client. Privilege is just an extra edge he went a few more years to college to collect. You never heard of insider dealing? If you make money into the sole criterion of success, everything else takes second place: morality, ethics, honour, loyalty, even pure professionalism. Lawyers are no different from anyone else: just more so.' Tiredness was turning me philosophic.

'You're telling me what Wainwright's hold on Andrew was. Big deal. Blackmail is blackmail. They're all scum. If you're right, and Wainwright was blackmailing Andrew, I'm glad he's dead. I'll tell you something, son,' he could be philosophical too: 'We've all got things to hide. Our bad actions are as much a part of us as the good. When they get hold of what you want to keep a secret, they steal your soul. I hate them, every one of the bastards.'

'I don't get it, Tim. I'm giving you a, lot of good material: motive, conspiracy, drugs, freemasons, you name it. You can get headlines for a month, your picture in the papers, your children can sell your autograph to their chums at school. How come you don't want to know?'

He looked glum:

'What've freemasons got to do with it?'

'Andrew is, Stonefrost was, Wainwright was, maybe de Peyer was: Jesus, man, it's staring you in the face. What is it about it?'

'It scares me,' he admitted, more easily than I would have expected: 'When you first asked me, I told you what I knew about 'them was enough to make me want to steer away from the subject. Unless you force me, I'm not going down that road.'

I snorted;

'And so the tax-payer gets value for money out of another of Britain's fearless finest? You're really that frightened of them?'

'If there's anything, any proof, I'll follow it as far as it goes, I will.' He sounded like he was trying to convince himself more than me: 'But I'm not stirring that pot of shit unless I'm certain I have to. Besides: how?'

'NG, Tim, no good. I've done some reading: since 1985, 1986, it's been their policy to co-operate with official enquiries. That used to mean just your lot, then there was that enquiry at Hackney which they co-operated with, and since then they've said they're willing to co-operate with other public authorities. You could find out if you wanted.'

'Yeah, and the minute after the minute I asked, someone at the Yard would know and want to know why. Like Woolard.'

I knew the case he meant. Woolard was a detective inspector investigating corruption in Islington. Freemasons were amongst his suspects, and some of them knew it. According to his own account, one day he received an unsolicited 'phone call from a man in the office of the Director of Public Prosecutions, enquiring how the case was going. It was unprecedented and totally out of order: in England, lawyers aren't involved in the police investigation, unlike America where the prosecutor is often briefed from the beginning.

Woolard accordingly went down, unforewarned and without the permission of his superiors, to DPP headquarters, and interviewed the official who had rung him. His belief was that there was a masonic connection: that a suspect had asked the man at the DPP's to help him find out, as a fellow-mason in distress, how close the police were getting. Within hours, Woolard was in trouble; within days, off the case; within weeks, off the squad and transferred — proverbially — to traffic control in Wembley, a part of London only marginally more relevant than Purley.

Woolard never 'gave up. He tried legal action, press statements, television appearances, even a parliamentary petition. He became obsessed with it, and it finished his career. Dowell wasn't willing to follow the same route to loss of pension rights. Fear of freemasonry is insidious and effective: there has always been precious little hard evidence of actual corruption within it, or of abuse of membership. How can there be if no one is willing even to investigate?

In the same vein, I'd read in the library since the case started a book called *The Brotherhood,* an expose of freemasonry. Its Prologue contained an account of how the book had been commissioned, and completed, before a change of ownership of the publishing company led to cancellation of the contract. The new owners were embarrassed, but open about their motives: their father was a freemason, and it would cause him concern if they published the book. He hadn't read it, or asked them not to; he didn't need to; they were prepared to side-step the issue rather than run the risk.

'What I told you about Stonefrost — that wasn't new, right?'

Dowell has a problem where I'm concerned. He likes me, so he doesn't like to deceive me. But he likes deception, in its own right, just as much. Instead of answering, he said:

'You asked about James Mather. Remember?'

'Gee, thanks for reminding me. I would've forgotten. What'd you find out?' I up-ended the rest of the coffee into the metal waste-paper basket behind my desk, in case I was tempted to try it again.

'The long-departed, much-travelled uncle,' he introduced: 'Is still wanted here, on a warrant thirty-five years old.' There is no Statute of Limitations in English criminal law.

'Apparently, he was in business with a fellow named ...' He paused to refresh his memory: 'Kenneth Richardson.'

'Sort of business?'

'Import/export. The years after the war contained rich pickings for those who weren't too concerned about the rules.'

'I remember.' Believe it or not, I did: I remember rationing; some things didn't cease to be rationed until the early fifties. At least, that's what my parents said. Now I thought about it, probably for the first time in twenty years, it may just have been a ploy to keep our sticky little fingers out of the cookie jar for a while longer than the law rendered absolutely necessary.

'Anyway, things went a bit badly wrong, their vessel was impounded and the partnership was dissolved without the usual formalities; Richardson was found in little pieces in the back of a lorry. It seems, James Mather wasn't available to assist the police in their enquiries,' he used the traditional euphemism for being questioned under suspicion.

At the point where they actually go so far as to admit that someone is a suspect, they have to give him a caution, let him see a solicitor, and engage in other kinds of unhelpful, enquiry-obstructing exercises like producing the accused before a magistrate. So they have this preliminary stage. It's extremely British. The same evasion goes on all over the world, but in this country it is institutionalized to an extent that has its own formal standing.

'The odd thing was,' he continued: 'It was very hard indeed to get in and out of the country in those days. You couldn't just hop a 'plane to the States. And don't forget their ship had been snatched. The files just come to a dead end, like someone ordered it shoved in a drawer. We didn't even try to find out how he got away.'

'Has he surfaced since?'

'Not here. But he's well-known across the ocean. There's an open RICO file on him.'

'Rico?'

'It stands for racketeer-influenced corrupt organizations. It's a law they've got that allows them to indict the people behind the people behind the people, if you see what I mean.'

'Mafia-type thing?'

'Yes, though I think that must be the most abused word in American law-enforcement. I've heard it used for Colombians, Cubans, Costa Ricans, Canadians, even Polish. Did you hear the one about the Polish mafia?'

I waited. He sighed:

'I can't be bothered. It's extremely complicated and I don't understand it either. Something to do with having a contract notarized. But he's not considered active now, more like retired and protecting his investments. Lives in Miami. Not Miami Beach. They're different cities. Everything's a city over there: two men and a dog's a city; McDonald's and a petrol station's a city. Pardon me, gas station.'

'You're sure about not active now?'

'Listen, it's not easy getting information. Over there, they only give it out in trade. Hands across the ocean, special relationship, don't count for nothing. You have to half-hint the Queen's personally at risk before they give you anything. Anyway, it seems this guy has been into everything: drugs, yes, prostitution, yes, gambling, yes, pornography, yes, numbers ... You know what numbers is?'

'Nope.'

'Me neither, but they always say it. At one time, this guy was the only. non-Italian operating out of New York. It seems like,' he dropped his voice like Marlon Brando as Don Corleone: 'People showed him a lot of respect.'

'And all this you managed to get since today ... yesterday? I would've thought it took you that long to find the files?'

He looked at me doe-eyed and sad:

'No, Dave, I didn't say I got it today, or yesterday.'

I had to extract one answer from another. Nothing I was telling him was news. He'd known about James Mather, and he'd known about Stonefrost. I played back my conversation on the first of these topics, and realized he had just fallen short of lying to me.

Pratt came back in, looking pleased with himself, like he'd finally found us after a long time looking:

'We've got one, guv.'

'Yes, Pratt, I daresay you have. Which one?'

'What? Oh, Martin Mather, guv.'

'Any trouble?'

'Nah; like a lamb, they said.' It was quite a long sentence for Pratt, and certainly more graphic than I'd come to expect.

'What about the other?'

Pratt shrugged: it wasn't an attractive sight.

'I dunno, guv. He's not there, is he.' His sole saving grace was that he did not add, though it would have suited: 'know what I mean?'

I looked at my watch: it was nearly six o'clock in the morning. Ali was still asleep in my bed, and I wished I was beside her. Dowell asked me:

'You want to say hallo?'

'Are your forensic people finished yet?'

'They should be. Why?'

'I was wondering about a wee trip to Hampstead,' where Ian Mather lived: 'Someone's got to break the glad tidings to him. Another assistant solicitor terminated without prejudice, who happened to be blackmailing one of his sons for leaking privileged information, with a background in drugs. Another son in the clutches of the constabulary. Maybe another on the lam. I should think it's the sort of thing he'd rather not read about in the papers.' I decided to try it out for size: 'Know what I mean?'

He grimaced: he didn't like it either.

'Next thing, you'll want a police car to take you up there.'

'Well, uh, it would help, at this time of the morning, y'know.'

I followed Dowell down after pausing to check an address in my files.

Martin was sequestered in his own office. That way he wasn't quite so legally in custody. But a uniformed officer was standing inside the door, not outside. He looked up, surprised to see me:

'I'm not sure my sister will appreciate your sense of priorities, Woolf.' For a slice of *sang froid,* it wasn't bad.

Dowell was conferring with the arresting officers — pardon me, officers who had invited Martin to assist in their enquiries. They left, I took it to go fetch Andrew. Dowell joined us before I could reply to Martin's quip. He cleared his throat, then said:

'Sir, I understand you were here earlier this evening. From ten o'clock. Is that correct?'

Martin said nothing, nor even acknowledged the question. He might be only a civil lawyer without experience of criminal law, but he knew enough form to stay *schtum*.

'Are you willing to inform me of what time you left here, sir?'

'About,' I corrected: 'Inform about.'

'Thank you, sir,' Dowell said to me, looking both grave and murderous: 'I think you understood my question, Mr Mather.'

Martin smiled pleasantly:

'Am I under arrest? This is fun: I've never been arrested before.'

'It's not a joking matter, sir.' On balance, I'm fairly sure Martin had managed to get under Dowell's skin.

'Yes it is, officer, if you've done nothing at all that merits the attention of the law. Do you propose to tell me what's going on, or do you not?'

'You are of course acquainted with one Christopher Wainwright, sir,' Dowell spoke slowly. Both the uniformed bobby and the uninformed Pratt were writing down every word of the exchange. I wondered if they'd included my intervention, and how a judge would feel about it.

'Did you see him this evening, sir? After you returned here at ten o'clock?'

Martin had gone pale, but did not reply.

'Will you tell me what time you left here, sir? Can you produce someone to confirm where you were between midnight and when my officers arrived at your house, sir?'

Martin bit his lower lip; for a moment, I thought he was going to say something, but he suppressed the impulse. Dowell shrugged: if that was how Martin wanted to play it, he could play too.

'I am informing you, sir, that Mr Wainwright was murdered, on these premises, at some time after midnight, and that I am arresting you on suspicion of complicity in that offence. I have to tell you that you are not obliged to say anything, but that anything you do say will be taken down and may be used in evidence against you. I also have to inform you of your right to consult a lawyer and to have him present during questioning, so long as I do not consider that this will interfere with my investigation.'

'Her,' Martin said: 'Have her present. I want my sister. She's my lawyer. Will you tell her that, Dave?'

I nodded once. They led him away. Only after he had gone did I realize I couldn't telephone Ali: she was at my home, and the answering machine was switched on.

House didn't quite fit what Ian Mather lived in. Palace overdoes it. Mansion is closest. He lived on Redington Road, in Hampstead, where the midget properties start at a million. He owned a three storey, double winged building which when I looked down the sides dipped sharply enough to tell me there was a fourth storey in the back. I could just about see the end of the garden, past the swimming pool, where the tennis court was. I didn't blame Andrew: if I'd had the choice, it was where I would have lived through college.

I rang at the bell and, eventually, a middle aged Latin woman, probably Italian, came to the door, opening it on the chain. Her eyes widened at the sight of the police car in the drive. I decided to keep it simple, and let her believe it belonged to me, or I to it:

'I'm sorry. I have to see Mr Mather. Would you wake him, please.'

Like most citizens; she believed that a request from the police superseded orders from the Holy Ghost. She shut the door to unhook the chain, and as she re-opened it to let me in, I saw her finish crossing herself. After a minor hesitation, because the social rule book doesn't spell out where to dump a policeman who comes calling at six thirty in the morning, she showed me into the dining room and left me there while she went to wake the master.

A quarter of an hour later, she brought in a tray of tea and toast. I didn't wait to be invited, but helped myself. French pancakes are filling but, like Chinese food, don't last. Ten minutes later, as dapper as ever, the man himself joined me. I admired that he had taken the trouble to dress properly, and to shave, before descending. He apologized for keeping me waiting, acting for all the world as if it was the most normal way to start the day.

'I'm sorry to have to wake you,' I swallowed a 'sir'. I was beginning to like the guy, and to be seduced by his manners.

'I rise at seven in any event, Mr Woolf.'

'Shall I pour?' It would be my second cup.

'That would be most kind. Thank you.'

I could see where Martin got the *sang froid* from. He wasn't going to ask until I was ready to tell him. I said:

'I'm sorry to have to tell you this, Mr Mather. The police rang me.' I decided against explaining in whose company I had been at the time: it was another life. 'There's been another death. Another murder.'

'Yes.' He took his cup in both hands and fumbled to raise it to his lips. He had worked that much out for himself.

'Christopher Wainwright,' I put him out of his misery.

His hands were shaking so bad, tea was spilling everywhere except into his mouth. Gently, I took the cup away from him and replaced it on the saucer. He said:

'I see. It's a great shock.' Then, in a moment of uncommon honesty, he said: 'A great relief.' He'd expected me to announce the death of one of his children.

I let him sip tea for a while before I told him he wasn't that far off: 'I'm sorry. I also have to tell you, Martin's been arrested.'

'For … ?'

'Yes.'

'It's ridiculous. Ridiculous. You must see that? You see that, don't you? Tell me you believe that,' his voice raised: 'Tell me,' he demanded.

'I believe it, Mr Mather.' I don't know whether I would have said it anyway, but as it was true, it seemed churlish to withhold his reassurance.

'Yes, yes, of course you do.' I wasn't sure he was going to survive my visit. It was worrying. I'd never killed one of my own clients. I'd once given a landlord a heart attack under cross-examination, but he survived and we lost the case. If Ian died, would any of the others be willing to keep on paying?

'We must get him a lawyer, a criminal lawyer, at once. Let's see, there's …'

'He asked for Allison,' I nearly said Ali: 'He was most emphatic he wanted her. You see,' I paused before plunging on: 'Wainwright came in expecting to see someone. That suggests someone sent for him. Both he and Randolph were at the office late. I don't think Martin had anything to do with it, Mr Mather, but I wouldn't swear he had no relevant information.'

'What are you saying, Mr Woolf? Are you suggesting that … Randolph?' His eyes bulged unhealthily, but he didn't go into the same song-and-dance routine about his older boy. I figured the wily old goat had a better idea about his children's quirks than I would have anticipated.

'I'm not suggesting anything beyond what I said. I think Martin wants Ali ... Allison ... because he wants to keep things in the family for the moment. I think he should be allowed to follow his own wishes for the time being.'

'He's not your son, Mr Woolf.'

It wasn't my house of cards, either.

'Yeah. OK But things aren't always What they seem. There's something suspicious' about the speed with which Dowell latched onto Martin. You have to understand, Dowell doesn't really deal in anything simple, not even simple murder.' His Adam's apple bobbed: I don't think he had hitherto appreciated that murders could be classified as simple.

'And anything he does, you have to work out what he's really doing.'

'What do you think he is really doing in this case, Mr Woolf?' He wanted to believe me.

'How much do you know about Cross Course, Mr Mather?'

'Martin's investment company? Why? What has that got to do with it?'

'I don't know that it does. But what I'm thinking is, what Dowell wanted wasn't Martin, but a warrant on Martin's premises: home and offices. He gets them automatically now. He didn't want Martin; he wanted grounds for suspicion.' Of course, he could always have broken in, like he had to my home and, once, to Sandy's office; but Dowell could tell the difference between us and a Mather.

He muttered:

'I never liked it. I' never approved. I always said it would get him into trouble. People should do what they are good at, and stick at it. Have you ever noticed, Mr Woolf, how all the lawyers who get into serious trouble — sometimes, even criminal — are those who have been involved in other enterprises?' I didn't like to point out that this was tautologous: as a licence to practice law doesn't include a licence to commit crime, it follows that a lawyer involved in the latter has of definition stepped outside his job description.

Otherwise, though, I knew what he meant and agreed. They see their clients coming in, with all their problems, and they begin to think they can handle things better, without all the problems; they get cocky; they confuse knowing law, and being legal.

'Where is Randolph? And Andrew? Has anyone telephoned Allison to go and see Martin?' He wanted his sons around him.

'Uh, there's no answer from Allison's home number. Perhaps she's taken a sleeping pill.' Not bad on the spur of the moment.

'Randolph wasn't at home. And, er, I believe that Inspector Dowell has made arrangements for Andrew to be informed.' I paused to congratulate myself on my delicacy.

He wasn't fooled:

'Is he under suspicion, too?'

I took a deep breath, then said:

'I'm sorry, I'm very sorry. Wainwright was blackmailing Andrew. I knew. I had to tell Dowell. I hope you understand ...'

He brushed my apology aside:

'Yes, yes. You have to do your duty. Why wasn't I told about Wainwright? What ... ?' He stopped suddenly and shuddered. He didn't want to know.

'I only learned last night.' I waited. He waited. Then he nodded for me to go on. 'I think it's possible ... It's likely ... I think Andrew leaked the information that made the News have to settle the Stonefrost litigation. Wainwright, er, found out about it.'

His shoulders were shaking. I wondered about calling for medical help. His hands were over his face. I said:

'Mr Mather? Mr Mather? Are you alright, sir?'

He wouldn't remove his hands. There was a strangled, gasping sound from within. It took me a long time to realize: the old man was crying. I got up and walked to the window, looked out at the police car still waiting to take us back into the City. The driver looked at me hopefully. I shrugged: not yet. When I turned around, Mather had brought himself under control. We neither of us made any reference to it. He said:

'Do you have more to tell me? I don't want you to conceal anything from me, Mr Woolf. Do you understand me?' But his tone was conciliatory; I think he heard me call him 'sir'; it could be the slip of my tongue that kept me on the case.

'Wainwright was, er, having an affair with the de Peyer woman. Wainwright told her about her husband's property. I suspect she told him about Andrew helping Stonefrost, to persuade him to help her.'

He was shaking his head from side to side, slowly, in disbelief:

'They are lawyers, Mr Woolf, lawyers. I brought up my sons to be lawyers; this is my firm. And … And people have breached privilege for their own, private ends. I cannot … I do not understand how it could happen, Mr Woolf. Do you?'

I poured out the last of the tea, equally: we each got half a cup. He gestured towards a bell on the wall and I got up and pressed it. The woman came at once with a fresh pot, without needing to be told. He waved away her offer to pour, and himself topped up our cups. Before she left, remembering he was a host, he asked me if I wanted more toast. I hated to say it, but:

'I've been up all night. Yes, please.'

'I asked you a question, Mr Woolf. It was not rhetorical.'

'What do I know, Mr Mather? I'm just a private eye scratching around for information. It's not my job to put it together.'

He snorted:

'Yes, I sensed your modesty as soon as I met you.' He was capable of sarcasm, too. 'Tell me something else, then, Mr Woolf. Do you know how the other leaks happened?'

'I've got a lead on one of them,' which reminded me I still hadn't been down to Companies House in accordance with Orbach's oblique instruction.

'And the other?' He wasn't going to eat evasion for an answer.

'I, er, yes, I have an idea. I'd say it was what we call a "bleeding heart leak", a sympathizer, someone who didn't like the idea of the parents remaining uncompensated.'

He met my gaze deliberately:

'And you are not planning to tell me who that was, are you?'

I'll leave the question-mark at the end of the sentence, though I'm not sure to this day whether it was a question, or an injunction. I said:

'No, I'm not. If you'll take it on trust, it won't happen again, and there is no reason to pursue it. It has nothing to do with anything else.'

He licked his dry lips, though whether with relief at the position I had so willingly taken, or because it was totally out of character to take anything on trust, I similarly don't know.

'Mr Mather, there's something else I want to ask you. Was Wainwright a freemason?'

'Yes.' He didn't shilly-shally about confidentiality: the question of a man's membership is his own; he is, contrary to popular belief, entitled to disclose it, in appropriate circumstances and provided it is not for the purpose of self-advancement; once a man is dead, the knowledge may be made public by another.

'The way I remember it, it never used to be a big deal who was and who wasn't. I seem to recall when I was a kid, they used to list people attending Lodge-nights in the local paper.'

'Yes. That's correct. After the war, we became — I'm not really sure why — somewhat introspective, even secretive. It has done the craft enormous harm; it has generated suspicion without cause or purpose.' He filled in a gap: 'Andrew introduced him. I was opposed to it. I did not think he was the sort of chap we wanted. I thought he was joining for unworthy motives. I did not believe he would achieve the standing of a man in good repute. It seems, I was right.'

'But Andrew insisted? Could he do that - over your objection?'

'Freemasonry is Lodge-based, Mr Woolf. I belong to four Lodges, myself, and Andrew is also a member of two of those. But he was a member of a third, and it was into that Lodge that he introduced Wainwright. Now, at least, I understand why.'

'Would you be able ... Would you know, or could you find out for me, about Lodge memberships: different people, who is or was in whose Lodge?'

'Why?' He snapped: 'What are you suggesting now, Mr Woolf.'

'Not a lot. I'm not suggesting a masonic conspiracy. But I think a few people have been a bit too connected to each other. I need to understand who and how much.'

He waited for me to elaborate. I didn't. He said, swallowing the discipline of a lifetime:

'I would need good reason.'

'Alright. I'll talk to you about it again. What about Chapters?'

He froze:

'That is an entirely different issue, Mr Woolf. I am not a companion of the Royal Arch.'

'But the Grand Secretary of Grand Lodge is also Grand Scribe Ezra in Grand Chapter, right?' I tried to keep a straight face as I gave the silly old scribbler his titles: 'And all the obligations, they say "Murder, treason, felony and all other offences of the realm being at all times most especially excepted".'

He was impressed:

'You've done your homework, Mr Woolf.'

'It's your time, Mr Mather.' Time and money.

'I, uh, I will have to think very carefully about this, Mr Woolf; I shall have to take advice.' I guessed who from: the ghoulish Gauldie.

It was time to go. I asked to use a 'phone, and tried my own number, just in case Ali picked it up. If she did, she wasn't admitting it, because I asked if she was there and nothing happened. When I got home, I'd get a recording of my own voice saying 'Allison, Allison, are you there? Pick the receiver up' over and over. I took a ride from the police car into town, but as we approached Oxford Street I asked to be let out. I reminded Mather I hadn't yet spoken to Allison, and he promised to contact her to go to Holborn police station where Martin was being held. I had another Mather to go meet first.

CHAPTER NINE

I'd taken down the address before I left the office. She lived in Mayfair, a block of flats in South Audley Street where only Arabs could now afford to rent or buy, but that had probably been in some part or another of her family for years of rent-controlled privilege. Though costly, it was run-down: impoverished gentility. There was no porter and I made my way up to her fourth floor apartment unhindered. I rang and rang at the bell; it was loud enough to wake the dead, and my thoughts were beginning to drift in that direction when she opened the door on the chain, enough to show herself enticingly alive.

'I'm sorry to disturb you, Mrs de Peyer,' I started the way I meant to carry on, by lying. 'I work for Mather's, and I need to have a word with you.'

'Do you have some identification?' Her voice was gravelly, from sleep and cigarettes, not sexily so.

I produced the bland and uninformative introduction letter I'd had Marion Mortimer type up for me when I began, and taken down for Ian Mather to sign. It was a shame he wasn't around at the time, but most solicitors' letters are in any event signed not with a real person's name, but that of the firm. One hand-written flourish — mine — looks much like another.

She let me in. She wore only a light dressing-gown and no evidence of anything beneath. I could still remember what beneath looked like. She led me into the kitchen and put on a coffee percolator with one hand, while she lit up with another. One of my hypocrisies is that while I smoke like a chimney, I ain't that keen on women who do. (My most 'profound residual sexism is: I can't stand women smoking cigars. It'd be like French-kissing my father.)

'What's all this about, then?' She asked boredly.

'Christopher Wainwright's been killed,' I said deadpan and determined to dent the don't-give-a-damn tone.

Her teeth clenched, but that was it. Her hands didn't tremble as she poured coffee -for both of us. Her voice was level as she asked if I wanted milk and sugar.

'You don't seem very shocked.' She shrugged, bringing half a breast into view for just long enough to make me want it to come out altogether.

'He's a casual friend. That's all. I'm very sorry. You said "killed"? What happened?'

'You knew about the other death at Mather's?'

'I can read.' She absorbed my answer: 'Do the police have any idea yet?'

'How would I know?'

'Because that's your job. I know who you are, Mr Woolf. I've been told about you.'

'No, not yet. I daresay they'll be round to see you.'

'When did it happen? Do you think they'll want to check on my alibi?'

'I should think so. It happened late last night. After midnight, anyway. Do you have an alibi?'

She laughed prettily:

'Sure. It's still asleep inside. Shall I fetch it?'

There was a smug twinkle in her eye: she wanted me to see who it was. I would have liked to have refused, on perverse principle, but I didn't professionally have that option. He was who I had come to see. I needed the visible proof that he was as greedy, as insatiable, as unconcerned for anyone else — ultimately, as out of control by any recognizable criteria — as I had suspected, and as almost everyone had, in one way or another, hinted.

As he entered, I picked up my coffee cup in a 'cheers' gesture:

'Breakfast with members of your family seems to be the order of the day.'

Randolph raised half an eyebrow while he poured his own coffee and then, unexpectedly, refilled mine. I returned the hospitality:

'I just left your father. He's gone in to the office. I should think he'd like you to come in. I know the police would.'

'Yes,' was all he said.

For all the aplomb, I'd shaken his cool, though it was yet unclear whether with news of Wainwright's rapid removal from the rolls or my discovery of him *in flagrante* with Anabelle de Peyer. I wanted to know what he had that could attract so many women, some of them extremely delightful. Maybe there was something to masonic mystique after all; being had in a hood might be fun.

'Did Wainwright know about you two?'

'I've known Anabelle for many years.' That much coincided with what Katrina. had said: he and Andrew had both claimed to be too close to handle the divorce for her ex-.

'What you're saying is, this isn't exactly the first time?'

'Correct. I would have to say, I don't think Christopher knew we still occasionally slept together. It, er, it is not what you would call a serious relationship, and of course neither of us is currently married.' He was saying he couldn't be a suspect either on the grounds of jealousy or to keep the affair secret.

'You were at the office late last night. With a secretary?' If I'd thought it might annoy Anabelle, I was wrong; she chuckled throatily and amused.

'Working, you know,' he waved a hand airily: 'That sort of thing.' We weren't supposed to believe him; if anything, he was admitting my accusation, bragging about his capacity.

'When did you arrange this — well — arrangement?' They exchanged a glance so fast I almost didn't catch it. He said:

'You still haven't told me where Christopher was killed.'

'At the office. He came in around midnight, expecting to meet someone, looking cheerful. My guess is, you rang him, and told him to meet you there; Mrs de Peyer said she was tired — not to come back. Is that about right?' It was a similar trick Katrina said Martin had once played on Tony Galucci; I began to wonder exactly what Ian Mather had taught them when he gave them each his version of the birds and the bees.

'That's what you say. Why would Mrs de Peyer need an excuse to tell him to leave?'

'I don't know,' I watched her while I answered him: 'But maybe he wasn't that easy to get rid of. You know? After all, she had what she wanted out of him a long time ago: since the divorce settlement; but she was still seeing him.'

They both understood what I was implying. She paled, but didn't let me draw her into it.

'I think you had better leave now, Woolf. I'm sure this is most distressing for Mrs de Peyer.'

'Yeah, sure, she looks distressed.' I was curious about something: 'Tell me, though. If you two have been such good buddies — bosom buddies, you might say — how come you didn't let her know about hubby's land in the Bahamas?'

He couldn't resist:

'That would be a breach of privilege, Woolf. It would be unthinkable.'

I met his mocking gaze:

'Yeah, right. Why didn't I think of that?' I waited a second: 'So you did know about it, then?' I'd flushed out an answer; he flushed right back at me. He mumbled:

'I didn't, as it happens,' knowing how non-credible it now sounded. He tried to bolster his answer: 'That's the sort of thing I might have found out, that led me not to conduct the case. Conflict of interest. There's no evidence to support what you're hinting about Christopher either. You're guessing.'

He was fumbling.

'Whyn't we ask Anabelle?' I turned to look at her; she was better to look at than Randolph.

'I said, you'd better leave, Woolf. I meant it.'

I was too tired to fight. I got up to go. Something else puzzled me, but I wouldn't get an answer this time around, even by default: if he wanted me to know he was with Katrina shortly before she was killed, albeit apparently reluctantly, why not admit he'd called Wainwright in? There is absolutely no better defence than an innocent explanation of the truth. Unless the difference was: he hadn't expected her to be murdered.

By the time I arrived at the office, Ali had been and gone, to Holborn police station where they were holding Martin. By the time I arrived at Holborn, she had gone with the police to Cross Course, to witness the search. I asked whether I could see Martin; they called Dowell at Cross Course and — still suspiciously helpful — he agreed. We were allowed to talk alone in a bleak, barred interview room.

He didn't look so chipper. No longer the swinge-breech. He needed to shave; his eyes were bloodshot, his shirt wrinkled, he wasn't wearing a tie. I said:

'D'they take it away from you?'

He held up a foot. He was wearing loafers:

'I think they were disappointed there were no shoelaces to remove.'

'How's it going? They feed you?'

'Now I know why they're called pigs; the swill they eat.'

'You going to court?'

He shook his head:

'Tomorrow. You took your time getting Allison here,' he complained.

'Problem. She was at my house; answering machine. Sorry: I had to go see your father.'

'How is he?' He asked anxiously.

'He's a tough old buzzard.'

'How much did you tell him?'

'All I know, more or less.'

'What was the less?'

I shrugged:

'No reason to tell you either.'

'I thought you trusted me, when you came to see me last night?'

'I did. Until you lied to me.'

'How did I lie to you?'

'Well, I can't recall exactly if you lied. Same way you said Andrew wouldn't've leaked. What's the expression that guy used: "economical with the truth", is that it?'

He smiled thinly:

'If it's good enough for the government, it's good enough for me.' The man who had brought the expression back into contemporary usage was the former British Cabinet secretary, who happened to be giving evidence in a court at the time: this is what is meant by the integrity of the civil service; they don't deny being a bunch of lying shits.

'Andrew's more deeply in trouble than you said. Right?'

He didn't answer.

'You were too easy, Martin. You rolled over on his leak like you were doing me a big favour. But a squirt who knew Andrew'd leaked a bit of information on a case wasn't worth eight or nine grand, was he? Especially not to Andrew, with his affection for Mr Green,' a Hill Street coinage. 'While I was waiting for your father to come down this morning, I tried to work out what he needed to live like he does. I've got a fair idea of all your earnings: it isn't nearly as much as I expected. You've all had to pay your way into the partnership, by deduction from profits.'

It was the usual way to buy in to a practice. If Ian hadn't also been so tight, I would've been more surprised he'd made his children pay their way in. 'Anyhow, it didn't leave a lot of change to host weekend parties and buy a lot of drugs to keep the guests happy and high. You — I know where your extra loot comes from. And Randolph ain't spending money getting his kicks — quite literally — so I don't know what he's worth. But where'd's Andrew's come from, Martin?'

He still didn't answer, so I told him:

'He was more involved with Stonefrost than you allowed. That's why he had to stop it getting to trial, not 'cos he might've been implicated as an occasional user, but as a dealer: I think Wainwright found out about it somehow: I don't know how; yet, but I will.'

'I don't know what you're talking about,' he said flatly.

'Never drink coca-cola?' I asked.

He looked at me like I was crazy; maybe he ought to call a guard before I flipped completely. I ignored the expression on his face:

'Did you know: ever since they changed the formula for coca-cola, there's been a shortage of cocaine? They produced a lot of it — a hell of a lot of it — before, and it was processed and sold to the medical industry. It was of course perfectly legitimate, indeed a helpful by-product. Don't forget, cocaine became known to the developed world as a medicine: it was nearly Freud's first major breakthrough, for use as an eye anaesthetic, though someone else got it just before. Then he discovered its other qualities: he used to put his whole family on it, when they got depressed. I guess he didn't have the time to spare to analyse them out of it.'

'What has it got to do with the price of eggs?'

'A lot of that legal coke got ripped off. Along the way, or at end destinations. It wasn't in itself one of the major sources, because most of them are sewn up, but it was a side-line source. It used to get into this country via Haiti, until they deposed the Duvaliers. Since then, the Bahamas is a favourite route. People coming in from the Bahamas are like diplomatic bags, they don't hardly get looked at. My guess is, de Peyer's Bahamian property was bought with drugs money: that's why it was never declared anywhere. It shouldn't even have been on file at Mather's. It's why it couldn't come out

in a court case.'

I waited to see if I had yet scored a reaction. In a way, I had. He leaned across the table, picked up my pack of Camels and extracted one for himself. I asked:

'How come none of you smoke openly? You're the third one to bum a fag off me that way.'

'Father didn't approve. His father died of cancer.'

The funeral his uncle couldn't come back for.

We sat in silence for a time, while he savoured the cigarette. Prompted by the reference to his grandfather, I said:

'Tell me about James Mather.'

'What's to tell?'

'Why is Dowell interested in Cross Course?'

'You tell me.'

'My thinking is, maybe it's a laundry for your uncle's dirty money?'

He laughed out loud:

'You're crazy, you know that, Dave?'

'So tell me,' I persisted.

'Why not? It's something to talk about while we wait.'

When he'd finished his long period of articles, he had inveigled his father into funding a summer sabbatical in the States. The only condition had been that he not look for his uncle. Martin said:

'I didn't have to. He was waiting for me when I came off the 'plane.'

'How? How did he know you were coming?'

'I asked him just that. He's the one gave me that line about not asking how someone found something out but working it out for yourself.'

'And did you? Work it out, I mean?'

He shook his head:

'No, I was just a kid, really.' America's fate is to be excused as a youthful folly. 'It was all so exciting, I was tired at the time, it never seemed important to know. Someone told him, but I don't know who. I suppose, it wasn't that big a secret; it could've been coincidence. Maybe it's what you said: it wasn't because he was good at finding things out, just that he found a way to use it.'

'Go on about James.'

'Well, as I said, it was exciting. I was what — twenty-two, twenty-three? I'd stayed up the night before, then my first really long 'plane flight. I spent it chatting up a girl in the seat next to me; I didn't have enough experience to realize how common that is when you're travelling, how you can get to feel really close to someone that quickly, because, after all, you're going to go your separate ways as soon as you arrive. So I was very turned on when I arrived, and as I came through customs I was suddenly being hustled towards this old guy — and I knew immediately who he was, the resemblance is marked — and a limousine.'

He stopped for a moment, perhaps reluctant to share a story he had savoured in secret for such a long time. 'We drove into town. He had an apartment in the Dakota — the place where Lennon lived; oh, not then, of course. But it was his New York home. And he took me up and there was, you know, well a girl there, he said was looking after the apartment for him. And he told me to get some food, have a shower, get some sleep if I could — he'd come by for me the next day. That was what she was for: to help me sleep. It was unbelievable, it was like out of a movie. She was young, she looked like a college girl, not a hooker; but she was good, God was she good. Everything before, well, I wasn't a virgin — none of us were in those days — but it was like I'd been chewing someone else's stale gum.'

He paused to enjoy the memory, his face alight:

'It was the best time of my life, ever. He wanted me to stay with him: I don't mean in New York; he wanted to travel around with me. We compromised, and I agreed to spend about half the time with him — I was there for four months, but in the end I did spend most of it with him. It was just so easy: everywhere we went was first class; he had friends everywhere — you also know he isn't exactly a conventional businessman, but his friends were all sorts. Once, we went to a party on the Cape, I met this guy everyone thought was going to be the next President: me, I was standing talking to him.'

His face shone still with the thrill:

'He had a family: a common law wife and a daughter, they lived in New Hampshire, and either she deliberately didn't know what he did for a living or they really didn't: the wife, I mean, the girl was still in her teens; she certainly didn't know. He didn't spend a lot of time with them. No one else was supposed to know about them: just me; I was his nephew; I was also family. And we went out to the West Coast: you know, we'd arrive, he'd make a 'phone call, there were people coming through the door before he hung up; tables at the best restaurants, the best seats at the ring, anything. And girls: for him, for me — they'd just appear. We went to New Orleans. You ever been to New Orleans, Dave? It's fantastic, maybe the most fantastic city of all: it's like all the best of Europe, condensed, but with all the historical hang-ups discarded. You cannot, you simply cannot have any idea at all what it was like.'

'It sounds like a dream?'

'A fantasy, more like.'

'How did it end? How was it left?'

He shrugged indifferently:

'It ended. He drove me, himself; usually when we drove he had a chauffeur, only I think the sort of machines he was best equipped to handle had triggers, not wheels. So he drove me down to Kennedy, from New Hampshire. And on the way, he made this big, long speech — sort of in bits, but I remember it as if it was one speech. About how the world was divided into three types of people. The bossed, the bosses and the bosses' bosses. He said no matter how high up you go, and how far back, when you come to someone who seems to be in charge, there's always one more behind.'

People behind the people behind the people.

'I think he was telling me, well, I know he was saying that's what he was: one more behind someone else. He was telling me to make my choices. I could live my father's way, according to a tight set of rules and with a narrow set of expectations, or I could live his: the hell with the rules, the whole world and nothing less was what I could expect.'

'And?'

He stopped to look for the right way to tell me. He went in at an angle:

'You read much, Dave?'

'Comics?'

'Do you know John O'Hara?'

'Maybe. Why?'

'I read this article about him. About how fed up he was because he'd never won the Nobel prize for literature.' I sympathized: I'd never won it neither. Know what I mean? 'Anyhow, the article was by this journalist who'd gone to O'Hara's home one night, uninvited. It was some kind of anniversary, or his birthday or something. And he looked in the window of this big, country house, and what he saw was a ballroom orchestra, and there were no guests, just O'Hara and his wife, dancing alone.'

I shook my head to clear it: I hadn't slept; I was tired; that was probably why I couldn't see the connection.

'The way O'Hara was, that's the way I used to see my parents. All alone in the Hampstead mansion. It's been more acute since mother went into the hospital. What I'm trying to say, look at my choices. I could be like my father; big, rigid man, a freemason but no real friends; just rules, bloody rules. You don't want to know what it was like being brought up by him. Did you ever think what a coincidence it is we've all become lawyers? We were never given a choice, Dave.'

'You found James attractive?'

'Absolutely. Randolph-was already well-set in his way: also a mason, heavily so, into the Royal Arch crap too, and ...' But he didn't finish the sentence. Instead, he said: 'Following Gauldie: now there was another role model for me. Gauldie loves, in the following order: himself, money, power; himself, money, freemasonry. Randolph's admired him all his life. He loves hierarchy, authority over others, the ritual, the mystery.'

He quoted: '"We three do meet and agree ... in love and unity ... the sacred word to keep ... and never to divulge the same ... unless when three ... such as we ... do meet and agree ... agree ... agree ... agree." That's a bit of Royal Arch, but I don't know much, because Ian isn't.' Maybe Shakespeare was though.

'So you went the way of James?'

He shook his head:

'No. That's the point I'm trying to make. I didn't want to be like James either. There's something weird about the Mathers, Dave, it gets to us all. Something to do with my grandfather, I think. Trying to live up to him, experience what he experienced. He had it tough when he was a boy; he was the ultimate self-made man. He was hard. Insecure, I suppose, but they didn't use terms like that in those days. And Andrew ... He was also Andrew,' he explained: 'And Andrew begat James and Ian and James begat Randolph and Martin and Andrew ...'

'Ali? She appeared under a bushel, maybe?'

'I'm sorry, Dave. I'm not being very helpful. I'm just trying to explain. I did not take up James on his offer. Though, for a while I thought I might: it was probably part of why I set up Cross Course.'

'Why'd'he make the offer?'

'At the time, I believed it was affection: he had his wife and daughter in New Hampshire; but he didn't live with them, and no son. I thought he wanted a relationship with me, for its own sake, you know?'

'But that isn't what you think now?'

'No, nor for a long time. I think he wanted a relationship with me not for its own sake, but in order to get back at Ian. He wanted to hurt Ian, by bringing me into his way of life and out of Ian's. Revenge. And, you know, I was tempted, I could so easily have done it. But that's what it would have, done: hurt Ian, more than I could stand.'

'Revenge for what?'

'That's something you'll have to ask Ian.'

'Why'd'you go to the office last night?' I shot at him.

'I rang Randolph at home; he wasn't there. I rang his private line; he answered. I wanted to talk to him, about Wainwright, about what you told me.'

'What'd he say?'

He didn't answer.

'He already knew, didn't he?' He still wouldn't tell me.

'How'd I do otherwise?' I meant my earlier analysis of Andrew's activities.

'Ah,' he said sadly: 'I won't lie to you anymore, Dave. It's gone a bit too far for that. But ... Well ... There may be no love lost, but they're family. All I'll say is, you weren't wrong, but you weren't that right either.'

'For God's sake,' I snapped. disgustedly: 'People are dying, Martin. It isn't like sneaking on a school-fellow.'

Maybe it was though: to care about life and death, you gotta care about people; the thing about the English upper classes is — they don't care, period; sneaking on a school-chum betrays the code, which is far more serious than whatever might happen to the fellow himself.

I didn't get any answer because that was when Dowell returned. He wanted the key to Martin's house: that was where they were going next. Martin gave it him without argument. It was easier than having the door repaired. I told him:

'I'll talk to Allison. I'll see you later.'

Tim said:

'She's meeting us at the house. I don't want you there, Dave.'

'I've got other things to do.'

They didn't have an underground station marked Beat Kelly, so I got off at Bank instead. No one had been lying when they told me it was only a small set-up. There was a reception counter within the main, outer office, and from the number of desks and computer terminals, I figured most of the staff worked in one, open-plan environment. They were busily sorting out files into drawers: replacing them after Dowell's descent. There were only two doors off. One was ajar, and I could see it was a conference room. The other was shut. That was where Beat Kelly would work.

'Could I see her?'

'Do you have an appointment? She's been very busy this morning.'

'Yes, I know about that. And, no, I don't have an appointment. Tell her it's Dave Woolf. I think she'll know the name, but if not you can say I was a friend of her sister.'

I was shown in with a minimum of ceremony. Martin had said she was beautiful. He hadn't lied about that either. For a moment, I could hardly believe she was Katrina's sister. Her hair was much lighter, almost blonde. She was about two inches taller, and several inches smaller around the waist and chest. If her skirt had been a millimetre shorter, I could tell how the thighs compared

'Yes, I've heard about you. From Katrina. And from Martin.' I sat down without waiting to be asked. She looked confused: 'The police took a lot of papers. Can they do that?'

'I don't know. Allison Hoyt was here with them, wasn't she?'

'Yes. But, well, she didn't seem to know either. We made them list everything. Is that what you came about?'

'It just seemed like time to talk.'

'Would you like some coffee? Or a drink?' She glanced at her watch; I didn't bother glancing at mine but said yes to the second. She didn't ask what I drank, but poured it out for me, and the same for herself.

'The first thing I remember Kat ever telling me about you was how much Southern Comfort you could put away.' There was the slightest accent in her voice. Notwithstanding the Irish name; I knew she wasn't, anymore than Kat had been Italian. She confirmed: 'I was married to an American called Michael Kelly. We're divorced now, well, isn't everyone?'

'I was never married,' I answered. I remembered: Allison said she had lived in the States.

'That's not smart. Marriage is the quickest way to someone else's bank balance.' She grinned and when she grinned she looked like her sister's twin. I felt a warm glow of belated recognition. Kat wasn't dead after all; just reincarnated with a lot less weight to carry about.

'Do you miss her?'

'I'm supposed to be the one asking the questions. But, yes, I do miss her, which is stupid because I hadn't seen her for a long time until just before she died.' I found myself telling Beat about the last evening together, and admitting out loud, as I hadn't admitted to anyone, why I felt guilty: 'I didn't have to go. I could've just stayed on 'till she was finished talking. It wasn't like I had a job to get up to in the morning. I could've slept on the couch. But I wasn't comfortable about some of the things she'd told me.' I didn't elaborate.

She was only barely listening to my expiation. She said:

'I can hear her. "Play bodies" was one of her expressions. You can't live for other people. We've all got the right to make our own mistakes.'

'What are yours?'

She got up and poured us both another drink. When she returned, she took a pack of cigarettes from the bag hanging on the back of her chair, and offered me one. I was about to refuse when I realized they were Camels. I thought about asking how she'd like to get her hands on my bank balance.

'Michael, I suppose. No, that's not true. We had a time, for a while.'

'Why were you over there?'

'I went to work there.' She was surprised I didn't know. People think their mutual friends and acquaintances talk about them more than usually proves to be the case.

She explained: she was — as I knew — Kat's older sister; she was also bright, and ahead of her years; she had qualified as an accountant early, and decided to take a couple of years in America rather than go straight into practice here. She wasn't qualified to practise as an accountant in the States, so she worked in business.

'What kind of business?' She shrugged:

'Things a bit like this. Kat never said?'

'No.' Kat had been holding back; I thought because of Beat's connection to Galucci.

'Did she know what you did?'

'I got around a lot. I was in Colorado, I met Michael. I couldn't believe an Irishman in Colorado, but there were plenty. We went down to Nevada together, got married in a hurry, I was just a kid, I didn't know what I was doing: that's why, you know, I don't really like to go back over it all.' Another one to write America off as an adolescent indiscretion.

'What happened with Kelly?'

'Nothing. After a while, nothing happened; that was the main reason for getting divorced, so I came back here.'

'How long were you there?'

'Three, four years. It seemed like longer.'

'And then?'

'Then I met Martin, and Tony, and I liked their ideas and the way they were beginning — just beginning, then — to approach money and the market: don't forget, we're talking years before Big Bang.' De-regulation of the stock market.

She warmed to her theme: 'We've been so totally conservative about money in this country, that's why the early Americans to make money here could make so much so easily. Martin and Tony, they saw the way things were going, how much mileage could be made out of diversification, how much money could be made out of an enterprise that didn't give a damn about tomorrow, just wanted in and out. It's all like that now, but in those days it felt — oh, I don't know — I mean, being an accountant isn't exactly an adventure, and it had been exciting working in America so I was looking for something like this. The idea of conventional practice was anathema.'

'You said "early Americans": like Latimer?'

'Sure. But he wasn't the only one. Though, I guess, he made his start here, while others came over already successful in the States.'

'Some did it the other way around,' I probed cautiously.

'What do you mean?'

'I was thinking of Martin's uncle, James Mather. What do you know about him?'

'Martin's talked about him.'

'How did Kat feel about you and Tony?' I shifted gear suddenly enough to catch her with her guard down. (I think that one goes on the funeral pyre with the other mixed metaphors.)

She shrugged:

'It was no harder for her to cope with than Tony having to cope with Martin and her.' But she hadn't told me about it, and in the context of that conversation it was a distinct, not a casual or accidental, omission:

'Did you and Martin ever, er ... ?'

'No. And to save you asking, I'd rather die than do it with Randolph Mather.'

'But you knew about his, er … ?' Talking to her sister made me coy about the details.

She blushed, bringing back more colour than she'd lost a couple of questions ago:

'Yes, she told me.'

I couldn't find it in me to ask her; as I'd asked Martin: what had she done about it? I wanted to think that it wasn't an entire irrelevance. I tried to construct a theory that linked his behaviour to her death: she was telling people; people minded; they were going to get him for it; he got in there first. It didn't make a straight line.

'Another question?' She nodded permission. 'Who do you think killed her, Beat?'

She shuddered:

'I haven't the first idea. I've thought about it; of course I've thought about it. If I thought I could pin it on Randolph, I'd kill him myself. I heard: you feel the same way. But he's alibi'd, and he's not concealing he was with her just beforehand. She never harmed anyone, Kat: she was bright, and chirpy, and I loved her more than anyone else.' There were tears in her eyes so maybe she was telling the truth; at least, she wanted me to believe she was.

I waited for them to subside, then I asked:

'Obviously, you know about Wainwright?'

'What about him?' The temperature dropped to somewhere below freezing. This time, I got up to pour the drinks. She grasped her glass with both hands, the way Ian Mather had been holding his tea when I gave him the news. She was younger; she made it all the way to her mouth without spilling a drop.

'Any thoughts?'

She shook her head:

'I didn't know him.'

I took a wild shot: they're my best. When I stop to think, I invariably get it wrong.

'What if I told you it was the same person that killed Katrina?'

If I'd had a camera in my hand, I could have convicted her; I didn't have a camera, and she was beyond confession. She slumped back in her chair, stared at me for a full minute, then hissed:

'Get out of here, Woolf; get out of here.'

I didn't move. Her eyes were bulging. I was an inch away from all the answers. She knew who had killed Wainwright, and now she believed she knew who had killed her sister. I waited for her to calm down. I waited for her to tell me.

'I can't,' she whispered: 'I don't know, I don't know. It was just a shock. It brought it all back, you see it brought it all back. That's all; that's it. I loved Katrina, Dave, I did, I really did. I wouldn't hurt her for all the world.' She made about as much sense as a masonic ritual.

'Beat, you have to tell me what you know. She was your sister, for Christ's sake. You owe it her.'

She shook her head violently:

'It won't bring her back, will it? I didn't know, I'm telling you, I didn't know anything about it.'

'I know, I believe that. But you do know now. What about the police? They're going to be round again. You might as well tell me.'

Time was operating against me. Every exchange allowed her to recover herself.

'There's nothing to tell. I'm sorry. I'm sorry,' she repeated dully: 'You have to leave now. I insist.'

I shrugged:

'I'll go, now, but it isn't that easy, you know. It — whatever it is you know, whoever it is you're scared of — it isn't going to go away like walking out the door.'

'I know,' she said dully: 'Don't think I don't know that much.'

I got up to go. I sighed:

'No, I'm sure you know that much, I'm sure you know more. You're cut from the same cloth Kat was, Beat. I want to help you, if I can, if you'll let me. People are getting killed for what they know, Beat; I wouldn't like you to be one of them.' I like to end on a subtle note.

She looked like I was discussing the arrangements for her funeral. Shaking, as I left the room, she was already reaching for the telephone, probably to call Tony. Or, a travel agent.

CHAPTER TEN

I had been lying to Beat Kelly from start to end: I did not know that the person who killed Wainwright had also killed Kat. The evidence pointed in the opposite direction.

'Person' wasn't really what I meant.

This is close to what I mean:

'The Juwes are

'The Men That

'will not

'be blamed

'for nothing'.

'Juwes' is not a misprint for Jews. 'Jubela, Jubelo and Jubelum — known collectively as the *Juwes*. In masonic lore, the Juwes are hunted down and executed "by the breast being torn open and the heart and vitals taken out and thrown over the left shoulder"', according to the author of *The Brotherhood,* the book that had almost not seen the light of day thanks to unfortunate fatherhood.

The subject was Jack the Ripper, who murdered a handful of prostitutes in London's East End in 1888: there's every kind of theory who done it, including the then Prince of Wales, but no one was ever caught or convicted of the killings. One theory is that freemasons were responsible. The relationship to freemasonry is evidenced by the eradication of the above nursery rhyme from a wall near one of the murders, by no less a personage than the Commissioner of Metropolitan Police of the time, a prominent freemason and a member of the Royal Arch.

In 1981, a scandal broke in Italy, America and all points between. It was known as P2. Not to overstate the position, a gaggle of Italian freemasons had put themselves in virtual control of the nation. (This doesn't mean as much as in a normal country: they change governments in Italy somewhat more often than underwear. But it's still something.) The implications rippled through the western world: they had three cabinet members, a few former prime ministers, several football teams of members of parliament, half the command of the armed forces, the judiciary, the police and the media, and a number of bankers.

The names have gone down in history: Gelli, Sindona, and Calvi, the man who liked to hang about Blackfriars Bridge. But the details have quickly been obscured. This isn't a history book so I'm not going to spell out the whole story, but these people were running the whole country, and everything that the wealth of a nation could buy. Ian Mather had scorned my conspiracy theory at its inception; but at the end of P2, the Americans decided not to act to replace all its involved officials, because of the effect it would have had on NATO (them what keeps you and me safe in our beds at night). That's how big it'd grown.

I made two more stops before I went back to the office. The first was to Companies House where I learned I was wrong about Westmoreland House: Cross Course played no traceable part in it. The second was to Hackney Town Hall. I'd tried to find the report about freemasonry at the council that Orbach had mentioned, but it wasn't in any library or bookshop so, undaunted, I decided to go to the source.

It was about five o'clock when I arrived. No one stopped me at the door, but there weren't many people around. English local government doesn't like to work late; it's not a rule, just a convention. I wandered down long, bland corridors, poking my head into unlocked rooms. If there was anything to steal, I could have stole it blind.

I was just emerging — fortuitously empty-handed — from a room marked 'Chief Executive's Secretary' when a woman came out of the next door office.

'Can I help you?' she asked politely.

I was surprised. She was smart, attractive, in her mid-forties, and spoke with an accent more polished than I would have expected of a secretary in what is variously referred to as the People's Republic of Hackney, 'Ackney, and the Lodestar of the Lunatic Left. I don't normally go for older women, but she could prove the exception.

'Uh, yeah. You had an inquiry here, a while ago, about freemasonry. D'you know anything about it?'

'I seem to remember something of the kind,' she said dryly: 'What about it? It was a long time ago, and not very significant.'

'I was wondering — how does someone go about getting a copy of its report? I understand it was made public, is that right?'

'Yes. But why would "someone" want a copy? It's very lengthy, and extremely tedious.'

'I'm, er, interested in the subject.' I felt like I was being hauled up to explain myself to the headmistress.

'Do you live in Hackney, Mr uh … ?'

'Woolf, Dave Woolf. No, I don't.' I swallowed a 'Thank God'. No one wants to live in Hackney. The worst thing is the road-planning. Most people born there are still trying to find the way out.

'Does that matter?'

'Hackney residents are entitled to a copy free of charge. Others have to pay.'

'You've still got a copy, then?'

'Good lord, yes. Hardly anyone was interested in it. By the end, I don't even think the author was. There were hundreds of copies printed, and most of them are now used to prevent subsidence in the basement.'

'Listen, I've been looking for somewhere I can get one. Can you help me?'

'The Council's Secretariat receives requests for copies. But I'm afraid there'll be no one there at this time. You'll have to write to them.'

'Aw, shucks,' I batted my eyelids: 'I still have trouble making the loops on all those letters.'

She was not impressed. I tried again:

'Listen, I'm a solicitor. It's really important to something I'm working on, not against Hackney,' I hastened to add. 'Is there any way I could get a copy now?'

She sighed:

'I suppose I ought to seize the opportunity to reduce the stocks; it probably won't come again. I still have half a dozen in my room. You'll have to pay, though.'

Oh, yeah, I got it: everyone's on the take. Reluctantly, I pulled out my wallet. She shook her head:

'A cheque please. Payable to the London Borough of Hackney. I shall give you a receipt.'

That was when she led me into her room. Not, as I expected, the room marked 'Secretary', but the one next door, without a marking. She walked behind a huge desk and familiarly opened a drawer, from which she extracted a key, which she used to open a cupboard. She pulled out a massive, yellow-bound volume and offered it to me. She must've been stronger than me, because I could only just carry it. She sat behind the desk while I wrote my cheque, and scribbled a receipt on a sheet of headed notepaper. Curiosity got the better of me:

'You're not the Chief Executive's secretary, are you?'

'The word "secretary" is redundant.'

'I suppose it happens all the time? Sorry.'

'Oh, no, Mr Woolf: it never happens. I do not allow it to happen.'

I left the room backwards, bowing courtly: ma'am, your 'umble servant.

When I got back to Mather's, Allison still hadn't returned from Martin's house: there was a message to ring her there, or go over, she'd wait for me. Dowell must have left if I would now be welcome. I wanted to see Ian Mather first, but he was in. conference with Andrew. I was glad not to have to be present. Marion brought me two mugs of coffee, as she had done ever since that was what I asked for the day Dowell came to see me.

I was having difficulty thinking straight. That had been the morning after I'd first slept with Ali. It felt like a month ago, but it was only the day before and I hadn't slept since.

The atmosphere in the office was thick enough to cut with a medieval sword. Randolph, apparently, had been questioned by Pratt, and released: he had an alibi that Pratt would much prefer to spend several hours interviewing. I knew it would stand up. I sent Marion out for a fresh cream donut before I starved to death.

While I waited for Ian to finish with Andrew, I leafed through the report. As Orbach had accurately summarized, most of it reflected its author's concern with the want of organization within the authority, rather than his commission to discern how much of it was rotten with freemasons. I am no more interested in local government than in any other kind of organization that tries to tell me what to do. For this reason, I flipped quickly through to the part of the report that concerned the ancient ('antient') order of freemasons. I paused at a few passages.

One of them described the initiation ceremony in terms by now familiar. There was also an explanation of Jabulon. He was said not only to be a secret God, but secret even to most of the membership. The name was apparently a composite of Jehovah (the angry God of my youth), Baal and Osiris, the Egyptian God of the dead. I don't know who Baal was: maybe he dealt dope.

My eye was caught by a heading 'Donkey Whipping. It is not generally believed, however, that there is any basis in the rumour that Freemasons whip donkeys, give poisoned sweets to schoolchildren, or drink boiled nail-clippings.' I wasn't amused: I was still eating.

Freemasons claimed to be 'men concerned with moral and spiritual values, who accordingly can be regarded as having taken it upon themselves to cultivate their own moral improvement ... The notion of "good citizens" recurred ... They ... invite men who they considered to be "of good reputation" ... to join.' I was out.

The contradictions were reflected in a passage which referred to John Poulson, who represents corruption in English local government about the same way Mayor Richard Daley does in America, subject to the minor difference that Poulson got caught and the major difference that a lot more money was up for grabs in Chicago. 'Commentators will commonly remark upon the membership of Freemasonry of Mr Poulson; yet one of the principal judges who condemned and sentenced him for his activities was himself also a Freemason, and prominently so ...'

Relevantly, the report recorded: 'It is hard to resist an impression of Freemasonry as constituted of generals and their foot-soldiers ...' This was the description Orbach had lifted: it did my heart good to realize that even he could sometimes stoop to plagiarism.

The analogy fitted with the conclusions I was beginning to form for myself. The way I saw it, the real danger was not the institution itself, but what men made of it. People with an attitude to life that relished ridiculous robes, raunchy ritual and obscene obligations, nonetheless enjoyed access to alleged secret powers and esoteric mysteries. Boys will be boys; it was a recipe for abuse and corruption, and ultimately and inevitably for evil.

Marion buzzed me to say that Ian was free. I wandered down the stairs. Andrew was just coming up, ashen-faced. Our eyes met; his were bloodshot; he had been crying. For a moment, I thought he was going to strike out. He raised a hand then, suddenly, thrust it towards me. Nervously, I took it. He said:

'I have to take a year off. Then he'll decide if I can come back,' he laughed uneasily: 'If I was anyone else, I'd be out on my ear.' As Kat said, even Ian could not resist spoiling him.

'No hard feelings, then, Andrew?'

'No,' he shook his head: 'To tell you the truth, it feels like a great weight has been lifted off me. I've been here since I left college; I know I've let him down; it's been a strain. I don't know how Marilyn will take it, but for myself, I'm just relieved the deception is over.'

'Is it?'

'What do you mean?'

'Your father's suspended you for leaking, right?'

'Yes?'

'I just hope he doesn't have to suffer anymore unpleasant surprises, Andrew.' He stared at me, trying to work out how much I knew. He said:

'I don't think ... I won't treat you like an idiot, Woolf: you've proved you're not, whatever we thought of you when you arrived. Obviously, there are things yet to come out: I didn't kill Wainwright, and you still haven't solved Katrina's death. But whatever else there is I think I've seen the worst of what I will have to take the blame for.' He was only following orders.

'I don't suppose you'd care to enlighten me? Tell me what other surprises there might be?'

He went white as a sheet:

'I would, Dave. I would. But ... I can't betray ... Oh, hell. No, that's all, no.'

'The brotherhood? Is that what you were going to say?'

He shook his head, his lips pursed:

'I wasn't going to say anything. Just, well, as you said, no hard feelings.'

We shook hands again — normal, not masonic — and I proceeded to the old man's office. Old was right: he'd aged twenty years in the short time I'd known him. I wasn't sure I hadn't too. He gestured me to a seat. He said:

'Would you like a drink, Mr Woolf?'

It was uncharacteristically generous; I hoped he wouldn't deduct it from my bill:

'Sure.'

'What would you like?'

'I, er, drink Southern Comfort. No ice. No soda.'

He looked puzzled:

'I don't believe ... Uh ... I don't think I've ever heard ... That is to say, I don't suppose we ...'

'Sure you do. Marion Mortimer's been keeping stocks since I arrived.'

'I'll try.'

While we waited, I told him about Southern Comfort, the peach-based American liquor that made it out from the mountain stills. We both needed a few moments away from the trauma.

His secretary brought in our drinks. He was drinking scotch, of course. Her legs hadn't improved in the intervening decades, but then again, they were no worse than I remembered. I sighed. He said:

'I understood, uh, that you were presently seeing, uh, someone.'

I studied him carefully to try and discern how he felt about it: was it a warning, or a blessing? He smiled wanly:

'Mr Woolf, if one of my children is a little bit happier since you arrived, I am not going, to object. After all ...' He tailed off: the rest weren't. 'The first day you came to see me, I said some things of which I am not particularly proud. I hope you will accept my apology.'

'Why?'

He looked surprised. It wasn't the answer he expected. I explained:

'I don't mean why should I accept it: thank you. I meant, why are you apologizing?'

'At the time, I said there was no one left for me to trust. So I had to trust you. I'm not pleased by everything that has happened. How could I be? Another young person is dead. But sometimes it is necessary to cause pain, in order to cut out the cancer.' Given how he felt about his father's death, I was taken aback by the metaphor, but at least it wasn't mixed.

I pressed my luck:

'Earlier, you said if I gave you some names, you'd find out about their masonic connections.'

'I said I would think about it. I said I would take advice about it.'

'And?'

'I was advised that it would be inappropriate, Mr Woolf.'

'Without even hearing my reasons?'

'That was what I was advised.' I saw the twinkle in his eye: 'I didn't say it was what I would do.'

'If I told you ...' He'd suffered a lot for one day, and the next piece of news wasn't going to act like a balm: 'The final leak was Westmoreland House.'

He nodded for me to go on:

'Because they had to settle, the landlords were way out of their depth. They were next to bankruptcy ...'

'Liquidation,' he corrected. People go bankrupt; companies go into liquidation.

'Yeah, great. The point is, suddenly, they were available — and were bought up — at a snip.'

'I see.' He picked up his drink and sipped it before gesturing for me to go on.

'The company who bought it, they're a Latimer enterprise. Topcent. Heard of them?'

'No,' he was genuinely surprised.

'Well, it's a property holding company, and one of the few that doesn't carry his name. But there is no doubt at all he owns it.'

'I see,' he repeated, absorbing the information. This time, he didn't ask me to carry out any analysis: he could manage on his own. The point Martin had made in his defence was the point I was now making: the leaks we knew about were no more than the tip of the iceberg.

'Who do you want to know about, Mr Woolf?'

I passed him the list. Most of the names would by now come as no surprise: his oldest and youngest sons, for example — I wanted full lists of their Lodges, and Chapters; Stonefrost, de Peyer, the Wainwright brothers; John a.k.a. Ron Fitzpatrick; Gauldie; Latimer. I included Galucci, too. There was one name guaranteed to cause something more than a mild frisson: James Mather.

'What has my brother got to do with this, Mr Woolf? He left this country almost forty years ago. I have had no contact with him since.'

'Except when he wanted to come back for your father's funeral; I gather you were the reason he couldn't.'

He picked up his drink again, but put it back down without touching a drop. I watched admiringly: it was something else I've never been able to do. He waited for me to go on.

'I don't know ... There's a lot I still don't know ... But you and your brother fell out pretty badly, didn't you?'

'Yes,' he was having difficulty breathing.

'Would you care to tell me why?'

'It's not necessary.'

'I think it is, Mr Mather.'

'It's painful ... for me to talk about.' I waited. He sighed. I wasn't going to let it go.

Most of what he told me I already knew. He had looked up to James, since they were children; it had never occurred to him that his brother was in any way dishonest, not even his exemption from military service during the war.

James' youth had passed at a time when their father, though not poor, was still a long way off rich. James had made it for himself, independently, and Ian admired that. When he established the practice, James made sure they got the early work that made the difference. Ian was glad to get it; proud to be trusted by his successful older brother.

Most of the work generated by James was handled by Gauldie; some of it by Ian; some of it by assistant solicitors — that which was of no real significance. Ian himself never had a clue that there might be anything amiss with his brother's business. Then, for Ian out of the blue, a ship was seized, and Richardson — James' partner — disappeared. James alleged that the ship had been seized for minor infractions of the regulations. That wasn't what the police intimated.

'James came to see me. He was trying to make everything sound like a misunderstanding, or that it was Richardson's fault, he'd been duped by his partner ... But it didn't add up, and I kept finding flaws in his case. It was my job, Mr Woolf, he was coming to me as a lawyer, not as his brother. He, well, he didn't take it well: perhaps he didn't like the idea that I could find fault with his ... Reasoning overstates the case ... He took another tack.'

I didn't like to tell him he had created a nautical pun, splendid in the circumstances:

'He admitted there was a lot he had never told me about his business, and he, well, he wouldn't deny he was implicated in

Richardson's death. I wasn't a criminal lawyer, Mr Woolf, and this was not a criminal practice. I told him we would not act for him. It was, perhaps, wrong of me, but I had begun to build up a clientele who would not wish their solicitor to be seen acting in a case involving smuggling and murder and much more, especially not when the accused was the solicitor's brother. Soon afterwards, James disappeared abroad. That's all.'

'You always call him your "brother". He was your half-brother, though?'

'Yes, but we were like brothers, we were very close. That was why ... He was upset when I wouldn't accept his account, and angry when I wouldn't act for him; he felt betrayed. I think ... I know ... He talked to our father, but he adopted the same attitude as I, as James — anyone who knew him — should have expected.'

'James was a freemason, wasn't he?'

'Yes,' he whispered: 'He introduced me into my first Lodge.'

'The police investigation, at the time, it came to a sudden end; they made no real attempt to track him down — or even to find out who helped him get away. Did you use any influence?'

'Certainly not, Mr Woolf; that is not my understanding of what the craft is about.'

'But he wanted you to, didn't he?'

He sighed heavily:

'Yes. By that time, I had the connections, amongst my clients ...'

'You've always been craft masonry, but he was Royal Arch as well, wasn't he?'

'What are you saying, Mr Woolf?'

'It's possible ... Someone else ...'

He knew who I meant. He didn't deny the possibility. The full implications were only just beginning to dawn on him.

Though his brother's activities had come as a shock to Ian, they could surely not have constituted news to the man who regularly conducted his affairs: John Gauldie. But all Ian said was:

'How could it have anything to do with, uh, recent events, Mr Woolf?'

'Someone told me, well, he was quoting your brother.' I saw no reason to tell him who; one more shock for the day. might finish him off. 'There's always people behind people behind people. D'you understand what I mean?'

'I don't understand what you're saying.'

'Everything that's been happening, it's connected, it has to be. It would beggar imagination to believe it was coincidence. Things don't happen in threes as the saying goes,' I suppressed the temptation to wise-crack 'except Royal Arch ceremonies'. 'We're talking about a lot of things that have been happening here; drugs are involved — Stonefrost,' I added quickly, since he still did not know of Andrew's added involvement: 'Cross Course — the police are definitely suspicious, and so am I. Now Latimer behind Westmoreland House. Two deaths, sir.' It didn't hurt so much the second time I said the magic word. 'Your brother, well, let's just say he's been as crooked over there as he was here.'

He nodded once, to say he knew: I didn't doubt he'd kept a distant eye.

'James swore he'd get back at me. I never believed ... I always thought ... Just bluster ... I always thought ... We were so very close once,' he repeated. The fullness of his brother's revenge, and the extent to which he had himself been played for a patsy, had finally sunk in.

'You shouldn't leap to any conclusions, Mr Mather,' I tried half-heartedly to reassure him: 'I may yet be wrong. You've got to understand, I can't work it out without asking the. questions.'

His voice was clear, though his skin looked like the clerks could use it if they ran out of parchment:

'Leave me now Mr Woolf. Leave me alone to think.'

I didn't want to; I wasn't sure that he didn't mean 'Leave me alone to die', and if I'd been him, I might have been feeling the same way: I was telling him he'd been betrayed by his two oldest connections — Gauldie and James. He waved me out without allowing any more argument. But he kept the list that would allow me to make my case.

I wasn't tired any longer. Beyond tiredness. High. Spaced. At an entirely different level. I spent a couple more hours at the office, sorting my thoughts, and then went over to Martin's house where I found Ali. She had been waiting for me, sitting in front of the phoney fire, nursing what I didn't think was her first gin and tonic, and that's where she went back to after she let me in.

'Pretty neat, huh?' I pointed to the fire.

'It all is,' Ali slurred, meaning the house.

'Mind if I look around?' It was no more than idle curiosity, to understand Martin better.

'Why not? Everyone else has.'

'D'they take anything?'

'Documents. Just documents. I made them list them out, one at a time, sheet by sheet. Your friend wasn't amused. He gave the job to one of his officers. He seemed to have some difficulty knowing how to write.'

'But I bet he gives great cosh.'

'Huh?'

'Never mind. You going to show me round?'

'Sure.'

She took me on the grand tour. It was a big house for a single person. Two upper floors each with its own bathroom, and between them three bedrooms. The attic access cover had not been replaced, which gave me an excuse to clamber up the steps and poke my head inside. It was completely empty: not even the old cartons, bits of broken furniture or empty cases that most houses would have. A man without waste.

On the ground floor, in addition to his study there were a large knocked-through living room that also served as a dining-room, a cloakroom and an open-plan kitchen, utility and breakfast area that made me think that maybe it wouldn't be all bad to have money and a real place to live. Steps led down to the boiler in the basement.

I had not expected to see or find anything; after all, Dowell had spent half the day searching. I asked Ali:

'D'you ever stay here?'

'Once. For a short time during the breakup.'

Married people do that. It's not 'my' breakup,' but 'the' breakup; the big moment, the big one they presume everyone they ever talk to knows about and understands. It's sad. Life stopped, and had to start again. It spells out the whole story of how stupid it is to get that tied to someone else.

We were in the kitchen. She opened the refrigerator to get more ice for her glass. I said:

'Don't you think you've had enough?'

Her eyes flashed, and for a moment I thought she was going to start yelling at me not to tell her what to do. Then they glazed over. She placed her glass in the sink, and came and put her arms around me, right around mine, the way she had that first night.

She leaned against my chest, and nibbled at the buttons of my shirt, sticking her tongue inside to lick my chest. She removed one hand from around my body, and placed it between us, gripping me to tell me she knew how I was responding. I had a flash of Randolph and Katrina, fucking in his father's office. This seemed equally inappropriate, and for that reason equally exciting. I whispered:

'Do you want to go upstairs?'

She shook her head, moving backwards into the breakfast area, pulling me with her, until she was standing right up against the solid-oak table. As we kissed, she put her hands behind her, to lift herself up so she was sitting on the table edge. Her skirt was no more than an inch below her waist. I slid my thumbs inside the band of her tights and panties, and lowered them, following them to the floor until, kneeling between her legs, I could slip off her shoes and remove her underthings altogether.

She put a hand on the back of my head but I didn't need any encouragement. She was wet and warm and welcoming. With one hand, I undid my own trousers and when I stood up I went straight into her hard, fast and furious. She fell back onto the table, flinging her arms out to grasp its edges while I tore at her buttons and roughly pushed her bra up over her breasts.

From the moment I entered her, it was a fight against time, we were both on the verge. It went on like forever, until neither of us could stand it any more and we came together, gasping and screaming and — dare I think it — full of love.

I stood there feeling eminently foolish. My pants were around my shoes. I was sticky and sweaty. I could see oozing out of her the evidence of our intensity. Usually, I hated to see it. I'm not into the natural, animal aspects of sex: I like the high, the tension; and the release, but you can keep what comes after. Yet now what I felt like doing was collapsing to my knees and burying my head in her again until I had licked her clean and we could start all over.

Instead, she pulled her knees up to her chest, and rolled free of me, trotting straight to the cloakroom before I could catch hold and tell her what I was thinking. Her one glance into my eyes told me she knew, maybe she liked it, but she didn't want to hear. With a fixed, foolish, wry expression on my face I stood in front of the kitchen sink to wash, and used sheets of kitchen-towel to dry myself before I pulled my clothes back up. I had to watch out: what I was beginning to feel about Allison Mather Hoyt didn't fit into any chapter of the teach-yourself tough-guy manual.

I heard the toilet flush, and then she emerged, smiling, from the cloakroom:

'Your turn.'

When I came out, the kettle was boiling.

'Tea?'

'Sure. Why not?' It was true. I didn't need a drink; I didn't even want a drink.

'What d'you want to do?' I meant, for the rest of the evening.

'Come home with me. I'll make us some supper. You're tired, you need to sleep, have a bath, we can go past your place first to collect some clothes, I'll look after you.'

She meant she didn't want to be alone. I didn't blame her. One of her brothers had been flung unceremoniously out of the firm; another was languishing in jail. It wasn't what was normally meant by a hard day at the office.

CHAPTER ELEVEN

At Mather's, whenever someone spoke about Latimer the man, as distinct from Latimer as shorthand for one or all of his enterprises, they always said, 'himself — pause — himself' in awe, like they couldn't believe he really existed.

I didn't get in to work the next day until after midday. Ali went in earlier; she had more to steal, so she left me a spare set of keys big and heavy enough to gratify a prison warden.

The atmosphere in the office was alive with tension, gossip and intrigue. If you wanted to know what people were thinking, the two places to bug were the women's and men's lavatories.

It was not surprising. Everyone now knew that Andrew Mather had 'withdrawn' in disgrace; they also knew that Martin was under arrest, and what for. There were journalists and photographers camped outside the door though, unflatteringly, none of them asked me for an interview nor took my photograph. Martin had already been arraigned, and returned to police custody while further enquiries were made, rather than sent to Brixton on remand. Whatever the outcome, he personally and the firm as a whole would suffer irreversible damage.

As if this wasn't enough, Ian Mather had disappeared. He had gone from the office the night before to the nursing home, where he had spent a private hour with his wife. It made me appreciate that Ali had skipped her visit, waiting for me at Martin's house instead: would her mother even know? Did she know Ian had been to see her?

Afterwards, it seemed he had driven home, asked for a suitcase to be packed, made some 'phone calls and departed in a taxi without leaving any forwarding address or contact number. Enquiries of the other Mather offices achieved nothing more than to spread insecurity and concern.

I had a number of options how to proceed, but I didn't yet trust my judgement, I was still tired, and shell-shocked. Instead, I asked for and was provided with a typewriter, and I put my head down to the tedious task of writing up everything I knew to date. Before I took my next step, I wanted there to be a record.

Late afternoon, Marion Mortimer told me I had a visitor. He wouldn't give a name but she insisted he was harmless. Reluctantly, I agreed to see him; I wasn't wearing my bullet-proof vest.

'Mr Woolf?'

'Yes. You are?'

He took a card from his pocket and handed it to me.. He was from the United Grand Lodge of England and had a title something like Grand Dragon or Grand Vizier; I only knew it wasn't the Grand Secretary a.k.a. Grand Scribe Ezra.

I was disappointed: he didn't look evil. He looked more like a salesman, or a clerk. If he had come to put the frighteners on me, they'd have to send someone my own height.

'Last night, Mr Woolf, I received a telephone call from Mr Ian Mather.'

'Where from? What time?'

'I don't know where he was telephoning from. It was about nine o'clock. He telephoned me at home.' It didn't need all my skills as an interrogator to draw the details out of him. 'He gave me a list of names, and some instructions. I should say, he asked me to speak with the Grand Secretary before I complied with them, and I have of course done so. The Grand Secretary was unavailable last night.' Probably wearing an apron while washing up the ritual tools of the craft.

He continued: 'The Grand Secretary has confirmed Mr Mather's instructions, and I am accordingly authorized to give you the information which I believe you need. I do so, Mr Woolf, on the strict terms, which Mr Mather assured me, that you will only use this information so far as it proves necessary for your enquiry, and will reveal it to no one, other than Mr Mather, or the police should criminal charges ensue. The Grand Secretary personally asked me to confirm this.'

'Yes,' it wasn't the time to be funny: 'Why, though? Why are you going to tell me?'

'I am going to tell you because I have been instructed to do so,' he avoided blandly. He was not, however, a mere Grand Messenger, so he couldn't help asserting himself. 'Mr Mather told me that you are investigating most serious matters, possibly criminal. It is our policy to co-operate with the police and public bodies in such enquiries. In the circumstances, and as it is Mr Mather for whom you are working, it seemed appropriate to extend that co-operation to you, on the terms as I have relayed them.'

'Put another way round, if I'm right and there's a masonic link, you're going to carry the can anyway; you might as well seek the credit for co-operation in completing the case. Right?'

'That is a cynical view; the craft does not encourage cynicism. I have the list of all the names you asked about, and of the members of their Lodges. They are complete lists, Mr Woolf: the names of many people with nothing to do with your enquiries are included.' I got the feeling he wasn't too keen on this extension of co-operation.

'And Chapters?'

He licked his lips nervously, then his head tweaked as he agreed he had brought me Chapter connections too. I held out my hand. Reluctantly, he extracted from his jacket pocket an envelope which he passed over the desk to me. I grabbed it before he could change his mind. I hardly noticed him go.

Before I left for the day, I took a call from Dowell.

He refused to meet me for a drink, so I knew he was serious when he asked me: 'Do you know where either Beatrix Kelly or Tony Galucci are?'

'Nope. Why?'

'They seem to have, let's say, taken offence at my visit to their office yesterday. I wanted to ask them some questions. They are "unavailable".'

'They don't seem relevant to what Martin's been charged with,' I observed.

'Really? Surprise me.'

'Ian Mather's done a bunk, too. You think he's run away with Beat? Or Tony?'

'I thought they would have gone off together.'

'Where did you learn that? During the course of your enquiries? You're not supposed to ask him anything about what he's already charged with.'

'Says who? His sister was here, I can ask what I like.'

'Not for a date, you can't. Was it?' To do with what he was charged with.

'I used to think you were just an idiot, Dave; now I think you may be an *idiot savant*.' Once in a while he liked to flex his education; in his job, the opportunities did not come often. I wanted time to think over what he was saying, so I let him explain.

'An idiot has an I.Q. of 25 or a mental age of two; an *idiot savant* is the same, but he's got one or two exceptional additional skills. Like mental arithmetic.'

I need a calculator to add up change from a pound.

I decided he might not thank me if I told him maybe someone — and maybe that someone was me — had put a scare into them that would send Superman into an otherwise unplanned orbit around and around and around the world. Instead, I said:

'You know you got the wrong Mather, don't you, Tim. Either one of them could have let someone in.' I'd said the same thing before, but maybe he hadn't heard me.

'Golly gosh, I wish I'd thought of that.'

'You will, Oscar, you will. So why're you holding him?'

'There's two things I could say. I could say: if I've got the wrong Mather, which one do you think I ought to have? Or: it depends on what I want him for. Then again, maybe I could say both. 'Night sweetheart, sweet dreams.' He put the 'phone down suddenly, either to taunt me, or because someone else had come into the room.

Sometimes, I get a lucky break. As I was leaving, I saw himself himself in the hallway, talking urgently with Gauldie and Randolph. It was too good an opportunity to pass up. I approached; Randolph rapidly left.

My first impression was wildly inappropriate. He brought to my mind a humourless Russian revolutionary bureaucrat: steel-rimmed glasses, closely shaved, cropped greying hair, thin and small. He was about twenty years older than me, approaching sixty.

'Mr Latimer, I'm Dave Woolf.'

'Yes?' He didn't look at me, but at Gauldie for explanation. Gauldie muttered something unbrotherly beneath his breath, and then said:

'The matter of Miss Pankhurst.'

'Mrs,' I corrected in spite of myself: 'That and related incidents. I was wondering if I could talk to you,' I hurried on, before Gauldie could deny me thrice: 'I think it's quite important for me to do so.'

Latimer cleared his throat to give himself himself time for reflection. He looked again at Gauldie for guidance, but, remembering what Ali had told me about the real repository of Latimer's confidence, I quickly contributed:

'I work for Ian Mather, Mr Latimer. Last time I heard, I still had his full confidence.'

He nodded almost imperceptibly, and said:

'Tomorrow morning, my office, seven o'clock.'

I swallowed, gulped and was building up the courage to explain that I couldn't stand up straight at that time of the morning, let alone think or talk, as he left.

'What do you want to trouble Mr Latimer for?' Gauldie snarled.

'That's my business, isn't it? I report to Ian Mather, not you,' I retorted. As you have gathered, I like and respect Gauldie an immeasurable amount: immeasurably small.

He looked down at me, nostrils flaring, eyes glaring, like he wished for nothing so much as. to put me on an altar for a ritual sacrifice.

'What is your game, Gauldie?' I asked, as innocently as if I was offering him a drink: 'There's something going on with you, and I wish the hell I knew what it was.' I didn't want him yet to appreciate just how much I'd already managed to put together.

'You're ridiculous, pathetic,' he snapped, turning on his heels and returning to his office where, I assumed, Randolph was waiting for him.

It was a good thing I was seeing Ali again that evening, not only because she could fill me in on the line of questioning which had been followed during the day, but also because I had forgotten to find out where Latimer's office was.

I knew Central Towers well, from the outside. I remembered when the concrete and glass monolith had been built, and then when it was left empty for years as it anticipated and patiently awaited the boom in commercial property values. At one time, it had been occupied by protesters drawing attention to insufficient and inadequate housing. On another occasion, anti-nuke activists let down banners, and floated ten thousand balloons, from the roof.

I suppose I was vaguely aware that it had been brought over the years into commercial occupation, though in ignorance of by whom, and overwhelmed by indifference. I had not known that almost half of it was occupied by Latimer International and its related companies. I had not known, therefore, that the top floor was given over entirely to Sterling Latimer personally, as both office and living space for his visits to the United Kingdom.

For once, I wasn't late. At least, when I arrived at the main entrance to Central Towers, I wasn't. It took me five minutes to get permission to use the elevator, ten — including a frisk — in the top-floor security lobby, another ten minutes in the outer office and quarter of an hour in Latimer's own waiting-room, while he finished his previous appointment. At what would have been seven in the morning, I was not the first.

No one apologized for the delay. He operated like the legal system, where more work is listed before a judge than he can handle, to make sure that if a case falls short, not a moment of judicial time is wasted, even if it means wasting everyone else's.

I'd been brought two cups of coffee to keep me occupied. By the time I was shown in to Latimer's office, I badly needed a leak.

I'd never seen an office so big, not even Ian's. We were in a corner of the building, and two walls were solid glass. Crossing the room was more exercise that I'd taken all year.

Latimer was seated behind a desk — entirely bare of papers — so big I couldn't even stretch across it to shake hands. He didn't look as if he wanted to mingle fingers anyway. There was something fastidious about him; his hands were finely-structured, his skin was sallow and his movements as considered as his words.

'Sit down, Mr Woolf, and tell me how I can help you.' He was being what Americans call 'old world courteous'.

'D'you mind if I ask you a personal question?'

'I'm listening.'

'How much are you worth? You see, I never met anyone as rich before, and I'd like to be able to tell my grandchildren that I once met someone like you.'

'Are you married, Mr -Woolf?'

I shook my head.

'Well, then, you're unlikely to have grandchildren,' he declined to answer my question. 'Now I'll ask you a personal question. How much are you worth?'

'You want to tell your grandchildren you once met someone that poor?'

He chuckled pleasantly:

'*Touch*é. Tell me why you don't want to make more money, Mr Woolf. Your income in the past year has been less than the staff on this top floor alone earn in a week. It has been considerably less than I earn in a day. Yet I'm told you are very good at your job.'

'Who said that?' I protested. I'd sue for slander.

He waved a hand airily:

'Never ask how someone knows something, Mr Woolf; it shows you couldn't do it; work out for yourself how they could have found it out, and next time you'll be able to do it to them. You still haven't answered my question.'

'I guess, well, I'm sort of choosy about the work I do. And a lot of the time, my clients don't have much money. Anyhow, what's it to you?'

'I like to know the people I deal with.'

'Apparently,' 'I was thinking of the access he had obtained to my accounts.

'Now tell me what you really want?'

'Sure. It's just one question, really. I want you to tell me who told you it was Katrina Pankhurst who leaked the LCP report.'

He stared back at me evenly and calm:

'What makes you think anyone told me that? What makes you think she did?'

'She didn't. I asked who told you she had. What makes you think someone told you she had is she's dead.'

He absorbed my ass-backward answer:

'I understand she was a friend of yours?'

'Yes. A close friend. As a matter of fact, a sometime lover and I wouldn't have minded resuming the relationship. She was a fine woman, Mr Latimer. Not perhaps the most beautiful, and probably not the most brilliant. But she was the sort of soul who makes living almost bearable. Did you ever meet her?'

'Once or twice in conferences, I think. And I agree with your description: not that beautiful, not that brilliant, but a good person.'

I expelled air: he was responsive.

'You just said, she didn't leak my report. Are you sure of that?' His eyes narrowed.

'Yes, one hundred per cent.'

'Will you tell me who?'

I shook my head:

'It's someone I like.'

'Mr Woolf, if you did not have the confidence of Ian Mather, I wonder if you realize just how dangerously you would be behaving?'

'Sure. I'm saying you're responsible for Kat's death. That's what you're referring to, right?'

He frowned and nodded. I added:

'I didn't say you had it done, did I?'

It was his turn audibly to exhale.

'A lot of people would say you're not making a lot of sense, Mr Woolf.'

'You don't, though.'

'I might. It depends what you think.'

'I think ... Let's see: I'd like to continue putting things obliquely, it's more fun, isn't it?'

He struggled to suppress a smile, and failed:

'I can see why Ian relies on you, Mr Woolf.'

I raised my eyebrows:

'I can't. Nevermind. I think I've worked some things out, and I think they make such a pretty fit with Kat's death that I can't resist the connection. It starts years ago, doesn't it? When you first came to this country, as a front-man for James Mather. It took me a long time to get there, and more than time — I had to do quite a lot of reading. Suddenly, there's this young Yank, without a penny to his name, and he's doing business with too many people who used to do business with James Mather. How'm I doing?' I shot at him, suddenly beginning to lose confidence in my own theory as I rehearsed it aloud for its very first performance.

'Go on, it's fascinating,' he said; 'perhaps my publishing house could give you an advance ...' For fiction.

'You've got his name, money from America, names of people to talk to here, and above all, probably his one true commandment, you're to use Mather's as your lawyers. Right? He says: don't trust anyone else; and when push comes to shove, if there's a real issue you need real advice on, don't settle for anyone less than my brother. Right? He also says: my brother's straight, straight as a die; but you'll get plenty extra help from Gauldie. He's greedy; don't be put off by the formal front; he'll bend the rules. Especially for a "brother". After all, he used his contacts to get me out of the country. Right?'

That was three rights, so I paused for confirmation. I settled for absence of denial and continued:

'My guess is — and I admit I am guessing now — you were far more successful than either James or you ever dreamed. You were ahead of your times in your attitudes and approach. You arrived maybe twenty years before other American businessmen and corporations; they really started to eat up England after the International Monetary Fund had to bail out the Labour government in the mid-seventies and made external investment a condition.

'Anyway, your style took off like a freaked-out firework. You went public, probably because Ian Mather advised you to so strongly you couldn't resist without creating suspicion; you bought in Europe, you even made contacts behind the Iron Curtain. You had some wonderful breaks from Gauldie, too: for a slice of the action, he could be disgustingly indiscreet about his other clients, and things he picked up on the masonic vine.

'All the time, there's James Mather lurking in the shadows. I'd say, he's probably become an embarrassment to you. You certainly don't need him now, and haven't for maybe ten to fifteen years. When the companies went public, there was an additional problem. It's quite one thing to use a private corporation like a private bank, but next to impossible when it's subject to the sort of scrutiny Latimer International and its offshoots have to suffer in the name of stock market flotation.

'That's where something like Cross Course could be useful, only it wasn't called Cross Course then. Beat Kelly was pushed in the right direction ...' I held up a hand: 'She didn't tell me anything. I don't want to read she's also been giving a blow-job to a bullet.'

He said softly, speaking for the first time since I began to lay my jigsaw pieces down on his desk:

'I thought you said you accepted I did not have Katrina Pankhurst killed?'

'I do. It's not you I think had it done. I don't actually think you knew what was going to happen to her, or even guessed, though whether a jury'd feel the same is a different question. But it definitely wouldn't be true now, if anything happened to the sister, would it?'

He curled his upper lip inside his lower teeth and scratched nervously:

'Go on. You understand, I am not admitting to anything you say.' He didn't deny knowing Beat; but he didn't seem to know she had beaten it.

'Sure. The way I see it, Mr Latimer, you probably haven't broken any laws in this country that I give a damn about. I don't know about your past, or care beyond curiosity. If you got a start with dirty money, I couldn't care less. I'm not even sure money comes dirty and clean.

'I think Gauldie made a mockery of professional privilege in your interests, but that's a matter for my client and I don't suppose he'll want to broadcast it. I'm curious, though: how much of it had to do with freemasonry?'

'Both the Mather boys were freemasons, and I joined too when I arrived, on James' advice. It was an easy and quick way not only to meet people, but also to create a conservative impression.'

'How involved was James?'

Latimer laughed:

'James Mather is involved in everything and nothing. He's a rogue, a complete, charming rogue. I should say: a dangerous rogue, but I think you've worked that out for yourself. He belonged to freemasonry for the same reasons he told me to join: front, image, contacts. In those days — don't forget, we're talking about the forties and fifties — it was a very respectable organization, everyone in the City and commerce, too, belonged.'

'You're being very candid about it,' I lied: 'Don't you get excommunicated or something if you tell an outsider?'

'You have to be a mass murderer to be expelled, Mr Woolf, and that's only if at least half your victims are fellow freemasons. I haven't been to a Lodge meeting for more than a decade. I would describe myself as having left the freemasons, because I've long ago stopped needing them, but rather like the Catholic Church, once a freemason always a freemason. They don't let you leave.'

'You've been talking about craft freemasonry, right? You said: you haven't been to a Lodge meeting for years.'

He met my gaze from a new dimension. My next question remained as yet unspoken, but the conversation was being carried on notwithstanding. He dared me to ask it. He was right: since I'd read the material brought me by the official masons, I'd been shitting myself. One of the names by which the freemasons refer to God is 'Great Architect' (of the Universe): he was currently working up a design for my tomb.

I cleared my throat:

'*Ammi Ruhamah*.'

When he didn't answer, I said:

'Didn't I pronounce it right?'

The new, and noticeably less accommodating Latimer said: 'Why do you think it won't be the last thing you ever pronounce, Mr Woolf?'

'Aw, shucks, you were supposed to answer "Jabulon".' When he didn't smile, I thought it opportune to mention: 'There's nothing we're talking about that isn't already written down, and copies where even you don't own. And they are all signed, and marked by me, as written in contemplation of death.' As I was talking my own ritual language, I explained: 'Statements made in contemplation of death are admissible in an English court of law, Mr Latimer.'

'Go on, Mr Woolf, go on with what you say you've got written down.'

'The Prolistic Chapter of Improvement is one of the oldest Chapters in Royal Arch. You were exalted — that's the phrase, isn't it? — a member in ...' I consulted my notes: '1967. Gauldie was a member; so was James Mather. Later, both Randolph and Andrew Mather were introduced to it; so also Maurice Francis, Viscount Stonefrost, and two others who I'm concerned with — Robin de Peyer and Stephen Wainwright ...'

'Wainwright?' He asked before he could help himself.

'Stephen, not Christopher. He was, is, was Christopher's older brother. That's how Christopher knew a lot more that he ought. There are a lot of other members — only, they're called Companions I think. I was barking up the wrong tree: I thought at first it was all to do with Lodges, but it's Chapters that matter. What is it about the Chapter that leads it into conspiracy?' Warren, the Commissioner of Police who'd covered up for Brother Jack, was a companion of the Chapter, and therefore maybe Jack too; Prolistic was reputed to have enjoyed closer contacts with P2 than any other English masons.

To my considerable surprise, he answered me:

'It's the belief that the only real power is secret power. You put your finger on it a while ago, by accident: you said that once Latimer was a public corporation, it couldn't channel Mather's money. Public power, public money — they're the same thing, of course — is publicly accountable: people can see how you use it. But the power, the money, that people don't know you have ...' He didn't need to finish the sentence. 'Ian, on the other hand, is committed to freemasonry as a moral influence. That class of freemason positively craves the respectability that open wealth brings.'

'How much did — does — James Mather really believe in it?'

'I don't really know, Mr Woolf. He might; he might not. It depends on whether he found it useful. James never needed an excuse to chase money or power, or anything like freemasonry to encourage him.'

'And you?'

He struggled:

'What do you mean by "believe"? Some people use the word to refer to a religion, some to a system of government or economics, some to refer to whatever they hold most dear. I joined first craft masonry, then Royal Arch, because that was the way ahead for me. It was expected of me.'

'How much has it got to do with your business now?'

'Nothing that matters.'

'That's what I figured. How come you never broke free of it, or of Mather?' A shadow passed over his face like a cloud: 'You think you know who had Katrina Pankhurst killed, don't you, Mr Woolf?'

'You're frightened of him, right?'

'You don't cross James Mather, not so that he'd know. I'm a very rich man. I could afford to hire bodyguards for twenty-four hours a day. He could still reach me.'

'The police? You must have enough on him?'

'Presuming the police are to be trusted, which would be a foolish presumption, I still doubt it. He's not what you would call candid about his activities. But weigh it up. All I have had to do for the last ten or more years — and you were extremely accurate about that — is to continue to treat him as a friend. And why not? Where would I have been without him? I was running a small time nowhere business when we met. Look at me now. I made my devil's pact, Mr Woolf; you've read Faust.'

Faust? Batfaust? Superfaust? Faust Street Blues? L.A. Faust?

'How come he knew about the leak? How come you gave him a name?'

'I think it was pride, mainly. He knew about the leak because he likes to stay in touch. It's always been part of my job to keep him in touch with his family.' Hence, Martin's good old welcome to the good old U.S. of A. 'He's a very old man, now, Mr Woolf. He doesn't have much to do but his mind is still as active as ever.

'He lives in Florida, in an apartment at the top of a block he owns, part of which contains a hotel he owns, in which there is a bank he's not supposed to own but does, with shops, lawyers, accountants, a sauna and massage parlour he also owns. He has the bodyguards, not me. He has to have his apartment and 'phone lines swept for bugs every couple of days, not me. He sleeps a lot; he isn't allowed to drink much anymore; he can't eat anything but totally bland food; I don't suppose he can still have sex.

'So he calls me often, to stay in touch, to talk, to feel part of it all. And I tell him things, things that are harmless but sound important. And I told him there'd been a leak; he had to know something was happening, even Latimer International dropped a couple of points when the size of the settlement was announced. And he asked where the leak had come from, and when I said Mather's, he demanded to know more, who.'

He lowered his head:

'I had no idea he would take it the way he did. I had no idea until I read about the Pankhurst woman's death. It ought to have been just business. He took it personally. Mather's is still his main point of connection. He has no family over there.'

'I thought he had a wife and a daughter?'

'He had a wife and a child — I don't know a daughter. They lived somewhere in New England. They were kept very separate. I never met them. The way I heard, they never knew what he did. After the wife died, he wanted to bring the child into his life, but as soon as he — she — realized what her father really did, she cut him off totally. Much like Ian.'

I shook my head slowly, in awe:

'You're making me feel sorry for the guy. Jesus, we're talking about a killer. A gangster. Someone who has just had a friend of mine murdered. And I'm sitting here, feeling sorry for him.'

He smiled:

'I've described him well, then. He has that quality. He's very hard to hate until he turns on you, and then it's probably too late for you to do anything about it. It's all over.'

I shuddered:

'I think I'll be happier leaving him out of my life. How do you feel about Ian?'

His lips twitched, as he thought about the answer:

'Sorry for him, really. He is a moral man, the sort of moral man he thinks everyone ought to be and if everyone could follow craft masonry they would be. I feel sorry to have participated in a degree of deception on him. For all of these years, he's been helping his brother without knowing it, and against his declared wish to have nothing more to do with him, and I have been one of the two main agents of that.'

'Two? Right, Gauldie.'

'Correct. Mr Gauldie. Since I like Ian, and admire him, I naturally regret that. But that's been business, too. To do as much as people like James Mather have done, and people like myself — though I hasten to add that my style is very different in the respects that concern you — we cut personal corners to suit commercial ends.'

'I'm not sure I completely understand Gauldie.'

'I'm not sure anyone does. You can't go through life, Mr Woolf, treating people as if they can all be reduced to a set of rational rules or a logical progression. People do one thing, and that's where they start the next step from. Gauldie went along with some sharp deals in James Mather's early days, and when he came to whatever was the next choice, it wasn't such a big step more. Isn't that what we all do? Did you plan to quit law when you snorted your first gramme of cocaine?'

He was re-asserting himself by displaying the extent of his knowledge about me. I sensed the interview was drawing to a close. There were a few more answers I needed. I said:

'Let's talk about Beat Kelly, and Tony Galucci. I've been very slow about it. The way I see it, I think the way you're telling it: James ain't a man to take no for an answer?' He nodded, curious to see how far I could take it on my own. 'Once he failed to seduce Martin to his way of thinking, to make. his deal like he made with you — Faust, was that the guy? — he still wanted Martin's ... What? Soul? Integrity? Name? Whatever it was that would give him his revenge over Ian. He could've broken Ian, by influencing business away from him, but that wouldn't have been nearly as good.

'So he directed Beat at him. Maybe he thought Martin would fall into bed with her. I would, given half the chance. I don't know how much Beat knew: maybe it was casual to begin with; I've got this nephew, don't mention my name -there's a family estrangement. But take a look at what he's into, he and his partner Galucci, it's right up your street. Then, when he needed her, he found out she wasn't so enchanted with him: he'd gone for her sister instead of her; and he'd picked the sister up and let her down over and over like a yoyo. Better yet: the partner now had solid reason to hate him — don't matter how modern you think, no one can stand being cuckolded. I learned that in my last big case. I didn't believe Kat when she said Tony didn't mind.

'I didn't think about it, though, because I was looking at the wrong bits of the puzzle. Also, though I thought I recognized Matheson, at the Clairmount, I didn't bother to follow it up. I'd seen him before, chatting with Galucci at Cannons: people look different dressed for sport, you notice different bits of them.

'Putting it together with they've done a disappearing act, which Dowell asked me about today, I think what Dowell's interested in is illegal, external, racketeer influence in gambling. I think they've set it up so no one's going to believe Martin didn't know the deals they were conducting with his own uncle. Gimme a break, willya, tell me how I'm doing?'

'I'd say,' he choose his words carefully: 'You've said nothing about James Mather that is out of character.'

It was as good as I was going to get. I didn't bother spelling out about how Matheson had rung Beat or Tony to tell them what he'd told me about Andrew and Wainwright. One of them had rung James. He had reacted much as had Martin: he'd take care of it. I still didn't know how he'd arranged to get Wainwright to attend his own funeral, but I had an idea:

'This notion, this revenge, is there any reason why it should be confined to Martin?'

'Not that I'm aware of,' he said dryly, sensing my direction.

'I'm told he's not active any longer, pretty much like you said. But, oh, say ten years ago, would it be an astonishing proposition he could have dictated whether supplies of a certain illegal substance saw their way into certain hands?'

He held up his:

'I've never known anything about that, and I never want to. I couldn't say it was impossible, or to use the same expression, out of character, but I refuse to comment further. I'm sure you understand.'

'Oh, yeah, I understand. I'm not sure I respect it a whole bunch. But I understand. You said: it's part of your job to keep him in touch ... Yeah?'

'I, or that of my understrappers,' he had an affection for obsolete, English words too close to my own for comfort: 'I never met Wainwright, Mr Woolf.' So it didn't matter he had set him up by passing the message from James back to Randolph. There could be no suspicion attached to such a call, from a businessman to his lawyer.

'Tell me something else, then: if you're so frightened of him, why are you telling me so much now?'

'I'm not telling you anything. I'm electing not to deny things you think you've worked out for yourself. That could be,' in a court of law, 'because I don't think they're worth denying.'

'And perhaps because?'

'Perhaps because ... As you said, Mr Woolf: Mrs Pankhurst was a fine woman.' Sounding like: it's gone far enough.

'And perhaps because it suits for someone like me to come along and get rid of the monkey on your back for you?' I was doing what he was too scared to do for himself; James couldn't attribute any of it to him.

He asked me:

'How sure were you when you came in?'

'Not a hundred per cent; maybe ninety-nine. I knew there were connections. But I'm a lawyer, I know a case can seem unanswerable until you hear the other side. Then you confirmed it for me.' I went on without waiting for him to ask how: 'When you said that crap about not asking how you found something out, but working it out for myself. That's a James Mather line. He told it to Martin, years and years ago.'

He winced: more, I think, because I referred to the line as crap than at what it had given me.

'There's something you ought to think about, then, Mr Woolf. As you've astutely observed, none of this ill-suits me. But it ill-suits James. It's not his style to throw away money or power, not even for the sake of letting Ian find out what he's done to him.'

'What are you saying?'

'Someone lit the touch-paper, Mr Woolf. I have to ask: who?'

Before I could take him up on it, he glanced overtly at his watch:

'I have now spent three appointments with you, which has probably cost Latimer International more even than your weight in worth ...'

Why does everybody find it necessary to point out I'm over-weight? I got eyes; I look in the mirror. Occasionally. If have to.

'I'll go, Mr Latimer, as soon as you answer my question,' I said without making a move to leave.

'Which question was that, Mr Woolf?' As if he didn't know.

'Who told you Katrina Pankhurst leaked the report?'

He hesitated before he told me, but probably he intended to all along:

'Randolph Mather. I told Gauldie I wanted the name. I told him I wanted a name within forty-eight hours. That was as long as James Mather gave me. Randolph rang me and that was who he told me. That was who I told James.' Randolph had given Latim-er Kat's name, instead of the name Kat had given him — that of his sister. 'I'm sorry. I'm very, very sorry. I hope you believe that?'

As a matter of fact, I did. But looking at him, remembering just how rich he was and it wasn't kosher, remembering how many got hurt to help him make his start, even if he had nothing directly to do with it, I couldn't for the life of me think of one good reason to tell him so.

CHAPTER TWELVE

Now I had everything, except a client to tell the story to. I felt like end of term jollies, but no one to share them with. There was, however, some unfinished business. Not on behalf of my client (which wouldn't stop me charging for it) but for myself.

I was still in the office before my normal hour of arrival. So was John Gauldie. Marion was waiting for me, to tell me he wanted to see me and to pour coffees down my throat. I checked that Ian had not re-appeared and when she confirmed it, I guessed how the interview would open:

'I want you out of this building, Woolf.'

'I work for Ian Mather; I'll leave when he tells me to. Unless, of course, you've got some reason for thinking he won't be coming back ...'

'Where from? Do you know where he is?' I was pleased he didn't.

'Of course I do. Listen, you might walk out on a partner, a law-firm or a wife: but you don't walk out on Woolf.'

He sneered:

'Bravado, Woolf. You've no more idea than I have.'

'You a gambling man, Gauldie? Let's make a little bet: you write down your guess, and place it in an envelope with your cheque for, oh, let's say, five grand, and I'll write down mine and do the same. OK?'

This was real bravado. I've never gambled five pounds, and you could ride a car on my cheque for five thousand. I did not for a second believe he would take me seriously. To my astonishment, he licked his lips greedily. Through sheer stupidity, I'd named a sum of money large enough to excite him. It was a cold day: I was sweating like a sauna. It was more money than I'd earned on the case. If I lost, I'd have to drag it on for another month; the way things were going, that probably meant half the rest of the staff would get wasted.

He shook his head to clear it:

'I'm not playing with you, Woolf,' but he was a little reluctant: 'I want you out of here.'

I shook my head:

'You're the next senior partner; but you don't own that big a slice of the action. Andrew's out of it for the time being, but he's still a partner and I think I'd carry his vote for now; same for Martin. I know I'd carry Allison's. I don't know the exact figures, but my guess is that even if you can tell Randolph what price to sell at, you'd need to call a full partner's meeting to have a majority.'

'What do you mean? Tell Randolph what price to sell at?'

It was just an expression, like the price of eggs, or the time of day: I'd struck a nerve. Even if it was irrelevant, I couldn't have resisted putting pressure on it.

'You trying to say you don't know what Randolph and his prolific Prolistic prelates are up to?'

He absorbed the incidental reference to his Chapter of Improvement. If there was any evidence he ever went in for anything as mundane as breathing, he would have been breathing shallow. He was between the horns of a masonic symbol. I don't think he did know what I meant; but he didn't want to ask. I said, equally casual:

'You set a crooked example, kids are going to play crooked games too. Know what I mean?' I had finally found a use for Lewis' favourite phrase. All I needed now was to be able to distinguish between a phrase and a clause.

I told him anyway. I don't care if he knew beforehand or not; it's an idle detail. The important thing was that I knew. I prefaced it with the same assurance I had given Latimer: nothing I would tell him wasn't fully documented.

'The way I see it, there's two layers of activity through the Chapter. One is you, Uncle Jim, Sterling, let's work out the next rip-off, just like the good old days when you could deal face-to-face, before you got him out and your friends decided it wasn't in the public interest for the police to probe too closely how you did it.

'It's an odd thing, Gauldie, but lawyers rarely get as rich as people on the outside think: it's all income, not capital. The trouble is: they're arrogant. Since they think they're so much more clever, they think they ought to be that much richer too. But you, you're real rich: I wouldn't like to guess what you're worth, but a lot richer that Ian, who you've always been jealous of, and you did it without a rich daddy to help. You must be very proud: to have conned all those people to trust you with their privileged information and plans.

'The other layer is Randolph, who got a bit impatient to run his own show, and maybe he wanted to prove he could make his own money too, uninherited. What it makes me think of is that old legal maxim, when an employer is not responsible for the acts of his employee, 'cos he's said to be 'on a frolic of his own'. Fizzy drinks, fuzzy memories, funky sex and frankly indiscreet.

'You brought too many kids in, Gauldie: you thought they'd all serve willingly as foot-soldiers in your army,' like Orbach, I stole the line from the Hackney report: 'But some of them wanted a commission of their own. Secret money of their own. Secret power of their own. Maybe just secrets of their own. They wanted to make that old masonic black magic work for them, not you. They wanted to see if it could be applied to modern methods of turning a dishonest buck, not boring old back-scrubbing business deals. Deals the way my generation means the word; crooked deals the way your generation always did it. It's the only way to stay ahead of the money game nowadays.

'You know the irony of it all? I'll tell you: it's all so damned small, so petty. You wanna know how much coke they ran in from the Bahamas? You wanna know how much money they made out of it? They've jeopardized your cosy little set-up for less money than you've spend on medieval weaponry.'

There was one. more thing I could've told him. I could have said that behind every — including this — scam skulked the omnipresent James Mather. I didn't think he'd dare do anything about it if I did so. I don't want to claim more credit than is due. I didn't know exactly how he'd react. But I only had to look at the horror on his face and in his eyes to realize it wasn't going to be fun for someone else. If the game was over for him, it was going to be over for everyone.

It wasn't going to be fun for me either. It was a bad day, the worst of all. Nothing happened. Nothing at all. You ever tried to wise-crack about nothing? What I had to do was to update and finish the report I'd started the day before, to give Ian on his return and to post safety copies off elsewhere.

Now that the case was coming to an end, the rest of my life started to come back into focus and a bit of it was missing. It was a long time since I'd seen or spoken to Sandy. If I'm honest, even now I can't claim that my loins were aching; or, if they were, it wasn't with passion for her, but a result of the excessive strain put upon them by unaccustomed antics with Ali. I punched the number I knew as well as my own, as indeed once it had been.

'Can I talk with Sandy?'

'Who's calling, please?'

'Dave. Dave Woolf.'

'What's it in connection with, Mr Woof,' as in dog.

It's great to feel well-remembered, loved:

'Uh, it's personal. She'll know who I am.'

'Oh. I see. Just a moment, please, I'll see if she's free.'

She sounded surprised Sandy should get a personal call. At what she does, Sandy's more thoroughly professional than the reputation the Mathers were about to lose.

'Hi,' she sounded brisk.

'Bad time?'

Pause.

'No.'

'Uh, well, you're obviously glad to hear from me.'

'Of course I'm glad to hear from you, Dave. I've been meaning to ring you. We ought to meet.'

'That was what I was thinking, kid.' She was four months older than I: 'I'm just about wrapped up here, at Mather's. 'Nother couple of days.'

'Yes.' Her enthusiasm and curiosity knew no bounds: they weren't even acquainted.

'Sandy, what's up?'

'What's up?' her voice raised: 'You let me walk out of a pub, on my own, in the middle of the day, without trying to stop me; you let me walk out of your life without even saying so long; you ignore me for weeks, then you ring up 'cheerful as a sand-boy, and you ask me — what's up already?'

I hadn't said 'already', had I?

'Look,' I said, calming and conciliatory: 'This hasn't been a lot of fun ...' She hadn't even asked who done in our ex-employee.

'What's the matter? Weren't the high-class bimbos falling over themselves to hop into bed with you?'

Well, uh, yes, as a matter of fact.

'Oh, shit, we always argue on the 'phone. We'd better meet,' she conceded reluctantly: 'How about the twenty third?'

If 'phones could see, I'd've boggled down the line:

'Sandy! That's nearly three weeks away!'

'Well,' she sulked: 'I'm pretty busy right now.'

You love someone in as many different ways and for as long as Sandy 'n' I've loved each other, there's some things don't need spelling out:

'You're seeing someone, aren't you, Sandy?'

Silence. Then:

'I don't want to talk about it on the 'phone, Dave.

Maybe I could make next Thursday, later on in the evening ...'

'Tell me, Sandy.' Tell me Sandy: I love you; I know I'm a jerk; I know I've been fucking around with someone else, but I always thought, you know, you understood the way I was, am; I always thought you, you loved me anyhow, at any price. That was what I wanted, Sandy; that's what I needed; someone to love me more than life itself; someone to love me as much as Robin loves Mick.

She said flatly:

'I warned you, Dave.' And so she had.

'You take care, Sandy. You take care, you hear? Doesn't matter how long; I'll still be here, well, there anyhow. Y'know: I'll still be around for you. You've only got to call: it'll always be true.'

I replaced the receiver gently before she could catch me start to cry. I'm ugly on a normal day; you don't want to see how ugly I get when I cry. It only happens once in a while: like when something sad happens on Hill Street, or Benny the lovable idiot is especially cute on L.A. Law, or every episode of Cosby and half the episodes of MASH You know: the really serious things. Or when I see someone's mother dying. Or when I forget I don't really give a damn about anything or anyone, and for a brief moment someone else seems to matter.

I was so depressed and lonely, I bought Marion a farewell lunch. In a desultory fashion, I tried calling Ali, but if she wasn't with Martin, she was catching up on clients. Someone had to keep the firm fruitful. I didn't mind: now she wasn't icing on another cake, I wasn't so sure how I felt about her. On the way to the restaurant, I popped into the post office, but I didn't let Marion see where I'd addressed my envelopes.

'Go on, have a drink, what the hell, there's no one left to complain.'

She laughed nervously, I was asking her to act entirely out of keeping:

'Alright, then, I'll have a glass of ...' I waited for her to say white wine or a spritzer: 'Beer. A pint, I think,' she said firmly. 'If you gotta break a habit, break it good.'

'That's my girl.'

'What's going to happen, Mr Woolf?' The greatest failure of the case to date was my inability to persuade her to call me Dave.

I shrugged. Cases aren't like a TV. programme. You never see the detective poring over files, going home to his wife and children and fighting over who does the washing-up, making 'phone calls to people who just aren't there, or getting a constant busy signal. It all happens, crammed into an hour. I wonder how they ever charge enough to make a living. The big bucks come when the case takes several days longer than you see on screen.

'You're going to find out, though, aren't you, Mr Woolf?'

'Oh, yeah, I know most of it anyhow.'

It wasn't her place to ask, so she didn't. Not directly. She said: 'Everything that's happened, it's ... It's frightening. Mr Andrew, Mr Martin. You see, well, I'm sorry,' we were now on our second drink: 'I'm frightened ... I don't want to hear ... Well, that Katrina ...' I got her point: she didn't want to hear Kat had also been bad.

'Listen, Marion: don't you worry 'bout Kat; she's up there in heaven, jiving to jazz happy as a cloud.' Can you jive to jazz? 'Everyone else in this whole saga stinks like ...' I was going to say 'shit', but I remembered who I was talking to: 'Well, just stinks. But she was good, Marion, and she didn't do nothing to hurt anyone. Whatever else comes out of this, it won't be nothing bad about Kat.'

She smiled wanly:

'I don't think I believe in heaven, Dave, but I want to believe she didn't do anything bad, and ... that she's listening to jazz now.'

She'd called me Dave at last. I'd finally won.

We got so pissed at lunch neither of us could work during the afternoon. Nothing continued to happen, but it was easier to cope with than in the sober morning. I punched the digits for Dowell about twenty times, and half of the time got the right number, but he was never in, or not in to me.

I was about to quit and go home for the day when Ali burst frenetically in to my office. Remember Ali? Until a while ago, I'd've crossed mountains, walked through fire, swam an ocean for the privilege of laying down just once more to lick between her legs. Then I'd spoken to Sandy. She was about to fail to restore the gloss. She said, breathlessly:

'Dave. I've just had a 'phone call from Heathrow. My father's there. He's, well, he's in something of a state; they said he wasn't making a lot of sense. The thing is, I've got to see a client in ten minutes, it's really important, especially now. Could you? Andrew's gone out to Oxfordshire, and, I can't find Randolph,' and Martin wasn't doing time as a chauffeur: 'Could you go and collect him, Dave? They won't put him in a taxi, I asked. They want someone to go and collect him.'

Last night, I'd lain on one side, resting on an elbow, and watched her drift off to sleep. It was warm in her flat, and we'd thrown off the duvet. I thought: I've never been this close to someone as beautiful before. I looked at every inch of her, parts of her I'd touched and that had touched me, and been filled with wonderment. I didn't know now what was different: what I was seeing, or the eyes I saw with.

I shrugged off my mood; I'd lost one girl-friend that day, I could scarcely afford to lose another. I said:

'Sure. I'll go. Where is he?'

I took the tube: I was still on expenses, but even four hundred a day couldn't compensate for an hour or more of inane prattle. I found Ian, as instructed, in British Airways' hospitality suite, attended by a ground stewardess. She looked relieved to see me:

'You've come from the family?'

'Well, maybe. Or the firm.'

She looked almost as confused as he did, but I didn't elaborate:

'I'm a friend. I've come to take him home, OK? You want I should sign for him?'

So I led an old man, uneasy on his feet, his eyes vacant, to the taxi-rank. I sat him in the back, whispered to the driver that he was sick in order to shut him up, and put his baggage in the space next to the driver's seat. S'far as I could tell, he hadn't bought any souvenirs, nor even duty-free. I gave the Hampstead address; I didn't think it would do much for the firm's flagging morale to see him in this state, but he wasn't yet bad enough to take to the nursing home.

'What happened?' I asked gently.

He didn't answer.

'When you saw James,' I promoted: 'What happened?'

'James,' he said dully.

'Yes, James. You went to see James.' This wasn't only my educated guess; they'd confirmed where he'd come from at BA. I would have won my bet with Gauldie.

'James,' he repeated.

'You went to see your brother. Did you see him?'

'Yes. James.'

'You went to see him about your sons, didn't you?'

After a while, he said:

'I knew where he was. I've always known where he was. He was angry, but I was hurt.' I wasn't sure if he meant during the visit, or when they'd broken up all those years before. 'He didn't think of that. He didn't think about how hurt I was.'

'People don't, Mr Mather.'

I don't think he heard me.

'He's an old man; I'm an old man; we're all old, Mr, uh, Mr ...'

'Woolf,' I supplied helpfully.

'Even John's old, now.'

I hoped he wouldn't get much older.

'Did you see him — James?'

'He wouldn't see me, Mr, uh ...' I don't like it when people forget my name, but he wasn't people anymore. 'He sent men to me. They took me away. They took me to an airport. That's all.' There was probably a lot more, but it was all that mattered.

I waited with him in Hampstead until Ali appeared, around nine o'clock. The Italian woman made us a meal, but he wouldn't eat anything and I wasn't hungry either. Ali ate for us all and asked for a bottle of her father's wine which I helped her with. She gobbled her food, intermittently talking about an important new client she thought she could keep notwithstanding everything that had already begun to break; Martin was going to be alright — they didn't have nearly enough to convict on the murder charge, and criminal charges would probably not stick on the Clairmount either; she'd reached Andrew — Marilyn was angry, but Andrew sanguine; Randolph was nowhere to be found.

This was an Ali I hadn't seen before. I'm not sure what I really felt. I didn't feel loving, or horny, but that was hardly surprising in the circumstances. I didn't feel sympathetic, either: she was too much in control — -of him, of me, of the firm, of herself. I suppose it's sexist: I couldn't cope with her when she was so patently capable of coping with everything for herself. I must be sentimental: I expected her to be shaken by what had happened. I was; I resented that she wasn't.

I left around eleven o'clock. Initially, I planned just to go home. But in the minicab, I remembered I'd left in the office a copy of my final report. There were two reasons why it made me uncomfortable. For one thing, I wasn't sure yet who I wanted to read it; for another, I didn't know there was anyone who was going to pay my account. I told the driver to change route; he argued — I was booked to Earl's Court, and Holborn wasn't Earl's Court, he was sure of that; well, pretty sure. I told him I'd pay the full fare to Earl's Court anyway.

I stood outside Mather's, looking up at its floors all the way to mine own attic. It was a depressing sight. I pressed the night-bell: at least I'd wake up the watchman, that would be a positive achievement for the evening.

He answered quick enough to deprive me of even that gratification. I had met him before. He was not a reserve policeman. He was a rotund, unfit, elderly man appropriately entitled Ernest.

'Good evening, sir,' he touched his peaked cap, recognizing me and my right to enter at this ungodly hour, re-locking and bolting the door behind me.

As I signed in, he said:

'You're not alone, sir. Mr Randolph is in his office.'

'On his own?' I tried to sound casual but that wasn't what my heart-beat said.

'No, sir. He came in with a gentleman. He said it wasn't necessary for him to sign in,' Ernest added, pre-empting my next question. I had the impression he was glad there was someone with some sort of authority to whom he could confide his concern that the rules had not been obeyed.

'What did he look like?'

'I didn't see, sir. As I let Mr Randolph in, the other gentleman slipped past and went straight up the stairs. I didn't catch a look at him. I'm sorry, sir.'

'Not your fault. I'll go up and see him.'

I walked up the stairs, remembering the first thing they teach a policeman: don't run into trouble, walk. I was on the first floor, turning towards Randolph's office, when I saw the man. He was hooded. I had time to recognize it as a mason's hood and the weapon in his hand as Gauldie's much-prized medieval sword, now dripping with blood, before he charged me, roaring at the top of his lungs the way soldiers do to scare the enemy: he needn't've bothered; I was already scared shitless.

We went backwards together and almost toppled down the wide, main steps. Upside down, I saw Ernest's astonished expression, then heard him cry out in a classic of understatement:

'Oy, you, what do you think you're doing?'

It was distraction enough for me to fight back. I clung onto his sword-carrying arm. We reeled from side to side while Ernest clambered wheezily up to assist me. At the last moment, my assailant broke free and charged him in his turn, knocking him against, then over, the banisters. He was at the main front door at the same moment as I rose too late to save Ernest from the fall.

He fumbled with the door, but couldn't get it open. He turned and waved the sword at me, daring me to come down the stairs. He didn't need to wave twice. He knelt down by Ernest to search him for the key. While he was distracted, I stepped backwards up the stairs until I reached the landing, and once out of his sight darted down it: if he wanted a part in the movie of the Wars Of The Roses, I did too. I grabbed from the wall opposite the vacant space where the sword had hung its sister spear. It was astonishingly heavy.

When I got back to the stairs, he was already at the door. The key was in the lock, but he hadn't undone all the bolts. I howled:

'Stop. Stop.'

He swung angrily around, as I staggered down towards him hefting the spear in my hand. He swung the sword wildly about him, to keep me back, danced a couple of steps forward, a couple of steps back. We froze for what seemed an eternity, but was only ten or twenty seconds. He thrust at me again; I jumped back and, without thinking about it, without intending to do it, with all my strength, I flung the spear straight at him.

He screamed just the once as it drove through his chest and pinned him against the door. Blood gushed from the mouth-opening in his hood. I stared at him horrified. He stared back at me, still alive but only just. I said:

'Who? Who sent you?'

I could see his lips move but only just. He mumbled what sounded like:

'Hyram Abyss.'

Then every limb twitched the once, like a single sharp pull on a puppet, and he slumped dead, still affixed to the door. I picked up the sword where it had fallen, and went to see how Ernest was doing:

'You alright, old chap?' I sounded more like a Mather or a mason than myself.

He didn't look alright. He couldn't speak. His eyes were yellow with pain. I muttered that I'd get help and was half-way to the telephone before I remembered Randolph. I hesitated, but I knew what I'd find and my methodical mind told me it would be preferable to be able to announce all in the one call.

The poor little bastard was still alive, though I daresay he'd rather already have died. He didn't have long to go. He'd been cut open from his throat to his waist; naked, bloody flesh hung off him like raw meat in a butcher's. His eyes, pleading, met mine, then moved slowly down to the sword in my hand, as if asking me to finish the job. I gagged back the rising vomit and clung to the side of the door, whimpering:

'Oh God, oh God, oh God.'

I couldn't stop it. Lunch, coffee, wine and what looked like a large chunk of my own guts poured out of me. From some point on the edge of life, Randolph, still conscious, watched, as incapable of speech as Ernest, but a lot closer to final relief; the last thing he would ever see was me throwing up.

I couldn't stay in the room with him. I couldn't touch him. I couldn't offer him comfort. I staggered into the next office and, for the first time in my life, rang the emergency service, gasping into the receiver that I needed police and ambulance, now now now now now ... I went back down to wait with Ernest. He had maybe a rib through a lung, one or two broken bones sticking out through his skin: nothing compared to Randolph. He was gradually achieving coherence. His hand reached out to grip mine. He wanted to say something. I leaned down so he could whisper in my ear, without breathing into his face: the state of my breath might have finished him off.

'I'm sorry, sir. I'm sorry. Tell Mr Mather, won't you?' Mr Mather meant Ian Mather.

I don't know how long we waited like that before the police arrived. Later, Dowell told me the time lapse between logged call and officer on scene was less than ten minutes. When

I think about it, it still seems like it was most of my life. The officers had to ring at the bell and bang and bash at the door before I heard them.

I couldn't open it properly. I got it open maybe about an inch, but then the man's body jammed it. I was pulling and sobbing and screaming in frustration. A voice was saying:

'Take it easy, sir, take it easy.'

'There's a body, on the door. I killed him,' I whispered.

I tried extracting the spear but it wouldn't come out. In the end, the police had to ram the floor to get it to open another few inches, enough for them to squeeze through. I fell into the arms of the first one in and he half-carried me back inside, leaning me against the reception desk and not letting go until he realised I wasn't actually wounded.

He was followed by other officers and an ambulance crew. I pointed to Ernest, holding onto the police officer's arm with my other hand:

'Take him first. He's alive.'

The police officer took one look around him and had already switched on his radio to call for more back-up. I said:

'First floor. Office off to the right. Another. He's probably not alive anymore. He's been cut open. I warn you. He's been cut right open. He did it,' I gestured at the body on the door.

'Take it easy now, sir. Sit down here.'

He jerked his head to one of his mates to go upstairs. The pounding in my head and chest that had begun when I arrived was beginning to slow down. I was beginning to breathe fairly normally again. I said:

'Ring the Yard. Get D.I. Dowell's home number. Get him here. It's his case. Tell him I'm here. Tell him Randolph Mather is the body upstairs.'

For once, a police officer didn't give me back-chat. He just asked:

'What's your name, sir?'

I told him, then leaned back in the chair and closed my eyes as they carried Ernest out on a stretcher. I think they had given him a shot of something, because he was completely unconscious. I envied him. As I sat there with my eyes shut, I thought: I'm going to have to tell Ali. Then I thought: I'm going to have to tell Ian. I didn't know which prospect caused me more pain.

I half expected Dowell to be angry. I don't know why: I suppose I felt guilty, responsible. I'd kept the pressure on and the pimple had popped. He wasn't angry. He ignored me when he came in and went straight upstairs to see the body. As I'd expected, Randolph had been dead before the first policeman found him. Dowell came back down, his face ashen. He went out to his car, and returned with a hip-flask. I remembered it from before, during Disraeli Chambers. He took a slug from it first, before he handed it to me:

'Go on. Deep now, Dave. Go on.'

I didn't need telling twice. It was the straight stuff. There must have been a quarter pint. I drank it all. It burned its way down insides raw from puking, but it stayed down. I grit my teeth to stop them chattering as I thrust his hip-flask back at him:

'Have you got any more?'

He nodded and threw his keys to one of the many policeman now milling about Mather's main hall:

'Car. Boot. Bottle.'

He looked at me wryly:

'I don't normally keep it in the car. But Sheila was still up when I got home.'

I smiled weakly. Sheila was his wife. Dowell was scared of her disapproval. I thought: what a wonderful life; to be able to enjoy the disapproval of a loving and loyal partner. It was the sort of sublime fantasy I needed to bring me back to reality.

'Tell me,' he ordered.

'There's a Chapter — a freemasonic Chapter ...'

'Lodge,' he corrected wrongly.

'No, Chapter. This isn't about craft freemasonry, Tim. It's Gauldie's. It's about as old as freemasonry itself, and it's completely, utterly bent. D'you remember Jack the Ripper was supposed to be a freemason?'

'I've heard the tale,' he said dryly, not particularly eager to extend his enquiries that far back in history.

'It's the Chapter he was supposed to be a member of. They're the ones with the international links. I've been doing a lot of reading, Tim. You wanna know how many books there are on freemasonry? It doesn't matter. Ian got me the information from the freemasons. That's when it all came together.'

He pulled up a chair as the police officer arrived back with our bottle. He took a swig, then passed it to me, muttering I shouldn't finish it all too, then said:

'Go on.'

'Not much more to tell, really.' I told him where he'd find the envelope containing the final report I'd come back to collect. I outlined what he would read.

Dowell whistled:

'Gauldie? That dry old stick?'

His eyes met mine.

'You already knew, didn't you?' I accused.

'Not as much as you told me. But some of it, maybe.'

'Who's Hyram Abyss, Tim?'

He smiled thinly:

'It's possible, just possible, mind you, he said "Hiram Abiff". He was an ancient master of the freemasons who was said to have suffered terrible tortures to try and get masonic secrets out of him, but who died rather than reveal them.'

'Oh, yeah, you really did know all along.'

He said:

'I'm going to have to take you down to the station, Dave. You understand that, don't you?' 'What about Gauldie? You've got to arrest him.'

'What for? I've no evidence yet; maybe after we've identified the door handle.'

'Ali. Ian. Who's going to tell them?'

'Sorry, Dave. I've got to take you in now.'

I was at Holborn Police Station for the rest of the night and much of the day. I wasn't charged; just assisting the police with their enquiries. A doctor examined me, and gave me a pill. They fed me: Martin was right; it was pig-swill. In the afternoon, I asked if I could see him. Dowell said:

'I don't think so, Dave. He's still got a murder charge to answer.' He'd let me the day before, though; or was it two days ago?

'Haven't you read my report, for God's sake?'

'It's not up to me; most of what it contains is guesswork or opinion.'

'What about Kelly and Galucci? Did you pick them up?'

'Ah,' he sighed: 'It seems they flew away. To Switzerland.'

'Extradite 'em,' I protested. He could bring them back on the Clairmount charge, but what I wanted them for was to give the evidence that indicted James Mather on Wainwright, and cleared Martin.

'Sorry, Dave, can't do it.'

'Why not? They'll talk.'

'I don't think they will, sunshine,' he said sardonically. I got the message. 'Car crash, as they left the airport. That fast, mate, that quick. These people have got what shall we call them? — branch offices? — all over the world.'

'Which people,' I asked bitterly: 'Masons or James Mather?'

'Your version is Mather did Pankhurst and Wainwright ...'

'But not Randolph. Randolph's his nephew. Can't you see, especially now, he only hits the ones around the family, not the family themselves? Have you identified ... ?' I couldn't bring myself to say who I meant, but he knew.

He coughed apologetically:

'Wainwright, Stephen Wainwright.'

'He's a mason, he was wearing a mason's hood, he said Hiram Abiff,' I said urgently, trying to reinforce my case at the same time as I realized how stupid it sounded: 'That proves it.'

'He's the brother of the second dead man; Randolph was potentially in the frame, and anyway the brother of the man we'd arrested for it. Revenge. That's all. What does it prove if he dressed in a bit of masonic regalia at the end; what does it prove if he mentioned — if, mind you, I'm not saying he did —if he mentioned a famous old mason at the last moment of his life? He would have been deranged by then.'

'What was your commission, Tim? Keep the masons out of it?'

He didn't deny it. He said:

'I told you if you brought me proof, I'd follow it down. But the proofs lying in the morgue, isn't it? Where you put it.'

I licked my lips. He poked his head out of the door and asked someone to bring me some more tea. I said:

'Are you going to proceed against Martin on the Clairmount?'

'No, not with the other two dead. Matheson will lose his licence. We can't prove complicity by Martin. It would've been a bit more difficult for him if the others were still alive to deny it, but now they're dead, he can lay it off on them too easily to be worth the trouble. It wouldn't've been that serious a charge, anyway.'

'But you want to go ahead on the murder?'

'Want to? No. But we've already charged him for it, there's no new evidence and that means it's got to be left up to the courts now.'

On the table between us lay a pad, onto which my formal statement had been recorded. I said:

'I've got something to add, Tim.'

'What?'

'Randolph was still alive when I saw him. I asked him, he told me he'd set Wainwright up.'

'You're lying, Dave. You would've told me before.'

'I had a shock, Tim; and these drugs they've given me, know what I mean?'

'You really gonna do it, Dave? You gonna stick by it?'

I nodded.

'What else did Randolph tell you? Did he tell you he did it for the freemasons, maybe? Or for his uncle? Did he tell you what he'd like for dinner when he arrives at the Pearly Gate?'

I thought about my answer. If I said freemasons, it was too easy to undermine; a lot of pain for no great gain. If I said James, he'd hit me before I hit the street. I said:

'That was all; just that.'

Pratt brought in a paper cup of tea. Dowell took it from the tray. Without any warning, he flung it in my face. It wasn't hot enough to burn, just enough to hurt and humiliate. The tranquiliser helped. I wiped some of it off my face with my fingers, and licked them dry, wetting my lips. Dowell said:

'Bring him a towel, for God's sake, Pratt. Can't you see the man's wet? Then take his further statement and let him go.' I wasn't going to be charged: I never was; the last thing that would have suited to keep the masons out of it was to give me a public platform to tell my tale from.

When he was at the door, I said to Dowell:

'You played me for a fool, Tim. It won't be easy to forget.'

He shrugged:

'We're all fools someone else is playing, Dave. I tried to warn you, enough so's you'd understand, not so much you wouldn't do what you were supposed to. We're just there to sweep up after the party's over, Dave. We can't either of us control what happens. Haven't you learned anything, Dave?'

'Sometimes you can try, Tim, sometimes you got to try.'

'Right,' he mocked: 'A man's got to do what a man's got to do. Shove it, sunshine. Grow up, Dave.' Just like Sandy had said.

I went straight from the police station to Central Towers. The security men wouldn't let me go up at first, but after I'd made enough of a fuss they called someone to tell himself himself I was there. I was escorted upstairs and given a more thorough frisk than the last time. I was shown in. He already had his overcoat on. He said:

'I have to leave in one minute, Mr Woolf.'

'Going abroad? Business?'

'Right.'

I said in a monotone:

'So I'll say what I have to say.' I paused one last time to get the words into the right order: 'He'll want to know who to blame. He'll want a name. You'll give him a name. If you don't,

I'll whistle every tune I know about you until I find someone you don't own who's prepared to broadcast the whole damned opera.'

'What name?' He asked in a tone as flat as my own.

'John Gauldie. I'll know whether you've done as I asked, won't I?'

'I should think so.'

My last place of call was Mather's, where I expected to find Allison, as I did, settling into her father's old office. He wouldn't be back.

'Does it feel good, Ali?'

She had the grace to blush:

'Someone has to carry on, Dave.'

'I should think you'll be a bit busy for a while, won't you, All? Probably won't have time for — er — an old friend?'

'I could use a good solicitor, though,' she tacitly confirmed she had no other use for me.

'Forget it. You've got Martin. I should think he'll be grateful enough still to have a career to come to work for his little sister. Tell me something, though?'

'Go on,' she said tersely.

I was only going to get the one shot: 'How much of it did you know in advance? Just how bad did you expect it to be? How much damage were you prepared to do so you could get your hands on the firm? How much of it did you actually plan when you cracked the surface by leaking the LCP report, the way everyone else was leaking to serve their own interests? That was clever, taking me to see your mother: I really bought it, didn't I?'

I didn't expect an answer. And that's the one I got. I walked out before I was asked to leave. I didn't ask if she'd enjoyed playing me too for a patsy, or how much of our love-making had been acting. I didn't ask if she'd've sneaked out of my bed while I was asleep, to read my notes, if Dowell hadn't conveniently summoned me into the office the night Wainwright died and let her read them at her leisure. I didn't even ask if she was going to pay my bill.

I took one last taxi home. The driver said:

'You look tired, mate. Been hard at work?'

'You might say.'

'What do you do, then?'

This was advanced cab psychology. Most people pay more for the pleasure of talking about themselves. I said:

'I look into things for people with problems.' Not very well, of course; sometimes, they had more problems at the end than they started with. I rephrased it: 'I'm the one they call in to iron out all the loose ends.' At least that was something I wasn't bad at; that and mixed metaphors.

THE
JUDGE'S SONG

For J.R.F. and M.F.S.,
Members of Manzi's Lunch Club

'Six nights ago a very good friend of mine got beaten up; five nights ago the flat I just moved out of was firebombed and there ain't much of it left; four nights ago some people came to this club and gave the owner – the then owner – a very hard time during which he dropped dead of a heart attack; three nights ago I had to move into a squat without curtains on the windows. Don't tell me about hurting, It's already been done.'

I let her wrist go. She stood there shaking, her mouth open. She had no idea how grisly was the game being played around her father-in-law. I wanted to get up and stroke her gently back to where the most frightening news she can think of is that Harrods' sale has come to an unexpected end. She looked as if she was going to speak, but she bit her lip to stop herself and left, still shaking, without another word.

CHAPTER ONE

'Hallo, just arrived, have you?' A chubby, balding little man in his early sixties, wearing horn-rimmed glasses and with a bare patch of lobster-pink belly bulging out where his shirt didn't quite button up over his knee-length safari shorts, rolled towards us, holding out a hand. 'Uh, *bonjour?*' he added, in case his assumption that we were English was incorrect.

Ever more able at the social amenities than I, Sandy was out of her deckchair before I could manage to get up from the upright at which I was sitting drinking coffee. The sun was hot and the time was early. I was unused to both.

'Hallo, I'm Sandy Nichol,' she introduced. 'This is Dave,' she added, omitting my last name. I finally got my limbs to work and, after her, took his clammy hand.

'Martyn Pulleyne,' he said. 'Your first visit?'

'Yes, we're just here for the week.'

'Friends of the Prestons?'

'Er, yes,' I said. 'Sort of. Friends of friends.'

'Lucky you. They usually rent the apartment out for the summer, then come down at the end of the season themselves.'

'They'll be here next week.'

'Shame, we'll miss them. Well, be on my way. See you at the beach?'

'Fine, fine.'

He waddled across the gravelled forecourt and turned right between the low privet hedge which was still high enough to conceal all but his gleaming pate, as he set off towards the main road and thence the beach.

'That's a High Court judge?' Sandy gawped once he was out of earshot. 'He looks like an accountant.' For a long period in her life, her steady lover had been an accountant: she knew no greater insult.

'That, my dear, is Sir Martyn Pulleyne, Mr Justice Pulleyne, no less.'

And I, Dave Woolf, neither knight nor judge but sometime solicitor turned private eye, was being paid the highest fee I'd ever earned in order to get the dirt on Pulleyne with which to destroy him.

I had been surprised to receive Orbach's 'phone call. We were not friends; perhaps we had never been friends, but certainly since the Disraeli Chambers case, friendship was the last thing I wanted (although I admit that, stuck for a way forward during the Mather's mess, I had turned to him for help). He had once been friends with the members of Disraeli Chambers — indeed, he was one of its founders — and his friendship had proved more than passing prejudicial to their health.

'I want to see you,' he said without preamble. 'I've got a job for you.'

I was too surprised to think of a witty answer and I didn't like to tell him that I didn't want to see him. As I've grown older, I've decided, albeit only on a balance of probabilities — a much lower standard of proof than beyond reasonable doubt — that there are sufficient good things in life to keep on playing at it. Those who incur the wrath of the almighty Orbach do so at risk of any future at all.

'Well?' He bellowed down the 'phone.

I held the receiver at arm's length to give myself space to think. There was, as he ought to have known, no possibility at all that I would work for him However well-intentioned, indeed however well-paid it might be — and however badly I might need the money (as I did) — I would never really know what I was doing or why: I would be the puppet and he would be pulling my strings. My experience at Mather's had left a sour taste in my mouth; the way I'd been played by others had cost me a lover, a friend and most of my residual illusions.

I didn't mind about the lover. Sandy Nichol — the great on-off love of my life — and I had resumed our relationship soon after; just a few weeks before Orbach's 'phone call we had dined out to celebrate six months' unbroken companionship. I would not have been at home to receive the call if Sandy hadn't wanted to spend last night alone. Normally, I stayed at the house she owned in Kentish Town. It was a considerable improvement on the dark and damp Earl's Court basement I had rented since my student days.

'Well?' he repeated, a decibel quieter.

'I'm, er, not really taking on any work — not that sort of work — anymore, Russel. I'm, er, thinking of going back to Nichol and Co.'

Nichol & Co is the name of the North London legal aid law-firm that Sandy and I had set up many years before, when we first qualified. You will note that it is not called Nichol & Woolf. It never was. This gives you some idea of the balance of power between me and Sandy.

At the time we set the firm up, we were not lovers. We were still not lovers at the time she threw me out of the practice with a nominal pay-off that didn't cover my outstanding debts to bank manager or dope dealer. The latter was the reason she threw me out, not the former. We didn't become lovers until years later, during Disraeli Chambers, since which time she had been trying to persuade me to return to what she describes as 'real work', as a solicitor. Recently, she had been trying to tempt me with the offer of a decently redecorated office and my own assistant. I would say that it's a woman's prerogative to change her mind, but the last time I said it to Sandy she hit me so hard I couldn't see straight for a week.

It was not true that I was thinking of doing what she wanted. Occasionally, I would help out in the office, but with administration, or drawing up bills of costs to serve on clients or the legal aid fund, not proper legal work. Drawing up bills is a task I'm good at: I've always had a creative bent. Over the years since I left, the firm had more than trebled in size, in turnover, and in both qualified and unqualified staff. Nonetheless, Sandy ruled solitary and supreme. It was easy to imagine the resentment my return would cause.

I only said it because it was the first thing I could think of to get rid of Orbach. Inevitably, it had the opposite effect.

'Good. That suits what I want you to do very well. Now, I take it you are willing to come and see me?'

When I had asked to see him during Mather's, offering to buy him dinner, he had abruptly terminated the conversation by identifying an extremely expensive restaurant — Frederick's in Camden Passage (which is, naturally, in Islington, not Camden) — stating a time and date, before hanging up without waiting for me to agree. It was worth a try. I said, 'Frederick's. Tomorrow night. Eight o'clock.'

He snorted. 'Tonight. My home at nine. I've moved. I'll give you the address.'

I was even more shocked that he had moved than that he had called me. For years, he had lived lonely and alone in a ground-floor flat in Highgate, sitting at the French windows overlooking his garden, his chair angled so that he could look out without seeing any other buildings. He used to share the flat with Margot McAllister, the MP, but they had split up when she went into Parliament so he could savour in peace and quiet the bitterness of his experiences at Disraeli Chambers, undisturbed by the constant demands made on people in public life. Their relationship had proved less important to him than his pain and anger.

He was altogether a strange man. He spent his holidays in Oslo, with a family of friends the female head of which he referred to as 'Mor', meaning mother, examining the new Munch Museum exhibits — they change them around every year — or going to concerts. He had no friends I knew of. He worked in an area of law well out of the limelight, but he was a Queen's Counsel and reputed to earn something between a quarter and a half million pounds a year. (This is not as extraordinary as it sounds, for one of the best English QCs was once paid a million pounds on a single brief, to appear in Hong Kong.)

I had heard no suggestion of a woman friend since McAllister left him, but so far as I knew he was not gay. I had once described him as aiming to hurt with every two things he said out of three. He nursed his loneliness like a jealous lover.

The news of a move was decisive. Even if I was not going to work for him, I could not resist the opportunity of finding out what had brought it about. I still hadn't agreed to the meeting when he hung up, taking for granted that I would come.

No sooner had he done so than the 'phone rang again.

'Hi, it's me.' This is a universally accurate opening, but in this case it meant Sandy. 'Are you coming up this evening?'

'Am I allowed back in?' I asked dryly.

I could hear her smile down the line. In the case of anyone else, this would be a universally inaccurate proposition, but not when it's Sandy.

Every time I finish up with someone else, and go back to Sandy, I can't remember why I left. There's no one who's a patch on her, or with whom love-making comes as close to transcending isolation. If I say there's no one who's as good as her I don't mean that she's invariably kind, or sensitive, or moral, or unselfish. She has the sharpest tongue of anyone I know, can be intolerably demanding in the most irritating, petty ways, can cut someone down to size swifter than a samurai's sword and when she wants something, heaven help anyone who stands in her way. What I mean is: no one else I know has got all their appealing and unappealing qualities in such perfect balance.

'Dave, I'll leave the office on time — get here early?'

'Can't, San. I've got an appointment at nine o'clock, though it won't be a long one and I'm not going to be far away.'

'I want to talk to you, Dave,' she insisted. Sandy has several variants on 'I want to talk to you'. One is: I don't want to talk to you, but you need talking to. Another is: I think maybe it's time we had a talk about things. Yet another is when she feels lonely or insecure, but doesn't want to admit it. The fourth is the eleventh commandment. 'Can't you change it?'

'Would you believe — Russel Orbach wants to see me? At his new house?'

'Ah.' Sandy knew Orbach too. She put up no new argument. 'Try to keep it short, then. That shouldn't be difficult.' Few people find an evening in Orbach's company a relaxing experience; most would rather back blindly into a fast-moving freeway. It's less dangerous.

'Sure. I won't be late.'

I was just about to hang up, when she said: 'Dave?'

'Yup.'

'Oh, nothing.' And she hung up.

Why does everyone find it so easy to hang up on me? Maybe they don't expect me to say anything worth hearing.

After this intriguing start to the day, I went back to bed. I do my best thinking in bed. Besides, it wasn't yet noon.

I had just the one chore that day. Following Mather's, I had for once done something sensible. After I had — not without a degree of hesitation — billed Allison Mather Hoyt for my outstanding fee, and after she had — with yet greater hesitation — paid it, I had splashed out on a piece of serious equipment instead of dissipating the loot on booze. I had bought a car.

What is more, I bought a good car, a car to last. I bought a Volkswagen Passat, a car so large I could sleep in it if I was evicted for non-payment of rent. It is a family car, designed for obedient Catholics. Like Orbach, I am a Jew and I do not have a family, but once I'd been for a test-drive, I fell in love with it.

My chore for the day was to pick up the car from the garage where it had been undergoing therapy. It was located not far from Orbach's new home. The trouble was that it shut at six-thirty and I could not make the trek across London twice in one day. I telephoned and asked if they would mind leaving the car out for me; I would send them a cheque. They were still laughing when I hung up. Accordingly, I found myself two and a half hours early for Orbach and about five minutes away.

There was only one answer. There only ever is. I drove to his street, parked, and found a pub. The Crown was on the other side of the road from his house, less than a hundred yards away. It had a forecourt, and I settled down outside with a large Southern Comfort to enjoy an unusually warm July evening and to watch the healthy, well-preserved, middle-class young mothers of the area bouncing tantalisingly by.

Cloudesley Road is at the heart of gentrifying Islington. One can walk to Frederick's if sufficiently well-heeled. It is a most attractive street. Though the pavements are unusually wide, the road itself is narrow; the way that cars are parked at an angle instead of parallel forces drivers to proceed at a crawl. Furthermore, as I had found to my confusion, it is part of a complex traffic system which means that, although not itself one-way, it can only be entered from one end. It is accordingly very quiet, almost as peaceful as the country.

The houses are flat-fronted Georgian terraced, one side with wrought-iron balconies, all of them with curved front-windows on the ground floor. The Volvos, Volkswagens and Peugeots testified to house prices I didn't dare dream about. The interiors were white-painted, with unframed pictures on the walls and Liberty print curtains, knocked-through from front to back;

most of the kitchens are in the basement, with mandatory stripped-pine table, microwave and dishwasher.

I was returning to my seat with my second drink when I saw a sight that made me toss it back in a single gulp and race inside for a third to calm my nerves. Orbach emerged from a car accompanied by a small black child in jeans who ran to his house crying 'me, me', attacking the front door with its own key. They disappeared inside. A few moments later the child — I now saw it was a little girl, maybe eight or nine years old — emerged and ran across the road. Orbach stood in the doorway and called after her, 'Half an hour, Frankie. That's all.'

'All right, Russel,' she shrieked without turning around. 'Promise, Frankie.'

'I promise,' she called out before disappearing into a house on the same side of the street as the pub.

Orbach shut his door. I waited patiently. I waited for half an hour. Nothing happened. I waited for a further quarter of an hour. Nothing happened. After one hour, Orbach emerged and crossed the road, intent on collecting the Frankie thing. I shut my eyes. Though I hate children, I'm squeamish. There was a serious likelihood I was about to witness murder or at the very least child abuse elevated to an art-form.

That would make it difficult for me to find out who she was. I knew she couldn't be his daughter. Not because she was black: one of the few epithets I never heard flung at him was racist. But one of those odd bits of information that had lingered in the faculty I laughingly like to call my memory was that Orbach couldn't have children. I don't remember when I heard it, or even if he told me. It was possibly something that had come up in the pub after a meeting in the old days; or something someone had offered in explanation of his antipathy towards the world at large.

Instead, a few moments later, the two of them went back over the road together, hand-in-hand, laughing. I could die a happy man. I had seen something no one else had ever seen. I had seen him laugh. I never thought he knew how.

It was still only eight o'clock. There was another hour to waste. I faced a dilemma. If I continued to drink at the same rate, I would probably not be coherent enough to confront Orbach; if I went across early, he would probably be incoherent with anger. I compromised. I had one more drink and ventured forth. Before my courage could flag, I was standing at his door, ringing the bell. I heard the child shout delightedly: 'Visitors!'

I would probably be the first one she'd ever seen. 'Hallo.'

She had opened the door before Orbach yelled from within the bowels of the house: 'Frankie, wait!'

'Hallo,' I replied. Children bring out the witty conversationalist in me.

'Who are you?' she asked. She'd obviously learned her tact and reticence from Orbach: 'What do you want?'

'I want to see Russel. He's expecting me. My name's Dave.'

Orbach appeared at the end of the hall corridor wearing an apron and brandishing a spatula. Beneath the apron, he still had on the trousers of his pin-striped court-suit and a collarless shirt. He was a tall, heavy man — I'd say fat, but he might not like it — with a bushy, grey beard and a shock of equally grey hair. It was a sight to behold.

'You're early,' he accused.

'Sorry. I didn't dare be late.'

'You've been drinking,' the monster said from far below my knees.

'He always drinks, Frankie,' Orbach said dryly.

'How do you do, Frankie.' I thrust out my hand hoping she wouldn't bite it.

She took it timidly and snatched hers back as if she had a similar suspicion.

'Are you going to eat with us?' she demanded.

'I wasn't planning to.'

'You can if you like,' Orbach said. 'Come on.' He led the way down to the half-basement open-plan kitchen that led through French windows onto the garden at the back.

'It's a nice house,' I said lamely, trying to keep up my end of this unexpectedly civilised conversation. 'When did you move?'

'Last year. Frankie!' He caught a milk bottle before it fell from the kitchen table. 'Get a glass, there's a sweetheart.'

While she reached into a cupboard, I gestured towards her: 'This is why?'

'Yes. She's my ward. You don't have to worry about talking in front of her. Explain to Dave, Frankie,' he said as she sat down to a glass of milk so big I didn't think she'd be able to lift it.

'Russel's my guardian,' she recited. 'My mummy and daddy were his friends. They died in a 'plane. So I came to live with Russel instead.'

I'm not sure which was the greater shock: that Orbach had friends, or that they would appoint him her guardian. Perhaps the two explained each other; they were obviously stark, staring bonkers.

'It must be a shock to the system,' I said.

'For both of us,' he admitted.

The whole time, he had been working at the range. Now he served up a stew with new potatoes and mange tout, in three huge, steaming helpings. I stared at mine aghast. I normally try not to eat too much to interfere with my drinking. He must have read my mind because he laughed.

'It's changed my habits, too. Shall I open some wine?'

The question had to be rhetorical. He drew a bottle out of a rack inside a cupboard and uncorked it. After he'd filled our glasses, Frankie picked up his and stuck her tongue into it, pulling a face. He bent down to kiss the top of her head before sitting down again.

'Not a boozer, are you, Frankie?'

'You drink too much,' she scolded. 'Daddy drank too.'

'So he did, so he did.'

'Who were her parents?' I helped myself to a refill

'You probably knew him. Mick Mellor?'

The name rang a bell so faint I could hardly hear it tinkle. I shook my head. He reminded me. 'He was a surveyor, he used to do a lot of housing work.'

I remembered a boyish, good-looking half-Irish quarter-Italian pure mongrel who gave evidence of disrepair on behalf of tenants against their landlords. I didn't know him well, or know that he had married, let alone that, presumably, his wife was black.

'How come you're her guardian? Didn't they have any family?'

He smiled thinly.

'You mean why would anyone let me bring a child up?'

Frankie had finished her stew, and her milk. She slipped down from her chair, and went round the table to hug Orbach. Although he had said we could talk in front of her, she was upset. He leaned down so she could whisper in his ear. I heard her say: 'I love you.'

He beamed and kissed her again.

I felt nauseous. It might have been the combination of booze and food, but more likely it was the sight of Orbach as loving father. It put me in mind of black-and-white newsreel-movies of Hitler kissing babies.

I finished the wine while he put her to bed. I didn't hear a door shut after he told her good night and the first thing he said when he rejoined me was. 'Keep your voice down, Dave. She still has nightmares.'

'What actually happened?'

He shrugged. "Plane crash. No one's fault, really. They were planning to emigrate — to Bolivia. They wanted to learn to fly for over there. I decided to do so at the same time, just for the fun of it. We bought a small Cessna together; I was going to buy them out when they went. There was never a definite answer — something shorn through, but it could've happened when they crashed.'

'It still seems odd,' I mused, wondering why they should have left her to Orbach.

'I can't have children of my own. Did you know that?' I nodded. He continued. 'Frankie's my godchild. A Jewish godfather for a Catholic child; one of those progressive priests. Well, I suppose a lot of that suppressed parental instinct went into her; when they said they wanted to name me as her testamentary guardian, you know how it is, you don't think it'll ever happen. Anyway,' he hurried on, 'you aren't here to talk about Frankie.'

'True.' I held up my empty glass and studied it pointedly. 'Was that the only bottle?'

We adjourned — with wine — to the living-room. There were signs of Frankie everywhere. I remembered Orbach's flat as a model of method, everything in its place — except me.

'What would you say if I told you there was a High Court judge who was corrupt?'

I duly gagged on my wine.

'I know they're all bent, politically; they'll stand on their intellectual heads to find for the establishment. But that isn't what you mean, is it?'

'No,' he said, 'that isn't what I mean.'

In America, bent judges are as commonplace as Kentucky Fried or MacDonalds. Just as there is a gas station for every five cars, there's a crooked judge for every five head of population. But America is America. For one thing, they elect their judges, which is a sure formula for corruption; people vote for those who behave the same way they do. For another, ever since they up-ended the tea-bags into Boston Bay, they've relished contempt for law — it's written into their Constitution.

In England, however, the judiciary derives its authority from the Crown. There's no Act of Parliament that says how judges are to be appointed. They are appointed by the Lord Chancellor: it's a question of the right chap appointing other right chaps.

Oddly enough for an erstwhile radical, I've always believed it is right (no pun intended) to appoint conservative judges. Law is something judges should uphold, not make. It is about maintaining the status quo. Changes in the status quo ought to be brought about by Parliament, which is elective. Thus — at least in theory — the will of the people remains supreme. So I am totally unmoved by judicial conservatism; I rather approve of it. The fact that it is morally and philosophically corrupt and corrupting isn't news.

But the idea of a really bent English High Court judge is something else. I could imagine the occasional magistrate on the make; they are drawn from the lay population. And there was the circuit judge whom they caught smuggling from the continent, but circuit judges apply for their appointments, normally because they can't cut it in the higher echelons of practice, so no one takes them seriously.

In the past, there have been more senior corrupt judges. Francis Bacon, Viscount St Albans, and Thomas Parker, Earl of Macclesfield, both Lord Chancellors, were dismissed for bribe-taking in 1620 and 1725 respectively, and Richard Bethell, Baron Westbury, also Lord High Chancellor, resigned in 1865 over the prospective appointment of his son as Chief Bankruptcy Registrar of Leeds. But there has never been a case of a High Judge known to be a crook. The skies would fall in on the authority of the law itself. How could judges sentence villains if they were capable of the same sins themselves?

Naturally, I asked; 'Who?'

He shook his head. 'Are you taking the case, Dave?'

'Ah.' He wasn't handing out free gossip with stew.

'More articulate than usual, but, yes, I'd say you've summed it about right. "Ah", he repeated sarcastically, 'as in "ah, I don't get to find out unless I accept the job".'

Another reason Sandy didn't object to my visiting Orbach before I came to see her is because he is the only person either of us knows whose tongue is more acid than hers. In the aftermath, hers doesn't sound so bad.

'What's your interest in it?' I asked guardedly.

He shrugged. 'You know how I hate hypocrisy.'

I shook my head. 'I'd have to work for you full-time. Even you couldn't afford it.'

He frowned, but not at my answer: he was putting his thoughts in order. He said, 'A few years ago — soon after I took silk,' he meant when he was appointed as a Queen's Counsel, 'I did a case — a commercial dispute —in front of this judge. At the time, I thought I was on a sure-fire winner. There was no way I could lose, unless the judge found my client to be so dishonest he might as well be up on fraud charges — and he was as straight as a die.'

'Which is what happened?'

'Right. At the time, I wrote it off as just one of those things. You know how it is, there's no such thing as a certainty; judges are the most unpredictable beings on earth. It's a formula: take the irrationality of human conduct, mix it with the irrationality of a judge, and at the end of the day you've got something that sounds like a rational account of the facts.'

'You could have appealed?'

'No. All the Court of Appeal would have said was that the trial judge saw the witnesses, formed an impression of them, and so on. They couldn't interfere unless his decision flouted all reason.'

'Well, you must've lost before — and since.'

His eyebrow twitched. 'Not often.' Nor did he. 'Nor ever for a reason I simply could not understand. Still, at the time, I didn't think any more about it. I was disappointed, but even if the client never came back to me, his solicitors continued to instruct me. They still do. Recently, though, I heard of a fairly similar business: same judge but the company involved was —is — related to the company I'd been against.' He paused again to collect his thoughts. 'I happen to know one of the barristers in the case quite well. He was junior for the defendant company.'

'Was he led by a silk?' In heavy cases, a client will retain two barristers to represent him in court. The more senior is known as the leader; the other as junior. Usually, a leader will be, like

Orbach, a QC, but there's no rule that says he has to be. My question wasn't important, merely idle professional curiosity.

'Yes. The same one I was up against before. I've led the junior two or three times myself. We get on all right. On a couple of occasions, he's come to me for advice.' It is part of the collegiate tradition of the bar that its members make themselves available to advise one another.

'Did he tell you about it?'

'We spoke at first on the 'phone, then met for a drink. He wanted to meet away from the Temple.' This is where the Inns of Court are, and all the barristers in London practice. 'Obviously, I agreed. The details don't matter for now, but he told me more or less what I told you, the difference being that he was appearing on the winning side. There was this further difference: he had wanted, time after time, to advise the clients to' settle the case, because he didn't think they stood a chance. But his leader wouldn't. Notwithstanding the state of the evidence, his leader was always quite confident of victory.'

I picked at the obvious pimple.

'So your friend had got it wrong. That's why people hire QCs. The leader was right all along — he thought they were going to win, and they did. Your friend thought they were going to lose, and he still doesn't understand how they didn't.'

'No. With a lot of junior counsel, I'd agree that's a possibility. But this man has his head screwed on tightly; he's one of the best juniors I've led. The point is, he could never get his own leader to tell him why he was so confident.'

'Freemasonry?' I asked automatically. Freemasonry had featured at Mather's, and the case had given me an understanding of how the secret power elite operates, overriding — and often excluding — the formal establishment itself.

'I don't think so. One or two of the players may be Masons, but the judge in question has spoken out against it.'

'Let's assume you're right, for a moment. Why are you pursuing it? Your case is stale, you said it's a few years old. Why doesn't your friend do something about it?'

'Ah, there's the rub. He can't take it further himself.'

'Why not?'

'Three reasons. First of all, what he knows is mostly privileged. Secondly, his own father is on the bench and I don't have to tell you just how awkward that would make it. Thirdly, his own future. As things stand, he'll get silk himself within the next couple of years and be on the bench within ten. If he's identified with even the suggestion that a judge is bent, he's finished.'

'And you? What will it do to you?'

'Ah, Dave, the establishment never forgets. I've got my silk. They had to give it me in the end because my claim was just too strong; but no one has a claim to a seat on the bench. They'll never give it me. I've got nothing left to lose.'

'Because of Disraeli Chambers?'

He had not broken a single law; he had done nothing for which he could be indicted; he had done nothing a newspaper would dare print. But I knew what he had done; others at the bar knew what he had done; the police — in the person of my former friend, lackey of the establishment, Dowell — knew what he had done. Quietly, the Lord Chancellor's Office, with responsibility for judicial appointments, would have been told.

'Why me, Russel? I know more barmen than High Court judges; it's not exactly the sort of circle I hang around in.'

'You've got a feel for lawyers, Dave; you can spot the discrepancy, the inconsistency, in a lawyer's reasoning the way a layman can't.'

'These two cases — this is all I'd have to go on?'

'There's a bit more that may fit. But if I tell you now, you'll be able to get too close to it.' He reminded me I still hadn't agreed.

Nor was I planning to.

'Look, Russel, I won't say I'm not flattered to be asked. And I won't deny I'm interested.' As a feat of investigation, it would be like solving Jack the Ripper. 'But as I said, I'm thinking of going back to work with Sandy and, well,' I looked for the safest way of saying it, 'I, er, I don't think I'd be too comfortable working for you.'

'I expected that. You might not be comfortable, but you'd be rich. I'm willing to pay twice what you earned at Mather's.'

My wallet got a hard-on: what I'd earned at Mather's was well over the odds. A couple of weeks at twice would exceed my average annual earnings over the preceding five years.

'Do you know how much that is?'

He shrugged modestly: Orbach the omniscient. I knew that the one thing I would never learn would be how he'd found out.

'Think about it, Dave. Don't reject it out of hand.'

I arrived at Sandy's considerably sobered. She, on the other hand, was a wee bit pissed — squiffy, she liked to call it. I didn't ring at the bell, I had my own key to her house.

We kissed and hugged and wriggled against each other homily. Someone I knew once referred to bad sex like chewing someone else's stale gum. Sandy was rare fillet steak cooked at the Savoy Grill. I bore down on her and we tumbled onto the sofa. We both like it that way: sudden, urgent, half-dressed, just the bits that counted.

Afterwards, while she went to wash, I poured us each another drink.

'Did you eat?'

I told her I'd eaten with Orbach, 'And, wait for this, his ward. He's got a child living with him. Her name's Frankie, and she's the orphan of …'

'Mick Mellor.' She clicked her fingers. 'He and his wife were killed in a car crash. I did hear about it. I'd forgotten. Poor kid. How awful for her.' She meant living with Orbach, not her parents' death. 'What's she like?'

'It was a 'plane crash actually.' She brushed the correction aside. 'Well, you know, she's a child. Isn't that enough? I mean, she's black, she's smart and she's incredibly beautiful, but she's a child all the same and you know how I feel about kids.'

'Oh, yes, I know,' she shut her eyes for a moment. 'But it's all a pose, isn't it, Dave? You don't really hate them, do you? I never thought you did.'

'Well, you know how it is. If I ain't got one, I don't see why anyone else should.'

'Did you never …' she hesitated, but plunged on, '… didn't you ever, just once, think it might be nice if you did?'

'What? Me? Have a kid?' I laughed so hard I nearly fell off the sofa. 'What if it turned out like me?'

'I know,' she said gloomily. 'That's what's worrying me.'

CHAPTER TWO

'But, San, you're forty!'

'Gee, kid, you say the most romantic things. I know I'm forty. So are you. So what?'

'But I thought ... Well, you know. Shit.' I got up and went into the kitchen to fetch more ice. I turned the tray over and the cubes spilled out onto the floor. 'Shit,' I said again, 'shit, shit, shit, shit.' I flung the tray after them.

The reason I always remembered Orbach couldn't have kids is because for a long time I thought maybe I couldn't either. I got so curious about it I had myself tested, and while it is true I have a low sperm count, it wasn't low enough to rule it out on that ground alone — only on the grounds I'd told Sandy. What if it turned out like me?

I started to pick up the ice-cubes but I couldn't. Either they kept slithering about the floor, or else I couldn't see straight. I was kneeling on the floor, grabbing at ice-cubes, crying like someone had died.

I didn't hear Sandy come in until she knelt down beside me and took my head in her hands, kissing my wet eyes until they were clear enough to see she was crying too. She said, 'I'm sorry, I'm sorry. I had no idea it'd upset you like this.'

I pushed her away. 'Don't be stupid, San, I'm not upset. I'm happy, you schmuk. Can't you understand? I never thought I would be. Listen,' I gabbled. Because Sandy knew that it was difficult for me to have children, I could ask the one, otherwise unthinkable question. 'I promise I'll only say it the once. It is mine; I mean, it's definitely mine, isn't it?'

'Oh, yeah, it's yours all right; the blood test'll be fifty proof,' she said laconically.

'What do you want, Sandy?' I asked, once we were sitting down again. 'How do you want to handle it?'

She knew exactly what I was asking.

'I want you to come back to work; I want us to live together; I want us to do it all right. That's all,' she concluded calmly, as if she hadn't asked me to give her everything I had.

I shuddered.

'It's spooky. First thing tonight, I see Orbach with a kid, like an omen; now I'm going to have one. You think, maybe, we're all growing up? Just before our last bust-up, she'd said: 'grow up, Dave, just grow up'. A few days later, Tim Dowell had said the same thing, as he reluctantly ordered my release from custody. I hadn't seen him since.

'You don't want to, well, get married?'

She shook her head firmly. 'No way. That's the last thing I want. I told you, I want us to do it right; if we get married, we won't last a month.'

'This's why you didn't want to see me last night? Why?'

She couldn't meet my gaze; she'd spent last night wondering whether to keep it. I got up and went and sat on the sofa with her, putting an arm around her shoulder. In the end, I just whispered, 'Thanks, San.'

We didn't decide anything that night. There was plenty of time, and she wanted me to reach the key decisions for myself: like giving up Earl's Court and quitting investigating. But she didn't argue the next morning when I said that, one way or another, I was going to take Orbach's brief. At that money, there couldn't be a choice now; and if it was going to be my last case, it might as well be a good one. I arranged a meet with him for the same place, same time, that night.

'But this time, don't arrive until nine,' he added.

With unerring instinct, he omitted to ask the one question I had the answer for: why did you change your mind? Instead, he led me into the living-room and produced a contract for me to sign.

I read it through carefully, then tossed it back at him. 'I can't sign that. It says you're retaining me as a solicitor. You're not.'

'If I decide I am, I am. There is no law that says what you can and can't hire a lawyer for, but there is a law that says what you tell a solicitor, or what a solicitor learns on a client's behalf, is privileged.'

'Which there ain't necessarily for a private eye, right?'

It's a grey area of law. In the States, private eyes have got legal privilege, but so do priests, hookers, doctors and barmen. In this country, only lawyers, and only when acting as such. I've told people I had privilege in my earlier cases but the claim has never been tested in court. Orbach wanted to be sure he owned what I found out, and he wasn't going to rely on either my word or my interpretation of the law.

I explained why I couldn't sign.

'I don't have a current practising certificate; I don't have professional insurance. Hell, I don't even have an office.' Though I worked from home, there was neither planning permission nor permission under my lease to use it as an office.

'Do it through Nichol & Co.'

'You paying?'

'I'll pay for the certificate; the added insurance is nominal.'

He was, of course, correct.

'Say Sandy don't agree?' In that case, the insurance would have to go in my own name and would add thousands to his bill.

'She'll agree,' he said calmly, 'you know she will.' I did too: she'd figure, once she got me back on the notepaper I wouldn't get taken off it again.

He handed me back the contract and I signed it. Then, and only then, did he tell me: 'Mr Justice Pulleyne, Sir Martyn Pulleyne.'

I knew of him. What I knew I didn't like. Primarily a criminal judge — though all High Court judges do both civil and crime from time to time — he invariably handed out the maximum. Didn't matter if you were a bank-robber, a baby-batterer, a drunk driver, a petty thief, a bent copper, a rapist, an inside dealer or someone who'd claimed a bit more social security than the rules allowed. There used to be a judge on the High Court bench called Melford Stevenson who was said to have named his house 'Truncheons' and who similarly enjoyed a reputation for harshness. Maybe Pulleyne's house was called Kalashnikov.

What I knew of him suggested someone rigidly upright: sentencing to a year a traffic cop who had accepted a fifty pound bribe for overlooking a speeding offence, he had reportedly described his crime as more damaging to society than a bomb in a crowded market. On another occasion, he had sent down a pregnant mother of five for the same number of years, for receiving stolen property, remarking that at least she wouldn't be able to have any more babies for a while.

Sometimes, though, he was right. There had been an outcry when he jailed a woman who had murdered what the press portrayed as her brutalising, incestuous father. During the appeal, however, it emerged that her principal motivation was the transfer of his affections to her younger brother, whom she had helped hold down the first time his father had fucked him. The press had missed the evidence first time around: it came out between two and three in the afternoon when all good journalists are still in the pub.

While Pulleyne was at the bar, though, he had acted for some of the most violent villains of his day. Remember the Reddins? A family of four Forest Gate brothers who enjoyed puzzles — which limb to stick back onto which torso. Two of them walked away from a twenty year minimum thanks to Pulleyne's advocacy and, with others of their generation, moved into the netherworld where big business meets crooked finance. The two who went down enjoyed a standard of life inside that is not normally associated with deprivation of liberty. He had acted for armed robbers, gangsters, murderers, and more of them had been acquitted than had gone behind the bars where they belonged. Exactly where he was now sending them.

Russel said: 'It's not that unusual. You get it on the civil side. Treasury Devils often turn soft once they get on the bench. Gamekeeper turned poacher.' Treasury Devils are the government's own barristers, who represent all their interests in court. After a while, they are rewarded with a High Court judgeship. Having acted for the most oppressive agency in the country, once on the bench they like to flex the muscles of their long-suppressed liberalism. It doesn't last long, just a year or two, until they remember there are yet more senior appointments available.

'Do you know what a High Court judge earns?' Orbach asked.

I shook my head. I only knew it was more — much more — than me, but less — much less — than Orbach.

'Eighty-five and a half. With pension rights, and no expenses, it's about the same as a hundred thousand for a barrister.'

I wasn't surprised. I've long known that judges in England aren't highly paid — relative to the rest of the profession. After all, Members of Parliament only get twenty-two grand which similarly, though more than most of the populace, isn't in the stockbroker league. The idea is to keep out of the higher reaches of the establishment anyone who isn't already financially a member. It's a sort of reverse Groucho — they only let people into the club who already belong.

'Now think what Pulleyne would have earned at the bar.'

'He did mostly crime, didn't he? They don't earn so much.' Not so much as civil lawyers, like Orbach; liberty and reputation are much less valuable commodities than property rights.

'Ah, well, they do and then again they don't.' Sometimes, Orbach was more Egyptian than Jewish: sphinx-like.

'How did your clients pay you, Dave?'

'Legal aid, of course.'

'Oh, yes, right. Just legal aid.'

I grinned, 'Well, er, maybe a wee sample, just to understand the charge better,' I punned. Most of my clients dealt dope.

He snorted. 'The rules say that if you act on legal aid, it can't be topped up by private money, right?'

I nodded. Legal aid means that the state pays a private lawyer on behalf of the client, but what it pays doesn't compare to what lawyers can charge a privately paying client. Unsurprisingly, the best lawyers are often not available on legal aid. Furthermore, there are limits on what can be done. Special permission is needed, for example, for experts or private investigators, or to have both a senior and junior counsel appearing in a case, which can be essential when there is a vast mass of documentary evidence.

Legal aid is means tested, so theoretically if you qualify you don't have the private means with which to attract the better-known lawyers, or to circumvent its limits But in criminal cases the means test is crude and rarely scrutinised and someone crooked in the first place won't hesitate to declare a falsely low income. This provides an opportunity to the sharp villain or civil litigant: by topping up legal aid payments, he can get the best lawyers and maximum facilities, plus a substantial subsidy from the state.

'You're saying Pulleyne took top-up money?'

'Don't sound so surprised, Dave. A lot of barristers do, *and* a lot of solicitors. The practice is so widespread, the Lord Chancellor had to issue a reminder just a little while ago. The money comes in envelopes, in cash, and the Inland Revenue doesn't need to know about it. What's more, you don't even need to pay your clerk.' Barristers' clerks are paid on a percentage basis.

Take a clerk's fee of, say, 10%, as it would have been when Pulleyne was in practice; take top rate tax — at the end of Pulleyne's time at the bar, it was 60 per cent, although in the 1970s, when Labour was in power, it rose as high as 90 per cent; out of £1,000, the barrister keeps only £360. Which would you rather have: a declarable cheque for £1,000, or five hundred in cash?

Orbach added, 'The bar's a business, Dave. The integrity's just a part of the mystique — for which you have to pay extra. What businessman lightly ignores a little tax-free cash on the side?'

'Say he took top-up money, then. Just for the sake of argument. As you say, a lot of people do.' My 'samples' provided a nice additional earner; even allowing for what I personally consumed, there was plenty left over for 'friends'. This was one of the pernickety, petty complaints Sandy had levelled at me when she broke up our partnership; the partnership she now wanted me back in. 'It's the same sort of thing as tax-dodging, and that's hardly a crime.'

Russel raised an eyebrow. 'I can think of people who have been to prison for similar payments or other sorts of tax evasion.'

But we both knew that white-collar tax fraud was crime without stigma, which is what I meant.

'It's still a long way from the sort of "crooked" you're talking about.'

'And it's a lot of money I'm paying you to make the connection,' he answered calmly.

'I still don't get what's in it for you, Russel.'

'You don't need to.'

In a similar situation, at the beginning of the Mather's case, I'd told Iron Ian Mather it was up to me to decide what I needed to know. I could have called Orbach the same way, but my heart wasn't in it. I was still bemused by the previous night's news; because of it, I wanted the money much, much more than ever before; and Ian Mather, for all his power, didn't have Orbach's air of authority.

Orbach had brought back for me a file on the case he'd lost. In addition, he had photocopied a number of law reports and a couple of unreported transcripts of cases in which Pulleyne had presided, or from which he had been unsuccessfully appealed. They included the case his young friend had been involved in.

'How about the ones where he's been overturned on appeal?'

'They're few and far between; I'll send you a note, if you like, but I don't think they'll tell you anything. Where shall I send it?'

I sighed and admitted final defeat — by him and by Sandy.

'Send it to the office — Nichol & Co. Mark it personal. You can send my retainer with it. There's one thing, though — I'd like to meet the guy. Any idea how that can be arranged?' The judge and I didn't belong to the same club.

He smiled smugly and flipped an envelope onto the table. He was way ahead of me. I picked it up and opened it. It contained two airline tickets to Genoa and a Hertz rental slip. I frowned. I'm not that keen on Italy, they drive like lunatics and there are several places where you can't buy Southern Comfort. Perhaps the whole thing was a subtle plot to get me to kill myself. He made me ask. I did.

'Pulleyne has an apartment in Cap d'Antibes, that's in the South of France in case you don't know. He goes there for the long vac.' The long vacation is the two month break in August and September each year, when the courts don't sit except for urgent business.

'Which you know — how?' I couldn't see Orbach being on social terms with a High Court judge any more than me.

'My parents have some friends in the same development.' I never thought of Orbach as having parents: I imagined him born, fully grown and bearded, criticising the midwife for failing to tie the knot right. 'It's called Le Bouquet and it's supposed to be very nice indeed. They've had it for years. They lease it by the year, and rent it out for the summer season; that more or less covers the year's cost and gives them a free holiday —they're not rich. They go down for a few weeks just before the season, and then for a long break afterwards. I met them at my parents' home one Sunday a while ago and they mentioned

Pulleyne; you know, making conversation about lawyers, that sort of thing.'

'And?'

'And it occurred to me that it would be a good way to get close to a High Court judge. An accidental encounter on holiday, nice and relaxed. There's a private beach nearby which tenants of the apartments use, you couldn't but get to meet him.'

'Meet's a long way from bosom buddies. Why don't you go? You'd stand more of a chance.'

'I thought of it,' he admitted. 'But, well, there's a number of reasons.' This is another reason I don't like Orbach: you and me, we do something because we want to, or because we have to, or because we'll make money at it, or because we fancy her. He's always got a list. 'The apartment's only free for that week and I've got a professional engagement. It might be a bit too close, might make him too chary. And I, uh, don't have anyone to go with at the moment,' he concluded lamely. 'Frankie's going away with her sister.'

I felt sorry for both of them: Orbach without a friend to take on holiday; and Frankie, whom fate had cast as Orbach's substitute companion. All I said was: 'Frankie's got a sister?'

'Half-sister. Jada. Her father's still alive, so she went to live with him She's at art college now, but I've agreed to let her take Frankie to Wales that week. I think it will be all right,' he added, voicing his parental concern. 'It'll be better if I'm here though, just in case.'

'Why Genoa?'

'I couldn't get a direct flight to Nice. It's the nearest alternative. It won't be a long drive. But you should get some lire for the toll-booths. Well?'

'Who am I supposed to take?' Though my name was on one ticket and the rental slip, the other ticket was blank.

'I never noticed you having trouble before.' During Disraeli Chambers, I had encountered Orbach in Oslo. I had been led there, the willing but ignorant victim of a luscious young barrister called Marguerita Bradkinson. He might have been referring to her. Or he might have known that my relations with Allison Mather Hoyt had been just as unprofessional, and equally designed to lead me astray. 'Anyway, if you're thinking of going back to work with Sandy Nichol ...' He let the point tail off.

'Er, yeah, it'd be Sandy. I'll have to talk to her. See if she can get away then.' I didn't have much doubt: we were talking about a free week in the South of France, we had no other plans, and she wasn't yet showing — not, anyway, so's a stranger would notice.

It's only in fiction or on the screen that everything happens back-to-back. In real life an investigation —or a legal case — often happens in little bits and pieces, spread out over so long that not only would a reader or viewer lose interest, but the lawyer or investigator would do so too if he wasn't being paid for the job.

For the next two months, until our September flight to France (well, Italy), nothing much happened. Not only the High Court, but also the local county courts all but shut up shop. The legal profession — along with MPs and the press — departed en bloc in search of the sun. It was, as Sandy did not hesitate to point out, the ideal time for me to return to the office.

We argued good-naturedly about the terms of my surrender. I claimed I was only coming back because of Orbach's case, temporarily as a convenience, at most as a consultant; she reminded me that with impending child-birth — not nearly so far away as I needed to adjust to the idea of being a father — she needed someone to share the responsibility of the firm. If it wasn't going to be me, then one or more of the assistant solicitors would have to be made up to partner; then it wouldn't be her firm alone any more, or ours.

Over the vacation, then, I spent relatively little time on Orbach's case. An office was decorated for me, though my promised assistant was on study-leave. I moved most of my papers from Earl's Court and gave notice to quit. I had to familiarise myself both with Sandy's own caseload and the work of the firm as a whole. The assistant solicitors who had come in since I left were not pleased to see me; they did not hesitate to bring me their files, to ask my advice, to try and embarrass me with my ignorance of current law and practice. They succeeded.

I got a bit of work for Orbach done though. I read the case reports and transcripts he had given me. There were three which involved companies who were, as he had put it, related. Pulleyne had found for the company each time. This was not on the face of it suspicious. There was no evidence to suggest he was aware of their connections. Three was not a large enough number of cases to constitute a comparative study.

One advantage of basing myself back at Nichol & Co was that I did not need to go down to Companies House to requisition my own copies of records and pay for them in cash: I could call up the agents the firm used, and they would supply them and bill the firm on account. I had engaged in equally tedious research during Mather's, with greater success than now. Though a large private corporate group, most of the holdings traced back to accountants, lawyers or other nominees. There was no block of shares marked out to Sir Martyn or any other Pulleyne.

I also saw Orbach's colleague.

'I've only agreed to see you for Orbach's sake,' said Justin Papworth. 'I can't say I'm particularly keen.'

Funnily enough, keen was just the word for him that came most easily to mind. He came from a class with which I was familiar. His parents would not have been hugely wealthy, but comfortable; he undoubtedly went to boarding school — probably one of the second tier public schools, like Winchester or Marlborough, wherever his father and older brothers (if any) had gone. Then, like them, on to Oxbridge: which half didn't matter, though for some reason Cambridge seems to turn out more barristers than the other place.

Twenty years ago, the bar was riddled with upper class buffoons. They were too timid to go into the army, too ugly for the stage or film and too stupid to do anything else. The money they earned was incidental to the status. They regarded the hours between ten and five as a pastime. Nowadays, such people go into the City, especially since deregulation.

In their place arrived a breed of earnest, smoothcheeked, bespectacled barristers who crave rich rewards but recognise that they come only to those who are prepared to work for them. They are indifferent to the substance of their cases: they will act for anyone who pays enough. Their cases are superbly prepared. They select a social life that suits their profession, rather than the other way around. They are stable, married, old before their years. Many of them are very good indeed. They are keen.

Justin Papworth belonged to this creed. I imagined that he rose each day at six-thirty, and spent half an hour polishing his cheeks before retreating to his study where his wife or the au pair would bring him coffee while he pored over the papers for that day's trial.

At eight or eight-thirty, he would join the family for breakfast and cross-examine his children on their homework. At precisely nine, he would fold *The Times* under his arm and step outside to his Renault to drive into the Temple, where he would be able to park because he had joined the waiting-list for permits the same day he passed his bar finals.

Outside court, he would meet his client. He would appear enthusiastic, encouraging, confident. He would adopt the same attitude whether his client was a landlord or a tenant, an aristocrat or an immigrant, someone he inwardly admired or someone of whom he disapproved. In this sense, he was the impeccable professional — he displayed no human feelings at all.

We met in the Tara, off High Street Kensington. I had suggested a place away from the Temple, because that was how he had asked Orbach to meet him. It was discreetly lighted, and the walls lined with phony book-spines hinted that, as in a gentleman's club, the done thing was to ignore other punters. Now he complained that it had been difficult to find, it would have been much better if I had come to his chambers. It was the second contradiction; the first was his claim that it was Orbach who was keen, not he.

I said: 'Orbach gave me the impression you wouldn't be happy to meet around the Temple; I thought he said you wanted this business followed up.'

'Oh, well, you know how it is, too many people know Russel.' It was who he was meeting, not why that had led him to see Orbach away from the Temple. 'I don't know,' he admitted suddenly, disarmingly. 'I don't know if I want this followed up or not.' It was obviously an unfamiliar state of mind. 'Do I believe my leader knew something he wasn't telling me? Yes. Do I believe that whatever he knew rendered victory certain? Yes. Therefore, he ought to have told me: right?'

Junior counsel needs to know everything about a case. If he does not do so he cannot perform properly as a junior. If his leader has to drop out — perhaps during a case, because of illness, or more commonly on account of a conflicting commitment — junior counsel is supposed to take over, so that there is no need for delay or adjournment.

'Even so,' I played devil's advocate, the professional role I knew best, 'it's a long way from what's implied about Pulleyne.'

'Yes, sure. I thought it would all become clear during the hearing. But I'm still as confused as ever. There is no doubt to my mind, no doubt at all, that anyone listening to the two accounts of what had been agreed would have believed the plaintiff. How familiar are you with the issue?'

'I've read the transcript. Land — mixed commercial, shopping and residential development — initiator's fee —how much — based on how big a part of the package,' I recited the way reported decisions are introduced in the Law Reports. 'On the face of it, it's not so odd. The judge believed one side, not the other. But ... Well, it's difficult for me to know, isn't it? Orbach had already put me on notice, I was looking for an oddity.'

'Go on anyway,' he encouraged me to voice my own disquiet, to reflect or support his.

'Well, why? I suppose that's it, really — why would Long have agreed to such an appalling deal? He had the initial idea; he had options on most of the land that was needed; he wasn't a complete outsider, a down-and-out who couldn't have raised the money in any other way, or who didn't have the other contacts — designers, architects, a link into the local authority, press and publicity people and so on. He'd done similar deals before, if smaller. He could even have gone to a bank: the terms would have been substantially worse than he claimed had been agreed with your clients, but much, much better than the judge found had actually been agreed. So, at the end of the day, I'm asking why he would have agreed on those terms.'

Papworth scowled. 'That's my view exactly. Shall we get another drink?'

He signalled the cocktail waitress and pointed at our glasses to say same again. She was a tall but cute long, blonde American of the sort I like to fantasise about but never seem to meet. Notwithstanding her earlier blandishments, we had both opted for conventional drinks — vodka tonic for him, the usual for me —rather than the bowls of fruit salad with parasols to keep them dry that others were sipping through bendy-straws. 'I don't think the judgement holds up, for that reason above all.'

'Why didn't they appeal?'

'Ah, well, you see, that's it. It's been very cleverly done, hasn't it? The only way one can argue with the decision is if you rely on the proposition that the deal was bad from Long's point of view, compared to the deal that he might have made elsewhere. But to do that, you need evidence of the other kinds of deal he might have made. There were, I think, no more than five minutes devoted to that issue, and only by way of Long's own examination, not by way of independent evidence. They thought the point was too obvious to need testimony. If I'd been appearing for Long, I would have taken the same view.'

He dropped a Gold Card onto the waitress' tray as she delivered our drinks. She said, 'Shall I run a tab?'

'No, I don't think so.'

If he'd said yes, he would've been buying all the rounds which followed. I didn't mind. Orbach would pick up my bill. If anyone ought to be running a tab, it was me. On the other hand, just because I had a client to whom to submit an account for expenses didn't mean it was going to get paid, especially when that client was Russel Orbach, so I didn't object to taking turns.

'Without the evidence at trial, he couldn't appeal. He would have had to get leave to introduce fresh evidence, and that could only be on the grounds that the evidence wasn't available at an earlier time. Well, it would have been available if he'd called it. No, it was only needed with hindsight.'

'You knew in advance what witnesses they were calling, right?' In a heavy case, that would be normal. He nodded cautiously. Once I began asking about what he knew before the trial we were getting close to privileged information even if not yet quite there. 'So why wasn't this the point your leader had up his sleeve?'

He banged the table. 'Because how could my leader have known that the judge wouldn't take the same view you and I are taking? He could not have known that for certain, and experience and instinct should have suggested the opposite. After all, Woolf, you've hardly got a long history at commercial transactions of this order, and you saw the point for yourself, hm?'

I wasn't enthusiastic about the insult to my experience — and instincts — but he wasn't wrong. I wasn't curious how he knew — the legal profession is not large; it's never difficult to find someone who knows about another lawyer, even a solicitor like me or a small firm like Nichol & Co.

'He might have guessed how Pulleyne would see it, though. Your leader — Charles Cushing, yes?' I knew the name from the transcript. 'Pulleyne was in your chambers when he was in practice; they must have known each other?' It was common for a junior to be in the same chambers as his leader. There was nothing unusual about a barrister appearing in front of — or even against —a member or former member of his own chambers. Chambers are not partnerships. Barristers share only facilities — like a library or the new technology — and services such as clerks and typists.

'Well, I suppose they knew each other, but not well. Cushing wasn't that senior when Pulleyne was appointed to the bench. And Pulleyne originally practised on circuit ...' by which he meant in the provinces. 'It was only in his last few years that he built up his London practice. In addition, don't forget, Cushing's mainly civil, but Pulleyne did mostly crime. Of course we both knew Pulleyne wasn't an experienced commercial judge, but the point didn't require experience,' he repeated.

'Why did you take it to Orbach? How did you know he would be interested? Had he told you before about his own experience with Pulleyne?'

'I didn't take it to him,' he corrected. 'He rang me. Very soon after the decision. I assumed he'd been watching out for a repetition. Did he tell you I'd approached him?'

I laughed uneasily. 'You know Russel. I thought that was what he said, but I'm not so sure now.' I sipped my drink. 'Have you discussed this with anyone else?' He shook his head. 'Not even ...' I hesitated, 'what about your father?'

His forehead creased. He didn't like my mentioning his father, Mr Justice Papworth.

'Have you ever heard anything — in your chambers —about top-up fees?'

He shook his head. 'I know what they are.' He, too, referred to the recent circular on the subject. 'But since Pulleyne's day, we've become more and more a civil set. I doubt we do ten per cent crime now. And — well I know the chaps who do the crime; there's no chance at all any of them would touch anything like that; they're as honest as the day.'

'Have you ever heard of Pulleyne in that connection —or anyone else in your chambers?'

He flushed. 'No, not at all.' We both knew he was lying, and he was finding it difficult. 'I wouldn't tell you anyway,' he equivocated.

'Justin,' I said gently, feeling I was losing him, 'what do you want out of this?'

'Nothing,' he said bitterly. 'I wish I'd never told Orbach. I wish it would just go away.' Orbach had told the truth in one respect: Papworth was frightened; not physically frightened, but frightened for his career. After a while, he added: 'You'll leave me out of it, won't you?'

It was a stupid thing to say, like a red rag to a bull.

CHAPTER THREE

'Hallo there,' he called as we walked down the steps to the private beach Orbach had told me about.

'Hi.' We hesitated, looking around for the beach-hut with our apartment number on it.

'Darling,' he addressed the woman stretched out sunbathing beside his deckchair, 'these are the new people I told you about. Staying in the Prestons' apartment.' She rolled over lazily and looked up at us through her sunglasses. She was in her fifties, younger than her husband, and visibly fitter. 'Isabelle. Dave and, uh … ?'

'Sandy,' I said quickly, before she did; I knew what tone of voice she would use to remind him what her name was. So far as she was concerned, Mr Justice Pulleyne was now next door to dead meat.

'How nice,' Isabelle said, languorous and indifferent. She rolled over again.

'And out there are our son and daughter-in-law.' Pulleyne waved in the general direction of the water. There were only forty or fifty people in sight. Were we supposed to guess which ones were his? 'That's your hut. Got the key?'

It was two huts away from theirs but the ones between were currently unused. We unpadlocked it and extracted a sun-lounger and a rolled-up beach mat. I'm uncomfortable lying down on the beach: covered with sticky cream or oil, the sand gets all over me, I can't find a position in which to read, and I burn too easily. Sandy, on the other hand, likes to stretch out and acquire a tan I'd kill her if she revealed in its entirety to anyone else. Accordingly, we ended up imitating the Pulleynes.

Though Isabelle Pulleyne was wearing a full costume, most of the women on the beach were topless. Sandy wasn't wearing anything beneath her t-shirt and I watched appreciatively as she pulled it over her head. She has good, full breasts. I wasn't the only one watching — Martyn Pulleyne's eyes were popping out of his shorts. As we settled down, his son and daughter-in-law came out of the water. She was also topless. I only just managed to suppress a low groan. If we found nothing else to talk about, Pulleyne and I could swap ogles.

As we were introduced — Henry and Caroline — one of the waiters from the bar above the private beach came down carrying an empty tray and an order pad. The French know how to do these things: it might be blazing hot but he was still a waiter and dressed accordingly in dark slacks, white shirt and polished black shoes. The only concession was a short-sleeved shirt.

Orbach was unlucky. The waiter approached us first. *'M'sieur?'*

'Can we offer you a drink?' I called out.

'Very kind,' Pulleyne replied, cutting off his wife's shake of her head. 'You sure, dear? I'll have a beer. Henry?'

'Same for me, thanks. Caroline?'

'No, thanks all the same.'

She had joined her mother-in-law on the ground but, thankfully, lay on her back.

I had the picture. Pulleyne senior was bored. He had been in Cap d'Antibes for almost two months. He had no one to talk to, no audience: for a High Court judge, it must be like cold turkey. Though I didn't know how long his son and daughter-in-law had been with them, his son was similarly prepared to leap on new faces, new company. The women on the other hand were quite prepared to keep themselves — and their menfolk — to themselves.

We too had beers: four quarter-litre bottles, sixty francs — with tip, seventy. Even with a good exchange rate, roughly seven pounds. If I didn't have an expense account, I'd have a heart attack. The Pulleyne men came over to drink theirs with us, Henry carrying his father's deckchair, but sitting himself on the ground, about six inches away from Sandy's thirty-eight.

'So you're just here for the week,' Pulleyne repeated what we'd told him earlier. 'Fly in last night?'

'Yes, to Genoa. Couldn't get a flight to Nice. Rented a car. Terrifying journey; all those tunnels, and the way the Italians drive.'

He chuckled. 'The French aren't much better. You'll get used to it. Where are you from?'

'London. You?'

'Yes. Though Henry's just come back from two years in New York. That's where he met Caroline.' I hadn't picked up an accent when she'd been introduced.

'What were you doing over there?' I didn't want to appear too exclusively interested in the father. As a matter of fact, other than professionally, I wasn't at all interested in the father, or frankly the son — just Caroline.

'Henry's a banker,' his father answered before Henry could get a word in edgewise. 'It's all very international these days, isn't it, son? Not like when I was young, when the banker meant someone in a dull suit refusing you an overdraft. And what do you do, uh, Dave?' I guessed he was deliberately savouring the moment when I had to ask him about himself.

'We're both solicitors.' I decided to include Sandy, before she swiped someone with her bottle.

'Really?' It must have pleased him no end: as members of the profession of which he was one of the bosses, his authority over us was unlimited; he was the school prefect and we the first years; if he wanted company, we would have to provide it; if he decided it was time to be alone, we would be sent on our way. Speak only when spoken to. 'What firm are you with? Would I know it?'

'I doubt it. We have a small, legal aid practice in North London. It's mainly crime.'

'Ah, good, that's what I like to hear. That's what I used to do you know, when I was in practice, mainly crime.'

'Oh, you're a lawyer too? I didn't realise.' What Orbach was paying me was some compensation for having to play straight man, but not enough.

'Didn't I say? Martyn Pulleyne,' he spoke the name firmly.

His son was expected to complete the sentence for him: 'Mr Justice Pulleyne.'

'I say, I'm awfully sorry, I didn't make the connection,' I laughed nervously embarrassed. 'You don't look like a judge,' sitting on the beach half-naked in the South of France sun. 'Sandy ...' I said, as if she ought to apologise too.

She smiled sweetly up at Pulleyne and said, 'Really?'

On the third day we were invited to join them for a meal.

'You haven't got enough time to find the really good places; come with us this evening; we'll show you.' I didn't think he was offering to pay; I was more concerned in case he expected *me* to do so. The bar behind the private beach was someone's nice little earner. Who could object to being brought a cold drink every hour or so without having to get up? So what if each one cost more than at the bar, and if you drank far more than otherwise? What was one pound, or two, or three, until I totted up how much we had spent, and how much of it I could reasonably expect to get back from Orbach?

But we agreed of course; we were duly grateful and invited them to join us for a drink in our apartment beforehand. We went back early from the beach to spend some time alone. We showered and stretched out in the bedroom, on top of the sheets. I turned on my side and kissed Sandy gently on the forehead, she was beginning to doze off. I placed a hand lightly on her hip, then started to lick her shoulder, her breast, I rolled my tongue inside her belly-button. Then I stopped, to listen to her even breathing. She said insistently, 'Go on,' without breaking its rhythm.

In London, there was too little time for such gentle, slow love-making. In London, there wasn't enough time to do more than try and remember each day that we were part of a couple, that we had each other to come home to, that there was something or someone else to consider. Sex was seized when opportunity and energy coincided, or when too drunk to go straight to sleep, or when it had simply been too long since. The occasions were few and far between that we spent two or three hours not needing just wanting to know each other physically.

I did not find it, however, an entirely unqualified experience. We had now been together nine months without a break. She was five months pregnant going on six. For two months, I had been getting used to the idea that I was going to be a father. Also, that I had to give up the Earl's Court flat, live full-time with Sandy — we had agreed we would have to find a larger house — and at least work from the office, which I knew in my heart meant that I would have to give up detecting and go back to law.

It wasn't easy. Perhaps the last few years had not been easy either — materially or psychologically — but at least I had been doing what I believed I wanted. I accepted what lay ahead, but I was sobered by it. I could see the love; I could see the peace; I could even see the joy; I just couldn't see when the hell I was ever going to have a chance again to be me.

As we showered a second time together and dressed, Sandy bitched about the forthcoming engagement.

'He makes me feel like a law student, I'm not sure he really accepts that I am a lawyer — I don't think he approves of women lawyers. I'd hate to be a woman in his court. I want to go to St Paul de Vence,' she reminded me non-consequentially.

'We're not paying for the holiday,' I reminded her. 'And we can go to St Paul tomorrow — if you drive.' St Paul de Vence is the small fortress town in the Alpes Maritimes behind Cannes and Nice — between which lie Antibes and its Cap — where many famous artists have lived and worked. That much I had read. I worked out for myself that mountain town meant winding mountain roads and there was no way I was going to drive.

Sandy's reluctance to spend the evening with them meant she spent longer getting ready than was customary or necessary. I had to entertain them alone. She was going to be even less happy when she came out and found that Henry and Caroline had used us as an excuse to opt for an evening alone, so a concentrated dose of judicial attention awaited her. I made her apologies, and mixed drinks: G-and-T for them, Southern Comfort for me. I had taken no chances and bought a bottle at the airport. As my concession to the heat, I added ice. I prayed no one I knew would notice.

'Of course, we've often been in here, when the Prestons are down. Though, I suppose, we tend not to overlap for long each year. How did you say you knew them?'

'They're friends of a friend. It was just one of those lucky accidents. He'd been thinking of coming down but he couldn't get away. We had nothing planned. He rang them for us. It seems they'd intended to come down themselves, but postponed it on account of, er, a bridge tournament. He's apparently a well-known bridge player.' Orbach had given me sufficient details to survive at least a minor cross-examination.

'That's right. We've played a few hands with them, but they're well out of our league. Charming couple.'

'Well, we just met them when we went up to collect the keys.' I cut off any further questions.

He asked, 'How come you hadn't made any plans? Young couple like you, I would have thought you'd be planning your summer holiday all year.'

This was the patronising Pulleyne — I could cheerfully have throttled him. 'Young couple', my ass. I gritted my teeth and said the first thing that came to mind: 'Well, er, we're going to have a baby actually.'

Sandy came in on cue and I heard her grimace (I *mean* I heard her grimace): she had yet to tell her closest friends. It was still a secret; we were still working it out together. It worked like a charm then though. Isabelle threw up her hands in pleasure and he raised his glass.

'Congratulations, congratulations,' he boomed. 'Dinner's our treat.'

We drove along the sea road, halfway to Cannes, to Golf Juan, to a restaurant called Chez Christiana just after the turn-off to Vallauris. It was still warm. We sat outside and watched the harbour as he selected the meal for all of us the way he doubtless did when he was out with his wife and family. I ought to tell you what we ate in complete detail, and probably how it was cooked as well. The truth is I've forgotten the former — except that it was fish — and wouldn't have a clue about the latter, but it was very nice anyway.

'Do you have other children?' I tried to avoid calling him by name. Once or twice I had called him Judge, or Sir Martyn, and he had corrected me. Nonetheless, it wasn't easy for me to call him Martyn. Sandy, on the other hand, used his first name as often as she could.

He and Isabelle exchanged a glance. She said, 'We've a daughter. She was up at Oxford, but she dropped out.' She laughed unhappily. 'So often the young have to make all the mistakes there are to make. We were luckier with Henry.'

'He's doing very well, you know,' Pulleyne switched subjects. 'They think very highly of him. And, well,' he smiled boyishly, 'we hope you won't be the only ones, uh, producing in the near future. That reminds me,' he clicked his fingers for the wine waiter and, over our faint protests, ordered a bottle of champagne.

When it came, he asked, 'How long have you been in practice together?'

'Fifteen years; it's about fifteen years, isn't it darling?' Sandy held my hand beneath the table and dug her nails into my palm until I all but cried out in pain.

'That's right ... darling. Doesn't time fly?' I had been in the practice a little more than five years before our bust-up and back not much more than five minutes.

'It's surprising I haven't heard of you. I've only been on the bench for ten years; before that, I knew all the criminal firms in London.'

'Did you never do any civil work when you were at the bar?'

'Oh, a little bit. In my day, silks did everything; the civil silks did some crime, and we did some civil. That's died out over the years, everyone specialises now. But I never enjoyed it. Our criminals were supposed to be the wicked ones, but some of my commercial clients were just as dishonest — perhaps more so.'

'But you sit in civil cases now?'

'We all have to do some of each; it's a requirement of the Lord Chancellor's Office. It's supposed to prevent us becoming stale, especially to prevent the criminal judges becoming too prosecution-minded.' He grinned disarmingly. 'Which, as you well know, I'm supposed to be.' He didn't wait for us to comment: 'But the only effect of the rule is to slow up the court lists. I'm sure a good civil lawyer could get through my High Court cases twice as quickly as I do, and I know I could get through their criminal list faster than them.'

He was drinking heavily. 'We'll have another, all right?' No one said no. 'Never change horses in mid-stream,' he added as he told the waiter to bring *'la même'* in an accent about as gross as my own. The waiter winced, but said nothing — I imagined that the Pulleynes were good, regular customers. When we had come in, table reserved, they had both shaken hands with the owner and we were formally introduced. He asked after Henry and Caroline. Pulleyne asked after his wife and daughter.

'Do you still think that — about commercial litigants being as crooked as criminals?'

'Absolutely, more so. I would say, ninety per cent of the issues in criminal courts have their origins more in economic problems — albeit sometimes far removed —than criminal inclination, and ninety per cent of the issues in the High Court are about one person attempting to rob another.'

The statement would have suited me — or Sandy — or, in his early, radical days, Russel Orbach — much better.

'Forgive me for saying so ... Well, you referred to it yourself a few minutes ago ... What you just said isn't quite what I'd expect from ... Er... Given some of the things you're reported to have said,' I gabbled the final words and took a deep breath while I waited to see if I'd be allowed to finish dinner before he sentenced me to hang.

Sandy smiled disarmingly and took my hand where it lay on the table-cloth.

'What Dave means, Martyn, is that what you just said sounded liberal, while you've got a reputation as an extreme reactionary.'

Isabelle laughed and hiccoughed. She reached out and covered both our hands with hers. Her long nails were painted bright red. I withdrew my hand before they bled all over me. She said to her husband. 'You see. That's what I'm always saying. Now don't get angry, we're on holiday and they're our guests. Besides,' she added, 'I like them.'

He smiled easily.

'I'm not angry. Not at all. But I'll watch out for you in court, and I'll double the sentence on the first of your clients to come up before me.'

He stopped joking.

'I'm a blunt Yorkshireman.' I had wondered about the slight accent. He noticed the flicker of interest cross my face and explained. 'In my day, we were all expected to lose any regional accent before we went to the bar even if we still lived and worked locally.' Then he went back to his account. 'I tend to speak my mind. The press like easy quotes, so I'm often reported. I've never believed that crime is a way to protest inequality. All the evidence shows that it's counter-productive; the more crime there is, the more people are willing to elect a repressive government. Like Reagan in America, or Thatcher,' he added, enjoying the expressions of amazement on our faces.

He allowed us a moment to absorb what he'd said, then he went on.

'I was interested in politics when I was younger. I was a local councillor for a time. An independent. Of course, local government reorganisation has all but abolished the independents — it's all parties, party-line, party-whip, nowadays. No good for me. I don't like being told what to do or what to think.'

I shook my head to admit defeat.

'You young people see everything in such simple terms. Good and bad. Left and right. Right and wrong. And all judges must be rabid conservatives or they wouldn't be on the bench, right?'

'Something like that. But you've hardly used your position to say the sort of things you've been saying tonight.'

'No more I have. That's not what the job is about. Do you know what happens to a judge who gets a reputation for being soft? Well, I'd better not say, but you can imagine. But I'm not soft; don't get me wrong; I believe in people taking responsibility for their own actions; I believe what I just said — that it does damage when people resort to crime.'

'You used to defend some exceptionally violent criminals yourself?'

'You know the rules: everyone's entitled to a defence.'

'You had an outstanding track-record,' I reminded him. 'Above average.'

We were on our third bottle. We were all tipsy. Isabelle said, fiercely, proudly. 'Martyn never did anything by halves. Martyn was the best.' She smiled at him loyally and lovingly. I wondered if Sandy would still smile at me like that after thirty years or more; I wondered if she would ever smile at me like that.

We spent a lot more time with them before we left for home, and although the senior Pulleynes didn't want to go up to St Paul de Vence — which they'd visited many times over the years — we took the trip with Henry and Caroline. Just like at all the great sights for tourists who want to see what the old and simple days were like, we had to park miles outside the town and couldn't take a photograph within its walls which didn't include at least part of a car. It was an enjoyable day nonetheless. Following convention, we swapped partners as we strolled; I was a swap away from heaven.

I had one conversation alone with Pulleyne. Bored and fed up with sitting on the beach, we strolled around the Cape and sat on a fallen tree where we shared the bottle of beer he had thoughtfully tucked into his carry-all, but that was already getting warm. It was Sandy's and my last full day, and the Pulleynes would be leaving only a couple of days later.

He went back to the dinner-table discussion. 'I have said other things, though. I'm as hard on the police as I am on criminals; I've criticised the establishment often enough. I once said judges shouldn't be Freemasons, which is enough to prevent me ever being appointed to the Court of Appeal.'

'Yes,' I admitted, 'I knew about that. I wondered why.'

'I'm surprised you remember. It was a long time ago.'

'Someone mentioned it, I think.' I hoped he'd let the point drop. It was not consistent with someone who, only a few days before, had failed to recognise his name. 'Anyway, it rings a bell.' I waited for him to answer my question.

'I waited longer for silk than I ought to have, you know, and perhaps also to be appointed to the bench. I was told outright, if I'd joined "The Brotherhood" I could have advanced faster. But that's not why, not really. I suppose it was for the same reason that I used to quite like some of my criminal clients. At least they were doing for themselves.'

I smiled and took the bottle from his hand, saying, 'If I was a journalist, I'd have a hell of an article when I got home.'

'I'd deny it all,' he said. 'Anyway, most of them wouldn't understand, would they? That's what I like about you — you and your lady — it's what I like about a lot of your generation, more than my own. If I had my time over, I'd do everything differently. I'd do the sort of work you do; legal aid, for the very poorest people. The choices were different, much more limited, in my time. Do you understand?'

'I think so,' I said, a little sadly, though I wasn't sure why: perhaps because, somehow, what he was saying made what Orbach alleged that much more credible than I'd begun to believe over the last few days; or, because he was an old man who couldn't have his time over, and one day that was going to be just as true of me too.

Soon after we returned from Cap d'Antibes, I went back to Earl's Court to clear out the rest of my flat. I had little furniture worth keeping and what there was could be stored in Sandy's garage until we found a larger house. It was the end of an era.

This also made me sad. For some bizarre reason, even my landlord — who would reap the considerable benefits of vacant possession or might find a tenant who paid his rent on time for a change — claimed to be sorry to see me go.

None so sorry, though, as Lewis, my fagotty and fat old villainous friend who suspected, not without cause, that my visits to his club on the Old Brompton Road were about to become a part of its history, instead of a regular comic feature. Sandy recognised what a loss this would be for the both of us, and excused me for a long, drunken night of Southern Comfort and vicious gossip.

'You, Dave, a father?' He gawped when I broke the news. 'You sure it's you?'

I shrugged. "S'what she says, Lewis.' I was already so drunk it came out Lois. 'It's only about three months away.'

He waved Malcolm over to join us. Malcolm ran the club for him. They used to be lovers, though Malcolm was forty years younger, forty pounds lighter and — as he used to say — could keep going for forty minutes longer. Lewis had mellowed with age. When Malcolm finally gathered up the nerve to tell him he had found someone else, he had lived to tell the tale and even to keep his job. Delightedly, he clapped his hands together and cried with glee: 'Champagne!'

Lewis grimaced: he knew who would be paying.

'Tell you what, Lewis,' I compensated, 'you can be the honorary godfather.' He liked to think of himself as a godfather — in the Marlon Brando mould.

'Why only honorary?' He bitched and belched and pronounced the silent 'h'.

'We're not married,' I explained gently, 'and you're not Jewish.' We don't have rabbis as progressive as Catholic priests.

The thought connected back to the job I was supposed to be doing for Orbach.

'Lewis, d'you ever hear of a bent judge?'

His eyes narrowed. 'What do you want to know for?'

I shrugged. 'If I'm going back into legal practice, I might need the extra edge.'

He fell back into his seat. 'You, Dave, legal practice?' He was more shocked than when I told him I was going to be a father.

'Why do I come here, Lewis? Why do I come and tell you all my innermost, darkest secrets? You only ever mock me.' And, occasionally, save my life.

He belched again. 'It's 'cos you haven't got any other friends, Dave, that's why,' adding his habitual: 'Know what I mean?'

'No, I know,' I sighed, raising my glass in defeat. 'Cheers, Lewis, I'll miss you.' I meant it. 'Now tell me what I want to know.'

He shook his head. 'I've heard of a beak or two, magistrates you know, not judges, not proper bent.' I understood his qualification to be the same as I had entered when Orbach first raised the idea with me ... they're all bent in one way.

'I have,' Malcolm said suddenly but with an apologetic glance in Lewis' direction.

Malcolm has beautiful eyes, a strong Glaswegian accent, looks like he wouldn't harm a fly, but the only reference Lewis needed when first he employed him —about an hour before they became lovers — was that he'd done three years for assault with a deadly weapon when he ought to have done ten.

He said: 'When I was at Parkhurst, I knew one of the Reddins.' He looked again at Lewis, I wasn't sure why. He didn't ask if I knew who they were; even if the name hadn't cropped up in connection with Pulleyne, no Londoner needed reminding.

Lewis shuddered but didn't say anything. It wasn't a pretty sight; it started at his head, rippled through his neck and by the time it reached his belly it felt like an earth tremor had hit the club.

'Tony, I knew Tony. One night, we were drinking in his cell, he got talking about his brothers — the ones outside. We were talking about how things are different in America. He said they weren't so different after all. He said his brothers had more legitimate interests than anything else, they belonged to city clubs, they had stockbrokers, bankers and lawyers in their pockets. Then he said, "A judge, too. A red judge." That's a real judge, isn't it, Dave?'

'Oh, yeah, that's a very real judge.' High Court judges wear bright red robes in court, to distinguish them from lesser immortals. 'I don't suppose he gave you a name?'

Malcolm laughed, 'You've got to be kidding.'

'But you believed him?'

'Tony Reddin doesn't need to brag, Dave. No one leads a comfortable life like him. Not since Len got Grendon eyes.' The other brother who had been banged up had finally gone bonkers, and been moved to Grendon, the high security criminal mental hospital, although his alleged insanity was popularly believed to be no more than a ploy to secure the parole that was otherwise still denied them.

'Do you know the Reddins personally, Lewis?'

'I've had a run-in in my time,' he admitted reluctantly.

'And it isn't something you'll forget?'

'Right.' He was torn between shining and confessing —as the shudder had already disclosed — that he had come out of it the loser. 'It was a long time ago; a very good friend, a very dear friend, met with an accident — a very horrible accident.' He didn't add 'Know what I mean?' so I could tell how much it still hurt.

'So they're not, er, exactly friends of yours?'

'Friends like that, you don't need.' He thought for a moment, then he asked, 'You're not going back into legal practice, are you, Dave? This is one of your cases, isn't it?'

I nodded. I wasn't happy saying so in front of Malcolm but I can't lie to Lewis.

'Well, I'll tell you something, Dave. If the Reddins are involved in it, I ain't going to help you.' He got up, with difficulty but with dignity. 'I'll miss you, Dave,' he held out a flabby hand. 'Keep in touch. Know what I mean?'

Malcolm and I watched in silence as he wove his way through the tables to his office. Malcolm said softly and flat, 'He's old, Dave. In the last few months or so he's aged ten years. It happens you know. Towards the end. They start to go in fits and starts. Sometimes, he doesn't remember a customer's name. Or he'll ask me who someone is who he's known for thirty years or where something is he's just put down.'

'He remembers the Reddins, though?'

'He's scared, Dave. And I don't blame him,' he added dully. 'The Reddins make the Kray Twins look like good-time girls. Remember that film, the one about the gangster and the IRA?'

'*The Long Good Friday?*'

'Right. If the Reddins had been against them, the IRA'd've lost. His friend, the one Lewis was talking about, he was his lover, before me. Danny — did you know him?' I shook my head — before my time. 'Lewis and the Reddins fell out over what you might want to call a property deal. What you have to understand, the deal was legitimate. It wasn't crooked, anyway not really. What you might want to call a bit sharp, but Lewis could've been Lloyds Bank The thing was, they weren't going to lose out to another — well, villain if you want —though Lewis has been more talk than tough for a long time.'

'What happened?'

'What do you think happened? They'd done things together in the old days. They asked him to drop out of it. Lewis told them to piss off. He didn't understand. Things are different now,' he repeated what he'd said at the beginning of the story, when he'd told us about Tony Reddin in jail. 'He thought: well, it's like any other legal deal, I can do whatever I want that's legal. On a crooked deal, OK, he'd know to stay out of the way of someone that heavy. He didn't understand that there isn't a dividing line any more, between legal and crooked; people need deals to feed their funny money into.'

It was the longest speech I had ever heard Malcolm make. I'd always liked him but I listened now with respect. He finished off. 'They snatched Danny. He was never seen again.'

Lewis came out of his office and returned to our table. He didn't sit down again. He steadied himself with a hand on Malcolm's shoulder. He cleared his throat.

'I'd be honoured to be your kid's godfather, Dave.' He handed me an envelope. 'That's for the nipper. It's just in case. I'm not so young no more, know what I mean?' Before I could thank him, he strode out the door and I saw him stumbling down the stairs. I didn't go after him. If he didn't want me to say anything, that's what I'd say. He'd be all right: one of the bouncers would drive him home.

I didn't know whether to open the envelope in front of Malcolm. He said, 'Go on then.'

It wasn't sealed, so I pulled out the flap and extracted a cheque, in my name. It was for a thousand pounds. I turned it round to show Malcolm. He whistled through his teeth.

'Looks like you said the right thing, Dave. He was touched, you might want to say.'

'Do you mind' Malcolm was Lewis' heir, or had been when they were lovers, and if Lewis had forgiven him enough to let him stay on at the club, he probably hadn't changed his will either. He had no one else to leave it to.

He shook his head. 'He can afford it, Dave. He made his money a long time ago, and he didn't spend it on fast women, you know.' He wouldn't, would he.

'Do you think I should take it? I mean, what you were saying, you know — about his mind.'

'You'd do his mind more harm giving it back than keeping it. Besides,' he grinned as he rose to go back to work, 'it might still bounce.'

We both knew it wouldn't.

CHAPTER FOUR

'Might Mr Papworth be free for an urgent con?' I meant conference, not confidence-trick. For some reason, when a solicitor sees a QC it is called a consultation instead.

Michael, Papworth's clerk, said suspiciously; 'What's it about?'

Barristers' clerks only have one name: Tom or Ken or Vernon or Gary. Their parents, wives or friends may know their last names but their solicitors don't. It's always just, say, Gary, Mr So-and-so-Hetherington-Cowdray-Joliffe's clerk. Clerks have no education whatsoever, most of them are illiterate, but they can add up faster than a Chinaman with an abacus.

All of them swill beer, love football, wear shiny polyester suits and hob-nailed boots, and invariably live in Essex, within an easy commute of London, where successful East End villains and others with too much money and no taste buy mock-Tudor farmhouses to decorate with plaster ducks on the walls, a private bar, cheap-print Constables and a matching three-piece suite with stretch-covers from a chain-store. They join the local masonic lodge, fish with ever more expensive equipment they have to get their children to assemble for them, watch rented pornographic videos with their mates, sleep with their own wives on a Sunday and someone else's on a Saturday.

Clerks run the chambers' office, organise a barrister's diary and negotiate the fees. They allocate any work that comes in which is not already designated by name — and switch some that is. They are accordingly extremely powerful and can make or break a career.

Barristers' clerks are also consumate liars. They get a barrister out of one low-paying long-standing commitment in order to free him for a new but high-paying case, offering some inadequate substitute with half as much or no relevant experience, who will be 'just as good, if not better' and 'knows all about the case', the papers in which he has not yet read. At the same time, they persuade one of their other barristers to take the poorly-paid case by saying that the solicitor insisted on him by name, implying many more briefs to come.

Clerks used to take ten per cent of the earnings of all the barristers in their chambers. Those were the days when barristers were too polite to be seen arguing about money. It wasn't on; this was the way it had always been done; my father paid his clerk ten per cent, so it must be the right thing to do. The modern barrister — the Papworth clone — is not at all shy of negotiating and renegotiating his clerk's contract and few clerks of an average chambers now earn more than five per cent. Even so, a good clerk in a good set will still earn into six figures a year.

A good clerk can accordingly afford to be choosy about who he deals with. Papworth's clerk was a good clerk. Nichol & Co had probably only ever sent work to his barristers once or twice in the entirety of the firm's existence. I think I had briefed someone there — I can't remember his name — very early on, but as that was more than ten years before my current call, his clerk couldn't remember me either.

'It's a private case,' I told him the most important news first: civil legal aid is not only badly paid but the cheque takes years to arrive. 'A rather heavy property dispute, as a matter of fact.'

'Ah,' Michael's voice lit up. 'When did you say you had to see him?'

'This evening if at all possible.'

Barristers are usually in court during the day. They have conferences after court, at four-thirty or five. After the conference ends, a good barrister will settle down to do paperwork: a written advice or a pleading in litigation. He is poorly paid for out-of-court work. It is part of the tradition of the English legal system to ensure that no one is properly prepared for the actual hearing and this is enforced by low fees for all work apart from appearance in court.

'Mr Papworth has a conference at five. But if it's really urgent, he could see you afterwards. It won't go on long, say — six o'clock?' Michael would go to the pub a happy man if I started a privately paying con with Papworth at six o'clock. He would look up at seven or eight with a gleam in his eye as he realised that he was still earning a percentage of someone else's effort.

'That would be fine. I'm very grateful. There won't be any papers, I'm afraid.' Normally, a solicitor has to send down written instructions, which tell a barrister what the case is about and encloses copy documentation.

'That's quite all right, sir.' Michael couldn't care less about the work involved, just the money. The reason I had insisted on seeing Papworth the same day was in order to give myself an excuse for the absence of papers—the case was that urgent. 'What is the name of the matter, sir?'

'Er, Passat, like the car. That's our client's name: Passat. It's not clear yet who the opponent will be, that's partly why I need to see Mr Papworth.' I'm unimaginative when it comes to names, and the name of a client was one part of the conversation I had not prepared for; what the case was going to be about was something else I had yet to invent.

'This is unethical,' Sandy said.

She was tucked uncomfortably behind her desk. I had not arranged the conference with Papworth until nearly a month after our return; she was already nearly seven months pregnant and in the last few weeks had billowed. It was cold; she was wearing a heavy-knit sweater over her maternity dress and is on the short side anyway. She looked like the Michelin man.

'I know. But I've tried everything else.'

This was an exaggeration. I had tried nothing. I meant I couldn't think of anything else to try and it was way past the time when I ought to do something. There was no way I could get the real names of the owners out of the nominees who held the majority of the shares in the Hackney Marsh group which controlled the three litigant companies in whose favour Pulleyne had found. It was a group without a single apparent common theme. They functioned in entertainment, packaging, transport, land, dishwashers, gardening shops, furniture, used cars and condoms and anything else that made money.

I thought of them as a parochial, poor man's imitation of the Latimer group I had encountered during Mather's, but if there was a Mr Hackney or a Mr Marsh to equate to the amusing, affable, inscrutable and unscrupulous Sterling Latimer, I had yet to identify him. The name came from the group's first company, a used car lot backing onto the Hackney Marshes in East London. The only thing this told me was that I was operating at the other end of the class structure than I had been during Mather's. All that Hackney and Hampstead have in common is that they start with an 'H', which Lewis would drop in the first case and over-emphasise in the second.

Nor was there any room for investigation so far as the solicitors acting in the litigation were concerned; two firms had acted in the three cases, and both of them had partners who featured in the schedule of shareholders. If any part of the network that led to Pulleyne fed through lawyers, the solicitors would not be likely to lead me to it.

But I remembered the most singular feature of Papworth's case — on which Orbach had also commented — that Cushing had been so confident throughout. He had to be the link. I had ransacked everybody's case-files to find a job of work that might be considered sufficiently significant to brief him; none of Nichol & Co's work came close.

This was why I decided to invent a case. And because it was invented, and because there would accordingly be no documentation unless Orbach was prepared to run to the high cost of forgery, I had decided that the best way to Cushing was through Papworth. If we could isolate points of law on which we needed Cushing's advice, it might not be so exceptional to address them, so my reasoning ran, without the supporting papers he could rely on junior counsel to have read. I did not deny that the wheeze was weak, but it was the best I could do for the time being.

Sandy's opening criticism had been that what I was proposing was illegal. Under pressure, she admitted she could identify no criminal offence. Hence, unethical.

'How's it ever going to get out?' I asked lamely, knowing that everything can get out and usually does. 'All right, even if it does, what're they going to do to us?'

'"Us"? How did us get into this? You, Dave, just you. I don't know about it, and I don't want to know about it. As far as I'm concerned, you've returned to the practice and brought some cases with you, and maybe just maybe some of them fall into your past line of work, but you aren't going to tell me and I'm not going to know, OK?' Pregnancy definitely didn't agree with her; she was distinctly nervous.

Sandy had been to see Lewis. When I showed her the cheque the next day, for a second I had thought she was going to refuse it. Then she had asked for the address of the club. I presumed she would write. Instead I came home a few nights later to find a message on the answering machine asking me to collect her. She was several Moets over the limit. I wasn't allowed any. I had never seen her so drunk; I had never seen him so happy.

Orbach refused to discuss my investigative method with me. He wouldn't even meet me unless I had something solid to report, but my claim for Cap d'Antibes had been paid in full and without complaint. I could guess why he was so uncharacteristically taking a back seat; he didn't want to be implicated in anything that went awry. I didn't ask if he would mind me using Papworth instead — using people was his addiction.

'Dave.' She hesitated: 'Dave, suppose Orbach is wrong? You know, by the end, I really did like him a bit,' she meant Pulleyne. 'And her.'

I shrugged. 'So what? I liked them too. That's got nothing to do with it.'

'But what if it's not true? Imagine how much damage it could do him if it got out he was being investigated. It could destroy him.' Her gaze held mine, and I knew what she was thinking — the thought had also occurred to me. What if Orbach was lying? What if it was all a plot to discredit the judge — regardless of the truth?

'How does that square with Papworth?'

'You don't know him. His reluctance could be a cover. They could be in it together.'

'No way. I've met him. He doesn't even like Russel that much; well, no one does. What I mean is, they've nothing in common.'

'So why did he talk to him?'

'You know Russel. He gets what he wants. No, it's Papworth that makes me think there must be something in it.'

'Still,' she pressed, 'even if it's not deliberate. What if you're all wrong, and it gets out?'

'I look pretty stupid. No one'll notice the difference.'

'Not you, maybe, but him. He's ... Well, he's almost a friend.'

'Holiday friendships are like holiday romances: it's a different thing.' I was making excuses for myself. 'Look, I'll take it easy; if I'm getting nowhere, then I'll drop it. OK?'

She said, 'Would you ... You need someone to talk it over with, Dave. I don't mean me. Someone more detached. Would you consider talking to Tim?' she added in a rush. It was what she had been building up to.

She knew how I'd react and I didn't disappoint her.

'No way. He's the last person I'm going to talk to.' I still felt angry — humiliated, betrayed — about Tim Dowell's role in my last major case. 'Besides,' I added, 'you were the one worried about it getting out. If the police know about it, the world'll know the next time anyone in his court is acquitted.'

'Fat chance.' Of an acquittal, not a leak.

I left her to go back to my own office, neither of us reassured by the conversation. With the exception of the reference to Tim Dowell, nothing that had been said had come as a surprise. Now that I had begun, at least part-time, to work as a lawyer again, I didn't want to do anything that would result in suspension. Despite myself, I was enjoying it. Furthermore, and regardless of whether or not Martyn Pulleyne classed as any kind of a friend, I was not indifferent to the idea that I might innocently — innocently, at least, on my own part — and accidently damage or destroy him.

But she had given me an idea. The idea of talking the case over with someone. Not Dowell, but someone else. Someone with the sort of relevant experience who might help me make up a sufficiently convincing case to feed to Cushing through Papworth. Someone who owed me: I was the reason he had never been charged with murder. My statement to the police was convincing and could not be contradicted without a telephone link to the hereafter. It was also wholly untrue.

I was thinking of another Martyn, Martin Mather. I had no doubt he would take a call from me.

'Any chance of lunch today?'

'Sure. Things aren't so busy any more. The gym?' He meant Cannons, the city gym club of which he was a member and which also sustained a first-class restaurant at which I had once eaten as his guest.

He did not express any surprise that I had rung, even though it was our first contact since his father's funeral a few weeks after I had finished my investigation.

'How's Allison?' I asked over pre-prandials. He smiled as I ordered Southern Comfort — no ice, no soda; he liked the idea that some things don't change.

Allison was his skilful and sexy younger sister; she ran the firm and for a while had run me.

'Happy at work; unhappy in every other way, but you know her, that doesn't count for anything.' His eyes tried to read mine. 'You wouldn't want to even if she did,' he said.

He had read me wrong. I told him so.

'Sandy's going to have a baby; mine.'

He shook my hand across the table. 'I'm really pleased, Dave. Really.' He grinned maliciously. 'I suppose you'd like me to let her know?' Allison.

'If I can be a fly on the wall.'

This was the only conversation about the past. We did not mention either of his brothers, or Sterling Latimer, or John Gauldie, his father's lifelong partner, who had also recently died, in a freak accident while gardening, electrocuted by his lawnmower. Nor did he say anything about his sudden release from custody shortly after my own, though he owed me the credit for it. He looked much better than I had expected — as fit as ever: I was glad he had not been beaten by the experience.

'I want to tell you something in total confidence. OK?' I trusted his word. If he had misled me at all during Mather's it was for understandable motives and never amounted to a breach of confidence.

'Yes,' he agreed instantly.

'Although I've gone back to Nichol & Co, I'm still working on an investigation.'

'Gee whizz, what a shock, golly gosh, you do surprise me.' I had forgotten what a sarcastic sod he was.

'Why will no one believe I might just have decided to resume my career as a solicitor?'

'Lots of people'll believe it, Dave, just no one who knows you.'

'The investigation is into a judge, a High Court judge.' I waited to give him an opportunity to tell me he didn't want to hear any more. He didn't bat an eyelid.

'Not to put too fine a point on it,' I lowered my voice yet further, 'it's being said that he's bent.'

He pursed his lips thoughtfully. 'Difficult. What sort of cases are we talking about? Crime? Civil? Family? How would it get into his list?'

Of all of these principal categories of litigation, a divorce or related family dispute would be the easiest to keep in front of an identified judge. Normally, English judges do not maintain personal lists; it is another element in the commitment to minimal preparation.

Even if the parties are told long before a case begins who the judge is expected to be it can be switched to another at the last moment, and for any one of a number of reasons, most of which will be outside anyone's influence or control — because an earlier case has taken longer than expected, because a judge falls ill, because a judge who is more suitable for the case becomes unexpectedly free, because a High Court judge is suddenly needed to make up the numbers in a three-man Court of Appeal, even because a court-room is being repainted and there is literally nowhere for the judge to sit.

Short of opening and adjourning a case, so that it is part-heard, the only time when a party knows for certain who will hear an action is if there has been some sort of interim or interlocutory application, during which either the parties have requested or the judge has ordered that it be reserved to himself — for example, because the issues are complex and he has already spent time beginning to master them, because he makes an order subject to a condition which only he can decide has been complied with, or because he has formed a view of the honesty of a witness or its absence.

'Good point — unless ... What about a listing clerk?'

'Highly unlikely. The listing clerks work for the court not the judge. So now you have to be talking not only a bent judge, but one willing to be known as such to a court official — in the High Court.'

'Wasn't there a fuss in the papers, a while ago, because court clerks were sending out to credit agencies the names of companies put into liquidation, or people made bankrupt? Something like that?'

'Both. But it was public knowledge — they were only facilitating the information and no judges were involved.'

The waitress brought out wine. He sipped it cautiously, then nodded approval. After she left, he asked, 'Are you going to give me anything more to go on, or do I have to guess it all?'

'You don't seem that shocked?' I prevaricated. I supposed that he more than most people had reason not to be surprised by the idea, but I would still have expected him to make a few of the right-sounding noises.

He settled back in his chair. The chair groaned. He was not a tall man, but a big, beefy man, heavy with muscle; I had seen him stripped to swim; he didn't carry an ounce of fat. If there was any justice in the world, he would be an underpaid private eye daily risking violent attack, and I would be the fat city solicitor growing fatter by the client.

'I'm not shocked,' he said eventually. 'I've heard a very vague rumour before.' He had been weighing up whether or not to tell me, or keep it in trade: I was flattered he had decided to come out with it.

'And does that rumour have a name?' I pressed.

'Yes and no.'

'Gee, thanks Martin. Remind me to do you a favour some day.' I stuck my knife upright into my meat like a dagger. Instead of quivering threateningly, it fell over into the béarnaise sauce. I extracted it disdainfully and licked my fingers clean.

'What I've heard is that there might be a barrister you might do well to go to if you haven't got much of a case, and I don't mean because he's brilliant. I know that what it's supposed to mean is that he has a judge he can talk to. I don't know how — uh — widely available this facility is, and I've never heard the name of a judge, not even a whisper.'

'We're talking civil actions — contracts, commerce, land, that sort of thing?' I answered his earlier question before it died of old age and asked one of my own.

'Yes.'

'Are you going to give me the name?' I asked.

'I think,' he hesitated, then plunged into independence: 'Perhaps you'd like to tell me what you think?'

'Charles Cushing, QC?'

'Yes.' He'd tested me to see how much I trusted him and wasn't going to play any more games.

We were onto coffee and liquers by the time I broached the idea of a sting.

'There's a barrister I think might help me out. He's in the same chambers. I was thinking of using him to take me to Cushing.' I explained why.

'No. It's too risky. Cushing's only got to ask to see one piece of paper and you're sunk and your mole with you. You need a real client, a real case; at least you need real papers. Haven't you got anything — good lord, Nichol & Co aren't that tinpot, are they?'

'We don't deal in the sort of case that would concern Cushing,' I answered defensively. 'We do unimportant things, like people getting thrown out of their houses, or fired, or picked on by the police because they're black, or shafted by ... Oh, hell, you know what I mean — just people getting shafted.' Like he'd nearly been, I reminded him Like I'd saved him from being. He was not by any stretch of the imagination a man pregnant with moral zeal; on the other hand, he knew when a debt was being called in.

'You're going to make me pay, aren't you, Dave? You're really going to make me pay.'

'We act,' I said to Justin Papworth, 'for a man with a Passat.'

He absorbed this important information with equanimity. He was still absorbing my presence in his office without. When his clerk told him he had a late conference, in a case called Passat, he had mentioned the firm of solicitors but not my own name; the connection hadn't registered. He was not pleased to see me.

We were in his chambers in the Temple. Even a lot of Londoners have never been into the Temple or don't know of its existence. Opposite the Royal Courts of Justice, between Fleet Street and the Embankment, it has the architecture and atmosphere of an Oxford college, but is considerably larger, with splendid, beautifully kempt lawns, statues, and its own church. Most of its entrances are discreet: you would not notice them if you were not looking. The Temple contains two of the four Inns of Court to one of which all barristers have to belong: Middle Temple and Inner Temple. Lincoln's Inn lies between Chancery Lane and the other side of the Royal Courts; Gray's Inn is at the top of Chancery Lane.

Barristers cram into the Temple, working two, three, four or even five to a room, sometimes sharing desks. Only QCs and senior civil practitioners have their own rooms. This again reflects the emphasis on advocacy as a barrister's only really important work. When a barrister has a conference with a client all his room-mates have to move out and find other desks to squat. When they are merely working on papers or preparation, they do so against a background cacophony of other people's telephone calls and casual conversations. Concentration is neither called for nor respected.

Papworth sat behind an antique desk more solidly than his word-processor sat upon it. All the bright youngsters use word-processors these days. They understand how pressing two keys at the same time is more effective than one; also, they have the co-ordination for it. I still can't understand where the words go when the machine is switched off. I'd be a Luddite if I wasn't frightened of getting a reputation as a progressive.

Finally, he asked; 'You needed to see me urgently because someone bought a duff car? You needed to see me because someone bought a duff car?' He was insulted. They don't make cars that cost enough to justify consulting a barrister who charged what he liked to earn by the hour, however badly they go wrong.

'Well, er, no. Not exactly.' I smiled what I hoped was disarmingly. 'No. Not at all,' I corrected myself. 'But I thought you'd like to know. I drive a Passat, too,' I added to give myself a little more time to find the right way to break the news that what I was really talking about was an entirely fictitious case, with a fictitious client and an effectively fictitious opponent.

'What do you want, Woolf?' He recovered his composure. 'This is about our last little discussion, isn't it? What's Orbach up to now? I'll save you the trouble: don't tell me; I don't want to know; I'm not going to play any part in it.' As he by now knew that he would not be charging a fee for the conference, it was a surprisingly lengthy sentence. 'Get out' would have done just as well.

I sighed. I hate blackmail. I'm so vulnerable to it myself, I don't like to encourage its currency.

'Justin,' I began, using like a weapon the first name he'd denied me, 'there are some things that, once you start, you can't stop. After all, Justin, no one made you talk to a QC about your doubts, about your challenge to the probity of a member of the High Court judiciary. I mean, it's a very serious suggestion. It's an impossible suggestion, Justin; it's an unprofessional suggestion. A senior member of the bar — one of Her Majesty's Counsel,' I used the archaic, full version of the title, 'a QC might feel obliged to report it; just the fact that it was said.'

He expostulated: 'But he approached me!'

'It depends whose version you believe,' I sighed. 'His — a QC whose honesty has never been doubted, even though his manners, dress-sense, suitability for parenthood, politics and taste in art might be — or a junior counsel who made a bit of a fool of himself trying to persuade his leader to bully the client into settling a case the client went on to win handsomely.'

He drew his breath in so sharply I was sure it would come out the other side, but if it did he was too well bred to let me know.

'Who could he report it to?' He struggled within the spider's web.

I shrugged.

'I don't know much about these things, you understand. I mean, it may qualify as conduct bringing the bar into disrepute — what do you think? So that would mean taking it to the Bar Council. Or Orbach might feel inclined to take you half-seriously, and allow caution to militate in favour of telling the Lord Chancellor's Office what you'd said. What is it they're in charge of — judicial appointments, oh, and appointment to silk, isn't it?' The silk appointment which was the next logical step in his logical career. 'Then again, if he was a decent chap, and the other chap had a father who had some sort of decent position in the profession, perhaps he'd think it the decent thing to do to go and have a decent word with the chap's decent father. Do you think Orbach's a decent chap, Justin? Do you think he even knows how to spell the word?'

It sounds as if I was enjoying myself, but I wasn't. The poor little sod was being squeezed harder than Orbach would have done for himself; he was being squeezed as hard as I believed Orbach might do. There's a world between. He had never done me any harm, nor anyone else that I knew of, doubtless other than professionally. My hold on him derived solely from the fact that Orbach had been able to tap into his better, more honourable, instincts. But, as he no doubt reassured himself when he put the boot in for one of his clients, I too was only doing my job.

These reflections gave him time to think. There is only ever one answer to an attempted blackmail. It does not matter how bad the thing you did that someone else has now found out about, or how serious the consequences, nor even how sincerely you fear that the blackmailer will use it on you, or believe naively that he or she won't come back for a second bite of the cherry. The only answer is to tell him to fuck off.

Papworth said sullenly: 'You'd better tell me what you want me to do.'

CHAPTER FIVE

It was impossible to associate the austere, robed figure imposingly high above us, his bald head covered by a wig, with the knock-kneed, lobster-pink, rotund dwarf we had seen on the beach at Cap d'Antibes and got drunk with at Golf Juan. Even his spectacles were different: he was now wearing half-glasses, designed to let him both read the papers before him, and peer at barristers across the court-room.

It was strange to be back in court. I had almost forgotten what it was like. The barristers in their own wigs and gowns, the ushers scurrying about looking for litigants and law reports, the stenographers at the table below the bench where the judge sits, the registrar also in wig and gown; on the press bench to one side sat a bored, besuited, pimply youngster with a reporter's notebook, not covering our case in particular, but just seeing whether anything of interest was happening. After about five minutes, he left. I wished I could've too.

'Mr Cushing,' Pulleyne interrupted learned counsel for the defendant, who was opening the hearing of the motion in a voice that could've substituted for Mogadon. 'Isn't this really a Chancery matter?'

Because Cushing was a QC, he stood in the front row of the bar. Junior counsel, like Papworth, have to sit one row back. As Papworth's instructing solicitor, I sat behind him, in the third row. I was too far back to see Cushing's expression as he answered. I could, however, imagine how smug he would look as he said, 'M'lord. Of course, that is a matter for m'learned friend. They are his proceedings.'

I heard a snort behind me, in the fourth row, where my lay client would normally be sitting, or members of the public. The snort did not come from my client: I did not have a client. The snort should have come —if it had to come at all — from my side, because its author was a member of the staff of Nichol & Co, entitled to sit with me in the row behind counsel. When I saw her waiting for me outside the courtroom, in jeans and a cracked-leather blue bomber jacket, a matching blue hedge standing upright in the middle of her otherwise close-cropped, dyed-platinum blonde head, I didn't have the heart to discourage Justin Papworth any further and declined to introduce her as such.

Her name was Carson. Just Carson, so far as I had been told. I still didn't know if it was her first name, last name or a name she had adopted for the occasion. She was about five feet nine, and as such a couple of inches shorter than I, but I nonetheless felt like she was towering over me. She was built to carry a couple of surfboards at a time and if she ever smiled she was saving it for someone else. She was in her mid-twenties, with an Australian accent which she applied in a gruff, low growl that sounded like she had sat up the night before chain-smoking.

'This is Carson,' Sandy had said, as she brought her into my room. 'She's just got back from holiday,' she added. I knew that before she had been on holiday, she had been on some kind of study-leave. She was the assistant I had been promised.

Innocently, I asked, 'Where did you go? Did you have a nice time?'

'What's it got to do with you?' she snarled.

'Now, Carson,' Sandy said from somewhere far below but a pregnant half-mile away, sounding like 'down, Carson, heel'.

'I went to Corsica,' she sulked. 'It was all right.'

'Carson is going to assist you,' the love of my life declared sweetly. 'She can clerk, and she can type.'

'Where'd'you learn to type? Holloway prison?'

'Fuck you, buster,' she swung around and stormed out of the room. It probably wouldn't cost much to have the door replaced.

'Carson,' Sandy shrieked in a voice more like a fish-wife than I'd ever heard from her before. 'Come back here.' Reluctantly, she returned.

'I just knew you two would get along,' Sandy said firmly, 'and you're going to. Got it?' She glowered at each of us in turn before she, with marginally greater decorum, left us alone.

'Sit,' I said.

Carson placed her hands on her hips and stood there like she was waiting for me to reach for my gun first. I sighed and sat myself down instead. She said, 'I'll tell you right off, if you ever touch me I'll kill you. I've done karate, tai c'hi, kung fu, won-ton, all that stuff, so I know what I'm talking about, OK?'

I raised my hands in horror.

'I promise not to touch you. Now will you please sit down?'

Still reluctant, she pulled up a chair the other side of my desk.

'Sandy says I've got to work with you,' she disclaimed all responsibility or joy in her new position. I noted: not for me, but with me. 'She says it'll be good for me and she says it'll be good for you.'

'How long have you been employed here?'

'A year.' She wasn't offering any hostages.

I remembered. I remembered Sandy mentioning she had taken on a new outdoor clerk who was a former client. I remembered Sandy giggling, and explaining she was a bit different but she had refused to elaborate at the time beyond telling me she came from Australia — it had been sufficient explanation at the time.

Carson, I now learned with less difficulty than the inauspicious opening would have suggested, had been in England since she was nineteen, was now twenty-seven, and had been in turn an art student, drama student, graphic designer, truck-driver and fence. Also, she had killed her uncle.

'Ah,' I said, as if that explained everything.

Sandy had represented her on the fencing charge, and she had been acquitted. Sandy had not represented her for killing her uncle, as that had happened when she still lived in Australia, but she had been acquitted anyway. Her uncle was a mad, bad, drunken Ukrainian mechanic; he lived with her, her two younger brothers and their father. Her mother was dead. Her father was partially paralysed from a mining accident. Her uncle had attacked her father with a meat cleaver. She had grappled with him, and won. I was not surprised. She was fifteen at the time. The court had called her a brave girl; she had snarled then, too, and told them she was a woman. They released her anyway.

I did not need to ask why Sandy had allocated her to work with me; even without Carson's threat, there was no risk of misbehaviour. Sandy has a monopoly on my capacity for forthright females; I like the others at least to appear compliant. The course had been a short course for legal workers, at a North London college. I had not known there were courses for legal workers who weren't also law-students. It was, I learned, the imaginative scheme of an administrator looking for new ways to bring in paying students, because of the cuts in government spending on higher education.

'And what did you learn?'

'Nothing I didn't know,' she snapped, reverting without warning to the surliness with which our encounter had begun.

'Carson,' I began patiently, 'either we're going to do what Sandy wants — which, I ought to tell you, is what I've found I always end up doing — in which case we ought at least to make an effort to get on with one another — or we might as well go and see her straight away and tell her it isn't going to work.' I thought an appeal to her sense of responsibility and maturity might help.

'Oh, why don't you just shut up,' she said, 'and tell me what you want me to do.'

What I wanted her to do was to go down to the High Court and issue a writ in the name of a man called Peter Passat — the alliteration appealed — against a company called Cross Course. This first step was the outcome of my discussions with Martin Mather and Justin Papworth.

After I had extracted from the latter the concession that he would help me, I had said, 'I want you to prepare a case and your opponent's going to be Charles Cushing.'

'Does Charles know he's being instructed?'

He might have been a weak man but no one said he was stupid.

'No. Not yet. He's going to be instructed by Mather's.'

'Mather's?' He raised an eyebrow frostily. 'Oh, yes, you had some involvement in that business, didn't you? And what is this case going to be about — buying a car from a Freemason, hm?'

'No. I'll tell you in a moment. I want you to tell me something first. In your case, were there any interlocutory applications?'

'Yes, of course. There usually are these days. If there's enough at stake, everything gets fought: discovery, accounts, points of privilege, the status quo pending trial and so on. Why?'

'Did Pulleyne hear an interlocutory?'

'As a matter of fact, yes.' His eyes widened, I like to think with respect. 'He reserved the matter to himself. Good lord,' he added as my point finally dawned.

'Once a High Court judge is sitting — doing a period in civil — everybody knows about it, yes?' I checked. 'And it's not nearly as difficult to select a particular judge for an interlocutory application as it is to get a particular judge for the full hearing, isn't that right?'

'I've never thought about it that way, but — yes. A notice of motion is usually fairly urgent if the full hearing itself is not to be delayed. You'd ask your clerk to get it on in the next few days; that means you already know what judges are over the road.' By 'over the road he meant the Royal Courts across Fleet Street from the Temple. 'If I know who's sitting, I might well say to my clerk: "Try and slip it on before old so-and-so". You know, because I think he'll be sympathetic on the point. A good clerk can manage that all right. It's not difficult.'

'How obvious would your clerk have to be?'

'Not very. It's a combination. He might say to the listing clerk that the judge in question would probably handle it quickly, is familiar with the law or case in question, or won't let anyone talk too long. That's the main thing that concerns court clerks, how much judicial time they have to spend. Say I'm after Judge One. My clerk asks around until he hears that Judge One is likely to be at least one of the options, even if there are others. We might not issue the motion until he's in the running. Then my clerk says it'll only take half a day in front of Judge One, but a full day in front of Judge Two or Three. This is the sort of thing that goes on.'

He paused to reflect.

'Of course, if that doesn't do it, my clerk might have to get a little bit more obvious. He might mention Judge One by name. As long as it doesn't happen often, no one will be suspicious. Cases are tactics as much as law and the notion that particular barristers prefer particular judges for particular cases is uncontroversial. Everyone rubs along or maybe my clerk has to buy the court clerk a drink or two. It goes on all the time.'

'How many interlocutory applications were made by your side in that case?'

'Three or four, I can't remember. Why?'

'How many of them were strictly necessary?'

'Strictly? Who's to say? In my view, possibly two.'

'And Pulleyne heard the last one? And reserved it to himself?'

He swivelled in his chair and stared long and hard and lonely at an oak bookshelf lined with old, leather-bound law reports. They started in the 1850s and continued up until the preceding year: the current year's reports in that series would still be in loose, periodical parts, and at the end of the year these would be sent off to be bound in a matching cover. He was looking at 130 years of unbroken tradition and history.

When he returned his attention to me, he summarised, 'It keeps going until you get the judge you want on an interlocutory application and then you ask the judge to reserve it to himself.

You didn't ask, but I'll tell you anyway: yes, Cushing' — a few moments before it had been Charles — 'was the one who suggested that it might be appropriate for Pulleyne to keep the case. Once one side asks, it's difficult for the other side to object — almost impossible. It's easy to say that you particularly want a judge for a case; on the worst construction, you're insulting everyone else. But how do you say to his face that you don't want a judge?'

We sat in silence contemplating the idea of telling a High Court judge that he was not suitable for a case. After a while, he said, 'You still haven't told me what the case is going to be about.'

'No more I have. I told your clerk it was a property dispute so we'd better stay close to that. Also, we might as well keep the name Passat. Martin Mather has a company of his own. It's not active any more, but it's still in the process of being wound up; it's taking time, because there are executors involved. It's an investment company called Cross Course. What we've got in mind is cooking up an argument about whether Cross Course owns a piece of property in its own right, or whether it was purchased on our client's behalf. We get an order freezing dealings in it; Martin Mather instructs Cushing to apply to discharge the order.'

'I think I see. Our client gave, um, Cross Course money to invest. They say it was invested generally, doubtless with some of the return reflecting their purchase of the property in question, while we say the whole of it went into that particular purchase. I can say one thing, Cushing will certainly enjoy that sort of thing. But wouldn't it normally go into Chancery? Pulleyne doesn't sit in Chancery.'

I hadn't thought of this. The Chancery Division of the High Court is highly specialised and Papworth was correct to point out that this was where it belonged. But, 'It doesn't have to go into Chancery, does it? We would be allowed to take it into the Queen's Bench Division,' the other part of the High Court. 'What do you think?'

He smiled for the first time since the con began. 'Well, all right. But you issue the writ with a general endorsement before you take my advice and get me to settle the statement of claim afterwards, eh?' What he meant was, if we were going to issue the proceedings in what would be viewed as 'the wrong Division' it would be my mistake not his. He still had his professional pride; mine didn't matter.

Now Papworth stood to explain to Pulleyne that the proceedings had been issued by his solicitor in Queen's Bench and he had decided that it would cause unnecessary delay and cost to transfer. He did not expressly say that the proceedings had been issued by me before his advice had been sought — that would have been an outright lie. But it was clearly implied.

This was the first time Papworth had spoken in these proceedings and accordingly the first time Pulleyne had more than glanced in our direction. I saw him look at me, as Papworth blamed me for the error of judgment, frown and scratch his head just underneath his wig. He was not frowning because of the mistake, but because he half-recognised me; he was trying to work out where he knew me from. I looked as different as he did. If he solved the puzzle, he gave no sign of it.

'Very well, Mr Papworth, it's your choice. Now, Mr Cushing: Mr Papworth obtained an *ex parte* order freezing any dealings in this property. What is the property?'

'It's an office building, m'lord.' Cushing rose as Papworth sat down again, like tweedledum and tweedledee. 'It's a fairly old building and not that valuable in its current condition. But there are development proposals in the neighbourhood and every prospect of realising a much higher price at the present time if we can enter into free negotiations. We're asking for the first order to be discharged. There's application for an account in any event, but of course we'll give the appropriate undertakings.'

This was no more than an outline. It said all that needed to be said on an interlocutory motion but QCs don't get rich saying things once that can be said ten times over. It's embarrassing to charge — say — a couple of thousand pounds for no more than ten minutes' visible effort.

Besides he had — or believed he had — a client to impress: doubly so, for Martin Mather was, as his solicitor, his professional client, and as owner of the company also the lay client. Martin was not sitting in the same row as I: there are seats in front of the QCs' row, to allow their instructing solicitors to instruct them during a case. We had only exchanged one look since we entered court; a quick, unsuspicious grin between temporary opponents who might well be personal friends.

As Cushing droned on, I half-turned and whispered to Carson, 'How much of it are you following?'

'Sounds like a load of rubbish to me,' she said loudly. I shuddered. Comments like that in open court could cost. I hushed her; she snorted. I had learned that a snort was her usual alternative to a snarl. 'Anyway,' she went on, admittedly a fraction quieter, 'it is, isn't it? You don't care if you win, do you? It makes no difference, does it?'

'Now what makes you think that?' I asked softly, turning around again without waiting for her answer, before she could see me smile. Maybe she wasn't entirely Sandy's idea of a joke.

True to skill, Cushing sat down at twelve-thirty. No barrister knows exactly what time he will begin speaking. Even if he is opening a case there will usually be one or two matters listed beforehand and they are of uncertain duration. The best barristers accordingly keep in their heads not one speech, but a range of submissions designed to permit them to select the most appropriate point in time to shut up and sit down.

Twelve-thirty was an excellent choice from his point of view. The application had been listed for half a day. If he had continued until too close to the one o'clock adjournment for lunch, he would be responsible for pushing it into the afternoon and Papworth could take as long to reply as he had taken to open. By sitting down now he could force Papworth to reply briefly or else take the blame for the extension beyond estimate.

In the event Papworth had much less to say than Cushing. Cushing had introduced the facts fairly. He had advanced his argument against the earlier order and it was convincing. The putative Mr Passat didn't give a damn about the building itself, and an account of the profits would do as nicely as American Express. The only valid reasons for preventing Cross Course conducting negotiations would be to put pressure on them to settle our action, or if there was any basis for suspecting collusion between them and the prospective buyers, who were of course as fictional as Passat.

'I don't think the order can stand, Mr Papworth,' Pulleyne said promptly at twelve fifty-five, 'unless you have anything else to say. I'll hear you, of course, but really the sensible thing seems to be to allow the defendants to sell. There's a real risk that the value will drop if they can't reach agreement soon enough for the building to be incorporated into the development. At least as I understand it, there are two other sites which would suit the developers just as well. Isn't that right?'

'M'lord,' Papworth said, 'if that's your lordship's view, I don't think there's any more I can say that is likely to change your lordship's mind.'

'So be it, then. Order discharged on the draft undertakings Mr Cushing handed up. Is that everything, gentlemen?'

Cushing rose. 'I was wondering, m'lord, since your lordship has already spent half a day mastering the facts in this matter ... Would your lordship consider reserving it to himself?'

Outside the court, along the corridor, Martin Mather and I went into a huddle. Opposing solicitors usually have a chat after a hearing to agree the next stage or two.

Once we were sure we could not be overheard I congratulated him, 'Like a dream. How did you do it?'

He shrugged modestly. 'I told him I wanted Pulleyne. I told him I'd had another matter in front of him of a similar nature and the client had been most contented. He pushed me a bit, floated a few other names he said might do as well. I expected him to. I said I wouldn't feel as confident in front of anyone else. Was that OK?'

'Sure.' I didn't care how he'd sown the seed just how it grew. 'What next?'

'I think we should leave it for a week or two then I'll go and see him again. Maybe point out that as it's my own company, we could reach an arrangement as to how he's paid — Cushing, I mean. Let him nibble on a bit of cash he doesn't have to declare. It'd be a good opening.'

'What if he won't?' I could see that if he did it was a much shorter step to broaching another payment that would not turn up on anyone's income tax return.

'He's not going to refuse. You should have seen the way he stared at me when I insisted on Pulleyne and told him to get it reserved. He knows what I meant; I know he knows,' he said fiercely.

'You scared, Martin?'

'Not yet,' he admitted, implying that we were swimming into troubled waters. 'How about you?'

I looked down the corridor to where Carson was impatiently waiting to go back to the office with me. 'Nah. I've got a minder.'

She and I were just leaving the building when someone brushed past me then turned and grabbed my arm. 'Dave?'

It took me less time to recognise him than if I had not spent the morning staring at his father. 'Henry? What are you doing here? How's Caroline?'

'I've come to have lunch with the old man. She's fine. You? Sandy?'

'Wonderful. Not that long to go. They say January. I've just been in front of your father. I don't think he knew who I was though. He kept looking at me as if he was trying to place me.'

'Join us for lunch, why don't you?'

'No, better not. Not quite on, really.' One can socialise with a judge provided one does not discuss a case he is involved in, but the same day as a hearing was pushing the limits of propriety. 'Anyway I ought to be getting back to the office.'

'Yes, that's right.' Carson interjected, thrusting a hand at Henry. 'I'm Carson,' she said without any greater explanation. 'I'm all right too.'

Henry winced as she released his right hand and massaged it with his left. 'Good, jolly good. Well, it's nice to see you, Dave, give our love to Sandy. Listen, we're going to have a bit of a bash soon. Won't you come, oh do say you will.'

I laughed. 'Sure, why not?'

'I'll send you an invite, then. I know the old man will be jolly pleased to see you; mater too.'

He waved as he hurried into the building, now late for pater.

'Come on, then, Dave. Let's go have a pre-lunch drinky-poo, oh do say you will,' Carson mimicked his accent perfectly.

I looked her up and down, saying, 'You don't like anyone, do you?'

'Yeah, I know,' she sighed her first candid answer. 'Sandy said that's why we'd get along.'

We tried for a drink in The George, opposite the court, but it was packed with lawyers and litigants. Instead, we wandered down to the Embankment and went on board the *Tattershall Castle*.

Once we had settled down I asked her, 'How did you know the hearing this morning didn't matter?'

I phrased the question ambiguously; she may just have meant no more than that all law was a game.

She was drinking lager, a pint. The glass looked small in her grasp. She took a long, deep draw before she replied.

'Is it usual for one side to have original letters which ought to have been sent to the other years before? Is it usual to draw up an attendance note of an interview with a client, lasting two hours, at a time when you were at ante-natal with Sandy? Is it usual to date a note of conference with counsel one week after you actually had it? I mean,' she concluded, 'I know I'm just an unqualified idiot, and all, so I'm just asking, you know, if it's usual.' She thought for a moment, then added, 'Anyhow, don't treat me like a mug, all right?'

'How did you know I got the original letters from Mather's?' Martin Mather had had to provide them on Cross Course headed paper, together with a back-dated and ambiguously worded investment agreement.

'You had a delivery from them by messenger service marked confidential. You threw the envelope in the bin. The letters weren't in the file the night before but they were when I looked at lunchtime the next day.'

'How'd'you do when it isn't your own boss you're spying on?'

'Not bad. When are you going to let me show you?'

'Buy me another drink.'

'Give me the money then.'

I thought about it while she was pushing at the bar. She knocked two city gents to one side, flipped a Sloane Ranger over her shoulder, trod on a little old lady and attracted the barman's attention by picking him up by his shirt-front and breathing our order into his face.

'Sandy ain't going to like it,' I warned her when she returned quicker than anyone else had been served. 'Were you always like this?'

'Like what?' She'd almost finished her second pint already.

'Aggressive.'

'Assertive it's called now,' she said in a tone a notch less butch than usual. 'It's not your business anyway,' she repeated more or less what she had said at our first meeting, but it meant something else now.

'Yes, it is. You want in, I'm entitled to know who and what you are. I never worked with anyone else before.' I meant as an investigator, rather than as a solicitor. Then, I never worked at all.

'Are you going to stay in the firm?'

'I set it up, you know.'

'Yeah, I know. But are you going to stay?'

'What do you think?'

'I think you don't know.'

'Do you think I ought to?'

'If you don't know, how should I? It's your business, Dave. Sandy wants you to stay; we all know that. Just about everyone else — anyway, the solicitors — they'd rather you dropped dead. Quitting wouldn't be enough for them, you might change your mind and come back. They all want to be partners and you're in the way.'

'What about the rest of the staff?'

'D'you know how Sandy's managed to survive so long without having to make anyone else a partner?'

'No. Well, she's smart; she could do that if she wanted. What do you think?'

'Everyone on the staff loves her like crazy. All the non-qualified people. Well, Naomi's qualified isn't she, but she doesn't count.'

She wasn't insulting Naomi. Naomi was at the College of Law with Sandy and me. She practised for a while but, like a lot of people, she found the strain of doing the job properly a bit too much for her own health; unlike most of them though, she chose to quit instead of doing the job badly or half-heartedly. Later she married and had kids, and now she came in two days a week to do the office books and some of the bills.

'So? What does that mean?'

'It means the solicitors have got no support; it means there's an atmosphere in which people find it easier to love her than fight her — no one wants to rock the boat too hard. It means if anyone gets a bit too stroppy, all their typing starts taking too long, or files are mislaid, or there's no outdoor clerk available to go to court for them, or the juicy cases get allocated to someone else, so they aren't earning as much as they used to and their claim to partnership is weaker. It means people stay longer than they might do otherwise and then quit without a struggle.' She had it all sussed out.

'How does that answer my question?' I meant how they felt about me.

'Sandy's in love with you.'

'I know that.'

'No you don't. You know Sandy loves you. I mean Sandy's in love with you. So if you're good together she's up, and if you're not she's down. She's like a little kid where you're concerned. So people've got mixed feelings about you. They've known her when she's unhappy because of you, and other times when it's been going well, and now she's going to have a baby with you and you're working back in the firm so she's really happy like most of us have never seen her, so they want you to stay.'

'And you? You want me to stay?'

'I couldn't give a shit,' she reverted to form.

'Hey, come on. It's not necessary, you know. If we're going to work together, talk to me.'

'I've been talking. Maybe you haven't been listening,' she said truculently. 'Ah, shit. 'Course I want Sandy to be happy. You know how long it is since I last worked somewhere for a year? You wanna know the names of the people who took the trouble to think what might be good for me, and then doubled the trouble to make me do it despite myself? You wanna know how many other people I talked to about my uncle, and said: "I'm sorry". That's all she said: "I'm sorry". I've had people say, "Wow, good for you", and I've had people draw back — you know, physically draw back — and I've had people who're turned on by the idea of a tough, violent woman, and I've had the worst of all, people who say "I understand" when they don't have a clue what it felt like. Sandy's the only one just looked at me and said "I'm sorry" just like that.' It wasn't easy to keep up with her: either she said next to nothing or she couldn't stop.

'So?'

'So if you stay in the firm 'cos you want to that's OK.; but if you're unhappy, if you just stay 'cos you think you ought, then it's going to be a strain, and Sandy'll be unhappy, and maybe she'll be more unhappy than if you buggered off, y'know?'

'What makes you happy, Carson?'

She snorted. 'This time *I mean* it's none of your business.' She waited to make sure I wasn't going to argue, then said, 'Well?'

'Well, what?'

'You know.'

'I know I want another drink,' and time to think whether or not to let her into the scam.

As I returned from the bar, having taken twice as long as she did to get served but presumably quicker than she expected, I caught her staring longingly out of the window over the Thames. I might not know what made her happy, but I knew what made her unhappy — she was lonely.

I banged her drink down on the table to attract her attention and said: 'I want you to find out everything there is to know about a group of companies called Hackney Marsh. And I want you to find out everything there is to know personally about the barrister this morning, Cushing.' I thought for a moment, to see if there was anything else, and remembered, 'Oh, and I want you shouldn't tell Sandy anything about it. She doesn't want to know, and I don't want her to know. Right?'

She said, 'Is that all?'

I began to feel sorry for Messrs Hackney, Marsh and Cushing, they weren't going to know what had hit them.

CHAPTER SIX

The invitation from Henry Pulleyne arrived within days with a scribbled note from Caroline: 'Longing to see you both. C. XX.' I hoped at least one of the Xs was for me.

The younger Pulleynes lived in Wimbledon, which is south of the river and therefore only theoretically London. The party was on a Saturday. It began at nine but, as we wanted to arrive on time, we left home just after tea, in case there was a long delay at passport control. We took the Passat because though I drive like a pig Sandy was now too big for comfort in her Peugeot GTL

In a moment of rare — perhaps unprecedented —honesty I said, 'I still can't relate to the idea of being a father.'

I saw her smile out of the corner of my eye. She said, 'You think I feel like a mother?'

Did I say Sandy is also Jewish? Her preferred answer to a question is another question.

'Well, I suppose I thought, you know, carrying it around all the time ...' We had been offered the opportunity to know its sex.

I wanted to know. She didn't. I wanted to know so that I could prepare for what was in store for me. She didn't want to know in case they said it was a boy. She thought I would probably only love it unreservedly if it was a girl. Who needs the competition?

'I don't know, Dave. What I feel is a big, heavy weight, which could be a blob or a child but is somewhere between. It's a heartbeat, not a human yet. I think, well, I don't know what a mother's supposed to feel like, do I? Maybe this's how I'll feel when it's born, too.'

I snorted. I was catching the habit from Carson.

The sound connected. She asked, 'How're you two getting along? She hasn't been in to complain about you for a few days.'

'She's a lovely woman. She's clever, and sad and thoughtful, and she's lonely and she's damned if she's going to let anyone know and I think she was the perfect way to get me to feel comfortable back in the firm. So, thanks.'

'Yup. I didn't think it'd take you long to find out,' she said as smug as a senior barrister. 'And I think she's a little bit in love with you, too.'

'Ouch. What's that about?'

'I saw her smile coming out of your office yesterday. 'Course, she was scowling till she shut the door. But she shut it. That's a lot for her.'

Late yesterday afternoon was one of the few occasions Carson had checked in since I awarded her field commission. The reason she hadn't been in to complain was because she had hardly been in at all. I suspect the reason she was smiling when she left was because she knew she had done a bloody good job, even if on principle I declined to admit it. What she'd come up with spelled a whole new ball game. I was glad it was a Friday and, by the time we finished, too late to do all the things the information called for. Next week would be soon enough to pass the news on to Martin; I could use the break first.

'Let's start with the poofta.'

'Who?'

'The poofta; you know, the fairy ...'

'I know what poofta means, Carson,' I sighed. It's tiring being treated like a moron. 'I just don't know who you're talking about.'

'Cushing, or cushion as I daresay he's called by some of his mates,' she grinned cheekily to emphasise the point. 'He's a three pound note. Likes landlord and tenant law: rent boys, the sort who hang around Piccadilly Circus offering a not so secure tenancy up ...'

I held up my hand.

'Enough. One day, you may have to make contact with a character called Lewis, or his mate Malcolm. They are both as queer as can be and very good friends of mine; if you go in talking like that you might just come out a corpse no one can tell which sex you used to be. I appreciate that all Australians are butch, faggot-hating lads and lassies who get a hard-on at the mention of a person of the opposite sex, but we're in England now, where homosexuality is the national sport, leading only by a short — uh — head the howls of hypocrisy which follow when anyone finds out about it.' Just because I slag people off on any grounds — including sexual preference — didn't mean she was entitled to.

'I've got nothing against pooftas,' she sulked. 'Some of my friends are; all of my friends are. Those that aren't lezzies. You don't know what I call myself.' She was daring me to ask, just so she could tell me that was none of my business either.

When I didn't, she continued her account.

'He's got two main squeezes: a bloke he shares his house in Kensington with who's an accountant, about his own age and as sexy as a pregnant snake; and a feller in a flat in Kilburn who likes to hang about leather bars when Cushing isn't hanging about him and who looks as if AIDS ain't got him he's going to get AIDS. He provides the boys, too: they like to party. I don't know what, if anything, this guy does for a living. He's out all day, going into shops and offices and bars and restaurants, but no one place in particular. My guess is Cushing keeps him, and probably keeps quiet about him to his house-mate.'

'Tell me about the accountant.'

'David Newton; partner in a big firm — one of these firms with so many names they don't put them on the letter-heading but tell you where you can look it up instead.' The phenomenon of partnerships too large for all the names to go on the notepaper was new to the legal profession but slightly older in accountancy; also, some of the practices were now international and the names wouldn't print in the Roman alphabet.

'Does the name lead anywhere?'

'No. Neither the firm name, nor any of the individual names checks out with Hackney Marsh, through any of its companies.'

She picked her nose ostentatiously and went on: 'I had a drink with his junior clerk.'

'How did you manage that?' Junior clerks are clones of the senior clerks they serve, adore, emulate and will one day stab in the back. However long they have been working they never look older than fifteen, the seats of their pants shine, they use hair-grease and they all have BO.

They do not, however, normally hang around with people who look, sound or behave like Carson. Perhaps the mohican-style blue strip in the middle of her head was pinned on like Bo Derek locks. I tried to imagine her in a dress with make-up and earrings; I shuddered; a nose-ring would be more appropriate.

'I followed him home to Surbiton. Ten minutes after he went inside what I found out was his parents' house, he came out in high-heel boots, silk trousers and a floral shirt I wouldn't bury a dead dingo in. It was wicked.'

One advantage of my insular Earl's Court existence was that for years I had lived in sublime ignorance of the slang of the young. Everything was now 'wicked', 'gross', 'brill' or 'mega', or 'well wicked', 'way mega' and so on — unlike the sensible and straightforward language we used to use, such as 'fab', 'far out', 'gear' and 'groovy'.

'So you picked him up in the local disco?'

'Nah, pub. There's a pub where all the kids go — it's so plastic even the glasses aren't real. I was the oldest person there. He's a snooty little shite. He was with a gang of his friends who were all giving me the eye; it was no problem to give him the eye back. He couldn't wait to tell me how much he earned and how powerful he was and how one day he was going to run his own chambers. He would've told me anything.'

I was waiting for relevant information but I didn't want to shut her up, I wanted to hear how the evening had ended. I wanted to hear and I didn't want to hear. I didn't want to hear she'd fucked a barristers' junior clerk. In the whole of the profession there is nothing so low. They are student leeches and openly so. They have made a lifelong commitment to becoming like the senior clerks I have already described in terms more charitable than they merit.

She giggled. It wasn't a sound I associated with her. She said, 'He told me he lived with his parents; I said he could drive me home if he liked; so he nicked his father's car and drove me back to Islington,' where she lived in an illegal squat belonging to the local council and in a very different part than Orbach. 'I got out and said thanks and was inside the house with the door shut before he could undo his seat-belt.'

'Any richer in information?'

'No, but I can always pick him up again, can't I? I could pick him up in town next time, now I'm supposed to know where he works.'

I didn't like to disabuse her: even if he'd spent the best night of his life between her legs, he'd run a mile rather than be seen with her around the Temple.

'Does he know Cushing is gay?'

She shook her head. It was considerate to check. As a last resort we could always threaten to reveal all to his professional colleagues as well as to the numerate Mr Newton.

'How've you done on Hackney Marsh?'

'All right. I've found out who owns it.'

'Good girl,' I said before I could stop myself. 'Pardon, good chap.'

'D'you remember a boxer called Trentino?'

'Sure, who doesn't?' He had been the best thing at his weight for several years. The Prime Minister nearly had to resign when he lost the world championship.

'The real owner of Hackney Marsh is a man called Trent who's his cousin, without the eytie-ending. The money comes from Trentino though; the cousin's just a front.'

I frowned. I was trying to remember something. 'I thought Trentino was supposed to be owned by the East End?'

She scowled triumphantly. 'Exactly. Trent's a front for Trentino: and Trentino's a front for ...'

'The Reddins.'

Bingo.

The party was in full swing when finally we arrived. A marquee in the back garden was visible from the street. All I could see was low-cut gowns; all Sandy could see was lounge-suits. I was wearing crumpled slacks and my leather jacket; she was in a pyjama suit bought at an Auschwitz closing down sale.

'Dave! Sandy! Splendid!' Henry all but hugged us. 'You didn't dress! Thank goodness; you'd think it was an evening in The Mansion House instead of a party.' The English educated classes have one redeeming feature: they know how to embarrass a guest. 'Have a drink before anything else. What will you have? We've got everything,' he rolled his eyes and the last word.

'Dave! Sandy! How wonderful to see you!' Still in the lobby, Caroline kissed a spot about five feet from Sandy's cheek; I didn't let her off so easily but kissed and hugged everywhere I could reach until I felt the heel of Sandy's flat-bottomed shoe shoot into my shin like a stiletto. What I could see was less than fifty per cent of what I had already seen — why was it more exciting now?

'You rogue, you,' Henry clapped me on the back. Then he helped me to my feet. 'And with a wife about to become a mother!'

'We're not married,' Sandy said abruptly, 'didn't you know that?'

There was an equally abrupt silence. They exchanged a look. Caroline said, 'I knew that. No one's married anymore, except us,' she sounded bitter, 'but you know them.'

'It's just a question of law,' Sandy's eyes flashed as if Caroline was criticising instead of defending us.

'And he am de judge, he am de law,' Caroline responded in a stage-negro accent.

'Yes,' Henry added. 'Don't say anything. They're so beastly old fashioned; living together is what the criminals he sends to prison do.'

'We never said we were married,' I interjected lamely. I knew they'd thought it. I had wanted them to presume in France that my name was Nichol, a considerably less suspect character than one called Woolf, though if asked directly I would probably not have lied and it wasn't necessary to sustain the deceit now that a substantial connection had been made. 'It can't be that important, not in this day and age. Surely?'

'Oh, Dave, you know my father. Have they talked to you about my sister?'

'No. Why?'

We didn't get an answer. The man himself emerged from the living-room, glass in hand, wife in tow. He had a tawdry purple cummerbund around his ample waist and a matching bow-tie all but lit up.

'Nichol! Two Nichols! Nearly three!' The scale of the Yorkshire accent worked better than a breathalyser — he was already well over the limit.

'Sandy! Dave!' Isabelle took one hand from each of us in hers. Even she was wearing a low-cut gown: it was lower cut than her swim-suit. I'd thought on the beach, and thought harder now, that she really was a most attractive woman. I've only ever met one older woman I fancied and I was afraid of her too. 'It's wonderful to see you.'

More bits of airspace got plopped.

'Well, rascal, turning up in court, eh? What do you say? Ha, thought I didn't recognise you, didn't you? Ha!'

'Henry — help — drink!'

'Bubbly! Coming up! Tell them why, pater,' he commanded his father. 'Come on, break the news!'

'If we can do it, anyone can?' Sandy guessed.

If you're going to put your foot in it, do it firmly. Caroline extricated her.

'No thanks, not yet. I'm too young to give up enjoying my-self. Henry's been promoted. We're off back to America; he's got the Chicago office.' We knew enough about his work and his bank to appreciate that this was truly something to celebrate. 'Sandy, come freshen up. Come on,' she took her by the hand and led her off.

Martyn Pulleyne didn't take my hand but it felt as if he had. He led me into the melee, looking for his brothers whom he wanted me to meet. There were more people in the house than I had pissed off in the last ten years. It was packed solid. You couldn't move for suits and tits and smoke without fire and darlings and drinks and deals.

'We really shouldn't at a social gathering but while we're here what do you think of ...'

'This stock ...'

'This man's prospects ...'

'That outrageous appointment ...'

'It'll ruin everything they've done in the last ten years ...'

'Let's sell now while we can ...'

'It's a double celebration, Dave,' Martyn explained. 'It's forty years to the day since I was called to the bar. Think of that — forty years.'

'Are congratulations or commiserations in order?' I asked as finally I caught up with a tray of drinks and took off two. 'One for me,' I downed it quickly, 'and one for the kid.'

'Are you excited, Dave? Are you thrilled?' It could have sounded sarcastic but from Martyn Pulleyne it seemed sincere and wistful.

'Scared, Martyn ... It is all right to call you Martyn, isn't it? I mean, here?' It had taken me long enough to adjust; I'd only begun to feel comfortable with his first name on the last day or two of our holiday.

He, too, had helped himself to a drink. He held it up in a toast. 'Of course. I wish you well, young man, in everything you do. Only,' he paused for effect, 'try not to call me Martyn in court,' he exploded with laughter and sprayed me with his champagne.

In the marquee, a band was playing. They were playing safe, gentle, familiar tunes people could hum or dance to. I wondered what would happen if they suddenly burst into something real. Would they listen — or even notice — if Keith Jarrett stepped up to the keys or Randy Newman started melodiously to mock them? I was getting drunk too fast and having thoughts that didn't work. Sandy arrived, a nearly empty glass in her hand; neither Caroline nor Isabelle was with her. While someone with a heavy cold barracked Pulleyne about the commercial conservatism of the British bench, she whispered in my ear: 'They're on the edge, Dave, on the very edge.'

'What're you talking about?'

'Henry and Caroline. Didn't you see that look when we were talking about marriage? She told me, upstairs; she didn't want to get married so soon; it was the only way they could be together.' Sandy was talking urgently, as if what she was saying was important, real business not merely superfluous gossip. 'She was going to leave him if he hadn't been sent back to America. She told me, she's never coming back here to live.'

I shook my head to clear it; it had nothing to do with anything. What the hell did I care? Why did she care? 'Why are they having this party, then?'

'For Martyn; it's some sort of anniversary for him.' I explained what apparently had not merited explanation by Caroline.

'Henry's henpecked by his father, Dave.' She told me nothing new. 'He's just doing what he thinks he ought to do. Tell me, Dave,' she hissed, 'we're not doing it just because we ought to, are we? You're not, I mean, are you?'

I shook my head and put my arm around her waist. 'No, Sandy, I'm not, we're not.' I leaned down and kissed her cheek and felt unaccountably sad. 'We're doing it because probably we didn't ought to.'

She turned her head and right in the middle of the party we did what no one is suppose to do at such an occasion: we kissed full on the lips, just as if we loved one another.

At one in the morning, I found myself in a distant corner of the depleted marquee, still sipping champagne and wondering where Sandy was.

'Ha! There you are, Dave.' Martyn pulled up a chair and settle down beside me. He was carrying a new bottle, which he placed between us on the ground.

'Wonderful do,' I said politely. 'Have you enjoyed it?'

'They like this sort of thing,' he evaded.

They were doing it for him; he was doing it for them. 'You'll be sad to see them go back, I suppose?' I took a stab at a less controversial line of idle conversation. He ignored me. He said, 'If my father could see this ... I don't know what he'd think. Well, I know exactly what he'd think. He'd say: the waste, the waste, it's all a terrible waste.' He waved a hand around at the debris of the party: half-finished glasses of wine, half-eaten plates of food; on a cloth-covered table nearest to us was a salmon mousse, formerly in the shape of a whole salmon, now suffering the effects of nuclear attack. One leg of the table was standing in a bowl of strawberries, god knows why or how. There was a salver of petit fours; someone had nibbled a little bit out of each.

He poured us both another drink. 'I never told you anything about my father, did I, Dave?' He didn't wait for me to answer. 'He was an extraordinary man. He was a clerk in a mill, laid off before they had redundancy payments and unemployment benefits and social security. I was the oldest; I remember it all. There were five of us. People had much larger families in those days; that wasn't considered so big. But he went out looking for work and he found it, too. He did a bit of this and a bit of that and he scrimped and saved and he wouldn't let my mother work, and we all did well, you know: we went to university, and into the professions or the army.'

I had earlier met a Major-General Pulleyne and a surgeon, both of them as half-pint as he was and as three-quarters crocked; I still hadn't encountered his youngest sister, although he insisted she was present with her husband, a Permanent Secretary. The middle girl had died young, of cancer.

'He was a proud man, a tough man, a strict man.'

'You were obviously very fond of him.'

He chuckled, 'D'you think so? I was terrified of him. I said to you in Cap d'Antibes ... Once, just once, we took my parents to stay in the apartment. They were already very old; this was — oh, nine or ten years ago, the year before he died, just after I was appointed to the bench; she died last year. Anyway, we thought it would be a good thing to do for them. He hated it, and insisted on flying home the very next day. He couldn't understand having a second home, even a holiday home; he couldn't understand the waste.'

'What were you going to say about Cap d'Antibes?' I prompted.

'Oh, yes, I said that if I had my time over I'd do it differently. Remember?' This time he did wait for me to answer. I told him

I remembered. 'I felt a lot of pressure to do well, to prove to my parents it had been worth all their effort, to pay them back in a way. And that's the thanks I got,' he concluded bitterly. 'He flew home the next day.'

'Did you come back with them?'

'No. Isabelle refused. She was right.'

'Children can't please their parents, can they? We all try, and it's never right.' My father and I hadn't spoken for over a decade.

We were — finally — talking about his daughter, too. I knew her name was Julia, from a chance remark by Caroline in St Paul de Vence that I had chosen not to follow up at the time. Julia was Henry's older sister by two or three years.

'She had a child,' he said suddenly. 'She wasn't married to the father, she never even lived with him, I'm not even sure she knew his name. I didn't.'

I gulped. Now I understood why Henry and Caroline hadn't wanted us to say anything about not being married. I felt torn: my job was to encourage him to continue confiding in me, to get as close to him as I could; but I liked him, and I didn't like the idea of deceiving him on such a personal matter.

He had surprised me before, and he surprised me again then.

'You're not married, are you — you and Sandy?' I shook my head.

'I suppose Henry told you I'd be angry?'

'More or less.'

'He can be such a fool, that boy; for a clever lad, he can be such a fool.'

'You only mind where they're concerned? Only where Julia's concerned? Isn't that — forgive me, Martyn — a little unforgiving?'

He barked: 'I forgive her the child. It's what happened afterwards I don't forgive.'

I waited; he was going to tell me; it was better not to ask.

He shared out the remainder of the bottle between us. It was strange to be drinking champagne during such an unhappy conversation; there was nothing else left. I understood what had provoked the reference to his father: the waste, the waste.

'She's living with another woman. She put her own child out to adoption so that she could go and live with another woman. The other woman wouldn't have a child in the house, she said.'

I shivered: stated baldly, it was a tale of unmitigated self-indulgence. Of course, there would be another side to it; doubtless Julia would try to justify her decision in terms of what was good for the child, her child. But it was impossible to imagine the excuse that would stand up.

He smiled wanly and continued.

'You see, we didn't know about it until afterwards, too late, when the child had already been adopted.' There was a bit more to come. 'It was the way we found out, too. The judge who approved the adoption is an old friend, we did our pupilage together,' the year of practical training. 'He didn't know for certain, not during the hearing, but he suspected. He almost adjourned it of his own motion, to find out.'

'So he didn't tell you till afterwards?'

'Right.'

I would've liked to ask which he minded more — not being told for themselves, or, that a colleague on the bench knew of the disgrace.

'I gave them everything, everything any parent could've given them. They had the most expensive education in the top schools, holidays all over the world, the best clothes, ample pocket-money, sports, and when they were old enough I bought them each a car. I wanted to do everything for them that my father couldn't do for me. It wasn't easy: in those days, when you started out at the bar, there was no legal aid, so a lot of people went without lawyers or you acted for them for free — charity work. You had to wait for the briefs; it took years to build up to a full-time practice. Once I was qualified, there was no more help from my father — there were the others yet.'

I'd heard the stories. Lord Denning, the former Master of the Rolls, head of the Court of Appeal, and possibly the most legendary figure in English law in this century, had waited seven years for his first case. You had to pay your pupil-master for the privilege of doing his work for him. You had to pay chambers' rent even when you weren't earning. You needed books, suits for court, wing collars and bands, wig and gown, to travel a long-distance on circuit for the smallest case at a fee that wouldn't cover the rail-fare.

'Isabelle worked until Julia was born; I still wasn't earning enough. When she came of course she had to stop, so it was a considerable struggle for a few more years — I got deeper and deeper into debt, we all did, that was how it was done if you didn't have family money. You borrowed: from banks, from friends if you could, from anywhere. That's why the bar was such an upper class club for so long — only the wealthy could afford it. But I persevered, I did every case I could, I all but stole, I wanted my children to have it all. There was no point to it otherwise, was there?'

'It's all long ago, though, Martyn. Don't you think, well, sometimes we have to step back from what we are, from how we got there, ask if what we are is really what we want to be, or if it just seemed that way while we were getting there.' I was trying to say, not very clearly: you don't have to be the hard man any more.

'But think of it,' he said gloomily, 'if it came out.' He meant Julia: he had finally answered the question I hadn't dared ask him before — it mattered more that his colleague at the bar knew about her than the loss of his grandchild. In a way, I was glad. It made it easier for me to answer when he asked, 'You mustn't tell anyone, Dave, you wouldn't? I can trust you, can't I?'

'Of course I wouldn't, Martyn; of course you can.'

The 'phone was ringing as we came in just after three o'clock. The answering machine cut in after the second ring, so we couldn't stop it. Almost as soon as it started to play the outgoing message, before either of us could lift the receiver which would also have turned it off, the tape stopped: whoever it was had hung up.

'Shit,' said Sandy, 'that means they'll try again later. Shall we leave it off the hook?'

We dithered for a few moments, but neither of us dared take the plunge. A 'phone call at that time of the morning could only be one of two things — serious personal bad news or a client in trouble. We would not want to know about the latter but we could not have slept for worrying in case it was the former.

'I'll sit up,' I volunteered, 'just in case one of us has to go out. Go to sleep. I promise I'll wake you if it's necessary.'

She smiled and gave me an awkward hug that was more baby than anyone else. 'Whatsa matta big boy; tired of doing it from behind? Used to be your favourite.'

I slapped her bottom but could only reach her hip. We could afford to joke. I don't understand the psychology of it but I was increasingly turned on sexually as she expanded, and not because I liked doing it from behind, which was the only way we could both be comfortable. It was probably because it was a novel experience and like a lot of my generation I'm addicted to novelty.

I sat down to wait with a book and a Southern Comfort to sober me up after all the champagne. When I'd moved my stuff out of Earl's Court, Sandy had commented on the absence of reading matter. I told her my books were packed up in cartons for storage. She said: 'Both of them?'

She was a hundred per cent out. I had four books. One was *Judaism As Creed And Life*, which I'd been given by the synagogue on my barmitzvah and still hadn't got around to reading; another was *A Guide To The Professional Conduct Of Solicitors*, which was in equally unread, mint condition.

Ever since, I had been studying assiduously to increase my literary quotient. I was working my way through the classics: Robert B. Parker, John D. MacDonald, Ross MacDonald, Lawrence Sanders, Elmore Leonard, Ed McBain, Loren D. Estleman, James Ellroy, Ross Thomas, Honore de Balzac.

I didn't have to wait long. The call came half an hour after we'd returned. I'd already switched off the machine so I could take my time to answer, to be able to claim I was asleep if I needed an excuse to hang up or time to think.

'You bastard, you fucking manipulative bastard,' said a voice I knew well.

'Oh, hi, Ali,' she hated being called Ali, 'it's nice of you to call; super to hear your voice. 'Specially at this time of the night.'

'Martin's in hospital,' she hissed. 'He's hurt, badly hurt. What've you got him into, Dave?'

'Hold on, Allison, what makes you think I've got him into anything?' She wasn't leaving me a lot of room to ask the polite questions like how had it happened and how bad it was.

'He asked for you; he told me to call you, to keep calling you till I got you.'

'Where is he?'

'The Charing Cross,' she answered automatically. The Charing Cross Hospital is in Fulham, nowhere near Charing Cross.

'What happened?'

'I don't know. He was mugged. They called me from the hospital. I'm still there. I've been ringing you for the last two hours.' She wanted to ask where I'd been, but it wasn't her business.

'How badly is he hurt?'

'I don't know. They're still doing tests.'

'He's conscious then?'

'He was a little while ago.'

'I'll come down.'

'I'll wait,' she said dully. She wanted me to come.

It took less than half an hour in the middle of the night with next to no traffic on the road, most of the lights in my favour and no one to see me ignore the others. Allison was waiting in the main foyer; she wasn't dressed for an occasion, but she was still a stunning sight. It was difficult to believe that, under whatever false pretences, for a short period she and I had been lovers.

'They've just taken him back to his room. They've given him an injection. He told me to come down and see if you were here yet. Come on.' She led the way to the lifts. 'I don't know if they'll still let him speak to you. What was it, Dave? What's it about?' She no longer sounded angry but I knew her well enough to avoid an answer which might amount to an admission that I had involved him in anything.

'Maybe he wants me to find the mugger?'

'Oh, right, highly likely; what're you going to use for a weapon this time?'

I replied with like sarcasm. 'Who knows, Ali; maybe I set him up so you'd get in touch?'

We proceeded in silence: further exchanges were unlikely to help either of us get over the strain of seeing the other again.

There was a nurse outside the door of Martin's room, talking to a uniformed police officer. They watched us expectantly as we came down the corridor.

'Dave Woolf, solicitor and friend,' I introduced myself. 'Is he still conscious? Can I see him?'

'He's conscious; he's resisting the injection; he wants to talk to you,' the nurse said. 'The doctor said I should let you go in; it'll be better if he goes under peacefully.'

'How badly is he hurt?'

'He's taken a beating,' the policeman answered. 'He's got a couple of broken ribs, and a fractured leg. He's been hit pretty badly about the face,' he warned me what to expect. 'He's tough but concussion's a possibility. He says he doesn't know anything about his attackers but it does seem, well, he wanted to see you so badly ... If you learn anything, sir, please tell me.'

'Sure, absolutely,' I swore on my father's grave. The one he didn't yet occupy.

Allison came in with me, but as soon as Martin saw her he shook his head as emphatically as he was able and she withdrew without argument. She was more shook up than I had realised.

He could hardly speak. His head was heavily bandaged and his mouth could only barely open. They'd left his nose uncovered though; current thinking is in favour of open wounds. It might be good for the patient, but I wished they'd spare a thought for his visitor. The rest of his body was hidden by a tent-like construction. I sat close so he could whisper. Now that I had arrived he had stopped fighting the effects of the drugs they had given him and was already starting to slip into unconsciousness. He spoke in shorthand.

'Had warn you. Call … Said friend Tony …' Tony Galucci was his former partner. It was a clever ploy —Martin was bound to be interested. It told me whoever had organised the call was extremely well-informed in certain, criminal respects, but that didn't come as a surprise anymore. And if they knew about Galucci, they also knew that Cross Course didn't trade anymore. 'Baron's Court … Two them … Jumped me … Special service … Said I getting a special service … What I'd asked for … D'you unn'stan?' I nodded. He wasn't asking me to explain. He understood too. 'Be careful, Dave. Look out for … self.'

'Don't worry about me. I'm sorry, Martin; sorry this happened; sorry I got you into it.'

But he was finally asleep and could no longer hear me.

I wasn't worried. I hadn't liked to say so: it would have sounded I'm-alright-Jack. The fact that they knew about his attempt to get a special service for a client — of the sort they had a monopoly on — didn't implicate me. I was supposed to be on the other side and therefore untainted. Allison was entitled to be angry. I'd let him take my fall. The only comfort was that he hadn't suffered worse, even terminal, harm; after what Lewis and Malcolm had told me, it's what I would have expected.

CHAPTER SEVEN

Monday started badly and ended worse.

I arrived at the office to find Detective Inspector Running Dog waiting for me with his new handler, a beetroot-faced sweating primeval beast whom he introduced as Sergeant Wadd, and who hovered threateningly over the weasel-featured Dowell like Pisa over a souvenir stand.

'Waddayawant?' I punned cruelly.

'Let's talk inside,' Tim Dowell said.

'You got a warrant?'

'Fuck it, Dave. You think I've got nothing better to do than hang around listening to your insults?'

'Tell me about it!' I relented. 'Come in. Don't sit down,' I added too late.

'Dave, you're in trouble again,' he announced without permission or preamble.

'Me? I've come back to work at Nichol & Co. This you can see for yourself. You may therefore believe it. How could I be in trouble?' I was still standing behind my desk.

'I don't know,' he admitted. 'But last night someone fire-bombed a basement flat in Earl's Court. Fortunately it was empty — the last tenant had recently quit and it hadn't been relet. It probably needed fumigating. Now who do you suppose the bomb was gift-wrapped for, Dave?'

I sat down with a thump they may have heard in Earl's Court if anyone'd been listening.

'What are you working on, Dave?'

There was a hint of concern seasoning his pan-fried duty.

'How'd you hear about it, Tim?' I played for time while I waited for my stomach to re-settle.

'You're flagged to me,' he shrugged, like I shouldn't be surprised. I wasn't. 'The landlord gave your name to the officers on scene and when it went through the computer I was automatically notified.'

'Was anyone hurt?' A fire could easily spread upstairs even in one of those well-constructed, older buildings.

'No. A fire-bomb does most of the damage when it goes off; it's not like deliberate arson. What are you working on, Dave? You're going to tell me.' He sat back in his chair and put his feet on my desk. He wasn't going to move till I did.

I cast a glance at Wadd.

'Wait outside, Walter,' he said.

I could barely wait until he'd shut the newly-repaired door before I exclaimed, 'Walter? Walter Wadd? Wally Wadd?' His previous assistant had been named Pratt. 'Do their parents give them these names because they want them to become policemen or do they become policemen because of their names?'

'Are you going to tell me what you're working on now?' When I didn't answer, he said, 'Let me put it another way. What are you going to do about it, Dave?'

'Do? I'm going to find someone to kick and I'm going to keep on kicking him and whoever comes after until something or someone breaks. What the fuck do you think I'm going to do?' I asked indignantly. I was a grown up now, with grown up responsibilities: it was the way grown ups always behaved.

'You, Dave,' he sounded like Lewis. 'Kick?'

'Well, er, maybe not me, but — you haven't met Carson yet. She's my new — well, sorry, — side-kick.'

'So tell me what it's about.'

'There's, well, a couple of teeny tearaways — sort of minor hoodlums — who I think believe I'm getting a bit too close to a bit of muscle they didn't ought to flex. 'Member Martin Mather?' At least I now knew why he had suffered no worse than a beating; they, correctly, didn't consider him the main man. 'He's been helping me out; he took a thumping last night. He's in the Charing Cross.'

He pondered this information. He knew Martin Mather almost as well as I did. He also knew that Martin was no pushover. The reason Dowell had booked him for murder was mainly because he was the only involved party with the physical strength to turn the corpse's head through an exact one hundred and eighty degrees. If Martin had been beaten that badly, Tim understood we were dealing with some extreme nasties. He played for time in turn.

'Does this place serve coffee?'

'Sure.' I rang for two cups for us and a plastic beaker for Wadd in case he dropped it. A few minutes later, coffee came in carried by the senior partner. She beamed at Dowell: 'Hallo, Tim. I told Dave he ought to give you a ring.'

'You're pregnant,' he accused, accepting a cup of coffee and kissing her on the cheek at the same time. Once, they'd held hands across a hospital bed I was lying in the middle of. Between them, they had put me there; left to myself, I would've been lying in a coffin. I hadn't yet fully forgiven either of them. 'Who by?'

'Wonderful, wonderful. No one believes I've gone back to lawyering; no one believes I could get Sandy pregnant.'

'What's new, Tim?' she asked.

He caught my warning grimace and said, 'I'm waiting to be told.'

'He's in over his head this time; he'd better tell you; if he doesn't, come see me.' She left us boys to our plots

'Tearaways? Hoodlums?' he prompted.

'Tee hee. Ho, hum.' I gulped my coffee down still too hot. It helped bring a little colour back into my cheeks. 'Uh, yes, well.' I didn't want to tell him, because I knew how he'd react. 'Er, they're called Reddin.'

'What the fuck? You stupid schmuck.'

'It's schmuck as in cook,' I corrected, 'But otherwise not far off. Listen, I didn't know what I was going up against; I've got a client, paying me a lot of money. Though if I'd've known who was at the other end of the piece of string, I'd've asked for double.' Which was exactly what Orbach had offered.

'Who client?'

'Privileged,' I said automatically.

'You're crazy, Dave. What're you in the middle of — an East London mob-war? Who's hired you? Them to fight for the other side?'

I stared unhappily past his head at the door to my room; maybe I could make a run for it, and just keep on running. He was right. I was crazy.

'Uh, you know, lotta money; and, well, I suppose you could say — lotta case.' I was going to tell him. Despite myself. 'It's not mobs. Bent judge. Red judge.'

'Who?' he rasped.

'Ah. Why don't you tell me?'

I meant — go out and see what you can come back with; then we'll trade.

'What makes you think you'll be here to tell? I take it you've got nothing hard to trace last night back to Reddins?'

'Just a good hard hunch. Was it bad, Tim?'

'Yup.' The monosyllable was intended to tell me that I wouldn't be alive if I'd been in at the time. I felt sad for the flat in which I'd spent so many years; then I felt curiously glad — no one else could live in it after me.

'What'd you do if I could make my case?' My case was Pulleyne; the Reddins were his. A lawyer to catch a lawyer and etcetera.

'As much as they let me,' he shrugged. His brief last time had been to spray air freshener upon the flatulence of a powerful, well-connected Freemason. I hadn't been awfully amused; I'd wanted him taken to trial. 'I'll go see Mather' That didn't worry me; Martin didn't need to be warned not to talk to Dowell. 'Who else is involved?'

'No one.' I couldn't tell him Justin Papworth; he would give up Orbach as soon as say hallo. I didn't count cushion Cushing. He was on the other side and ranked with Pulleyne as a name only available in trade.

'At any time — this is on the record Dave — at any time you're prepared to turn it over to me, I can arrange protection. For you and Sandy. It can't be long before they catch up. Think of her, Dave; her and the baby.'

'I do, Tim.' I meant it. I was thinking of them almost as much as I was thinking of myself. Nonetheless, 'You remember what you accused me of last time I saw you?'

He grinned sheepishly. 'Playing the cowboy, you mean? A man's gotta do. That?' It didn't sound so stupid at the time.

'Yeah, sure. Well, you see, I haven't changed.'

'No, he sighed, 'I didn't think you would've.'

'That's it?'

'That's it,' Carson confirmed. 'That's the shiny bright headquarters of hamlet-famous Reddin enterprises.'

'The Shell Building it ain't.' The Shell Building it wasn't: the Reddins operated from a warehouse/office prefab in Forest Gate. We were parked a hundred yards down the road.

'What d'you want to do? Go in and beard them?

'You crazy, Carson? I'd like them to think I'm Kentucky Fried for a while longer yet.'

'I could go.' When she was tense, her Australian accent got much more pronounced.

'What are you going to say? You going to walk in, say hi, how're you doing, what're you doing? Hope your hair-style scares them?' It was probably our best bet.

Obviously it was precisely what she intended, as she couldn't find a sarcastic answer. The profound intellectual power of my argument must have persuaded her because she shifted gear. 'We need another sting.'

I shook my head. 'I'm still smarting from the last one. No. We need a whole new angle. We've gone in from one end, and come up against a brick wall. So let's review the problem as a whole and see what other ways into the maze there might be.'

She understood exactly what I meant. 'It's a bit early for a drink but all right.'

Before we could move, the doors on both sides of the car swung open simultaneously. What looked in the instant like two times two pounds of meatloaf reached in and drew us out like a pair of potato chips. I couldn't see her, nor she me. We were both concentrating on our new dance partners; we were about to be led around the floor.

'Wot are you doing 'ere?' mine growled. "Oo are you?'

'What's it to you?' I played for time, waiting for Carson to put her much-vaunted martial arts into practice, chagrined to realise that he was at least three inches shorter than me and about half my weight.

He drew me down by my jacket lapels towards his unshaven, sweaty face, vinegary breath billowing from his mouth and nostrils into mine. I'd rather he hit me than kissed me. Across the car similar intercourse was in play, but I imagined her orang-outang was more scared of being kissed by Carson.

'I said 'oo are you?' he repeated. "Oo are you, 'oo are you, oo are you?' He said it over and over again as he bounced me back and forth against the car.

'We're from the council,' I squeaked. 'We're from the local council.' Since he found it necessary to say everything four times, I thought I'd say it twice to give him half a chance to understand.

He was troubled by my answer. It wasn't one he expected.

'Look, I've got identification. In the car. Let me show you?'

He thought about this for a while. Carson still hadn't gone into action. Maybe she needed anti-freeze. He let go of my lapels and nodded. I ducked into the car and poked around in the glove compartment. After a second, I slid right inside and called out: 'Where's the ID, Carson? I can't find it.'

Her jackal presumably didn't resist as she pulled free and leaned back in to help me search for what wasn't there. I had one hand through the wheel next to the key. I whispered, 'On three.'

Her scared eyes registered. I counted off. In unison we kicked our doors backwards and she jumped in as I turned the key, blessing my garage out loud when the engine caught immediately. I stuck the stick into first and rammed down hard on the pedal. The hoods grabbed the doors and hung on as I tore away. Hers let go first and the door slammed shut on the bumper of another car; instinctively I swerved, sending my guy tumbling. I grabbed at my own door and pulled it shut — you wanna know what a respray costs? Just as we were about to turn the corner, I heard a bang and the rear window shattered.

I kept on driving. It wasn't a gun. The guy who'd held her up had flung a tyre-iron straight through it and it lay now in the back in a flood of glass. It wasn't till we rejoined the main road that I slowed down. I wished my heart would too.

Out of the corner of my eye I could see her biting down hard on her lower lip, hard near to bleed, like she was trying to keep everything inside from bursting out. I asked, 'What happened to all that karate and stuff, for chrissake?'

'I never said I finished the course, did I?'

We were both still giggling nervously when, a couple of miles further on, I saw — like an oasis in the desert —a sign that read 'Car Windows' bang next door to a VW centre. I pulled in.

A West Indian came out of the office: 'Closed f'lunch.' Then he saw the condition of the car. He walked around it twice in complete silence. He said, 'Open again. Pub that way.' He pointed to the next corner. 'Key.' He held out his hand. I gave it to him through my window and leaned back against the head-rest. What I really wanted was sleep.

It was nearly five before we finally emerged, three halves pissed, taking full advantage of the new licensing laws which allow pubs to stay open all day like every other civilised country in the world.

Part-way through, I went back to collect the car; there was nothing on the back seat but the tyre-iron, wrapped in yesterday's *Daily Mirror*. There was no way to tell what had happened to the window. I settled up in cash and courteously omitted to ask for a receipt. As I got back into the car to drive it around the corner, he said nonchalantly, 'Damn council, damn roads, all sorts things fly up 'n hit the car. Hey?'

I smiled wanly. 'Right. Damn council.'

But he'd given me an idea.

'We need something to fly up off the road, Carson, that's what we need.'

She looked at me bleerily like I wasn't making sense and hiccoughed.

'The biddy's got a daughter, a dyke. You know, lezzie, lezbo ...'

'Yeah, yeah. And I've gotta coupla bull friends'll take your two queens apart. Which biddy?'

'Pulleyne. Daughter: Julia. Disenfranchised. She must be, oh, thirty-two, thirty-three, lives or lived with another woman. She was up at Oxford, dropped out, had a kid by who knows who or what or how and maybe she doesn't, gave it up for adoption to go live with her girlfriend who doesn't like kids, and daddy — her daddy, that is, not the kid's — doesn't love her quite the way he used to any more.'

'Then she'll hardly be in his confidence, will she, ducky?'

I winced. I was supposed to be her boss. She was supposed to show me unrelenting respect.

'Right. But for one thing she's an embarrassment to him and for another who knows what she knows from way back when, which maybe she feels the same about him as he feels about her and will be more than happy to talk about. Find her, Carson, good dog, find her and let's talk to her.'

'You or me?'

'Find her first. Find out all you can, about her and her fairy friend.'

She looked at me curiously and asked: 'Are lezzies fairies too?'

I had to confess. I didn't know.

I dropped her back in town and parked near the Temple. The damage to my car-door reminded me I hadn't yet dealt with Papworth and he was entitled to a warning. Though it was already six o'clock I was confident he would still be at work. He was not.

'Ah, yes, Mr Woolf,' said Michael dryly. 'Another brief for us have we, sir?'

'Er, no. I thought Mr Papworth might be in — any chance of a quick word?'

'No, sir. Mr Papworth isn't in. Mr Papworth is unwell, sir. He's not expected in for a while, sir. He spoke to me and suggested you might like your brief back. I understand there's to be no charge for the work to date.' There was more to come; I waited patiently. 'Mr Cushing, sir, also mentioned you might be in. He was under the impression you might want Mr Mather's brief back as well. I've got them both here. Here you are, sir.' He thrust them at me as if they smelled. Which, of course, they did.

I looked up Papworth's telephone number, but there was no answer. I drove to his home, and there was no one in. Neither surprised me in the light of what his clerk had done: the last thing a clerk ever gives to one side's solicitor is a brief containing the papers delivered to counsel by the other side. Everyone who mattered knew everything that mattered. I only went on looking for Papworth out of habit, like a chicken without its head — he didn't need warning.

Driving north I thought: not bad, even by Orbach's standards. One hospitalised, a flat fire-bombed, a car badly damaged, and a career in ruins. And all of it had happened to people who were on his own side. It was time to ask him why.

He seemed genuinely surprised to see me. Fortunately, the outrageous infant was over the road playing with her friend again so he let me in.

'I hope this is important. You've got ten minutes maximum.'

'Gee, it's nice to feel welcome. Yes it's important, Russel. Anything that nearly gets me cremated without my consent is important. Someone fire-bombed my flat last night.'

'I thought you'd moved out?'

'That's why I'm still rare steak. They didn't know I'd gone, but they knew everything else.'

'But I don't,' he reminded me calmly: he'd refused to be told.

'I want a drink, Russel.'

'You've had enough,' he retorted.

'Yeah? You also wanna know about two thugs with more muscles than you've got brains or I've got beauty who tried to take down me and my, er, assistant merely for passing the time of day admiring the architecture of their bosses' warehouse? And when we declined to hang about and discuss it with them flung a tyre-iron through the back window of my Passat? You'll be getting a bill for that, and for damage to the nearside door, and you dare quibble 'cos I forgot to ask for a receipt and I'll tyre-iron you.'

At last he looked like he believed me. Enough to fetch me a drink. My suspicion of him began to subside; he'd bought in a bottle of the best.

In as few words as I could muster I brought him up to date. I told him: I didn't care whether or not he wanted to hear; I wasn't offering a choice. I outlined the scam and the extent to which it had been successful before — the way I saw it — someone somewhere decided to check out whether Martin Mather was as crooked as he claimed. It was Cushing, presumably, who had told the Reddins about the approach, belatedly but better than never.

Orbach shook his head. 'No. Not late. If Cushing was going to check — and I'm sure he did — he would have done so before the case got into court. You have to ask why they let it run that far before they reacted.'

'I thought Pulleyne might be going back to crime, so they had to get it on in a hurry and took the risk.'

He shook his head again. 'Pulleyne's sitting in Queen's Bench for most of the rest of the term. They're shorthanded since Bowne died and Kline was promoted to the Court of Appeal.' It is an oddity of the English legal system, or an acknowledgment that they need the talent, that at least half the High Court and Court of Appeal bench is Jewish.

'Why d'you think then?' He was supposed to be the brains; Carson was the brawn, I was the elegant flab.

He frowned as he pondered the puzzle but, incapable of admitting 'I don't know', finally came up with a possibility: 'It bends Pulleyne a bit further over the barrel.'

'Come again?'

'If they reacted before the case was heard, and in effect stopped it happening, Pulleyne was wholly out of it, uninvolved; by letting it go one step further, he's at least potentially implicated in what came after.'

I was about to say that it all sounded a bit too clever by half when I remembered to whom I was talking, and the sort of people we were talking about. The Reddins — for all their emphasis on muscle — had nonetheless enjoyed the foresight, presumably years ago when they knew Pulleyne as their counsel, to put him into their pocket. They also controlled Cushing. It put them on a par with the city financial analysts who saw well ahead of time the trend towards American economics in the UK and, correspondingly, an American attitude to related professional activities. I had under-estimated Hackney Marsh from the outset.

'What comes next?' he asked.

'You want to go on with this, Russel? Do you really want to? Why? How much of this did you know before, or even suspect? What else have you got up your sleeve? I'm not going on blind, Russel; I'm not even sure I'm going on at all.' I was bluffing; he knew I would as well as I did and Dowell did. 'Listen, Russel, you don't know this, but Sandy's going to have a kid, my kid,' I pre-empted the usual sarcastic question. 'I wanna be around to see it. Just think, a whole new person who's never heard any of my jokes before!'

On cue, his girl let herself in the front door. He used the excuse to avoid an answer and went to help her off with her coat. I heard them talking in the hall, then she came in and said hallo to me while Russel went down into the kitchen.

'Hi. How're you?' I asked. I was practising how to talk with little people.

'You're Dave.' She didn't remember; Orbach had reminded her. 'Are you going to eat with us again?' She emphasised the last word. For the second time, I thought how nice it was to feel welcome.

'No. I've got my own home to go to. My, er, my wife's going to have a baby, you know. Maybe you'll be friends?'

'That's stupid,' she observed astutely, 'it'll be far too young.'

Russel saved me from further humiliation. He emerged from the kitchen carrying a tray with a glass of milk and a pack of chocolate biscuits on it. I hoped they weren't for me. He explained:

'Frankie's going to watch television in my study for a bit so we can talk. But we mustn't be long, must we, Frankie?'

She shrugged. She didn't care; she'd probably prefer watching TV and eating biscuits to dinner with Russel. I know I would.

When he returned, he poured himself a drink — his first — and topped up mine without needing to be asked.

'I obviously suspected there had to be something or someone serious involved and I admit it occurred to me that the Reddins might be it. My guess is Pulleyne took top-up money from them when he was at the bar and since then they've been squeezing him. I don't know where or when Cushing came in. I don't know how widely they use Pulleyne or how widespread the problem is. He might not be the only judge involved; they might not be the only villains either.'

What he told me I could have guessed for myself.

'It doesn't say why you want to pursue it though.' I sipped my drink. As I had been drinking solidly since about midday I ought by then to have been semi-comatose but I was sober as a judge; the alcohol was stopping me choking up from within It numbed the internal tension generated by the day's two attacks. Oh, yeah, and by the one on Saturday night on Martin Mather too. Probably.

'What do you think would happen if the establishment suspected what was going on, Dave? If they even get a whisper they'll whisk Pulleyne off the bench so fast he won't have time to change his robes. He'll be put where it doesn't matter: the Law Commission, the Court of Human Rights, somewhere totally irrelevant. It'll be brushed under the carpet like your Mather's affair but quicker and even more firmly. They'll nip it in the bud at the stage before anything can be said with sufficient certainty to publish or — most important of all — to generate pressure for a prosecution. Actual prosecution itself is out of the question, they'll never let it happen —they couldn't.'

'You want it sewn up so they can't bury it?'

'Something like that,' he said elliptically. 'Don't you?'

I knew what he meant. Neither of us belonged to the English establishment. Tim Dowell once said as we boozed at Lewis' club during Disraeli Chambers before our credit was cut off that I identified with Orbach because we were both outsiders. Orbach's estrangement had led him to triumph from within, to sneer at them from the heights of their own institutions; my reaction had been to poke a finger at the whole circus, stuff my nose with cocaine and hide away in my now burnt-out basement flat. Nonetheless, we had trained as lawyers, we had worked as lawyers, and some feeling for the law survived our contempt for its proprietors.

'I suppose I do or I wouldn't go on. Not even for the money. But I'm ambivalent. I'm scared, and I'm not convinced that however much evidence we get they won't still find a way to cover it up. By the way, Dowell knows: not Pulleyne's name, nor yours of course, but what I'm up to. I had to tell him,' I tailed off lamely. After a second, I added defiantly, 'Well, maybe I didn't have to tell him but I was shaken up when he saw me about the flat and I did tell him, so there's not much we can do about it now.'

He didn't like it but my addition had forestalled attack or objection. He asked: 'Has he got enough to work on?'

'He's got Reddins and an invitation to trade information if he can get hold of any in exchange. It's worth finding out from our point of view just how widely known the situation is within worlds I don't have access to. But I don't think he'll be able to take it far unless we want him to.' This was a hunch — another hunch — and I hadn't yet fully worked out why.

However much Orbach didn't like my having told Dowell, he had already accepted it as a *fait accompli* and was thinking forward to how we might be able to use it.

'Keep in touch with him. Play it by ear but don't give him any of it without talking to me first.'

I nodded. He who pays the piper says who can sit and listen. 'Anyone else know?'

I shook my head: he didn't know, or know about, Lewis and I wasn't about to tell him. He was my edge. 'Well of course Sandy.'

He already knew about her because of the trip to France.

'And Carson. She's the assistant I mentioned.'

'That's up to you.' Assistants and employees, like clerks, aren't real people. 'What's your next move?'

'I've put Carson onto Pulleyne's daughter — there's a story in it but I don't know how it'll read; you want to find out what's happened to Papworth?' He was much better placed to pick up bar gossip.

'I'll let you know. What else?'

'I don't know.' I was suddenly very, very tired. 'Maybe we should see what their next move is. My guess is they didn't know who we were this morning. I doubt they got the licence-plate; I doubt they could read. Also, I wouldn't've thought they'd attack Sandy's house. One try is one thing and it was just me; they'll call down all hell if they try the same thing again with someone else involved.' I wished I felt as confident as I was trying to sound. 'I'm going home; I'll give you a call in a couple of days. When I've got an estimate on the car door.'

'You didn't ring Tim, did you? He came looking for you,' Sandy growled as I came through the door.

'How'd'you know?'

I was tired, too tired even to argue.

'Your landlord rang. He seemed to be worried about you. It wasn't difficult finding out why.'

'Ah.'

'How's Martin Mather?' I had told her only that he had been in an accident. 'Met with any more accidents — an accident in hospital perhaps? Have you eaten?' Heritage will out.

'No,' I admitted, 'not a thing. And, yes, I could eat a horse,' I was surprised to hear myself say.

'Well you can either go out and eat in a restaurant while you're looking for a hotel to sleep in or you can start telling me the truth. Right?'

There is a certain refreshing bluntness about Sandy's debating technique.

For the second time that evening, I told my tale. Her reaction surprised me.

'You've got to go on with it. There's no choice,' she said venomously. 'Can't you see? It makes a mockery of all our lives: well, maybe not yours,' she reclaimed her wit. 'You've managed that on your own. But the rest of us: what's the point been of everything I've ever done if it can be set aside by people like Pulleyne or the Reddins?'

I admitted my surprise, and how scared I was of continuing. She said, 'Don't get me wrong, I'm scared too; for you, for the baby, for me. I think, well, maybe we ought to move out of here for a bit, go and stay somewhere.' She waved away my objection that they wouldn't try the same thing twice. 'Maybe, maybe not. You wanna gamble on it? At the very least you ought to stay somewhere else for a bit; I agree next time they'll try to make sure that they've got the right place first; it'll take them a bit of time to find out this address and it wouldn't be a big deal to put it about that we've already managed to have another row and you've moved out again. Anyone'd believe that,' she added unnecessarily. 'We can find somewhere for you.'

'Where?' My brain was tired; my body was tired; I wanted to focus on the unimportant, undemanding details instead of the awesome issue itself.

Sandy wasn't to be distracted. 'That doesn't matter; we can think about it tomorrow. But it does matter you should go on with it, it's too important to stop.' Her eyes shone: I was finally engaged as an investigator in a case and a cause that she could respect. Ironies would never cease. 'Just one thing: you've got to trust Tim — don't trust Orbach at all, and if push comes to shove sell him out to Tim.'

I shrugged, 'I know what you're saying about Russel; but don't forget what Tim did at Mather's; he's the sweeper-upper; he said that once — he was just sweeping-up after someone else's party.'

'Yes,' she said softly, 'but don't you forget either: his insistence on sweeping it under the carpet is probably ninety-nine per cent of why you're still in one piece. I told you, Dave, I want to do this right,' she patted her sexily swollen belly.

'Me too. How about some food?'

'Right,' she rose from the sofa with difficulty. 'One more thing: if we're going to find you somewhere to stay, it ain't a licence to stray. Right?' She gripped my arm like a vice. 'Right?' she repeated.

'Right,' I conceded while I still had two arms with which to fend off anyone else who was interested. I wondered where Sandy had plans to put me.

The telephone rang. She said: 'I'd better get it. And if it's Allison Hoyt I'm going to tell her I won't let you come out to play — even if she's in hospital herself,' she added tartly. She was well aware how close Ali and I had been during too much of Mather's. She'd still be well aware of it when we were ninety-five.

I said, 'Use the recorder.' Sandy had an answering machine that doubles as a tape recorder for conversations you want to keep without anyone knowing.

I heard her answer suspiciously: 'Hallo?' Then: 'He's not here. He isn't staying here any more. Who is this?' She looked worried; I was too. 'Yes, I can give him a message but not till I get to the office tomorrow. No, I don't know where he's staying.' I wished I could lie as fluently as she has always been able to do. 'Oh, God,' her voice dropped and began to break. 'Oh, God, no.' She handed me the 'phone. 'It's Malcolm, Dave. Lewis is dead.'

CHAPTER EIGHT

Tuesday afternoon, I got a telephone call at the office. This was more surprising for a solicitor than it might seem. I wasn't supposed to be working as such.

The call came from Caroline Pulleyne.

'I thought you'd be in the States by now?'

'I'm flying over after the weekend. I want to speak to you before I go.'

Hm.

'I was thinking about lunch,' she added, before I could suggest a long, loving lie-in.

'OK.' I'd take her whenever I could. 'Tell you what, come to my club.'

'I, well, uh, maybe that wouldn't be, you know, such a great idea.'

I laughed, adding, 'I don't think it's the sort of club where you'll bump into anyone you know. And when I say "my" club, I don't mean a club I belong to; it's mine; I own it.'

I gave her the address on the Old Brompton Road and we fixed for Friday. The funeral was on Wednesday; things would be near back to normal.

To say that I owned the club was in strict law correct; it was in every other respect a lie. Lewis had left a handwritten will, and one he had based entirely on legal advice he had snatched from me in bits and bobs when I was drunk, without my realising they were his own affairs he was gradually putting into what, if it ever came to court, no Chancery lawyer would ever describe as order.

His will began:

'THIS WILL is made by me LEWIS ALEXANDER ALTONSPRITZER being of sound mind but a bit overweight and I don't think I've got long to go. I'm not sorry. I've had a good time. Know what I mean?' It was dated not a month before.

'Altonspritzer? Alexander? No wonder he never let anyone call him anything but Lewis.'

Malcolm smiled pathetically and went behind the bar. We were alone. Sandy had wanted to come with me, but after some hesitation we agreed she would be safer staying in. I rang Tim at home in Ealing and told him about Lewis; also, that I would move out of Sandy's within a day or so; he promised to ring the local station and ask them to keep an occasional eye on her house in the meantime.

The problem was that Malcolm McCafferty—as I for the first time learned was his last name — would not be able to obtain a licence to run the club until his conviction had been spent; it would be a while yet before he could legally claim to have no criminal record. Without a licence the club didn't exist — he would have to sell it.

Lewis' solution, squeezed out of me god knows how long before, had been to set up a secret trust. The club had been left to me in the will without qualification but in a private letter, of which Malcolm had the original, he explained that once the conviction had expired, I was expected to transfer it to him outright. As a matter of law I would have no choice but to do so. In the meantime, Malcolm would run it and keep the profits.

Well, most of the profits.

'I ought to add something about how I trust you and you've been my friend but I'm not that good with words in writing. I've left a little something for your nipper in the will proper, and I'm sorry I shan't get to see it. If it's a girl, call her after me. If it's a boy, give him a kiss. Tell your Sandy I liked her and she's too good for you. The other part of all this is so long as you own the club, you get to drink free. I thought it was better this way than leaving you some money. You'd only piss it away. Know what I mean?'

The 'little something' was ten thousand pounds. It was a lot more than the Passat I'd be passing on. I was glad there were only the two of us in the club and that the lights were dim.

The other major bequest was an annuity to Danny's mother whom he'd been supporting since Danny's undignified demise. Apart from minor gifts everything else, — 'the reservoir of my estate' as he called it — went as expected to Malcolm. Malcolm came out from behind the bar with a bottle of champagne.

'He'd be angry at anything else.'

'Not if he was paying.'

'Well, he isn't. I am. Or you are. I don't know. Which is it? What do you think?'

'Is there any family alive to challenge it?'

Not that he ever mentioned. There aren't any Altonspritzers in the 'phone book.' This was not a surprise.

He'd put a tape on the cassette player while he was behind the bar but I'd only been half-listening. In response to a screech from the speakers I shrieked back: 'What the hell is that?'

'Opera. Mozart. Sometimes after everyone was gone he'd sit here in the dark, listening for hours.'

'It's awful.' I gulped my drink.

'Yes. But it's art. That's what he said.'

Suddenly he lurched over the table and started to bawl. I didn't know what to do. I filled his glass and pushed it towards him but his head was on his folded arms and he didn't see it.

'Here, Malcolm, here.'

He looked up, still not seeing the glass but, hearing what I said, put his arms around my neck across the table and wept against my shoulder instead, knocking the glass onto the floor without noticing or caring. I only just caught mine in time. It wasn't what I'd meant but there was nothing I could do about it. I patted his head awkwardly until his sobs subsided and he sniffed back his tears.

'He was like a father to me,' he explained.

I stifled a wry remark about incest.

'You're not gay, are you, Dave?'

'Uh, no.' I shuffled my chair backwards — fine time to make a pass.

'Don't worry.' My reaction amused him. 'I meant, you don't understand.' I shook my head. 'With an older man, it's like being a kid again, like when you're a little boy and you climb on your dad's knee and hug him and he's warm and rough and smells of booze and most of all he's big, so big you know no harm can ever come to you. Which isn't what it's about when you grow up.'

'You never met my father. If I climbed onto his knee, he'd knock rent off my pocket-money.'

'When I met Tom,' his current lover, 'Lewis was never angry. I suppose he knew it'd happen sometime, like growing up.' Actually, Malcolm had done a straight — well, direct — reversal of roles: I'd met Tom; he didn't look old enough to be legal, but twice as cute. I'm not sure what my answer would have been if Tom, instead of Malcolm, had asked me if I was gay.

'You still haven't told me what happened.' It was way past time to change the subject.

'Right. I'll get us another bottle, shall I?'

I shrugged: 'It's your profits, Malcolm.'

'You'll do it, then?'

I am a Jew; he a Scot. We had our priorities. I said, 'Yes. But there's things to work out. Books to keep; I don't want to find I'm liable for a whole lot of tax on money I never saw or for people who accidentally fall down the steps after they fail to pay their bill. You can't even formally be the manager, so we'll have to hire someone clean.' I'd have to set up a holding company. 'I'll have to charge for the time I put into organising it all.'

'Fair enough. It's not that long, anyway: five more years.'

I scowled. 'Only five? I'll be hard-pressed to get more out of it than my kid does.'

'You'll manage. I'll put these on your tab.'

We raised our glasses.

'Lewis,' we said simultaneously and solemnly. 'Lewis,' a voice said from the doorway.

We swivelled around — Malcolm angry, me scared: he had relocked the door downstairs after I arrived.

It was Dowell. He was tie-less and unshaven, in a mood for a wake and holding up an empty hand as if he was clutching a glass.

'Welcome to my club,' I said. 'Have a drink on the house.'

His eyebrows shot through the roof. 'Your club?'

"Till Malcolm's conviction is spent.'

'Ah. Is that legal?'

He fetched himself a glass from behind the bar. 'I don't know. Is it?'

'I'm sorry about Lewis, Malcolm,' he offered his free hand.

'It was quick,' he said curtly, but accepted the handshake. He didn't trust Tim; well, no one in their right mind trusted Tim; but he didn't know him — not like I did, and Lewis had.

'How'd you get in?'

Tim held up his picks. It was his proud boast there was no door in London he couldn't get through in five minutes without needing to knock it down. He'd broken into both my home and Sandy's office. He would patiently explain that as he had no intention of stealing or damaging anything, what he did was only a civil wrong for which we could sue, not a crime for which he could be prosecuted; and he didn't do it when he was looking for evidence to use in court. In those cases, he kicked the door in to support his claim to have entered in an emergency to prevent a crime in progress and 'stumbled upon' the evidence 'by accident'.

Malcolm was grudgingly impressed.

'Is it?' I repeated.

'If no one knows about it, I should think so.' He wasn't going to tell. 'Of course, if anyone did know about it, they'd expect to be able to drink free any time they came by.'

Malcolm groaned, 'First him, now you. There won't be any profit.'

'It's a tough life. Besides, he left enough else.'

'What do you mean?' I asked when Malcolm didn't.

His will had not listed his assets other than the club. 'Well, let's see. There's his houses, of course.' 'Houses? Plural?'

'Then there's a row of shops in Fulham. There's a boat. There's a villa in Spain.'

'Sicily,' Malcolm muttered. 'He sold the one in Spain and bought in Sicily instead. Said he liked the food better, but he wanted everyone to think he had Mafia connections.'

'Costa Nostra?' I quipped.

Tim grinned but it escaped Malcolm.

'How'd'you know so much about it, Inspector?'

'Lewis and I go way back. Went. I always liked to keep a close eye on him. Never knew when it might be useful.'

Dowell's capacity for information he could use as a lever never ceased to amaze me. Lewis liked to know things others didn't but if he used them it was in self-defence or to help a friend — like me — not for the sake of power itself. Dowell had said that Orbach and I had things in common: maybe him too.

Dowell recited: 'Massive coronary; here at the club; no witnesses, no one present; twenty minutes for the ambulance to get here, five minutes from here to St Stephen's. They say he went out like a light. Not even time for a final blow-job so far as I can see.'

'You're a pig, Tim,' I glanced at Malcolm to see how he was taking it. To my surprise, he was grinning widely. 'You rang the hospital?'

'Yup. Now, who was with him?'

'The police said they weren't interested,' Malcolm said.

'They're not; I am.'

'Why, Tim?' I asked.

'I don't know yet. But he's a friend of yours, and it's a hell of a coincidence, wouldn't you say?'

'Oh, come on, Tim.' I splashed more champagne into all our glasses and over half the table. 'Lewis was due to go: he was showing all the signs; overweight, memory fading, irrational actions — like giving me a cheque for the kid.'

'He's right,' Malcolm said suddenly. 'It's not coincidence.' He looked at Dowell questioningly. 'I'm not making a statement, am I?'

'With that caterwauling on the radio I can't hear a word you're about to say. No wonder Lewis had a heart attack.'

'Tape,' I corrected unnecessarily. 'Malcolm?'

Saturday night, the night I was first partying at the Pulleynes' and subsequently making whoopee with Martin Mather, Lewis had received a couple of unexpected visitors. He told Malcolm about it afterwards. They wanted to know where to find me. What he told them was the same they could have found out from the 'phone book, but even if they knew how to read it wouldn't've been as much fun for them as forcing it out of a friend of mine. What he didn't tell them was that I had left the flat.

Malcolm said: 'He meant to ring you; he said he was going to; I suppose he forgot. He forgot a lot recently.' I'd been paid back for my own failure to ring Martin Mather before the weekend.

Last night — tonight — they'd come back. Malcolm was out for an hour. He returned soon after they arrived and heard about the shouting match in Lewis' office from a waitress a second before he could hear it for himself. He could guess why they were angry; the purpose of the parcel they'd left at my apartment had not been to permit my former landlord to redecorate courtesy of his insurance company. He was about to go in when the door burst open and they flew out of the room, throwing him to one side, and out of the club too soon for Malcolm to buzz down to one of the front door gorillas to stop them.

It was plain they hadn't touched him. He was still sitting at his desk slumped back in shock, but nothing was disturbed nor was he in any way marked or dishevelled. From what Malcolm had been able to make out, and from what all three of us could in any event be certain of, Lewis hadn't talked.

'Well, now,' I said softly, 'this puts a whole different complexion on things. It seems I've got a lot of scores to settle with someone.' I was working two cases: Orbach's and my own; whatever happened to Pulleyne was only of personal interest so far as it helped make something bad happen to the Reddins. I don't mean I wasn't scared: just that I had no choice.

'Dave,' Tim cautioned, 'leave this to me. We agreed: they're my case, you get the judge.'

'That was before,' I said with a lot less hesitation than I felt.

'You can't handle it; you're way out of your league. And don't start telling me about your Australian amazon.'

After her performance in Forest Gate the previous morning I wasn't about to. It wasn't necessary. Malcolm said, 'It's not out of my league, Dave. In fact, it's right up my street.'

What he said told me he was the man for me: he could mix a magnificent metaphor.

'This is yours?' Her mascara doubled the way I could remember her breasts doing when she breathed deeply on the beach.

'Well, sort of. It's been left me by a friend but I'm really holding it for someone else.'

'Till they grow up? Will they want it? It's a bit, uh, seedy.'

'You should see where I'm living.'

On the Tuesday afternoon, when finally I reached the office, hung-over from the private party Lewis had omitted to attend and before Caroline herself had rung, Carson had been in to see me.

'I hear you need a place to crash.'

My wits were dulled by want of sleep.

She said, 'Sandy suggested you might come and stay at our house for a bit.'

I groaned, 'But you're a squatter.'

The house she shared with an unknown number of other youngsters, all of whom probably wore their hair a different colour, was in Islington, belonged to the local council and had been left empty by them pending redevelopment proposals frozen by government spending cuts. The same sort of cuts that had caused the course she had attended. Carson was doing well out of cuts: the house had been taken over illegally but they were likely to be allowed to remain for two or more years yet.

I had not at that time visited. I imagined the worst. There would be holes in the roof, cardboard to cover up missing or broken glass, bare wires but no usable electricity, there might not even be plumbing. Milk would stand on the window-ledge half-way to yoghurt. Also, squatters don't wash. This is a well-known fact. They all take drugs and are constantly the subject of dawn raids by the police hoping to catch them in the middle of an orgy but content to cop the inevitable pair of uncovered tits. This is another well-known fact.

In the name of peace, harmony and anarchy squatters pass the time of day raping one another, pillaging and looting like Vikings of old. Since they have none themselves – which they are therefore happy to share – they do not believe that anyone else should own property. None of them work, even those in highly-paid employment. They draw social security in two or three names, none of them real. These, too, are also well-known facts. I keep stressing that I am only giving you the facts in case you think I'm prejudiced against squatters.

This was the sort of accommodation my loved one and the mother of my as yet unborn heir had selected for the period of my cower. It was difficult to discern whether it was to punish me, protect me or to prevent any penile-misplacement.

Carson sympathised, "Course, you'll have to do your share of the household chores. Let's see, you can have the Sunday rota for emptying the bog-buckets—they're always full after Saturday night. And on Tuesdays, you can cook stray dog over an open fire in the yard. Oh, yeah, Friday night'll be your turn to stay in your room in case anyone wants to avail themselves of your body. At least you'll get a good night's rest.'

'I, uh, well, you shouldn't take offence at this, Carson, but I've been thinking of staying in a hotel. It's very kind of you, but, well, you know, I don't think if I was staying in the same house as you ... You know ... It'd be very difficult to resist.' I smiled sweetly and added in tribute to the late Lewis: 'Know what I mean?'

The thing I like about Carson is the dual standard. She can dish it out, but she can't take it.

'Don't do me any favours. Find your own fucking accommodation.' She stormed out slamming the door. It had only just been repaired after our first encounter and there didn't seem to be much point having it repaired again.

That night, she came to Sandy's with me, where I collected a suitcase of clothing, and took me home with her after we'd eaten what would probably be my last hygenic, home-cooked meal for a while. Although I'd only been living full-time at Sandy's for a few weeks, I was downcast about leaving. I was going to miss the enormous expanse of taut-stretched skin lying beside me in the bed; I was going to miss lying out comfortably on the sofa watching TV while Sandy made my dinner; I was going to miss the fridge, the washing-machine, constant hot water, someone to do my ironing; I was going to miss Sandy for all the right reasons.

There was no one else in when we arrived. I couldn't form much of an impression from outside. The house was on Ambler Road just around the corner from Finsbury Park station, in such a depressed portion of Islington you could spit across the border into Hackney.

It was a three-storey terrace with a back-addition bathroom: the kitchen and what was used as a living room were on the middle floor. Carson shared the top two rooms with a friend whose sex and on what terms I still didn't know anything about. Another couple of friends shared the ground floor but one of them was doing academic work in Holland on sabbatical from his college and it was his room I was to use.

The interior was much cleaner than I had expected; it was in better condition than my old flat in Earl's Court, even before the fire. There were rugs on the bare floorboards; I stared long and hard at the mattress on the ground and nothing inside it moved; the door shut and only one pane of glass was cracked. A long trestle table ran the length of one wall, bearing a range of electronic equipment that I couldn't understand. Carson explained that the usual occupier was building his own computer from second-hand parts.

It took me a while to realise what was wrong: there were no curtains. I was in the front room, hidden from the street only by the overgrown privet on which I'd scratched my face as we came through the gate.

'Nick likes to wake up with the light,' she explained, 'don't you?' And left me to my public exposure.

I wondered now whether Caroline Pulleyne would like to lend me her house when she went to the States. Before I could ask, she announced: 'Henry's not coming with me. He's not coming over till the New Year.'

'How come?' I wondered what a flight to the States could cost.

'I don't know.' She fidgeted with her cocktail glass while we waited for our food. The club didn't serve much to eat at lunch-time: a selection of plain dishes that wouldn't distress the stomachs of the hung-over members who called in at that time of the day for a hair of the dog. It didn't serve much to eat in the evenings either. 'I thought you might tell me.'

'*Moi?*' I was still thinking of when I first saw her in France. 'Why me? I haven't seen Henry since your party.'

'Something's wrong, isn't it, Dave? With Martyn. You had a long talk with him on Saturday; he likes you, but you're not a close friend. I just had an idea he might've told you.'

'Have you asked Henry?'

'He won't admit anything's wrong; he says his office wants to keep him here for another month, but I don't believe him.'

'Why are you going to the States now?'

'That's part of why I don't believe him.' The waitress — one of my employees, ha ha — brought our meals. Caroline was having quiche and salad. She stared at her plate aghast; I could see why. The quiche looked like it'd been bought second-hand and the salad fished from a waste disposal plant. 'Can I have some wine?'

'Good idea.' It would dull the pain while I chewed my steak. I tried to snap my fingers for attention but it's something I've never been able to do and she had to do it for me. I ordered champagne, neither out of ostentation nor because I was entitled to drink for free, but because it was the only wine I thought might be reliable. 'So why do you think there's anything wrong?'

'Well, when he told me, I said, uh, I still wanted to go over before Christmas, you know, to spend it with my parents. That was the original idea, you see. He wasn't due to start till the New

Year anyway, but we were going to have some time in New York first and maybe do some skiing in Vermont together, too.'

I listened carefully, trying to spot the clue to what she wanted to tell me. It was well-hidden.

She went on: 'I thought there'd be an argument, but he didn't argue; he didn't argue at all. In fact, he encouraged me; said I should go after the weekend just as we'd planned. If it was anyone else, I'd think he had another woman.'

'No, I don't think so either.' I sometimes think Henry's pretty stupid but he's not mad. 'Why should this make you think there's something wrong with Martyn?'

'It's just part of it. Call it instinct. He's worried —Henry, I mean. He's spent two evenings with his father this week; that's not normal and he won't tell me why. Of course I've asked if Martyn's ill, or Isabelle, or if it's something to do with Julia, or investment difficulties, all the obvious things.'

'OK, fine, let's say something's wrong. Why me? As you say, I'm not close. I'm just a holiday friend, you know?'

She studied me with those big, brown, beautiful eyes as if she was trying to decide whether I was stupid, innocent or just lying. She explained: 'I was transferring names and numbers into a new 'phone book before leaving. When he came in on Monday night I said, "Shall we put Dave and Sandy under W or N?" He went white then red like he was about to burst but he wouldn't answer or explain. That's what made me think somehow you knew something. I don't know. How'm I doing?' she asked impishly, raising her glass. 'You're some kind of detective, aren't you? Am I detecting well?'

'Not bad. But now of course you're going to have to tell me how you knew about my detecting.' Like it was a shameful habit. Which maybe it is.

She pursed her lips.

'Henry found out about it a few weeks after we came back from France. His bank used to use Mather's, the solicitors, for quite a lot of their work, but they moved, of course, when everything broke up. You came up in that connection and Henry worked out that Dave Nichol was Dave Woolf, if you see what I mean.'

'Did he tell his father?'

'Sure. I'm sure he did. Why? Is it a big deal?'

'No, just, you know, uh, now I'm back in practice, I don't want people thinking of me in those terms. When did Henry mention it to Martyn?'

'I don't know.' She held up her hands. 'What is this? Why's it so important? It wasn't that long, ago: maybe two, three weeks or so. You know, like you said, you were just a holiday friend. I think maybe about the time Henry bumped into you at the court.' Martyn knew about me after, not before, the mock-hearing. Orbach was right, Pulleyne was being set up. But he did know about me when he'd talked to me at the party. And I had still been invited.

She went on: 'I don't ... Oh, hell, I don't even truly like Martyn. I told you that, sort of. I like her, though, and Henry's crazy about his father so I have to care. D'you see what I mean?' Nervously, she reached over and lifted one of my cigarettes. There's an unbelievable number of people who smoke just occasionally ... most of them smoke mine.

'I can see what you mean,' I said as I lit her cigarette for her. 'But I'm not sure why you're telling me.'

'Because something's going on and I want you to tell me what. Oh, hell, I want to go to the States. The last thing I want is to spend Christmas here, with them. But, you know, well, if

Martyn's in some kind of trouble and Henry's upset, I guess, well, I want to be with them anyway. D'you understand?' She didn't even inhale ... I wondered if she knew how much a pack of Camels cost.

'No, I'm sorry, I can't help you. I don't know anything.'

'Not even why your name's mud in my house?' she asked softly, disbelievingly.

My eyes met hers and gave her the answer she already knew.

'You don't trust me, do you Dave?'

I smiled. 'I can't even spell trust. What did you come here to tell me, Caroline?'

She stared at me blankly. She hadn't expected me to call her bluff. She thought that if she flirted with me, batted those lovely eyelids at me and thrust out her chest, I'd do anything she asked. She'd never know how close she came.

She stood up suddenly, picked up her handbag from where it hung on the back of her chair and leaned over the table towards me. She hissed: 'Don't hurt Henry, Dave; that means you don't hurt Martyn either. If you do, I'll find you; I'll hurt you too. D'you understand?'

She turned to go. I grabbed her wrist. There are some advantages to a meet on your own terrain — no one came over to tell me to let her go. I replied, 'Six nights ago a very good friend of mine got beaten up; five nights ago the flat I just moved out of was fire-bombed and there ain't much of it left; four nights ago some people came to this club and gave the owner — the then owner — a very hard time during which he dropped dead of a heart attack; three nights ago I had to move into a squat without curtains on the windows. Don't tell me about hurting. It's already been done.'

I let her wrist go. She stood there shaking, her mouth open. She had no idea how grisly was the game that was being played out around her father-in-law. I wanted to get up and comfort her. I wanted to put my arms around her and stroke her gently back to where the most frightening news she can think of is that Harrods' sale has come to an unexpected end. She looked as if she was going to speak, but she bit her lip to stop herself and left, still shaking, without another word.

I called after her: 'Caroline. Go home to the States. Do it. Go. It's the only thing you can do that makes sense.' But I'm damned if I knew how what I was saying made sense and if she heard me she showed no sign of it.

I gave her a few minutes' start and went to get my own coat before leaving. As I reached the stairs Malcolm caught up with me, thrusting a bill under my generous nose. I protested but to no avail. He said: 'You drink free. This is for the food. You're lucky I haven't charged for what she drank.'

The week ended as it had begun with Tim Dowell at the office. I was not pleased to see him so late on a Friday afternoon.

'Make it quick, sunshine; Sandy'n'I're going to her parents for the weekend.' We had thought of booking a hotel out of town, but what I wanted was to catch up on my sleep. I'd been awake by seven every morning and it was killing me; her parents' would be perfect. No stimulation of any kind. We would even sleep in separate beds.

He was accompanied by Wally Wadd. He said: 'I'll let the Sergeant tell you.'

Wadd read from his notes: 'Since Tony and Len Reddin went down, there've been seventeen Crown Court criminal cases involving known associates of the gang. You probably know that since that trial, neither of the other brothers has been charged with anything more serious than traffic. Nine of those cases came up before one High Court judge. That's interesting in itself, because four of them qualified for either High Court or Circuit judges.' Offences in England are arranged in bands: leaving aside the minor cases in magistrates' courts, at Crown Court the middle band will be heard by a Circuit or a High Court judge, depending on severity. It is not always certain in advance how a case will be classified.

He continued to recite monotonously and stoney-faced: 'Those nine cases involved sixteen different accused. The charges include grievous bodily harm, affray, VAT fraud, handling stolen property and a conspiracy charge involving obtaining by deception from mortgage companies — multiple mortgages on the same houses. There was also one rape charge, incidental to the affray but a lot more violent. With the exception of the rape and one grievous bodily harm, these cases all led to acquittals.'

'What was the acquittal rate in the other cases?' The eight that had been heard by other judges.

'About half and half. There's one more statistic I haven't given you, sir.' I hate being called sir; I know it can't be true respect so it has to be sarcasm. I also knew why Dowell was allowing Wadd to take the glory. He wanted me to know I had been wrong to dismiss him because of his name. I didn't mind. It was the smallest error of the case, paling into insignificance beside some of the others. 'Twelve of the seventeen cases were on the same circuit and the High Court judge involved is in charge of the lists on that circuit.'

'But he didn't take them all?'

'Which raises a question,' Tim interrupted. 'Was that because he didn't want it to appear too obvious, or because the Reddins wanted to do down the others?'

'The former. He couldn't guarantee conviction elsewhere. If they wanted someone convicted, they'd also want it in front of him.' Like maybe the rape.

Thus far, no one had mentioned his name.

'Well done,' I said to Wadd. 'Police National Computer?'

He glanced at Dowell who nodded permission to tell me: 'No, sir. Mr Dowell's own programme.'

I suddenly understood how Tim managed to retain and retrieve all the information he accumulated that didn't belong anywhere else, that meant nothing to anyone but himself — like the property Lewis owned. I asked Dowell, 'Would you let me see a print-out of my file?'

Wadd sniggered. Dowell ignored the question and frowned at Wadd.

I asked instead, 'What now?'

Tim said, 'It would take very little additional work to produce a comparative analysis of other senior judges on their own circuits. I would've thought we would then have enough to take to the Lord Chancellor's Office.'

'More than that,' I admitted. I could see no advantage in concealing the information and he was entitled to something back in exchange. I told them about Trent, Trentino, the Hackney Marsh group of companies and the High Court civil actions which had not reached the conclusion that the facts justified. I did not tell them about Cushing QC, although as Wadd wrote down the names of the cases it could not be long before they found him for themselves. The reason I didn't say was because Malcolm and I needed a wee time alone with Cushing. 'So take it to the Lord Chancellor's Office,' I challenged them, which was the last thing I wanted them to do.

'Ah, well, yes, we could,' he admitted. 'I don't know a lot about how these things work,' he lied, but I think it would be a good guess he wouldn't be sitting in court much longer.' I waited. He sighed. 'You know as well as I do it wouldn't be enough for a charge even if he wasn't a judge. Not against him, and not against them. Stop playing games, Dave.'

I grinned. Wadd grinned. Dowell scowelled.

I knew why I was grinning; Wadd was grinning out of good nature.

'This is the first time in all the time I've known your boss I've had the upper hand,' I explained. 'If you take this a step further, up just one flight of stairs, you'll be told to walk it straight over to the LCO and though he's off the bench he and they have got away with it. That means you can't move, you can't do a thing; above all, you can't spend any more time on it that has to be accounted for; you certainly can't get warrants to look at people's offices, homes and banks, and you can't go around busting heads till someone bleeds red. It's a complete catch-22. You move; you lose. You don't move; you don't win. That's right, isn't it, Tim?'

He nodded dourly. I went on.

'But of course there's your private computer programme that I daresay isn't registered under the Data Protection Act. And you've got a lot of contacts you can talk to without a warrant. And you've got muscle on tap if the situation gets heavy enough to justify using it in its own right.' I was thinking of me; oh, uh, and Sandy and the ubiquitous unborn.

I sighed with pleasure and with power. 'So the only thing you can do is sit back and wait for me to provoke them into a wrong move. Right, Tim?' I repeated, rising to show them out of my office without needing confirmation. I was going to enjoy my weekend.

Still no one had mentioned his name.

CHAPTER NINE

In the tiny available space, far too small for two, I was sweating, mainly with embarrassment. Malcolm was equally hot, but with resentment. We were squeezed up in the walk-in cupboard that served as a dressing-room to what had been Lewis' bedroom.

Over the weekend, two holes had been cut in the wall. They were covered by a Peruvian rope wall-hanging. With a tripod on our side, we had set up a home-video camera against one hole; there was just enough space to watch through the other. I was glad Malcolm was hogging it to himself. I didn't want to look.

It had taken Tom, Malcolm's tasty toy-boy, only two nights — Wednesday, the day of the funeral, and Thursday — to track down Cushing at one of his haunts and let himself be taken back to the Kilburn flat Cushing's clandestine boy-friend lived in. Tonight, as instructed, he had sought Cushing out and told him he wanted to be with him alone. The thought of refusing never passed through Cushing's mind.

It was late on Monday night. We had left the lights on, which rendered the holes behind the hanging unseeable without close inspection. The lies Tom had to tell were small ones, easy to carry off: he lived here with his lover; the lover ran a drinking club; he was never in before four or five in the morning. Malcolm gritted his teeth as we listened from the cupboard to Tom and Cushing laughing and drinking in the living-room before they got down to the serious business they had come back for.

Any guilt I might have felt about the set-up was overridden by the reminders of Lewis that still littered the apartment. It was a large, comfortable, luxurious apartment, contrasting cruelly with the squat in which I was living. Were it not for the use to which we were now putting it, I could have moved in for a while; as it was, none of us would be wise to go anywhere near it until the war was over.

When they came into the bedroom, Tom put one of Lewis' operas onto the compact disc player in the bedroom, which served to conceal the quiet whine of the camcorder. During my one brief opportunity to watch, while Malcolm set the machine in motion, I concentrated on Cushing. He was old and fat — fatter even than me — as fat maybe as Lewis — and out of condition; he was extremely hairy, except for on his wrinkled stomach, but the hair was all grey.

I nearly blew our cover laughing out loud when he undressed to unveil sock-suspenders. I've only even seen them in films from the forties and fifties. He was in the baggy, loose boxer shorts I thought only Americans ashamed of their masculinity ever wore, and when he climbed into bed neither he nor Tom yet had an erection. It didn't remind me at all of my father. But as amusement receded, embarrassment grew and I wasn't sorry when Malcolm shoved me to one side to get a clearer view than through the lens.

We let them carry on for ten minutes or so. Tom had been instructed to look frequently at the wall-hanging, to make sure we got his face in the frame, which can't have made it any easier for Malcolm. In fact, he was one year over the legal minimum, but Cushing wouldn't know it, and Malcolm had thrown together a couple of unimportant documents which suggested the contrary.

Though they would not stand up under proper police scrutiny, they would convince Cushing.

Malcolm touched my arm. I nodded. He was holding the remote for the music system and handed it to me so that as I came out of the cupboard I could switch the sound off. It was entirely accidental but as we emerged Cushing came, his eyes squeezed tightly shut, roaring like a bull pricked by a picador, so that he neither saw us nor appeared to appreciate that the future Mr and Ms Figaro had suddenly ceased screeching at each other about where to put the bed after they got married. We stood there politely waiting for him to recover his senses.

Tom, of course, was aware of us throughout. He was straddling Cushing. He witnessed our entry and grinned as he rose and fell against the flabby old silk's stomach until it was over. On my nod of instruction, he stepped off leaving Cushing's diminishing prick — cautiously condomised —totally exposed. It was the most unerotic thing I had ever seen.

Tom made only one mistake. As Cushing lay there, eyes still shut, breathing wheezily, he blew him a silent, sarcastic kiss. Malcolm's arm flashed and Tom fell back against the wall as the crack across his face finally brought our presence to Cushing's attention. Unimaginatively, his opening words were: 'What the hell?'

He struggled into an upright position but before he made it Malcolm — fully clothed — straddled him in his turn and started pummelling his face and body until the man was shouting for him to stop. Just too late, I screamed at Malcolm that it was enough: blood streamed from Cushing's nose as he howled and grabbed at it.

'God, God, it's broken.'

'Get us a drink, Tom,' I said, my voice shaky. His nose probably only felt broken, I reassured myself.

Surlily, he left the room. When he returned, he was wearing a short silk dressing-gown and was carrying three empty glasses and a bottle of Scotch. I hate Scotch. At my insistence, he went back out to see if there was anything civilised. On second thoughts he must have felt sorry for Cushing because he came back in carrying not only my bottle but also a fourth glass.

Malcolm finally stepped off Cushing, sneering and wiping his clothes like he was wiping off dirt. Cushing made as if to get off the bed and Malcolm hit him back onto it again with much greater force than necessary. There was no fight left in the man. I reached out a restraining arm which Malcolm brushed off like an irritant. Instead, I picked up a towel from a chair and chucked it to Cushing to hold against his nose. As the bleeding slowed down, he raised himself into a sitting position and accepted the glass of whisky I gestured to Tom to give him.

Eventually, he asked flatly; 'What do you want?' He was intelligent enough to appreciate this was no ordinary roll for what he might be carrying in his wallet.

Malcolm pulled back the wall-hanging and pointed in at the lens. Cushing snorted, 'So what?'

'You sit as an Assistant Recorder, don't you?' I asked as calmly as, in the circumstances, I was able. Most QCs and many senior barristers sit as Assistant Recorders; they are part-time judges appointed for a limited period of three years during which they try minor criminal cases for twenty working days a year. The fact that they are part-timers and that many grovelling hacks are allowed to undertake the task does not stop the newspapers writing up their indiscretions as if committed by a proper judge.

'Oh, come on, so I have to resign.' Another QC, also an Assistant Recorder, had been the subject of a blackmail attempt which he had resisted, and which led to the publication in one of the gutter newspapers of a picture of him sitting up, apparently naked, in bed together with a love-letter to his young, male lover. He had merely resigned his position as Assistant Recorder and carried on practising, earning enough respect for the way he comported himself to make up for his few lost clients.

I took out of my jacket pocket the two documents we had prepared: one was a social security claim card, the other a driving licence. I tossed them onto the bed and Cushing picked them up and examined them closely. Notwithstanding his bloodied nose, he went white as a sheet. His colleague had committed no criminal offence — buggery with a minor remains illegal. Before he could stop himself he said, 'They'll kill you for this.'

'Who will?' I asked innocently.

He didn't answer my question. Instead, he said, 'How do I know these are his?'

'You don't. You'll just have to take our word for it.'

He snorted.

I added, twice as confident as I felt, 'There's a way to prove it. In all civilised societies a system exists for proving this sort of thing.' He turned away, knowing what was coming as I concluded: 'They're called courts.'

'All right, tell me what you want. How much?'

Almost off-handedly Malcolm removed from his back-pocket a small curved knife and unsheathed it. He used it first to clean his fingernails. Disgustingly, he picked something out from between his front teeth with it. I wondered if he also used it to pick his nose. He said: 'Tom, go next door.'

While Tom left, I pulled up the chair from which I had removed the towel and sat down fairly close to the bed.

'Let's agree some ground-rules, Charlie,' I said, trying to sound cheerfully in command of the situation. 'This ruins you. You're out of the bar. Also, David Newton ain't going to be too happy, and you're not going to have enough money to keep leather-jacket in the style or nose candy to which you've accustomed him. What's your best bet? Maybe the Reddins — that is who you meant, isn't it, when you said "they'll kill you"? — the Reddins'll let you work in one of their companies, if — and mind you it's a big if — they don't decide you're too much of an embarrassment to keep around.'

I paused to let it sink in before I continued: 'As they've already tried to kill me once, you'll understand why I'm not impressed by your threat, and why I'm sceptical they won't consider you suitable for similar treatment. But if they don't, that's some life you're looking at — being treated like an office-boy by scum like that. And that's after you come out of jail. 'Course, in jail, it won't be you putting it into little boys; everyone'll want a taste of plump pink barrister's bum.' I recalled Carson's evocative expression: cushion Cushing.

'You're Woolf,' he muttered. 'I thought I'd seen you somewhere before. While you were waiting to see that creep Papworth.'

'What's happened to him?'

He shrugged. Malcolm jabbed the knife at his belly, lightly, not even drawing blood. It wasn't part of the deal to use a weapon on him; just to threaten. I was beginning to worry how honourably Malcolm proposed to keep the bargain.

Cushing said, 'I'm the senior man. He knew no one would believe him. He ran like a scared rabbit when I confronted him. There was a job in Brussels that was his for the asking; they're desperate for British lawyers at European Economic Community headquarters. He went on leave until it was sorted out. He can probably come back in a few years. He can come back now if you like,' he offered.

I shook my head. 'I don't care; I was just curious.'

'Who're you working for, Woolf?'

'You don't know?'

'No, I don't. It's one piece of the puzzle no one seems to know.'

'That's too bad. But you can take it as read whoever it is won't be bought off; I'm working for me too now. I don't like people who threaten my life; I don't like people who threaten my friends. The man who owns —owned — this flat was a friend. The Reddins' messenger boys gave him a bit of a rough time and he had a heart attack.'

Suddenly, unexpectedly, I felt sick.

'What in the name of fuck, Cushing? What in the fuck are you doing? You're a barrister, for Christ's sake. You're a QC. You're supposed to believe in law and civilised behaviour. You're supposed to be a clever man. You're supposed to be the crème-de-la-crème. You're supposed to be responsible and upright. For god's fucking sake! Look at you!'

He flushed. 'It's easy for you to talk with me lying here like this. I'm easy to laugh at. A fat old fool. Your generation, you had it so easy; no one cared if you were gay; I've even seen barristers with ear-rings, flaunting their homosexuality in the courts. In my day, well, it was still illegal, you know, until 1968. I was thirty-five before it was legalised.'

'Is that how they put you in their pocket?' It was a question that didn't need an answer. 'But that's long ago. You've been paid for what you've done since —topping up payments, I presume, but of a rather larger order than usual.' This didn't need confirmation either. 'I should think your life-style is expensive even on a QC's income.'

He glanced down. His shrivelled penis was still inside the condom. I said to Malcolm; 'Give him the duvet.'

Malcolm said, 'No.'

'Give it him, Malcolm,' I pleaded. Cushing's humiliation was beginning to sap my resolve.

'No,' he repeated stubbornly. It had nothing to do with the case, and everything to do with Tom. It wasn't rational: he'd known what Tom would have to do; he'd told Tom to do it; he'd given up a bit of his current love for the sake of a dead one. Now it had been done, he wanted reparation.

'Sorry,' I said to Cushing, meaning it but at the same time appreciating how effectively Malcolm and my hard cop-soft cop routine was working.

'It doesn't matter,' he leaned back against the headboard. 'I'm sorry, too,' he added, meaning he was sorry for what he had done to his position, to the profession, to the law, to the trust others had reposed in him. I was the only one there, the only one available, the only lawyer to whom he could say it. I was probably the only one who would ever believe it. All the others would read it as regret at what he had done to himself. 'What do I get out of co-operating?'

This was the difficult part: his opportunities with cooperation were not that much greater than without. Nonetheless, there were things I could offer that would make the difference.

'This part of it doesn't come out. Tom disappears, the film disappears. You don't go to prison. You keep Newton. If the case is made, there's no reason why your name should come into it, is there? We'd be talking guilty pleas; they'll move heaven and earth to make sure of it. That means you'll get a job, a decent job; there's a market for silks in the city. Maybe you can do a swap with Papworth, go to Europe. They don't find these things so surprising there.' We had moved on from homosexuality to corruption.

'And what does co-operation consist of?' He was recovering his wits: so far, he had said nothing that could convict him of more than buggery. It was all ambiguous, and as referable to a deal to avoid that charge as anything else.

'The Reddins and Pulleyne,' I said softly but firmly.

'I don't know what you're talking about,' he said immediately. 'And I'm discussing nothing further until you turn the camera off and I check for myself there's only the one.'

'Fair enough. Come on.' I led the way into the cupboard and switched off the machine, unscrewing it from the tripod and placing it, facing away from the bedroom, on the floor. Malcolm was behind him in case he made a grab or a run for it.

When we went back into the bedroom, he asked: 'Can I get dressed now?'

I was about to agree when Malcolm shoved him so that he fell again onto the bed, but this time face down. He hit his arse hard with the flat of his hand to make him turn over. Then, as if he hadn't made his point clearly enough, he took Cushing's cock in his hand and, without a second's hesitation, with a single swift swipe sliced off the head of the condom. It happened so fast I hadn't time to protest before it was over.

Cushing, when his heart started to beat again, turned his head to look at me. Our eyes engaged in silent conversation. He was saying to me: 'This price is too high to pay to go on living. Give me the strength.' I was trying to tell him 'I'm sorry; I didn't know it would be like this'.

As he turned back to face Malcolm, his eyes fixed on the doorway. I looked around. Tom was standing in it, his hand grasping his semi-erect prick, masturbating. From the horrified look on his face, he had seen the flicker of Malcolm's knife across Cushing's penis. He was not excited — what he was doing was a nervous, primal reaction.

'Get out of here,' I screamed, 'get out, get out, get out.' I was losing it. I couldn't breathe. I was drowning. It brought back what had happened at the end of Mather's. Coupled to the fear I had felt since Dowell first told me what they'd done to my flat, I reacted in exactly the same way and without any warning threw up the contents of my stomach. Some of the vomit hit the bed and instinctively Cushing drew back, though none of it would have touched him anyway. I did it like it was the most natural thing in the world to do or no worse than a deep, welcome burp.

Throughout, Malcolm was wholly unmoved. He tapped the end of his knife against his neatly clean fingernails. He had done no more than glance around at Tom. He too understood that Tom was not excited but terrified; that was what Malcolm wanted. It was grossly unfair. He was still revenging himself on Tom for what he'd made Tom do. I wanted to weep. I had never experienced anything like it — the need to be evil to fight evil or sick to fight sick.

Malcolm said, 'Mon, you're going to have to tell my friend what he wants to know. This's what you might call upsetting him. I hate to see him upset.'

Cushing looked at him with low, sad eyes, then at Tom who had yet to obey my injunction — for a split second, he remembered how good it had felt with the boy and perhaps for that moment it all seemed worthwhile — then at me. He half-smiled, saying, 'Your friend seems very determined. I suppose you are too. What is it you want?'

I swallowed a shot straight from the bottle to rinse out my mouth and spat it into the pool of vomit between us.

'I want the connection between the Reddins and Pulleyne. I want to know the why of it, how it worked, and I want it us-able: cases, dates so far as you are able, what the pay-off was and what for.' I wanted to hear it all the way through once and then record it on a new film after we let him get dressed and cleaned up his face. It couldn't be too obviously blackmail, or the result of violence — both would invalidate the admission.

'I can't really help you, you know,' he sighed as he hefted himself up by his elbows into a sitting position, ignoring Malcolm's slight shift towards him. 'You see, all I've ever been asked to do is to try and get a case before a particular judge. That's not illegal; it's not even unprofessional. Perhaps one doesn't read about it in the text-books but from the start of pupilage you hear people saying: "We'll be all right in front of so-and-so". This was what Papworth had said, so I was inclined to believe it; hell, I'd said it often enough for myself. He said: 'So what if a client asks me to try and get it in front of a judge? All it means is the client is — what shall we say? — court-wise. None of it will be enough for you to prosecute on.'

'It's a start. It was always the Reddins?'

'I don't know that. In these cases, they're companies. I don't see their memoranda and articles of association or ask for a list of shareholders,' he said sarcastically.

'But you check with the Reddins? That's how you knew about Mather?'

'I checked about Mather,' he admitted easily, 'but that's because of who he was. In other cases, my instructions have come from one of two particular firms of solicitors. That's who I've relied on.' It was what I had guessed. I asked him for the names of the firms, for the record, and he told me the ones I already knew.

'What about crime? You've done some criminal cases in front of him too, haven't you?' It was a guess. If Wadd had analysed the barristers involved in the cases either they hadn't told me or the results had proved inconclusive.

'One or two. Same solicitors.'

'Who did you talk to about Mather?'

'Ah. This is the key point, isn't it. When I answer that question, I'm condemning ... Let's just say someone ... Aren't I? That's the point at which I start to find it hard to get life-insurance, wouldn't you say?'

I was trying to think of a duly sarcastic reply when Malcolm did so: 'No, this is the point,' and drew with the tip of the blade up from Cushing's belly-button to the base of his throat.

It was so casually executed and caused Cushing so little pain he did not even cry out. I was surprised to realise he had cut through the skin at all. I watched, morbidly fascinated, as the trickle of blood welled up along different stretches at a different pace, hampered by different thicknesses of matted-grey hair, only gradually forming into a complete line.

Cushing said calmly, 'You sadistic bastard. Why don't you go the whole way? Kill me. Come on. I don't care.'

'I might yet,' Malcolm answered equally evenly, though I sensed that he realised Cushing meant it. 'Dave told you about Lewis. He was the best thing that ever happened to me. I don't care about going down for you either.'

'Now, now, boys, let's behave like gentlemen,' I said.

Malcolm snorted but Cushing was amused. My admiration for him was growing by the second: it was as dangerous and dispiriting as when his excessive humiliation had earlier threatened my capacity to carry on.

I said to Malcolm: 'Let's have a word outside.'

He shook his head. He knew what I wanted to say. He wasn't interested. For a second, I toyed with walking away. But only for a second. I was already too deeply implicated. I was in the game despite myself.

'You still haven't told me who you checked Mather out with,' I resumed.

'No more I have.' He sighed: 'Oh, well, as you say, I don't have a lot of choices, do I? I checked him out with Henry.'

'Henry?' The two Reddins on the outside I knew about were Pat and Ralph. 'I've never heard of Henry.'

'Of course you have; you were on holiday with him. Henry Pulleyne.'

I counted to fifty before I let my breath out. Malcolm was looking at me, as confused as I. I said quietly:

'Start explaining.'

'Henry's the link. Henry's who they pay. Henry's who pays me. Even when he was in New York; I've only ever dealt with Henry, for years now.'

I got up from the chair and turned my back. I paced up and down, looking out of the window across the dark roof-tops;

hardly anyone else was still awake. I wished I wasn't. I wished it was only a nightmare.

It made a degree of sense. Neither Pulleyne nor Cushing himself would want brown paper bags of cash delivered to chambers. Henry had ample ability to move money. Even from America, he would be able to check the same day if a deposit had been made to an account virtually anywhere in the world, and if he wanted he could move it from there, also to anywhere in the world. He could pay Cushing off the same way. He was probably formally in charge of his father's investment portfolio. Caroline had mentioned investments as something he and his father might be worried about, needing to meet to discuss twice in one week.

'When did you speak to Henry Pulleyne about Martin Mather?'

'Before the hearing, of course.' He was offended I might think him careless enough to leave it until afterwards. Orbach had appreciated he wouldn't take the risk.

'And what did he tell you?'

'He just told me to go ahead. I admit I was surprised when later I was told it wasn't for them, bloody surprised.' I presumed he meant he was later told by Henry Pulleyne.

'I bet you were,' I muttered. 'You have always known it was the Reddins for whom you were expected to deliver this — what's the expression they like to use? — oh, yes, this "special service"?' He nodded. It was no more than formal acknowledgment that we had already passed his point of no return. 'Tell me, how long has your contact been Henry Pulleyne?'

'About six years or so.'

'Before that?'

'Originally, I dealt with Len. He was who ... He had ... Oh, lord, a long time ago, I was, er, involved with a young man. He'd been a client, it was stupid, I always knew it was stupid, before it began. But I was only young myself. A young barrister, lonely, pretending to be straight, borrowing my sister's friends to take to chambers' parties and dinners in the Temple, aloof and austere towards my solicitors and clients. This boy, he knew at once. You're gay,' he turned to Malcolm, 'so you know what I mean.' If he was trying to win Malcolm over it didn't work. Malcolm showed no sign of acknowledgment let alone sympathy.

Cushing continued: 'I won his case; it was just a stupid trial in the magistrate's court, shop-lifting or car-theft, I can't even remember. As we left court, he shook hands with me and said he wanted to find a way to thank me. His solicitor was still present and didn't even realise what was going on. I said something like "nonsense, it's just my job, if there's anything I can do, perhaps to help you find a job, give me a ring", and gave him my number. As we walked away, the solicitor kept saying over and over how decent I was to try and help him. If only he knew.'

He sighed at the memory.

'The boy's father found out. I don't know how. He went to see Len Reddin. I was the middle class, public school boy leading his lad astray. For God's sake, that boy had slept with more men than I'd been at school with. He frightened me, Reddin, I mean. I was naive and as I say it was criminal then. I could see my whole career disappear, that used to happen, you know, not just at the bar — one incident and a man was finished for life.'

'What happened then?'

'Nothing much for a while. He was a clever man, that's why I believe it's probably true what they say, that's he's shamming at Grendon. He's got the ability, believe me. He let me stew, then he let me relax, then one day he asked me to stand alibi for someone. I didn't have to go to court, I just had to tell the police he had been doing building work in my house at the crucial time. Reddin even had someone come round and replace a window.

After that, there was no chance of a prosecution; no jury would believe a barrister could lie.'

Malcolm sniffed. 'You're all liars; all of you.'

'Yes, perhaps; and perhaps as time went on, and I performed other little services for them; I thought I was doing no different than other lawyers. The line between what it is fair to do to get someone off and what it is not is not always as clear as you might think But the key time came when one day — oh, now, about ten years ago — I was asked to make sure I got a case listed before Pulleyne. I can tell you when — it was just after he was appointed to the bench. I can tell you too; it shocked me. After all, I'd known him in chambers, and never suspected anything.'

Not even top-up payments?'

'No, not at all. I knew he'd acted for the Reddins, of course, in their trial.' He meant the main trial, when Len and Tony went down, but Pat and Ralph whom Pulleyne represented got off. 'But I never suspected Martyn. He was always, always so upright.'

'You probably appeared the same way to him.'

'Perhaps. You want to know who I dealt with before Henry Pulleyne. Well, Pat at first, there were a few meetings with Pat. Then a man called Trent, whom Pat introduced me to. Then after a few years I met Henry with Trent and that's when the circle was complete. I have to say, I've never made a lot of money out of it; there were never great sums involved; they didn't have to pay me that much, did they? They already owned me,' he concluded bitterly.

I was not surprised by his claim to have been poorly paid. Even without their additional hold on him I knew that most corruption was for trivial gain. Even the grand corruption scandals of English local and central government — those involving Poulson, for example, or more recently the Property Services Agency — had involved petty benefits: a holiday, some work to a house, a weekend in London with all the trimmings and without the wife.

'Tell me about Henry.'

'The only link I can make for you is between Henry and Trent and Trent and Pat Reddin; none of it necessarily implicates Martyn Pulleyne himself.'

'But you know?'

'What does "know" mean? I believe so, but I've never discussed it with him nor has Henry ever expressly made a statement that would incriminate his father.'

'What do they have on him? How did it start for him? He wasn't into little boys as well, was he?'

'No, of course not. I don't know. That's something you're going to have to find out for yourself. I've told you all I know; the rest is all detail.'

Malcolm glanced at me to see if I was satisfied. I nodded. He re-sheathed his knife and almost tenderly said to Cushing, 'Come on; let's get you cleaned up. You've got one more performance tonight.'

It took surprisingly little time to complete. We sat Cushing in a chair, and used some of what I supposed was Lewis' makeup to conceal the damage that couldn't be washed off his face. Lowering the lighting, there was no way any of the pressure showed.

I acted as interviewer. I began with the date and exact time and went on: 'My name is David Woolf. I am a solicitor. With me is Charles Cushing QC. I have been investigating an allegation of corruption on the part of a High Court judge. The judge's name is Sir Martin Pulleyne. The statement which Mr Cushing is about to make is of his own free will and does not result from any duress. Is that correct, Mr Cushing?'

'Yes,' he answered hoarsely, but as rehearsed: 'I can no longer keep to myself what I have been involved in. I am deeply ashamed but the interests of the law require me to make a complete confession. It is the only way I can make amends for the damage I have done to it.'

I concluded with a restatement of the exact time, so that the absence of editing could be proven.

After it was over, I offered to drive him home. Malcolm refused to let me. I didn't want to leave Cushing alone with them. While we were making him up he'd said, either with regret or relief, I wasn't sure, that the accountant Newton was away at a conference. I wasn't convinced by Malcolm's sudden about-face at the end of the first stage of the interrogation, before we recorded the confession for the camera.

I said, 'We still need him, Malcolm.'

'Do we, Dave?' At least he had the courtesy not to lie to me outright.

'Yes, yes. I don't know if the film will be admissible in evidence without him. I doubt it. Remember: it's only a part of the evidence, not enough on its own.'

He said, 'Statements made in contemplation of death are admissible, though; I remember you said that once.' I had said it, and relied on it for my life, during Mather's.

'This wasn't in contemplation of death, Malcolm.' I managed to say his name instead of 'idiot', which was what I was thinking. The knife was still in his back pocket. If either Cushing or I had to be spared for the sake of a prosecution, I was the lesser loss. 'Look, Malcolm, he's finished; you've had your revenge; you've hurt him enough.'

He shrugged. 'Nothing that mightn't have happened in the course of a kinky scene that went a bit far. Happens all the time. Amongst us faggots, you know.'

I ignored the sly insinuation in his choice of expression. I said: 'There's been enough damage done and there's a lot more to come.'

He smiled strangely. 'I know, Dave, you're right. Don't worry. I won't touch him, I promise.'

I searched his eyes to see if I could read anything extra into them but I couldn't and I had done as much as I could to protect Cushing; if we ignore the fact that I had set him up in the first place. I didn't think it was an excuse that would satisfy Sandy, or a court of law, or even Tim Dowell; I didn't fool myself it would satisfy me tomorrow, but it satisfied me for then.

I drove home sombre, exhausted and depressed. I didn't know with whom I was more disgusted: Cushing, myself, or Malcolm. Tom seemed to my eyes to be the sole innocent, despite the grotesque image of him in the doorway playing with himself while his steady lover nearly cut off the prick of his pick-up.

It was five o'clock by the time I arrived back at Ambler Road. I undressed in the dark but even before I got into bed I knew I would not sleep. I lay there hugging a pillow as a substitute for Sandy, the duvet pulled right up to my neck, a little cold and aware that in a short while dawn would bring up the light. I didn't want to be — couldn't be — alone. I wanted to get up and drive over to Sandy's, but there were too many reasons why not, not least the belief that she would be as ashamed of me as I was trying not to feel myself, and that I didn't trust myself behind the wheel again.

Nervously, like a cat-burglar, I crept through the house dressed only in my underpants. I don't own a bathrobe or dressing-gown. I stopped to piss and brush my teeth for the second time, then proceeded to the top of the house. I hesitated between the two top floor doors. I had seen into them and knew they both contained beds, Carson's a double or large single — I hadn't been allowed in long enough to be sure. I still didn't know what her relationship was with Natalie, the other occupier of the top floor.

Natalie was a sharp-featured, five feet two inch, dark sometime dancer of Jewish-Russian extraction with a waist I could enclose in one hand and tits I couldn't enclose in ten, now gaining further experience as a waitress before buying her own bistro. If she and Carson were lovers I was jealous of at least one of them. I tapped gently at Carson's door. To my surprise, I heard her call out at once: 'Come in.'

I did. She was alone.

She said, 'I heard you come home. How did it go?'

By design she did not know the details but she had a fair idea what I had been up to. It had been her information which I had used and she had briefed Malcolm directly on Cushing's hangouts and the best times to find him where.

I sat on the side of her bed. She must have sensed something was up because she took my hand and squeezed it without trying to break any fingers. I wanted to tell her and I didn't; I wanted to talk and I couldn't.

She shuffled over to one side: 'Come on, get in, get warm. You need to get warm, Dave. Just warm.'

CHAPTER TEN

Iwas between the privet hedge and the dark, empty house thinking that the street-light which kept me awake was for once and thankfully out when a blow to the back of my head swung me around.

I cursed and fell back into the remains of a wild rosebush fortunately out-of-season but still not completely devoid of thorns. They caught on my leather jacket and then, as I lost my balance altogether, my hands and face. A boot went into my stomach as I sought to struggle free. I couldn't see my assailant's face but it was neither of the bullies from outside the Reddins' office.

I curled up as if to protect my genitals and face, reaching inside the jacket for the gun Malcolm had given me at my request, after Dowell left us the night of the wake, against just this eventuality. As I extracted it, hoping it was pointing the right way, my attacker kicked my hand and sent it flying into the undergrowth.

He said, 'You stupid fuck, you stupid, stupid fuck,' and I knew I was going to be all right.

Dowell let me get to my feet and then, still fuming, pushed me against the bay where he went on dancing around me, senselessly and without doing serious harm punching at my body until, sighing, he stepped back. 'Ach, this is pointless.'

'You can say that again.' I lowered my head as if in defeat before, suddenly, I kicked out at his balls, catching him off-target but near enough to cause him to collapse to the ground, avoiding the rose-bush and clutching at himself, grunting and gulping short, deep breaths to counteract the pain.

As if it had been waiting for this moment, the streetlight flickered and came on a mere six hours after it was due. We looked at one another foolishly then he started to laugh even though not yet free of pain: 'I didn't think you'd have the, well, balls.'

He knew how unadept I was at fighting, especially hand to hand. It was why I had insisted that Malcolm give me something to protect myself with.

We scrabbled around to find the gun, which he pocketed, and I let him into the house. We sat in my room just the other side of the bay sipping Southern Comfort as he told me why he was angry.

'We found Charles Cushing. He's the one, isn't he?'

'Yes.' I knew what he meant in both respects: Cushing was involved with Pulleyne; and Cushing was dead. 'How'd it happen?'

'Shot himself. His boyfriend found him. What'd you do to him, Dave? He'd been badly beaten, cut too. Gorbals' steak-knife, I'd say.' He meant the Gorbals, in Glasgow, where Malcolm came from. 'He left a note.'

'Saying?' I was silently cursing Malcolm, and myself, for failing to follow instinct and insist I accompany Cushing home.

I was also prepared to bet money Malcolm had kept his word to me. He hadn't touched Cushing; he had made Tom do it.

'It said he'd been in a scene, a gay scene, and afterwards sought you out and made a statement to you on film. He gave the exact times of the film He said everything he'd told you was true but he didn't say what he'd told you. He said he'd had enough. Where's the film, Dave?'

'Film.' Malcolm wasn't stupid. He'd managed to get him to write enough to salvage its integrity as evidence. The written statement was in clear contemplation of death; arguably, it would shroud the film itself with the same authority. 'I need more time, Tim; the moment I give it you it's over, isn't it?' It would be technically enough for an investigation and perhaps even for a charge, but if Cushing was accepted as a suicide — and therefore unreliable — the scales of interest would still come down with a bang on the side of cover-up. Neither suicide note nor film would emerge at an inquest. They only stood a chance if there was a trial, and that meant a trial of the Reddins.

'Don't blame me, sunshine; you're the one pushed it over the edge.'

I shook my head. 'I didn't want ... well, this. Will there be an investigation of Cushing's death?'

'Sure. But unless someone's been very stupid, it'll stand up as suicide. It doesn't matter, does it, who pulled the trigger? It's your fault; if you run around with people like that, you've got to expect how it'll come out.' He hefted my gun in his hand as if to make the point.

'Give it back, Tim,' I pleaded, 'I need it. Especially now.' I didn't mean I was planning to use it, as a weapon, just to bolster my confidence.

'Yeah, I know you need it. Which is maybe why I won't give it back to you. Who d'you think you are, Dave? God almighty? Clint Eastwood? Dirty Dave giveth and taketh away?' I shut my eyes as if I couldn't hear him. 'I said I'd help you but not for this for Christ's sake. It's vigilantism.' I hadn't left Cushing with a lot of choices; he couldn't have needed much persuasion.

Before I could answer I heard the front door open and then a knock at mine. As Tim slid my gun out of sight back into his pocket I called out: 'Come in.'

It was Natalie. Her face followed her into the room ten minutes after her body began. She said, 'Hi. No one else's in. I wondered ... Oh, I'm sorry.' She hadn't seen Tim sitting on the mattress on the floor behind the open door.

'It's OK; come in; Tim, Natalie,' I introduced them. Tim re-started the regular, deep breathing from before. He was hurting for a different reason.

'D'you know where Carson is? I was going to make some coffee,' she added. 'Do you want some?'

'I was just going,' Tim made as if to get up.

'Please. I'm sorry,' she repeated. 'I didn't mean to disturb you.'

'No, it's OK,' I said. 'Yeah, sure, I'd like some coffee; I'll come up in a minute.'

We waited until we could hear her moving about in the kitchen. Tim reminded me: 'Film?'

'Can't you lose the note for a while?'

'No way. Too many others.' It would require an instruction from higher up for it to be forgotten and that would only come in connection with an order to forget it for good.

'Uh, say I posted it? For safety?'

'Where?'

'Abroad. I'll get it back. In the Christmas post we're talking a couple of weeks at least.'

'Is that the best you can do?'

He wasn't arguing; he was allowing me the extra time. He knew what we were fighting as well as I. He still wanted his Reddins.

'For now. Gun?' He finished off his drink and rose to go without answering. 'Tim, for God's sake,' I begged. It wasn't until he was half out of the door that with a sigh of reluctance he turned around and thrust it back into my sweaty hand.

'Remember last time, laddie.' At the end of Disraeli Chambers, when I'd bought a gun from Lewis and Lewis had snitched in time for Tim to save me from my own worst efforts. 'Lewis ain't around now. Be careful.'

Upstairs, I said to Natalie, 'I'm sorry. I've got to go down to Trafalgar Square,' the 24-hour post office.

She looked disappointed.

'D'you want to come too?'

'Sure. I'll leave Carson a note where we've gone.'

Alfie, the fourth occupant of the house, had left that day for Holland for a few weeks over the holidays to join the man whose room I was living in. It ought to have been the ultimate fantasy: I was alone in the house with two women. Why is it always the wrong time? Nothing had happened between Carson and me the night before; nothing would happen with Natalie; I just wanted to go home to Sandy.

In the car, Natalie asked, 'Is Carson OK?'

'Sure. Why?'

She shrugged; bits of her wobbled; I swerved just in time to avoid crashing into a parked car. 'She's excited, she doesn't get excited.'

'How well do you know her?'

'Pretty well. We were at drama school together.' I didn't know Natalie had done drama as well as dance. 'We've waitressed in the same places; this is the second time we've lived together. I don't get on so well with most people. You know how it is. She's different.'

'You can say that again.'

'I'm just being nosy,' she laughed nervously.

'It's what we're working on,' I answered her question. 'You wait in the car?'

'As long as they don't ask me to move it; I can't drive.'

I posted the package to some old friends in Pelham, Massachusetts; it's the next door town to Amherst where all the universities are. I knew Karen and Chuck Smith from years before when they both lived in London and we wrote or spoke frequently. I was always promising to visit but never got it together; they also yearned to come back but two children — Noah and Abraham, of whom I was periodically sent photos— put the prospect financially out of the picture. It was probably only because we never met up that we had remained friends ... no opportunity to annoy one another.

I had rendered true my lie to Tim Dowell with one omission. The film I sent abroad was not the film with Cushing's confession on it. It was the now valueless film of his last stand. There's only one certainty: you can't blackmail a man beyond his grave. I started a note telling them not to watch the video, or at least not in front of the children, but I remembered them telling me that American and British videos aren't compatible and didn't bother finishing it.

As for the real film, it was already with the one person who could I suppose be called its rightful owner. I had delivered it to Orbach's chambers during the day with a short explanatory memorandum, telling him it was too early to use yet. Tomorrow, I would let him know that the police knew of its existence, but not of its whereabouts.

Natalie and I drove home in silence. She'd found out what she wanted to know; I still didn't know why it was important to her.

Carson didn't come home that night or over the weekend which, once again, I spent with Sandy out of town, but this time in a hotel. When I got into the office on Monday after a second night innocently alone in the house with Natalie, there was a message to ring a number in Devon. When finally we connected she told me she had traced Julia Pulleyne to a cottage outside Sidmouth.

'Where're you?'

'I rented a flat in the town. It's a holiday flat belonging to a builder and his wife.'

'How'd'you find it?'

'The wife owns a kiddies' clothes shop.' She hurried on before I could ask what she was doing in it. Some women are small enough to fit children's sizes but not Carson.

She must've been looking for a present for someone —I wondered who. 'I happened to ask if she knew a good place to stay and she said the flat was empty. They live next door; they're good people; I ate with them over the weekend.'

I waited for her to finish before I explained I wasn't asking for an account of her every movement. 'I meant, how'd'you find the cottage?'

'I tracked down one of her old college chums who knew she was living in the area but didn't have an address. It's taken a while.'

'She with the other woman?'

'Yup. Eleanor Millett. She's giving a talk tonight, the local literary club. It's at the library, open to the public. Well?'

'OK.'

I picked her up at the flat just after seven. She was nattering to her next-door neighbour, the builder, a small man with a nose as long as he was short.

'Dave Woolf. Ken Mortimore. Dave's my boss,' she hastened to explain.

'Oh, yes.' Ken didn't believe her. 'You'll be staying here, then?'

'I guess.'

He grinned comfortably saying; 'Come in and have a drink?'

His wife came out of their own house. She was even smaller than he but considerably more dainty. Shirley. She, too, extended an invitation to join them for a drink. I was tired from the drive and a drink would've set me up for a boring talk about books: I like listening to them even less than I like reading them. Carson said we didn't have time. There are times when I don't like her either.

'Are you going like that?' I asked.

She had forksaken her usual leather for a tatty old parka. She explained her jacket wouldn't fit over the sweater she needed against the bracing winter country air, so she'd bought the parka at a local jumble sale.

'Twenty-five pence,' she said proudly, waiting for the inevitable 'looks like it' that I accordingly denied her. 'They don't make 'em like this any more.'

'No,' I told her, 'it's probably against the law.' The law of good taste.

I settled into a corner of the library hoping there would be enough of an audience to disguise my snoring. Most of them looked old enough to die without anyone noticing. I still hadn't seen any posters announcing what the talk was about. Being broad-minded and unprejudiced, I anticipated a six-feet deep bull-dyke pronouncing on sexism in seventeenth century soliloquies. The sort of subject the Sidmouth citizenry loved to sit up for.

To my surprise a tiny, peach-faced woman with a bundle of blonde hair perched atop her bird-like head began in a clear, firm voice: 'The main difference between the English thriller and the American thriller is the gun.'

I shot upright.

'In the modern American thriller — it doesn't matter whether we're talking about police procedural, private eye, gangster, political or spy, or even of the semi-humorous "mood" or "atmosphere" school — the pace is set by violent death. The plot never lags because if it threatens to do so, someone gets killed. Raymond Chandler put it succinctly: enter man with gun. Because of the proliferation of guns, death is much more credible; in an English thriller, anything more than the occasional murder strikes a chord of disbelief in the reader. We are still a society in which, until a few years ago, a single violent death was front page news for weeks on end.'

On this analysis, the Pulleyne case was about to make the headlines. Fortunately, she equivocated.

'Of course, we have become much more used to violence in the last decade or so and rationally we know that guns are in widespread use in this country both by the police and by criminals. But it takes a long time, much longer than a decade or perhaps even two, for such a development to sink sufficiently into the unconscious —from where we derive our sense of fantasy: and fantasy is what thrillers deal in. Thrillers fulfil the same role that comics used to when we were children, so there's a significant time-lag before credibility catches up.'

She put her hands into the pockets of her baggy trousers, the sort I always associated with Diane Keaton in *Annie Hall*.

'What I want to do tonight is to compare a small number of plots that are theoretically similar, perhaps even identical, in American thrillers and in English thrillers.'

It was worth the drive.

It also gave us our opening.

After the talk, we waited behind until the rest of the audience had left. I let Carson lead. She introduced herself.

'And this is Dave.'

Eleanor Millett shook hands with her but made no move to take mine

'We were very interested in what you were saying. You see, we are private investigators. In fact, we're down here on a case.'

Millett's eyes lit up. 'Really?'

'Really,' I said dryly. I guessed why she was so excited. 'You write thrillers, don't you?'

'Yes,' she admitted. 'I'm a lecturer, but you're right, I write as well. Under a pseudonym,' she added, laughing pleasantly, 'and no, I won't tell you what it is.'

'Would you like to go for a drink, Ms Millett?' Carson asked.

'Eleanor. Yes, all right. Oh, no, I can't; I promised my, er, friend, I'd go straight home; we haven't eaten yet. Urn,' she hesitated, but the carrot of a free plot dangled vividly before her eyes. 'Would you like to come back to my house? It's outside town, but not far; I'm sure we could make the meal stretch. I mean, if you haven't eaten.'

My stomach rumbled. I doubted any meal made for two could stretch far enough to fill it unless she also knew how to walk on water. I said: 'We haven't but we don't want to put you out. Perhaps we could go and eat somewhere and come out afterwards, if it wouldn't be too late.'

It was only eight-thirty and in London early enough to fit in another dozen encounters during the evening. Country folk are different; the want of street-lighting makes it seem much later than it really is.

Carson frowned. She has no sense of priorities. Eleanor drew a map for us. I was sceptical we'd ever find it, but she insisted that if we followed her directions carefully we couldn't miss the cottage where she lived. She also suggested the name of a pub in town where we would be able to get a filling meal quite cheaply.

I said, to remind her: 'It's OK, we're on expenses.'

It was nearly ten by the time we arrived. Eleanor and Julia lived in a plump, squat thatched cottage in a turning off the road from Sidmouth to Otterton, leading to Newton Poppleford. It was on a mound opposite a farmhouse. When I switched off the engine and opened the car door I couldn't hear a single sound: not a cow moo nor a goose cackle. Even the air was clear and crisp and clean. It was terrifying. I was suffering withdrawal symptoms. I wanted to watch a mugging, witness a spectacular car crash or side-step a pool of drunk's vomit. Above all, I wanted a cigarette.

'I'm sorry, this is a no smoking household.'

I twitched uneasily. A no smoking injunction has the reverse effect on me — I crave nicotine at double my normal intensity.

'Carson and, er, Dave; this is Julia, my house-mate.' I studied her curiously. There was much of her brother about her though neither of them closely resembled their father; if anything they had drawn their features from Isabelle. She was tall — lanky was the word which came to mind — much taller than Eleanor who, according to Martyn, was the dominating influence, for whose sake Julia had given up her child. She had the same movements as her brother, on the border between gawky and graceful. Her face was leaner than Henry's but only just. They had the same mousy hair in almost identical waves.

If I hadn't known of the age gap I would've sworn they were twins. I knew she was in her thirties but she could have passed for ten years less. She was wearing a skirt, and when she settled down onto the same sofa as Eleanor she crossed her legs carelessly, showing an inch or two of bare thigh above the knee. She had beautiful legs. I regretted that it was probably Carson with whom she was flirting not me. She exuded the ethereal aloofness of someone special and who knows it; an almost other-world sensibility.

We were seated in the main living-room. Though the ceiling was low and beamed it didn't feel at all cramped. There was a huge, open fire that in London would have been let out as accommodation for half a dozen tourists. To one side of the fireplace there was a deep alcove into which they had fitted all the modern accoutrements: TV, video, stereo, racks of tapes both audio and visual. I got up from the rocking-chair into which I had been placed to examine the tapes.

'D'you mind?'

As I suspected, the video tapes comprised a collection of films shown on television, the overwhelming majority of them violent in one extreme or another. Had it not been for Millett's talk, it would, in the setting of the cottage, have been as incongruous as I.

'Tell us about your case,' Eleanor asked with unconcealed greed. 'What could two private eyes want in Sidmouth? Unless it's to trace someone's elderly relative.' Sidmouth is a retirement town, rather like Bournemouth, with an average age in three figures.

'Nothing so exciting, I'm afraid. More a case of corruption, gangsters, a bit of murder on the side, and all of it against a family drama in which no one knows whose side anyone else is on — you know the sort of thing: the sort of thing that doesn't happen in England.'

Julia looked startled. Eleanor patted her hand and laughed. 'That isn't what I said and you know it.'

'I thought what you said made a lot of sense,' Carson chipped in unnecessarily. 'But I wouldn't want it differently. I wouldn't want to be able to carry a gun even if I was allowed to.' She was sitting about two feet away from the one I had seen no reason to tell her about. I hoped there were two rooms in the Mortimores' flat or she'd get a hell of a shock when we undressed. 'Don't you find it difficult, I mean living here and writing thrillers?'

This was wonderful. We were bearding the lion's daughter in her den and Carson wanted to talk about writing.

'Oh, well, we've both lived in the city. Did you mean what you said, Dave?'

I saw the core of steel. She went after what she wanted and didn't stop until she got it.

'Sure, why not? You know it can happen here.'

'But why Sidmouth? How in Sidmouth? Nothing exciting ever happens here.'

Suddenly, Julia started hyper-ventilating. For a moment we were all too shocked to do or say anything, then Eleanor pulled her to her feet with more strength than I would have thought her capable of, and placed her open mouth straight on hers, breathing air directly into the other woman. It wasn't the first time it had happened.

Carson and I exchanged an embarrassed glance. Eleanor helped Julia back down onto the sofa and went to the kitchen to get her a brandy. While she was out of the room Julia said nothing, but stared at us as if she was looking at a ghost. Eleanor brought in four glasses and a bottle on a tray.

'It's me, isn't it, isn't it?' Julia said just as her friend came back in the door. Eleanor stood there, shocked; the glasses rattled on the tray. 'I know it is, I know it.'

Carson said, 'I'm sorry; we didn't want to upset you.'

'Well?' Eleanor demanded, still standing in the doorway holding the tray. 'Is it true?'

'Yes,' I said flatly, 'we want to talk to Julia.'

'You bastards,' she hissed. 'Get out of here. How dare you?' But what was making her angry was that we'd conned her. 'Go on, get out.'

We rose to leave. Julia stopped us. 'No. I want to know. I want to know what you want.'

We stood as if in a tableau until Eleanor frostily nodded permission to sit down again. But she didn't offer us a drink. This was going to be one of the hardest interviews I had ever conducted: I couldn't smoke and now I wouldn't drink.

'Julia,' I said as gently as I could in these trying circumstances, 'I think your father's in a lot of trouble; maybe Henry is too. I think, well, I think that if the truth doesn't come out soon, however bad it is, one or other of their lives may be at risk. Two men are already dead; there's been an attempt on my life.'

'This is ridiculous,' Eleanor made a final attempt to regain control. 'If all this is true why hasn't Julia heard from Henry? Why aren't the police involved — or are they?'

'Well, you see, I don't think anyone involved dares go to the police; they've all got much too much to hide. That's about right, isn't it, Julia?'

Her face was as white as mine had been when Dowell told me about the arson attack on my former flat. She got up from the sofa and knelt on the rug in front of the fire; she poked at it and didn't draw back when sparks flew up from its red-hot logs.

Eleanor too got up from the sofa and knelt behind her, putting her arms around her shoulders and leaning her head against her back. She said, 'Maybe it's time, Julia, maybe it's for the best.'

'What do you want to know?' Julia asked dully without turning to look at us.

I figured I'd probably only get one main question. I asked: 'Why does Henry hate your father? Why would Henry set your father up to be exposed as corrupt?'

Eleanor shuddered but Julia was unmoved.

There was a very long silence until I began to wonder whether we'd get any answer at all. Then Julia extricated herself from her lover's grasp and stood up, turning finally to face us. The fire had brought back the colour to her cheeks. She was a singularly beautiful woman. She said, 'It's because of the baby. Because father made me give it away.'

I was confused. It was the exact opposite of what Pulleyne had told me. Before I could explain why her answer puzzled me, she added: 'I wanted to keep it; Henry wanted me to keep it; our baby,' she concluded defiantly.

I seized on the central point immediately. Before she had time to go back into her shell, I asked: 'Did he know? Does he know?'

She shook her head sadly.

'I don't understand, then.'

This time, she sat down with her back to the fire-surround. The light lit up one side of her face and left the other in shadow. Eleanor, dubiously, returned to the sofa. Without any explanation, as if it was the most natural thing to do, Carson crossed over and sat down beside her, leaving me the lone inquisitor in the rocking chair.

'I really need a drink,' I admitted while I waited for Julia to explain. Carson glanced at Eleanor who nodded, and she got up and poured us each a brandy. I don't like brandy that much more than Scotch but I couldn't imagine a bottle of Southern Comfort in such surroundings. A log cabin in Louisiana maybe; not a Devon thatched cottage in winter in front of a blazing fire.

When no answer was forthcoming I asked the same thing differently.

'Why did he make you give it away? I'm sorry, is it a girl or a boy?'

'It's a girl,' Eleanor answered dreamily. 'Her name's Alicia. She'll be ten now.'

'Don't,' Julia whispered. 'Please.'

'Martyn said it was because you wouldn't have a child in the house,' I addressed Eleanor. 'That wasn't true, either, was it?'

'God, no. I would have loved a child; she was a beautiful baby. I don't care, I didn't care, about its genesis. We can hardly have our own,' she added dryly.

It didn't seem time to start a discussion about the merits of artificial insemination.

I double-checked; 'You're sure he never knew?'

'That's why, don't you see? That's why Henry's so angry, but he can't tell him why.'

'But how did he do it? You weren't that young; in your twenties — it was after you'd dropped out of Oxford; you were grown up enough to stand on your own decisions.'

'Oh, you don't know my father.' I didn't interrupt to tell her she was wrong. 'It was shortly before he was due to be appointed to the bench; he thought if it came out it would ruin his chances;

the faintest whiff of scandal — that's what he said. How could I refuse?' she asked bitterly.

'Wouldn't this ... Uh ... You and Eleanor ... Wouldn't that have caused a scandal, too?'

'We didn't live together then. My mother took his side; Henry argued with him — but, you see, well, Henry couldn't argue as hard as he felt, couldn't tell him why he cared so much; we were terrified, well of course we were terrified it would come out. Henry, I mean; Henry and me. Don't forget, he was still at university.' She was watching the expression on my face and laughed. 'You're so shocked, Mr Detective. Incest, the greatest of all taboos. You wouldn't think it was fifty years or more since Freud wrote about it. It happens, you know, it happens between brothers and sisters — even in the best families. People accept sexual abuse in the family — with violence — so much more easily than sex based on ... love.'

'It's true,' Carson interjected. I didn't know if incest was a part of her own history; it would have fitted. It didn't matter. Arguing the relative effects of family scars is like debating whether it hurts more to have eighteen or nineteen breaks in a leg.

'I still don't understand why he told me you were the one who wanted it adopted; he gave me a long spiel about how the judge who heard the adoption was someone he knew. It was very convincing.'

'I bet,' Julia said sarcastically. 'He could convince you night was day. I think, sometimes, that he's schizophrenic. The honourable and upright Sir Martyn Pulleyne — but like you said, he's a crook. Do you really find it so suprising he could turn the truth about me on its head?'

'Maybe not. But why bother with the lie?'

'I don't know. Perhaps he felt guilty about it; they have to have some explanation for their friends, and for themselves; he could hardly tell them he'd made me give it up for adoption because he thought it would spoil his chance of elevation.' It was strange to hear the professional terminology from this woman, in this house, at this dark hour of the night: it reminded me that once, presumably, she had been the daughter of a lawyer, leading an ordinary life as such, accumulating a miscellany of its language. 'It also accounts for Eleanor.'

'What is happening?' Eleanor brought the conversation back to the present.

'I don't know,' I admitted. 'Quite a lot. I was asked to investigate an allegation that Julia's father has taken bribes since he's been on the bench. I have to say I believe it to be true; no, I know it now. I have evidence. He's involved with a very dangerous pair of villains. There was a barrister, a QC, also involved, who killed himself a few nights ago after making a statement to me.'

'I read about his death in the papers,' Julia surprised me. 'Charles Cushing. I think I remember him. He was in Daddy's chambers, wasn't he?'

'Yes. Were they friends?'

'Not especially; not that I knew. You see, I think perhaps that's why I wasn't so surprised when ... Well, that you're here. Who asked you to investigate?'

'I can't tell you that.' But I could add: 'I don't know how much of this he knows; he is very, very clever at acquiring information that causes others pain. But in this instance, of course, he's right.' It wasn't the most tactful thing to say; I wanted to excuse my acceptance of instructions. 'How did you know about your father's, uh, activities?'

'Henry found out. Someone came to see him, perhaps one of these people you're talking about. They wanted him, well, they needed someone in banking, you see. They threatened him with Daddy. He asked him outright if it was true. He didn't really have a choice after that. Did he?'

I frowned. 'If as you say he's that angry with Martyn, why did he help? Why didn't he let them expose him then? He appears to be on the verge of it now.'

Eleanor said, 'It's all so easy the way you see it. Black and white. Well, it isn't, in families you hate and love at one and the same time; sometimes more of one, and sometimes more of the other. Henry was shocked and upset and, yes, part of him wanted to say the hell with Martyn and especially perhaps to get revenge. But don't forget, he doesn't feel free of guilt himself either ... about Alicia, I mean.'

Unasked and unanswered was how Julia felt.

'You see Henry then?'

'Oh, yes, he and Caroline have come down here. They don't tell Martyn or Isabelle, of course,' Eleanor continued to answer on behalf of her lover.

'Does Caroline know? How much does she know?' Julia shook her head.

But she no longer looked defiant.

I needn't have worried how many rooms there were in the flat. Though it was long after midnight when we got back, Carson packed up at once, and wrote a note to the Mortimores to go with the cheque I made out on the Nichol & Co office account. It was less likely to bounce than my own.

We drove back to London in silence, both of us replaying the remainder of the interview like two people listening to the same tape on separate headphones. There was next to no traffic on the road; it was cold outside and we put the heating on full; we didn't stop even once; the journey took exactly two and a half hours; it was a perfect drive, almost blissfully so, exactly what we needed.

Just before we arrived back at Ambler Road, as we passed King's Cross Station, Carson broke the silence.

'Are there any ordinary lives, Dave?'

I thought of my own childhood and its parental strains still to an extent unresolved. My mother was dead, and they never could be resolved; my father to whom I hadn't spoken for so long; my sisters I could go a year forgetting to call.

I thought of my life: through law school; into practice with Sandy; sorting away the anger and the humiliation of the daily grind on behalf of people I couldn't win enough for if I practised a thousand years; secreting myself away in my basement flat, broke, boozing, beating myself up and off. I was rescued from it first by the revenge Orbach had taken on Disraeli Chambers, then by another family at war with itself at Mather's; during the last few years, Sandy and I had been on and off, on and off, on and off, and now we were to have a child together.

'No, I don't think there are.'

She said softly, 'It makes me feel ashamed.'

'Why?'

She had to work it out before she could explain.

'I suppose, just — was everything I did justified by what happened? I've always thought I was so different, behaved differently because of it, and now I think — well, everyone's got these terrible tales and they get on with their lives even so.'

I drew up outside the house. I was surprised to see a light in the middle floor, either on the landing or in the kitchen, not in the front living-room. Natalie must still be awake I thought, or else she'd left the light on because she didn't like sleeping in the big, empty, creaking house on her own. I'd rung to tell her I wouldn't be back; she said she'd double lock the door from inside, but she'd forgotten because it was only pushed shut.

'Cuppa?' I suggested leading the way to the kitchen. I was right, it was the kitchen light that she'd left on.

'Sure,' she followed me up the stairs.

'Ah,' I said, standing in the doorway, staring at our visitor. I gestured Carson to back off but another came out of the living room behind her and herded us both into the kitchen.

'I said you was lying,' the man standing behind Natalie said, reaching down with his free hand to squeeze her breast, not, I suspected, for the first time.

His other hand held a knife to her throat. She was tied to a chair. She was gagged with a tea towel. Tear-stains ran down her cheeks. Her blouse was half-open and on the floor beside her lay a sweater. There were no signs of anything worse but I didn't know. The man behind Carson prodded her further into the room, also with a knife. Me they didn't touch.

I recognised them: they were the men from outside the Reddins' office.

The one behind Carson gloated, 'Now we've got one each.'

'And 'im,' the other one replied. 'And 'im.'

CHAPTER ELEVEN

Untouched by human hand, our protests ignored on a street practised at turning a deaf ear, we were tossed into their car one after the other and tumbled pell-mell onto the floor of the back seat until we lay piled up on top of each other, me on the top. They knew how to make the others hurt. One of them got into the back and sat along the seat, his legs spread wide apart, one foot on my neck and another on my well-padded backside.

I was face down and facing Natalie whose gag they had yet to remove or the hole in whose outfit to close. After the car started, I bit her gag between my teeth and pulled it down. I wasn't planning to kiss her.

I whispered; 'Are you OK?'

Her terrified eyes answered yes but she was still too dry-mouthed to speak.

'Did they … ? Did they … ?' I couldn't actually ask. She shook her head.

Eleanor Millett had been right in one respect. People in England still don't think in terms of guns. No one had patted me down. Now all I had to do was summon up the nerve to use it and choose the right time and person to point it at. Meanwhile, it was pressing hard into Natalie's thigh. I hoped she hadn't done Mae West at drama school.

We were driven to the Forest Gate office/warehouse where we'd first met our new friends and herded inside. There were no more surprises. Two men whose business cards I didn't need to ask for awaited us. They were in tuxedos: we were the after-dinner assortment.

'I'm Pat,' the older one introduced himself without offering to shake hands. 'This's Ralph. We've been to The Mansion House, in the city. The Mansion House,' he repeated, in case we didn't get the point the first time around.

They were an ugly pair. In their fifties. Pat was thin and bald but for an obvious toupee; even when he smiled, he sneered; he examined Natalie closely with what we were obviously intended to think was anticipatory lust but looked like he'd never seen a woman close up before and was curious how they were constructed. Calmly, he undid the remaining two buttons of her blouse. Less calmly, she spat in his face. It was a dry, half-assed effort containing much more dignity than damp. He chuckled and twisted her wrist until she cried out and dropped to her knees.

Ralph was taller than his brother and a lot heavier. He too was balding, but his brother didn't allow him enough pocket-money to buy his own rug. Maybe he borrowed Pat's when Pat wasn't looking. His face was pinched and lined and whatever he said emerged as a plaintive whine.

'Sit them down,' Pat commanded. We were sat in a semi-circle around his desk, one thug behind each of the women and Ralph behind me like we were going to play musical chairs.

'D'you mind if I smoke?' I didn't wait for permission but drew a pack out of my pocket. 'Does either of you gentlemen indulge?'

Pat snorted and nodded once but not to say yes. Ralph reached around and snatched the cigarette out of my mouth before I could light it. I shrugged and put the pack and lighter away. Pat said dryly, 'Haven't you heard of passive smoking?'

'Look,' I might as well make the gesture; it'd look good on the record. 'Whyn't you let the women go. They've got nothing to do with it.' It was such a stupid thing to say even Ralph didn't think it worth an answer. 'All right. What do you want?'

Pat chuckled again. It sounded like he was throwing up.

'Nothing. Nothing at all. Nothing we haven't already got. We've got you,' he added to make sure I understood. Notwithstanding the harshness of the content and an East End accent he could use as a knife and probably did, he spoke without raising his voice, in a flat, level tone that admitted of no emotion whatsoever.

'And Pulleyne. But now you don't have Cushing to get to him with, do you?'

'I can buy another bent brief any day I want. You did me a favour. He was unreliable.'

'Well, if you just wanted to thank me ...' I made as if to rise and Ralph shoved me back down into my chair I was beginning to have some idea how Charles Cushing must have felt. It wasn't nice.

'Who knows what you know?'

'No one important. A detective inspector and his sergeant at Scotland Yard; a non-bent barrister whose name you don't know; one or two others you don't want to lose any sleep about.'

'That Scots boyfriend of Lewis's?'

'What Scots boyfriend?'

Ralph picked me up by my hair; I went on rising long after I left the chair; he didn't give me a parachute before he let go. I didn't make a sound until I was comfortably back in my seat then I said politely, 'Ouch.'

Ralph swiped me once on the back of my head and I tumbled to the ground with a genuine yell.

I was still lying there when Pat said, 'Take the girls next door. Don't touch them. Yet.'

Next door was a thin, untreated-plywood partition away from where my own interview was being conducted. Disconcertingly, I could hear as they were led in and thrown across the room. The partition shook. Then a spooky silence descended that would have sent my imagination into overdrive if I hadn't had my own problems to contend with.

Ralph helped me to my feet by the seat of my pants and flung me at my chair so hard it fell over backwards — and me with it. While I was still struggling to get up, Pat left the safety of his desk and came round to stand over me, prodding with his toe to tell me what was coming next. His shoes weren't nearly shiny enough for his suit.

'You're going to tell me what I want to know,' he prophesied flatly, not without foundation. 'Who're you working for?'

'Me,' I answered promptly. 'This is between you and me. It's for Lewis.'

He swung his foot back and I watched in slow motion as it drove into my stomach, taking too much breath away for me to let out even a tiny groan for some seconds after. I remembered Dowell's deep-breathing when I kicked him: I'd be thankful to be able to breathe at all. 'Next time it's your face, understand?

Mind you,' he did his rattle of a chuckle again, 'it'd probably be an improvement.'

'Dowell'd'gree with you,' I said through gritted teeth.

'Who's he?'

'The DI I told you about.' I didn't feel bad giving him up; he was paid to be a target for villains.

'Who hired you?' As I opened my mouth, he moved his foot back again to remind me he wanted to hear the truth. 'This began before Lewis copped it. It wasn't us anyway. Dickey ticker. Too fat. Bad luck was all.'

'Prob'ly,' I admitted, 'but it didn't have to happen.'

'It had to happen,' he contradicted me. 'You can't be that stupid. You know who we are. We've run this part of town since before you first wet yourself; we're an institution. Damn you, damn you,' he kicked me in the stomach again as repetitiously as he cursed. 'Don't you understand what you've done?'

I rolled over so he wouldn't kick me any more. I said, 'Yeah, sure. But don't you understand, you can't fuck with the law? You're on the wrong side of the tracks, Pat. The law's an institution, too. For every crooked lawyer you find, there's a thousand who'll come down on you like a ton of bricks. It insults them. D'you understand me?'

He looked at me, thoughtfully. He understood what I was saying all right, just not why I was bothering to say it.

He said, 'Lawyers; they're nothing special; they're in it for what they can get out of it — like everyone else.' He wasn't saying anything Orbach hadn't said.

'Yeah, sure,' I was enjoying the reprieve from being kicked too much not to try and draw out the conversation. I was finding it hard to concentrate. I thought I heard movement next door; I thought I heard Carson ask for a light. She didn't smoke, did she?

'And what we all get out of it is power; but lawyer-power, that depends on an integrity — oh, sure, it's only a myth of integrity — but without it, there's no power either. You're fucking around outside your scene, Pat.'

I don't know what he might have answered, because at exactly that moment the partition wall between the two offices went up in a sheet of flame. As the two of them gawped I rolled away from them and pulled out my gun. I screamed at them, the tremor in my voice a match for my trembling hand: 'Floor, hit the fucking floor.'

Pat started towards me wholly unintimidated. He was smart. It was me who was now outside my scene.

Ralph wasn't. He overtook his brother, pulling his own gun from inside his jacket. I hadn't stopped to think about them also being armed. I didn't stop to do so then. I didn't stop to think at all. I pulled the trigger twice. Even I couldn't miss. The fat man keeled over, astonishment on his face. I screamed hysterically at Pat: 'You next, you next.'

Reluctantly but thoughtfully, and without any show of fear, he raised his hands. His eyes read it exactly like it was: I was scared, horrified that I'd shot and maybe — yet again — killed a man. I wasn't in control and if he pushed me I was too frightened to do anything else but pull the trigger.

I glanced at what was left of the wall behind him. The fire hadn't taken beyond a single section of partition and was already flickering away. Through the hole, I could see Carson — her brand-new second-hand parka hanging off her in charred tatters — slugging it out blow for blow with one of their captors, while the other lay crying on the floor alternately clutching his crotch and face as Natalie swayed over him kicking him again and again without remission — in the face, in the balls, in the face, in the balls, in the face, in the balls. She hadn't lied about learning to dance.

I said, 'Tell him to give up.'

He had the wit to ask, 'Which one?' but he didn't wait for an answer. 'Dick, leave it out.' Then he said to me, 'I don't care if you call yours off. They're useless to me if they can't take care of a coupla girls. You're a dead man, you do know that, don't you, Woolf?' he added conversationally and emotionlessly, as if asking the time of day.

Trying to sound tough, I said, 'I'm breathing, Reddin.'

It took most of this last exchange for Pat's instruction to sink in to what passed for Dick's brain. Sullenly he dropped his hands to his sides and looked at his boss for further orders. While he was looking away Carson delivered the knock-out blow. He sunk in a heap to the ground, where she checked to see how effective it had been with a quick tap-dance, in the same style Natalie was slowly and reluctantly bringing to a close on his mate.

'Go on,' I gestured towards the space where the section of wall used to be.

'You didn't answer my question, Woolf,' he reminded me as he did as I bid. 'How'd's it feel?' I was holding the gun; he was jeering at me. It was more disconcerting than to be at his mercy.

'Ask your brother,' I said. 'Carson. Go see what's left of him.'

'Yes, boss,' she muttered without a jot of sarcasm, sidling nervously around me staring at the gun. 'Where'd' that come from?'

'I found it on the floor.' She snorted. It was nice to get back to normal.

We waited for several minutes until she croaked, 'I think he's alive, Dave.'

I was glad, and I was sorry. I was glad because maybe I wasn't going to have to live with his death. The only time I'd killed someone still brought me more than the occasional nightmare. But I was sorry because it confused the issue of what to do next. I had to take responsibility for whatever I did or failed to do.

Carson called out, 'Come and tell us what you think, Nat.'

Natalie had meanwhile been busy buttoning herself back up. I was less sorry than might have been supposed. I didn't need the distraction. As she passed me she said, 'Thanks, Dave.'

'Thank her. I didn't do anything.'

She grinned and stood on tip-toe to kiss my cheek all the same.

Again we waited. They returned together, Carson carrying Ralph's weapon.

'Sorry boss. She agrees.'

I needed time to think. I said, 'You know how to use that thing?'

'About as good as you do. We used to shoot rabbits in the hills when I was a kid.'

'Dingos?'

'Oh, all right, dingos then.'

Either way it meant she knew how to use a gun a lot better than me.

'Keep him covered. I've got to take his.' I put my own into my trouser band at the back. Feeling rather foolish I said, 'Stand up against the wall.' In the movies they say things like 'spread 'em', or 'assume the position'. I wasn't as much at ease doing this as I wanted him to think.

Only Pat was upright. The other two still lay on the ground: Natalie's groaning; Carson's unconscious. Pat said, 'They're not tooled. D'you think I'm stupid?'

'Right.' I extracted his weapon and stepped backwards towards the others. 'Me neither.' I frisked them on the ground but he hadn't lied.

'What are we going to do about him?' Carson tossed a head in the direction of the other office, where Ralph lay. 'He's in bad shape.'

'What d'you think we should do? I need time for a little talk with Pat first.'

'Dave,' Natalie said, 'I know it's not my business but well ...'

Carson abstained. I guessed we owed Natalie something. I thought for a minute then crossed the room to a telephone.

'How'd's this work?' I asked Pat after I picked it up and got not even an internal dialling tone. He didn't reply. 'It's your fucking brother,' I said.

'Press nine,' Carson said, 'it usually works.'

It did. I dialled from memory. A weary voice answered: 'This better be good.'

'It is. I'm pointing a gun at one Reddin and I've already pointed a gun at another. It went off. I'm in their warehouse where they brought me.' I was trying to do the honourable thing and leaving the women out of it.

Dowell said, 'Just you? What about a witness?'

'Right. Carson's here. I forgot.'

'Hm. She works for you.' Not so good.

'And Natalie.' So who needs honour?

'Bit better. Their gun was it? Grabbed it in a struggle?'

'How'd'you guess?' It was marginally more convincing than claiming to have found it on the floor. 'Listen,' I deliberately didn't say his name, 'I didn't have a choice.'

He heard the note of desperation in my voice.

'I believe you, sunshine. You'd better hope a judge does.'

He was beginning to have a reassuring effect.

'Oh, yeah, I've got just the judge for the job, waddayasay? Look, Ralph's hurt badly but he's not dead. One of the men got beat up by Carson. He's pretty bad too. I don't know about the other one, but he won't stop crying; I think he misses his mother.'

'Is that it?'

'Uh, right. Gotta go now, sweetheart. Be in touch.' 'Dave,' he was calling down the 'phone as I hung up. 'Now what?' Pat said. 'You've got about ten minutes.

'What d'you think I'll tell you in ten minutes?' He asked with apparently disinterested curiosity.

'We're going for a ride. I've got my own office I'd like you to see.' It wouldn't be open but I had keys. After all, it was technically my club.

'What about them, Dave?' Carson reminded me. Ralph wasn't going walkies, but either of the others might recover enough wit to put one foot in front of another before the police and ambulance got there.

'Tie'm'up,' I said. 'You were a girl guide, weren't you?'

While she was working on them, I kept my gun and my eyes on Pat. He had turned around, without waiting for me to give him express permission. He was still watching me thoughtfully, trying to work out how to tackle a gun-toting, trembling, lunatic lawyer. I was outside his experience; I was way outside my own. Though I couldn't meet his gaze, I didn't want to look anywhere else. I didn't want to see Ralph; I didn't want to see blood coming out of holes I had put in him

They weren't impeccable knots but they'd hold for the few remaining minutes that mattered. I said to Pat: 'Come on.'

He shook his head sadly. 'You're crazy, Woolf. You can't get away with this; you know who I am. You know what I am.'

His cool finally broke what little was left of mine I was as near as damnit to pulling the trigger again. Instead, and now Carson was in a position to cover me, I took my own gun by the barrel and wacked him straight across the bridge of his nose with it. It wasn't a cold-blooded act, but a substitute for what I might otherwise do. He fell with a surprised thud that sounded only marginally louder than the blow itself.

'Come on,' I hissed, 'we've got to get out of here.' I watched, horrified, as Carson and Natalie headed for the door. 'Come back. We're taking him with us for Christ's sake.' And for mine. Before we left the building, I flung Pat's gun into a corner.

We took the car we'd come in. A cab would've taken too long.

'You drive,' I told Carson. 'Sit in front Natalie,' I added. In his turn, I flung Pat face down on the back-seat floor and sat with my legs spread apart, one foot on his neck another on his backside. It felt better than the other way round. 'What happened in there? You managed to complete the fire-bomb course?'

From the front passenger seat Natalie explained, 'She asked for a cigarette and set light to her parka. It was brill. She fiddled with it like it wouldn't work properly then the flame shot up half a mile.'

I drew my breath in sharply.

'Shit.' The law I'd been thinking of when I saw her in the parka the first time wasn't the law of good taste but the safety laws. A bit belatedly I asked, 'You all right, Carson?'

'Sure,' she said cheerfully. 'I told you: it didn't cost much; you can buy me a new one.'

Natalie continued, 'She set fire to it then flung herself at the wall. There was a pile of old papers against it. They caught first, then the partition caught. I mean, for a moment it looked like an accident. That's what they thought. It was enough.'

'You didn't do so bad either, kid,' I said affectionately.

'I had a lot of encouragement,' she answered defiantly. 'He won't even want to look at another woman for the next five years.'

'All things being equal, he's unlikely to see one for at least that long.'

Beneath my feet Pat, recovering, said, 'Don't invest that idea in the bank. One of us isn't gonna come out of this the way we went in and it isn't me.'

I pressed down with my right foot to remind him he wasn't in a position to argue.

Natalie had half-turned and was watching. 'Are you enjoying this, Dave?' she asked, half with genuine curiosity and half in horror.

I shook my head slowly so's she saw but there was a good reason lying on the floor not to answer out loud.

It was fourteen hours later when I presented myself at the front door of Henry Pulleyne's Wimbledon house. It was just a few minutes after he came home. I know because I had followed him from his office. He opened the door nervously, and in a futile attempt to avoid the inevitable tried to slam it in my face. I rammed a foot into the doorway and, to my own horror almost as much as his, found myself pulling out the gun and threatening him with it.

'I've used this once today. It isn't going to make a difference if I use it again.'

He stepped back, appalled at the expression on my face as much as by the aggression. I didn't blame him. I must've looked like I stepped out of a Jim Thompson black novel or a Humphrey Bogart escaped convict movie. I hadn't shaved since Monday morning. It was only Tuesday night, but I'm not sure what week.

'Put it away, Dave; for God's sake; you're a lawyer not a gangster.'

I'd said much the same to Cushing. I did as I was told.

'I don't know the difference any more, Henry. Do you? Does your father? Did Cushing? Listen Henry, I'm scared. I don't mind saying it. I'm scared shitless. There's probably police looking for me. People've tried to kill me and maybe I've tried to kill people. I've got a baby coming, for God's sake. I can't live this way; but I don't know what else to do. I can't stop it. It won't stop until it's over.'

He took my arm and led me into the living room. He poured us each a drink and though it was Scotch I didn't argue but threw it down my throat too quick for my palate to object. I asked, 'Where's Caroline? Did she go to the States?'

'Yes. She told me she'd seen you. She told me you'd said it was the best thing to do. I said you were right; it was what I'd been telling her too.' He slumped onto the sofa without spilling his drink and stared gloomily at the wedding photograph on top of the piano. Then, as if it had given him the idea, he got up and went over to the piano and began to play —I don't know what — as ably as if he was in a concert hall.

Neither of us spoke during the performance but at the end, as he got up to pour us each another drink and before he returned to the sofa, he said, 'Julia and I used to play duets.'

'Oh, yeah, I know.' I didn't mean to say it out loud but I must've forgotten because he stared at me long and hard and afraid.

'Did she tell you that?'

'No. It wasn't what I meant either.'

'Yes of course, I see.' They'd spoken; of course they'd spoken. 'What happens now, Dave?'

'God only knows. I don't. The whole thing's out of control.'

'How much trouble are you really in?' He wasn't yet ready to talk about his own troubles.

'Not a lot I suppose; not with the police anyhow; no worse than I've been in before, I should think. I, uh, well, let's say I acquired the gun during a struggle with your friends and the rest is self-defence and there's no one to contradict me. There is a small matter of Pat Reddin.' He waited for me to explain. I didn't.

We had taken Reddin to the club on the Old Brompton Road and down to the cellar. It was, as I had expected, deserted — I almost forgot to switch off the alarm in time. It was all we needed: to be busted for burglarising my own establishment while in possession of firearms and a prisoner.

Carson drove Natalie to a friend's house and would come back for me with my car. Before they left, while she kept him covered, I strung him out like a sheepskin to dry across the front of several heavy metal barrels of beer. He struggled a bit but more for form's sake than with any real hope of release.

'It's funny,' I said, once we were alone. I found a case of Southern Comfort in a corner and helped myself to a bottle which I drank from direct. 'I'm a coward, really; at least, that's how I've always thought of myself. I just have this knack of falling into violent situations where I don't have the choice. I killed a man once before,' I added, forgetting momentarily that Ralph wasn't necessarily dead. 'Have you?'

He dignified my candour with an honest answer of his own.

'I had to do Danny. Lewis had to be made to hurt. You know about that?' He allowed me no time to answer the question. 'I know what you mean, though. I always thought Len was a coward. He hated being touched, physical contact, Len ... But he was the clever one, the cleverest of us all.' He had answered my question and now asked one of his own. 'How'd you get onto Pulleyne?'

'You made someone angry. He didn't like losing a case.'

'A brief?'

'No.' God knows why I was protecting Orbach; he hadn't done much for me that way. It was supposed to be about to be the happiest time of my life: my kid about to be born. Instead, it was the time when I looked least like enjoying much more of it.

He must have been a mind-reader because he said, 'I meant what I said; you are dead; even if you kill me, you're still dead. There's Tony and Len yet, and you can't reach them. There's no way you can escape. When you think about it, there's no other way really, is there?'

I understood what he meant; we all have to work it out within our own terms of reference. For him, there were no others. I didn't blame him so much as Pulleyne and Cushing who could've chosen any they wanted.

I shrugged.

'Until it happens I'm alive; when it happens it's over. Besides,' I added with more than a little bit of truth in it, 'I've never been that sold on life. There's bits that're good and other bits that're shit, you know what I mean?'

Now I had him, I wasn't sure what I wanted him for. I couldn't extract a confession that appeared free from duress. I already had enough detail. As a professional courtesy though, he filled in some of it for me; the bits that didn't matter.

'He was into some friends of ours for a lot of money. He'd borrowed legitimately, as far as he could, then he had to borrow from them to keep afloat — as soon as Len heard about it he took the debt over — so then he was borrowing from us. Len was the clever one, he saw where it could lead. It was the beginning: some cash on the side to reduce the debt, what you lot call top up payments; a few short-cuts to an acquittal; other favours came after. He didn't have a choice.'

He paused to remember how good it had felt to own their own briefs, like they believed American mobsters did. 'Mind you, we always thought it'd be the other one — Cushing — who'd become a red judge. He did the civil work. The most we expected of Pulleyne was a circus judge.' I didn't bother to correct him: he meant circuit judge. 'That's why we always put more effort into Cushing. But, well, you can never tell, can you?'

He told me where they got the idea. Len had once seen a directive by a Mafia financial front. It was perfectly legitimate on the face of it, if you didn't know on whose behalf the organisation operated. The directive took the form of an aide-memoire to representatives travelling to Europe from America. One instruction said that if there was any conflict with the law in England, representatives should seek to have their cases brought in front of a particular judge. Not, he hastened to add, a High Court judge.

'But Len said, why not?'

He explained how it had become impossible since about the middle of the sixties — 'when the Yanks got stuck in' — to manage a crooked business and enjoy its rewards without an apparently honest source of income — hence Hackney Marsh and a number of other quasi-legitimate enterprises fuelled by illegitimate funds.

He eventually told me — and this came as the greatest, perhaps the only real, surprise — that his brother Tony and Lewis had once been in partnership, and when his brother blew his share of the proceeds Lewis had cut him out cheap. It had been a fair thing to do so far as the ethics were concerned. They hadn't been big enough then to strong-arm Lewis — himself in the prime of his criminal career — in retaliation. Though he didn't say so, it was the real reason things had taken a turn for the nasty — especially for Lewis' lover, Danny — years later, over an entirely other incident.

There was something else Pat didn't say. He was talking about the past the way a man does for whom it is all over. Past victories; past glories; lost powers; ignoring the present like it wasn't happening because he couldn't handle it, couldn't control it.

When Carson came back, I left her to watch Reddin while I went to telephone Malcolm.

'Er, we've got a guest in the cellar. Pat Reddin. His brother Ralph's in hospital — or the morgue. It's all a bit heavy really.' I didn't expect sympathy from the man who'd offed Cushing mainly because — like a lot of other people before him — he'd been upside Tom's arse. He might claim it was for Lewis, but I'd seen the way he'd behaved at Lewis' flat, and I was the last person in the world who'd ever believe him

'Mon, you're something else.' He hung up; he was on his way over. The first thing he asked on arrival within a quarter of an hour was, 'What about your friend?'

'Dowell? He knows about the damage I've done and he can work out I've got Reddin, so all it needs is to put two and two together and he'll know where.'

'But will he get his wee calculator out?' To add it up.

'I don't know; to be honest I just don't know. What've we got that we didn't have before? A kidnap — of me and Carson and the other woman in the house; a bit of assault and battery maybe. Nothing that ties to Pulleyne and therefore nothing that ties to corruption. My guess is he won't want anything bad to happen to Reddin — not really bad — but he'll let me keep going for a bit longer.'

There was one part of it that needed additional explanation.

'Dowell doesn't like people taking too much of the law into their own hands, Malcolm. Not, anyway, when someone ends up dead. He's angry about Cushing. If I were you I wouldn't assume he'll give you the benefit of any doubt if anything — uh — excessive happens again.'

He grinned wickedly and tapped my nose.

'You don't need to tell me not to trust him: he's a copper. Lewis and he were sort of friends for a long time, a lot of years. But don't kid yourself Lewis ever trusted him.'

'Didn't he? Lewis saved my life once trusting Dowell. That cuts a deep bond, you know?'

He studied me curiously then laughed, so short it was almost a bark.

'You'n'I mon, we don't have that sort of bond, do we now.' It wasn't a question. 'So you'll understand if I what you might call remind you you're about as deep in the shit as me. Know what I mean?'

'Oh yeah, I know what you mean, Malcolm. Whyn't I remind you about something too? We're supposed to be doing this for Lewis, not our own pride, know what I mean?'

He barked again and clapped me on the shoulder. 'You're all right, Dave. What're we going to do with this one then?'

'I don't know. I need time to think. I need something more, something solid to connect him to Pulleyne in an evidential sense. I'll come back tonight. If Dowell doesn't get here first.'

'Where're you going to go, Dave? You can't go home; you can't go to your office. You need some sleep. D'you want to go to my place? Tom's there,' he added.

'I've got Carson with me. I don't think we should go there. What about ... I hesitated because it would hardly be conducive to peaceful slumber, but I couldn't think of anywhere else. 'Give me the keys to Lewis' flat.'

He extracted them from his pocket. I fetched Carson and she drove us the short distance to the flat. There was already ample traffic on the roads. I watched out of the window, gloomily envious of those with ordinary jobs to go to, ordinary concerns — the ordinary lives I had denied existed when Carson asked.

We stopped by the river and while she waited in the car I flung Ralph Reddin's gun far out into the Thames With the one we'd left at the warehouse, and one which I was still carrying that Malcolm had given me, there were two guns accounted for: two guns for two brothers, I say.

At the flat, we stripped off the bed and remade it. Then, while Carson showered, I rang Sandy. It was not a long conversation. There was not a lot I wanted to tell her on the 'phone. I said we were all right, it was moving ahead. It wouldn't be long till it was over. She didn't catch the ambiguity of the remark. I asked how she was. She didn't think it'd be long till that was over either. At the hospital they were still insisting the child would not arrive until after the holiday — she begged leave to doubt them.

I said, 'I'll be there; don't worry; I didn't go through all that stuff to miss the big day.'

We hung up without saying what both of us most wanted to say: I love you.

While I showered Carson worked out how to put our clothes though the washing-machine. I'd never have thought of it but she was right: we both stank. When I was finished I crawled into bed beside her much as I had done the night I finished with Cushing. We could neither of us sleep this time; we tossed and turned and at some point we turned towards one another and fucked fiercely, greedily, selfishly seeking orgasm, without love and without a flicker of betrayal of Sandy on either side.

Afterwards we finally slept, though it didn't feel like it or make much difference. It was mid-afternoon when we awoke. We could neither of us look each other in the eye to begin with and, unnaturally polite, offered to await the other's turn in the bathroom. I think we both would willingly have fled but we had yet to put our clothes through the tumble-dryer so there was another hour to kill before we could leave. We had black coffee — there was no milk of course — and dug some chops out of the deep freeze which we put into the microwave for a few minutes and under the grill for a few minutes more, eating them in our fingers like cannibals.

She said, 'Listen ...'

I said, 'About what happened ...' We both started to smile at the same time. She offered a hand across the kitchen table and I shook it.

We wrapped up our plans for the remainder of the day. She'd drive; I'd tail. She'd only met him the once; I knew him in every state from near-naked to dinner-jacket. I gave her his address in case — as it proved — he travelled by public transport. While I was listening to him play the piano she was waiting outside in the car. It was a comfort to have a partner I could trust.

'What do you want with me, Dave?' Henry asked at last.

'I only want what you want.'

'What do I want?' he asked unnecessarily melodramatically. 'I want the life I started out to enjoy. I want to go to work, love my wife — I've always been faithful, you know.' I wished he wouldn't talk about fidelity. 'Start a family. Whose grandparents come to visit,' his voice tailed wistfully away.

'Why couldn't you? No one knew about Alicia. No one knew about your father.' Not in his circle.

'I knew about both,' he coughed, embarrassed by such a direct reference to his secrets.

'Does Caroline?'

He shook his head emphatically.

'How can you have a decent life with her if you don't trust her, Henry?'

'I can't,' he said bitterly. 'That's what it's all about isn't it? I've always known; with others before Caroline and with her, I couldn't have a real life. I only really loved her though, you know.' He was on the edge. I didn't need him to go over it. He was my penultimate shot. If I couldn't make him give his father up all I had left was to barter Pat Reddin with Trent, the only other person who could and maybe would make the direct connection. 'It's been hell,' he admitted. 'Everything's been a lie for so long now.'

'I do understand.' Lying to myself was how I'd spent most of my life too. 'It's got to come to an end. Listen Henry, you know Caroline came to see me. I wish someone loved me that much. Well,' I laughed nervously, 'maybe Sandy does. It doesn't show the way it does with Caroline though.'

'Do you think so?' he asked hopefully.

'Sure. Sure. You should have heard her. She wants to share it with you, Henry.' I surged onwards: 'Everything. The good and the bad. I'm not saying she'll find it easy —but you'll survive; both of you I mean.'

What we were talking about was Alicia but the thing that mattered was his father.

'Henry. Listen to me. You believe what I'm saying; you know it's true; you can feel it. If you can't trust in your own feelings then can't you understand there isn't anything worth saving?' The therapy I was giving him I needed far more for myself.

'And Julia? Where does she fit in?'

'She's a very beautiful woman; she's got something special; it's elusive; I don't know what it is. But I suspect it's something that transcends normal feelings. D'you understand what I'm trying to say?' I wasn't sure I did.

'I think so. Do you want another drink?'

'No. I've had enough. Unless,' I hesitated, 'you wouldn't happen to have any Southern Comfort would you?'

'Right. I forgot that was what you drank. Sorry. Scotch. Brandy. Gin. Vodka.'

'Ah, go on. Vodka on ice.'

When he came back in he said, 'There's someone sitting in your car.'

'This is true. My assistant. Can I call her in? You met her before.'

'Good lord, the Australian. Leave it a bit, won't you?' I held up a hand, both to acquiesce and to receive my drink.

He wanted to talk more about his sister.

'I think that's right, what you said. I think there is something about her that isn't normal. I've not thought about it that way before,' he hurried on as if anxious to disclaim any intent to deprive me of my originality. 'Everyone worshipped her; I could never think of her as "just" my sister— she was someone different as well. D'you think it could be that simple, Dave?'

'Could be. Once Freud'd said about Oedipus and all, it didn't sound so weird.' This was heady material. I'd read Freud as closely as *Judaism As Creed And Life*. If it fits wear it. Tell me: did your father worship her too?'

'Everyone,' he repeated emphatically. 'Everyone. From when I was a child I can remember that whenever anyone referred to her it was always how special she was, how different. Good lord, you're not asking ... ?' His voice took off through the roof of his mouth.

'I'm not saying anything. I was just curious.'

But I'd given him something. I'd made a connection between his own incestuous activity and the possibility of incestuous intent on his father's part. The mere possibility, however little foundation there might be for it, was enough.

He said, 'I suppose you want your colleague in for the rest of this?'

'Er, yes,' together with the video-recorder we'd picked up at Lewis'.

It took not much more than an hour. There was so little now to say; it was only important that it be said. Henry approached by Pat Reddin. With Trent. Asked if he would move money abroad for them, under an account that belonged to the bank. He was outraged, threatened to call the police, told them to get out of the office. They'd thrown onto his desk a copy of his father's debt account; then a full statement of the subsequent arrangements between them.

He had, as I had been told in Devon, confronted his father with the allegations. He had gone in expecting his father to instruct him to call the police at once, to laugh at this pathetic attempt to blackmail his son into illegal activity. He had come out a different man. He wouldn't tell me what his father had said.

'Ask him yourself. I'm not going to make his excuses for him,' he stated bluntly.

'Why didn't you tell them to go to hell anyway?' He looked again at Caroline's portrait.

'I thought of it. Then I thought about my mother; I thought about what sort of life my father would have once it came out ... No, that's not true: I was thinking mainly what sort of life I'd have, in the City and otherwise, if it came out. The son of a crook. The corruption'd rub off. Especially, a crooked judge. It'd tear up the roots of everything; it'd be like a disease. And, yes, what Julia said is true; I had my own guilt. Perhaps I was frightened that would also come out in the wash; but that wasn't how it felt. More like I was being punished for it. That's all I can tell you, really. After the first step, the others aren't so hard.'

'I don't understand what happened about the hearing I set up with Martin Mather. You knew who I was before it happened, and you knew it was going to happen, and you didn't warn your father or Cushing, right?'

He nodded.

'After, though, you must've told the Reddins. Why?'

'No. They found out.'

'How?'

'I don't know. I supposed Cushing had talked to them direct. Is it important?'

'I don't know either.' I'd assumed Cushing had been told by Henry, but now I realised it wasn't exactly what he'd said. My stomach tensed. There was a point to it but I was damned if I knew what it was. 'After it came out then you told your father about me?'

'Yes.'

'Why? Did he need to know?'

'Probably not, the case could simply have disappeared. But I thought if he knew how close it was to coming out, he might resign.'

'Would they have let him?'

'Perhaps. I wanted to think so.'

'Was that all you wanted? Would that have been enough for you?'

'How do I know, Dave? It would've been a lot. Especially in his terms. It ought to have been enough. We would have been on the very edge of being found out. It's like drinking, isn't it?' He laughed unhappily. 'You don't know what's enough until afterwards.' An analogy I could understand.

'Why did you ask me to your party?'

'He still wasn't frightened by the business with Mather. It wasn't going to make any difference in the end. He said the Reddins would take care of it — which of course they did. So I asked you anyway. He didn't tell me not to. Perhaps the challenge of confronting you appealed to him Does that make sense?'

'As much as anything does.' Which wasn't much. 'Caroline said you saw a lot of him afterwards, that you were worried. Even before Cushing died. What was that about?'

'I was still trying to persuade him to quit. I was frightened; I felt responsible for what I'd let happen —the hearing. I knew about Mather. I was frightened what might happen to us. It all seemed to be out of control, as if it was coming down around us. It was, really, wasn't it?' Flip-flop. He'd done it for hate; he'd done it for love. It was a toss of the same coin.

We were just finishing when his telephone rang. He went to answer it and then, a surprised look on his face, came to fetch me. He warned me: 'It's Reddin. Pat Reddin.'

My knees were knocking as I went to the 'phone. They had an answering machine like Sandy's and I switched it on to record the conversation. I don't think I was expecting to get anything from him so much as I wanted someone, somewhere, to have a recording of what my beating heart told me was about to be a decisive exchange.

'I've got the Scots boyfriend, Woolf.'

'Where are you?' I asked.

I was not expecting an answer, so I was surprised when he said informatively, 'At his club.'

I didn't think it the right time to explain that it was actually mine in law. I wasn't certain that was what he'd rung up to talk about.

I glanced at my watch. The club would be fairly empty; we didn't even bring on a full complement of staff until midnight; many of them had already put in a short shift elsewhere. Because they were desperate for any amount of additional income and were working tired and only at half-strength, Lewis got them cheap.

'You still there?'

'I'm still here. How'd'you get out?' I figured he was in a mood to brag.

'Remember Cushing's other friend? He was one of mine.' I figured he was talking about lovelorn leather-jacket of Kilburn rather than number-cruncher of Kensington. 'He found Malcolm's little boy. We did a trade off.' Someone had put enough together: probably one of our temporary guardian angels from last night. Even in jail they could talk to a lawyer; passing messages would be the least of the sins his solicitors had committed.

Reddin's answer covered more than the question I had asked. I now knew who had told them about the phony hearing and why it had been important to know. He said they'd invested heavily in Cushing. They'd kept their investment under constant scrutiny, but I hadn't covered enough of the angles.

'Ralph's dead,' he said suddenly, non-consequentially. 'You've got to pay for that, Woolf; you know you've got to pay.' He didn't say it as if he cared about Ralph; just that I had to pay because those were the rules.

My stomach churned; I'd known all along Ralph was going to die; he had to; I couldn't be that lucky; I couldn't get out of it that easy.

'What do you want, Pat?' I didn't even bother to ask how he had tracked me down to Henry Pulleyne; he knew all the players and had all their numbers. For all I knew, he'd already rung Martyn and maybe Sandy too. The only one he wouldn't've rung to ask was Tim Dowell.

'I want you, Woolf. I want you here.'

'Why on earth should I come to you? Tell me that, Pat?'

'Because if you don't, Malcolm's seen his last dawn, if you see what I mean. Do you see what I mean?'

I choked with false laughter.

'What do you think I care about Malcolm, Pat? You want to hurt him, do it. He's given it and he's taken it. I told you, I'm a coward. Forget it. There's no chance.'

There was a long silence while we tried to out-wait each other. Finally it dawned on both of us that neither was bluffing. I felt sad. I liked Malcolm, notwithstanding our modest difference of opinion about who ought to live and who ought to decide who died. Lewis had loved him. He had done the decent thing for Tom; the decent thing I wasn't about to do for him. I could, and — when I hung up — I would ring Dowell. But Pat knew that and wouldn't wait around any longer than I had waited the previous night. There was nothing else I could do.

If I'm honest, I'll admit that I don't know how much I really felt about what was going to happen to Malcolm. What I'd said about giving it and taking it was true. He'd said it too — it was his league, his street. The only thing I'm certain I cared about was that I was recording the conversation and if Malcolm turned up dead we finally had the last of the Reddins in a box even he wouldn't be able to bully or bribe his way out of.

He said flatly, casually, like we were arranging our next date:

'I'll see you in hell, then, Woolf, won't I? I'll see you in hell all right.'

It was the only certainty. One way or another, it was bound to be true.

CHAPTER TWELVE

And then Sandy was screaming a meaningless noise and I was screaming with her and before I knew it a third voice had joined us. A tiny head, a tiny body, a squirming, squiggling, squawky little thing emerging half-afraid half-defiant from between Sandy's legs and somewhere back in the mists of time from between mine too. It sounded to my ears like it was crying: 'Gimme a Southern Comfort, wanna stay up for *Hill Street*, gotta Camel?' Then I can't remember a couple of minutes, maybe including that one, until a nurse was showing me the child saying: 'It's a boy', in case I couldn't tell the difference.

I leaned over him and kissed his tiny wrinkled head once for me and once for Lewis like he'd asked me to do; and to pacify all the available gods I baptised him with my tears.

If life had any sense of dramatic priority this would all have happened at the end — the end of the day, the end of the tale — and I could've sat holding hands with Sandy, relieved to be alive and revelling in the future. Instead, Wadd was tugging at my arm telling me we had to go and Sandy was looking alarmed and asking: 'Where're you going, Dave?' And my son asked: 'Where're you going, Dave?' So I told them: 'Back to jail; 'member, I'm supposed to be under arrest.'

It wasn't what I expected when I followed Tim's instructions to drive myself and Carson down to Chelsea Police Station where an interim command headquarters had been set up because — though the wreckage of my rampage was littered all over London — more of it was in or around Chelsea's patch than anywhere else. Just.

The instruction came in the second of the 'phone calls which followed Pat Reddin's. I'd caught him at the Yard and he told me to wait at Henry Pulleyne's while he put the machinery into motion. Then he rang back and told me where to go, emphasising that — whatever Pat's threat had been — he was not the sort of man in whose honour I ought to invest a great deal. My life and that of Carson would remain at risk until he was caught.

I said, 'What about Sandy?'

'Amazing. He's finally thought of someone else's safety. So'd I, sunshine. I've put someone on her house.'

On request, and for her safety, I told him where he would find Natalie.

I think it was his considerateness that led me for the first time ever to do what he told me. Nonetheless, we took the long way round to Chelsea. I wasn't taking any chances; I dropped the Henry video off at Orbach's chambers. There was no one in, of course, but I figured it was safer there than in police hands. Besides, it was still privileged.

We arrived at Chelsea to find Wally Wadd waiting for us. He held out a hand for the gun, which I gave him along with the audio-tape from Henry Pulleyne's answering machine. He dropped the gun into an evidence bag.

'So this is Woolf,' a tall, gaunt, moustachioed, uniformed inspector with more buckles than balls sneered from the other side of the desk. He could have stood in for John Cleese on a dark set. 'I wouldn't've thought he could do anyone any harm.'

I smiled sweetly and blew him a kiss across the counter. His face froze.

'Book him, Wadd. Bring him into my office. I want the pleasure of watching you charge this slime myself.' It was dispiriting to realise he got his lines the same place I did: off *Hill Street Blues*.

'Er, excuse me, sir,' Wadd had spent too long with Dowell to obey orders without an argument or to find polite refusal easy. He struggled to contain himself, and to express himself without acquiring his own set of charges — internal, disciplinary charges. 'Mr Dowell was quite explicit that Mr Woolf was not to be charged, sir.'

'And I,' the inspector leaned over the desk towards us, tall enough only to have to bend from the waist in order to speak straight into our faces; 'I, Wadd, am being quite explicit that he will be charged. This is my station, Wadd, and what I say is what I am accustomed to find is what happens. Send the gun out for fingerprinting,' he added as he turned and swaggered away from the desk-area, confident that his command would be obeyed.

During this exchange I had been studying the gun in its evidence bag. It was prettier to look at than the inspector. I began to think through the implications of having it printed. They would find my prints of course, but this was uncontroversial. I did not deny that I'd shot Ralph Reddin with it. They would also find Malcolm's but, given the course of events, this was similarly uncontentious.

What they would not find were any prints marked out to the late, unrepented Ralph Reddin himself. In view of my account that I'd seized the gun during a struggle with him this was perhaps not altogether appropriate. I worried about it until I remembered someone else whose prints would be found on the gun.

I whispered to Wadd as he hustled me and Carson into a corner for a quick confab: 'Your governor isn't going to like having that gun printed, Wally. He isn't going to like it at all.' As I already knew he wasn't as stupid as his name I wasn't surprised when he grasped the point immediately, much as Dowell had grasped the gun.

Before we could decide what to do, Larry-the-beanpole howled from an office down the corridor: 'Wadd. I'm waiting, Wadd.'

Wadd was so shocked he swung violently around and dropped the evidence bag. He and I jumped backwards: he in case it was still loaded; I because I knew it was. The inspector too ducked nervously out of sight. Carson, helpful as ever, and ever instinctively the domestic, swooped to her knees and picked the bag up, the wrong way. The gun fell out of it.

She stammered, 'I'm s-s-s-sorry,' as she seized it both by the handle and by the barrel, wringing it in her fingers and finding time to give the trigger itself a quick slither before she finally offered it to its wrongful owner by the trigger-guard with similar indiscretion. Nice touch, the stammer.

By this time the inspector had re-emerged. He witnessed the destruction of evidence and screamed apoplectic: 'Wadd. Stop her.'

'Stop her, sir? Stop her what, sir? Oh, I see. Here, miss, be careful with that, will you miss, it's dangerous you know, miss.'

'Right, sorry,' she let him take it from her and he, also apparently nervously, added his own prints and some dutiful smears to the mess that we could now be confident would end up in the report as 'a large number of unidentifiable partials'.

'Bring them both in here,' the inspector's voice had risen to a pitch to do Jessye Norman proud. 'I want them both charged, Wadd. Him with murder; her with ... Her with ... Put her on the same charge as an accomplice for the time being,' he added ominously, as if he might add the really serious charges later.

Wadd chewed on this for a while then shook his head. 'I don't think I can, sir. This is DI Dowell's, case, sir, and I work for DI Dowell. If I do what you say, sir, I'll be disobeying him, sir. Then I'll be in real trouble, sir.'

What he meant was: your threats won't survive Dowell's return.

A uniformed constable poked his head around the door.

'Got the girl, sir.'

I caught a quick glimpse of Natalie standing the other end of the corridor. I waved and saw her wave back before the inspector said: 'Tell the duty sergeant to come in here. Right away.' The duty sergeant entered seconds later. 'I want a charge sheet drawn up for these jokers. For the murder of Ralph Reddin.'

The sergeant looked even more confused.

'I thought, sir ... I thought they were assisting in the investigation, sir?'

'Don't think, Sergeant, do it.'

He sat complacently back in his chair, as if to say: what do you all think of that, then.

Wadd said; 'Excuse me, sir ...'

'No. Get out. Consider yourself lucky you're not on a charge yourself; I saw the way you handled that gun.' I thought it was more a case of failing to handle it, but I didn't suppose he'd welcome a correction from me any more than from Wadd.

As the duty sergeant led us down the corridor Wadd mused out loud; 'False imprisonment. Wrongful charges. What's it worth to a solicitor, would you say Sergeant?'

The duty sergeant grinned amiably; 'At least a cup of canteen coffee. Don't worry: it's often like this. I usually find that if I take my time, it's calmed itself down. D'you want an interrogation room?'

'I want to make a 'phone call,' I said. 'I'm under arrest. There's a gangster running around London trying to kill people, including me, and I'm under arrest. I wanna call my lawyer.'

'I thought you were a lawyer, sir,' the sergeant said.

Wadd explained: 'He's not a very good one.'

I looked at him balefully. I'd take that sort of remark from Dowell, if drunk, but not from his sergeant; there was no respect any more.

I told Carson to call Sandy, and I'd call 'someone else'. I was going to tell him about the latest video. Before either of us could call anyone, however, a telephone call came in for Dowell which was passed to Wadd. We were left sitting on a hard bench with Natalie but without a 'phone.

I knew why they wanted her. I wasn't worried. Neither she nor Carson nor the two goons they'd been beating up on at the time had witnessed the shooting. The only witness was Pat Reddin and in a conflict I'd bet even my word against his. Nor, if asked, would Carson or Natalie have to lie: they'd never seen me with a gun before the plywood partition went up in smoke.

'Come on, Dave,' Wadd grabbed me by the arm. 'That was the police from your lady's house: they're taking her to the Royal Free. She's all right,' he pre-empted my cry of concern, 'but your kid's about to be born the child of a jail-bird. Let's get out of here.'

He dragged me through the door as the inspector came out of his office yelling: 'Where do you think you're going, Wadd?' And Carson was yelling, 'Go, Dave, go; give her my love.'

I got a little calm time with Sandy before it happened: in between spasms of labour-pain we still weren't prepared for notwithstanding the classes. She said, 'What I have to do to get you to pay me any attention.'

Wadd had gone to fetch us both whatever was available to feed and fuel us. She started to giggle: 'What on earth have you done to your friend Karen?'

'Why?'

'She called up. She said you'd sent them a video and it'd been intercepted by the US Customs. They're being charged with importing immoral materials. What's it all about?'

'It's a bit nasty. It was, uh, related to Cushing. I thought they couldn't watch it on their system.'

'You know, they can transfer tapes across from one system to another, Dave; they're quite technological these days; even in America. You'd better ring her.'

'I'll speak to Tim first.' He'd have to sort it out. If I couldn't ring with a few reassuring noises I was the one who'd be importing immoral material — what she'd have to say to me down the 'phone line.

After I'd brought her up to date on the events of the last two days, she said, 'Is Carson all right? Are you all right?' She wasn't asking about either our physical or legal condition but about the things we'd been forced to do.

'It's been heavy,' I admitted, my eyes searching hers to see what else she might be asking.

The intermittent outbursts of agony left her calmer than normal between.

'I'm glad. Glad she was with you, Dave. Glad I found her for you.'

I nodded.

'There's things you do that I know I'm not a part of. I know I can't be; I don't want to be. But over the last few days, I've been thinking: maybe that's for the best; maybe that's part of why I've gone on loving you when you've given me a million reasons not to. I do love you, Dave, I do.'

I squeezed her hand in reply.

'And ... And I know you love me too. So I'm glad you had her to share it with. It makes me a bit a part of it too.'

I didn't get to ask her exactly what she might have meant, because that was when it finally started to go down. As they wheeled her to the theatre, Wadd returned from a 'phone call, telling me Dowell was back at Chelsea and wanted us there right away. I didn't even bother telling him that for once Tim'd have to wait.

On the journey back, Wadd gave me the news: Malcolm McCafferty was dead but Pat Reddin still at large. Dowell had been all over town. At Malcolm's flat they'd found Tom in a state of shock, but alone and unhurt. They'd almost caught up with Pat Reddin on Hackney Marshes. He was accompanied by Trent and two other henchmen. They had been in the process of burying Malcolm in a vacant lot a few hundred yards away from their own property.

Wadd caught the shame on my face.

'There was nothing you could've done.'

'If I'd done nothing, he wouldn't be dead.' I'd killed him as much as Ralph Reddin.

Reddin and his cohorts had fled to their car for a chase through Hackney's malevolent one-way system. I was surprised anyone had found anyone else, let alone found their way out again. Reddin did; the police didn't.

When we arrived, Dowell was in conference with the John Cleese clone. A police surgeon was in attendance. He'd examined both Natalie and Carson and now had to pay for the privilege and examine me too, in each case more in order to check out the consistency of our stories than to see whether any of us had suffered serious harm. He was able to confirm that I had been badly beaten within the last twenty-four hours. He also noticed some older bruising, but I diplomatically declined to identify Dowell as my assailant.

Natalie and Carson had been lodged in a cell for the night, the latter still, like me, uncharged. I was put into the interrogation room where not long before dawn Dowell joined me. He was grinning broadly.

'Stupid poof.'

I gathered that these two words were intended to convey that I was a free man at last. Free in theory, but not in practice.

'Reddin's on the loose; you've got my gun; what now?' He shrugged.

'What can I say? These things happen. At least we've got him on Malcolm's murder, if we catch up with him. You'll see your kid grow up.'

'He, uh, gave me the impression he or his brothers might have arms that stretched beyond walls. Waddayathink?'

'I doubt it. Who'd be interested? What I hear, if the other two ever get out they'll be too old to shuffle to the post office to collect their pensions. Why would anyone want to preserve Pat's position for him? I'd say, once we've got him, the next six months, maybe a year, take it easy, look over your shoulder, just in case, while the vultures're carving up the territory between them.'

'How'd it happen, Tim? How'd I do it?'

I didn't try to fool either of us I'd put the Reddins into the history book by any sort of design or skill.

'Same way you do most things, Dave: the bull in a china shop school of detection.' He wasn't kidding. 'You were the unexpected, Dave; no one had their guard up against an utter nutter. Look what happened with your sting —they saw through it in no time. It was a rational attempt on your part, so they were prepared for it — or something like it. But since, you've been acting wholly irrationally —even or especially in their terms. No one but no one would expect anything like it. If you'd any sense at all, you'd've been scared off, given up, run away and hid — like you were supposed to do and like all the other professionals they've known when things got a bit rough.'

'Is that how it works, Tim? Is that how the Reddins and the other hoods manage to make it in the so-called straight world? By turning nasty on people who can't deal with it?'

'Something like that.'

'So why'd they let them get near in the first place? That's what I can't figure. Oh, sure, I know they want their money. But money can be had without inviting them into their homes. D'you know where the Reddins had been? They'd been at The Mansion House for dinner, for Chrissake.'

'Which is what they wanted as much as they wanted their money at work in the legitimate market,' he said. 'I'll tell you what it is, Dave. Those types in the City, they're bored. Look at them — it happens here now, just like in the States — they're doing coke, crack, every kind of crap they can get their hands on. You wanna ask why? These people're making more money than you or I ever dreamed of. But they get so hyped up doing it they can't unwind. They're excitement junkies. People like the Reddins are exciting; the thrill of the forbidden and the unfamiliar. Then one day they find out they've let them get a little too close to the hearth and it isn't fun anymore: the Reddins want to play the party-games they're good at instead of the ones their hosts know best.'

These were the times when I recalled Dowell's university education and he forgot momentarily to play the part of the plodding policeman. I was glad it didn't happen too often. I said, 'So all I got to do is wait for you to catch him?'

'Yup.'

'Here?' In safety.

'Well, uh, yes, or no.'

He'd covered all the options.

'Waddayawant, Tim?'

His eyes shone.

'Wadd told me about the second video.' He meant the Henry video. 'This is our chance. Once we get Reddin, he'll offer up Pulleyne. He knows he won't be able to use him any more. It'll all be his best bet. He'll expect to be able to negotiate thirty a long way down and probably will. It'll all be in the hands of the lawyers. His lawyers'll talk to the Lord Chancellor's Office as soon as talk to us.'

'I thought you said your people would take it direct to the Lord Chancellor's Office anyway?'

'That was before last night, Dave. We've got the second video and we've got a murder on our hands. It's a different ball-game now. To a copper, murder's it, the big one, the hit parade. The psychology'll be completely different as long as Reddin's on the loose —no one's looking beyond the hunt, beyond the capture.'

'What are you suggesting we do?'

'Grab him now. If we move now, before we've got Reddin, no one can be a hundred per cent certain Reddin'll do a deal, even if it's what I or they expect. There's too much risk to participate in a cover-up until they've got Reddin's consent, it might yet come out later. I don't want to kid you.' He didn't want to be blamed if it didn't work like last time. 'Maybe it'd mean no more than a night in the jug. But it's something; we'd have him; the press'd get it, wouldn't you think?' Sure they would; he'd leak it.

The press were already all over Forest Gate and they were going to catch up with Hackney Marsh by midday. 'Waddayathink? It's perfect, Dave. We've got it; it's our one chance,' he repeated.

'What do you need from me?'

'The videos.'

'Ah, the videos.'

'Yeah, the videos. That one, and the other. The one you sent abroad,' he reminded me in case I forgot what lie I'd told.

'It's a funny thing, by accident I sent the wrong film. Which reminds me, there's another little problem I need your help with.' But I decided to leave the request to call the American authorities to one side for the time being. 'The one I meant to send was in this country all the time. It's with my client. So's the new one.'

'Yeah? Really? All the time. Well I never! Will your client release them?'

He still didn't know who my client was.

'He'll have to, won't he?' I meant, though Dowell still didn't know it, that they were evidence of a serious crime and he was a barrister.

I was shown into an office to call. I was told how to use the extension: like the Reddins' I just had to dial nine. I didn't. On a side-table there was a direct line; I rang him on that instead, at his home.

'Yes?' he answered testily.

'It's Dave. The police want the Cushing video. I also got Henry Pulleyne on film. He was the go-between for the last few years. They want that too. It's at your chambers. I left it there last night. It's a long and complex and rather sad, sick story; I'm at Chelsea nick. People're dead, Russel, more than you know about. Oh, uh, and Sandy had our child this morning.'

He was unaffected by the latter news. 'Congratulations,' he said flatly without asking whether it was a boy or a girl. 'I want to think about it. It belongs to me.'

'Yeah, well, sure; but without it there isn't a quarter the case we've got together. Listen, Russel, the police are prepared to run with it. Well, Dowell is.' I realised he had as little reason to trust Dowell as did Malcolm. 'Anyhow, you can make copies, to prevent a cover-up. Right?'

'Are the police holding you?'

'No.'

'I'm engaged this morning. I'll see you after lunch. We can talk then. I want to think it through first, fair enough?'

It's like that with a client sometimes. When I was in practice. I'd work really hard, creatively and aggressively, to screw a settlement out of the other side that was a lot better than the result we'd get if we won in court. Then I'd ask the client in to see me anticipating praise, adulation or at least a box of chocolates.

Instead, the client would start arguing with me: couldn't I do more? If they were prepared to pay up now, didn't it mean the other side thought they were going to lose in court? Perhaps they had more to hide than we knew about? Wasn't it worth pressing right to the door? Why was I so keen to give up, sell out, take a bum deal?

But I didn't see what more Orbach could want. I'd done the job for him. I had Martyn Pulleyne by the proverbial short-and-curlies, tighter than we'd any right to expect. All of it wrapped up in old newspapers with 'murder' in the headlines. Even if they wouldn't prosecute, he had the material to publish.

'It's a bit more difficult than that, Russel. There's someone still on the loose; he killed a man last night; he's killed before; he's the one who had my flat fire-bombed, and, uh, he's sort of still none too friendly. I shot his brother. I, uh, had him tied up for a while and I'm not sure he enjoyed it.'

'Then you shouldn't have let him go. My chambers, two-thirty, Dave, or no deal.' He hung up as if he'd said nothing more sinister than 'Frederick's, tomorrow night, eight o'clock'.

By the time I'd hung up too, Dowell and Wadd were gone. The day desk sergeant knew enough about my relationship to the case to tell me they'd run after a rumour about Reddin, but not enough for me to convince him to lend me a policeman, preferably one packing a pistol on his hip, to keep me company for the day. He did agree to hang onto Carson and Natalie once they awoke and not to let them leave. It simply didn't occur to me to stay there myself until it was time for the appointment with Orbach.

Once I'd left the station, though, I wondered what I was supposed to do with myself to kill time without allowing Ralph Reddin the opportunity to kill me. My Passat felt like a London-wide neon sign, visible from everywhere. I went back up to the hospital where at least I knew there was a police guard on Sandy and the kid — I still didn't think of it as a he — who might be willing to protect me as well. She was well enough to be thinking about work and I passed much of the morning on the pay-phone acting as her clerk, dealing with matters mundane. I told them where they'd find me in the early part of the afternoon and that I'd ring them again later.

I made it to the Temple alive. I was late and I wasted more time deceiving and dissembling my way into the car park, promising I'd be no more than ten minutes. The car-park attendants at the Temple probably have more influence within the legal profession than clerks — they certainly do more to earn it. I had to park at a distance from his chambers. I walked through the open-air car-park, past the rich old buildings and the wantonly spacious gardens, drinking in greedily the collegiate atmosphere, thinking to myself what an incongruous combination it made with the circumstances that brought me there.

There was an odd, unsettled mood in Orbach's chambers. Things were happening, important things, like someone had received a six-figure cheque or a Hong Kong brief. I was placed in the waiting-room, where I could neither hear nor see anything, just sense it. At about three I was led in to see Orbach by his grinning clerk.

'Sit down, Dave,' Orbach too was smiling.

'What's the fuss? D'you finally win a case?'

'This,' he slid across the desk a slip of embossed paper that contained the following announcement:

'The Lord Chancellor announces with regret that he has accepted the resignation of Mr Justice Pulleyne. Sir Martyn has suffered ill-health for a number of years and the Lord Chancellor wishes to express his profound gratitude for the way in which he has nonetheless continued to discharge the onerous duties of his office.

'The Lord Chancellor announces the appointment to the High Court vacancy caused by the resignation of Sir Martyn Pulleyne of ...'

I didn't need to read further.

'I should've seen it coming. I've never known you need time to think about anything.' I cursed myself for my stupidity. He'd given away our trump card. 'I've been running all over London, being shot at,' I was exaggerating but only just. 'I killed someone for you, Orbach; a friend of mine died pretending he didn't know where I was; his friend was carved into little pieces last night for you ...'

'McCafferty?' He was fully informed. More than I would have expected if his only contacts were with the Lord Chancellor's Office. 'Hardly for me. He was no lily-white innocent.'

'No, he didn't do it for you and I don't think he did it for me. But he did do it for Lewis, and he did it for a friend of his who would've been dead otherwise. At least he did it for principle, Orbach; so did I.'

'You did it for money, Dave.'

I shook my head violently. There was no way I could accept that everything I'd done was simply in order to repair the hole in my pocket.

'I cared about getting Pulleyne, Russel. I cared about what he'd done. Sandy cared — Sandy encouraged me to go on with it when I was beginning to think maybe not. She said he'd made a mockery of our lives, but it's you who's made the mockery.'

He sneered: 'You're so naive, Dave.'

I asked, 'What happens when they catch Pat Reddin? What happens if he decides to talk at his trial instead of settling for a shorter sentence?'

'It's not very likely, is it, Dave?' His lack of concern was too casual so he added, 'They've got a lot of room for manoeuvre. All that's needed is to confine the charge to McCafferty. That means there's no reason for a recommendation.'

The difference between thirty served in full and a life sentence without a minimum recommendation was about twenty years — he might only have to serve ten. He could do less if he behaved while he was on the inside. A few hours ago I had been reassured I would get to watch my kid grow up; now I'd be lucky to see him into secondary school.

'How much of this is the Lord Chancellor himself?' The Lord Chancellor was a man popularly perceived to be so proud of his integrity he'd prosecute the Prime Minister rather than participate in a cover-up.

'None of it. I haven't even been in to see him yet. It's been, er, arranged.'

'He's not a fool; how'd they manage it?'

'Dear Dave, you're so innocent. Civil servants have centuries of experience; no politician is ever a match. Besides, don't forget that I'm highly technically qualified and the Lord Chancellor's a man who positively doesn't want to hear bits of undocumented rumour and gossip about a man's past, all that establishment tongue-wagging. All they've done is to give him what he wanted — nothing but the relevant, professional truth.'

'And who are "they"?'

'Ah, well, no one in particular really. You see, no one needs to know the whole story. If the right different people — in the different departments of government —know the right different bits of it, the outcome can be utterly predictable.'

He couldn't resist showing off just how well he knew how to play the system.

'It's the way government works. You know, most civil servants are basically honest, so all you have to do is to structure the information each of the ones you talk to has available until their honest reaction to it fits the end you're looking for. Bear in mind: the first thing — perhaps the only thing — that concerns them has been to make sure the Pulleyne story doesn't break.' He had manipulated the government and its civil servants — both in and beyond the Lord Chancellor's Office — much the way he'd manipulated me.

Which reminded me to ask, 'What about me; everything I know?'

'It's privileged, all privileged, Dave. Unless you're subpoenaed by a court you can't say a word to anyone.' And if I did, he'd have me, as we quaintly like to call suspension of a solicitor, struck off the rolls. 'Which doesn't augur well for your return to practice, or the contribution you'll be able to make to your child's upbringing.'

'You had it all worked out from the beginning.' It was supposed to be an accusation, but I daresay Orbach took it for admiration. 'All along, you never intended anything more than this. You let it all happen: just for this.' The judgeship they'd never otherwise have given him.

'You're lucky, Dave, you always have been.' To my surprise, he sounded envious. 'Nothing ever came easily to me, Dave, you know that; nothing ever fell into my lap; they've always hated me.' Both the establishment and the opposition. I didn't feel sorry for him; he'd brought it on himself. 'Anyway, I didn't do it for me, Dave.'

I waited. He folded his hands across his stomach and continued sanctimoniously.

'You see, Dave, I have Frankie to think of now. It's no good for her, my working late, overwrought about some case. I get just a month in the long vac, a couple of weeks at Christmas, to take her somewhere. She needs and deserves more than that, Dave. You'll understand soon enough. She's worth everything, Dave, everything. There's nothing too good for her, or too great a sacrifice. This way, I can lead an orderly life, a conventional life, a respectable, responsible life, be there for her whenever she needs me. I did it for her, Dave, for Frankie. I hope you'll believe that; I hope in time you'll understand.'

'What am I supposed to say, Russel? Well done? Congratulations?'

'Just send me your final account.' He rose to indicate that the audience was at an end.

As he came around the desk, I thought: I've always wanted to hit a High Court judge. Well, I'd never actually thought of doing so before, but it felt then as if it was something I'd always wanted to do. He didn't think of it at all. So he didn't see me hesitate as he held the door open for me, the courteous way the powerful and possessed like to do, to remind you they haven't left their manners behind even if they have left you, nor did he understand when I dropped into a crouch. Nor, therefore, was he prepared when I came up with my forehead into his chin and both my fists clenched together into his belly.

I slammed the door behind me just in time for no one else to hear him howl or see him fall to the ground. I didn't want him heard or seen: it wouldn't be a dignified way for Sir Russel, the Honourable Mr Justice Orbach, to find his way onto the High Court bench.

I was heading for my car when a voice called out: 'Mr Woolf, Mr Woolf.'

I turned and saw Michael, the clerk to Pulleyne's former chambers, hurrying to catch me up. I waited for him He said: 'Sir Martyn would like to see you, sir. He asked me if I could find you. He's at chambers, sir. It's very sad, sir,' he added, presuming that I by now knew.

Members of the judiciary, according to convention, formally maintain a seat in their old chambers and their old clerks carry out a number of minor tasks for them, as a courtesy and in consideration for the valuable good-will their elevation brings to the chambers as a whole. I was surprised Michael was still bothering to be helpful to Martyn. From the way he'd put it, he didn't know the full story, but he was nonetheless much more polite to me than the last time we'd talked.

I dithered for less than a second. There was nothing left to gain, or to lose. It seemed appropriate. Besides, I was curious and it was less than a two minute walk. If it'd been three, I might not've bothered. As we strolled back together I asked how he'd found me. He told me he'd rung my office. They told him I was with Orbach but he'd just missed me there, so thought it was worth the effort of chasing down the Temple to see if he could catch me.

Michael went through to tell Pulleyne I had arrived and when he returned told me I'd only have to wait a couple of minutes, he had a quick call to make first.

I used the time to ring the office from the clerk's room. They told me Dowell had been trying to reach me, so they'd told him the same as Michael. I rang Dowell, but he was still on the road and they wouldn't patch me through. Wadd was back, though, and we exchanged a few words, coded for want of privacy at my end, in which I managed nonetheless to communicate where I was, that it was all over bar the shouting and that Sir Martyn Pulleyne had resigned from the High Court bench on account of his health. He told me he already knew the last. I was glad I wouldn't have to be the one to break it to Dowell.

Pulleyne was carefully folding his red robes into a battered suitcase as I walked in.

'Sit down, Woolf. Would you like some coffee?' He picked up the 'phone and asked, 'Michael. D'you think Mr Woolf could have a cup of coffee? Oh, and, er, could I have one with him?' When he hung up, he explained, 'You probably have more influence with him now than I.' Former judges can't return to practice; Michael had lost two fee-earners in as many weeks; which was why he had to start being nice to solicitors all over again, even one like me.

'The mighty fallen. You don't act like it, Martyn.'

He settled back behind the desk. It wasn't his own desk. Once on the bench, they do not maintain the facilities; they have no regular use for them; but facilities are made available when necessary. As the room contained only the one, large desk, I guessed it belonged to the head of chambers.

He waited for one of the junior clerks to bring in our coffees before he answered.

'I've learned to take what fate has handed out. You've seen the announcement, I take it?'

'Yeah, sure, sorry to hear about your health.'

'Were you surprised, Woolf?'

'It's what I always thought we were fighting against. I've lost battles before. How's Henry?'

'Ah, yes, Henry.' His eyes glazed over. 'He's gone to the States, this morning.' He glanced at his watch. 'Concorde. Should be there by now.'

'He came to see you last night?'

'Yes, of course. What else would he do?'

'And Isabelle? How's she taking it?'

Unspecified was: what were we talking about? Martyn's disgrace, or that of his children?

'She's gone up to Yorkshire. I'm joining her for a few days. We're thinking of flying down to Cap d'Antibes for the holidays. Of course, the flats aren't really intended for winter-use but it's very mild there now.' He was so sanguine I almost expected him to invite us to join them.

'Did you know?' About Henry and Julia.

'Know? What does know mean?'

The last person'd said something similar to me was Cushing. It was almost an admission.

'Who would have expected them to appoint Orbach?' he said. 'That was a surprise. But not, I should think, to you. Would that be accurate?'

'I didn't know what he was about.' I was damned if I'd cover for him any longer. 'But it doesn't excuse ...'

'There is nothing to excuse, Woolf. I never had a choice; not if I cared about my family.' Like Orbach, he'd done it for all the right reasons. 'I've been a barrister for forty years. They've been good years; more good years than I was brought up to have any right to expect. Of course it's sad when things slip away from you, but it doesn't mean they didn't happen. All things considered, some might say I've done rather well to protect the position for this long.'

'Is that what it's about — protecting the position?' He shook his head sadly.

'You're so naive, Woolf.' Now where had I heard that before? 'You still don't understand, do you? What do you think I did that was so terrible? There are secrets amongst the judiciary just as elsewhere in every walk of life. Do you think we don't lie and steal and cheat: on our friends, on our wives, on our financial associates? It's a short step to cheat on our litigants. It's only laymen and fools who think we're actually innocent of any wrong-doing: we're not even supposed or expected to be. It's the image that matters, not the man but the office. It's about the role, Woolf, not the reality.'

He picked up a volume of the Law Reports from his desk and flicked it over until he found a passage which he recited:

'"If one judge in a thousand acts dishonestly within his jurisdiction to the detriment of a party before him, it is less harmful to the health of society to leave that party without a remedy than that nine hundred and ninety-nine honest judges should be harassed by vexatious litigation alleging malice in the exercise of their proper jurisdiction." The House of Lords, in a 1985 case,' he noted. 'Of course, it's not quite the same but as lawyers, well, you know this as well as I do, Woolf, we're used to applying a principle from one area of the law to another. Eh?'

'Do you think that answers it, Martyn? Is it enough in the face of the evidence?' I decided to put it into terms that he might, just, be familiar with.

'What evidence?' He joined the tips of his fingers in a spire then began to lay it out for me, the way it would sound if the push of my word ever came up against the shove of his. 'The film Henry made with you?' Cushing's wasn't even worth considering. 'The film you made him make?'

'There's no question of duress.'

'That depends on what you mean by duress, doesn't it?'

'You tell me what kind of duress I put on him, then.'

'Your threat to expose the truth about Julia's child.' I remembered what Julia had said about his ability to turn the truth on its head.

'You came to Henry with a cock-and-bull story about me, playing on his position as a banker, and he went along with it under your threat of exposing his relationship with his sister,' he stated blandly. 'It was natural for him to think of protecting her first. In the circumstances.'

'About which you'd say you've always known, I daresay?'

'Of course. That was why I wanted her to have it adopted.'

I started to laugh. I couldn't help myself. I meant it to be mocking laughter but it sounded real. I no longer knew what was true. If he *had* known about them, as he implied, then maybe that was really why he made her get it adopted. I told him why I was laughing. He mused, apparently not at all eager to bring the conversation to a close.

'That's the job of a judge, you know, to decide what is true and what isn't. To decide what the facts are. Not, mind you, to know what the facts are; no one can know, can they? No, our job is to take two sides of a story and chose one side as true, even though we might be getting it wrong. Because we say it, it becomes the truth, or the facts. It's that aspect of the job — that almost god-like function — that I always found the hardest to accept. It's what made it all so unreal.' And as something unreal, so also easy to treat with contempt.

I was tired of fencing.

'You abused it, Martyn; people trusted in it and you abused their trust. You can't get around it with philosophy.'

'I wonder. I wonder if I did. What I was trying to say just now — it doesn't matter what's decided, just that something is decided. How it's decided doesn't really matter. Look at some of the men who've been appointed in the last few years.' I knew some of them he was talking about: a generation of judges who'd come to their professional peak during an age when the only constants were the stars of cynical capitalism, and some of whom continued to adhere to them assiduously once they were on the bench for want of any other article of faith. 'What criteria do they apply to their decisions? It's all self-interest.'

'Why did you want to see me, Martyn?'

'I thought you'd want to see me. I thought you'd want to ask me.'

'I've been asking; you haven't been answering.'

'Haven't I, Woolf? I thought I had.'

'No, all you've really told me is you're not ashamed and that if it ever comes out it'll be your word and that of your family against mine. But there's Pat Reddin yet,' I reminded him. 'No one yet knows what he'll do or say.' Once — if — they caught him.

'The mad meanderings of a criminal. A futile attempt to blacken the name of a member of the High Court. A man whose name is above reproach. I, I Woolf, I am above reproach.' He had stopped playing games. I was reminded of Caroline's 'he am de judge; he am de law'.

'Then why resign, Martyn? If you've got all the answers ready, why resign?'

'Why? Because it's the right thing to do, isn't it?' I shook my head in defeat.

'How the hell would you know, Martyn? How in the hell would you know?'

It wasn't much of an answer but, then, it wasn't much of a conversation. I was disappointed, like at the end of *A Man For All Seasons*, when Thomas More finally speaks. Instead of an impassioned plea for the rights of conscience, what he offers is a lawyer's quibble about the validity of the laws and procedures as a result of which he is about to part company with his head. All about form; nothing of substance. The meeting hadn't been worth it — to me or to him. I still didn't understand why he had bothered.

He glanced at his watch again, saying, 'I have to catch a train, Woolf. I'm sorry. You'll have to excuse me now.'

It was already winter-dark when I emerged.

I went back to the car and found that, notwithstanding the permission to park I thought I had procured, instead there had been secured to the windscreen a caution that if I parked there ever again in the entirety of my life my car would be towed away and probably crushed to the current size of my ego. I busied myself trying to clear it. I had to rub and spit and scrape until my fingernails were jammed with it and threatening to break. It was almost pleasing to have something unequivocally useful to do at last.

'I wouldn't bother if I was you,' the familiar, flat voice spoke behind me. 'You're not going anywhere.'

I swung around to see Pat Reddin watching me from a few feet away, leaning against the railing of the gardens, calmly pointing something at me through a raincoat pocket that I didn't think were fingers. He tossed his head towards a path that led around the side of King's Bench Walk and came to a full-stop. In my turn, I leaned back against the car and shook my head.

'I think I like it here, Pat.'

'You think I'm scared to shoot you right here?' He pulled a gun — yet another gun — from his pocket and strode the few remaining feet without hesitation.

On the pavement, barristers in three-piece, pin-striped suits, their polyestred clerks, the occasional client arriving for a conference with counsel and the odd secretary or typist watched, amazed, disbelievingly, thinking it must be a movie in the making, too stupid or stupefied to notice there weren't any cameras.

From between the other cars, half a dozen plain-clothes police emerged, waving guns back at him, shouting at him that they were armed. I remembered how casual Orbach had been about the threat of Reddin breaking ranks, and his admission that the people he'd talked to hadn't only been in the Lord Chancellor's Office. It wouldn't've mattered if Reddin had dropped his gun and put up his hands in surrender. As he would himself have said, he was a dead man. I felt sad: we'd both tried to buck the system; the difference was, he'd come closer to success than had I.

The deafening roar of their gunfire shattered the contemplative calm of the Temple. His own shot went wild through what was left of the warning on my windscreen. It seemed somehow appropriate. He collapsed to the pavement, smiling with contempt.

I knew now why Pulleyne had wanted to see me. Dowell, who'd not been present, had seen the point of the interview that I, who had been, had missed. But Dowell had an advantage. It was the same reason he wanted me out on the streets instead of in the safety of a cell. Neither of them had any purpose other than to place me where Reddin could reach me.

ORBACH'S JUDGEMENT

What was it about Orbach?

He was a big man, not physically but in emphasis and effect, a man of gothic proportions, a man of mystery, a man of apparent – but I emphasise only apparent – total command not only of himself but of everyone around him, a manipulator; at times I thought the word that fit best was monster; at other times, despite myself, I still liked him, sensing that one day the lid had to come off, and when it did it would cause him a lot of hurt.

Above all, he was an arrogant man. He was a brilliant man. His arrogance was surpassed by his single-minded ability, and his ability by his extraordinary ambition. He had enjoyed supreme professional success, and corresponding wealth. But he was probably the loneliest and unhappiest man I ever met, and certainly the most cruel. He made enemies first thing in the morning the way others made their beds, and left them just as tidily ordered.

Through patently a driven man, with a centrifugal energy that swept lesser mortals out of his way, I had struggled long and hard to identify his code and his direction. He lacked any identifiable morality. In this sense he was, of course, the perfect lawyer and an even better judge; but he was a wholly imperfect human being.

*For long-suffering,
long-complaining Ruthie: A long overdue dedication!*

CHAPTER ONE

I was exhausted by the time I finished the manuscript. It was nearly three o'clock: a cold night early in the new year. No one was left in the club, save Natalie, a waiter and a couple who didn't want to go home to their separate apartments and separate partners.

I was sitting behind the desk in the office, as I had been since I had started to read, some five or more hours before. I had drunk the best part of a bottle of Southern Comfort and either I had hardly smoked at all or I was on my second pack of Camels. I felt like I'd run a marathon, got up before ten in the morning, made love twice in a month or done something else equally exhausting but exhilarating.

I couldn't at first work out why, but the mood I was in reminded me of Bob Dylan's 'Desolation Row'. I remember the first time I heard it: the first time, the second, the third and on and on until I was equally exhausted. Exhausted, yet relieved, as if I had just discovered that a secret wasn't as dark and as dirty as I'd always believed. There was something about the song that made it for me the greatest Dylan of all. It was a glorification of depression; an exuberant celebration of despair; an anthem to the awful; a theme tune for the intense loneliness I then suffered from, and continued to suffer from for many years after; a song about people driven mad by loneliness, the mad I was often on the verge of, the mad that sometimes made me think I could murder for the sake of feeling someone's warm body next to mine

Sometimes I would listen stoned or drunk, on occasions with a companion, too often alone. It didn't always bring me relief. Sometimes, it made things worse. Nonetheless, it reflected and gave a tangible form to the balance of my own mania. In those days I saw only the downside of life. Moments of joy nestled uncomfortably and unnaturally between visions of hell. If it wasn't going to beat me — and there were many times it came close to doing so — I had to be able to relate to it other than out of a bottle of pills. That's what the song did for me: it spaced out my despair.

Times changed. Me too. I grew up — some say less than others, everyone says less than I ought to have. I could find what I wanted in music instead; jazz, classical, recently, thanks to the private tapes Lewis left in the club, I've even begun to listen to opera, which gives you some idea of how old I am and comparatively settled. Thanks for the latter go mostly to Sandy, and of course always and above all to Alton.

Sandy is the woman I loved and the mother of our son, Alton, the child I'd never believed I was going to have, in part for reasons medical, in part because it had been an article of my faith that the kindest thing I could do for the world was to leave nothing of myself behind.

Alton's odd name derives from my friend Lewis, who owned the club before me and who had died in the middle of my last case. Fat old faggot, ubiquitous usurer, conniving club-owner and erstwhile gangster, he had been a shoulder for me to lean on, a source of information when others had dried up, a name to get me through doors, and once or twice the principal reason I hadn't achieved my main objective in life: to take up residence as a handful of ashes in an imitation Grecian urn.

Lewis was only ever known as Lewis. I found out why when I read his will. His full name was Lewis Alexander Altonspritzer. The way the club came to me is long and complicated and — as a matter of fact — I'm not the person he intended to get it. A lot of people played a part in its devolution onto my shoulders: Malcolm, Lewis' ex- and the then manager of the club, who was supposed to benefit but didn't stay around long enough; Tim Dowell; and Tom, Malcolm's tantalising toy-boy. Tom was the only one who might've objected to the chicanery that left me in charge, but it wouldn't have benefited him anyhow: the club would have gone to some obscure relative in Malcolm's native Glasgow, no friend of Lewis, nor Malcolm, nor even of mine. I gave Tom a job in the club and the club was paying for him to go to private classes to get some paper qualifications with which to help Natalie keep the books.

Natalie? Well, that's another part of what'd been happening but if I tell you about it now, I'll never begin. This is supposed to be about how come my sons got a weird name like Alton.

In a separate letter to me which was with his will, Lewis said of our then unborn child — if it's a girl, call her after me; if it's a boy, give him a kiss. He had also left him ten thousand in the will itself. 'It' was a boy, and I gave him a kiss, but it wasn't enough, so Sandy suggested we give him half Lewis's last name as well, as a sort of compromise. We couldn't call him Alexander: that was a name already appropriated by Alex Keenan, one of

Sandy's former lovers. I had protested about encumbering our child with such an awesomely awkward name. Sandy said:

'You wanna call him Spritzer?'

Lewis itself was out; it would've been tempting fate. Liberals we might well be but we wanted OUR son to be NORMAL. I suggested lamely:

'Elton?' She'd been known not to turn the radio off.

'Alton,' she repeated, and that was the end of the discussion. Sorry, kid, I thought: you'll understand when you're older.

It had begun just a few days before. I was at work. This itself would once upon a time have been cause for comment, but in the year and a quarter since Alton had been born I'd gone back into and stayed in practice as a lawyer with Sandy. She was now only working part-time. The practice was the same one I'd set up with her after we'd finished all our qualifying stages, more years ago than she'd forgive me for telling. It was called Nichol and Co. Nichol is Sandy. My name's Dave Woolf. Sandy's authority over the names we use goes back a long way.

I'd been in it at the beginning for maybe four-five years before she kicked me out. Seemed to think I ought to be paid in cash instead of coke. When all our debts and assets were totalled up, I got less back out of the partnership than I'd put in. I set up as a private investigator. After a while getting by on process serving and divorce work, I ran out of steam altogether.

I picked up a big case: Disraeli Chambers, the serial killings of a bunch of loony-tunes lefties. That was when I met Dowell: he's a policeman, then a detective sergeant, now a detective inspector. It was when I re-encountered Russel Orbach, the barrister, who I'd known years before in a much less tortured lifetime when he was himself a member of those Chambers. It was when Lewis saved my life.

It was also when Sandy'n'I'd made up our long-standing dispute, discovering as I'd long suspected that the aggro between us all those years before had Freudian undertones. For a while after that we were on and off. She wanted me to come back to work as a lawyer. I was always finding an excuse not to. The excuses ran out when she told me she was pregnant, and my last case as a private eye finished the day Alton was born. I'd been going straight since.

Mostly what going straight meant was legal aid work. Our practice is in North London where a lot of people are still tenants of private landlords, or employed on terms and in conditions that would make Edwin Chadwick, the nineteenth century public health reformer, shudder; many of them, maybe a majority, are black and in that part of London this is a criminal offence in its own right, which gave me a lot of time in the magistrates' courts.

It wasn't boring work in itself, but it bored me. It was routine, and I hate routine. It was a time-warp. It felt like I'd gone back a decade or more. It was the same sort of work I was doing that had driven me to dope. We made a profit out of young, fairly recently qualified solicitors we didn't make up into partners, and outdoor and articled clerks who couldn't be; we made some too on conveyancing and out of a couple of housing associations who wanted, as public landlords, to show whose side they were really on when they got us to evict one of their tenants in rent arrears.

What we didn't do was commercial work, heavy landlord activity, setting up or advising companies, patent, copyright, shipping, tax or anything else that made real money — or libel.

'Why does he want to see me?'

'I think he'd rather explain that himself. We'll pay for the interview, of course.'

I shrugged, but as this was a telephone conversation, his secretary couldn't see. I said:

'Yeah, sure, why not.' And made an appointment for Nigel Morris, managing Director of Aldwych House, the publishers, to come see me. My best guess was: when he saw the location and state of our offices, he'd turn right around and go back to the city solicitors his firm usually hired, where the carpets come up to your knees, the coffee is freshly ground, they've even got a couple of law-books and the opening 'how are you?' cost three figures.

Three days later, after the weekend, at the end of the day, the first man ever to make me feel physically insubstantial was ushered into my room.

What I mean is that he squeezed through the door sideways while my receptionist shoved from one side and I pulled from the other. He was six four, weighed at least twenty stone, his belly so big I thought he might be pregnant; he had a nose my grandfather would've been proud of; he was close-bearded, a light brown, almost ginger colour; his face formed a perfect circle; his shirts were made by a marquee manufacturer; he wore boats on his feet and that part of his girth that didn't overlap them was contained in *schmatter* enough for three pairs of normal trousers.

'Sit there,' I quickly pointed to a chair I'd long hated and was looking for an excuse to get rid of: 'We take no liability for physical injuries to our clients. Is that clear?'

He chuckled knowingly:

'Are you trying to make the point that I'm f-f-fat?' I retreated around my desk. He said:

'How much has this cost us so far?' He held up a hand: 'No, I know, lawyers don't like to talk about money. Ah, it's so different in the world of publishing where our der-der-derisory emoluments mean we can't afford to do anything else but engage in baroque conversations about it. That's why all publishing deals take place over lunch: it's the only way we can eat. This,' he placed his hands on his stomach: 're-re-represents fifteen years of expense account.

'Have you ever been to F-f-f-frankfurt? Of course you haven't. Why should you have? Everybody hates it. It's become a major st-st-status symbol not to go. There's a huge hall, like a giant who-who-whorehouse for coal-miners who haven't seen the surface since they were Bevin boys at the beginning of the wa-wa-war . . .'

I held up my hand:

'Stop.'

He jerked back in his chair. The back cracked. At least, I think it was the chair's back, not his own.

'I di-di-digress. You're a busy man. You don't want to hear about Frankfurt. You probably have a hundred hungry clients desperate for you to take their cases: criminals with con-convictions as long as your face; wives dr-drooling at the prospect of divorce; pa-pa-paternity suits; ha-ha-half the city needs you to ha-ha-handle a merger; it's an exciting life as a lawyer. Publishing. People think it's exciting. They thinks it's d-d-deals made in exotic parts; mi-mi-millions of p-p-pounds . . .'

The stammer was brilliant. I hesitated to interrupt again, because I couldn't be sure what was coming next: something interesting, something relevant; or just more of the same.

'Lunch in M-m-maxims, a flight to New York, a Ca-ca-cadillac to a writer's Con-con-connecticut estate, a black butler serving di-di-dinner to a li-li-liberal conscience, the publisher's cheque-book tucked neatly into his tuxedo . . .'

'*Genug,*' I could guess from the nose and the verbal diarrhea what we had in common; it might be more effective than English.

'That's very cl-cl-clever of you. Very few people g-g-g-guess that I'm Je-je-jewish. I'm only half-Jewish actually; half-Irish. My mother was Irish. My father was a sp-sp-sports journalist . . .'

I lowered my head into my hands and began to cry.

'You w-w-want me to tell you what I'm doing here?' He seemed surprised.

For the barest second, he stopped. Before I could help myself, I asked:

'Have you always stammered?'

'Al-al-always. You should have heard me when I was y-y-y-younger. Wh-when I was about ten I . . .'

'I'm sorry. I shouldn't have asked; it was my fault. Please stop. I mean, you can stop, can't you? Is there some special trick to make you stop? It's late, I'm tired, I want to go home. I want to get home before my child goes to secondary school,' I pleaded.

'How old is your child? Is it a boy or a girl? Let me show you.' No one, but no one, carried pictures of their family in their wallets anymore. (In my part of town, they were well advised not even to carry wallets: I, too, digress). Nigel Morris passed over a picture of an admittedly pretty little girl, maybe two or so. 'This is Mimi,' I thought he was stammering again. 'Miriam really. The l-l-l-love of my life. June and I tried for a l-l-l-long time . . .'

'Do you want a divorce?'

'Good Lord, no. Why on earth should you . . . ?'

'Do you want to have your child adopted? Do you want to sue little Mimi? Do you want me to put a contract out on her? What's it got to do with anything?' I howled.

The door to my office burst open and Ruth, one of our junior solicitors, put her head nervously inside. Behind her I could see two others: James and Neil. They weren't stupid. Ruth said:

'Is everything alright?'

'Fine, fine,' I said wearily. 'Nigel Morris meet Ruth Binder. The two behind her are James Coatman and Neil O'Rourke. They're solicitors in the firm. They're all very good. Very, very good. Much better than me. Wouldn't you really rather discuss your problem with one of them? They're cheaper too,' I appealed again to common heritage.

'No, it's definitely you I want to see,' he said without the slightest hint of a stammer. 'Well,' he explained, 'it comes and then it g-g-g-goes.'

The staff backed out in unison, like an orchestration from the detective show *Blue Moon* that I'd taken up watching after the tragic demise of *Hill Street Blues*. They couldn't be less alike, which was good, because I couldn't stand to be reminded of what I was missing.

I leaned back in my chair:

'Mr Morris, so far I've cost you or your firm the better part of a hundred pounds, and I have not heard anything about what I can do for you.'

'Ah, yes, lawyers' legal charges never cease to amaze me: the der-der-derisory...'

'Derisory emoluments. We've done that bit already. And I know you're half-Jewish, half-Irish, and you had a child late in life and she's beautiful — which I freely admit — and named Miriam or Mimi affectionately and that sometimes you stammer and sometimes you don't and that it's a much harder life in publishing than people like to think and, oh, yeah, you've a wife called June and what else? Nothing else. Nothing at all. It's not that I really mind, I mean you're paying for my time, or your firm is, and if it's your firm why, why, why should they be paying? Please. Pretty please?'

I stopped, exhausted. It wasn't one of my better speeches but they rarely are before I get the chance to polish them for posterity.

He sighed. At that moment, I finally took to him He reminded me of Lewis. The room shook, the building shook. I hung onto the arms of my chair and held my breath until it stopped. When it did so, he began:

'Do you know the name Jada Jarrynge? Of course you do. Ev-ev-everyone knows her name.' This didn't stop him telling me about her.

Jada (long 'a', short 'a') Jarrynge (pronounced as in fat syringe) had bounced onto the airwaves only a year before. She was a tall, stunningly beautiful, black woman — Dominican in origin — who was still at art college at the time her first album was released.

I don't know what they call that sort of music. I've heard it called soul, but it's got nothing to do with the sort of soul I grew up with. I only listened to it to begin with because you couldn't turn on the radio or television without. Gradually, it grew on me like it grew on many others and when her second album (is a compact disc an album?) came out, I went out and bought it — not merely to leer at the cover — and, also like everyone else, including Nigel Morris, had to admit that it was even better than the first.

Most of this Nigel Morris told me, even though I already knew it, at far greater length than I've now set it out and interspersed with metaphor, allegory, personal reminiscence and miscellaneous observations I couldn't categorise.

He also reminded me that she had quit art college, and — wholly out of order for the normal career development of her peers, if there were any — had immediately taken the principal supporting role in a short-run television mini-serial to display an acting agility probably as substantial as her voice. She had since made a movie and though, of course, it was too early to be sure, it seemed as if she was here to stay.

What he didn't tell me was something else I happened to know about her, which I didn't think he'd know, so I told him.

Jada Jarrynge was the daughter of Eartha Mellor and step-daughter of Mick Mellor. Eartha and Mick had a child together, called Frankie. A few years ago, Eartha and Mick died in a plane crash. Under the terms of their wills, they had appointed as testamentary guardian Mick's best friend, the Honourable Mr Justice Sir Russel Orbach, High Court Judge, although at the time still plain Russel Orbach, Queen's Counsel. Jada had gone to live with her father; so far as I knew, Frankie was still living with Orbach, which is where and how I'd met her. By now, she probably ate ground glass for breakfast.

'You're wrong. I did know. That's why I've come to see you.' Another whole sentence without a stammer. 'I also know that you and Orbach er — how shall I put it?' It was the first time he'd been stuck for words, so I didn't help him out. 'Have a relationship,' he concluded uncharacteristically unimaginatively.

'It's one way of putting it,' I said dryly. 'A better way to put it would be that we enjoy a state of love-hate: one per cent love. Can you work the rest out for yourself or do you need to borrow a calculator?'

He didn't ask me why, which suggested he knew more about my business than he ought to have. But then, the affairs in which Orbach and I have both been involved, while never in their full glory making the front pages — where they belonged — made good gossip, maybe as much as ten or fifteen per cent of it accurate, and I'd long since ceased to be amazed by how many people had a slice of the story. Morris was a publisher: a lot of lawyers write. Aldwych House was part of a conglomerate which owned newspapers: journalists know a lot they can't print and don't hesitate to talk about it. He was my generation: I'd learned he lived in Hackney, during one of his conversational cul-de-sacs, and so did a lot of lawyers I knew; he would have friends amongst them.

Orbach had lurked like a moving shadow in the background of the Disraeli Chambers case. Had he killed any of them? Certainly not. Had he hired anyone to kill any of them? Certainly not. Had he conspired with anyone to kill any of them? Certainly not. Had he done anything in connection with any of those grisly deaths for which he could be indicted, or even subject to civil suit? Certainly not. Was he responsible for all of them? Waddaya think.

He'd done me a favour during the Mather's case, mostly — I thought at the time — to show off how powerful and knowledgeable he was: the aura of omniscience. I'd come to rethink his reasons a while later when he called up and asked me to carry out an investigation for him; the Pulleyne case. If he hadn't offered me so much money, really a ludicrous amount, at a time when — in anticipation of Alton — I needed it, I wouldn't have worked for him.

The fact that I'd worked for him and his elevation to the bench were a lot closer than kissing cousins. The last time I'd seen him, the day of his promotion, I'd punched out his lunch and taken a good shot at re-arranging his jaw line by way of saying good-bye, I'd hoped for the last time ever.

Now are you going to tell me why you're here?'

'Jada Jarrynge writes.'

This, I confess, came as a surprise. She'd been at art college, she was a singer and an actress. I would have expected her to sign her contracts with an 'x'.

'Jada Jarrynge writes bri-bri-brilliantly. She has written a book. Her ag-agent sent me the book. He wants half a mill-mill-million pounds for it. That's a lot of money. People think pub-pub-publishing is gl-gl-glamorous, we're always flying off to make mill-mill-mill . . .'

'You've told me. You've told me at least once. Maybe you've told me twice. You've also told me about Cadillacs in Connecticut, the Frankfurt Book Fair and Bevan boys. It's not fair. We were just beginning to get somewhere.'

'Bevin,' he corrected. He leaned back again and the chair cracked again and I held my breath again as this time he sunk slowly and surprisingly gracefully to the floor. It had obviously happened to him before. His arms were behind him to break the fall and he lay there, like Gulliver, his belly about the same height as my desk, in sublime and peaceful silence. For a moment, I thought he was going to doze off.

Fortunately, there was no one left in the office. I helped him up and, reluctantly, proffered the other chair in my room, one I was quite fond of. He sat on it gingerly, mentioning that I could add the d-d-d-damage to my b-b-b-bill. I waved a hand in the air as if I wouldn't dream of it, and made a note on my pad to do just that. Aldwych House was a big enough publisher in its own right and the group as a whole qualified for the description multi-national. They could afford the hundred quid I'd charge for a chair I'd've paid someone a fiver to cart away.

'What're we talking here? Autobiography? I mean, ain't she a bit young to write her life-story; she's only just out of diapers?'

'It's not just an autobiography. At least, it says it isn't. I'm not sure how to describe it. It's called "Where I'm C-c-c-coming From". It's a co-co-collage, in a way. There's poetry, songs, drawings, a play, stories, re-col-col-collections.'

'Sounds yuk. You really wanna publish it? A bit pre-pretentious, isn't it?' Now he'd got me stammering.

Actually, I found it quite attractive, and above all disarming. I couldn't escape the idea that he'd deliberately adopted a stammer to compensate for his weight. Big people are quite intimidating to most of us. They loom over us, invading the personal space we expect to be allowed around us, often not realising how far they're intruding and how much we mind

But I hadn't felt that with Morris and maybe the stammer was why. Who can feel threatened by someone with a stammer? It's a disability, isn't it? Like only having one leg or being deaf or diseased? I mean, basically, they're crips, ain't they?

'No, you're wrong. I do want to pu-pu-publish it. I haven't described it very well. The things that are in it flow into each other; they're extremely well cr-crafted, well connected; the theme, the title, flows through it like, well, like an air that flows through a group of medieval madrigals; that's what makes it a problem.'

I shook my head; he'd lost me. It wasn't the first time but it was the first time I thought it might matter.

'There's a part of it, a part of it she won't con-contemplate cutting, that pur-purports — but only thinly — to be fiction, in which she writes about the death of her m-m-m-mother, her mother and her step-father. She b-b-basically is s-s-s-saying it was m-m-m-murder.'

I raised my eyebrows but didn't say anything. My heart was beating, as if I knew where the conversation was going, and I knew where I'd go with it.

'She-she-she's accusing the man who her ha-ha- . . .'

'Who her half-sister — Frankie — went to live with, right?' There was no way I could wait for him to finish for himself. 'It's crazy, it's bizarre, she's mad, she must be, there's no way, I mean, I know he's a disturbed man, maybe a bad man, yes, I'd say he was a bad man, but this is too much.'

And I was protesting too much.

Orbach.

What was it about Orbach?

He was a big man, not physically but in emphasis and effect, a man of gothic proportions, a man of mystery, a man of apparent — but I emphasise only apparent — total command not only of himself but of everyone about him, a manipulator; at times I thought the word that fit best was monster; at other times, despite myself, I still liked him, sensing that one day the lid had to come off, and when it did it would cause him a lot of hurt.

Above all, he was an arrogant man. He was a brilliant man. His arrogance was surpassed by his single-minded ability, and his ability by his extraordinary ambition. He had enjoyed supreme professional success, and corresponding wealth. But he was probably the loneliest and unhappiest man I ever met, and certainly the most cruel. He made enemies first thing in the morning the way others made their beds, and left them just as tidily ordered.

Though patently a driven man, with a centrifugal energy that swept lesser mortals out of his way, I had struggled long and hard to identify his code and his direction. He lacked any identifiable morality. In this sense he was, of course, the perfect lawyer and an even better judge; but he was a wholly imperfect human being.

When I had re-encountered Orbach during Disraeli Chambers, he had been an isolated, bitter man, obsessed by age-old grudges, a man who had broken up with his lady friend in order to be left alone to pursue his revenge, living in his silent Highgate apartment and spending his holidays inspecting the Munch Museum in Oslo in company with a woman old enough to be his mother and who indeed he called 'Mor', which I'd learned was Norwegian for mother.

It was difficult not to contrast this with the fond father-figure I had met at his new house in Barnsbury, enjoying life with his adoptive daughter, who had finally found someone to love who couldn't hurt him back. A man who had discovered, at last, a way to live with himself and with someone else.

I remembered him telling me how Mick and Eartha had died in a small Cessna they'd all owned together, on which they'd learned to fly when Frankie's parents were planning to emigrate to Bolivia, and which Orbach had planned to buy them out of when they went. I remembered him telling me there'd never been any explanation for the crash: something shorn through, but perhaps it had been broken when or as they came down.

And I remembered something he had said during Disraeli Chambers, something so chilling that it had accidentally helped me fill in the missing pieces. I'd been at his home, still the flat in Highgate then. We'd been discussing the deaths: I can't remember now how many had happened by then; three or four or five. He had baldly stated that he had no objection to his former colleagues dying.

I had challenged him He stood his ground: they were hypocrites, they were scum, it was better they were dead. I'd got up to leave and as I did so I copped out of the discussion by saying it was a good thing we didn't have to make those decisions:

'Because gods and governments do it for us.'

He hadn't answered. He hadn't wanted to lie. I was quite clear at the time what he meant: he considered himself bound by the decisions of neither.

It was a dangerous starting-point for an investigator. A lawyer is supposed to believe his client, and not care how much of his account is true: he is only concerned with the probably untrue. But an investigator needs to start with an open mind or else he'll see evidence where there is none, and fail to spot the fallacy lying at his feet.

Morris left the manuscript with me. There were more reasons involved in his wish to publish than the book's alleged intrinsic quality. For one thing, even if it was garbage, it would have a guaranteed sale that would recover the advance being asked for several times over. Serial rights, as well as hardback and paperback rights, both in this country and in much of the remainder of the English-speaking world.

For another, it had become a matter of interest to the man who owned the publishing conglomerate. Morris had of course discussed the book with him; initially, he had been horrified. He saw his knighthood, ennoblement and eternal hotel reservation in heaven disappearing out the window. Morris had persuaded him to read the book and indeed to meet Jada Jarrynge privately before making up his mind.

'Do I get to do the same?' I grinned.

He held up a hand.

'No, he's not like that. Not at all.'

I got the impression it wasn't blind loyalty so I didn't push the point. 'He spent an hour with her. I don't know what went on. But he was moved by it; I mean personally moved. He's still frightened of publishing it, but tempted. Both as a book, and in one of the group newspapers, *The Sunday*. But he's scared of what the lawyers will say. You know your lot, by the time they've finished li-li-libel-reading a book, there's nothing left but the title.'

He'd reached an agreement with his boss. Before they reached a final decision on publication, it had been decided that they would carry out their own investigation, to see how much of it they would be able to support when the proverbial hit the air-conditioning. Morris'd asked around who might be suitable and my name had come up. It had come up in two different ways. For one thing, I was reputed to be the best, if not the only, investigator who specialised in the misconduct of members of the legal profession itself. For another, I was linked to Orbach.

'Are you saying you — or your boss — believes her?'

'I'm not sure. She clearly believes it herself. Something happened. You'll have to make up your own mi-mi-mind.'

For the sake of form, I told him I wasn't investigating anymore. I had to say that, or Alton would be enjoying life without father: Sandy'd kill me. But it was only form: I never had any real doubt I'd take the job: the notion had been planted in my mind; I had to find out, one way or the other.

The compromise we reached meant I would be retained as a lawyer, and that I would accordingly be paid on a hourly rate which, once I worked it out, meant I'd be paid more even than Orbach had paid me. Given time, the right mood and something to offer in exchange, I stood at least a chance of securing Sandy's consent. Sandy liked best butter on better bread.

I didn't take the manuscript home with me that night, or at all. I wasn't ready to broach it with her yet. Instead, I took it down to the club on one of the routine twice-weekly visits

I was allowed: allowed by Sandy, both for the sake of my liver and so I couldn't linger too long over Natalie; and allowed by Natalie, who'd finally got fed up with my interfering with her management of the club and threatened to quit if I didn't stop coming around so often. The only times I went more frequently were when I had to cover during her holidays.

Natalie was a friend of Carson, my former investigative assistant who was now in Australia. There were times when I had wondered whether they'd maybe been a bit more to each other but I never found out for sure and decided, wishfully, probably not. A beautiful Jewess of Russian extraction, a sometime dancer, sometime actress, commonly waitress, she'd been sharing a squat in Islington with Carson and a couple of others, in which I'd stayed for a short time while hiding out from some people who didn't like me anymore.

At that time, she had plans to open her own restaurant or at least a cafe of some sort. When I'd first asked her about the club, she'd refused. But shortly afterwards, they'd all been evicted from the squat and her meagre savings were going to have to go into house purchase if she didn't take up my offer, which came with a small flat at the top of the building on the Old Brompton Road where the club is situated and where once upon a time Lewis had seduced not only Malcolm but many of his other employees and not a few of his customers.

In the last years of his life, though, the flat had been used as a storeroom, or sometimes for a homeless member of staff to live in, and Lewis himself had an apartment elsewhere, considerably more opulent than this. We argued long and hard about it, and eventually I agreed she could spend a few thousand doing the flat up. She moved in, occasionally but never for long joined by a friend, and took control of the club.

She was surprisingly successful. Though Lewis was gay, and so were many of the staff and customers, the club was not exclusively homosexual. It's principal purpose was to provide people with somewhere suitably sleazy but not exorbitantly expensive to go after the pubs shut at the excruciatingly early hour of eleven o'clock. Lewis had kept it open during the afternoons as well, in the days when pubs also shut from three o'clock to five-thirty, but now they could open all day there was insufficient business and we'd quickly dropped the daylight hours.

In Lewis' time, the club was darkly-lit, gloomily-decorated and, until the last customer had gone, the music he played was what he thought contemptuously they wanted to hear. After they left, I'd learned the night of his death, he would often stay behind for what was left of the night, listening to opera, counting his money and brooding about his weight, his lost sexual capacity, gang-wars he'd won and a few he had lost.

I formed a company to run the club, made Natalie a director and appointed an accountant to serve as secretary. I told her I didn't care if it made a profit, but I didn't want to make a loss and I didn't want anything to happen that made us liable for any real damage, like poisoning a guest or physical harm from the condition of the premises or the customers. I didn't want to get sued for anything, not even non-payment of bills. I don't think she was robbing me, because there would have been a substantial excess income over expenditure but for what she was spending to make the place over into her own image.

I hate to admit it, but I liked it better these days. There were still pockets that were discreetly lighted, so people could enjoy their clandestine affairs or encounters which for other reasons they didn't want witnessed. She'd rewired throughout, and brought in a sound-engineer to restructure the music system so it could be heard evenly almost everywhere, without deafening some and leaving others straining to listen.

She'd also done amazing things with the menu. We had to serve food, by the terms of our licence, but during Lewis's tenure it had been so bad no one ever ate there twice. Now, I looked forward to my meal on my evenings at the club, and a couple of times when we'd found a baby-sitter and managed to tear ourselves away from the child who was going one day to rule the world, Sandy'd eaten there with me too.

Normally, I went home first and came down around nine o'clock, still before the place really woke up. I'd eat a meal with Natalie and we'd discuss problems that hadn't been serious enough to ring me about, the latest dilemma in her love-life, and what I thought of whatever she was wearing. Natalie'd look good in a nun's outfit so she never took much notice of my answer: it was just her way of reminding me she knew that if I wasn't straining to remain faithful to Sandy I'd be lapping at her heels. After we'd eaten, we'd retreat to the office for an hour or so to go over the books, before emerging, proud of our proprietorship, to see how many of our customers we could out-drink.

This night, though, I went to the club from the office and asked Natalie to go through the books with me as soon as I arrived. Then I asked her to send my meal in to eat alone and to make sure that I remained undisturbed.

Then I settled down to read what Jada Jarrynge had to say for herself.

CHAPTER TWO

If she was right, it was a tale of extravagant evil. A man who had selected his own happiness over and above the lives of his best friends. A man who had viewed as an object to be fought over and fought for, a child he claimed to love. A man who considered not at all what might be best for the child, only what was best for himself. Put like that, maybe it wasn't so different from a million other murders.

After I looked out into the club the first time, and saw Natalie still had company, I returned to the office for a final smoke and brood. When I came back out, only Natalie was left. Pointedly, there was a bottle of Southern Comfort on her table. In that subtle, reticent, coy style she had learned from her friend the sophisticated conversationalist Carson, she said:

'So what's up?'

I said, 'Tell me about Carson.'

Carson had been my assistant. She had taken off within a week of the end of the last case. She didn't tell me why. Just left a note at the office during the Christmas-New Year break saying she'd probably be back some day, with probably underlined.

I didn't know if it had something to do with all the deaths; or because during the case she'd begun to reflect on how she'd conducted her life and needed to sort some things out about it that were still in Australia; or because at one point of high tension we'd made love and she didn't want to face Sandy back at the office. I expect it was just because she felt like it.

Once during the past fourteen months, Sandy and I had received a postcard from Tasmania: it said 'down under but not down'.

'I see.' Natalie knew enough about what I used to do, and what I did with Carson, to understand that my question was also a sort of answer to hers. She'd been peripherally involved in our last case, and shown herself a solid trooper when it counted.

'Do you know the Dylan song "Desolation Row"?'

She shook her head. Of course not. She didn't draw a pension either.

'It's about loneliness, at least that's what I think it's about; about people driven mad by loneliness; mad enough maybe to kill.'

On another subject, she might've mocked my pretension. But she knew enough of loneliness herself not to do so now.

'What does it mean?'

'What do you mean?'

'What does it mean for you, now? This is a case, right?'

'Right. Have you been in touch with her?' Twice I had asked her if Carson had written or if she knew where she was and she'd denied it. Now I wasn't sure: 'Do you know where she is?'

She flushed.

The first period I knew Natalie, I fancied her so badly I'm still not sure why I didn't try: probably because I couldn't believe I'd ever get that lucky. When she moved into the club, the emphasis went out of it, partly because of Sandy and Alton, partly also because the club, like the office, had become a routine. Now, for no reason I could explain, I was sitting there as turned on by her as ever I had been.

She knew. She reached around the table and squeezed lightly. My turn to flush. She said:

'Thanks, but, uh, it's not a good idea is it?'

'You've grown old this last year or so, Nat.' For old read wise.

'It makes you, a place like this. They're not happy people who come here, or they wouldn't be here: they'd be at home, holding hands and watching television, listening to music, making love in front of the fire, the way it's supposed to be.'

'You haven't answered my question.'

'No more I have,' she admitted tacitly that she knew where Carson was.

'Do you have an address?'

'No, but I have a number where I can leave a message.'

'And, uh, are you willing to disclose this number to me? Why've you never told me before; why've you actually lied about it?'

She shrugged. The effect was as extravagant as when Morris did so, but much more erotic.

'She didn't want you to ring her for a while. But she wanted me to be able to make contact for you when you really needed her. I guess she thought you'd stay in touch with me,' she added with a broad grin.

It was late; maybe that was why I was confused. She explained:

'She thought you'd have a hard time of it, settling down at the office, settling down with Sandy and Alton; she thought you'd want her around because of that — not need her, want her —

but that if she was, it would actually be harder for you. I don't know, I'm not explaining very well. Maybe she meant you bring something out in each other.'

Oh, yeah, we do.

'But, of course, she knew there might come a time when you really needed her, and that would be different.'

'And that's now, right?'

'Well, that's what I'm asking you. It could be. I don't know, do I? You haven't told me what it's about.'

No more I had.

'Well? Are you going to?'

I had no doubts about trusting her. Nor did I want to hurt her by giving her the impression that I didn't trust her. But it was still all too fresh in my mind, I still hadn't worked out where I was going with it — or why. So I told her no, I wasn't going to tell her what it was about, and yes, could I please have Carson's number in Australia and yes, I'd probably tell her about it soon.

She sat for a while, evenly divided between agreeing and refusing, between demanding to know and trusting me that it wasn't time yet. Then she got up and went into the office, to her desk I suppose, and returned with the number written on a memo-sheet

'Tell her she can stay with me,' was all she said.

I got to meet Jada Jarrynge. I didn't get to meet her alone. I got to meet her in the company and at the office of her agent. I didn't know they made agents like that anymore. He was a prematurely balding, bespectacled, fundamentally slight man but with a middle-aged spread he wasn't prepared to acknowledge by wearing shirts and trousers quite big enough. He had a disproportionately large moustache and looked as if he ought to be behind the counter of a pornographic bookshop, picking his nose and pressing a buzzer under the counter to admit favoured customers to the back room where the really hard stuff was on display. He introduced himself by so many names I promptly forgot them all.

Jada Jarrynge was something else. She was at one and the same time the entire stock of the bookshop in question and an open-faced, innocent child, devoid of any make-up so far as I could tell, wearing faded jeans and a faded denim jacket with floral-patches sewn on, underneath which was an off-white, Greek-style peasant blouse cut just low enough so I could see where her breasts began to slope downhill into heaven. She was very tall indeed: maybe six foot, six foot one in flat running-shoes; her skin was rough yet lustrous; from her ears hung silver spirals and sprays; her hair was a natural phenomenon of wiry black spikes; she was alternately animated and sulky.

'I can see the family resemblance,' I said.

'With whom?'

Note: whom. I shouldn't've been surprised. I'd read her book. Nothing Morris had said about it was an exaggeration.

'Your sister. Frankie.'

'How do you know her?'

'I've been to Orbach's house. I met her there. Oh, this was a couple of years ago, a bit less.'

I started to light a cigarette.

'Please don't. It's bad for my voice,' she said.

I didn't argue but put the cigarette back in its pack. I once started to walk out on a case because the client didn't want me to smoke and only came back when he sent for an ashtray. Morris, the other night, during one of his detours, had expressed regret that I was trying to kill him before he could watch Mimi grow up to win the Nobel Prize for Peace, Literature and Science. His ambitions were, beside mine for Alton, so very modest.

'How old are you, Jada?'

'She's twenty-two,' her agent answered. He had to do something to earn his percentage.

'How old were you when your parents died?'

'It was my mother and step-father. I was nearly eighteen; just over four years ago. My father's still alive. I lived with him until last year.'

'I presume you bought your own place?'

'Of course,' the agent interrupted: 'It's very important for her to put as much as she can into property.'

'Advising her on other property deals, are you?' I snapped.

He looked startled, then laughed easily.

'No. It's what I tell my own daughters.' He made more points in one sentence than I had time to count so I let it go. Besides, I was more interested in the address. I asked. She said, with due suspicion:

'What do you need it for?'

'If I'm going to work on this, I may need to contact you urgently, to check something out or, hell, just to talk It through. I know you're not my legal client, but in effect you're the one whose hunches I'm working out.'

She pondered this for a while and conceded her 'phone number. If I failed on the case, I could probably make money selling it.

'I want to ask you about . . .' I withdrew from my briefcase the copy Morris had allowed me to take of the manuscript: 'Your mother's letter. On page eighty-three. The one to . . .'

'Yes. I know what you mean. It's the only letter that matters.'

I looked at her, wide-eyed and sad: it was maybe the first time I ever appreciated the naivety with which I had gone through my student years or the meaning of the phrase 'sublime ignorance'.

'Is it real?'

It was the key question.

She seemed surprised I should ask.

'Of course.'

The letter had been sent to Mick Mellor, then in Bolivia looking at land they might buy. It read, in part:

'He came around again last night. If he was anyone else, I think he was trying to get with me. He's been sitting as a judge. He was very tired.

'He was still going on about it, trying to change my mind, talking about Frankie, why it wasn't good for her, how he'd miss her, how he'd miss us. He's so lonely, Mick, I feel sorry for him, but he won't face it's his problem not us. He wants something from us he shouldn't ask. He wants answers from us no one else has. He frightens me. He can be so persuading, I can't answer him. He has hundred reasons why it's bad for Frankie bad for us all of which bad for him One time, I went for drinks, when I came back he was talking to himself — say, it won't happen, it won't happen. I say, don't take on so; you'll visit; we'll visit; you don't lose us, don't lose her. I feel frightened. Something's going to happen. I feel it. Come home. Please.'

'I'm curious about something,' I said to Jada.

She nodded graceful permission to ask.

'You write beautifully yourself. This is your mother's letter, your dead mother's letter. I don't know if it's word-for-word the way it was written. There's a lot of, well, bad English in it. Why didn't you clean it up?'

Her eyes flashed. I flinched.

'My mother was the best woman I knew. This was her English. Who says what's right and wrong English? She wrote like she spoke and she spoke like she was and a West Indian she was, I am. She had very little formal education, not until later when she went to college through her work.' Like Mellor, she had worked in housing. 'Did you have any difficulty understanding? Could you put it better?'

'No. I'm sorry. I just wanted to understand.'

'Try harder,' she hissed. 'You've got a hard job, you're going to have to work hard at it, all of it. Do you understand me?'

I grinned.

'Oh, yeah, I understand you alright. Maybe I understood already. Maybe my way of understanding wouldn't've been the same as yours. OK?'

She settled back on the sofa satisfied for the time being, both with her own answer and, I liked to think, with mine.

'Does Orbach know you're writing a book?'

'Sure. I told him. I told him he was in it.'

'Why?'

She beamed:

'I want him to read it; I want him to look forward to reading it.'

I nodded:

'Yeah, that I understand.' The greater the shock. 'But it's sort of dangerous: he's a dangerous man, you know.'

'I do know,' she whispered, 'I know, don't I?' Then: 'Do you? How do you know? What do you know?'

I made a decision. Perhaps I'd made it before I came, but I hadn't known it until then. I was going to break all the rules with her, for her. I glanced at the agent, then back at Jada. I said to him.

'Would you let me talk to Jada in private for a bit? I want to tell her some things. They're, well, privileged really. Things I shouldn't be saying. Things I want to tell her.'

They exchanged a glance and she nodded. He rose and said he'd go and make some tea. I asked for coffee.

I told her then the story of Disraeli Chambers. I told her too how Orbach had succeeded to the High Court judgeship of which he was so proud. Then I told her what mood her book had put me in and she knew the song and she knew what I meant. I told her I knew it was possible that she had written the truth. I didn't say I believed her, because I still didn't know if I did: just that it might be true that somewhere along the line his arrogance and his ambition and his loneliness and his pain had snapped into harmony, he had crossed the line between knowing right from wrong.

'You sound as if you're sorry for him — are you?'

'Maybe,' though it wasn't something I'd thought about.

'Will that stop you?'

'Sometimes I feel sorry for Adolf Hitler. There's no evidence he ever had a happy day in his life: to the contrary. But it wouldn't have stopped me killing him if I'd had the chance.' My courage is inexhaustible when my enemies are already dead.

The agent returned with two cups. She looked at me and it was my turn to nod assent. She said it was alright for him to come back in now. While he fetched his own cup, she said, 'You can smoke a cigarette if you want.'

I laughed out loud; she knew as much about handling people as I'd failed to learn. I lit up.

'How did you get the letter? If it was in Mick's things, surely . . .' If it went to anyone, it would have gone to Frankie — Mick wasn't Jada's father.

'I stole it,' she said without hesitation. 'I knew, you see, I knew when he'd been, the time she was writing about. My mother talked to me. I wasn't a child anymore. The letter was, well, I should say about six months before it happened. When it happened, I was already suspicious. Why did he buy the plane with them? Why had he agreed to learn to fly with them? Why was he helping them get ready to emigrate when he didn't want them to? I've written all of this in the book.'

'Yes, I remember.' There was nothing in the relevant parts of her book that wasn't already engraved on my memory.

'So when it happened, I took the letter. Before anyone else could do so, I wanted proof.'

It was a frightening picture; the seventeen-year-old child already plotting revenge for her mother's death.

'Did you never try and talk to anyone else about it? I mean, about your, well, suspicions.'

'I talked to my father. He . . .' She hesitated. She was looking for a way to say it that would not sound disloyal. 'My father told me not to say anything. He said no one would believe me. He said I would make a lot of trouble, and would be hurt by it.'

'Did he believe you?'

'Does it matter?'

'Do you know anything about what the letter says at the beginning — sitting as a judge? I think she must have meant as an Assistant Recorder, that's a part-time judge. A lot of barristers do it, especially if they're trying to impress the Lord Chancellor in the hopes of further promotion. Why would she have remarked on it?'

She shrugged:

'That's what I want to know too. When I've visited with Frankie, sometimes I've stayed in the house; once, no twice, we went on holidays together, he's talked to me a lot.' She meant that she'd used the opportunities to get him to talk. Who'd've believed it? The great manipulator outwitted by a girl less than half his age; that would be the greatest humiliation of all. 'He likes me; he trusts me. But I don't know anything else about it. Is it important?' She was intellectually concerned she might have missed something significant.

'I don't know. I can find out.'

'What do you think, Mr Woolf?' the agent asked.

'What I think is, Jada's father was right. There's a real risk involved'. I told Jada: 'I once did a job for Orbach. I learned something during it. They — the establishment — whatever you want to call them — the legal establishment, the government, the civil service, whatever — they'll go to any lengths to prevent any dirt attaching to a judge, especially a senior, a High Court judge; to prevent anyone finding anything out; and if it's getting close, to cover it up; even then, they'd let a judge get away with it — resign, disappear from public life — rather than see him in court, or a word in the papers. It's fundamental to the system: you can't have a crooked judge.'

When I had seen Orbach at his chambers, right after his appointment to the bench was announced, he told me that he had wanted to become a judge so as to not have to work the long hours of a successful Q.C., to have more time for Frankie: 'What I think now is — if Jada's right,' I entered the continuing caveat, 'if she's right, then the real reason would've been because he knew that a judge would be untouchable: not just from when he became a judge, but for always.'

'You're a practising lawyer, they could do you more harm than they could do Jada, couldn't they?' the agent persisted.

'I suppose so.'

'But you still want to take it on?'

'Yes, yes of course.' I was surprised by the question.

'Why?' Jada asked.

'I'm not entirely sure I can explain. I just need to know.'

It was complicated. It wasn't entirely to do with the fact that Orbach had — for a while — conned me during Disraeli Chambers. Nor that he had used me during the investigation I'd carried out for him. after all, he'd paid the piper, and handsomely. Nor was it about something Tim Dowell used to say, that Orbach and I were alike, two versions of the same difference. Nor, for sure, after the outcome of my last case, was it because of any residual commitment to the law and its integrity. These were the things it wasn't. Now I had to find out what it was.

Alton was fast asleep in the buggy that looked like it had been built on Mars — I was glad, he was far too young to meet him; Sandy was still enthusing about the house we'd been to see; I waited nervously to see if he answered the door, half-hoping he wouldn't.

Therefore, he did.

He was growing old and casual: he didn't bother to conceal his surprise. In days gone by, he would've felt obliged to act like he'd been expecting us.

'What are you doing here?'

He didn't invite us in immediately. Our last parting had not been a promising indication of future warm relations.

We had more reason for surprise than he: he had lost a lot of weight and had shaven his beard, though not his moustache; he reminded me slightly of one of the recent vice-chancellors, also moustachioed, who in turn used to remind me of Rumpole of the Bailey on the television. I had seen other members of the bar who had similarly lost weight when they went onto the bench. The law is an essentially sedentary occupation, but while in practice it calls for a lot of energy — usually generated by excessive food and/or drink. Once on the bench, there aren't the same strains; it is easier to follow a physically more disciplined life-style.

'Well, uh, we came to look at a house, down the road in fact, and I, uh, thought we'd come and say hallo.'

He studied me like I was also something from outer space totally ignoring Sandy until she said:

'Hallo, Russel. Or am I supposed to call you Sir Russel? Judge? God? You look better without the beard — or the belly. Less awesome.'

Despite himself he contrived a smile; he smiled rarely — he viewed it as a sign of weakness:

'Same old Sandy. You'd better come in, I suppose.'

'This is Alton,' she introduced. 'But knowing how you used to feel about children, I don't suppose you'll be calling him anything anyway.'

'It's different now,' he answered. He didn't query the name so things couldn't've changed that much — he hadn't been listening.

'Where's Frankie?' I asked as he led us down to the kitchen.

'Out. Tea? Coffee? Drink, I suppose, for you, Dave?' He said dryly. Ouch. I was tempted to remark that I, too, had changed, but it was asking too much of myself.

He knew what I drank. He hadn't finished the bottle he'd bought in during the time I was working for him. Nor had anyone else since. Frankie must be eleven or twelve by now: I was surprised she hadn't drunk it. Orbach was not himself what I call a great drinker but then there are very few people who I do.

'Perhaps, Sandy, a glass of wine?'

There was a time — maybe fifteen or so years before — when there would have been nothing noteworthy about us sitting around together, drinking. We'd all been part of the same, early seventies, so-called radical legal movement: fighting the landlords, the bosses and the police in the name of sixties' idealism. That was when Russel was at Disraeli Chambers, I was at Nichol and Co., and we as solicitors briefed them as barristers. So much had changed, barristers didn't even need to be instructed by solicitors anymore, but could take instructions from other professionals like accountants or surveyors and, soon, would probably be able to do so from lay clients direct.

Then Russel had left Disraeli Chambers; I'd left Nichol & Co.; Sandy had stopped instructing him; he'd become a Q.C.; the last time the three of us were together in one place our other companions were Alexander Keenan, Orbach's oldest and best enemy but Sandy's sometime lover, and a jittery German with a penchant for automatic pistols. Today, he was a judge. Orbach, that is: not the German.

'Sure.'

'I'll open a bottle.'

Sandy made a half-hearted protest, which he properly ignored. He said: 'Perhaps the living-room would be more comfortable.'

As we followed, both of us compared his house with the one we had just been to see. There were surprisingly many differences. His kitchen led through French-windows onto the back garden and his living-room was entirely separate. The one we'd seen was much larger and the whole of the ground floor was open-plan, with the kitchen in the front of the basement, an intervening dining-area and steps up to the living-room on the garden level.

On the ground floor in 'our' house, where Orbach's living-room was, there was a room at the front that would serve well as a study, and a second bathroom. On the middle floor, two more rooms, one for Alton and one for prospective Nanny. On the top floor, in a recessed attic addition, the bedroom that would be ours, with its own *en suite* bathroom. I don't know why; everyone's got their personal idea of luxury; mine's always been an *en suite* bathroom.

Once he had settled us into the living-room, he went to fetch a bottle of wine. He took a long time. Suddenly, we heard an anguished curse, a howl of protest at an inconsiderate, scatological deity, followed by the shattering of glass. Sandy and I exchanged a look. Neither of us wanted to go and see what had happened; for all we knew, he might've found Frankie helping herself to a glass of milk without asking. Reluctantly, I went down to the kitchen to see what was going on. Russel was kneeling down, brushing into a dustpan what was left of the bottle.

'Problem?'

He looked up surprised, like a naughty child caught in the act, then recovered himself to say:

'No, not at all. I dropped the bottle. That's all.'

But in the pan I could see the remnants of a cork still firmly ensconsed in the remnants of a neck, and by the sink I saw the corkscrew, with half a cork part-way up it. Also, the shattered glass and the spilled wine spread across not only the floor but the work-surface and into the sink. The cork had split, and so had Orbach's control.

I backed to the kitchen door, afraid despite myself. 'You don't need any help, then?'

'No,' he hissed between gritted teeth. 'I'll be right up. I don't need your help.' Yours or anyone's.

There wasn't enough time to tell Sandy what had happened before he finally emerged, glasses and new bottle in hand. He raised his own after he poured for her:

'Cheers.'

Nothing had happened. I had dreamed it. I said, ignoring the incident in the kitchen, 'No hard feelings, Russel?'

He smiled, 'You know me, Dave, I don't bear grudges.' I choked on my Southern Comfort.

'How come you're looking at houses around here?'

As ever, Orbach had put his finger on the contradiction.

The one thing we were not supposed to be doing was looking at houses around there.

For a start, they were far too expensive. Sandy might have money, but it was going to take me a while to catch up on the missing decade of my own earning career.

For another, who'd want to live near Orbach? It'd be like leaving school and moving in next to the headmaster, or getting out of a gaol and taking up residence as a neighbour of the chief warden: forever on parole. Every time I looked up, he'd be there, watching, knowing, disapproving; when I changed channels on the television, drank milk from the bottle, picked my nose, jerked off. Hell, no, not like parole at all — a life sentence.

But as a matter of fact we were looking at houses around there.

The answer — as to so many mysteries in my life — lies with Sandy. Sandy had not been at all impressed by my account of Nigel Morris' visit; she didn't even find my imitation of his stammer funny. Nor was she impressed with Jada Jarrynge's manuscript which, contrary to my express instructions not to show it to anyone, I offered her to read. Nor did she want her autograph. Nor even — most uncharacteristic of all — was she overwhelmed by how much money I would earn running up the hours of a private investigator, at the charges of a solicitor. I got the message. She didn't want me investigating — anyone, at any price, and especially not Russel Orbach.

My first attempt accordingly fell on deaf ears. My second did a little better. I resorted to our usual method of cohabiting. We were both lawyers. I offered a deal. Sandy had wanted to move out of her house since before the baby was born. In the way of these things, the actuality of Alton had overtaken the aspiration and she had been too tired and too busy and just too plain absorbed in him to pursue it. If she would let me delve a little way into the new case, I said I would make the time to go house-hunting with her; even better, if we actually found somewhere I could afford a share of — an important qualification — I might actually agree to buy it.

'Whereabouts?' she asked suspiciously.

What I had in mind was Crouch End, Hackney, maybe even North Islington — places you didn't need a computer to count your bank balance. But as we had been talking, I had an idea how to merge my interests.

'How about South Islington?' I said brightly. 'Barnsbury, for example?'

She shook her head in amazement.

'You're about as subtle as a child on Christmas morning. You can't afford it; you don't want to live near him; and, no, I won't let you use us as a coy excuse to happen to bump into him or pop in and say hallo.'

I smiled winningly She flung a pack of nappies at me.

'And change Alton for the rest of the week?'

I love my son, I hate his excrement.

Like most of my plans, this one had already begun to backfire. Two minutes after we went inside the house I had picked on his street — one of many with a For Sale sign up — Sandy handed me Alton and pulled out her calculator, looking pointedly at me as she began to punch buttons. She could do that: she used to go with an accountant. There was an irony lurking in the near-distance that was so sweet and so terrifying I knew it was about to take over.

'Which house have you been to see?'

Sandy told him. It was on the same side of the street as his, but closer to Copenhagen Street, and the Sainsbury and Marks and Spencer on the other side: about an equal distance from the Crown pub, but in the other direction.

'The one with the show-garden? I didn't know it was up for sale.'

'No. It's got a funny shaped garden, and I think it backs onto the show-garden at one point, but it's a few houses along. The garden's fabulous: walled, goes off in every direction, it may be the best feature.'

He explained didactically, 'There used to be businesses in the middle of what are now the gardens; some of them were stables; the properties went wholly residential at different times; it has led to some odd shapes; some of the gardens are tiny; I'm quite lucky, but if it's the one I'm thinking of, I can see why you're excited.'

It had been his area of practice: land, planning, development. He knew Mick Mellor because they worked on cases together. Orbach as barrister, Mellor as surveyor.

'You must be doing well,' he added condescendingly.

Sandy and I exchanged a look. I changed the subject quickly.

'Tell us what it's like, being on the bench.'

If you'd asked me the last time I saw him whether I'd ever again be willing to sit and chat politely, I would have sworn on the grave my father didn't yet occupy that it would never happen.

'It's pleasant, really, compared to practice. There isn't the insecurity of wondering where the next case is coming from, nor the lurking guilt when you get time off; we're supposed to be concerned about appeals, and about the prospects of promotion to the Court of Appeal, but I would have thought I've gone as far as I'm ever likely to, wouldn't you?'

He had already gone a lot further than he had any right to do.

'It can be hard work; it calls for a lot of concentration, and there's much more preparation than people realise, both before a case and when it comes to writing judgements. But on the other hand, it's not that difficult to know what decision to reach.'

'No? I would have thought that was the hardest thing of all: people are so unpredictable.'

'Rubbish,' he dismissed my sentimental proposition briskly. 'People are the most predictable animals of all. All you have to do is to work out what they wanted to do; people only do what they want; people can always be made to do what they wanted to do; once they start on a course of conduct, they can't get off it.'

'Still sounds to me like hard work — sussing out what they want to do.'

He stepped off his rostrum.

'I can't complain; it's what I wanted; it gives me time for Frankie.'

'How is she?'

'She's wonderful. She's doing brilliantly at school, she had the lead part in the play last year, she's on the running team, she's . . .'

Sandy shook her head in awe; 'Dave told me you'd turned into a doting father but I didn't believe him. Is it really you in there, Russel?'

He laughed mirthlessly.

'I've changed, Sandy, I've changed a lot. Before, well, I never really knew what happiness was, a normal life.'

'Margot?' I asked.

'Margot? That was an affair of the mind We were intellectual partners, and, of definition, that required considerable independence, separateness. I thought I'd lost all chance of knowing, well . . .' he laughed again, but this time nervously, embarrassed to talk of such intimate matters, 'Well, I mean knowing a way of life like others always seemed to manage to find.'

'When do we get to see this paragon?' Sandy asked.

'Not today, I'm afraid. I've let her stay with her sister. Do you know who that is?' He asked proudly, 'Jada Jarrynge. The singer. And actress. Of course, she's only her half-sister, and I had no part in her upbringing, but she's turned out very well and I like to think perhaps I helped a little. After all, her father,' he waved a hand dismissively. I couldn't remember what her father did, but I got the point.

'Does she write her own material?' I asked out of a bloody-minded refusal not to have some fun at his expense, not to feel in the slightest way that I knew something he didn't.

'Certainly. She writes very well. She's writing a book, you know, about her life; she says she's going to put me in it,' he beamed.

'Really?' I managed to sound surprised. 'That'll be interesting.'

CHAPTER THREE

There was one question left over from the investigation I had carried out for Orbach: whose side had Tim Dowell been on? I knew the facile answer — his own, as always. I also knew that the way things had ended might be considered proof that he, as much as Orbach, had been playing me for a patsy. He'd done it before. But it wasn't so clear this time around; certainly, it wasn't clear that he'd intended to use me until very late on, when perhaps there were no real choices left.

Between my second and my third major cases, I'd avoided Tim, angry at the way he'd conned me. This time I'd seen him a couple times. I saw him soon after we took Alton home. He came around to discuss the club. It wasn't his business, but that never stopped him interfering. In his will, Lewis had left it to me: I wasn't supposed to keep it; it was to be passed on to Malcolm — once an old violence conviction had been spent and he could qualify to hold the liquor licence. All of this was to be found in the side-letter. Tim had acquired the letter. Now that Malcolm wasn't going to see the time out, he proposed to tear it up. That left the club in my name without qualification.

We'd stood on the doorstep, arguing the ethics of what we were about to do, and in the end it was he who had torn the letter into tiny pieces and thrust them deep into the dustbin to be carted away. He'd come back once more, with a present for Alton: the pram that could convert into buggy and that was carry-cot as well. It was, for a copper, an expensive gift, and I'd read it at the time as some sort of apology.

'Nah,' he said now, 'I just thought, you don't have much family, do you. I mean, your mother's dead, you hardly speak to your sisters and you and your father haven't been in touch as long as I've known you. And, well, with Lewis gone . . .' He was about all I had left for a friend.

He wasn't far off.

I didn't say thanks. Sandy'd said it when he brought it to the house and I didn't want to spoil him.

'How's your zoo?'

He was a vicious, deceitful, hard-drinking, wholly incorruptible in any conventional sense, successful Detective Inspector, with a tiny head that wouldn't've looked big on a weasel and a university degree in law he didn't like too many people to know about. Most of the time he was kept on stand-by for the dirtiest jobs, where neither the Marquess of Queensbury nor the Judge's Rules had anything to do with how the case was handled. Nonetheless, or perhaps because of it, he was happily married, to the best of my knowledge and belief never unfaithful, and from the occasional remark a thoughtful and sensitive father.

'Good. Sandy'? And Elton?'

'Alton's fine,' I corrected, ignoring the deliberate slip. 'Sandy's headaches have started again, but otherwise she's alright; she's working part-time now.' As long as I'd known her, Sandy had suffered from occasional headaches. They weren't at the front of the head, nor at the sides like a migraine, but at the back, at the top of her neck. They didn't last long and for the first year after Alton was born, they went away, but recently they'd returned.

'She should see a doctor.'

'You know Sandy.' Bad news happens when you go looking for it.

He eyed me suspiciously, this desultory chatter was not why I'd called him up.

'Well?'

I sighed:

'Don't you want another drink?'

We were at the club. In the past, we'd spent many hours there, alone or with Lewis. He hadn't been in since the night of Lewis' death. When he arrived, he sniffed around, like a dog marking out his space. He had been surprised to see Natalie, but polite and had yet to make any of the more obvious remarks I would have expected of him. Perhaps he was growing up too.

'Alright.' This was what he and I had in common, Southern Comfort. He always drank it with me — his wife wouldn't let him keep it at home. 'I'll do you a favour.'

'Do me another? Could you get me the police report on a plane crash?'

All plane crashes which result in deaths, whether or not of the pilot or passengers, and whether or not involving commercial aircraft, are investigated by the Civil Aviation Authority. Save where the crash involves the Royal Air Force, or when there is litigation as yet unresolved and one or other of the parties injuncts to prevent it, these reports are published. They are obtainable through Her Majesty's Stationery Office, and I had already read — though barely understood — that concerning the Mellors.

The police will also normally conduct an investigation, on behalf of the coroner. That report will not be made public, save insofar as it produces evidence in a case, whether in front of the coroner or otherwise. The verdict returned by the coroner — accidental death — was itself valueless. It wasn't conclusive that there had been no human intervention. It was merely the most probable explanation in the absence of any other. Jada had reproduced the local newspaper reports of the inquest: they were neither of them more than two paragraphs, and contained no useful information at all. The crash didn't make the nationals.

'What do you know about planes?'

'Nothing.' This was true. I know they used to have four wings and now only have two, which is terrifying enough in itself. I know they go up in the sky with lots of foolish people in them, and whenever I can I make sure I'm not one of them.

I once flew to America, by *Loftleidir*, the Icelandic airline which in those days was the only cheap service. It was a night flight and I didn't see the aircraft as we boarded. But we had to touch down in Iceland. Though it was by then after midnight, it was spring or summer and very light. That was when I realised the plane ran on propellors: they had to give me a tranquillizer and carry me back on board to continue the journey.

The Mellors' plane, I had learned from Jada's book, was a Cessna six-seater, a single span light turboprop they'd bought with Orbach, second-hand, and parked — if that's what you do with a plane — at Southend Rochford where there were private club facilities. I knew they got tuition there too, and that by the time of the crash, Mick — a faster learner than either Eartha or Russel — had secured his licence. I knew they had filed a flight plan to Pontoise, outside Paris, but were barely across the Thames Estuary when they crashed.

'So? What would you do with the report? Get Alton to explain it to you?'

'Uh, let me rephrase the question: could you get me the police report and someone to help me understand it?'

'You want something more than the usual, bland, C.A.A. guff, huh? This is a personal injuries case, right? A death claim? Manufacturer's negligence? That sort of thing? I mean, it must be, 'cos you're a solicitor now, Dave, and that's all. Right?'

'Uh, yeah, right, definitely.'

He sighed and downed his drink, but hung onto the glass.

'I wondered how long it'd last.'

'Is that why you've been keeping away?'

'Could be.' Like Carson, we brought something out in each other. 'Then again, could be I wasn't sure what you were thinking.'

'About Pulleyne?'

'Yup.'

He was asking me the left-over question I was supposed to be asking him

'I'm not sure. I believed, I believe, right up until the end, you wanted the same thing I did. After that . . . I don't know. Do you?'

He thought about it for a while then shrugged.

'I think, at the end, I knew we wouldn't get everything, so I settled for something. That make sense to you?'

'About.'

'Will it do?'

While I was still an investigator, the roles were reversed: he wasn't supposed to care what I thought; I was supposed to curry his favour; that's the way it's always been between the police and a private eye. Now he wasn't sure whether to treat me the same way, or as a solicitor. Me neither.

I didn't answer.

After a long silence, he said, 'Are you going to tell me about it?'

'An old friend of ours. Now a High Court judge. That make any difference to you?'

'Orbach.' He and Orbach went way back. A lot of people went way back with Orbach — few of them went forward. I nodded.

He blinked about a dozen times:

'You never learn, do you? You working for him or agin' him and is there a difference?'

'Agin.'

'Why're you doing it, Dave?'

'I thought you might tell me, Tim.' I held the bottle out to him, but he shook his head.

'You've got a very destructive streak, Dave . . .'

'Tell me something new . . .'

'I thought, maybe, you know, with a child . . . It'd have an effect.'

'Some,' I conceded. 'Just not enough. So?'

'I'm not your shrink . . .'

'Never stopped you before . . .'

'It isn't funny, Dave. You could do yourself a lot of harm. And Sandy. And Alton. You just can't accept . . . the idea of someone you can't understand. It frightens you; he frightens you.'

I pondered this for a while, and poured myself another shot while I did so, though he again refused.

'Hell, there's lots of people I don't understand. I don't even understand myself half the time.'

'That's exactly my point.'

I half-understood but was too proud to admit the other half.

'So? You gonna help?'

'Like I said, Dave, you never learn.'

He put his glass down on the table, got up from his seat, turned casually as if looking to see where the door to the lavatory now was, and walked out of the club.

I couldn't do anything for the next couple of weeks. A Crown Court trial came suddenly into the list and I had to spend most of each day at court, sitting behind a barrister who knew less about the case than I, who'd been handed it at the last moment when the woman I'd originally instructed couldn't get out of another case she was in. Despite his worst efforts, we got an acquittal, but they'd allow me on legal aid only the same low rate for my constant attendance as they'd allow for an articled clerk.

I rang Carson once, the day after Natalie'd given me the number. I got through alright: it was nine hours ahead of us. I got through to a man with a middle-European accent who sounded old enough to be her father if I didn't know her father was dead and who told me Carson had gone on a trek into Gibson and couldn't be reached. No, he had no idea when she'd be back; could be a week, could be a month. Did I want to leave a message? Sure: tell her Dave called. She didn't ring back.

I went down to the Temple on a conference in another case, which I'd deliberately allocated to a barrister in Orbach's old Chambers. His clerk seemed surprised to see me: we hadn't briefed any of his barristers for many years. As I went in to the con, I said, 'If you're around when we finish, have a drink?'

'Certainly, Mr Woolf. It'd be a pleasure.' He was yet more surprised. Usually, clerks cruised solicitors to come for a drink. Gone were the grand old days of Marshall Hall when solicitors had to persuade barristers to accept a case: with a few exceptions, most of the bar now touted outrageously for work, themselves or through their clerks, and it was a rare conference which didn't end with an offer to me of a drink from one or other. Most sets of chambers found an excuse for a party half a dozen times a year, to which they invited all those solicitors they hadn't seen since the one before.

We went to a wine bar, itself called Chambers, above the Witness Box pub. Orbach's former clerk was called Edward. Neither Ed nor Ned nor least of all Ted or Teddy. He wore a suit more expensive than that of the barrister with whom I had been in conference, and a watch-chain of solid gold. He was balding, pompous, in his late forties and lived in Essex. It is unnecessary to say more.

He selected carefully a claret at the top end of the price range. I thought about asking for a Southern Comfort but it would be interesting to see what the rest of the world drank. I even quite liked it. He asked me:

'How did you find Mr Davies, sir?'

'Alright,' I said grudgingly.

Theoretically, all barristers are supposed to be equally brilliant, distinguished, absolute masters and mistresses of any area of law on which they are asked to advise and advocates to the gentry who make their services available to the general public out of the goodness of their hearts rather than for fees the size of which most clients didn't complain about because they had been stunned into shocked silence.

Solicitors and barristers' clerks know better. 'They know that cases have to be switched around at the last moment. They know they can't always have the barrister of choice. If he was that available, he wouldn't be that good. So a lot of the time, by silent agreement, we settle for someone with an average degree of competence rather than start over in other chambers, again and again, looking for a brief with more positive qualities. 'Alright' was praise enough for a Davies. Edward nodded gravely. He wasn't looking for more.

'Do you see much of Sir Russel?' I asked idly.

'You knew him quite well, didn't you, Mr Woolf?' I presumed he had some idea of the state in which I'd left Orbach the last time I'd been at his chambers — maybe he'd even helped him up off the floor.

'No, we're fine, a little misunderstanding was all. I was at his home the other day.'

'Camden, isn't it?' I forgot to mention that barristers' clerks are also the most suspicious people on earth — because they are themselves so thoroughly untrustworthy, they don't think anyone can be trusted.

'Islington,' I corrected dryly, so he poured me another glass of claret. 'Thanks. Cheers.'

'Your health, sir. He doesn't come into chambers often. He had a party at his house after his appointment. Naturally, I was invited.'

'Yes, but did you go?' I chuckled maliciously.

He smiled forlornly, but judges don't bring their former clerks any income, while solicitors do, so he shifted gear into a broad grin intended to look boyish but that would've made Boris Karloff look amiable.

'Have you ever seen him in court?'

'No, sir, I haven't. Too busy.'

'Not even when he sat before his full-time appointment? As an Assistant Recorder, I mean?' This was what I was after.

He shook his head. We were almost at the end of the first bottle and he'd drunk more of it than me. I offered to buy another.

'Let me, sir.'

'If you insist.' It wouldn't stop me claiming it on expenses from Aldwych House.

'Where did he sit in those days?' I asked when he had returned and refilled our glasses.

'South-Eastern Circuit, if my memory serves.'

'Yes,' I said: 'I think that's what I remember, too.'

She didn't return my call, but when I arrived home for dinner after my drinking session with Edward, she was sitting in the kitchen, Alton on her lap, Sandy fussing to feed her.

'You called, master,' was her opening remark.

I sat down opposite her. We'd neither kissed nor shaken hands. We were still sizing each other up.

'I might've called to check you were still far enough away.'

'You wouldn't've spent the money. Unless of course,' her eyes glinted, 'you had a client paying expenses.'

'You've already talked to Natalie,' I accused.

She pointed with her foot to the rucksack behind the door: she'd come straight here.

We examined each other openly and curiously. I never had a partner in an investigation before Carson — assistant, partner, it was all the same and not always clear who was in charge or, at least, in control. The first time I'd seen her, she'd terrified me. From her reaction, I wasn't sure it wasn't entirely mutual. Most of the time she was surly if not downright sour, scowling instead of speaking, or mumbling monosyllabically. Then she would switch mode and talk without end at as great a length as, but more to the point than, Nigel Morris. Initially, she'd been secretive with me. Now we were secretive together.

'Lost the mop, I see.'

'Wearing contacts, are we?'

When I first knew her, she had a blue hedge standing upright in the middle of her otherwise close-cropped, dyed-platinum blonde head, and wore a blue leather bomber jacket to match. Her hair had grown out, and it was now somewhere between blonde and mouse, maybe even its natural colour; her jacket, too, was now a boring and undistinguished tan.

She was about five nine, a couple of inches shorter than I, but even without heels walked so tall I always felt she was hovering over me. She was built big, too, and every inch of it was solid. Her Australian accent came and went with her moods. No one would ever call her beautiful, or pretty, nor maybe even turn a head to watch after her on the street; they were the ones who were missing out, not her.

'If you two want to go outside and punch each other for a while, that's fine — dinner'll be a bit yet,' Sandy said.

Alton started to cry. He didn't like violence.

I've never been sure if Sandy sensed what had happened between us. She was jealous enough to suspect I slept with anything less macho than Rambo. I think she usually assumed I had unless and until the opposite was proven beyond any doubt at all; reason doesn't come into it. But there'd been a hint or two beyond the generality, coupled to the slightest suggestion that she might even understand and, in this one, exceptional case, excuse.

It was a balmy spring evening so we took our drinks and doing half what Sandy suggested, took them outside. We leaned against the fence at the end of the garden, not talking, until she put her drink down on the grass, stood up and came and put her arms right around me, almost as if she was pleased to see me. I got no opportunity to put my glass down, so I drank it over her shoulder, lowered it as far as I could, and let it plop straight down, base first, to the dewy ground where, as I had hoped, it didn't break. We held each other's face in our hands and grinned and giggled and kissed just once, mainly chastely but mouths a fraction open, on the lips.

We didn't speak about that other time. We'd agreed after it happened that it wasn't necessary, and in the brief period before she'd disappeared to dingo-heaven we'd hardly seen each other. It was just after Alton was born and I had other things to occupy my mind — like, where to learn to be a father, and quickly. We both began to speak at once —

'It's great to see . . .'

'It feels like coming . . .'

Then we hugged again, picked up our glasses and went back inside. Sandy examined us critically: as Carson never wore makeup, she couldn't've been looking for lipstick; she must've been looking for blood. She bit her lower lip, nodded once in satisfaction and gestured with her head to the table, where Alton was already belted into his high chair.

We didn't talk about the case over the meal. Conversations at the dinner table, one of life's few true pleasures, were a sacrifice to the child. We couldn't complete a sentence without a howl from Alton, or from Sandy as food dribbled disdainfully down his chin. As often as not he needed changing half-way through, which didn't do much to enhance my appetite.

After, Alton decided suddenly it was bed-time which meant also that we were only going to get a quarter of a night's sleep. We retreated to the living-room while Sandy took him upstairs, graciously waving away an offer to do the honours I hadn't made.

'How was it?' I asked.

'OK Better than I expected.'

'Whose 'phone was it?'

'He was a sort of third cousin five times removed.' There was not much left of her immediate family. 'I stayed there mostly.'

Our eyes caught. When you know someone that well, the most banal sentence can carry a host of meaning. I just said: 'Weird.'

She shrugged:

'I never did old before.'

'Thanks,' I broke our rule.

She giggled. She can do that, giggle without seeming silly or childish or, worst of all, girlish. That was something else no one would ever call her.

I didn't mind. I suppose what I'd learned most in the time since she'd been gone was that I could handle the one thing that had always terrified me: compromise. I got it off Alton, I guess. I found I couldn't always have my own way, but that it didn't matter anymore. I'd never been faithful to a woman before Sandy, nor indeed for the first years with Sandy, because I couldn't reconcile the need to do so with the inevitable and not-so-occasional sexual desire for someone else which, being of my generation, it never used to occur to me didn't necessarily have to be acted on.

'Stay here tonight; move to the club tomorrow,' I urged. I wanted her under the same roof.

'OK,' she said unquestioningly. 'You gonna tell me what it's all about?'

'Sure. They have electricity in Australia yet?'

'A bit.'

'Steam-radios?'

'Trannies.'

'Television: like, uh, radio with pictures?'

'Moving pictures?'

'Yup. Moving pictures.'

'No. But it's coming soon — in the next ten, twenty years, soon as someone kills Kylie Minogue.'

'They got Jada Jarrynge?'

'Right. What're we doing for her . . . Or should I say to her?' Which'd you rather?'

'For. I like her music. I like her.'

'You ought to. You've got a lot in common.' I meant they both had a childhood experience that threatened to take over for good. At fifteen, Carson had killed her uncle, who had attacked her crippled father with a meat-cleaver. It was part of what she'd gone back to Australia to sort her head out about. It was what she meant when she said it'd been better than she expected.

'What's the scam?'

'She thinks someone killed her parents.'

'And did they?'

'The man she thinks did it goes by the name of Orbach.'

'Yuk,' she observed intelligently. 'Really?'

'Really what? Really does she think it or really did he do it?'

'Whatever.'

'Really she thinks it. I don't know about the other. 'Talked to Tim — seems to think I've got a bit of a bee in my bonnet about Orbach, some reason. What do you think?'

'Where do we start? When?'

It's all and always and only about connections. There's no crime that isn't. That's why the perfect crime is said to be the murder of a complete stranger. Even then, there's a momentary connection, however fleeting, however distant, as, for example, between the random sniper and his victims. They are still together in a connected place, and the connection takes tangible form as a bullet. Similarly, the person who poisons a stranger, a number of people, or a whole city. They're connected too.

One difficulty lies in how deeply the connection is buried; the slighter the connection, the shallower the grave it calls for. But the main problem is knowing where to dig. I knew approximately from when to when: a six month period in Orbach's life, when he was still a barrister, sitting some of the time as an Assistant Recorder, between the letter Jada'd quoted in her book and the day the Mellors' Cessna came down. I knew he'd still been living in Highgate, because he moved to Barnsbury on account of the space needed for Frankie. I knew therefore there would be little purpose plodding around his private life of that point in time: he had none.

Assistant Recorders sit mainly in the criminal courts. That is to say, the Crown Court, not the magistrates' courts which don't have real judges. They also sit in county courts, where minor civil actions are heard, and very occasionally in the High Court itself, where Orbach was now a permanent, full-time judge. Mostly, though, it is the Crown Court. That's where the volume work is, and where the backlog that matters builds up. The law has always regarded as far more important whether a person should be fined tuppence-halfpenny for stealing a bottle of milk — which is the sort of petty offence part-time judges try — than whether or not he should be evicted from his home.

They especially tend to put people to sit in crime when someone has, or has had, a left wing reputation, as Orbach was tagged because of his one-time membership of Disraeli Chambers. They want to see just how liberally they will perform on the bench. Usually, they're the hardest bastards of all. They are motivated not by such paltry considerations as justice, fairness, or the economic or psychological deprivation of the accused, but by the really important matters, like how quickly they can achieve their own professional advancement which is bound to be of greater value to society than letting off another little villain.

In an unfair division of labour, I sent Carson to play with airplanes, and concentrated myself on pinning down Orbach's professional activities, on and off the bench.

Perusing the law reports helped: he had appeared as leading counsel in a long-running building contract dispute for much of the time. My mind winged tangentially to the moon: builders are Freemasons; Freemasons are, as I had discovered during the Mather's case, at least potentially a criminal and invariably a conspiratorial crew; builders also have the opportunity to bury people in concrete, so I'd read in a hundred thrillers and seen in many more movies.

The trouble was, the Mellors had died in the air, not at the bottom of the sea-bed, and what I knew of builders suggested they would be wholly incapable of doing anything technical to an airplane. Especially if they were Freemasons, who rode on their broomsticks instead.

As for Carson, she didn't do a whole bunch better. There was a flying club at Southend Rochford Airport, which I already knew; there were several flying clubs at Southend Rochford, which I didn't know. Tuition could be arranged at any of them. So could parking space.

She finally tracked down the club through which the Mellor-Orbach Flying Circus had functioned, but the man in charge of tuition was new, and could neither remember who his predecessor of that time would have been, nor where his records were. An outside firm did their small plane maintenance; he knew little about them. She rang to ask whether it was worth the cost of staying in an hotel to make further enquiries. I told her to cash in her return ticket and hitch-hike back to town.

I wasn't too worried. For a change, even absent the assistance of the cowardly Dowell, I had alternative resources. I rang Nigel Morris.

'You still thinking in terms of running this in one of the newspapers?'

'Uh, yes. *The Sunday.* Did you see last week's ed-ed-edition? There was a full-page story about a country I'd never heard of. I'm not su-sure if it even exists. It was ab-about . . .'

'Nigel,' I cautioned, 'I'm charging for this call.'

With his usual lack of direction, we discussed the possibility of tapping into the investigative resources of the paper. An hour or two into the conversation, he confirmed that he could ask whether they could be made available to me. An hour after that, still in the same conversation, he confirmed that he would so ask.

The next day, he rang to give me the name of a contact, Brian Battle. I didn't try ringing straight away; it was twelve o'clock and if he was any good as a journalist he'd already be in the pub. I left it until four and we arranged to meet that evening at the club.

For the duration of the case, and of Carson's stay with Natalie, the usual restrictions did not apply: I could go as often as I liked, provided I did not interfere in club management more than usual. Someone told me it is profoundly sexist to surround myself with women who tell me what I can and can't do; I understand the theory — it means I'm worth their time, trouble and attention; the difference is, my lot mean it.

Battle was a tall, lean, gangling man, in his thirties but already greying, with a wrinkled shirt and a stain-spotted tie, but smartly pressed slacks which, he explained, he had bought that afternoon to replace those over which he had spilled his liquid lunch. I told him he could order food if he wanted, but didn't tell him he wouldn't have to pay until after he'd selected what he wanted. I chose the wine for him — chateau cheapo.

'This your place, then?' He asked, licking his lips as he watched Natalie return to the bar with at least one unnecessary, sarcastic tweak of her backside. 'Nice.'

'The place is; not the people in it.'

'Pity. How did you come to own a club like this?'

'It's a long story. You wanna join?'

'What's it cost?' His eyes narrowed.

I told him. He barked. I wasn't going to be able to compensate the accounts for what my extra visits were costing the club.

'What do you know?' I asked.

'Nothing. Memo from the chairman. Find an investigative journalist; lend him to Aldwych House. Then I got a call from a man named Morris: talker, stammerer . . .'

'I know. Don't remind me. He told you what?'

'By way of his ignorance of new technology, his honeymoon on a canal boat, a bestseller he'd failed to buy and his daughter's medical history, to take a call from you and do whatever you asked me that was legal. He said you were a lawyer, so I should worry a lot and consult the group's legal eagle if in doubt.'

'You know what an Assistant Recorder is?'

He nodded.

'How would you go about finding whether and where he was sitting at a particular time?'

'Ring the Lord Chancellor's Office?'

I shook my head.

'Chat up his clerk.'

'Tried it.'

'Ask him.'

'They say tomorrow never comes, but I don't see why I should make it a sure thing.'

'This got anything to do with Pulleyne?'

Another one with a name, a slice of a story and a shot at the annual 'What The Papers Say' award.

'Who?'

He grinned:

'Worth a try.'

'You've tried. Now try to answer my question.'

'They sit on circuits, don't they? You know which?' I told him.

'And you said you know when?'

'Within six months...'

He groaned.

'Do you know how many local papers that means I have to plough through?'

'Start in Southend-on-Sea.'

CHAPTER FOUR

'It's, er, hardly the best way to choose a neighbourhood,' I proffered lamely. 'I could understand better if it was his house you wanted to buy.'

Sandy was still going on about the property in Cloudesley Road.

I understood well enough. I liked the place about as much as she did. I could remember the impression the street had made on me the first time I'd visited Orbach's, waiting for him sitting outside the pub nearly opposite his house. Very few streets in London have what can properly be called a discernible ambience. Cloudesley Road did. It was a light street, with double-width pavements but a narrow road that could only be entered from one end so that there was relatively little traffic. In the middle, next door to the pub, there was a general store. People wandered casually from their houses almost as if they weren't going outside at all.

It was a village and as such it was as close as people like us ever got to the ideal of the sixties like it was sung: back to the country.

Sandy said, suddenly serious:

'Sometimes I get frightened, Dave. I get frightened by the things you do. I get frightened you won't be here all that time ahead. I want us to have some of the good life now, instead of saving it up for a future which isn't there when we arrive. You know what I'm saying?'

'Not a chance; I'll outlive the lot of you.'

We were in the kitchen. B.A., the kitchen was not the focal point of our home life. It was used for its specific purposes, but we'd sit and talk and often eat in the living-room. Since his fall to earth, the increase in kitchen chores — cooking, feeding him, washing clothes — meant there was often so little time left at the end of the day it wasn't worth moving to another room.

This was another reason for buying a new house. The kitchen was not designed for living in. The house was the one Sandy had bought, years and years (and years) before and done up for the lifestyle of a single person. There were plenty of work-tops but not enough places comfortably to put our bottoms. She'd always assumed that if she ever had a family, she and whomever would find somewhere together that would be theirs not just hers. She hadn't reckoned the whomever might be me, with attendant problems like absence of capital, a mortal fear of commitment and a concentration span too short for England's archaic convey-ancing process.

'We can't really afford it, can we?'

I hadn't a clue what we were worth. I drew cash from the firm, to spend, and everything else was handled between Sandy and Naomi. Naomi was at the College of Law with us but after practising for a while, she'd quit, married, had kids and now came in two days a week to do the office books and accounts and some of the bills. If I was short, I borrowed from the till at the club. If I was really short, I borrowed from petty cash at the office. No one had caught me yet.

'We'd have to borrow most of it. I mean you will.' She grinned comfortably: 'I can afford my end.'

'I thought I could too,' afford her end, I meant. 'For richer and poorer?'

'We're not married.'

'For Alton's sake?'

'Precisely.'

It was a straightforward, conservative proposition. If I invested heavily in property, a house I'd actually want to hang onto, I'd have a real incentive to stick at steady work.

'What about Orbach? You really want to live spitting close?' Orbach could spit. 'We can hardly ask him to move out for our sakes.'

'We don't have to have anything to do with him. This is London. Do you know who lives two doors away? Hell, do you know who lives next door? Besides, if Jada Jarrynge's right, he's not going to be around for long, is he.' It was the first time she had conceded that there might be something in the accusation. I said so. She said, 'That's not what I'm saying. I said "if".'

'What do you think, though, San?'

She scowled.

'... Times I have to tell you ... ?' Not to abbreviate her abbreviation. 'I think ... I think you have to find out; I think you have to satisfy yourself one way or the other; I think, maybe, you're going to come a cropper, but as long as you don't get hurt too badly, well ...' she smiled sweetly and didn't finish her sentence.

'You think it'll teach me a lesson?'

'Something like that. Either way, he's not a problem.'

'He won't go to jail,' I said flatly. 'He'll still have to live somewhere.'

She shook her head.

'If he's disgraced, he'll move away, somewhere he's not known, people always do.'

'Orbach ain't people.' Nonetheless, she was probably right: his temper tantrum over the broken cork confirmed what I had always believed — that somewhere deep inside was a man scared of shame. 'What if you're right and I don't prove anything, or I actually prove her wrong?'

'Then he'll never know you even tried,' she said smugly.

'Bullshit.' These things always come out. Orbach was a man who had made an art-form out of knowing things he wasn't supposed to. 'He'd know.'

'He's not God, Dave — just a High Court judge,' she sighed.

'You tell him; I shan't '

'You'll do it, then?' She ignored my objections.

'Do I have a choice?'

'That's good. They accepted our offer.'

I should have known. She'd already bid on the house and for all I knew had exchanged a binding contract to buy it.

'No. The surveyor's going round tomorrow.' She didn't mean Mick Mellor.

'What about this house?'

She shook her head sadly.

'You're some detective. Really.'

I guessed then, or else I had unconsciously noticed as I came in, that there was already a sign outside.

'What if you don't sell it in time?'

She shrugged, 'I'll bridge. These houses go like hot cakes.'

'And you're a jammy bugger,' I muttered.

On the baby-mike, we heard Alton begin to cry. I smiled. I was a jammy bugger too. I loved him and I loved her and they both knew it better than I did. One way or the other, I had about a month to finish off the case if I was going to be able to see Orbach on the street without crossing to the other side.

During my discussion with Brian Battle, Carson had been watching from another table, at an angle, from where she could see him but where he wouldn't see her unless by chance. Battle stayed until after one, until my third offer of another cup of coffee told him I wasn't good for anything stronger. As soon as he left, she joined me. Never the dissembler, she said:

'Don't trust him.'

'Why?' I didn't, instinctively, but I wanted her to tell me the reason.

'I don't know. The way he was looking at Natalie, maybe.'

'On that basis . . .'

'Yeah, I wouldn't trust anyone. Including you. Hey: it's me. Remember? I don't.'

Thanks, I thought.

I wanted to go home. With a bit of luck for me, less so for Sandy, Alton would wake up just before I got back. I wanted to hold him for a while, then I wanted to hold Sandy for a while longer.

I pondered Carson's remark — her opening remark, not the sarcastic ones that followed — and told her to go back to Southend herself, hang around the local newspaper back-issue libraries, pick up on whatever he did, shadow him. I suppose I could've told her to do the job herself, now Battle'd given me the idea, but she wouldn't've been grateful and I could see no reason to look a gift horse in the mouth.

While she was in Southend, I went to see Alex Keenan. Keenan and Orbach had been friends long ago, then enemies. Keenan had been a Q.C. many years before Orbach; he was some years more senior. But now Orbach was a High Court judge and Keenan still only a barrister. I didn't imagine Keenan minded — to the contrary, he'd lose whatever little credibility he had with the left if he accepted an appointment.

He wasn't happy to see me. On the other hand, he could hardly refuse an interview. I knew far too much about him. He wouldn't come to the club to talk. I had to go to his new chambers late one evening, not just after court but after he'd already finished a lengthy conference on another matter. It was so late there weren't even any clerks around. It was so late there weren't even any other barristers around. I got the point: he didn't want to be seen talking to me.

'Have you ever seen him since?'

Since meant since the night at Sandy's house when we'd last been together.

'No.'

'Not even in court?'

Keenan did mostly crime, but he got a little High Court work too.

'I think . . . It's generally known that I couldn't appear in front of him. Not why, of course.' He added: 'Just that there's sufficient proper cause to keep my cases out of his list.' On such understandings did the law tick over.

I toyed with asking him about the Lady Helen, his wife; I'd heard a rumour they'd split up. I decided uncommonly in favour of discretion.

'Did you know Orbach moved house?'

'I heard,' his eyes narrowed. 'What's this about, Dave?'

He wouldn't descend to use of my surname alone: it's part of his man-of-the-people pose. But it didn't sound any different than if he had called me Woolf.

'We're buying a house in the same street as him. You knew about ...'

He nodded curtly:

'I heard. Congratulations,' he said dryly.

I tried to keep the smug, superior, winner's grin off my face. I didn't succeed. But then, I didn't try very hard.

'Is that what this is about?'

'No, of course not. I want to ask what you know about Mellor, Mick Mellor. His child went to live with Orbach after he died.'

'I heard,' he repeated. 'I knew him. Why?'

Mellor had originally been a housing surveyor, doing legal aid work for tenants who wanted their landlords to indulge them in such luxuries as windows that shut, tiles on roofs, floorboards you could walk on, working lavatories, an absence of rodents and of algae.

'Did you know they were that close?'

'Yes. They were friends for a long time. As long as I can remember.'

'You said you heard; did it surprise you?'

'Yes and no. Yes, because Russel always professed not to like children — but no, because I always thought it was an act, because he couldn't have them himself. He could be very good with them. Talk to them seriously without being condescending, take time to listen to them, get them to express themselves better, clearer, so they understood themselves more. I think it was a great shame he couldn't have children. I think ... More than anything, I think that's what made him such a bitter man.'

Despite my intended discretion, I said:

'That and the way his friends treated him '

His lips puckered.

'That made it worse. Perhaps what I meant was, that's what made him such an unhappy man; the way he handled his unhappiness antagonised people; they felt put down by him, when really he was putting himself down; so then they turned on him. The bitterness followed.'

It was an acute analysis.

'You still haven't told me what this is about, Dave.' The Dave didn't sound quite so four-letter this time.

'I'm . . . Well, let's just say I'm curious — why should anyone have named him testamentary guardian? Given what you've said: he was a single man, whoever's fault it was by then he was also a bitter man, he was very unhappy, he was very lonely too. I remember visiting him at home.'

'He was always lonely. As long as I knew him.'

'What does he do for sex? I've never really figured him out that way.'

'That may be true of him too. I don't think he's gay; anyway, no more than most of us are capable of. When he was younger he went out with a lot of women. But I don't know. Russel keeps a lot to himself, or at any rate he doesn't let it show to those around him '

He didn't used to, but the mini-incident in his house, when the cork wouldn't come out of the wine, suggested to me that he was on the turn. I said nothing, so he continued:

'I think, because of his sterility, he was incapable of seeing sex as anything other than fun, a game, a hobby — ultimately, therefore, an indulgence and, as such, a weakness to be despised. It was hard, especially in the late sixties and early seventies, to imagine sex as a love-medium that could last as such in its own right. Once you also have to rule it out as a means of procreation ...' He tailed off.

'Tell me more about Mellor: did you know his wife?'

'No, I never met her. Not that I remember. I don't know what to tell you. He was a good-looking man, amusing, very dedicated, serious about his work. Perhaps that's what he and Orbach had in common: a sense of professionalism, setting themselves the highest standards. There's an implicit arrogance in it: only I recognise the true standards that are capable of being achieved; only I strive hard enough to attain them. Perhaps that could account for appointing him his child's guardian, so it'd ...'

'She.'

'So she'd be brought up by someone with the same sort of approach to life, at least to work.' Then he thought about my correction, 'She? You're not suggesting...'

'No. She's only eleven or twelve years old.' That didn't make it impossible, but Keenan knew it was highly unlikely. 'Do you think ... I know he wouldn't, probably couldn't, forge a will or anything like that. But do you think he'd be capable of ... well, finding a way to make them appoint him the guardian, as it were against their better judgment, against their true wishes even?'

'I see. You're working for a relative? Someone else with a claim to the child?'

'Something like that.' I could afford to go this far with Keenan — he was the last person who would run to Orbach with the tale.

'Well, you know as well as I do, from Disraeli Chambers, he's a skilful manipulator. So I'd have to say yes, but not I think in any way that could be proved in law, especially not against a High Court judge. To upset a will like that, you'd need to show such a degree of undue influence, or blackmail, or drugs, that the court recognises that the will does not express the intentions of the testator; it's not enough just to show that someone influenced someone else, or persuaded them; after all, most of our decisions are not wholly independent, we don't exist in a vacuum; other things and other people bring us or help bring us to our answers.'

'Would he be capable of that, then? Not drugs: there're two wills involved, Mick's and his wife's. But — what about your example? Blackmail, say?'

He thought about it for a long time. Though he and Orbach were enemies, and both had ample cause to despise the other, neither of them had ever, to my knowledge, descended to cheap insult or unfounded criticism. They were respectful foes.

'I'm trying to think about it objectively. I think I would have to say that in the right circumstances, given the right incentive, Russel is capable of blackmail. Wouldn't you?'

I nodded. A nod cannot be taken down and used in evidence.

'But I can't imagine what that could be. I mean, to blackmail or even bully someone into naming you as your child's guardian — well, what would be the purpose anyway? It's only going to be effective if they die. I've been presuming that they didn't both have some deadly illness at the time. They died in a car crash, right?'

'Plane crash. And, no, they didn't have a deadly disease either.'

'So what's the end gain, if it will not and cannot be rendered effective except by chance? That's what I'm trying to say. It's a game without a winner. Isn't it?'

I didn't say anything. I wanted to see if he filled in the missing link for himself. He, more than most, had reason to do so. Gradually — much more slowly than he would have done in years gone by — he saw the point. The blood drained out of his face. His eyes looked haunted.

'Good Lord,' was all he said though.

I said:

'And could you believe that?' Even though what 'that' was remained unspoken. 'Suppose — take your thesis — unhappy man, because he can't have children, lonely man, somehow becomes testamentary guardian — throw in: this is the closest thing he has to family — they're planning to emigrate, far away, South America — could a combination of circumstances like that trigger something off in him, something as extreme as . . . that? I ought to say: he was a part-owner of the plane; he had access to it he was learning to fly with them.'

He shook his head.

No. I don't think so. As you know, I have more reason than most not to be impressed by his respect for human life. But I don't think he's capable of violence himself, not personally. He's a complex man; what he does is to play on others' weaknesses, perhaps encourage things to happen, perhaps even make them happen — but only at second-hand. You could call it hypocrisy: I would; but don't forget what a good lawyer he is — and a good civil lawyer — he understands everything there is to know about cause and consequence, and I don't mean only legally. Without someone in the middle, a buffer if you like, to absorb the responsibility, I don't think he'd go that far.'

As if it had suddenly dawned on him that we had been discussing the possibility that a High Court judge was a murderer, he rose firmly:

'I don't think I can help you any further, Dave. I'd have to say, no, I'm sure not.'

He might have to say it: I still wasn't convinced he meant it.

We met him on the street during the Saturday after we had exchanged contracts and thus irrevocably committed ourselves to the purchase. We had gone to the house with our builder, to decide what works to have done before we moved in. The current owners had already moved out, and were, unusually, permitting us access for works before completion so we'd be able to live in the house without being surrounded by plaster, paint and the smell of turpentine.

He was with Frankie. They were walking back from Sainsbury, guiding a supermarket trolley, each of them pushing with one hand. I saw others who lived on the street also pushing their loaded trolleys home, or returning empty ones to the store car-park facing Cloudesley Road across Tolpuddle Street and which, because it was a flat, open car-park, contributed to the street's atmosphere of light and space. Soon, we'd be doing the same.

'Frankie. You remember Dave, don't you? And this is his friend, Sandy. And, uh, er . . .'

'Alton.'

'You're serious about the house, then?' he asked.

Frankie was much taken with our child; but he was asleep and didn't care enough to wake up to talk to her.

'We exchanged on it this week,' Sandy said. I'd never heard an announcement of a house-purchase spoken with such defiance before.

'Well, well,' he wasn't going to pretend he took easily to the idea of us as neighbours. But he knew how to be a gracious loser even if he didn't like it. 'Would you like to come in and have, uh, a drink?'

'Sure. Why not?' I accepted before Sandy could plead want of time.

We walked the remaining hundred yards to his house and followed him in. He put the food away, and Frankie was bribed to return the trolley on promise of keeping the one-pound coin refund. We chattered idly until she came back and, not without considerable hesitation, allowed her to carry Alton up to her room and even, as a part of the game, to take up the carry-bag of Pampers, powder, juice and the remainder of the paraphernalia he insisted we take with us everywhere we went.

'I saw an old acquaintance of yours the other day,' I said as if still merely making pleasant conversation: 'Alex Keenan.'

His face clouded like a sudden summer storm. It looked the way I saw it in the kitchen last time I was there, just before he realised I had come in. Then it passed.

'You never forgive, do you, Russel? Doesn't it get tiring?'

He brought us our drinks without mishap or tantrum and sat down opposite us in the same leather armchair in which he used to sit, staring out of the French-windows of his Highgate flat, looking at the trees and the sky, at an angle that brought no other houses or people into the line of his vision. He took the question seriously.

'Perhaps, but it's always safer not to forget, don't you think?'

'Forewarned and all that? Who do you think still wants to hurt you, Russel? Hell, who ever really wanted to?'

'You know better than that, Dave.'

'Perhaps. But which came first, the chicken or the egg?'

'Yes, I know,' he conceded the point Keenan had made: he had provoked much of the animosity that had been directed against him 'Then let me put it a different way: why give people a chance?'

'You've got such a pessimistic view of the world,' Sandy interrupted. 'You think that everyone's bad, everyone's selfish, everyone'll do you harm if they can. People aren't like that, Russel.'

'Aren't they?' He treated the question as seriously as if he had been asked for his legal opinion on a subject. 'I think most people are capable of doing some pretty bad things. Once bad things start to happen, they go on. That's been my experience. I agree people aren't basically good — or basically bad. They're both. But they remain capable of being bad, and they remain capable of being made to behave badly: it's only a question of knowing which you want from them.' He dismissed free will as an irrelevance. 'If I don't suffer from it, it's only because I'm ready for them, I'm ready,' he added grimly. 'And I win.' He challenged either of us to deny it.

Daring life and limb, Sandy asked, 'Is it, well, the best way — the best atmosphere — to bring a child up in?'

He shot her down.

'You mean, instead of addicting her to cigarettes, Southern Comfort, lying in bed until midday and, as I recollect, spending a small fortune on cocaine.'

I laughed hollowly. I didn't know what else to do; it was all too true.

Suddenly, unprecedentedly, before Sandy could come to my defence, he abandoned the attack.

'It's too late. I won't change. I'm fixed now.' His massive mind had been brooding on the dark side for far too long. 'I can't compromise,' he added, without explaining what he meant. 'I'll stay on the bench until Frankie's left school and college and doesn't need me anymore. Then I'll retire.'

'And do what?' I asked before Sandy decided to throw the apparent olive branch back in his face.

'I'm not sure. Go abroad to live, I should think.'

'Where would you go?'

'It doesn't matter. Norway, perhaps.' Where he had his friends. 'Or Switzerland. I'll want still to be accessible to Frankie. If she wants...' He didn't want to think of a time ahead when she was so independent she might choose to keep as far away from him as possible. The way everyone else had done.

'Is that why you don't want anyone living in, to help you with her I mean?' Sandy asked in a neutral tone.

I'm not sure I understood the logic of her question, but he did. He looked at her thoughtfully:

'You mean so that no one takes her attention — affection — away from me? Perhaps. But she's increasingly close to her sister; I don't discourage it. On the contrary, I encourage it. Family's important. If you've got it.'

'Why did they choose you?'

'You asked me that before, the first time you were here.'

'So I did.' But then I had been working for him so I hadn't really listened to the answer. 'What did you tell me?'

'I can't remember,' he laughed almost pleasantly. 'We were friends. He was my best friend. I was close to Eartha too. It wasn't her first marriage. Well, of course you know that. You know, when a friend gets married, it's not uncommon to lose him. But there was never any jealousy on Eartha's part; she accepted me as his friend, and encouraged us to keep up our friendship. She became my friend too. I don't think she and I ever had a cross word or an uncomfortable exchange.'

He didn't know, then, how she had felt about his visit. He continued:

'I think I was the only one of his friends who stayed close after their marriage. She had friends, who stayed friends, and family but most of them weren't that well-off, and I think most of them, perhaps all of them, had their own children. By then, I was, well, successful, financially too. Besides, you know, you never really think these things are ever going to happen. People don't care as much what they arrange for after their deaths.

They think they do, but because one's own death is really so unimaginable — I don't mean the fact of it, but what it means as a state of mind — they don't apply the same criteria they'd apply to a decision while alive.'

'Sometimes they use it to do things they couldn't do when they're alive,' Sandy observed. 'Revenge wills, and the like.'

'Yes. I think I'll leave all my money to my good friends and colleagues at the bar,' Orbach said in what was for him a rare moment of self-deprecating humour.

Frankie brought Alton back down.

'I changed him,' she announced proudly.

I had to restrain Sandy from grabbing Alton out of her arms to see how much damage she'd done. She said tersely:

'Shall we go and see if you've done it right?'

'I've done it right,' she insisted.

Orbach beamed. Of course she had; she was his girl. While Sandy and Frankie were out of the room, I asked if he still flew.

'I didn't for a while but funnily enough I missed it so I started the lessons again when I had more time.' When he went on the bench. 'I don't want Frankie to grow up with a phobia about it.'

'Fear of Flying?'

He didn't get it and it wasn't worth explaining.

It only took Battle a couple of days to ring in and confirm, as instinct had told me, that Orbach had sat as an Assistant Recorder in Southend, and that he had done so during the period that mattered.

'Sentencing him, Assistant Recorder Orbach said ...' was how he found it: Assistant Recorder Orbach and Assistant Recorder Llewellyn Evans and Assistant Recorder Smith and Assistant Recorder Papworth and Assistant Recorder Uncle Tom Cobley and all.

He had sat for a two week period, during which he fined members of the local population a total of four thousand two hundred pounds, placed fourteen villains on probation, put two away for six months each and another one for a year but suspended, and made a dozen or more community service orders.

'What else do you want me to do while I'm down here?'

'Nothing for now. Thanks. That's very helpful.'

'You sure? It isn't much. A fool could've done it.' I wasn't sure a fool hadn't. 'I mean, I know you don't want to tell me what this is about, but we both work on the same team, you know. I could be a lot more help.'

'Yes, sure. But I need to talk to Nigel Morris first.' I was stalling — talking to Morris was a great way to stall. 'That'll take forever. Suppose I give you a ring back in London, what, tomorrow?'

'Fine. I'll come back now.'

But he didn't.

After he hung up on me — although Carson didn't know to whom he'd been speaking — she followed him back to his hotel. He didn't check out. It was already too late in the day for any other kind of office-hours' investigation. She was staying in the same hotel. She didn't think he'd connected her: there was no reason why; he hadn't seen her in the club; she was reaping the rewards of her post-Australia, less flamboyant style. He spent an hour in his room then emerged and strolled down to the front. He seemed to be wandering aimlessly, popping into pubs, drinking alone, only a pint in each.

At about half-past eight, it seemed like he found who he was looking for. He sat down in a booth.

'Mind if I join you?' He asked its solitary occupant, a greasy-haired, sour-faced, sallow, middle-aged man in a crumpled, polyester suit who was nursing a pint of lager in a tall glass.

Carson couldn't overhear anything more. She stayed at the bar, chug-a-lugging Fosters Fermented Fly-piss or some similar Aussie brew that she had felt since her return chauvinistically bound to buy even though she liked it about as little as did I. But she could see. And she saw when he passed something under the table that looked suspiciously like a bundle of brown notes.

'More than you pay me,' she added when she reported.

Battle left soon after the exchange. His companion stayed where he was, looking furtively around until he was confident no one he knew had seen him He came up to the bar to get himself another pint. As he picked it up, Carson bounced into his back, apologising almost before his drink was spilled. She insisted on buying him another; unaccustomed to being accosted by a woman, he stayed up at the bar to drink it with her. It cost her two more rounds, and more patience than she used to have, to find out that he worked in the local Crown Court.

'Nothing fancy. Just a clerk. Just a job.'

'We've all got to live,' she'd said profoundly.

'That's life. Would you like another drink?'

She was learning patience. She made a choice. If she pushed further, there was a risk she'd scare him out of doing whatever Battle was paying him for. If she left it until it had gone down, she could scare him into giving her the same information — and for free.

She went back to the hotel and ate there, her back to the table at which Battle was sitting, now in company with a travelling saleslady he was regaling with tales from the Fleet Street front to what, from her sarcastic interjections, Carson guessed was little effect. Nonetheless, the woman went with him into the bar and subsequently they went upstairs at the same time though she neither knew nor cared whether to one, other or separate bedrooms.

I didn't ask what Carson'd done — she didn't tell me, so it wasn't my business.

The next day, she was up before him but not before his prior night's companion. The latter looked in worse condition than the evening before, but as, according to Carson, the beds in the hotel were less comfortable than the bunks at Chelsea Police Station, that didn't give her any additional information. By the time Battle came down, Carson had packed, loaded her bag in the car I'd let her rent and checked out.

She didn't leave town. She followed him again, on foot, this time into the town centre. In a coffee bar near to one of the local newspaper offices, he was joined by a young woman Carson recognised from inside it. She in her turn was the beneficiary of a handful of notes —

'But only fivers.'

I waited for another crack, maybe how it was more my scale, but she knew how to let me down, and let it pass. Instead, confusingly, she asked, 'Journalists don't share sources, do they?'

'Not if they can help it. No more than a copper shares a snitch. What're you thinking?'

'My guess is, she's a secretary or maybe works in the cuttings library or something like that. He got the name of someone else's source out of her, and whereabouts he might be found. This was the pay-off. It's a small enough town; I doubt there are a lot of real secrets; just things people think are secret.'

At lunch time, Battle had met up with his and Carson's drinking companion, and a buff envelope changed hands the opposite direction the notes had gone the night before. She followed our man back to the Law Courts on Victoria Avenue and, with a little bit of disingenuity, to his office. He did a double-take when he saw her, but his first — extravagantly vain — reaction was that she'd come back to chat him up.

'I came to apologise to you for last night,' she said softly.

'That's alright. You don't need to apologise. I mean, that's life.'

'What I mean is, I'm apologising for lying to you.'

He slouched back in his chair, confused more than frightened. But fear was beginning to rise; he'd left Battle only a little while before; he was still feeling guilty.

'I told you I was on holiday. I'm not. I'm working down here. Carrying out an investigation.'

She had his full, bated-breath attention. She said:

'Whatever you gave him, I want copies of. All of it. I'll get my hands on his copies, soon enough. And I'll know if you've left anything out.' I know how intimidating Carson can be. I still commonly feel intimidated by her, and she's supposed to be my friend. I could imagine how he felt.

He didn't argue. He hardly spoke. He was sweating so badly, Carson was positively relieved when he told her he couldn't get the material until later in the day and that there'd be trouble if she stayed in his room. She couldn't wait to get away. Before she left, she leaned across the desk, snorting into his face, trying not to breathe, telling him how long the last person to cross her had spent in hospital. He probably thought she didn't mean it. I knew she was telling the truth.

She spent an uncomfortable afternoon moving around town, not looking for Battle for any reason other than something to do, nor finding him: as we later learned, he'd come straight back to London. She thought every policeman she saw was after her, whatever the clerk had done wrong for Battle didn't make what she was doing any better. But he showed up on schedule, at the pub they'd met in the night before, with an envelope that looked no less full than the one he'd given the journalist. Oddly enough, once he'd handed it over, he refused her offer of a drink. She had a feeling he wouldn't be drinking in that pub — or the two or three Battle had looked in first — for a while to come.

I had been wrong. Battle was not a fool. He knew we were looking at the activities of a judge. He'd known enough to ask about Pulleyne even if I hadn't given him any answers. What he'd paid for was a full set of charge sheets and court records for the cases Orbach had sat on during his stint in Southend, whether or not they had been reported in the local papers. The court records included, where relevant, the previous convictions of the accused — whether or not on this occasion found guilty.

There was one case that hadn't made the papers. The court had sat unusually early, and a plea of guilty had been entered to a charge of indecent assault involving a couple of local youths. The assaults had not involved violence — the boys were willing hands. But it was assault because they were under age. It should have merited prison time, because there had been a similar previous offence some years before, albeit in a different town. Orbach had, however, suspended the sentence and let the man go.

The man's name was Walker. He was twenty-eight, married, and his occupation was aircraft mechanic.

CHAPTER FIVE

'You could have knocked me over with a feather when I saw who he was. I didn't know if I should have said something. But he didn't and I thought, well, it's his court, he's the judge, you know?'

Stephen Walker was not so open when first we approached him. To the contrary, he denied he was Stephen Walker, denied he'd ever worked at Southend Rochford and even denied he cared that it would be a criminal offence if he hit me with the wrench he was hefting from one of his grease-blackened hands to the other throughout the first five minutes of what may sardonically be described as our conversation.

We didn't get back to Southend for a few days after Carson's return to civilisation. There were other jobs to keep up with at the office and then the weekend intervened. I know private investigators aren't supposed to take weekends off, but Carson had already arranged to go out of town to catch up on some friends and I couldn't persuade Sandy that the way she most wanted to spend it was to pay a visit to the seaside in the early spring, cold enough not to be sure we weren't still in winter.

There was a surprising number of Walkers in Southend-on-Sea and its surrounding area. He had moved from his old address, which was a council tenancy so the new occupier didn't have a clue where he now lived. She directed us to a neighbour who'd lived in the area for enough years, but in turn she could only tell us that Walker had moved elsewhere in the town. She thought he'd changed his job at about the same time and perhaps that was why he'd moved. She wasn't too precise about dates, but give or take a decade, it fit.

I wasn't too bothered. The weather had improved. It was even a little sunny. It was better than being stuck in the office in London. Carson insisted I buy her an ice-cream cone with all the trimmings and we sat on the front looking across the water at Canvey Island while it dribbled down her fingers. We'd had no joy out of Battle. When we rang the paper, they told us he was on leave. When Morris rang his editor, he confirmed that Battle had taken some time off, long overdue, but was cagey about when he had booked himself out. I had learned a new rule of detection: when a gift horse looks you in the mouth, rip his open by the teeth, wrestle him to the ground and break his legs.

We had also gone out to the airport, just north of Southend, off the A127. Walker had never been employed by the airport; it had been possible that he was, but equally possible — and in context probable — that he had worked for one of the aircraft maintenance companies who serviced the clubs; the airport carried no employee records on the private companies. We strolled around, pretending with difficulty to be interested in joining a flying club and learning to fly, but our access was limited and we met no one who remembered him. There were other Walkers, we were told, but none who matched in age.

There were not, however, too many Walkers with an initial 'S' to be found in the 'phone book for resort to the oldest, most tedious routine of all.

'Hallo, is Stephen there?'

'Who?'

'You got the wrong number, mate.'

'Fuck off.'

'You've got a nice voice. How about meeting for a drink?'

'What number do you want?'

'Why don't you learn how to dial.'

Click.

'He doesn't come home for lunch. You'll find him at the garage,' a woman's voice told me. I could hear a child crying in the background. It was still only a long-shot, but I asked nonetheless:

'Have you got the number?'

'Who is this?'

'An old friend.'

Click.

Carson helpfully pointed with an ice-cream sticky finger to an entry for Walker's Classic Car Repairs. It was worth a try. Using our brand new town map, we found the address. I was surprised it was listed in the 'phone book. I was surprised the 'phone company had lines running down the long and unpaved alley that led to what looked like an abandoned Nissen hut until we turned the corner, cursing the damage to the suspension of Sandy's Peugeot and our own backsides, to find there was a door on the other side, facing the wrong way but open.

Inside was the man we eventually established was Walker, working on a Morris Minor in the best condition I'd seen since I hopped up to the window of my mother's car and kissed her good-bye when she went off to have her hair done and, I for the first time in my life, was left alone in the house for a full hour, aged nine or ten.

'You Walker?' I asked.

He unfolded himself from beneath the bonnet and scowled. He was a big, beefy man, with a weak face and too many chins to count, wearing what had once been white overalls but now couldn't be seen in the dark and with thick, hobnailed boots on his ample feet. He had a wrench in his hand. I waited patiently and politely for his answer and for him to put it down.

'Who're you?' He flipped his head at the car: 'I don't do modern.'

'It's beautiful,' I gestured to the Morris Minor. 'We live in London so there's no point: it'd get ripped off in ten minutes. How'd they manage to keep it in such good nick?'

My friendly interest provoked exactly the response you would expect from someone who had already received a warning call from his house:

'Go away. Go on, go away.'

Carson tried next.

'Listen, we just want to talk to you, Mr Walker. We just want to ask a few questions.' He responded to her own tentative foot forward with a step towards us of his own, considerably less tentative.

'I've got nothing to say. Go on, go away, this's my property.'

'Uh, no, it isn't actually.' I was guessing — but it was an educated guess. 'Your lease is only of the hut.'

He relaxed for a second:

'You from the landlords?'

'Uh, yes, right.' This time I took a pace towards him. 'We've been asked to pop down and have a chat with you.' He bristled at my movement.

'You got identification? Who are the landlords?'

'Ah.' One step forward, one step back.

I took a deep breath.

'You're Stephen Walker. You used to be an aircraft mechanic working at Southend . . .' And I claim my five pound reward for spotting the newspaper's mystery man on the sea-front.

'You've got the wrong bloke. You want to watch what you're saying.' He raised the wrench. 'Why can't you people leave me alone?'

'You've already got one criminal conviction you don't want anyone to know about. You don't want another . . .' I cautioned him.

'I don't bloody care . . .'

'Least of all your wife and children.' I took another educated guess: 'We don't . . .'

Wife and children were the wrong references. He roared like a bull and charged at me with about as much grace. He might have been a midnight gay but during the day he was as sexist as the next man and forgot about Carson until she stuck a sneakered foot into his path and as he went down jumped him from behind, twisting his wrench arm up around his back.

'Get off, get off . . .' he pleaded.

'Drop the wrench,' she suggested pleasantly.

He did as bid, so she did too. He got to his feet slowly and awkwardly, looking sheepish as he did so:

'I'm not a violent bloke, really.'

He could've fooled me.

'It's OK,' Carson said.

He turned to examine her with curiosity. 'Where'd you learn to handle yourself like that?'

'Dave — that's Dave, he's my boss — he's useless; one of us had to learn.'

Thanks, Carson. It wasn't strictly true, either. I'm not great with my fists, or with my feet except for running away. But give me a big enough human target less than a couple yards directly in front of me, and a gun that someone else has loaded, I can usually do enough damage. Also, I'm not bad with medieval weaponry.

'Can we talk now?' I asked gently.

He nodded.

'How about closing up the shop and coming for a drink?'

'I'll close up and come with you, but I don't drink, not anymore. Not since . . .'

I got the point. It's not news anymore, but I can remember a time when each day's papers, especially the local papers, carried an account of how this or that reputable, often middle-aged man, usually married and/or a vicar, had been arrested in a public lavatory, drunk as a skunk and down on his knees chewing gristle. 'But officer, I thought it was wafer.'

He slipped out of his overalls, locked the door of the Nissen and got into the back of our car, directing us to a pub where we would be able also to get a bite to eat. As we bounced back down the alley to a real road, I said: 'I'm surprised you get any business down there.'

'I get enough. It's just me and a part-timer. Mostly it's word of mouth. The classic car owners know each other.'

'Do you ever do any of the really old stuff, antique cars?'

'No. I haven't got the equipment.'

'It isn't exactly the safest spot I've ever seen,' Carson contributed to keeping the conversation casual.

I've got it wired up well. I'm good with electricals. That's what I mostly did on the planes. It's safer than you think '

We pulled into the pub car park and piled out of the car. He took my arm and held me back as Carson led the way in. 'Do we have to talk in front of her?'

"Cos she's a woman?'

He nodded miserably.

I shrugged. 'We don't have to. But she's, uh, pretty broad-minded and, look, Steve . . . Can I call you Steve?'

'Stephen.'

Diminutives had gone out of style.

'Stephen, then. I don't want to know about what happened. Not why you were in court. OK?'

Reluctantly, he agreed that I didn't need to send Carson to eat at another table. If he'd ever seen her gobble a ploughman's while slurping lager, he might not have given in so easily. When we were settled at the table, I summarised:

'You used to work at Southend Airport. You were a mechanic. You had a conviction, some years before, for, uh, the same thing you got caught for again. You were married?'

'Not when . . . Not the first time.'

'Right.' It added up. 'You worked for one of the private maintenance firms, on private planes, usually through the clubs, right?'

'Yes,' he sipped his St Clements: orange juice and bitter lemon. Then he swallowed whole a quarter of a cheese and onion sandwich. I wouldn't like to be the engine he was breathing into that afternoon.

'Then you got picked up again. The case went to the magistrates' court first?' It would have had to.

'Yes. But it was all very quick. Over and done with. I pleaded guilty. I mean, I was guilty, wasn't I. Because of the time before, I was sent up to Crown Court for sentencing.'

'OK. Was there any publicity at the magistrates' court?'

'No. I was lucky. It was the same as when I was in front of him; it came on before the court really started.'

'Why? How?'

He shrugged. It was an ambiguous shrug that could've meant he didn't know, or that he wasn't going to tell us.

'So what happened at Crown Court?'

'Like I said. It came on the same way, early. We all stood up. He came in. I didn't recognise him for a bit, because, you know, he had his wig on and one of those funny collars . . .' Wing collar; barristers' bands. 'Then I recognised him and he looked straight at me and I know he recognised me too so I thought it's up to him to say anything. He just said he'd read the reports and he was going to give me a year but suspend it for two years and did my solicitor want to say anything. Then I was told if I got into trouble again in the next two years I'd go to prison and that was it and I was free to go. It took less than five minutes.'

'Tell me about the Mellors.'

'Who are they?'

'Orbach — the judge — he was learning to fly at Southend, right?'

'Yes. He had a plane. A Cessna. It was a six-seater . . .'

'Single span turboprop. Yes, I know.' I knew it off by heart, even if I didn't know what it meant. 'He owned it with some other people. A man and his wife. She was black, does that help you remember?' I shouldn't think, to this day, that it's a common combination: white man, black woman, learning to fly.

'Yes, I remember,' he said excitedly: 'She was a decent sort.' As if it was a surprise. remember. What about it?'

'What do you know about the crash?'

He frowned:

'What crash? Did the plane crash? When? How?'

If I could've answered the latter, I would've been out of a job.

I remembered what his former neighbour had said:

'You left your house about the time of your case? And your job?' If so, he would no longer have been employed at the airport.

He nodded: 'My dad thought it was the best thing to do. You see, my wife knew about the first time, the old one, I'd told her. My dad was mad at me, he said I shouldn't tell anyone. But I couldn't do it, you know, I couldn't marry her without telling her. But, well, when it happened again . . .' He paused to try and find the distinction between needing to tell his wife before they were married and not telling her when it happened afterwards.

He couldn't put it into words and I didn't push him. It wasn't relevant, and besides I understood all too well: the past is past; the past isn't an infidelity; the past didn't reflect on her. He continued: 'I didn't say anything. I knew, well, I knew I could go to prison, but my dad told me not to worry, I wasn't going to.'

By then, I knew better than to ask whether he in his turn had asked how his father could be so sure; Stephen — even now, in his mid-thirties I guessed — took for granted that his father could fix anything.

'My dad bought me the lease on the hut. He wanted us to leave Southend, but Gina — that's my wife — she wouldn't go. Her family's all here. But he put me off the job and he lent me some money and he got us a transfer to another house, in Raleigh.' Raleigh and Southend ran into one another. To a stranger, and to the 'phone book, they were one and the same town. 'I always wanted to do this anyway: it was always a hobby. I've made a go of it, you know. You'd be surprised. Next year I'm going to get a proper building. And we're buying our house from the council.' The law required local authorities to sell their houses and flats to sitting tenants, at a substantial discount.

'You said your father "put you off the job." What do you mean?'

'Where I worked, it was his firm see.'

I saw.

There was something else I asked Walker about before we left him alone.

'Why was your wife so suspicious on the 'phone this morning? Why did she ring you to say I'd called?'

I merely wanted confirmation.

'There was someone else came around a couple of days ago. She knew I'd had a stranger visit; she thinks it's something to do with the business; she knew it'd worried me

'Tall bloke?'

'Yes. Brian Battle. He was from the papers. He threatened . . .' He choked up on the memory. 'He threatened he'd write about my conviction.'

There was no way he could get a word into a national newspaper, or probably even the local paper, about a four-or-more-year-old conviction of a nonentity for indecent assault, but Walker wasn't to know it.

'What did you tell him?'

'I didn't know what to do. I rang my dad. He told me to send him to his office.'

'Did you ring your father about us?'

He shook his head.

'I didn't know what you wanted. I would have.'

Carson asked:

'Are you going to ring him now?'

His shoulders slumped.

'Well, I've got to, haven't I?'

She said, 'Stephen, we want to help you. Really we do. Battle's trouble; we can take care of him. We can shut him up. But if you bring your father into it, I don't know if we can.' I could count three lies and one non-sequitur in her statement.

'What do you want?' He asked dully. 'What's all this about?'

I had to give him something:

It's about the plane crash, the Mellors, you see.'

'I don't know anything about that. I told you. I never even heard of it till you told me. What's it got to do with me?'

'We think . . . Look, we'll trust you . . . But if we trust you, you've got to trust us. OK?'

It was a deal simple enough for him to understand. He nodded quickly. He'd grab at anything that left him out.

'We need to find out, well, how honest a man Orbach is. We think he may have had something to do with the crash. We think what you've told us, well, you must have thought — your father — Orbach — the way everything was handled — you know what I'm saying?'

He was on the verge of tears: 'I never asked him to . . .'

I went on quickly, 'It's alright. You see, we're not interested in that at all. We've got what we need now. But if your father knows we're, well, snooping around, he's going . . . he's bound to think we're, uh, after, I mean interested in him, isn't he?'

'But you're not? You're saying you're not?'

'That's right. We can leave him out too.' It paled Carson's lies into insignificance: but I'm a qualified lawyer while she only trained as a paralegal. 'Do you see what I'm saying?'

'I think so.' He was blinded by how badly he wanted to believe us. 'What about Battle?'

'I told you. We'll take care of that. How long ago did he come round?'

'Before the weekend.'

'What happened between him and your father?'

'I don't know. Dad rang me later and told me not to worry, he'd seen to it.' His eyes shone, 'He always does.'

'Are you an only child?'

'I've got a sister. Why?'

'Just curious. What about your mother? Is she still alive?' The curiosity was genuine, but probably not enough to have bothered asking if I hadn't wanted to distract him from his father-idolatry.

'I don't know.' His eyes clouded over. 'She left us, a long time ago, when we was kids. It's always been Dad and us.' So much for my distraction. It hadn't been a total failure though: 'I won't tell him you came round. I want, I need, I ought . . .' To make up his mind what he wanted to say? 'I don't want to keep going running to him. In a way, what you're saying, it'd be doing something for him, wouldn't it?'

'For sure.' I restrained myself from patting him on the head and telling him he was a good boy.

We drove back to London, less chatty than on the way down. Things about parents have that effect on both of us. I never got along with mine, and Carson's strained relationship with her father had taken a plunge between the time she'd saved his life and — soon after — when he had himself finally let slip away what little was left of his broken spirit. He'd felt humiliated that his daughter, still a child in everyone's eyes but her own, had to save him. Her mother, too, had abandoned them when

Carson was a kid, which was another point of identification with Stephen she could've done without.

Sandy on the other hand hadn't had a day's trouble with her parents in the whole of her life, except when they were still bullying her to get married and settle down. They'd accepted half the cake: settling down with me; she still spoke most days with her mother, and there were few weeks that went by without some gift or other for Alton arriving on our doorstep or notified by this savings institution, that broker or the Premium Bond people. To be fair to my father, he'd also sent a present when Alton was born: a cheque for twenty-five pounds. It contrasted well with the ten thousand Lewis had left him in his will.

'What're we going to do about Papa Walker?' His son had given us his proper name, Nicholas R, known as Nick.

'I'm not sure. I think a little bit of company research first, just for form.' Stephen had told us which was his father's firm. 'Check out the local government year-books, see if he was a councillor.' I had forgotten to ask when Stephen said his father had arranged his tenancy transfer; it's less easy to do than many people believe and suggested considerable local influence. 'Maybe he's a magistrate himself — they've got books'll tell you that too. I want to know more about him before we beard him.'

Especially now Battle'd queered our pitch. I was going to have to catch up with Battle before long. He might be aiming for the British equivalent of a Pulitzer, but unless he got out of my way he was going to be out of a job.

It wasn't a good time for me to have to spend so much time away from the office. Sandy was hardly ever in. She was organising the move, supervising the builders, looking at one and the same time for live-in help or else new child-minding facilities in the area, showing people around the old house and pretending she was taking it all in her stride.

She wasn't; though she was, unusually, not taking it out on me, it was making her headaches worse and I was worried about her, although there was little I could do to help apart from take as much strain at the office as the case allowed me and occasionally suggest that she go in for a medical check-up.

We went out to dinner that night, just to get away from it all. Carson babysat. For some bizarre reason, Alton had taken to her like I felt about Southern Comfort. It was mutual: Carson had fallen in love with him too. Sandy wasted an extra half-hour fussing and telling her ten times over where everything was — much of it already boxed for the move — and where we could be found. Just in case.

We had a drink at the club and I caught up on business with Natalie, then went to a restaurant off the King's Road we hadn't been to for a long time — not since I lived in Earl's Court — that we were pleasantly surprised to find was still in the same hands. Restaurants in the area change owners, theme, cooking ethnicity and price range more often than the cooks change boyfriends.

'How're you doing?' I asked once we'd settled back and ordered. I like going out with Sandy. She doesn't drink too much. There's no dispute over who's driving home. It means that one time in twenty I'm not gambling with my licence.

'It's OK. I feel less, well, out of control than I expected.' This I had already appreciated. Sandy out of control makes Woody Allen look laid back. 'How do you feel?'

'Strange.' It's not every lawyer who can reach his forties with a newborn child, an overdraft, not even the smallest share in a house but the owner of a drinking club instead. 'It's easier than

I thought it'd be. To settle down. 'Course, it's different at the moment.'

They brought our starters. We are unimaginative eaters. Exotic dishes terrify us. She had a prawn cocktail; I had parma ham and melon. We'd crossed town for a meal we could have bought at any half-decent restaurant within a ten minute walk.

'But I can't deny I'm pleased. I never thought, you know, all those years, well, maybe the reason I kept on like I did . . .'

'Like an asshole?'

'Yeah, right.' She has a charming tongue. 'You know, I couldn't see anything that far ahead in the future. I mean, when you're young, you can't be that excited about something as conventional as . . . well . . . having children, buying a house, you know, stuff; even making money.' Sandy hadn't had that problem, she'd always lusted after material security. 'But if there's nothing else that excites you instead, it adds up to not a whole lot of things to live for. You know?' For once, she didn't want to take over the conversation so I went on: 'It's sort of touch-and-go. Which comes first — blowing yourself out or finding something worth keeping going for?'

I was talking about myself, though there was a moment I wasn't sure if I was also talking about Orbach.

'Just luck you made it, huh, kid.'

I grinned and took her hand and, unexpectedly and entirely possibly unprecedentedly, brought it to my lips to kiss her fingertips. After letting them linger for a bit, she snatched them away ostentatiously, with a phony drawl:

'Husht, honey, someone might see.'

I poured us both more wine. We held our glasses up. 'Cheers.'

Someone had seen us. The manager came over to welcome us back. He joined us for a glass of wine. I liked him He was a

Spaniard whose English was not much clearer now than when he came over, long before we first met him; his children, about whom we'd heard over the years, were growing up; his daughter was qualifying as an accountant. I'm sentimental. I found the idea appealing that the daughter of a Spanish waiter could become an English accountant.

The moment had passed. She asked: 'What do you think really happened, Dave?'

I knew what she was asking about.

'I don't know. If I'm honest, I admit I still don't know, and I still have difficulty believing it — even of him. But I can see how it might have happened.' I gathered my thoughts. 'I know we always see Orbach as a great planner and manipulator, but I'm not sure it's all that true. I think it's more a case of finding a use for everything that comes his way. The way I see him — he wants something, and he can't stand it when he can't have it, so he pushes and shoves and doesn't give up and doesn't take no for an answer and somewhere along the line someone or something gives . . . and that's why and when what he wants happens.'

'When he visited the mother . . . What's her name? Eartha. You don't think he had anything planned?'

'No. I'm certain of it. Otherwise, why would he still be trying to talk them out of emigrating? I don't think . . . I can't see him working out how to do it, and then trying to change their minds to save him from having to carry it out. Anyway, I don't think he could have set it up that early. No. At that point, he just wanted them not to take Frankie away from him . . .'

'Frankie — not to keep them from going away themselves?'

'Obviously just Frankie.' As usual, it took a moment to sink in that she might have a point. 'Well, maybe not so obviously, maybe he would've liked it best if they'd all stayed, though of

course she'd never have come to live with him. But you're right;
he didn't necessarily want that much.'

'And then he gets his main chance?'

'Only chance, it would've seemed.'

'And Daddy was willing to pay the price, just for seeing
sonny boy walk free? It's a hell of a price. Couldn't he have cut
a deal with the prosecution on the basis of what Orbach asked
him to do?'

'I doubt he'd think of it; I doubt he'd be sure they'd keep his
son's name out of it. I doubt Orbach would have told him outright what he wanted back, or even necessarily that he'd want anything back, though a man like Walker must know that nothing
comes free. A lot of corruption's like that. It isn't a straight swap.
It's scratch my back 'cos I itch now, and I'll scratch yours when
you start to itch.'

'I would've thought . . . the scratches had to match.' She can
mix a good metaphor.

The main course arrived. Grilled fish, asparagus, boiled
potatoes for Sandy; steak and chips for me; another bottle
of rosé.

'Yeah, but you're running ahead of yourself. By the time
it came to it — to the "favour" — it wouldn't've been that
straightforward anymore. First of all, Orbach could still leak
about the boy: it was recent enough then to be a story in its
own right. Secondly, the fix had been in at the magistrates'
court and someone at the Crown Court also had to rig the early
hearing; the police had to be involved; maybe Orbach knew
about the house transfer; he would've been in a position now to
bring down father as well as son for a hell of a lot of local fixing.
Finally, it'd be difficult to prove Orbach himself actually did
anything wrong; there were reports; he made a lenient decision;

that's all. That's how it could've worked: he let Walker build it up until it was a much bigger debt available to call in.'

'What are you going to do about Battle?' We'd arrived back in town too late for me to catch Morris.

'Sell him to Colonel Sanders?'

'What's he up to?' A bone got stuck between two side teeth and she couldn't get it out. I reached over and extracted it for her. No greater love hath man. Then I replied: 'He thinks there's a good story in it; he's taking a hell of a risk with his job. At least,' the thought occurred for the first time, 'maybe he is. It's possible his editor knows what he's up to, in which case they're both about to be deep-fried.'

We were silent while we considered dessert. After we'd ordered, she shook her head:

'I don't think he could've done it. I mean, I know him. I just don't see how he could kill his own friends, his best friend, his godchild's parents, too. Mind you, I've never understood how anyone could kill someone else.' She caught the look on my face and remembered it was a subject I was still sensitive about. 'I'm sorry, Dave.'

'It's OK. Mine were when there weren't a lot of choices.' It was true of those I'd killed. But was it also true of others whose deaths could be laid at my door? There was one in particular at whom I had knowingly and coldly pointed someone else's trigger finger. Was that the point Keenan had been making? Was it why Dowell kept telling me I was too like Orbach for my own comfort? Was it why, according to Sandy, I had to satisfy myself about it? Or was it why she accused me of thinking he was God?

I shrugged.

'Hell, I don't know. You say we know him; do we? Would you have said he was capable of other things we know he's done, before he did them? How many times do you read about people — or have we acted for people — who those who've known them best would've said, or did say, it isn't possible? Who knows the depths of anyone else's dark side, or even their own? Maybe there simply is no bottom to it — it's a question of cross the line once, find out what you can do that isn't as unthinkable as you believed it to be, then keep going.' It wasn't what Orbach had said, but maybe what he meant.

She said: 'This is different, it's so much worse.' The manager came back over.

'Mr Woolf. There's a 'phone call for you.'

We nearly knocked each other over as we scrambled to find out what disaster had overtaken Alton; we did knock over both the manager and the table. Sandy got to the desk first and grabbed the 'phone.

'What? Carson? What is it?'

There was a prolonged silence while, I could tell from the glow in Sandy's eyes, Carson reassured her. Then said, 'Here he is.'

To me she just said, 'He's fine.'

'Yup, Carson?'

'Boss?' She sounded shaky, Sandy hadn't noticed, in her anxiety about Alton. 'We got problems, boss. I got problems.' Shaky, hell — more like on the verge of tears.

'What is it, kid?'

'It was on the news, just now: the local news.' I glanced at my watch: it was ten thirty-five. The Regional News would have just finished on ITV. 'They found a body; like, a clerk from the local court, y'know.'

'Cool it, Carson. It could be coincidence; might not be the same one.'

'Yeah? Well, seems like it didn't take them any time to i.d. him: the bobby who found him recognised him from the court. And they showed his picture. Oh yeah, and something else . . .'

'What?'

'They're looking for a woman in her late twenties or early thirties, sort of a big, economy size woman, seen in his office with him the other day having some kind of an argument; seen in town with him, y'know. They showed a photofit: it's not a bad likeness, boss.'

CHAPTER SIX

When we got home from the restaurant, we found Carson sitting in the living-room, without any lights on, but wearing a pair of my sunglasses, a scarf of Sandy's and one of Alton's (clean) potties on her head.

'Waddaya think? Think anyone'll recognise me?'

Sandy didn't let us stay at the restaurant for coffee, so as soon as she had been up to see that Alton was unaffected by an evening in the hands of a murderess, she went to make up a jug while Carson and I went over what we knew.

There was not much to add to what she'd already told me. The body had been found in the early hours of Sunday morning. He was found on the beach on a strip the gays cruised and it had at first been taken for a fag-bashing: 'homosexual killing', the newsreader had said marginally more politely. Enquiries during Sunday and Monday had apparently convinced the police it was something more though there had been no explanation why. And those enquiries had thrown up a mystery woman, whose visit to his office at the court had apparently caused him some consternation.

Also, she had his name — Arnold Waterbottom.

'Jesus, someone did him a favour. Maybe it was suicide?'

'Maybe that's where they got the fag-killing from. Actually, I didn't think he was a fag, either. Not the way he was looking at me in the pub.'

'What does that mean? Sexy Stevie's got two kids. I don't suppose he found them in the back of a Morris Minor.'

She shrugged:

'I just don't think so, is all. Which means the police're going to go on looking for me until I show up.'

'Let's be calm about this,' I poured us each a drink to go with coffee when it arrived. 'I figure, plead guilty to manslaughter, provoked by bad breath and dandruff, you'll probably be out in ten years, with good behaviour — so, OK, twenty,' I corrected myself: it was unlikely Carson would behave herself for ten days let alone ten years in Holloway. 'Look on the bright side: we'll be living within walking distance; I can come sing to you outside your window some moonlit night.'

The coffee arrived accompanied coincidentally by Sandy. She heard my last remark and grimaced: 'Ask for an inside cell.'

Singing is a misleading description of what I do in the shower. In hotels, people've been known to call the manager and, once, a doctor.

I said two words people don't like to hear, the second one of which was 'in'.

Sandy said:

'You know what I'm thinking, kids?'

No one knows exactly what Sandy is thinking so the question had to be rhetorical.

Carson guessed: 'He's had too much to drink?' Meaning me. A safe guess.

I guessed:

'Carson didn't do it? Nah. The police never look for someone if they haven't done something wrong.'

'I'm thinking . . . How many deaths were involved in Disraeli Chambers, Dave?' I had to think for a moment before I could tell her. 'And at Mather's?' That one was harder: exactly how many to include was an open question. I erred on the side of modesty and gave her the lowest possible figure. 'And last time?' Carson totted it up out loud for her.

'That's one hell of a lot of dead bodies, Dave. Now there's one more.'

'You're thinking it ain't gonna be the last?'

'Right.'

'So you're thinking,' I knew her this well, 'I gotta talk to Tim before it gets any worse?' She had an image of Tim as my guardian angel that accorded not at all with my own perception of his role.

'That's one option: the other is to get out.'

'Hey,' Carson protested. 'What about me? You want I should go back to Australia?' She spent her days with me, with Sandy, with Natalie: you should be surprised she was beginning to sound Jewish?

'You've got an alibi,' Sandy answered calmly. She's a lawyer, too, and a better one than I. 'You were with friends at the weekend. It isn't about whether you did it or not; it's just a question whether. and when you go in and give yourself up to clear yourself.' Which would still call for explanation about her connection with Waterbottom and was therefore no different than if we decided to tell Dowell directly.

'I offered Tim in. He didn't want to know. I go talk to him now, or Carson walks into Southend nick, we've got to give up Battle, the Walkers, and what do we get out of it?' One of my greatest failings in life is my tendency to ask questions which I intend to be rhetorical but others expect an answer to.

I continued, as if I'd always meant to do so: 'First, maybe it's coincidence, so we blew it for nothing.' I paused to let them snort their derision in harmony. 'Secondly, one of 'em's got something to hide about Waterbottom. You sure that was his name? Maybe you misheard? Maybe you made it up?' She didn't dignify either alternative with an answer. 'If it's Walker, what it does is put him out of our reach which correspondingly means we don't get to find out anything more about Orbach. If it's Battle . . .' I shook my head, unless he was a psychopath there was nothing in it for him; he might be bad news, but he wasn't a baddie.

'I'd say that made three possibles.' Carson contributed: 'Or back to two if you acquit Battle.'

It was a thought, but: 'Orbach doesn't get his hands dirty; that's not his style.'

'I think what Carson's saying,' Sandy translated, 'maybe you'd get Walker acting on Orbach's instructions. That'd be enough, wouldn't it?'

'Nah. It's the same deal. To get Orbach, you'd have to get cast-iron evidence; hell, even in the case of an ordinary villain, the uncorroborated evidence of an accomplice doesn't count for much, you know that.' A jury can convict on it, but the trial judge has to warn them that it's risky. 'Waddaya think it'd count against the word of a High Court judge?'

'Then what sort of evidence are you looking for, Dave? What sort of evidence will be sufficient?'

'You're forgetting. I ain't trying to find enough to convict him; just enough to justify them publishing the story.' As of tonight, the story's value to my clients would have doubled. 'What I'm saying is, as soon as I give Walker to Dowell, he's out of my hands, off the street, out of touch. Then you've either got to talk criminal conviction or nothing. That's so whether it's just Waterbottom or the Mellors as well. And criminal conviction — of Orbach — you ain't gonna get; not even prosecution. Nope, I need Walker outside.'

'Where you think, maybe, he'll write it all down for you and have it notarised?'

'You know me better than that, Sandy. I can't think that far ahead. I'm only thinking a step at a time; let me get Walker into a corner; then we'll work something out.' But she had an idea: like Walker or Orbach on a wire, or Orbach with his hand in the proverbial till to pay Walker off. I had but one article of faith, and it was Orbach's own — keep on pushing, keep on shoving, something'll give. It was my singular contribution to the philosophy of detection.

'Right now, I'd say your priority's to find Battle,' Sandy said. "Cos, the way you see it, Battle gave Waterbottom up to Walker — right?'

'You see any other way to spell the story? That's my guess. You got a better?'

Carson shook her head.

'It doesn't add up that way.' She's so contrary, she can't even use my metaphors. 'I know what you're saying — you see Waterbottom as one of the links in the chain.'

She got up to pour herself another drink but when she made as if to pour me one too she caught a scowl from Sandy that sent her scurrying back to the sideboard to put the bottle away.

'But he's not a link in his own right; I don't know, you don't know, if he had anything to do with the original fix; I doubt it, I've met him; he didn't have that sort of clout. His only value was in conjunction with Battle, because of the information he gave him '

'What you're really saying is, Sandy's right, he's not the last. It's gotta be Waterbottom and Battle or neither?'

'Looks that way,' Sandy agreed with her protégée's reasoning, proud it was a jump ahead of mine, her partner's. It was Sandy's. original idea — and, boy, was it original — to bring us together as a team.

'Have a headache,' I snarled. 'You're all so clever, you go solve it.'

'Uhuh, Dave; the difference is, I'd let it go, and I daresay Carson would — if I asked nicely. You're the one so damned determined to pin it on Orbach.'

Which is why first thing the next morning I drove Carson — well out of my way, but for some reason she wouldn't take the tube or a taxi — to the club, where everyone who could see at all saw double, and then I drove to Southend.

There was one consolation. It meant I had Sandy's car for another day, and she had to make do with my beat-up Beetle. After my Passat had been cruelly and unnecessarily beaten up during my last case, I'd sold it. I gave up on decent wheels. There didn't seem any point. My relationships with cars didn't last as briefly as my relationships with women used to. Carson had her own car before she went back to Australia, but hadn't time to replace it since she returned. I was too mean to let her rent one except on specific occasions I could charge a client for. So on long journeys I took Sandy's.

I couldn't go into Southend with any ostensible connection to Waterbottom. I could with a connection to Battle; the police weren't looking for him, so they had not, at least so far as I was aware, made a link between them. From the club, I rang Morris. I needed another favour. His first effort to bolster my investigative team had proved a disaster so I knew better than to ask for another journalist. But — surmounting the usual linguistic hurdles — I persuaded him to speak to Battle's editor and in turn authorise me to look for Battle on behalf of the paper. I rang in when I arrived at Southend and was sent to a fax-centre to pick up a written letter confirming my commission.

There were three places where Carson had been that counted. Though she'd been seen with Waterbottom in the pub, I figured it for incidental intelligence. She'd been at the court; she'd been at the hotel; she'd been with me when we visited Stephen Walker. I started at the court, arriving before it opened for business — at least, before the time it opened for ordinary mortals without anyone to pull someone else's strings. I was in time to hear the judge deliver a brief oration:

'You will all have heard that over the weekend, our Mr Waterbottom died, and in the most unpleasant circumstances.' I tried to envisage a pleasant circumstance in which to die: I could only think of how Phil Esterhaus went out in *Hill Street,* humping Kate Gardner, and I'm not convinced it didn't too closely resemble strenuous exercise for my comfort. 'Mr Waterbottom had worked in the court system for nearly twenty years. He was a valued member of the court staff. It is a relief that he left no family to mourn him, but we in this court will miss him, and mourn him instead.' I gotta get this judge for my funeral — he'd have everyone who wasn't already in stitches busting their sides.

The judge asked for one minute's silence and everyone else stood, though he remained seated, stroking his side-burns with affection. There were limits; Waterbottom was only a clerk. I didn't see anyone crying; I didn't see a collection hat passed around; I didn't see anyone open a book on who was next in line to die.

'Next case,' the judge said, to signify both the end of this over-lengthy period of tribute to the dear departed and his wish to get on with playing God himself.

'Police and Everard, for sentence, Your Honour.'

I don't know why. Maybe because I was tired and courts are good places to rest; maybe because I wanted to see a bit more of this joker judge; maybe I still wasn't sure how to handle the next step and needed time to think. I didn't leave. My mind drifted away and was only brought back, just after the judge pronounced sentence, when the prisoner in the dock screamed at him.

'You *cunt;*you fucking cunt.'

The judge was unperturbed. He signalled the police to wait a moment before taking the prisoner down. He said:

'Everard. In a few hours' time, I shall leave this court in my comfortable, three-and-a-half-litre Rover, and be driven to my home in rural Essex. When I arrive, I shall kiss my wife, pour myself a large gin and tonic, and settle down in front of my twenty-six-inch colour television until my dinner is ready. I believe I shall be having a roast tonight: rare roast beef, dripping with blood, microwave crisp vegetables, a bottle of fine wine — I shall spend the journey home deciding exactly which. Later, I shall retire to my custom-made bed, luxuriating in my silk pyjamas, and read until I decide it is time for me to sleep.'

He paused to let others envisage the enjoyable evening ahead of him. Then he continued:

'You, on the other hand, will be going to prison, where you will be strip-searched, given second-hand, rough garb to wear, and fed slops before you're put into your cell, where to toss-and-turn in an uncomfortable bunk, lights out when the warden decides. Now who's the cunt? Take him down.'

He was the sort of judge who used to refer to hanging as a suspended sentence.

I went out to see Stephen Walker next. As I drove down the dirt track to his workshop, an ancient bronze Jaguar in condition good enough to kill for, its bonnet emblem proud as a ship's prow, passed me going the other way. There was only just enough room, so I slowed to a near-halt to let him squeeze by. Age and beauty. I'm talking cars, not drivers. As our front windows drew parallel, we looked directly at each other. He didn't know who I was, but I was fairly sure I'd just met Nick Walker for the first, but undoubtedly not the last, time.

Walker's part-timer was on the job, so I stood in the doorway until Walker looked up from the engine they were working on. He was startled to see me. I glanced at his colleague, still bent over inside the hood, and he nodded that he would join me outside.

'What do you want?' he hissed. 'You promised you were going to let me alone.'

'Was that your father I passed?'

'Yes.'

'And?'

'And what?'

'And did you tell him about our visit?' I tried to keep the impatience out of my voice.

'No. I said. I said I wouldn't.' He was getting angry. I'd for-gotten what a big man he was. I was glad there was someone else within hailing distance; I didn't have Carson to look after me today. At worst I'd only get beaten, not killed. 'Why are you here?'

'Have you read a paper today?' I asked, trying to sound no more than idly curious. He shook his head. 'What about the TV last night?'

'I watched. What?'

He wasn't as thick either as he looked or as he sounded. It began to dawn on him why I'd come back to see him He looked crafty:

'That was her, wasn't it? That was your girl, your mate. And she knew how to handle herself alright.'

I could see no advantage in lying.

'It was her. But she didn't do anything. She was away at the weekend.'

'Then what are you worried about?' he jeered. He was human enough to enjoy having the boot on the other foot. It was, on him, a very big boot.

I smiled sweetly.

'You're absolutely right, Stevie sweety. We'll just go in and explain what she was talking to him about. We'll tell them we were suspicious of a case a long time ago, a case that got a bit rigged, you know. You see, that's the connection, Stephen: you want that's what we should do? Especially, given where they found him. Yes, you're right: I should clear her and let them go back to their original theory, together with that little bit of extra information, right?'

He shook his head numbly. He wasn't good at being a hard case. It brought him into the middle of it as much as us. Him and his dad. I left him, confident not only that he would not be reaching out to dial 999, but also that he was less likely than before to tell his father about our visit.

I called next at the hotel where Carson had stayed. I produced my identification from the firm and explained that we were checking up on employee expense claims.

It was routine, I insisted; we did it to all employees every once in a while. I happened to have some work nearby, so it was easier to call in than telephone or write. The receptionist did not take to me: I don't think she appreciated how much in an employee's interest it is to have their integrity occasionally verified; I think she thought I was a suspicious sow-turd. Nonetheless, she sent me through to the manager, who not only thought it was an excellent idea, one he might yet adopt, but also appreciated that I — as an employer — was a better bet for future business than the employee.

'Yes, well, certainly there's a record of her stay,' I confirmed the entry. 'But did you see her yourself? Could you describe her, so that I can know she was here in person?'

'I don't recollect her myself, Mr, er, Woolf. We do have a large number of visitors,' he smirked and stroked his moustache. 'Perhaps one of the girls?'

'Can I ask them?'

'Certainly. Now, let's see; the young lady you saw outside would have been on duty when she checked in and . . . Oh, you're in luck: also when she checked out. She ate here, I see from the account; you could ask the maitre d', but I can't tell from this which of the waiters served her. I'd have to retrieve the original bill. Would you, er, like me to. . . ? I have to say, sir, the restaurant's quite dimly lit in the evenings. It's very unlikely they'd remember.' For which read, it would be a lot of work to dig out the original bill.

I shook my head.

'I'll just ask the girl outside and the maitre d', if you wouldn't mind letting them know.' If God heard me refer to the receptionist as a girl, I hoped she wasn't a feminist. Sandy would've torn my head off and Carson would've done time for me instead of Waterbottom.

It was a risk, because the questions might've prompted someone's memory which hadn't yet, and mightn't otherwise, have clicked to the photofit. It also didn't produce any certainties, because either of the ones I asked might not even, or yet, have seen the picture. But both of them were emphatic they couldn't describe her or remember her face; just that there had been a youngish woman, paying with a firm's credit card; she remembered her bomber-jacket, though.

'That sounds like her alright. Thank you for your help. Have a nice day.' I got it in before she could. It'd only recently caught on in England: I'm sorry to have to tell you your mother just died, have a nice day; I'm afraid the car cost twice as much to repair, have a nice day; we're out of stock at present, have a nice day; gimme your wallet fuckface, have a nice day.

Finally, a little more secure that Carson had not been identified, and above all secure that she had not been identified back to me, I went to the police station. I produced the fax, and my own i.d., and explained to the desk sergeant that I was, on behalf of the paper, looking for one of its journalists, who had gone strangely absent. He was confused.

'Do you want to post him as missing, sir?' If so, why send a solicitor to Southend to do it?

'Not exactly. No, not at all. He, uh, how shall I put it?' I wished I'd spent more time thinking about how to put it before I'd started. But, as I'd said to Sandy, thinking more than one step ahead at a time was an excessive strain on what I — though few others — like to call my brain. 'He has something, uh, some information, belonging to the paper.'

'Are you reporting a theft, sir?' If so, why aren't you reporting it in London?

'No, I shouldn't say so. Uh, no, definitely not. I'm hoping, well, you see I'm hoping to find him and persuade him to return it. I think, my, uh, clients, would not want to consider charges, not at this stage. I'd say, they've got a lot of time for him. I'm sure it's a question of find him, forgive and forget.'

'The forgive and forget division's down the street and take the third turning on the left, sir,' he said dryly. 'Depending on your denomination, of course.'

'I was hoping, perhaps, a word with one of your detectives — to get some thoughts; perhaps he picked up a parking ticket?'

'Why do you think he's in Southend, sir?'

'Well, he was here for a while; he filed his expenses claim.'

'Did he claim for a ticket, sir?'

'Uh, no.'

'Well, then,' he said triumphantly, as if that explained everything. Which it did — whoever heard of a journalist with a parking ticket not trying to reclaim it?

'So, uh, there's nothing you can do to help?' I asked forlornly.

'I didn't say that, sir,' he sighed. 'If you want to speak to one of our detectives, I can't stop you. They're very busy, though, sir. You may have heard: a matter of murder.'

'Yes, I read about it. In the local paper,' I added quickly. A court clerk doesn't make the nationals; not for a mere bash on the head, however fatal it proves.

'If you'd like to wait there, sir.'

While I waited, I reflected on what I wanted most. If I gave them enough, I could get them looking for Battle. That might help him, but I was certain it wouldn't help me. So either I'd have to tell a few whoppers, which might just land me in trouble later, or else I'd have to tell them the truth, which was exactly what I was there to avoid. If I gave them nothing, nothing was what I could expect in return.

I was shown into an office, where a man sat behind a desk marked D.S. Ambleton. I was surprised; I thought they'd give me to a raw recruit.

'We're short-handed today. Murder.' It was obviously the high-point of the Southend police season. 'How can I help you?' He flicked over the pair of papers which allegedly confirmed my identity and my quest in life as if he never had doubts.

He was not an attractive man. In his early forties, with bouffant hair held in place by too much gel, his fingernails were bitten down but still somehow managed to suggest long-secreted dirt. He was wearing a cheap, black leather jacket to try to keep up with the younger street detectives, most of whom were in their turn trying to keep up with what the public saw on the box. Sergeant was as high as he would ever rise.

I played it like I saw him. Someone else, I might've played differently.

I gave him the same rough outline I'd given the desk sergeant. He gave me the same rough runaround. I asked him where he would start looking for someone like that: he was a detective, wasn't he? He suggested sarcasm wouldn't help me. After I'd apologised, he suggested the local paper, and the bars. I told him both local papers had been rung — which was true, though by Battle's editor in London, not by me — and would he, seeing as how it was lunchtime, care to join me for a drink in the nearest available alternative. He looked at me sceptically, but agreed.

I was relieved. The pubs had been open for an hour and I hadn't put away my first of the day. I treated him to a pint, and — unsolicited — a plate of sandwiches. Comfortably ensconsed in a corner, he asked first:

'Why are they really so concerned to find him? I mean, you're a solicitor, you lot cost a packet, it must be something they're desperate about: why not hire a private detective?'

'Well,' I sold out the brethren of my calling without hesitation, 'it is a sensitive matter; they're a crude bunch of buggers I think, perhaps the best way I can put it, there's a certain amount of internal dispute involved. This isn't news material we're talking about.' I didn't quite tap my nose but I conveyed nonetheless that any intelligent man of the world would understand precisely what it was about. It's a bluff that works ninety nine per cent of the time: people don't like to admit their ignorance.

'Still and all, it's odd. I mean, I know you are a solicitor like you say . . .'

'I showed you my firm's identification,' I reminded him, thinking he was indicating doubt in my *bona fides*.

He sneered: 'Anyone can make identification. No, I checked in the Solicitor's Diary.' All solicitors are listed in it, even me. 'What I was going to say,' he reprimanded me for interrupting him, 'I was wondering if perhaps you did some writing for the paper, whether you were interested in something else.'

'What might that be, sergeant?' I asked quietly, neither admitting nor denying it.

'Well, the only thing it might be is this Waterbottom business,' he munched merrily on the last quarter sandwich, which I'd been saving for myself. 'It's the only thing alive in this whole town.' He was implying he was superior to this provincial backwater.

I chuckled graciously.

'Very good. D'you mind?'

He was so pleased he'd tumbled my true racket he wouldn't've noticed if I told him I'd come into confess. Orbach would have been proud of me. There's nothing like stumbling on the truth, by accident or by skill, to disarm suspicion. If I'd walked in and asked him outright, I'd've been bounced on my buttocks back to Sandy's car.

'Why aren't the regular people doing it? I mean, you must have crime reporters? I don't read your rag, you understand; the Sunday one, isn't it? Bit too highbrow for me.' If that was his idea of highbrow, the Beano comic must've been a strain. 'You do have crime reporters, don't you?'

'Yes and no.' I got up. 'Another?'

'Alright.' He didn't offer to get it. Rounds of drink are the most common, the most acceptable, and possibly the most insidious, form of petty corruption. He hadn't forgotten his question by the time I returned, though: 'What d'you mean, yes and no?'

'Yes, we've got 'em; no, they don't dig deep enough. No offence now — but they do tend to be little more than police mouthpieces. Sometimes, it's more interesting to cover it from another angle. I've done legal writing for the paper,' I could lie my head off now I knew he'd never read it, and so long as nothing I said regenerated his suspicion. 'I thought it'd be interesting to see how the police go at it; never mind the actual crime, if you like; but a meaningless sort of murder like this, how the police work at it.'

The last time I'd posed as a writer, the person I'd been trying to deceive had seen through me in less than a minute: that was

Alex Keenan. Ambleton was a D.S. not a Q.C. He shrugged; if it didn't make any sense, he wasn't going to say so. He asked:

'What about this Battle bloke, then?'

'He really has been down here; we really don't know where he's gone; but all I want with him is, if I find him, he's going to work with me on this.'

'You're wasting your time, if you ask me. There's nothing to it.'

'What about the girl? The photofit? What's she about?' He frowned:

'I don't know. I'm not working on the case, you understand, or I wouldn't talk to you about it. But it's a small department, I've a good idea what's going on.' And an idea that a Fleet Street paper was worth a good sight more than a couple of drinks and a sandwich. 'Waterbottom has — had — a friend who's quite high up in the court system — they played chess together — he saw him with this woman — and he saw her at the office the next day, after which he saw Waterbottom later looking worried. He doesn't like the idea of burying Waterbottom with a bleeding backside. I think,' he hesitated and looked at his glass and sighed.

I did what was expected of me, hoping he wasn't using the excuse for time to change his story. When I came back, he wasn't in his seat and for a moment I thought he'd done a runner until I saw him emerging from the lavatory. I suppressed an audible sigh of relief. After he replenished his now empty bladder, he continued:

'This other guy — I'm not going to say who it is — you needn't try twisting my arm. He's also single; people knew they were friends; I think he feels that if Waterbottom's put down as a fairy, he will be too. And he's got enough clout — well, anyway, he could make things administratively quite difficult for us, you can imagine. That's where it came from.'

'D'you think you'll find her?'

'No way. He said a woman; it'll be a man. He said she was five feet nine or ten; we're looking for a midget. He said she had light brown hair; we're looking for a redhead, a blonde or jet-black. He said she was big-build, we're looking for an anorexic. You're a lawyer; you know how it works. They won't even show the photofit again: it was put out last night to show willing, but that's it and that's all.'

I pressed my luck.

'I presume you don't think he's actually lying?'

'I don't know. I doubt it. It'd be a bit rich; officer of the court wasting police time — like,' he added, as if he hadn't thought of it before, 'like you might be said to have.'

'Drink up, Ambleton. That's never a waste of anyone's time.'

He laughed pleasantly.

'No more it is. But I'll buy this round.'

It was by the book: not generosity or any genuine sense of wanting to show willing. I'd encountered it before. If the mark buys at least one round during a long session, it ceases to be corrupt: 'We each bought rounds; I don't remember who bought how many; I know I bought my share; ask the barman.' You find me a barman can tell exactly who bought how many rounds, I'll show you an undercover cop on the job. I took it Ambleton would know if the barman was an undercover cop.

'So?'

'No, I do think there was a woman; my guess is, he swung each way; he got turned on by her; when she didn't come across, he went out to get the other and bumped into a weirdo instead.'

I grimaced, which fortunately he mistook for a wry look of approval. Suddenly, he swallowed in what looked like one gulp the remainder of his pint.

'I've got to be getting back.'

I was puzzled; he'd bought one to my three — I owed him at least another half dozen.

He was pissed enough to confide.

'See that man over there, the one talking to the manager?'

I nodded. I saw who he meant.

'He's a council member on the Watch.' The Watch was the old name for a local police committee; the committee made up of local council members and local magistrate nominees who oversaw the police of every area except London, where the equivalent polite pleasantries were omitted by the Home Secretary. 'I don't want to be seen.'

He was more scared of being seen over a long, boozy lunch by a council member of his committee than by a magistrate: they saw enough of the seamy side to understand police tensions; politicians only understand their own. He'd saved Carson a trip to the library. 'You staying down?' He still had an eye out for the Fleet Street cheque-book. 'You know the Swan? It's opposite the puppet-theatre on the front. I go there for a jar after work; 'bout seven, seven-thirty. See you later?'

'Right,' I said absent-mindedly, but with no intention of showing.

I wasn't absent-minded because I had recognised Nick Walker. I'd recognised him as soon as Ambleton pointed him out. I was absent-minded because Walker was looking straight back at me — he had recognised me too. I couldn't say who was more concerned about the coincidence: him or me.

CHAPTER SEVEN

It was moving too fast to observe an ideal caution, or any caution at all.

I knew Margot McAllister from way back when, both as a result of her living with Orbach and otherwise. We'd been at the same occasional parties and the odd campaign meeting. She had been for many years the country's foremost welfare lobbyist, before she went into Parliament, where now she was one of the few responsible and respected members of Her Majesty's otherwise discredited and comprehensively non-credible loyal opposition. As Keenan had told me, she had recently married, another Member of Parliament — they were the only husband and wife team amongst the opposition spokespersons. I was surprised she had married at all: we were all getting old and our dearly-held principles had grown soggy with age.

It was not too difficult to arrange to see her, once I succeeded in getting through on the 'phone. She was a hard-working, quietly intense, excessively serious and — surprisingly for a politician or indeed for a lobbyist — an essentially shy person, who tended to presume that others did not want to waste their time anymore than she did hers. I said only it was a private matter, I'd be grateful if she could find a space in her diary. She invited me to come to the Commons, where she, as others, frequently had to hang around for long periods, waiting for this or that Division on a matter of underwhelming significance that interested her not at all.

I had to wait in the lobby for her to come down and countersign my day pass. I hadn't often been to the Houses of Parliament. I was surprised how small it was inside. I expected grandiose halls, sweeping corridors, magnificent arches. Instead, the central lobby couldn't contain an average company's annual dinner-dance, the corridors were long but narrow and several of the arches looked like they were held together with Polymix.

There were a lot of policemen, but they were older than those I was used to seeing on the streets, and less fit. The more serious offences were dealt with by Black Rod or a robed Speaker and punishment comprised 'naming' a member; their hardest task was pouring drunken legislators into taxis. If a trainee guerilla with a water pistol got past the initial security, I'd put my money on him, not them.

When I'd last seen Margot, her nearly-red hair had hung down to her waist; nor did she wear glasses, makeup or jewellery. Now, her hair was styled and barely reached her shoulders; it had been high-lighted. She wore blue-rimmed glasses behind which I saw traces of mascara, and heavy round earrings. Otherwise, she was unchanged. She was still slight and underweight, she had the sweetest smile of anyone I ever knew on those occasions she deigned to display it, but if she and Nigel Morris ever tried to kiss it would take a structural engineer to disentangle their noses.

'We can use my office; it's free at the moment.' This is something M.P.s have in common with another branch of the law, barristers. Except for leading members, or those who have been in Parliament so long they have acquired some elusive and ill-defined rights of passage, they are crammed into tiny offices, which they have to share normally with another member from the same party, though it is not unprecedented for junior back-benchers temporarily to have to put up with someone from another.

'I heard you married. Congratulations,' I offered.

'Thank you,' she accepted my good wishes gracefully. She had a low voice, one that when I'd called her I could've mistaken for that of a man. Her full initials were M and R — though I didn't know what the R stood for — and some of the correspondence which littered her desk was addressed to Mr McAllister. There was no trace of a Scots accent; as I recollected, the name was an ancient accident of history and she had no connections north of the border. She did, however, have a slight lisp, a hiss on the 's'. 'What was it you wanted to see me about, Dave?'

'Uh, it's delicate. It goes back to when you were living with Russel Orbach.'

She froze. The last vestige of her smile sunk without trace.

'What about him?'

She automatically assumed it was about him; all I'd said was that it related back to that time.

'Look, I'd better put my cards on the table right away.' It was going to be difficult to deceive her; she was by far the brightest of the people I'd had to deal with — Orbach himself excepted. 'Do you remember Mick and Eartha Mellor?'

'Of course. They died. I went to the funeral with Russel.'

'And Frankie?'

'And Frankie.'

'You know of course how they died?'

She nodded, waiting for the promised explanation.

'It's been, uh, suggested, suggested to a client of mine . . . well, that it might not have been an accident.'

She absorbed this information slowly, tasting for all its possible ingredients. I watched her hackles rise. Momentarily, she kept them at bay and, perhaps only playing for time, asked:

'Why have you come to see me, Dave? I'd left Russel well before then. I was no longer involved.'

'I never heard it . . . that you were the one to leave him '

'It's not important; it was no particular way round; we'd been "just good friends" for a long time beforehand; it was simply a matter of maintaining separate homes instead. You still haven't told me why you wanted to see me,' she added politely but firmly.

'Look, I want to tell you as fully as I can. I want to explain something first, though. You're right, of course, this does concern Russel. But if he knows I'm looking into it, well, you know him, you know how he'll react.'

'I shouldn't blame him,' she said frostily. 'He's a High Court judge now; any suggestion of scandal would be taken very seriously; besides which, if you're implying that he had anything to do with this . . . this alleged,' she emphasised, 'I repeat, alleged non-accident, he would be entitled to be very angry indeed. It's slander.' She might not have been a lawyer but she knew the distinction between slander and libel. 'It's very serious slander. It is also quite laughable. I don't understand for a moment why you think you could come to me, tell me such a thing, and expect me to remain silent about it — at least, that is, not to tell Russel.'

She half rose in dismissal. I shook my head with enough vigour to propel her back into her seat.

'I haven't said it's true. I said someone hired me to investigate it.' I paused to see if she questioned it as an unusual task for a lawyer. When she didn't, I knew she had remained close enough to Orbach to have followed some of my own activities since last she and I had met. 'Better me than someone who doesn't know him, who doesn't care if the investigation alone is sufficient to hurt him If Russel finds out, he'll kick up such a fuss he'll bring it into the open even if he's got nothing to hide. As you said, he's a judge now; mud'll stick; a lot of mud.'

A shadow passed across her face so fast I almost missed it; she could believe at least that much of what I'd said.

'I still don't know why you think I can help.'

'I'd say, you probably know him better than anyone else in the world: don't you agree?'

'Possibly. Until Horace . . . my husband . . . until he and I got married I stayed very close to Russel . . . Right up until then we met often, probably once a fortnight; even if it was an odd friendship for a High Court judge.' She meant because of her politics. 'After that . . .' She didn't complete her sentence.

I read into her remarks not that she would have objected if she'd remained close to Orbach, nor could I imagine her bowing to any jealous pressure on Horace's part, but that Russel hadn't wanted to continue seeing her. She confirmed my guess.

'We were sometime lovers, long-time friends. Nothing needed to be read into our continuing as friends so long as we were both unmarried. He was concerned that if he continued to see me, there might be an inference that might be, well, inappropriate for a judge.'

She looked up at a screen hanging from the ceiling which displayed the title of the current debate: the Doggie-doo-dah Bill, Second Sweep Up?

'I'm going to have to leave you shortly. I think, after all, perhaps I can help. You see, Mick — I knew Mick better, for longer; Eartha was his second marriage; Russel and I were already drifting apart by then — Mick was Russel's best friend. Excluding myself, no one understood or tolerated Russel so well. You know Russel; he is difficult; he was always difficult; Mick was perhaps the one person who never found him too much to handle. That's the absurdity in the allegation; it would have been for Russel like cutting off his writing hand. Self-destructive even by his standards.'

I often forgot that, as well as an extensive practice, Orbach had written a number of the leading legal texts on his subjects. For all I knew, many of them were still in use, although as a judge it was a convention that he did not write new books or editions, so as not to give a particular legal argument undue weight when it derived from mere research rather than the heat of adversarial advocacy. I knew Orbach so well, and on such idiosyncratic terms, that it was easy to forget that he was one of the small handful of true stars of the profession — both when he had been a barrister, and now as a judge. As a lawyer, a near-myth in his own life.

She shook her head again, as if to clear it.

'I must be going crazy. I don't know why I'm even discussing this with you, Dave. I hear what you say, I won't tell Russel; but you should lay the idea swiftly to rest if you don't want to do him, or yourself, serious harm. He was fond of you, Dave, in his own way; he'd be very hurt to think . . .'

I held up a hand.

'You said it'd be self-destructive. Of course that's right, at a lot of levels. Do you say he'd be incapable of it?'

'Of course; that goes without saying.'

She met my gaze and held it for what seemed like several minutes before she flinched.

She was a politician. A Member of Parliament. She had integrity, but she also had her career. Any serious scandal involving Orbach would do her harm too. She nodded permission for me to continue.

'You were around at the time of his break with Disraeli Chambers.'

'Yes. That wasn't why . . .'

'I know. You read about their deaths later.' I remembered that when she was a lobbyist, she used to read all of the newspapers, every day. I imagined she would keep equally abreast as an M.P. 'If I told you,' I selected my words with care, 'if I told you he had more responsibility for what happened to them than any other person, what would you say?'

'I wouldn't believe you,' she snapped. 'This has gone far enough, Dave. I remain very fond of Russel; he was a major part of my life for a long time. If you say another word, I will tell him everything you've said; I'll give evidence that you said it,' she repeated that I could be sued for damages.

'There wouldn't be a case; he'd never sue.' I sounded more confident than I felt. He was proud enough to think he might get away with it. 'I'm not a complete fool, Margot. I'm not without some evidence — about either.'

'Use it, then,' she snapped. 'Don't go around smearing him like this. He's a good man — look at how he's taken care of the child; he looks after her better than if she was his own.'

As when I had canvassed the case with Keenan, I didn't say anything. She went white; she had just seen the one, the solitary, motive Orbach might have to — as she had put it — cut off his writing hand. She got up to show me out, gesturing toward the screen that showed the countdown to a Division. I followed her back to the lobby. As we entered it, I took her arm.

'You'd gone; Mick and Eartha were planning to emigrate; what would he have had left?'

'God save you if you're wrong, Dave.'

'And if I'm right?'

'God save him, then.'

A burly, bull-headed man came up from behind and took her arm.

'Margot . . .'

'Hi,' they pecked at each other's lips. 'Horace, this is Dave. Dave Woolf. He's a solicitor. He's an old . . . friend of Russel's.'

He shook my hand cursorily.

'We'll be late.'

As they disappeared into the chamber, she gave me one, last, backward glance. I couldn't swear to it, but I was sure there were tears behind the blue-rimmed glasses.

'I want to get a better feel of them,' I justified my wish to see her again.

'You've read my book.' Jada didn't reciprocate.

'It's more about you,' I reminded her. 'There's very little about Mick. You never say anything about why they wanted to emigrate, for example.'

'Him. Not them. It was more his idea.'

'Well, there's something.' Not much, but something.

'We're recording this week. We work late. Call me at home around midnight; I'll see how I feel.' She hung up.

I used the excuse to go to the club.

It was around eleven o'clock when Dowell walked in. He didn't waste words.

'What've you got to do with the Southend killing? And where's the Kangaroo Kid?'

'Hi. Nice to see you too. Really nice. Sit down. Have a drink. Have two.'

He sat; I ordered; he waited.

'Why d'you want Carson? How did you know she's back?'

'I didn't till you just confirmed it. What I want her for is to take her down to Southend to stand still in a line-up.' He extracted a folded copy of the photofit they'd shown on the television but that I still hadn't actually seen. Carson was right, it was a good likeness.

'Carson wasn't in Southend at the weekend. She can prove it.'

He shrugged.

'Maybe. That's not my problem, or yours — yet. It's hers.'

Natalie came over:

'Hi, Tim.' Natalie was one of only two women I'd ever known to tempt his fidelity. He groaned inwardly so only his haemorrhoids could hear. 'Thought you two boys weren't playing together anymore?'

'Ha ha. Go get Carson, will you, there's a good . . .' he caught himself in time, 'uh, soul.'

'Right,' she instantly forgot that Tim was fuzz. 'That was dumb,' she said as she remembered. 'Was it terribly dumb, Dave?'

'Terribly, horribly and awfully — almost as dumb as I was.'

'Shall I get her?' she sighed. 'D'you want another drink?'

'Bring the bottle,' I asserted my rights of proprietorship. The first time I ever said 'bring the bottle', Lewis was still alive, and I was riding as high as a kite because I — wrongly — thought I'd begun to put two and two together on Disraeli Chambers. Only in new maths does it make five.

'We both drink too much,' Tim reflected while we waited.

'I knew a barrister, one of the best, terrific practice, wrote law books, novels on the side, earned a small fortune, beautiful home, everything going for him, drank a half-bottle spirits every night without fail, often with wine or beer beforehand — or both.'

'What happened to him?'

'Oh, he killed himself.'

'Cheers,' we held up our glasses. 'See you on the other side,' I added.

'Me too,' our fugitive from Southend joined us. 'Am I in bad trouble?'

'Depends,' I said. 'Don't open your mouth; you'll survive.'

She took off and gave me back my sunglasses:

'But tell Sandy I like the scarf.'

Natalie decided she too needed to put her feet up and sat down uninvited. She said;

'The thing I like about you guys, you've got such a great sense of priorities.'

She clicked her fingers at Tom, behind the bar; she didn't touch hard liquor. Her normal brew was a spritzer. Tom brought it over with a special swish for Dowell but didn't try turning it into a larger party.

'Well, is it you?' Tim demanded.

Lips tightly sealed, Carson nodded firmly.

'And are you alibi'd, like Perry Mason here says?'

'Up to here,' she broke her short-held vows of obedience and silence. 'I went up to Oxfordshire, near Henley, stayed with a solicitor I used to work for and his wife and two kids. He's a mean sod: we went out to dinner on Saturday night and I had to pay half; main courses for six — he ate two; the credit card record'll prove it; he wouldn't take my cheque.'

'Name?'

She gave him the name of the solicitor, and of his firm in Notting Hill Gate. He said:

'I know them.' They did as much crime in their area as we did in ours. 'They're good, but he might be honest anyway. Now it's time for another mean sod of a solicitor to give me some answers.'

I glanced over my shoulder to see who he might be, talking to.

'How d'you get it, Tim?'

'One day you're asking me about a plane crash out of Southend; the next day, people start dropping dead in Southend and there's a picture of Tonto on the tube. I'm supposed to be a detective, too, you know.'

'I never said anything about Southend,' I reminded him. He had, after all, followed up my initial enquiry. 'To get there, you must've done some work on Orbach; which means his name's on a file somewhere; which means . . .'

'Crawl before you walk. Of course his name's on a file; he was part-owner of the plane; how many of his planes you think crash every day? The man's a judge — not a major airline. Now,' he reminded me I had yet to give him a clue what any of it had to do with Waterbottom.

I shook my head and started to say:

'Sorry, Tim; privileged . . .'

As I opened my mouth, he was already adding:

'And don't give me any of the privilege bullshit . . .'

'It is, Tim; really.' In the past, I'd claimed privilege as a private investigator which, under English law, is altogether without legal foundation. Orbach had insisted on hiring me as a lawyer for precisely that reason, so that he could own outright everything I found.

'Crap. Material's only privileged if it's in contemplation of litigation,' he was citing someone else's legal opinion, or a text-book, or maybe something he remembered from when he did his law degree.

'Who's to say when litigation is contemplated? Didn't you say, just the other day, I could be working a civil suit for damages? We could even be talking private criminal prosecution.'

He shut his eyes to think about it. Natalie was distracting him He recited:

'Mellor's only relative was the kid who now lives with Orbach; hers — well, she had family — but in terms of damages, that'd have to be the noise.' Jada Jarrynge did not have a fan in this copper; still, he lived in Ealing where few people of any taste spend more time than it takes to drive through without stopping. 'I need to know, Dave, or I'm going to take Carson in and send her to Southend. Would you wish that on anyone?'

I exchanged a look with my assistant. She didn't give me a hint.

'And I need you not to know, Tim. She told you, she's alibi'd. Unless you can show any connection between what happened to Waterbottom and her meeting with him, you can't hold her, you can't charge her, you've got nothing except a coincidence to be eliminated from your enquiries. Which I happen to know is what they think it is anyway.'

'Yeah, from a loudmouth called Ambleton who thinks — thought — you were writing something for a newspaper. I disabused him; told him you had difficulty writing a shopping list. After I explained to him that if he didn't want to talk to me he could talk to his Superintendent, he told me two things I found interesting.' He didn't bother to list them: that I had i.d. from the paper, and that I was looking for a man called Battle.

'You've got a lot, then.' I pulled the half-empty bottle away from him, not to pour myself another drink but to tell him he'd had everything he was going to get out of me — liquid or solid — for the time being. Carson poured herself one; she was getting as good as me.

She caught the look on my face.

'If I'm going back to Southend, I'm going to need to be pissed.'

'Take the bottle. Hell, it's the least I can do.'

Tim gave it one last try.

'Do you know what you're doing, Dave?'

'Nope,' I admitted with false cheerfulness. 'But as long as I don't, you won't either.'

We waited for Dowell to call our bluff. I don't think any of us expected him to do it. He rose and gestured at Carson.

'Come on, then. I'd like you to assist me in my enquiries, if you're willing to do so, of course.'

And if she wasn't, she'd be busted for interfering with the police in the course of their enquiries into a murder.

'Mick was a gentle man. A gentle gentleman.' She stirred her herbal tea with a solid silver teaspoon that had a handle in the shape of a microphone. 'Gross, isn't it,' she sighed. 'My agent saw it in a second-hand shop and bought it for me.'

I too was drinking tea. This will come as a surprise. The explanation is simple — Jada Jarrynge didn't drink, so neither did anyone else; she kept the first dry house I'd knowingly been inside since I got out of short pants. Nor had she yet extended an invitation to smoke.

She lived in the architect-designed, high, top half of a converted, flat-roofed warehouse on the Isle of Dogs, with a vast expanse of clear glass overlooking the Thames far below. The rooms were on slightly different levels, ascending or descending into the main living area. Along the front of the apartment was a balcony, wide enough to sit out at a table, or sprawl to sunbathe in the unlikely event of a genuinely hot summer.

'My mother had a rough time when she was young. My father wasn't a bad man — he's a good man — and I don't think he was bad with her. But she used him up getting herself straight.' She sipped her tea carefully, cautious not to burn the inside of her mouth, or her solid silver tongue.

'It's funny. She was black; she was born in Dominica; she grew up here mostly; I'm not saying things are easy now, or that there isn't racism, but they're easier than they were; there's many, many more first generation blacks than in her time. When I was at school, it wasn't anything special, different anymore. We were maybe a majority, I don't know. So she should've felt she belonged less than him But Mick was the restless one; he did his job well; anyway, that's what I knew — he made a lot of money, he got a lot of big contracts, even though his reputation was originally based on small housing cases. So he must have been good?'

'He was good; he was good at the housing cases, and I don't think he knew how to do anything badly.' She wanted the affirmation.

'Yes, I thought he was good. But he didn't belong. He didn't feel he belonged. He didn't belong to the surveying establishment.' She laughed. 'Is there such a thing? I suppose so: there's an establishment for everything.'

'RICS — Royal Institution of Chartered Surveyors. Sure. That's the establishment.'

'Well, whatever it was, he didn't belong within it I don't mean he wasn't a member. I don't know if he was; but still he didn't "belong". He didn't have a university degree. I think he minded that. I think he felt left out of other sorts of institutions; he worked around lawyers, social agencies, everyone else had been to university. He came from a working-class background: my family, my mother's family, they were — are — working class, black working class of course; he got along well with them, but of course he didn't fit in with them either. I mean, you can't, can you? Not when you do an interesting job, a profession, highly-paid; they're driving cabs, working in the post office, a stall in a market. Do you understand what I'm trying to say?'

'I think so. I never felt — well, part of this country, I suppose. But it's easier in a way. I'm a Jew; I know a lot of black people don't think that's the same; hell, we've been here a lot longer; we're integrated, supposedly; we're white; one time recently, we had five members of the Cabinet — think of that; and at least half the High Court bench is Jewish. Like Orbach. But if you've got something onto which to pin the feeling of not belonging, I think that must be easier than just feeling it on its own, or for a lot of different, unconnected reasons.'

'Yes. That's what I'm saying. That was Mick. He was a hand-some man — do you remember? Shall I show you a photograph?'

I remembered, but I told her to show me anyway.

She went to fetch an album. The album was her mother's, because it went back before Mick, and to a time when Jada couldn't have lifted let alone operated a camera. The later pictures included shots of Frankie. There were several in which Orbach featured. I said:

'I'm surprised you keep them.'

She settled back in the peacock chair from which she had been conducting our interview. She was dressed, as the first time I'd met her, casually, with the confidence of a woman who knows she looks good in anything. When I arrived, she had been in the shower; she told me she was going inside to get into something more suitable; she meant it; I didn't even have time to fantasise what she might be wearing before she emerged in jeans so baggy I could have fit into them myself, and a sweater used in winter to keep a family of Catholics warm.

'They're just pictures.'

I pointed to one of her mother.

'Just a picture?'

She looked wistful; for a moment, the child she still — to me — was.

'She was so beautiful, so incredibly beautiful.'

I smiled.

'You ain't no wallflower yourself.'

'I know. But I had all the advantages; she gave them me.' Shelter, food, comfort, care and, above all, protection from the ravages of the social environment.

'Why do you think Mick and Russel were such good friends? People've said to me, because they were both perfectionists, but…'

'He puts a hold on people. It's seductive to be around someone who seems to know everything, have all the answers, who's right more often than not, and right more often than others. He's extremely perceptive, and when he wants to, he can use that in a constructive way. I remember conversations with him when I was young — before my mother died, Mick and my mother. I've seen him with Frankie. she is bright, she can do anything she wants — and a lot of that comes from Russel. In our house, he was almost an idol.' She smiled at a memory:

'When Frankie was two or three, just beginning to talk, she used to talk about "Wussel" all the time. The childminder — I don't remember her name — she asked, "Who's Russel?" Frankie couldn't say the word "god-father", so she said "God".'

I, too, had a memory, though not one I shared with her: the way people at Disraeli Chambers used to talk about him — with awe, the sort of fear-based respect that would be more appropriately associated with a mafia godfather; only, they thought he was the devil.

'Do you think,' I began another thought hesitantly, 'do you think Orbach, well, wanted your mother, was in love with her maybe?' Her mother had raised but dismissed the notion in her letter to Mick in Bolivia.

She shrugged; she didn't know.

'Tell me more about Bolivia.' I wasn't sorry to change the subject.

'There's not a lot to tell. It was his dream. She knew, my mother knew he needed it more than she needed to stay here; in a lot of ways, she was much stronger than he was.'

'Have you ever been there?'

'No,' she said gently. 'I wouldn't, would I.' It wasn't a question; she didn't pause to give me time to reply. 'But they talked about it. It's big, and they could have bought land — land like we can't imagine it here — for the money they had. A whole valley, where all you can see is your own; imagine.' She was a sensitive and intelligent, highly artistic woman; she didn't find it inconsistent with a developed sense of material values. 'Do you see the dream?'

I saw the dream and I saw something else. They were chasing their dream. It was only a dream, as transient as any other dream and as expendable as a night's sleep. Once they went they ceased to be who they were before; they could as well simply cease to be. The implications for Orbach, though, were entirely real — a man without his own dreams, he could not respect theirs. Put the other way round, he too was an outsider — why should they be able to escape if he couldn't?

The same sergeant as before was on the desk. He recognised me and scowled: Dowell of London's attention to the case had not gone unnoticed; the hicks had allowed themselves to be suckered; I needn't expect them to thank me. He didn't.

'What do you want?' He paused, a witticism rising slowly. 'I already told you we don't deal in forgive and forget.'

'This may well be true; but I am a solicitor — as I already told you; and I do have a client in custody, who I'd like to get out.' I gave him Carson's name, as if he didn't already know who I meant.

'I don't know if she's in our custody, sir.' He drew the 'sir' out so far I could've gone for a walk in it. 'I'm afraid you'll have to wait while I find out.' He smiled thickly and pointed to a hard wooden bench.

Once I'd sat down, he waited until he was sure I was watching him before he picked up from the desk the papers he'd been looking at when I arrived and started to study them assiduously, making the odd correction here, sighing, calling out to a constable to fetch him a cup of tea, picking up the 'phone to tell his wife what time he'd be home for dinner, going to the lavatory for longer than could conceivably be necessary, until I got the message the one thing he wasn't going to do was acknowledge they had Carson in custody.

I'd expected something like it. It was par for the course. As soon as they admitted they had her, they had to let me in to see her, and either charge her or let her go. I doubted they gave a damn about her; it was me they wanted to annoy. I was reassured: once they had finished playing games, I wouldn't have any real difficulty; there wouldn't be any point to the delay otherwise. It was eleven when I arrived, one o'clock before the desk sergeant said:

'Yes, we do have her, sir. I'm told she can go now.'

'Gosh, what a surprise.'

I got up and crossed over to the desk.

He said so softly I could barely hear him: 'You've got some of us into trouble; we'll get you too. Bank on it you bastard.'

'But officer — I'm not a bastard; I saw my parents get married,' I protested. He didn't smile. They didn't study the law of legitimacy at police college.

'Dave?' Carson stood behind me. 'You took long enough.'

'I've been here long enough, too. Come on, let's go.'

She filled me in.

'They brought me down here last night; I rang Alan at home.' He was the solicitor friend with the ambitious appetite. 'He came down first thing. He said 'cos he was a witness, he couldn't represent me, but that was it. They asked a few more questions after, but they had nothing to hold me on. Alan gave me this anyway,' she handed me a bill. 'For his time.'

It had to be a first — a solicitor charging for an alibi that was true.

CHAPTER EIGHT

I was at the office when I took the call:
'Mr Woolf?' asked a disembodied female voice, a secretary.
'Yes.'

'Just a moment, please. I'll put you through to Mr Schofield.'

I have tried to explain to the receptionist at the office that when a secretary rings for me, she ought to get the caller himself on the line before she connects me. Why should I be left holding on, while only his secretary's time is wasted? It's a game: who's more important than whom? But she seems to think that everyone's more important than me so persists in putting the call through without waiting. Or maybe she just thinks that she is more important than me? Maybe she's right.

'Mr Woolf?' This time the voice was male. 'Patrick Schofield. I'm an Assistant Secretary.'

'When do I get to speak to the real thing?'

'Excuse me?'

'Oh, never mind. What's this about? What can I do for you?'

'We, uh, have a common acquaintance: Detective Inspector Dowell.' He got that right — common as muck. 'He, uh, thought it might be a good idea if we, that is you and I, were to have a little chat.' I waited. After a moment, he said: 'Mr Woolf?'

'Uh? I'm still here. Chat on.'

'Well, I was rather hoping, if we could perhaps meet . . .'

'Are you looking for legal advice, Mr Schofield?' A client-referral from Tim Dowell would be a first; it must be his worst enemy.

'Oh, good Lord no. I am a lawyer myself. I work, well, with the Lord Chancellor's Department.'

'Well, that's alright, isn't it.'

'I was, uh, rather hoping, well, that you wouldn't mind popping in for a little chat. Uh, here.' When I still didn't say anything, he continued, somewhat more firmly: 'I'm quite sure it would be in your interest, Mr Woolf. Quite sure.'

'Yeah, well, if Tim Dowell suggested you ring, it could hardly be otherwise,' I replied.

The sarcasm was entirely lost on him He said:

'Oh, good, I'm pleased you see it that way. Would it be possible . . . say this afternoon? Say five thirty?'

'Put me down at Chancellor's Gate,' I told the taxi driver.

Chancellor's Gate is an archway into the House of Lords, where the Lord Chancellor's Department works. The end of the archway is barred to pedestrians save for access to an incongruous, prefabricated security building. I had to wait on line to pass through the metal detector, then again to talk to one of the two uniformed police officers behind the desk. Unlike those I had seen posted within the House of Commons, these were burly and intimidating. He seemed surprised to find my name on his list. I had to produce identification: he seemed surprised I had any. Then I was issued with a day-pass and told to wait in a tiny cubbyhole for someone to collect me.

'Mr Woolf? Would you like to come with me?' If I was a piece of paper, she'd have held me by a corner, at a distance from her body. She was middle-aged, blue-rinsed, bespectacled and nothing like what I expected of an Assistant Secretary. This was not a surprise. She was the real secretary, to whom I had spoken earlier. She dumped me in a waiting-room with copies of *Punch, London Life,* the *Lawyer* and the *Law Society's Gazette* just like at the dentist's.

After another delay we went on a wander through wonderland. I wasn't sure whether we were still in the House of Lords or the Commons. One of the corridors looked familiar from my recent visit to Margot McAllister.

'Come along in, Mr Woolf,' a thin man with a hawk-like face offered me a seat. 'We're pleased to meet you.'

I raised my eyebrows. He was the only one I could see.

'Is that the royal "we" or is there a midget in one of your drawers?'

He chuckled appreciatively, with the wholehearted comfort of a man in perfect control.

'Yes, I've been told you're something of a wag. Jolly good. No, I'm afraid it's just me.'

'I thought — I read somewhere — there's always at least two of you?'

'Oh, well, usually, but I'm sure you're not going to offer me a bribe. Are you? I'm dying for a couple of seats to *Aïda* — you wouldn't have any ideas, would you?'

'Chuckle, chuckle.'

He frowned. Sarcasm was a low form of wit. Too low for a senior civil servant.

There was only one of him because he didn't want a witness.

'Cigarette?' He pushed an onyx box across the desk towards me. 'They're our own brand, you know.' Houses of Parliament cigarettes, to help our legislators die of something other than boredom. I wondered if the original package carried a government health warning but refused his offer and lit up a Camel. 'Sherry?'

I shook my head.

'Scotch? We've all become rather fond of Scotch recently.'

Since they appointed the first ever Scottish Lord Chancellor, even though he did not himself drink any alcohol. His relations with the Bar since his appointment had been abysmal: they shared neither a legal tradition nor a social.

'Southern Comfort?'

'Who? Sherry or Scotch. Or tea?'

'Yes, alright, tea.' He buzzed and within minutes another secretary brought in a pot. I waited until he'd finished playing mother before asking: 'You wanted to see me. Why?'

'I thought it was time I met you. I'm, uh, rather familiar with some of your, uh, work, Mr Woolf.' He made it sound like he found it difficult to dignify my activities as 'work'.

'As in — Tim Dowell — Martyn Pulleyne?'

Pulleyne was the focal point of my last case, the one I had worked for Orbach. I knew that at some point Tim Dowell had gone to the professional authorities, or else they had come to him. I also knew from a couple of casual remarks — if anything Dowell says can ever be treated as casual — that his contact had not been technically a member of the Lord Chancellor's Department itself, but some sort of liaison group. It tallied with Schofield's description of himself on, the telephone as working 'with' the Lord Chancellor's Department.

'Something like that, Mr Woolf,' he confirmed. 'I thought it would be interesting to, uh, explore with you, uh, anything you might have to say in the same sort of area.'

I smiled. He had style.

'You mean Dowell thought I might tell you something I wouldn't tell him?'

He smiled too.

'I think we understand each other, Mr Woolf. And are you going to do so?'

I had never witnessed such a quick-step from polite dissembling to the point.

'No chance.'

'Then I wonder if you'd be willing to listen to me, instead?'

'Listening's what I do.'

'Really, Mr Woolf? I thought you were quite an active sort. I mean, you were quite active at Disraeli Chambers. And then again at Mathers.' I presumed he wasn't telling me how much he knew just for the hell of it. I wasn't surprised at what he knew; I would have been more surprised if he didn't.

'Why don't we talk about Pulleyne?'

'Pulleyne?' He repeated, as if he had difficulty remembering. 'Sad loss to the bench, eh?'

I shook my head in awe.

'You said that with a straight face. I wonder how it worked. Did you make him a deal or what?'

'Golly gosh, no. Nothing like that. More a question of helping him do the right thing, wouldn't'cha say?'

'For what?' I asked, suddenly serious. 'What was his offence?' I wanted to hear how he put it.

'Well, you know, being a bit too close, to, well, a couple of chaps, sort of, wrong type of friends. D'you know what I mean?'

I shook my head.

'Wrong. Pulleyne told me so. That was no crime. The crime was being found out.'

Schofield shrugged.

'Perhaps he meant the same thing as I did.'

His smug self-satisfaction began to irritate me.

'What about everyone else who got hurt?' There were many — Lewis, Malcolm, a couple of lawyers. 'What about his family?'

'I'm sorry, I'm not concerned with that. His family, well, if they were upset by what happened, of course it's always unfortunate for the family. But I'm a civil servant, Mr Woolf, and you have to understand that what concerned me was the welfare of the nation. Oh dear, that sounds more pompous than I meant it to. But it is my job, all our jobs as civil servants; be we ever so humble or ever so grand.'

I felt like screaming. I could see how for centuries they had managed to rule the world. Complacent calm confidence. There's no more powerful weapon.

'Pulleyne read me a bit out of a judgment. It was all about how one bent judge in a thousand is worth covering up for, for the sake of the other nine hundred and ninety-nine. What I want to ask you is — what about when we're talking two in a thousand, then ten, then a hundred like in the United States? At what point does it cease to be worth covering *up* or, rather, at what point does it become more important to sacrifice the judge for the sake of the office? Can you tell me that?'

'More tea, Mr Woolf?'

Despite myself, as if hypnotised, I saw my hand move cup and saucer across the desk. In penance, I piled into it several teaspoons of sugar from the silver bowl, sufficient to cause him to wince.

'I can't answer all these questions, Mr Woolf, they're for finer minds than mine ' I wondered if that was how he spoke to his wife when she asked how he would like the chicken cooked for dinner. 'That's a question for a finer mind than mine, dear.' 'I'd be interested to know why this, uh, old history should concern you at the present time, though.'

I sipped my tea. He was right: it was disgusting. I pushed it away from me while I pulled my thoughts into order.

'I'm curious to know just how far you'd go to prevent a similar scandal — or one that was worse?'

'There could be no worse,' he said flatly. 'It couldn't happen; it wouldn't happen.' He watched my face to see if I flinched. When I didn't he sighed. You don't get to be an Assistant Secretary by being extremely thick. He explained. 'As there was no Pulleyne scandal, as you call it, so also would and could there be no similar scandal, let alone one that was worse.' Five times nothing is nothing.

'In any circumstances?'

I waited.

He waited.

I said: 'Well? What's your answer?'

'I thought I'd already given it, Mr Woolf.'

'Is this what you wanted to tell me? Why you called me in here?'

'I wanted to be quite sure that you understood, Mr Woolf. I can be sure, can't I, Mr Woolf?'

I smiled and got up to leave.

He showed no sign of concern.

'Good day, Mr Woolf. More tea before you leave, Mr Woolf? A Houses of Parliament cigarette, Mr Woolf?'

I pulled the door shut behind me quietly as he picked up a telephone. I had a good idea who he was calling.

No sooner was I in the door than Sandy said: 'You had a 'phone call.'

'Another! I'm getting popular.' I presumed it would be Tim, reacting to the call from Schofield, ranting and raving because of my failure either to give up my information or to give up the case.

'I'm not sure that's how you'll feel. Russel rang. He wants you to call him.'

Which I did.

'Ah, Dave, good. Wondered how you'd like to come for a little trip tonight. Little flying trip.'

'Flying? Tonight?' The case was over. He'd finally flipped.

'That's right. Night-flying. Wonderful experience. Do it quite often when there's something on my mind; it's the best place I know to get my thoughts sorted out.'

'I hate flying, Russel,' I said firmly.

'No, no, you'll have a marvellous time.' When I didn't respond, he said, in a different tone of voice: 'Interesting, anyway. You'll find it interesting. I promise.'

I didn't have a lot of choice. There was no way it was co-incidental. There was no way I could turn down the opportunity and continue with the case. Sure I was scared, but only at the prospect of flying; it never occurred to me to be physically frightened of Orbach. Weakly, I agreed. He wanted me to meet him at Southend, at the airport. He gave me precise, detailed instructions how to get to the private club area, where to park, even what to wear:

'It's cold up there; wear something warm.'

I called Carson, she was out; Natalie offered to come with me; Sandy offered to come with me; Alton offered to come with me. I went — as invited — alone.

Though only a small airport, Southend Rochford was staffed twenty-four hours a day; even when there weren't any scheduled flights, private planes might want — or need — to land. Orbach had directed me not to the main building but to a side-gate to the airfield itself that would be open, near to which I could park. Over to my right I would be able to see a line of small aircraft. That was where Russel's plane was supposed to be waiting.

I pulled off the A127 onto a slip road, then as instructed onto a narrow lane, an external service road parallel to an unlit, internal strip. The warm weather had been deceptive: it was a cold night; it was dark. I could see the airport building in the distance, maybe a mile or more away. It was dimly lit, throwing off a hazy shimmer; signs of life were most noticeable for their absence. All but one of the runways were pitch black, with low night-lights picking out what I took to be the solitary, permanent, emergency landing-strip, designed to cast the minimum possible light into the surrounding area.

I could only just make out the line of planes Orbach had told me about. I was beginning to wonder if it was all a practical joke when he stepped out from between two planes and waved me towards him. I felt like I was walking through a minefield. I nearly tripped as I crossed the concrete of the first, unlit strip, that which was parallel to the mesh-fence. As he ushered me onto his plane, I looked around and noticed a light flicker briefly in the cockpit of the next plane in line but then go out. I asked him about it. He told me to get into the plane and made his point with a little shove, sliding the door shut behind me and leading me forward to the pilot cabin with a tight grip on my upper arm.

'Don't be frightened, Dave; trust me; there's nothing to it. Just pretend you're at the fairground.'

'Fairs scare me too, Russel.'

He chortled delightedly. He switched on the engine: it was just like a car in this respect, but there were far more knobs and dials. So far no sexy stewardess had offered me a drink.

He spoke into the microphone.

'This is Sir Russel Orbach.'

The control tower acknowledged and asked for his formal call-sign and confirmation of flight-plan. A few moments later, the lights of a small runway, connecting to the emergency runway that was already lit up, came on. I gritted my teeth and strapped on the seat-belt.

He drove the plane slowly and evenly onto the runway. Twisting my head, I could see that behind us the other plane was reversing in the opposite direction, onto the unlit strip. We were between it and the airport building. Our cabin was lit up, and so were our wing-lights, red and green for port and starboard like a ship or a pair of Kickers shoes. No lights at all showed from the other craft. It took me a while to realise what was happening. Our plane was the shill — the magician's way of distracting the attention of his audience — for the control tower, to cover the noise of its take-off and its movement.

I asked:

'What about radar?'

He shook his head:

'Not at this height. By the time they pick it up — if, that is, anyone's watching at this time of night — we could have come from anywhere.'

'So what's it all about, Russel? Why the Red Baron act? Who's in the other plane? Snoopy?'

'What other plane?' He asked, as if he had not just a moment before acknowledged its existence. 'Where's your assistant?'

'Who?'

'The Australian.' She had first worked with me on the case I had worked for him

'Went back to Australia,' I said gallantly. He didn't argue so I figured he didn't know I was lying.

I was less scared being up in the air in a small plane than I had expected. If it hadn't been for the circumstances, it would have been an exciting experience, exhilarating, even enjoyable. I was surprised how much I could see of the ground below. The accumulated lights of the towns extended from above to the fields around them; there were lines of road-lights well out into the undeveloped countryside.

The other plane came alongside us. My eyes had adjusted to the dark and I could now see the pilot, though not clearly enough to make out his face or any features. I had a fair idea who it was:

'That's Walker, I take it.'

'Who's Walker?'

'I suppose you never heard of Waterbottom, either.'

'Who's Waterbottom?'

'And Battle?'

He didn't say anything. I got the point. He would talk about anything other than what this was all about. Not yet. Not until he was fully settled into the pilot's role.

'Who's babysitting Frankie?'

'Jada. That's . . .'

'Yeah, I know. I just wondered if you might ask me who Frankie was too.' I don't know why but I found it reassuring to think that Jada was with Frankie.

He chortled again; it was out of character; it was the most frightening aspect of the adventure.

We were heading out over the sea. It grew darker. We flew through low wispy clouds of our own, then as we emerged we could watch the stars flicker between higher levels of thicker cloud. It was eerie, but not unpleasantly so. It was vaguely like I imagined might be the thrill of sitting beside a camp-fire in the middle of an otherwise dark forest. I could only imagine it; I'd never been camping: tents don't have TV. Notwithstanding my sweater, I realised it was getting cold.

'You wanna turn on the heating?'

It's not the same sensation,' he declined my invitation. I'd discovered what he did for — or instead of — sex. I flashed an image into my mind of Orbach jacking off while flying: it was suitably grotesque.

We flew in silence for a few more minutes until at last he said quietly:

'I want your help, Dave.'

'Sorry, Russel, only one client at a time.'

'Who's your client?'

'What client?'

He caught the crack. and smiled thinly

'Same old Dave. You're the one constant in my life.'

'I don't mean to be any part of your life, Russel; it's the last thing I want.'

'But you are, Dave. I don't seem to be able to shake you out of it.'

I looked down at the sky; I felt pretty shaken just then. 'What do you want, Russel?'

'I suppose, just for you to listen. Well, listen and think.'

Suddenly everyone wants me to listen.

'I didn't kill Mick and Eartha.'

'Did I say you did?'

I cursed Stephen Walker under my breath. Then I cursed my own stupidity, thinking I was clever enough to prevent him telling his father about our visit. Then I cursed Carson's stupidity for not coming up with a better way to keep him quiet. Couldn't she have done something? Maybe she could have seduced him. Maybe not.

'You've been investigating me,' he said flatly. 'I realised it the moment you turned up at my house. How did that happen? Coincidence or contrivance?'

'A bit of both. Started out as contrivance, ended up as coincidence when Sandy took an untarnishable shine to the house.' I laughed a lot more heartily than I felt. 'We're going to be such close neighbours you'll wonder how you ever got along without us. Maybe we can babysit for each other — waddaya think?'

'No, I don't think so,' he said sadly as if he truly regretted that we now could never be friends. 'I don't think moving in is that good an idea.'

'You know we've exchanged contracts. The builders are already in. You know Sandy. You tell her. I'd rather jump out of this plane without a parachute. It'd be safer.'

He didn't smile. He turned to stare at me, puzzled until he realised it was only another of my so-called gags.

'So what made you think I was investigating Mick and Eartha?'

'I didn't think it to begin with. I didn't know what to think. Just that you had to be up to something.' It was a back-handed compliment. 'But when you turned up in Southend, looking at the Walkers . . .'

'I thought you said you didn't know anyone called Walker?'

'I've just remembered,' he said dryly. 'There's a man called Walker who runs the maintenance company that services this plane. Nick Walker. Is that the one you mean?'

'Right. That Walker,' I tossed my head in the direction of the other plane. 'The Walker with the son who has trouble keeping his fly done up. The son you let — pardon the pun — walk. Gee, Russel, I'll never cease to be amazed by your powers of recall. Got any more tricks like it?'

'Well,' he said, 'I don't think that can be Mr Walker. I don't even know if he can fly. So far as I'm aware, he doesn't own an airplane, and he certainly doesn't own that one. It belongs to a local travel company. They don't use it in connection with their tours, at least not so far as I'm aware. It's more a promotion and hospitality job. Tax-free perk for the managing director, I daresay.'

'What sort of promotion are they doing out here now? Exploration of hotels on the moon?' That's how it felt; nothing between the earth and the moon — just us.

'What's out here now?' He contradicted himself inconsequentially. 'That plane can't fly; it's scheduled for a service tomorrow morning. Planes are well-documented. There are paper records, flight plans, logs, that sort of thing, and mechanical records too of course, and other ways of telling whether a plane has been in the air. My guess is, that plane you think you see out there is firmly on the ground — probably where you wish you were — and it will show no signs of having been airborne since it was last taken up by its owners.'

Walker would spend the rest of the night and its scheduled service in the morning personally stripping down the parts and cleaning them, turning the meters back, refuelling to precisely the correct level and eliminating every means of proving it had been up and out.

'You said you wanted me to listen,' I reminded him 'To what? To how clever you are? How you can make me think there's another plane up in the air with us and prove there isn't?'

'No. I hope that question won't ever arise.'

'What then?'

'You're quite right that I let Stephen Walker off with a soft sentence. You're quite right that I did it for Nick Walker. I'm not going to deny it: not to you, anyway. I won't take you for that big a fool. I won't be the first and I won't be the last judge who allowed a personal consideration to affect a sentencing decision. After all, most judges do, even if they don't realise it; the things that judges are soft on are the things they don't personally believe are that bad, and vice versa. I don't believe that what Stephen Walker did was that bad. The boys were only just under age, not little children. They knew what they were doing. For God's sake, Dave, don't be such a prude,' as if I had started to argue. 'Masturbation in a public lavatory is all we're talking about.'

I decided unusually in favour of silence. Let him talk it around for himself.

'But I sought no favour from Walker in return, let alone something as awful as what happened to Mick and Eartha. For God's sake,' he was invoking the Almighty a suspicious amount of the time — also uncharacteristically. 'They were my best friends. I was the godfather of their daughter. I had to take her in because of their deaths.'

'It was an accident, huh? Just an accident?'

'That's what I thought until recently. You see, well, I did have a little suspicion at the time; it is true Walker knew how unhappy I was at the idea of them leaving the country. Just from chatting, while we were waiting around in the hangar or what have you; I mean, not only from me but from them.'

'So he decides to return your favour by wacking them out? Come on, Russel. You said you weren't going to take me for a fool.'

'Walker knew about that, Walker knew about Frankie,' he recited the facts as if he was presenting a case in court. 'The thought occurred to me that he might have believed I wanted them dead. But I brushed it aside: it was too wild; people don't do that sort of thing; the CAA concluded it was an accident; the insurance paid out; at the time, I think I felt guilty — one often does when someone close has died — especially if something comes out of it that is, well, good, and you know how I feel about Frankie and my life with her. People feel the same way when they get an inheritance: well, in a way, I did get an inheritance, and I realised I was feeling guilty and that came out as the idea that Walker might have fixed the plane. But,' he hesitated, as if struggling at such intimacy, 'you have to appreciate, I'm talking about something I thought once or twice — a few minutes over a few weeks. That's all.'

'Until recently,' I reminded him.

'Until yesterday,' he announced.

'What happened yesterday?'

'Walker came to see me.' He half-turned his head, to see how much of it I believed. I tried to look expressionless. I don't know if I succeeded. I doubt it. 'You mentioned Waterbottom. And Battle. That's what he came to see me about.'

I tried to stay ahead of him so as to be able to pick holes as they appeared. He was clever. It was a neat fit. Walker comes to him and says he whacked Waterbottom. If Orbach goes to the police, he'll spill both the Mellors and what Orbach had done for his son. It would not be enough to convict Orbach, but enough to make him keep silent. Walker could — as Carson had guessed — only have wanted Waterbottom out of the way if he knew about Battle. Absent divine intervention, Battle had to be how he knew about Waterbottom. Which left the question:

'Where is Battle? Is he dead too?'

'Ah, there's the rub. Walker didn't mean to kill Waterbottom. So he says. Battle came to see him — Walker. He, uh, got Battle's source out of him . . .'

'How?'

Orbach grimaced.

'Walker plays rough. Well, that's obvious. He's still got Battle, as a matter of fact. He belongs to a gun club — it seems that a lot of people in Essex do. It has one of the highest per capita licence ratios.'

'Fascinating,' I said dryly. 'Let's say I go along with you for the moment. Walker beats up Battle, gets Waterbottom from him. What did he want from Waterbottom?'

'I imagine, to make sure he had told no one else.'

'Which he had,' I completed. Me. Through Carson. Hence his question about her. In answer to which I had lied. Which he knew. I was beginning to get very frightened indeed. He repeated his earlier question.

'Who's your client, Dave?'

'I told you. I don't have one.'

He snorted derisively.

'Ah, I see.'

'What do you "ah, I see"?' Even now, he had the most sarcastic tongue I knew, even including Sandy's.

'Ah, I see now why you had to get me down here, or perhaps I should say up here. All you've managed to get is a connection back to me.'

He banked slightly, following the other plane further out over the North Sea. I had been studying the dials, and I thought I'd worked out we were now flying at about fifty-five hundred feet. I asked him and he told me I was right.

'So what do you want from me, Russel?'

'I want you to understand. I want you to believe my account of what happened. I want you to accept that I am not responsible for Mick and Eartha — or for that matter for Waterbottom. I'd like to know who your client is, but it doesn't matter that much if you won't tell me. I'll find out. I always do.' It wasn't an idle boast.

Nonetheless, I derived some comfort from his ignorance. He was assuming that whoever had hired me was only concerned with getting Orbach rather than the truth of the plane crash.

'You want me to tell my client it wasn't your fault?'

'I want you to tell your client I had nothing whatsoever to do with it.'

'And Walker? What about Walker?'

'What about him?'

'What am I supposed to tell my client about Walker? Why wouldn't that bring you down anyway — if he's prosecuted for Waterbottom, even if they don't now prosecute for the Mellors.'

'How will they know about Waterbottom? Unless you tell them.'

'Which you don't want me to do. Right?'

'Right.'

I shook my head in disgust.

'You're a High Court judge, Russel. You're asking me to cover up three murders, for Christ's sake. Doesn't that mean anything to you?'

He shrugged.

'What can I do? It won't bring them back to life. If Walker is sure things will go no further, it's all at an end.'

'What about Battle?'

'Yes, that is a problem,' he said sadly.

Throughout this discussion, the other plane had been flying within our sight. Suddenly, it wiggled its wings in what I understood to be a signal to Orbach. Orbach hesitated.

'Do you believe me?' he asked.

'Does it matter? You're telling me what you'll say — if it ever arose — aren't you?' It was as close to denying him as I dared.

He sighed.

'I didn't think so.'

He wiggled our own wings in reply and pulled the plane into a climb, crossing over above Walker's and coming back down on the other side just as the passenger door slid back. The cabin was fully lit up. We were very close. There was a body within — a man's body — naked, stretched out along the deck, one leg at an angle that meant it had been broken, wrists tied to the seat-struts. Walker knelt down within to untie him I think I saw it happen in my mind's eye a split second beforehand. Stupidly, futilely, I lashed out at the window as if there was anything I could do. Orbach jerked me roughly back into my seat.

I watched, then, as Battle's body — I didn't know at the time whether or not still alive — flew out of the plane. He fell, turning over and over, faster and faster, arms and legs flapping wide, until we lost sight of him beneath us in the dark, descending like a bomb that would explode on impact with the water.

By apparent design, the two planes now parted company. My mouth was as dry as my eyes were wet. There was a soggy sensation in my underpants and I realised that, if I had not quite proverbially pissed myself, I had permitted a literal leak.

I wanted to claw off my clothes. I wanted to follow Battle to his watery grave. I didn't want to live with the memory of it.

Strangely, it never occurred to me that Orbach might be about to extend to me the same opportunity to re-establish that only birds, not men, can fly. I was shaken more through horror than fear for my own life. For the first time since the flight began I lit a cigarette, my hand quaking; it took the silver Dunhill Sandy had bought me for my birthday and that I hadn't yet managed to mislay, an unprecedented half-dozen strokes to catch. I placed the cold metal against my hot forehead with one hand while I dragged deeply on my cigarette held in the other.

Orbach was leaving me to work it out for myself. I wasn't doing very well. I was supposed to be investigating him for a past crime, one that at best would be hard to prove and that, hitherto, would be likely to have led to nothing worse than his resignation in disgrace. The odds were overwhelming against being able to tie him into Waterbottom, whatever the truth of his involvement in it might be. Nonetheless, he had now handed me the first-hand evidence of his complicity in a whole new murder.

I felt guilty; I felt responsible for Battle's death; if I'd confided in him, trusted him, perhaps he would never have gone off on his own, or at least he would have understood the nature of the beast he was tracking. I'd witnessed his death. His death had been orchestrated for my entertainment.

'For your education,' Orbach broke in, as if he could read my thoughts. For all I know, in the state I was in, I might well have been babbling out loud. 'Listen to me, Dave. You will give up this investigation. You will never suggest to anyone that Mick and Eartha's death was anything but an accident. You would do best never to mention them ever again. You will never say a word about what happened tonight; you can't prove it, but you won't even try. Am I making myself clear? Do you understand me?'

I understood alright, but I was damned if I'd let him off the hook of spelling it out. I looked blankly back at him as if I didn't know what he was trying to tell me.

He frowned:

'Alright, Dave, we'll do it your way. If you ever give me the slightest cause to think that you are doing anything about any of these matters — Mick and Eartha or Waterbottom or Battle — if you ever give me the slightest cause to think that you are investigating me, interested in me, writing about me, suing me, even thinking about me, the next person you see falling from a plane will be you or Sandy or your son.' And if not a plane, then a car, a mugger, a fire in the new house or ten hours locked up listening to Nigel Morris. 'You've threatened the life I lead with my child; I'm threatening yours,' he added flatly. 'You see, it wasn't that funny a joke after all, was it?' My earlier unfortunate crack about what I'd rather do than tell Sandy we weren't moving into Cloudesley Road.

I asked:

'Why, Russel? Why not simply kill me too?'

'Are you complaining, Dave?' He didn't wait for an answer. 'I like you, Dave; I've always liked you.' Margot McAllister had said something similar. 'I like Sandy, too. I don't think you've ever set out to harm me, not in the way that others have done; not until now. I don't want to have to harm you, so long as you don't make me.' I didn't believe his reason for a second, but it wasn't the time to tell him so.

We neither of us spoke to the other until we were back on the ground, though Orbach told traffic control we were coming back in. I guessed that Walker was flying the other plane the same way he'd gone out, but I didn't see it come down and it didn't come back to its parking space beside us, at least while I was there. Possibly, it was taken elsewhere for its service. The service would of course include a thorough internal clean, to remove also any traces of Battle's last battle. I didn't know or care about the details but I had no doubt that they had been worked out to the last degree.

As he let me out of the passenger cabin door, he patted me on the shoulder:

'As I said, Dave, I don't think you're a fool.' I could be relied on to do the sensible thing.

I looked straight at him I had a thousand things I wanted to say that would tell him he hadn't succeeded, he hadn't scared me, I could and would stand up to him. The trouble was, none of them would be true, and I badly needed a proper pee.

It was, I suppose, the most obvious answer of all; I unzipped myself, found with difficulty my shock-shrivelled prick and urinated on the steps and wheels of his plane.

To my eternal shame, he roared with manic laughter.

Then he reminded me of his warning:

'Remember, Dave, remember what I told you. You know me, Dave — I will know and I will do as I say.'

I did know him. And I believed him. I was finally scared — scared for my life and the lives of the people I loved — as I'd never been before, not even at those moments when I had directly confronted death. He turned away as my knees buckled and I grabbed hold of the steps to stop myself sinking to the ground.

CHAPTER NINE

'*Woolf against Orbach, for hearing. All persons having naught better to do draw nigh and enjoy the performance. Honourable Mr Justice Orbach presiding.' The clerk swished his gown around his shoulder like Zorro and kicked me in the shins.*

My counsel at the bar rose.

'M'lord, in this matter I appear for the plaintiff, Mr Woolf, and m'learned friends, Mr Tweedledum Q.C. and his junior Mr Tweedledee appear, well, as it happens, for your lordship. This is an action for a declaration, m'lord, that, not to put too fine a point on it, your lordship is stark, staring bonkers.'

'Mr Austin-Smythe-Filibuster,' who had taken the case at the last moment when the fifteenth barrister I had instructed found himself unavoidably professionally detained elsewhere, 'do you take exception to my hearing the case, in view of the fact that I might be considered in some sense partisan?' Orbach interrupted the opening.

'Good Lord, no, m'lord. I am sure your lordship's considerable reputation for impartiality is more than protection enough for my client.'

'Yes. That's my own opinion. Nonetheless, I thought I ought to mention it.'

'Your lordship is too kind. Too, too kind. I am much obliged. Would it be convenient to your lordship if I were to continue with my opening?'

'Is it really necessary, Mr Bumsucker? I have read the papers. I mean no disrespect to your client, of course, but it is hardly, well, a complicated matter.'

'Your lordship is quite right. I shan't trouble your lordship any further. Perhaps in those circumstances I can rest my case?'

'It's entirely a matter for you, Mr Lickspittle; please don't let me interfere in your conduct of the case.'

'What about me?' I hollered. 'Don't I get a say in any of it? It's my case, after all.'

'Oh, sit down, Dave,' Orbach said. 'You know you're a lousy lawyer, and a worse advocate. You haven't presented a case in court for more than a decade. Besides, you have most competent counsel appearing on your behalf.'

'Look, Russel,' I said heatedly.

'Mr Woolf,' he was horrified. 'In my court, you will address me in the proper manner. Everything must be done in the proper manner.'

'Right on, bro,' someone in the public gallery called out, sounding suspiciously like Carson.

'All rise,' mumbled the clerk in his sleep.

'Usher,' Orbach instructed. 'Open the window. Drop the clerk out of it.'

'M'lord.' The usher did as he was told.

'Look, Russel, this just isn't fair,' I protested.

'Fair?' screeched Orbach. 'Fair? Who said that? I decide what's fair. I know what's fair. Arrest that man.'

'Fuck it, Russel, this time you've gone too far. Even your sweet-talking counsel can't get you out of this one.'

'Tell us about it, Dave, tell us all about it. Come on, come on up here, sit on my lap and tell us about it. It'll be alright. There, there. Don't cry. Usher, bring Mr Woolf a Southern Comfort.'

'Russel, you killed your best friend. And his wife. Who you fancied.'

'Knickers. Prove it.'

'Prove what? That you fancied her? There's . . .' I was about to tell him there was a letter that proved it, but I remembered my duty to my client — privileged information.

'Not that,' he snapped crossly.

One of his counsel rose; it was difficult to know which one.

'M'lord, I must object to your lordship's tone . . .'

'Sit down, fool. You're supposed to be on my side.'

'Am I? Sorry, m'lord, m'learned junior's mistake.'

'I invited you to prove that I killed Mick and Eartha, Dave. Well? Well? What was my motive? It's ridiculous. They were my best friends. I was the godfather of their daughter. I had to take her in because of their deaths. So much for motive. Anyway, the crash report was inconclusive; the coroner returned a verdict of accident; the insurance paid out. Besides, how could I have done it?'

'Walker did it for you.'

The well of the courtroom erupted in laughter. Even I was laughing. Choking on my mirth, I went on.

'You let his son off from going to prison . . .'

'For a pathetic little wank with a couple of willing youngsters. Oh, really, you've got to do better than that, Mr Woolf.'

'I agree,' Schofield announced. 'This case is totally out of order.'
Behind me, Tim tugged at my gown.

'Sit down, Dave, you're making an ass of yourself.' I mooned
him and ignored him.

Alton began to cry.

Frankie popped up from behind the judge's bench demanding:
'Give him to me.'

In the witness box, Jada sang a few bars from 'Desolation Row'
which quickly descended into 'Rock Of Ages'.

I said:

'Then there's Waterbottom. What did you have to do with that?'

'Hang on, Dave,' Orbach protested. 'I ask the questions here.
This is a trial, not an investigation. Members of the jury, disregard
that last remark.'

The twelve cardboard cut-out men good and true flopped
forward as far as the floor and sprung back up into place with
nary a sound.

'Waterbottom's not even a runner, and you know it. Move
along, move along, get to your best point — if you have one.'

'Battle,' I said firmly. 'Brian Battle.'

'Who?' answered Orbach.

I tried to tell them but I couldn't get the words out. How could I
describe it? I had been there. I was, however unwillingly, however
unwittingly, an accomplice. My mouth opened and shut and
opened and shut to no effect. Someone else was tugging at my gown.

'I told you, Woolf, in no circumstances; the Pulleyne scandal
never happened; this isn't happening; five times nothing is nothing;
it's all in your head; it's all a dream.'

It wasn't Schofield tugging at my gown, but a uniformed
police officer shaking me by the shoulder. I woke up with a start

and banged my chest against the steering wheel. I was still parked on the side-road by the airport. It was just after dawn.

'Are you alright, sir?'

His car was parked in front of mine, preventing a quick getaway. He said:

'I wonder whether you would mind stepping out of the car, sir.'

Awkwardly, I got out. He didn't try to help me. 'Have you been drinking, sir?'

'What?'

'I asked, sir, whether you had been drinking.' He was extracting a breathalyser from its case.

I cackled crazily.

'No, officer, I haven't been drinking.'

It was true: the one time in my life a police officer asked to breathalyse me was the one time in my life when I wasn't half-cut.

There were two reasons I didn't drive back to London straight away. One was, I was still shaking so bad I wasn't sure I could handle the car. The other that I didn't want to face my family For a lot of years, I'd been pretending to be a tough guy, handling occasional but very real physical fear with gallows-humour. Just like everyone else. It wasn't easy admitting the truth was that I was far more coward than anything else. What Tim had said at the club was right. Orbach scared me. We used to say in the sixties, he scared me shitless.

I had a theory. Becoming a proper, full-time judge had been both Orbach's saving coup and his major error. Until then, though isolated in his personal life, he had contacts and influence, even power, principally through his work; information and circumstances and people he could use to his own ends; like he'd used others during Disraeli Chambers, maybe like he'd used to find something out for me during Mather's — I now firmly believed in order to put me into his debt — and like he'd then used me and others during Pulleyne. Like, too, he'd used his position as an Assistant Recorder to manipulate Nick Walker.

Once he was a full High Court judge, his access to people and his room for manoeuvre were restricted. His power and influence had been formalised. He couldn't call up anyone in the legal profession or any of the other established institutions without attracting attention to himself; there were fewer places he could safely go without a legitimate explanation; he had placed himself under the microscope of an abstract integrity which can only be sustained by minimal activity.

This was the trade off: he gave up his freedom of action for an effective immunity from prosecution, an immunity of which he'd tested the fibre during Pulleyne. Which threw up another question — why fight it? Even if, and I was still a long way off, I was going to be able to put together a package convincing enough and sufficient to justify publication, with the only consequence that he had to resign, wasn't that exactly the deal he'd made with himself?

The answer wasn't as obscure as it might have seemed to someone who didn't know Orbach: It was one thing for him to accept intellectually that there would forever remain a risk of discovery and to guard against it; it was another actually to confront it and admit it was happening — happening to him Perhaps there was another level to it, too; perhaps, though he'd theorised that he could accept push if it came to shove, in reality he was incapable of doing anything other than he had done all his life — fighting it, fighting back, fighting 'them', whoever for the time being might be his enemy. Like a *schmuk*, I'd stood up to be counted.

'So what're you going to do?' Carson asked with her mouth full of muesli.

I had driven to the club and let myself in. I had rung Sandy and told her I was alright, I'd be home later, I'd explain when I got back. She had been so worried she had even rung Orbach to make sure nothing had happened on the flight.

'What did he say?'

'He said it was fine. He left you in Southend.'

'To tell the truth, I feel asleep in the car.'

For some reason she believed me. She said in a small voice:

'Dave, are you alright? What's going on, Dave?'

'I said I'll tell you when I get back. Honestly. Go to sleep, San.' She must've been tired: she didn't tell me off. 'I love you. Kiss Alton for me.'

I replaced the receiver sadly.

After the local law let me leave, I drove back to London slowly, carefully and thoughtful. I tried to keep the image of Battle's final fling out of my mind I tried to put my fear and my guilt to one side. I set out to think it through.

The nightmare helped. It reminded me of the essentials. Orbach was the law. Orbach, with Schofield and Dowell in support. They were not there to protect the man; just his office. I knew and liked and respected Tim, and for all his manner sensed that beneath Schofield's callous exterior lurked an essentially decent man, one who would at the lowest prefer people not to be unnecessarily nasty to one another. If I could put a strong enough package together, I had a good chance of abridging the professional career of Mr Justice Orbach much as Pulleyne's had come to a premature end.

The difficulty was that I could not go so far as to put Orbach away. The Mellor charge depended entirely on Walker. Jada's instincts were not admissible evidence. Eartha's letter was ambiguous. Even in a court, Walker would not make a compelling case; a good brief would easily be able to get Orbach off. I knew, however, that there would be no trial, of either of them: Schofield had as good as said it; it was an essential premise. They would rather not charge Walker than have Orbach's name dragged into his defence.

So far as Waterbottom was concerned, there was even less evidence to connect Orbach. I was not certain in my own mind that Walker had been in touch with him beforehand. It was a messy killing, and probably unnecessary; I doubted Orbach would have sanctioned, let alone conceived of it. Again, however, if I — or anyone else — pointed the finger at Walker, he would threaten to involve Orbach and charges would have to be dropped as soon is they realised that it was not a wholly hollow hazard, that a sufficient connection to withstand superficial scrutiny could be sustained.

There was only one case where there was independent evidence. Battle. Me. My word against Orbach's. My word against Orbach's and Walker's. My word against an open journey taken by Orbach — foolhardy indeed if the purpose was a public viewing of a private execution — and a journey Walker would, so Orbach claimed, by the time I could cause any enquiry, be in a position to prove had never taken place. Once again, the conclusion was inescapable: no trial, no incarceration.

The most I could achieve, therefore, was the Schofield-style 'quiet word' that compelled Orbach to resign. This was not a solution that suited. The man had terrified me beyond terror; he had threatened the only things in life I have ever held precious enough to want to go on living for; he had a camel-like capacity to harbour grudges, a Sicilian approach to revenge, an elephantine memory, skill and money; he would know my part in his downfall, and Jada's when her book was published. Even if forced to quit, even if — as he had said he might do later on in life — he went abroad, I and my family would remain forever vulnerable. It was not something I was prepared to subject them to; it was not something I was prepared to subject myself to.

There were, it seemed to me, only two ultimate solutions. The first was to do what Orbach wanted: drop the case, forget about him and it, go back to being a lawyer and a father — as he wanted to remain. The second was to push the logic of the situation to its extreme: if Orbach was protected by his position, if Walker was too, why should it not extend also to me?

I was, however, not yet ready to confide my decision in anyone. I was about to embark on an extremely dangerous undertaking: I knew there were people — above all, Carson and Sandy — who would, once I had told them about the plane trip, go as far along the route with me as I wanted; while the choice to do so would remain their responsibility, it would also be mine — as I felt responsible for Battle. I did not wish to involve them unless and until it became necessary. I would not know whether it was necessary until I had worked out the details. Until I did so, it seemed to me that caution called for an apparent abandonment of interest.

'I don't feel I have any choices, Carson. I'm going to do what he says. I'm going to go back to London, and I'm going back to the office, and I'm going to tell Mister-mister Nigel-nigel Morris-morris it's a load of crap and I can't waste my time on it anymore, and then maybe I'll forget to bill him or maybe it'll be even more convincing if I do.'

'What're you going to tell Sandy?' Why did I have the idea she didn't believe me?

'I'm going to tell her the same damn thing. I'm going to tell her I'm convinced there's nothing in it and that's that.'

'What're you going to tell Jada?'

'I'm going to tell her to grow up. Just grow up and don't be so stupid: you can't do everything you want in this life; that's why there're laws; being gorgeous and brilliant and half-orphaned and a pop star doesn't make her any different.'

'And what're you going to tell Dowell?'

'How the hell did Tim get into this? I might've told him at the beginning but he told me to take a running jump.' I groaned — it was entirely the wrong expression to use and equally entirely accidental. 'So I don't have to tell him anything.'

She shook her head.

'Uhuh. As soon as Battle surfaces, he'll be onto you.' This was true.

'Who says he surfaces? The fishes'll eat him. How can they i.d. him? He had no identifying clothing — not even a watch.'

'I dunno,' she admitted. 'They do, though, don't they? Besides, someone's bound to report him missing sooner or later.'

'I don't know,' I said with false bravado. 'He was pretty much of a slime; I doubt he was married; his parents probably denied responsibility for him five minutes after he was born. With the current turnover in Fleet Street, no one's likely to notice at his paper.'

'Crap.'

'So, already, I don't have all the answers. I never said I did.'

'That's even bigger crap, Dave. You're not telling me the truth.' Her eyes met mine and glowered. 'How dare you call me back from Oz and then hold out on me?'

'*Chutzpah?*' I suggested lamely.

After I had talked with Sandy, telling her too what had happened on the plane, I crashed out. She left Alton off at the childminder so I could get some sleep and went into the office. I was only just in bed when the 'phone rang. It was Jada Jarrynge. She had rung the office and demanded my home number. When you're a pop star, you can do things like that; they wouldn't have given it out to the Lord Chief Justice in person. She omitted the courtesies altogether — perhaps Orbach had more of a hand in her upbringing than I had appreciated.

'This is Jada. What happened last night? What are you doing with him?'

'What do you mean?'

I forgot he had told her he was going night-flying with me. She reminded me and added:

'Why?'

'Ah, right. Well, that's about it. You know we're moving into a house near his. He was talking about flying and, uh, that was it: he told me he sometimes went night-flying and asked me if I'd like to go. I said sure, why not. It was something new, you know? That's all, just a new experience.' And then some.

She breathed heavily into the 'phone. If I had taped it, I probably could've sold it for a smash hit.

'What did you find out? What is this? I agreed to look after Frankie; I thought — this was something you were doing for me. I had to cancel a recording session. Just so that you could do something new?'

She sounded incredulous. I couldn't blame her.

'Listen, Jada, I was going to talk to Nigel Morris today but, uh, you know him, I didn't have enough years to spare.' She didn't laugh. Maybe she didn't know him that well. Maybe I wasn't funny anymore. I didn't laugh either. 'I've done a lot of work on this thing . . . I don't think it's going anywhere . . . You know, when you've got a certain amount of experience, you get a nose for it: I don't think it's there, Jada — you know?' If I said 'you know' once more, I'd scream.

More rhythmic breathing.

'Jada? You still there?'

'What did he give you? What did he pay you? Why are you backing down? You believed me; you told me about him; you know it's true. He buy you off, or what?'

'Hey, c'mon. Those're heavy things to say. Nobody buys me off. I don't have to take that kind of shit from you; you know, what are you — just a kid? I don't have to take it — you know?' I didn't scream. Even I couldn't rely on my word.

'Oh, yes, sure I know. I know what this is about. I know what all you people are about. Remember: if you aren't with me, you're against me.'

She hung up at about the same time I slammed down the receiver in my own unjustified indignation.

I figured I'd better get my version into Morris first. I called but he was in a meeting. I left a message. When he called back, he rang the office instead of the home number I'd left for him. He only tied up the main line for half an hour. By the time he got through to me, he'd already talked to Jada.

'Working at h-h-home?'

'We're moving soon; thought I'd do my share of packing.'

'I r-r-r-remember when we moved. I never thought, looking at my b-b-b-books on the shelves, how many p-p-p-packing cases I'd need. June w-w-w-went . . .'

I groaned. Unlike on earlier occasions, when I'd wanted him to get straight to the point, my aim this time was for him to let me do so. I started talking over him.

'If you've spoken to Jada you'll know I've come to the conclusion there's nothing in the case. You're not going to be able to publish. It's a libel — and I think it probably qualifies as criminal libel.' I knew not much more about criminal libel than the civil variety: but I knew it existed, and had been used once or twice in recent years, and if telling the world that a judge whacked off your parents didn't qualify, I had a hard time thinking what would. Queen eats baby for breakfast? Archbishop's silk underwear secret? Prime Minister's hair out of place? President tells truth?

'I s-s-s-see. Don't you think, don't you think we ought to discuss this. There's a v-v-very nice cocktail bar near then office: I could buy you one of their extraordinary con-con-concoctions. They do one that . . .'

'I don't want to. I'll write you a letter; you consider what I have to say; if you still want to meet and discuss it, OK, it's your money, your time.' I'd reached a compromise over billing: I wouldn't charge for any of the time I'd spent working on the case; just for all the tune I'd spent listening to Morris.

'B-b-b-but . . .' he was still protesting as I replaced the receiver: 'The co-co-co-cocktails are ex-ex-ex-exquisite . . .'

This is how I passed the next couple of days. Sandy was happy for me to take Alton to, and pick him up from, the childminder; she told me where to get cartons for packing; she even let me do the shopping though I got most of it wrong.

In my place, she went into the office for most of the hours it was open. I think she would have enjoyed the role reversal if she wasn't worried about me. It was more her firm than mine, and it gave her an opportunity to see how much damage I'd done during my tenure. We didn't talk much, though: she refused to ask what I was going to do, unwilling to be accused of nagging, waiting instead for me to tell her, and I decided there were a lot of programmes on the television that I was really quite addicted to.

Nor did I go to the club; nor did Carson ring me. She was sulking; I was skulking. I know she went into Nichol & Co, who were her theoretical employers, and Sandy said she was working on a couple of cases, to help out, to have something to do. She also said they'd had lunch one day, and a chat the other, but the way she said it was like a cross-examination where there's nothing left to lose, bluffing for an answer. I knew Carson was disappointed, maybe angry at me, but she would remain silent — for a while at least — to give me an opportunity to make up my mind

In the end, though, Carson's patience gave out and she called round, during the day — the third of my retreat — bearing a bottle for me and a bunch of flowers for the house.

'Got it bad, boss, huh?' She glanced at my already full glass and, ostentatiously, at her watch.

'Have you come to lecture me, or to have a drink?'

'Both.'

I got her a beer from the fridge as she stretched out comfortably on the sofa. Half the room was now taken up with boxes: we'd run out of elsewhere to store them. In another few days, there'd be a couple of rooms at the new house which would be sufficiently ready for us to start carting over the breakables we didn't want the removal men to handle, and a few pictures which it would be convenient to hang before the day of the move itself. We had seen too many friends move into half-decorated, half-improved houses, and live out of boxes for years, adjusting to their incomplete homes until, it seemed, they were happier than if the work finally came to an end. We didn't want the same.

'You looking forward to moving?'

'You mean what I think you mean?'

'Sure.'

'No, then. No, I'm terrified of it, terrified of seeing him, terrified, even, of seeing *her*,'Frankie. 'Terrified how I'll react.'

'Waddaya gonna do, then? Ask Sandy to leave you here for the new owners? Hide in a back room? Emigrate? Forget it,' she pre-empted any flip reference to going back to Australia with her.

I sighed.

'I suppose it's time.'

'Certainly is. Time for what?'

'Time to tell you what's on my mind.' I paused to gather my thoughts, to find the best way to tell her. Confident as I had been until then of her support, I suddenly realised that I didn't know her that well, that no one knew anyone else that well, to be a hundred per cent sure they would go along with the wildest and most dangerous scheme.

'I've been thinking about a lot of things. The choices're much less straightforward than you seem to think. In fact, I think there's only one that makes any sense.'

'Tell me.'

I was about to do so when — with impeccable mistiming — we were interrupted by a ring at the door.

He started talking before he was into the living-room:

'I don't believe it. I really don't believe it,' he howled. 'They had floods in Bangladesh, a war in the Middle East, dictators in South America; here, there've been tube crashes, train crashes, plane crashes, football crowd crushes — and yet you haven't been involved. I don't know why not. You're a one-man walking disaster area.'

'I resent that,' Carson piped up.

'Right. One-person,' Dowell snarled back at her. He could give as good as he got.

She started to tell him that wasn't what she meant when she realised it wasn't what he meant either.

'What are you talking about, Tim?'

'I'm talking about one death soon after you mention Southend to me maybe I could eventually have persuaded myself to swallow as coincidental; not two.'

'Who's the second?' I asked with sweet-toned innocence.

'Your friend Brian Battle, the one you said you were looking for in Southend, from the same paper you claimed you were working for. Seems he went swimming; correction, diving.' He was sufficiently at home to fetch his own glass before he sat down. 'Sky-diving,' he added unnecessarily melodramatically. 'From an airplane that maybe came out of Southend Airport. Without a parachute.'

'This Orbach's plane that Dave originally asked you about? The one that crashed?' Carson asked disingenuously, to remind him it wasn't a connection on its own.

'You,' he wagged a finger at her, 'you keep quiet. You're far cleverer than him, and if I'm going to trip him up I don't want you running interference, right?'

I wasn't sure if it was a mixed metaphor or not, so I asked:

'Start again, Tim. I've had a lot to drink. I'm taking a break from work.'

'Yeah, I know. Like a fool, I thought you'd be at work, went to your office first.' Where Sandy had told him I could be found at home. 'And to add to all these coincidences, you happen to decide to take a break. Really,' he exclaimed. He shook his head: 'Stop pretending, Dave. Stop pretending you don't know. Stop pretending it ain't serious, Dave.' His tone turned quite gentle, 'It's getting heavy again. How long do you think you can go out playing cowboy without somebody blowing your head off, Dave?'

I conceded nothing. I repeated:

'So far, all I know is that Brian Battle, you say, is dead, and I think you're saying he fell — but maybe you're insinuating he was pushed, as I say I don't know — out of an airplane that might've come from Southend Airport, which you think connects to me because I asked you about a plane crash which involved Orbach and that's where the plane he owned flew out of and Carson was down there recently but alibi'd for when Wetbum got it. Is that it? Even for you, it's pretty thin, isn't it?'

'That and he was helping you on the Orbach case.'

'Is that something you know or just a wishful guess?'

'Both more or less. His editor didn't know what he'd been working on, but he'd already filed his expense claim which gave me Southend. I was referred to a man called Nigel Morris, a book publisher who I'm going to put under arrest for speech impeding the police with their enquiries.' He was talking about my Morris. 'He claims he doesn't know what Battle was doing for you, but agrees he lent him you to assist. He won't tell me why until he's spoken to his boss — he says his boss is out of the country and, allegedly, entirely uncontactable. I don't believe him; everything I've read about his boss says you can contact him in the bath. But there's nothing I can do at this stage; he's consulting the group's own lawyers.'

'This ain't necessarily criminal, then?' Otherwise he'd be talking obstruction as he had with Carson over Waterbottom.

'Not necessarily, not yet. He was naked when he was found. Given the height from which he fell, we're talking a small aircraft. Probably five, six thousand feet from the damage.' I omitted to tell him how close he was. Broken bones, crushed vertebrae, he gave us a few other distasteful details which told me they couldn't be sure what sort of state he was in before he took a dive. 'But he died of a heart attack of course.' I nearly had, so why shouldn't he?

'And it definitely came from Southend?'

'No, it could've been Humberside, Norwich or Ipswich — or maybe even Cambridge or Stansted. Could have come from the continent, too. But Southend has five, six flying clubs, which is a lot, and it's nearest.'

'If he was naked, how d'you i.d. him? He was carrying his passport maybe?'

'There's a dental computer at Eastbourne. The Dental Estimates Board keep it; they've just got a new system up and running; when you've got a body you don't know who it is, one of the first things they do is X-ray the jaw and teeth and feed it in.'

Without thinking about it, I was gnashing my own teeth and stroking my jaw. I didn't like the idea they were on public record; it was an invasion of my privacy. Anyone could find out how I had neglected my gums

'If it doesn't kick anyone out, it's either a foreigner or someone with perfect teeth. Even private dentistry's on the records. Usually, it'll produce anything from one to half a dozen people it might be. From then on, it's relatively straightforward. In this case, because his record showed up his occupation as a journalist in London, they faxed a photo through to the Met. where it was matched with his press pass picture, from where it led to Waterbottom and you.' And Dowell.

'How long had he been in the sea?'

'Probably a couple days. The temperature's been volatile, which makes it harder to pin down. He was trawled the night before last,' he added, literally fished out. 'Now it's your turn to do the talking ' He tapped his glass impatiently but it wasn't another drink he wanted. 'What was he up to?'

'He was on what we like to call a frolic of his own, ducky.' A job on the side for which his employer would not have to take responsibility. Dowell, a former law student, might remember the phrase. 'He did a bit of research for me and then decided to do some freelancing; so how can I know what he was doing?'

I waited for him to argue. When he didn't I added:

'I don't know where he'd been or why. That's it. You can book me for interfering with an officer and all that jazz, if you like. But you haven't got the basis for it; you won't be able to hold me even overnight; it doesn't help you get any answers.'

He sighed loudly, satisfiedly. I thought he'd been taking it all too calmly so far. He had simply wanted to confirm I was going to lie to him. He had something else up his sleeve.

'Well, if you won't tell me anything, I'll have to tell you a bit more, won't I? I think I, er, forgot to mention, I've already got some information. Yesterday, they checked all those airports for private craft flights over the last few days and particularly for night-flights.'

He watched my face drop — to the ground, where I keep my brains.

'Another bit of odd coincidence,' he continued. 'Remember the name we mentioned before? Sir Russel someone? Had a flight out a few nights ago. I saw him at the lunch-break — pardon, luncheon adjournment — today. Naturally, I was most deferential, especially as he hasn't got such fond memories of me, apologised for disturbing him, genuflected, kissed the hem of his robes, touched my forelock. I explained we were making enquiries of everyone who took their planes out of certain airports — the ones I told you — whether they'd seen anything suspicious, whether they happened to lose any passengers, that sort of thing.'

'And?' I croaked.

Carson got up and filled my glass for me and, rather than miss anything by going into the kitchen for a beer refill, poured herself a shot. Dowell held his glass out but she shook her head:

'Not yet.'

'Mr Sir Russel Justice says he neither saw anything suspicious nor did he lose any passengers. He says he only had one passenger, who he assures me will confirm what he says, and who was definitely still with him when he landed. Get it?'

I was clenching so hard, the glass shattered in my hand. I've heard of it happening, but I'd never seen it and it's never happened to me before. I jumped up cursing. Fortunately, it had not cut me. As Carson went inside for a cloth, I started to lick the sticky Southern Comfort off my fingers — waste not, want not — when Tim grabbed my hand to stop me:

'Slivers,' he warned.

'Ta,' I said faintly.

After we'd cleaned up, Carson announced she was going to make coffee.

'This is no way for two responsible people to spend the afternoon.' She refused to say who wasn't.

We followed her into the kitchen.

My knees were weaker than when I'd left Orbach at the plane. This was why he hadn't killed me. They had to kill Battle — it was inevitable, possibly even from before Walker contacted Orbach, because he was already too badly damaged; it would all be superceded by harm done in a fall. Because they wanted to drop Battle, they needed a flight — and preferably a night-flight; a flight meant a record; a record needed an alibi.

I could always tell the truth.

My word against his. My life against his.

Tim babied:

'Talkie time, Davey.'

'Nothing to say. I was up with Orbach. Only me. We both came back. That's it.'

'And what did you see while you were up there?'

'Uh, stars, and, uh, clouds, and, well, more stars and clouds and of course we looked down at towns and the sea and stuff.' I gulped my coffee too quickly and burned my mouth. 'Shit.'

'Tut.'

'Tim, you're taking it all very calmly, aren't you? I mean, for you. Isn't this when you take out your rubber hose?'

He normally got quite pissed off when people got whacked. Quite but not very. But he was invariably furious if he thought I had anything to do with it.

'I know you, Dave. If something's going down again, I'm resigned to it; let's just get on with it.' It was the first time he'd ever admitted that, one way or another, we worked well together.

I snorted.

'You're snowing me, sunshine. I've got nothing to tell you and sweet-talk won't get it either.'

'Right, then. I'm going to ask you formally,' he took out his notebook. 'Sir, did anything strange happen, or did you see anything strange, while you were in the air with Sir Russel?'

'No.'

He shook his head sadly as he put his notebook away.

'Dave. I like you; I like Sandy; I don't want to see you hurt. I'm your friend, trust me.'

'Someone else told me the same thing just recently,' was as far as I would go. 'But I don't think you'd expect me to trust him either.'

CHAPTER TEN

We sat up most of the night, me and Sandy and Carson. In the middle, one of Sandy's headaches came on and she went to lie down for an hour or so, but still sleep would not release her and she got up again, around three o'clock, to re-join us in the living-room, in the middle of our boxes.

Sandy was the hardest to convince. She scrutinised every element of my reasoning and the details of my plan the way sometimes I would come across her examining Alton, inch by inch of the perfect body she could not believe she had built, for the slightest hint of flaw or potential problem.

What I was trying to do was handle it the same way Orbach would. It was simple: Orbach had hurt me, Orbach was enemy, Orbach must die.

I pointed to the boxes.

'And the new house? Just forget it? You love it, San; I love it. It's the perfect place for Alton. It's our house.' Nothing we hadn't said many times since she'd decided we were going to buy it. 'We can't move into it if he's there.'

She shook her head.

'Not good enough, Dave. You can't do this so that you can have the things you want, we want. That's as bad as him It's only an option if it's the only way to defend yourself, to defend us.'

'You should have seen,' I said also not for the first time, 'you should have seen Battle. Can you imagine how he felt, what he was thinking? Dowell said he died of a heart attack, of sheer shock; it may not have been for long, but he knew what was happening to him.'

'No, of course I can't imagine it. The closest I can get is to try and think how I'd feel if, say, Alton was ill, we took him to the hospital, and they said — well, he's dying, he's going to die in a few hours or days. I couldn't cope with it — it's the unmentionable, the unthinkable. That's why, I suppose, that's why despite everything — everything I've believed about violence, everything I've believed about law, everything I believe about civilised behaviour — so-called — that's why I can even sit here discussing it.'

After a lengthy silence, she asked, as if Carson was not present:

'What about Carson? Is it fair to involve her? Remember. . .'

Carson cut her off:

'I know what you're going to say.' For Carson to participate was inevitably to evoke the memory of all she had gone through about her uncle — the publicity, her trial, being shunned by some people and congratulated for all the wrong reasons by others. 'It's the same thing. It's not immediate, hot-blooded, spontaneous. But you're — we're — not dealing with a hot-blooded man. The opposite, really. It's the only way. It's an absolute certainty they won't prosecute him. Either we lie down under it, or we put him down. There's no middle ground. It's not our responsibility; it's theirs — because they won't use the power they've got.'

I said much the same:

'It's them, not us. This is a situation that doesn't fit concepts of "civilised society". In a civilised society, an awful crime is always punished — unless of course it's perpetuated by the authorities themselves, in which case — give or take — it's not a crime at all. What we're saying is that because the authorities won't take any real action against him, they've adopted his conduct, absorbed it if you like.'

'With us or agin' us?'

As Jada had said.

'I suppose. In a sense, no. In actuality, he is one of the authorities. What I'm saying is, we're right outside all the known rules now. This is what the judiciary are: above the law, part of the penal system, part of the process for enforcing law and therefore no part of those who are intended to be enforced by it.'

'*Quis custodiet?*'

'They made their devil's pact when they made him a judge. And unless there's any chance — which there isn't — that they'll admit their error, sacrifice some of their authority, the mystique of law that says a High Court judge can never be crooked, then that's their choice. I ain't paying for it; you ain't paying for it; Alton ain't paying for it. The whole thing is outside the law; what he was doing in that plane was outside the law; the law has abdicated responsibility for this particular game; therefore, we've got to play it the same way it would be if there was no law.'

Which is when she conceded I was right; there could be no other outcome. It was a question of survival.

It had to be done fast. Dowell was already too close. He was far closer than hard evidence permitted him to prove, either to the press-pack in hot pursuit and protection of their own or to his superiors, because he knew what people were involved and could probably guess how they were tied together. Once the destination of an investigation has been identified, it is twenty times easier to determine the route, to find the evidence that links the beginning to the end. In addition, we were now less than a week away from moving in as Orbach's near neighbour.

I didn't tell either Morris or Jada Jarrynge the full truth of what I was going to do. I didn't know how either would react. I told both of them that I was back on the job. I needed their help. But I told them only as far as they needed to know. If my cover-up theory was wrong, if anything went wrong with my plan, it was still not impossible that I — and maybe Carson, maybe even Sandy though I would not let her play any active part — would face charges, if only of conspiracy: I didn't want either Jada or Morris to be subject to the same risk.

Jada's main task was to convince Orbach; Carson's to enlist Stephen Walker; Morris's, despite what he claimed were his better instincts, to help me out again in the world of journalism: I had to remind him that he had hired me to provide sufficient proof to enable them to publish Jada's book; what I wanted from him would achieve that result.

I considered Orbach's four basic rules: people are predictable; they only do what they want; once they start on a course of conduct, they can't get off it; and, people are capable of being both good and bad. An Orbach plan meant confrontation, that was his forte; he liked to strip away the insulation and bring the bare wires close together, so close that the slightest tremor would cause them to touch and to spark; so close that, notwithstanding the danger, the thrill of the impact became irresistible, like a child reaching out to touch fire. All I had to do was to engineer Orbach and Walker into the right place, at the right time, and under the right conditions — nature, according to Orbach, would take over from there.

Jada rang in before lunch. She gave me an avowedly verbatim account of her conversation with Orbach. He had not suspected her for a second. Why should he? This was the half-sister of his ward, who admired and respected him so much she had already told him he was going to feature in her book. It was an encounter between the citizen above and the child beneath suspicion.

She went to see him at the High Court, in his chambers, before his working day began. She told him she had been telephoned by a man, who wouldn't give his name. The man was demanding money, under threat of disclosing something extremely damaging about Orbach.

'Disclose to whom?' Orbach had asked, immediately but understandably visibly anxious.

'He didn't say; I didn't ask. I'm sorry, Russel, I was stupid; I panicked. I know there's nothing he could do to hurt you, but I was frightened. He said he was watching, watching the flat, then, while we were speaking,' she had proven her acting ability in the TV mini-series, 'he said I should ask you: you wouldn't want me to go to the police.'

'Yes, you did the right thing. You see, Jada, I've told you this before, the slightest hint of scandal — people like to believe the worst, a judge, me — people have always liked to believe the worst of me.' His ego was all. 'Did you see him when you left your flat?'

'No. There isn't a 'phone box; it must have been from one of the other flats or houses on the wharf.'

'Not necessarily; it might have been a car 'phone. Is he going to contact you again?' He didn't doubt her for a moment.

'He said — he said he was going to come to the flat tonight. How did he get my address, Russel? What about my 'phone number? I'm scared.' She had appeared on the verge of tears. 'What's it about, Russel? Did you do something?'

'Yes,' he said tersely. 'I did. It was a long time ago. I'm not proud of it, you understand; it's something Mick and your mother knew about,' he invoked the uncontradicting dead. 'There were some people who had done me a lot of harm. They almost wrecked my life. Someone else was, well, threatening them. I could have warned them. I didn't. That's what he's talking about: it must be.'

Jada interrupted her account to say to me:

'It was what you told me about; the chambers. But twisted so it sounded like nothing serious.' She continued: 'I asked if he knew who it was.'

'Not for sure. It's possible, there are one or two people. You have to understand, Jada, I didn't do anything wrong. I just, well, I didn't go out of my way to help people who had hurt me.'

'I understand, Russel. I know you wouldn't do anything that was wrong. What do you want me to do? Should I go to the police?'

'No. It's impossible. What time did he say he was coming?'

'He didn't say. He just said tonight: anytime after seven. He said to have the money there.'

'How much?'

'Twenty thousand pounds. What do you want me to do, Russel? I want to help you. I want to do the right thing. Surely, if you talked to the police, if you explained . . .'

'I said, it's impossible.' He glanced at his watch. 'I have to be in court.'

'I've got a recording session tonight. I'll cancel it. I'll see him. I'll give him the money,' she had sobbed. 'I don't want anything to happen to you, Russel.'

'No. Don't be silly. I'll see him of course. I'll be there at seven. Don't worry. Keep to your session. Have you got a spare key?'

She shook her head.

'I can get one; I can drop it in here at lunch.' She did have one with her, but it would have been too obvious to admit it.

Before she left, he hugged her tightly to his robed chest.

'It'll be alright, you'll see. I'll take care of it. I always do, don't I?'

Carson had the harder task. And the most dangerous. We had to take the greatest risk to ensure her safety. I felt like an assassin who had only one shot in his gun, and only one chance to use it.

Walker was only a locally powerful man. He was not a rich man, but a big small businessman, a local power in an insignificant community, impressive to the likes of Ambleton but not otherwise. He did not have troops to call upon, nor Orbach's skill at manipulating others to do his will.

No one is more dangerous than his Achilles' heel. Walker had one weak spot that we knew about: his son Stephen, with whom we had already established something of a relationship, though from the conversation on the plane — when it touched on Carson herself — it was not one to be relied on. If we could manipulate Stephen, I had no doubt at all we could manipulate his father.

She waited until mid-afternoon before going to the workshop to see Stephen. Fortunately, he was alone again. He didn't look displeased to see her: like other clumsy and physically cowardly people, he admired unduly those with agility and fighting ability; she had taken much of the lead in reassuring him; though uneducated, he was a sensitive man, and she had shown him consideration. We had forced him to acknowledge that his father had fixed his case for him, and informed him who had paid what price. The bonds of secrecy between us were not insubstantial.

Carson, too, later provided me with a full account though I guessed there was a lot more re-creation in it than reconstruction.

'Why have you come here?' He sounded less surprised than he ought to have been.

'You said last time that you wanted to help your father?'

'Yes, I remember.'

'I think he's in trouble, Stephen; I think maybe he's in bad trouble.'

'You said you'd keep him out of it,' he accused half-heartedly but without challenging the assertion.

'We have, this far; we can only do so much. We're not responsible for everything he does.'

'What're you saying? What's he done?' He asked listlessly, a protest without conviction.

She had been surprised initially at how easily he accepted the details as she laid them out for him Later, as they drove together to see his father, he said he had read about Battle — it was a bigger story locally than nationally; without wanting to admit it to himself, he had sensed his father's involvement; he confirmed that he had — reluctantly, he insisted, only under questioning by him, not until after my second visit — told his father about us. He realised his father was distressed, he knew something was badly wrong — he just hadn't known what to do about it, or even how to ask. Without telling his wife how it had all started, he hadn't been able to seek her guidance. Carson was quickly his confessor. He was ripe for penance.

'I want to see your father, Stephen.'

'What for?'

'I told you — Dave told you — we're not interested in hurting him; it's Orbach we're after. But your father, well,' she shrugged, 'he's the key, the only key.'

He thought about this for a while, then shook his head:

'If it's like you say, then he's safe, isn't he? I mean,' he had the grace to blush, 'now.'

'Waterbottom didn't have anything to do with the original fix, did he?'

'I don't know.'

'Well Battle certainly wasn't anything to do with it.'

'So what?'

'So if it can come out once it can come out again. Don't you see, Stephen? It's not going to remain hidden forever. It's going to happen again and maybe again and again. There're some things, well, you can't keep hold of forever . . .' She hesitated, then plunged on: 'Some things have to be undone, Stephen.'

'What do you mean? They can't be brought back,' he said dully, halfway to her answer.

'Big wrongs, Stephen . . .' Require big rights.

'Right,' he muttered.

She said, almost tenderly:

'It's time for him to do the right thing, Stephen; you too.' She reminded him it was on his account it had begun.

'I know,' he said quietly. 'I know what you mean. What do you want me to do?'

'I want you to try to persuade him to help; I want you to fix it for me to see him '

'He won't see you,' he shook his head.

'Not on my own, no.'

'What's this about?', Nick Walker asked aggressively as soon as his son and companion were shown in. 'Who's this?' He studied Carson curiously, then snapped his fingers. 'I know you. You were . . .'

'Correct, I was; but I have an alibi up to here and I've already been eliminated from their enquiries by the police. Have you?' She went straight onto the offensive.

He paled but blustered:

'I don't know what you're talking about. Why should they want to talk to me? I'm on the police committee. I'm a councillor. What are you doing here?'

'Calm down, Mr Walker; I'm not here to do you any harm; I promise you.' Compared to what he deserved, it was the truth.

'Why were the police looking for you?'

'I'd been seen with Waterbottom.'

Nick revolved the swivel chair behind his desk and scowled at his son:

'Why've you brought her here? What's this about?' With difficulty and perhaps without precedent, Stephen stood up to his father:

'You should listen to her, Dad. Please. I know . . . I know what this is about.' He had flushed, then said in a rush, like he'd been rehearsing it in the car: 'I know about the Mellors, Dad. I know what happened at court. I don't . . . I didn't . . I'm sorry, Dad,' he tailed off in a gruff whisper. 'I never meant to cause you trouble; I never meant you to do something like that on my account.'

Walker was torn in two. He knew he ought to deny any knowledge of what his son was talking about, because Carson was present; if he denied it, he was also denying his son in his moment of shame. He said cautiously:

'You've never been a trouble, son; the things that have happened — well, they happened, right. I wanted . . . I've wanted to help you. You've nothing to apologise for. But, mind now, I'm not saying I understand what you mean about the Mellors, right.'

'Or Brian Battle?' Carson asked.

'Who's Brian Battle?'

'Don't you read your paper, Mr Walker? You recognised me quick enough.'

'The journalist in the sea, right. What's it got to do with me? I didn't know him I never met him.'

She snorted. It didn't require any acting ability.

Walker avoided his son's eyes. The son who could positively link him to Battle and who was on this woman's side. He was visibly shrivelling before Carson's eyes.

He placed his certainly sweaty palms face down on the desk as if he was about to use them to lever himself into an upright position. Carson said:

'I've got a proposition for you, Mr Walker; it's an interesting proposition and I think you'll regret it if you don't hear me out; maybe for the rest of your life. I know your son agrees with me.'

'Go on.' He struggled for an appropriate sarcastic epithet with which to cling on to his pride. 'Entertain me.'

'It's all about Orbach. All and only. He's all I'm interested in. If you help me get him, you can put all of this behind you.' She was unmoved by the overwhelming enormity of what she was saying; so apparently was he. She paused to watch his reaction; behind the scepticism lay a glimmer of hope. 'I'm working for someone whose name you'll know, the singer, Jada Jarrynge. You know her name?'

He shrugged indifferently.

'I don't listen to music much. I don't have the time.'

'Did you know Orbach has a little girl living with him? A little black girl. Her parents were the Mellors, who died in a plane crash; a plane you had the maintenance contract on.'

'I remember. Yes, there was a child. I knew she went to live with Orbach. Right.'

'The woman — Eartha — had another daughter — much older — that's Jada Jarrynge.'

He was more interested in hearing where this was leading than where it came from.

'Jada knows the crash wasn't an accident . . .'

'That's rubbish; there was an investigation; no one had tampered with that plane; people who fly, they know the risks . . .' The sequence of Carson's argument was too quick to accept without an automatic denial.

'The investigation was inconclusive. What is conclusive is that you rigged a soft sentence for Stephen, from Orbach, a few months beforehand.'

He still wouldn't look at his son while he challenged her: 'So what? It's a coincidence. You can't prove there's any connection.'

Carson shook her head.

'No. That's what I'm here about; to try to persuade you to help us prove it. There's no other way.'

'Yes, right, why should I do that? Even if it were true — which it isn't,' he remembered to add. 'I'd be putting my head in a noose.' As England has no death penalty this was not quite accurate, unless he meant he'd rather top himself than do time.

As in the law of physics, she was using the sheer weight of what he had done against himself.

'They won't prosecute. He's a High Court judge — you know that. It's what he's always told you,' she guessed. 'It's true; and if they can't prosecute him, they can't prosecute you.'

He shook his head slowly, bewildered.

'Then why should I? Why take the risk? What can you do with it?'

She said:

'I want you to talk to Jada, Mr Walker; I want you to make a statement to her; it's enough for her to get the child away from him; it's enough to get him off the bench, Mr Walker. That's what she wants; it's all she wants.'

'What would be in it for me?'

Carson had gone as far as she was able on her own. Stephen chipped in on cue:

'Dad. Listen. You can't get away with it. I've seen you, the last week; you're unhappy, Dad. It'll come out in the end and then, well, it's not just you, is it?' It was Stephen, too, who would be exposed, which would make all of it utterly pointless.

'Mr Walker, listen to your son, listen to me. Orbach's crazy. You must know that now. Do you think he's going to leave you out here, leave you alone, with what you know about him? How long for?'

'There was never any trouble before . . .' He meant after the Mellors died.

'He wasn't there, Mr Walker, was he?'

It was a significant difference from Battle.

'What about Woolf?'

'He's already made a statement to the police that he saw nothing: even if he changed his statement, they couldn't use it to prosecute because of the risk a jury wouldn't believe it. Mr Walker, what we're asking is for you to help us — all of us, Jada Jarrynge, Dave, hell England,' she appealed to his patriotism: he was, after all, a Conservative councillor. 'Help us get rid of him.

I'll be honest with you: there's no way we could ever link Orbach to the Mellors' death without you; not enough.'

His eyes narrowed.

'There's no way you could ever link it to me, either — without me, right.'

'Correct. Especially so long ago. But it's not the same for Battle. And who knows what'll come up about Waterbottom.'

Stephen shook his big head slowly, awed by the schedule of the dead for whom his father was responsible.

'Dad. Dad. I don't know what to say. I feel, like, well, I'm to blame, 'cos it started for me, 'cos I called you when Battle came. But I never, I never thought . . . I'd never have believed . . .'

'But you do?' Nick Walker snapped as he swung towards his son. 'Why? Why believe her? Why believe her instead of me — instead of your father?'

There were tears tumbling slowly and singly from Stephen's eyes:

'Tell me then it's not true, none of it; tell me, Dad; I'll believe you.' He sniffed: 'You know me, Dad, I'm not that clever, I don't do everything right, I don't see everything right, everyone always said I was stupid but you never did, Dad.'

They sat in silence for what Carson insisted was at least five minutes, but was probably about thirty seconds. Eventually, she broke it.

'Listen to me, Mr Walker. You're scared of Orbach. Everyone's scared of Orbach. He's used you, Mr Walker, taken you over; you're not your own man anymore.' There was a latent challenge in this: she wondered if he would spot it; it was the reason Stephen's support was so essential. 'Help us now and you're free of him. He'll have no power left; he'll be a broken man; there's no risk: no prosecution, Orbach finished, you're off the hook, Mr Walker — the hook he put you on.'

For a time she thought she'd lost but the imperative of his son's presence brought him to the otherwise unachievable pitch.

'It's true,' he mumbled. 'I never wanted to. I put myself in his debt; I never knew what it might mean. You've got to understand. Stephen,' he spoke as if he had forgotten he was there, 'it would have finished him, finished his marriage — she would have left him — the way his mother left me.' He buried his head in his hands and his shoulders jerked, but there was no sound of tears. His son got up and walked awkwardly around the desk, resting a meaty hand on his father's shoulders.

Eventually, he looked up, but he didn't brush his son's hand away.

'I lost my head. I didn't mean to kill Waterbottom, Orbach didn't know about that beforehand. I didn't hurt Battle that badly, not to begin with. I've never, well, never killed anyone before, not with my hands,' he corrected before Carson could mention the Mellors.

He hesitated again but now that he'd begun it was pointless not to finish: 'I've never even fought anyone really. I went to see if Battle was telling me the truth. To see if he'd told anyone else. Funny thing was, such a little man, he stood up to me better than Battle. I hit him too hard. I don't know if it killed him, the first time. But after that there weren't any choices left and, well,' he added apologetically, 'it seemed — just then, not now — it seemed as if it couldn't make any more difference.' Not to him; only to Battle. 'It was Orbach worked the rest of it out. No,' he looked Carson straight in the eye: 'I was responsible too. Right. I know that. I'm sorry for what I've done. I can't make it right any other way. I'll do it. What do you want me to do?'

The encounter between Orbach and Walker was over much quicker than I had expected. But, then, there was a number of aspects of it that I hadn't expected. For example, I hadn't expected Walker to be armed. Orbach, on the other hand, obviously had. The very first sound we heard, almost as the door opened, was some sort of thump, a howl of pain, a grunt and then the noise of furniture falling. For a couple of minutes, there was silence, save for a brief series of clicks I couldn't identify — maybe Orbach was doing rosary.

'What's happening?' Jada whispered.

I shrugged. I didn't know.

After a while, Orbach spoke.

'Come on, Walker, get up, I didn't hit you that hard.'

When he got no response, we heard him moving about the flat, then running water — the cold jug cure. My heart went out to Walker — Sandy sometimes did it to me when I O.D.'d on Southern Comfort; there's nothing worse.

'You bloody fool, Walker. What did you think? I'd wait patiently until you pointed it at me? Did you forget I knew you belonged to a club? I didn't, I never forget — anything.'

I cursed myself for my stupidity and carelessness. Walker was supposed to have believed he was going to see Jada, was supposed to have decided to help, but I ought not to have expected him to be entirely without suspicion. Orbach himself had told me that Walker was a member of a gun club. I hadn't warned Carson.

And what else did I expect Orbach to do? I had intended him either to suspect or even to feel sure that Walker was who he was going to meet at Jada's flat. I wondered what he had hit him with and where. It was difficult to imagine Orbach in the act of physical violence: I associated him exclusively with its planning; I had forgotten my own theory — he had no one left to do it for him.

It was possible the scene I had set was about to come to an unscheduled ending. I couldn't think about the implications while I was listening, but it might go beyond what even the silken Schofield would be able to keep a lid on, and in turn that would render my part of it more open to scrutiny than I had intended.

I was listening from the flat roof. The recording session Jada had planned for that night was in her own home. Friends from the music business had wired it as professionally as any spies might have done. We had wondered about setting it up for vision too: a remote or sound or movement-triggered video camera. But there was no way to eliminate a whirr within the apartment without the sort of sophisticated equipment it would have taken much longer to acquire. There would be no other sounds to cover it up. I didn't think Orbach and Walker would be playing music to dance by.

Stephen Walker had wanted to come with his father, Carson told me later. His father refused, ordered him back to his wife and children. Stephen had reluctantly obeyed. He had asked his father to ring him later and then, when his father was already in Sandy's car, as he walked Carson around to the driver's door, he asked her too to let him know. She squeezed his hand:

'It's the right thing, Stephen.'

They had driven in almost total silence. Once, Nick had asked what part of London they were passing through. Just once, he repeated what he had said at his own office:

'I'm sorry for what I've done; I am, right.' As if he was trying to remind himself.

She told me later: 'I ought to have been scared when he said he didn't want Stephen to come with him.' The man had personally and brutally murdered two men within the last few days. 'But I didn't even think of it until we were almost there.' Nor did she think of it when he went to fetch his coat — and gun. 'He was too pathetic; he was like a child who had been found out doing something wrong, being taken to his parents for punishment. It made me think — killers aren't so different; they're ordinary people, too; people like you and me.'

We looked at each other; we had disobeyed the same commandment. We belonged to the same club — those who had passed judgment on another human being. Orbach had done it; we were doing it to him.

As they reached Jada's door, Carson told him to go ahead alone, she had to go back to the car. He looked at her strangely, like he knew, but all he did was nod and point at the door to the flat to check it was the right one. She said:

'Go on in; it's open.'

'Put it away, Orbach,' Walker said at long last.

'Why did you do it, Walker? Did you really think she'd meet you here without telling me?'

'I don't know what you're talking about.' Then: 'You're the one who got me here. Is this what for?' In his shock, he believed Carson was on the other side, Orbach's side. 'Go on, go ahead, do it,' Walker dared. 'I'm not afraid, right.' I could smell his sweat glands from the roof.

'I said tell me why you thought you could get away with it.' Orbach's authority did not seem to have been undermined by the challenge. 'What were you going to sell her? How much were you going to tell her? How dare you? How dare you approach my family?' His voice rose in controlled anger.

Jada whispered:

'Shouldn't we do something?'

I shook my head. I wasn't armed.

'You can't do nothing,' she hissed.

'Watch me, Jada. Just keep telling yourself, it's your mother's killers talking.'

'Why did you bring me here?' Walker asked.

'What game are you trying to play, Walker? You rang Jada. You came here. You, were going to tell her about her mother, weren't you?'

Silence. I imagined Walker frowning with effort. The idea of Carson as Orbach's moll no longer rang true. Slowly, unsure of himself, Walker said:

'Yes, I was. Not for money, right. It's gone too far, Orbach. First the Mellors, then Waterbottom, then Battle. I was frightened. She frightened me. My son wanted me to talk.'

'Your son? How does he know? You told me you'd never ...'

'I didn't,' Walker said. 'Your woman did,' he probed.

'Jada? What are you talking about, Walker? Make sense, man'

'Not Jada. I never met Jada. I came here to meet her, right. So I was told,' he added.

'What do you mean — "my woman"?'

'The Australian. The one who was there before.' Which had led Orbach to me.

'Woolf's girl,' Orbach snapped.

It was a good thing Carson wasn't with us on the roof or there would have been another outburst of violence. She had gone back to the car to await the outcome and to cover the door to the building faster than we could if it proved necessary.

'Tell me exactly what happened, Walker? This is a set-up. Good Lord,' the point finally dawned. 'Jada? Jada's a part of it?' He sucked in his breath so loudly it registered on the tape-recorder. In a puzzled tone, he said: 'But I trusted her. I loved her almost as much as I love Frankie. How could she?'

'You killed her mother,' Walker said as if it was something he might have forgotten. 'We killed her mother.'

'Yes, yes, I know,' he brushed it aside as trivial. 'But she didn't. How could she know? Woolf. Woolf told her. Why would she believe him? When? Since the flight?'

'You said Woolf's a private detective as well as a solicitor, right.' Walker was surprisingly in command. 'Who was he working for, Orbach?'

After a moment, Orbach answered:

'Jada. Jada was who he was working for. It has to be. What has she told Frankie?'

There was another, much longer silence. Then Orbach again:

'She set this up. She set me up. She set you up. What for? I wonder. Yes, I see it.' His voice was clinical now, analytical. 'They thought we'd fight, perhaps they thought we'd kill each other, that's it, that must be it. What do you think?' He didn't wait for an answer. 'Perhaps they're right,' he mused. 'Perhaps that's right. I shouldn't trust you. I can't trust you. You've told your son . . .'

It was the wrong person for Orbach to mention. It made Stephen, too, vulnerable. As long as Orbach was alive, his son was as much at risk as Nick Walker. Orbach must have realised the mistake, because next we heard Walker.

'What are you going to do?' he asked, the pitch of his voice the only indication to us on the roof that the question might not be entirely disinterested. 'Here, Orbach? Here in her apartment?' Then: 'Go on,' in a calm, resigned tone of voice. 'Go on then. It doesn't matter. It doesn't matter anymore. I'd rather. Go on, Orbach, do it,' he shouted.

I had physically to restrain Jada during the prolonged silence that followed. Once I was sure she was back in control of herself, I crawled to the side of the roof and waved down at Carson to warn her it was coming to a head. She pointed at herself and then at the building's front door to ask if she was supposed to go in. I shook my head violently enough for her to understand that she was to stay in the car and out of sight.

When I got back to the tape, nothing was still what was happening. Jada was biting her lower lip. I lit a cigarette. She didn't tell me not to. Then I heard a chair scraping as it was pushed back. Orbach said crisply, as if announcing his decision in court on a point of law: 'No. It would be too easy, far too easy.'

There was a loud clank, like something thrown onto a hard floor or table top, then the sound of the door pulled shut behind him.

Jada rose. I pushed her back onto the roof-top and told her to pack the gear up and, to make sure it was done before I entered the apartment, switched off the tape-recorder myself. Unless she made a deliberate decision to turn it back on, she would not now be able to hear, which was what I wanted. Then I dropped back through the hatch into the corridor. Orbach had gone. The door was shut. I used my key to let myself in. I tried but failed to do it silently.

Walker was still sitting, presumably in the same place he'd been told to sit when he came in. He turned to look at me. He'd last seen me in the pub in Southend. He nodded, as if he was expecting me. He picked up the gun and pointed it at me.

'Ah,' I said brightly, but mostly because it was the only sound I could squeeze round the lump in my throat. 'I don't think that's a good idea,' I said eventually.

He said tiredly:

'You're full of good ideas you are, right.'

'I didn't start it, Mr Walker. You can't pretend it's not your responsibility.'

'No? People've got away with worse, right.'

'I don't know; perhaps. I'm sorry we tricked you.'

'You used my son,' he said flatly. 'You tricked my son too.'

'Only a little bit, Mr Walker. I promise you only a little bit.' Why did he snarl at my use of the word promise? 'You had to see for yourself, to see you'd never be safe from Orbach.'

'Why did I have to see? Do you think I'm that stupid? I believed your girl: she was working for you after all, wasn't she?' He rushed on: 'I knew it for myself. I've always known it would be me took the blame, not him.'

'That's not quite what I meant.'

'I know what you meant, right. Don't treat me like an idiot.' He didn't like it any more than I did. 'I've done bad things; I know that; I told your girl, I'm sorry for them; but I'm not a fool, right. I just wanted, always, I just wanted my son . . . I wanted my son to have a better home than I ever gave him. Can't you understand that? Have you got a kid?'

'Oh, yeah. And I want to live to see him grow up. I need your help, Mr Walker, to help me do so.'

He looked at me peculiarly. He was right to tell me not to treat him as an idiot. He was way ahead of me. He said:

'He won't go up.'

'I think I can make him.'

He shook his head slowly, still not lowering the gun.

'Until now, I would have said the only man I knew who could make him do it was himself. Maybe, I don't know. You've got this far.'

He was talking about the same thing Orbach had taught me: all you can ever do is make people do things that — at some level — they want to do. I said:

'The trick is to make him think he wants to do it.'

'How?'

I moved slowly, the gun following me, to the cane chair in which Jada had sat the night I visited her and extracted a small microphone. He smiled thinly:

'I thought of that. He didn't.'

'Why didn't you tell him?'

'I didn't want to listen anymore.'

'No. But he will.'

'I won't,' he said suddenly. 'Not to him, not to you.'

'Wait,' I said.

He turned the gun around and placed the barrel at his mouth. I said:

'If you do it, you leave your son to Orbach, Mr Walker.'

'It seems my son can take care of himself,' he said, though not without a measure of doubt. He gripped the barrel of the gun between his teeth.

I tried another tack.

'Fine. But you know what I want. If you won't help me — be there to help me — I'll ask Stephen to, Mr Walker. You know he will.'

His eyes widened, then blinked once to tell me he had understood; it hadn't made a difference.

I lunged across the room as he pulled the trigger. I fell into his lap as we both belatedly realised that nothing had happened: Stunned, he slumped back, the hand carrying the gun pointing loosely down at the floor. I crawled off him before he thought I'd confused father and son and took offence. He let me take the gun from his hand. I opened it. The chamber was empty and, when I extracted it, so was the clip. I realised then what the clicking noise had been after Orbach hit Walker: he had been unloading the gun; he had never intended it to be used — not by Walker, nor even by himself, not even at the very end when it seemed as if he was threatening to kill Walker. What the hell was he playing at?

CHAPTER ELEVEN

The next day was the last day. It was the beginning of our final weekend in Sandy's house. Completion was due right after the long, end of May, Bank Holiday weekend. Jada could not stay at her flat until it was over but was unwilling to stay away from town. Carson took her to the flat above the club overnight. In the morning, they all came over, along with Tom, to help Sandy in the final packing and other preparatory removals.

I had work to do, one more piece of the puzzle to put into place: it was the piece for which I had needed Nigel Morris. The meeting could not take place any sooner; nor could it be postponed. Reluctantly, Morris deserted the magnificent Mimi and met me by arrangement in a pub near his office. He was accompanied by a gap-toothed, black-bearded, bulky, ugly, unkempt man wearing a worn leather jacket, a battered hat and smoking an untipped Gauloise. Morris introduced us:

'Dave W-woolf, S-sean McCarthy.' He turned to McCarthy: 'D-dave has told me what he w-w-wants you to do; it's got the p-p-papal blessing.' Their mutual boss, the newspaper magnate who owned the book publishing company. 'I don't know exactly why D-dave w-wants things done this way,' he held up a hand to forestall any interruption by me, 'I don't w-want to know.' He was a shrewd man. 'I've sp-spoken to the l-lawyers: th-they can't see anything il-l-legal in it except l-l-libel and I have D-dave's w-word,' he looked at me balefully, as if there could be nothing quite so unreliable, 'It won't be shown to anyone who could s-s-sue.' This was true: it is not a libel if the person written about is the only person to whom you publish it.

He got up to leave. The floor creaked as he exited. McCarthy said, 'Did the earth move for you too?'

'Another drink?'

'Sure,' said Sean.

To gain a little time to get the measure of the man, I asked about his relations with Brian Battle. I had assumed they were friends.

'Lord, no. The man had no friends. He was a pig. That was why he was loaned out to Morris. That was why the editor agreed to his taking a break. Anything to get him out of the newsroom.'

'It was just an impression I got, from your piece on him.' An account of his death that doubled as an obituary: they didn't want to waste too much space on him.

'I took everything I thought and turned it on its head. Worked well, didn't it?'

I said:

'You couldn't care if they don't catch his killer, then?'

'Yes, I'd care. He took my bloody chance away.' His eyes narrowed: 'What's this all about?'

'What have you been told?'

'You want a story written — a dummy Sunday — tomorrow's date — it'll probably never get published properly.'

'Right.'

It wasn't completely correct, only in part. With Orbach dead, Jada's thinly-veiled accusation would be publishable. Though it would arouse press interest and possibly some modest investigation, none of the participants would be available to feed it or to keep it alive. Later elements of the tale would have to remain unpublished — I was doing this in order to survive, not to put my own head into a noose.

I selected my words with extreme care and prejudice.

'I have someone so important there is no prospect at all of his being prosecuted, nor of any paper — including yours — risking publication of what I have.' No paper would go ahead without their own research: authentication of tapes, sworn affidavits, they would be bound to give Orbach the opportunity to comment, and the sheer enormity of that exercise is what finally would persuade them to abandon it or turn it over to the authorities, which in the circumstances would be the same as spiking the story or, as they probably do nowadays, wiping the floppy disk.

He looked at me sceptically:

'I didn't think she went in for cold-blooded murder, not personally.' I took it he meant the Prime Minister not the Queen. 'So as it can't be published, you want to make it look as if it can be, has been. Right?'

I nodded once. He was stumbling preciously close to the whole point: the purpose Nigel Morris had the foresight to foreswear all knowledge of. The evidence of the confrontation between Orbach and Walker would not be enough on its own:

Orbach would laugh at a mere recording; would tell me I would never get it published. McCarthy asked me:

'Why?'

'I want to spook him. I think I can spook him into panicking. I think that might, uh, let's just say it might be a helpful thing to happen.'

'Help who? Help what?'

'Help make sure he doesn't get away with it,' I turned and looked him straight in the face. 'Or anything like it again.'

He understood I was saying it was in his own interests not to press me any further. He said:

'I know about you. I know a hell of lot about you.' He told me. He did. He knew most of what there was to know, informally, off the record, the same Fleet Street scuttlebut Nigel Morris had picked up but in much greater and more thorough detail. He said: 'And none of it ever gets printed, and no one ever gets into court. That's your style. Right?'

'Seems that way,' I admitted. 'Not of my choosing, you understand.'

'What you're saying,' he concluded, a crafty smile creeping across the black holes in his mouth, 'it's going to happen again. Only this time, you want me to help you control the outcome. Is that about right?'

'Something like that.'

'You've got nerve. You want me to set up the best story of my life, and never see it in print. You want me to trust you to know what the right outcome is.'

'I just want to be sure I've got it right.' He shook his head in mock disbelief.

'I want you to help make sure Battle's murderer doesn't walk free. And, well,' I shrugged, 'for what it's worth, your employers seem to trust me.'

He thought for a moment, then asked:

'What do you need me to do? When?'

I told him. He frowned, then nodded:

'Not much time. But it can be done. It'd be a change to write the truth for once. I just hope you're right; I hope it is the truth.'

'It is,' I said as I flashed him the tape. 'You got somewhere we can listen to this in private?'

Which is how, very late on Saturday night, instead of relaxing for the next-to-last time in our old home with my old woman and our young child, I was a few houses down from where we'd be living come Tuesday, banging at the door, waiting for Orbach to answer it, so I could play at newspaper delivery boy.

Nick Walker had gone straight back to Southend by taxi. I had no doubts about his commitment to the cause. Unless Orbach, too, had gone directly to the airport, Walker would be ahead of him. If he flew off without my final shove, I was so much the cleaner and that was so much the better. No part of what I felt involved the necessity for me to do it for myself.

I had spoken to Walker twice during the day and Orbach still hadn't shown up. Earlier in the evening, while they were still unpacking — by the sound of it, with the help of a couple of bottles of wine — at the new house, I rang for Sandy to pop into the street and she came back to confirm that there were lights on in his house.

He came to the door. He nodded at me, as if he had been waiting for me. He was wearing slippers, but was otherwise dressed. He had on the Norwegian cardigan with its steel buckles in which he had greeted me when I first went to his Highgate apartment during Disraeli Chambers, or one that looked like it. He was freshly-shaven, his customarily unruly hair tidily in place, his eyes shone brightly, excitedly.

I asked if I could come in and he held the door back for me. He put a finger to his lip as he led the way to the living-room. I knew from an earlier visit that Frankie still sometimes suffered nightmares from her parents' death, and accordingly slept with the door open. We didn't speak until we were out of her earshot.

Then I handed him the first, previous night's copy of the next day's paper, holding it open so that he could read the headline:

'MR JUSTICE MURDERER: POPSTAR JADA'S J'ACCUSE!'

He stood as he read the story on the front page, spiced with selections from the transcript of the tape we'd made, including Orbach's opening remarks, and the exchange between Walker and Orbach in which they'd said:

'It's gone too far, Orbach. First the Mellors, then Waterbottom, then Battle.'

'Your son? How does he know?'

And:

'You killed her mother. We killed her mother.'

'Yes, yes, I know.'

He tossed the paper aside as if contained nothing that interested him.

'I suppose it goes back a long way. I don't know. How far back does one have to go to find out who is the real self? A minute after birth, an hour, a month, a year? I was one of six children. Five of them, pouring over the cliff of my psyche like lemmings,' he repeated a pat phrase he had obviously used often before. The outrage was emphatic: 'my' psyche. 'That surprises you, doesn't it? You thought I was an only child, a spoiled only child. Or did you think I was born a bastard who wouldn't know if he had any brothers and sisters?'

He laughed briefly.

'Well, I wasn't an only child and I wasn't spoiled. Anything but. Oh, of course we had all our material needs taken care of, we wanted for nothing that way. My father wasn't wealthy. He was a doctor. The money came from my mother's side. But it was a big family to cope with, even for the times, though they both came from yet larger. My father was one of ten, my mother one of seven. My father suffered from his inability to provide for us all, to the high standards my mother expected. It made him broody, withdrawn, but subject to occasional outbursts of anger and affection in equally immoderate proportions. My mother, the princess: she saw no reason why so many children should interfere with her social life; that's what nannies were for. My father had a different idea of what nannies were for; we got through them fast; that was his revenge.'

He paused to recollect the point of his account.

'Yes, that was it. You see, from the very beginning, from as far back as I can remember, I always felt I was different, I was special, I wasn't like others — ordinary people. Does every child feel that way? I don't know,' and he didn't want an answer in case, belatedly, it undermined this all-important criterion by which he was to have lived the whole of his life.

He went on:

'I was disappointed; from the earliest years of my life: disappointed that I'd been born to these banal people, disappointed in the boring ordinariness of my siblings, disappointed I had to compete with them for my parents' attention and affection, disappointed I had to do all the things expected of me that I hadn't determined for myself, disappointed down to the last detail —

the hand-me-downs and small meannesses and ostensible gener-
osities that were never what I wanted but always what someone
else thought I wanted or thought I ought to want. Disappointed, too, that others didn't seem to understand my particular,
special position.'

He stopped for a full minute, then:

'I haven't spoken to any of my brothers and sisters in, oh,
five years — not since my mother's death, when we all went to
the funeral. My father died a long time ago,' he added paren-
thetically. 'We were such strangers, we weren't sure whether to
offer each other condolences. There's a lot of accident in life. I
thought, who is that man — the accountant with the balding
head, the paunch bigger than mine, the ill-fitting suit and above
all with the wife I had not met since his wedding and the adult
son I had perhaps met twice in my life. This is my older brother
I am talking about; I told myself I was supposed to love him,
care about him, care if ill befell him — but I wouldn't have noticed if he was no longer alive and I doubt I would have gone to
his funeral if it was inconvenient for me to do so.'

He was bragging about his uncompromising honesty.

'And the others — in their different ways, their different
identities, their different lives — meaningless. No love, no feeling, nothing. What offended me most was my middle brother —
I was second from last — he's a very successful man, in the city,
and he was making a big show out of us, out of the brothers and
sisters, a show for the wider family and friends, as if there was still
something there between us all, as if there ever had been. Well,
I suppose it's his trade: selling stocks and shares in companies
without assets.' Hypocrisy had always been his biggest bugbear.

I could and perhaps should have stopped him but I wanted to
know; before it was over, I wanted to know. He continued:

'They told me, later on, but when I was still a youngster, they told me I was always the one who was the worst trouble. As a baby, I screamed the loudest, I made the biggest mess. I was naughty — always naughty, they called me. But not a nice naughty, as you might use the word about an impish child, a child with spirit, a child who challenges the rules because he wants to understand them or even because he wants to beat them. They meant evil naughty.'

He spoke with pride of the profit he had extracted from this putative peculiarity.

'I'm not sure why. At least, not why it began. I don't believe in inherent qualities, or defects; I don't believe anyone is born bad or whatever word you want to use. But something in the aspects of my family cast a shadow over me from so early on I can't remember a time without it. I can't remember a single moment of happiness in my childhood; I can only remember always, always the bitterness of the struggle.'

'Struggle for what?'

'I'm not sure. To survive is the expression that comes easiest to mind, but survival was never really in doubt. Perhaps that's it. Perhaps I didn't want to survive. I think . . . I think I was always so damned disappointed, each day disappointed, and hoping against hope that something would happen to give me some sense of joy, or hope, but it never did. I think, above all, I was disappointed in myself. I think that's true. I think that dates from a very early age. I was disappointed in me.'

'What does that mean?'

'Just that I didn't admire myself, I didn't think I was making a good job of being me, of demonstrating how different I was from all the others. They weren't noticing, so I was failing. In turn, I grew contemptuous of myself, for my failure. Do you see?'

Again he did not wait for an answer.

'I went through phases. When I first went to school, for the first couple of years I was always top of the class. It was a great shock when one week someone else came out equal first. Then I stopped, just like that. During one term, I went from the top to nearly the bottom. They don't do it anymore, even in that sort of school,' he meant private, fee-paying schools; 'But then they marked us each week. What was I trying to do?'

I watched him speculate, visibly straining with the effort. He said:

'It's difficult to know, without discounting hindsight. I wanted to be liked. I'm sure of that. Perhaps I stopped working in order to make myself more popular. Why was I unpopular? Because I was always top of the form? Because I didn't conceal my satisfaction at it? Because I competed too openly for it? But if it wasn't there to be competed for, to be satisfied about winning, then what on earth was it there for?'

This was one I thought I could answer:

'To show you knew how to be a good winner?'

'How to play the game?' He smiled: 'Perhaps.' He wasn't interested in my interventions. 'Then there was the Jewish thing. I suppose I could put it like this,' he started to explain, as if he had forgotten that I was too. 'As an outsider, you think you always have to try harder just to keep up — it's their culture, their world, they belong and it seems as if it must all come so easily to them. But actually I didn't need to try harder. I was at least as good as them all along, probably better. So then I went to the other extreme in order to try and fit in; the desire for assimilation, the immigrant's traditional weakness. I was probably working harder to come bottom than to come out top. What do you think, Dave?'

This time he seemed to want me to speak.

'I don't know, Russel. I've never known; I mean, I've never known what makes you tick the way you do. I've only ever known that something was very badly wrong with it.'

'It's as good a definition of insanity as any I ever heard; fortunately,' he replied dryly, 'not one known to the law.'

Another prolonged pause. He got up from his leather armchair to fetch and place within easy reach the bottle of scotch from which he'd earlier poured himself an uncharacteristically substantial slug. I already had my bottle at my feet.

'I don't want to relive my schooldays. I think I've probably described the path enough for you to understand it. Veering between showing them what I could do when and if I wanted and showing them too how I could turn it all on its head, mocking them by failing as much as I was mocking them when I won. It was all so easy. They never understood: not my parents, not my teachers, not my brothers and sisters either. I could do whatever I wanted and they never found out how I was fooling them. They looked for reasons, psychological explanations, just some way to understand the way I swung to and fro. It was the same when I left school.'

I knew he had not followed the conventional route from school to college to bar course into practice. He had been at sea for a while, in the merchant marine — the Norwegian merchant marine, which was the origin of his relationship with that country and knowledge of its tongue. Then he had come back, done exams at a crammer and gone on to study law at university. I was to understand now that he had been poking two fingers at their system by leaving school when he wasn't supposed to, simply in order to come back and show them it was not for want of ability to master it.

A pattern was emerging. Thus, he had become a left-wing lawyer, which traditionally was a course followed by those lacking a marked academic bent — whether from want of interest or ability; accordingly, Orbach had also to show off by becoming a successful scholar in his subject. He was one of the founders of Disraeli Chambers: therefore he had to break up with them and prove he could make it at the straight, non-political bar. He had bettered law, so he had to better life without it. He had become a judge, an administrator of law; he had become its abuser.

I don't know whether it qualifies as schizophrenia. I ain't that educated. It reflects a profound root ambivalence, designed, I suppose, to isolate and protect his individuality from any possibility of routine definition or classification, and perhaps I could identify it because there lurked traces of it within me too — to belong and yet retain my independence; to enjoy the fruits of professional qualification but not to be constrained by its disciplines; to defy the notion that because you are good at one thing, you cannot be as good at its opposite.

Sensing the course of my reflections, he said:

'I must admit, I've never really understood why you made life so difficult for yourself, Dave.' He was trying to understand me; I was trying to understand him

'Me too,' I murmured, unwilling to have the spotlight shifted or to engage any further on any more personal a note with him.

'You seemed to have so much going for you,' he disregarded my reluctance. 'Sandy was a good, solid, reliable partner; you had between you enough spirit and cash to get your own firm off the ground without having to spend too long putting up with some-one else's way of doing things; then you blew it all. Why?' He'd envied me? Back in those early years, when I'd always envied him?

I said quietly:

'I just found, well, too much pain, too much human pain. It affected me; I couldn't ignore it; so I had to isolate myself from it. I thought you understood that; I always thought that was why you concentrated on civil law rather than doing crime.'

He shook his head.

'No. Crime was no challenge intellectually. That's all.'

After a brief pause, the bracket closed, he added:

'There's something else I wanted to say. It's been a burden, always a burden — being me I mean.' I wasn't surprised, but I didn't interrupt. 'I felt guilty — now there's another traditional Jewish trait for you. Because I was making such fools of them, I felt guilty; but I couldn't stop doing it; I've never been able to stop. I never could; I couldn't imagine what life would be like if I did; this was the only me I had built, that I knew; I couldn't let go of it, but I would have given anything to have it taken away from me.'

We sat up through the night. Snatches of conversation stay with me, though not in actual or logical sequence. Orbach saying:

'I had thought about it — we had even joked about it, how I half-hoped they would have an accident. Then he' — Walker — 'said to me: "I'll do anything . . ." to keep his son out of prison. And I thought, "anything". I wondered if he meant it. I wondered if he knew what it meant. I wondered if this mealy-mouthed mechanic had any idea of the things it could mean, of the things I had managed to make "anything" mean. I don't think, at the beginning, I planned to do it. It was more a matter of putting him into my debt, knowing the possibility was there. Then I suppose it took on a life of its own.'

'Why did you stay with Margot for so long? I mean, once it was clear that you were not going to continue as lovers, as a couple.'

'Why separate? We were each other's best friend. I have a higher regard for Margot than for anyone.'

'Didn't you think, well ... Didn't you perhaps want someone else?' In his early days at the bar, he had been powerfully attractive to — and commonly, almost indiscriminately, attracted by — women.

'I don't think I did, really. Perhaps it's why it didn't work out fully with Margot, either. I didn't really like the constant intimacy — especially physical: too much familiarity; too little respect.'

'Respect?'

'Yes. Respect,' he insisted. 'Respect for me, the real me, the private me. I think the period between Margot and my separation as lovers and her departure was the best: I had a sufficiency but not an excess of companionship; the fact that I still lived with her, that I shared a home with her, was an effective bar to a full, new relationship — we had lovers, we both did, but of necessity they were held at a distance, and of course, therefore, did not last. I was protected, insulated, but not isolated.'

Throughout he was detached, relaxed, occasionally sipping his whisky but showing no signs of being affected by it, nor of tiredness. I, too, was drinking much less than usual, seeking to keep a clear head. Though I was tired, I was not anxious to bring it to an end. I knew what I intended, but — confronted by his calmness — I was no longer so confident that I could cause it to come to my conclusion. I needed, but did not yet know how to compel, his co-operation.

'Were you in love with her?' Eartha.

'In a way; as an ideal; as a fantasy. But only in that sense.'

'Didn't you ever mind what you were doing to the law?'

He sneered.

'Their law? No, that was part of the point of it. Pulling down Pulleyne; putting myself up there in his place.' He chuckled with satisfaction. 'I've done things to them far worse than any one could imagine, and yet it still will not make any impact. You know, if this was Russia, they could at least wipe me out of the history books — the law reports is what I mean. But here, they can't do that. There's an irony for you: my judgments will be cited in argument in courts for decades to come; and only an inner core, a clique, will know. Who's the winner, Dave? Them or me?'

The word 'judgment' struck a nerve.

'It's an odd word, isn't it. Woolf's judgment: does it mean the judgment given by Woolf, or that imposed on him?'

I'd rather he substituted his own name.

'I still want to know, Russel. Why? How could you?' The Mellors.

'I could not believe they were going to do it. I just could not believe it. First they gave with one hand — bringing me into Frankie's life and Frankie into mine You know, it wasn't just a formal, distant, godfatherhood. I always saw a lot of her, they always involved me. They knew, well of course they knew I could not have children, so they were doing it partly for me but also for her. That makes them sound more selfish than I intend. I just mean, they could feel confident in her interests that I would have more time and energy and love and support to spare than someone who had his own children, or might yet.'

'Just not how much?'

'Yes, that's the best way to put it. They unlocked something I no longer believed existed in myself. They held out a hope for me, and they were planning to take it away. Explain that, Dave? How could they do that? It was cruel. Wasn't it? Wasn't it?'

'Ach, Russel, I can't say that. What about Frankie?'

'What sort of life would she have had? In Bolivia. For God's sake, whoever heard of Bolivia? What do they know in Bolivia? How much would I have seen of them in Bolivia?'

'Them?'

'Yes, yes, them,' for the first time, he sounded anguished, disturbed, confused. 'Yes, alright, I admit it, that is what you want, isn't it? Yes, I probably was in love with her. If you want to put it into little categories you can understand, Dave, I shall not contradict you.'

'No,' I shook my head sharply. 'It's you who doesn't want to admit it's that banal. You can't face the thought it was the mother, you wanted Eartha, it was that basic. God, why didn't you go to bed with her?' He'd slept with another man's wife once before. 'Hell,' I expostulated, 'why didn't you kill him? At least I could understand that.'

He laughed in short bursts:

'I should be recording you. Are you recording me now?' he asked, so many hours into the conversation it was as unimportant as he made the question sound.

'No. What for?'

'They might catch up with you yet. They can be such crafty buggers.' Crudity came uncomfortably from his lips. 'They might find a way, Dave.'

'For what? Tell me what my crimes are, Russel.'

He thought about them. Those which were identifiable were minor, certainly insufficient to justify the risk of scandal. Save one, yet to come.

Not for the first time, he could read my mind.

'You could even get off that too, couldn't you? Conspiracy's always such a difficult conviction.'

He knew all along what was planned for him.

I shrugged.

'If they charge, I'll plead.' Guilty.

'Why?' He asked idly.

'I don't know,' I admitted. 'It would seem the right thing to do. I've done things that are legally wrong — before now, too — but none of them have been morally wrong. At least, that's what I believe.'

Until the last moment, this was the only exchange about how the night was to end.

'It wouldn't have worked.' He admitted he had thought of killing only Mick. 'She wouldn't have had me. So I would have lost a friend, without gaining a wife or a child.'

'Why wouldn't she? Hell, you're not an ugly man; I remember a time, you had no trouble finding women. Why wouldn't she?'

'I think. . . I think she would have had too much delicacy.'

'What do you mean?'

'Can you see it? Mr Justice Orbach, highly educated, white middle-class male, with his working-class black wife?'

'You weren't a judge then,' I reminded him.

No, but she would have known that was what I wanted.'

There would have been no question of postponing, let alone abandoning, his ambition in favour of his wife.

'Do you think about them? About Mick and Eartha?'

'Of course,' he appeared offended I might think otherwise. 'Often, perhaps daily. Frankie and I talk about them. And Jada. Ah, Jada.' She was not someone he wanted to think about but he had to come to it. 'The book, it was the book, wasn't it? She said she was putting me in her book; this was what she had put in the book?'

'Yes.'

He held up the newspaper:

'They were going to publish it, but wanted proof first. Yes, I see. That was how it was.'

'Right.'

'But how . . . ? Why . . . ?'

He was having difficulty formulating his question, so I did it for him:

'Why did she suspect you? Well, she suspected her parents' best friend who didn't want them to leave, helping them learn to fly, buying a plane with them, apparently doing everything to facilitate it, and I suppose at some level she sensed what you felt about Eartha and then she also knew Eartha was frightened of you . . .'

'What do you mean?' he cut across my recitation. 'She was not frightened of me. She loved me too. I know that.'

'No, she was frightened of you. Look at the inside account.'

He picked up the paper he had thrown down earlier, after reading only the front-page — possibly he hadn't even noticed there was a follow-on inside.

The oddest thing of all that I remember is that he read it almost out loud, his lips moving like an ill-educated person reads. He could skim a law report and absorb ten pages in a minute. They invented speed reading so others could compete with Orbach. When he was in practice, he used to need to extract the essence from a hundred-page bundle of documents in no time at all, often well after a case had commenced, perhaps while it was continuing in court. He was expected to do the same on the bench. Now he read word for word, like each one was a struggle.

I knew when he came to the vital letter. Tears fell from his eyes, first in a slow dribble then in a flood, onto the newsprint, making it wet, so that when he put the paper down and wiped his face he left it streaked with black lines as if he had been wearing mascara. When next he spoke, it was to say:

'I'll get ready.'

I rose to follow him

He shook his head.

'There won't be any difficulty.'

While he was gone, I rang home. It was approaching morning, but I doubted any of them had enjoyed any real sleep, Alton excepted. Carson picked up the 'phone on the second ring:

'Boss?'

'Yeah. Where's Sandy?'

'She had another headache; I made her lie down.'

'Jada?'

'Oh, she's here. You wanna speak?'

'No. Go up and tell Sandy you're both going out, or if she's asleep leave a note. Then take my car and come here, both of you. Wait in the car till I come out.' I had Sandy's car, for the longer drive.

When he had not reappeared after fifteen minutes, I went up to find him. He was kneeling by the bed of the deep-sleeping Frankie, sobbing quietly into the sheets. I said quietly:

'Russel.'

He got up slowly, leaned over to kiss her cheek then covered her carefully with the sheet again. On the way down the stairs, he asked:

'Jada?'

'Of course.'

'She's young. You'll help?'

'We'll help.'

We waited in the hall for the sound of my car drawing up. At this time of the morning, it would only be Carson.

'Sandy's a good woman, Dave. Hang onto her. Don't make a mess of it again, eh? If I'd ever found someone like her, well . . . well, I never could have, could I?'

'Why not, Russel? Why not if you'd only let yourself?'

'Let thyself what? None of them ever wanted me, not really, not for more than a moment. They enjoyed the heat I gave off, the sensation of power, the man on the rise, but the last thing they'd ever have wanted was to stay with me. Margot was the only one strong enough to cope, and sometimes even she feared she was drowning under it.'

'You didn't have to . . . You didn't have to be so strong, so hard, not if it made it impossible for you to live with yourself, or with anyone else.'

'You should have been a shrink, Dave,' he laughed. 'No, you shouldn't. The first pretty patient to sob on your shoulder would end up with her legs apart on your couch.'

Though his earlier crudity had seemed so out of character for the Orbach I had come to know in this last round of our acquaintanceship that started with Disraeli Chambers, this second venture reminded me of an Orbach I'd long since forgotten, and that he had too; a man capable of humour, ordinary activity, a bit of banality, a glass of beer in the pub with the lads. It isn't an achievement to write books about; it's how much of the world lives; it just wasn't enough for him.

As we emerged from the house, Carson flashed her car lights to let me know she was there. I said to Orbach:

'The best thing would be for you to get into my car, let me give your house keys to Carson.'

I thought for a moment he was going to do what I told him Instead, he crossed the road to where she had parked, walking around the car to the driver's side. I followed. Jada looked terrified. Carson used the central locking. I signalled her to lower the window electrically, just an inch or two.

Orbach thrust the keys in at Carson then spoke across her.

'I'm sorry, Jada, I'm most terribly sorry.'

Jada wouldn't look at him. She stared straight ahead out of the windscreen. Then she said:

'It's too late, Russel. Tell it to my mother and Mick.'

'Take care of Frankie,' he started to say, but Carson had already put the window back up. It wasn't his right to say it.

CHAPTER TWELVE

As we left Cloudesley Road, I could see in my rear-view mirror Carson and Jada letting themselves into Orbach's house. I presumed everything had been left to Frankie; we hadn't talked about it, but there was a realistic possibility that my new neighbour would be a famous female pop-singer and actress. Sandy would be pleased, it would boost house prices.

With one exception, we drove in silence until we neared the airport. The exception was soon after we were on the road, when he asked:

'How much does Jada know, about . . .'

'I told her you would be leaving the house; not coming back.'

'That's all?'

'That's all I told her,' I admitted it was possible she would have guessed the rest. 'Why?'

He didn't tell me. Thinking back on it, it seems he was pleased by my answer, pleased she didn't know, pleased she hadn't sanctioned my solution.

As we turned off the A127, he asked: 'Do you understand yet, Dave?'

'I don't know,' I admitted. 'It's hard. I understand bits of it. Does it matter?'

'Try to understand, so some day someone can explain to Frankie. I did love her, I do love her, more than anyone. I know that does not sound well from me, and I know what you think about Eartha, but I loved Frankie more purely than I've ever loved.'

We turned into the airport. It was open for business. I drove down the road to where the flying clubs were sited.

He added:

'You've done well, Dave. This, not the alibi, was what I wanted to keep you alive for. You're a little on the predictable side, but that suited my purpose, and you don't let go. Now there's a final judgment for you: after all your efforts to be anything but, you're a reliable man. Lucky Alton, lucky Sandy.'

He got out and slammed the door, walking away, I thought, without another word. Then he returned to the car. I lowered my window. He said:

'I hope Jada or Carson will remember to pick up the paper before Frankie gets up. They shouldn't destroy it. It's a collector's item. Unique. It was very clever, but I'm not sure if it was necessary.'

'Wasn't it, Russel?'

'We'll never really know. I knew it was a fake, though, from the beginning.'

'How?'

Did he really know or was it one last claim to omniscience? It was punitive to demand an answer but until he gave it I would not know of whom.

'They would have been banging at the door, the telephone would not have stopped ringing, someone from government would have been there before you were, Dave. I know how they work; I know how they think; just as I know how you do.'

I had neither caused nor compelled his co-operation: it had been his choice; at the end, he had to tell me that he had done it, not I; that was his game.

I watched from the car as he boarded his plane.

From the hangar, Walker emerged, dressed in an overcoat. It looked odd. It was no part of the script.

I could not hear their exchange at the cabin door. Orbach tried to shut the door, Walker was holding it open. They were gesticulating at one another. Walker pulled out a gun and thrust it straight at Orbach's face, with no attempt at concealment. Orbach backed into the cabin and Walker climbed in after him I understood Walker's amendment to the agreed plan.

In a few minutes, the plane began to taxi onto the runway. I drove quickly to the small, fenced area between the terminal and the control tower from which spectators were able to watch. There was a handful of casual observers, commenting on the different craft, a couple of them with cameras.

I watched and I watched as the plane flew out towards the sea, smaller and smaller until I could hardly identify it in the distance.

At the last moment, the dot in the sky turned red and smoke billowed out of the craft as it floated slowly back towards us, clearer and clearer, confused only by the cries from those around me, until it fell out of sight beyond the hill.

I remember clearest of all the long, painful silence that followed its departure from our vision, then the solitary boom as it finally shattered on impact and we could neither see nor hear anything yet knew it all. I drove back to London.

Only Sandy and Alton were at the house. I had expected Jada and Carson to bring Frankie back rather than to remain in Orbach's house, but Sandy shook her head.

'Jada wanted to be there with her. I think she wanted to be alone with her but Carson insisted on staying.'

I nodded detachedly. I was not interested in the domestic details.

Sandy looked at me quizzically, critically.

'No, I suppose you aren't.'

'What's that supposed to mean?'

We were in the kitchen, now bereft of all but the basic amenities. I was tired; I wanted to sleep; I didn't even want a drink.

'Just what I said.'

'Hey, come on, Sandy, I'm hardly in the mood for a feminist analysis of my failures as a father and partner . . .'

She shook her head, also tiredly.

'That isn't what I meant.'

'So?' I asked irritably.

'Just that — you aren't interested in the details, the details of what comes after.'

'What're you saying?'

'Jada and Frankie have to go on living. It's hard to imagine a more difficult circumstance. But you wash your hands of it.'

I was stunned: after what I had just been through, the last thing I expected was one of Sandy's verbal assaults.

'You knew what was happening,' I protested, as if she was criticising what I had done with Orbach.

'I knew. That doesn't make it right.'

'Shit, Sandy, it's more than a bit late for this.'

'No, I don't think you understand what I'm getting at, Dave.'

I waited for her to explain.

She said:

'I'm not saying you — we — were wrong to go ahead with it; I agreed, it was the only thing to do . . .'

'Oh, hell,' I cut across her. 'It was what he wanted. He didn't have to go up. He guessed the paper was a dummy. It was his choice.'

She shrugged; the facts rarely concerned her.

'I'm not talking about his choices, Dave; I'm talking about ours.'

Maybe the reason I was still in love with her was because I still didn't understand five per cent of how her mind worked. The day I got to ten, I swore to myself silently, I'd leave.

'I agreed. I'm not denying that. I agreed so as to protect you, us. But it has to be an end, Dave, an end to the whole way of life you've been leading — and a beginning. That's what I'm trying to get at, I suppose,' she admitted she was almost as confused as I. 'The thing's done; it's time to face up to the consequences, and all that it's left behind, and to make sure the same things don't happen again. Do you understand?'

I understood, but I was still angry. There were times to talk, and times for support. I know what Sandy would say. She'd say she had to get at me when I'm weak and vulnerable because the rest of the time I just don't listen. So all I said as I got up was:

'You do choose your time, Sandy,' and swung out of the kitchen to head up to bed without waiting for her answer.

I crept into bed without washing and fell into unconsciousness without another thought.

When I awoke, it was late afternoon. The house was deserted. I found a jug of coffee and a note in the kitchen. It told me that Sandy and Alton had gone over to Cloudesley Road, to go with Carson, Jada and Frankie to the fair on Hampstead Heath, the lower fair, opposite the Freemasons' Arms on Downshire Hill. The note didn't suggest I join them, but the detail left it open to me to do so.

I took my time washing and dressing. I felt both annoyed and relieved. Annoyed, because though I understood the logic of taking the children to the fair, something else, something less raucous, seemed to be called for on this day; relieved because I didn't want to talk. I almost didn't go after them, but in the end what I wanted least of all was to be left alone.

It was a bright, sunny day. I found them without difficulty. They made a distinctive group. Alton was in the backpack, but Jada was wearing it along with huge sunglasses and a floppy hat that were almost completely effective to disguise her. Frankie was the star of the show, leading both Sandy and Carson by the hand. I was surprised but not displeased to find Natalie with them. My family. I felt proud.

I watched from a distance for a while. Then Frankie was dragging Sandy towards a whirly-gig, one of those infernal constructions made of cardboard and stuck together with glue that go round and round and up and down all at the same time and that she hates as much as I do. They were all laughing at Sandy. I ran across to say I'd go instead, but they were already ensconced, a metal bar across their waists, and they only just saw me as I arrived, Frankie giggling, Sandy with her teeth clenched in fear, before the machine began to move.

My teeth too stayed clenched for Sandy's strain as long as they went round. My beautiful woman. The others' attention had switched to the dodgems; they were still debating whether to have a go when Sandy's agony finally drew to a painfully belated close. I helped her off as Frankie, with barely an acknowledgement of my presence, galloped away to catch up with her sister. I put an arm around Sandy.

'Hi.'

'Hi,' she replied, neither her face nor her tone telling me whether or not she was yet ready to forgive and forego the morning's argument.

'Are you OK?' I asked, giving her the opportunity to answer whichever way she wanted to take it.

'I feel a bit giddy.' She clung onto my arm for support rather than to tell me what I wanted to know.

The others decided against the dodgems and strolled back to us via a candyfloss stand. Sandy called out:

'Not for Alton.' Then she looked at me wryly. 'Jesus, my head hurts. What a time for a headache. Jesus,' she screamed suddenly, grabbing the back of her neck.

'San? San? What is it?'

She sunk to her knees and keeled over face down on the ground. I dropped to the ground beside her, gently rolling her over.

'San? San?'

I don't know what happened next. There was a crowd and voices and then a St. John's Ambulance man and a police-woman and they were carrying her between them to the car park and thrusting her into the back seat of a police car and I was running after them and another car — a complete stranger's car, I don't to this day know whose — drove me the minimal distance — just a few hundred yards — to the Royal Free, where Alton had been born. At that moment, I didn't even know where Alton was. I didn't even care.

They raced her into casualty and I went along with her into the examination room. I said yes when they asked if she was my wife. So she was in all but law. I answered a couple questions then someone said she wasn't breathing and they pushed me out while they were shoving a tube down her windpipe; someone else was examining her eyes. Outside I found the people I had thought of a few minutes before also as my family. I snatched Alton and hugged him to me and hissed at them:

'Go away, go away, go away, we don't want you here.'

Jada covered Frankie's ears with her hands but that was the only movement amongst them until Natalie stepped forward to relieve me of Alton before he drowned in my tears.

'What's happening, Dave?' Jada asked.

Carson walked away to make her own enquiries.

'I don't know. Just . . . She has these headaches . . . You know that . . . no, I keep forgetting, you didn't really know her till just now . . . She's always had these headaches and then when she came off the whirly-gig, well, she said she felt giddy then she said she had a blinding headache then . . .'

Frankie started to sob:

'She didn't want to; it's my fault.'

I got to her before Jada and hugged her tighter than she'd ever been hugged:

'It's not your fault, sweetie, it's not your fault, I promise it's not your fault, don't ever, ever say it.' It was all pointless if she, too, was damaged by it.

Somehow time was slipping by and they wouldn't tell me what was happening. Carson came back and said they'd taken her to the neuro-surgical unit: we were lucky, it was the centre for neuro-surgical problems for the whole of the North West Thames Area. Then she disappeared again and I could see her at the 'phone bank but I didn't know who she was phoning.

It went on for what seemed like forever. They didn't let me see her. A doctor came and talked a foreign language to me.

'She has a ruptured beri aneurysm.'

I looked blankly at him. He thought I wanted an explanation but all I wanted was to be told my wife, my life, Sandy, was alive and would get better.

'It's a congenital malformation of the blood vessels around something called the Circle of Willis. Well,' he laughed nervously, 'I don't suppose that means anything to you. Has she suffered from these headaches for long?'

I'd told them when we came in about her headaches and that it wasn't the first, though self-evidently the worst.

'Forever,' I said listlessly. 'What does it mean?'

'The vessels control the blood supply to the brain. The malformation has probably been present since birth. I suppose, the only way to describe it is like a blow-out in the blood vessels. It's caused a brain haemorrhage in the internal part of the brain. Like a stroke in effect. We've been doing a C.T. scan.' At the raise of an eyebrow he elaborated: 'Computerised Tomography. Basically, this will show if there's a sub-arachnoid haemorrhage secondary to the ruptured aneurysm and, well, whether it's operable. It'll take a couple of hours to complete.'

He was beginning to wonder about examining my own pupils when Carson drew him aside:

'This's going to take a while?'

'I'd say so.'

They whispered together for a while then Carson came back:

'I'm going to send Jada and Frankie home with Natalie and Alton, Dave. Have you got the car keys?'

I handed them over without protest. They hovered around me, touching, kissing, murmuring: I hated them, they were all so fucking healthy.

Only Carson stayed.

'You got enough cigarettes, Dave?'

I shrugged. She reached into my jacket pocket and squeezed the pack.

'I'll go get some more, huh?'

While she was gone, Tim arrived. He was who Carson had been calling. I understood why: he was authority, but a bit of it that was — in the last resort — on our side. He sat down beside me without a word and we sat there for a moment until I looked at his face and he saw it coming and put his arm around my head and pulled it into his shoulder like he was my father. I didn't care what it did either for our future relationship or his jacket. Someone had to be strong.

'It's my fault, Tim. You know?'

'I know. I got it on the wire hours ago. As an accident of course. One thing's got nothing to do with another, Dave. There's no connection.'

'Wrong, Tim. I'll tell you how it is,' I said dully. 'I've been playing God, playing with death; this is his message back telling me who's really in control. Get it?'

He shook his head sadly.

'She's not dead, Dave. Don't give up hope.'

But his tone told me he'd already spoken to the doctors and hope was merely a way of bridging the time between love and death.

I can't remember much after that. I remember Carson coming back and she and Tim consulting quietly, first with one another and then with a different doctor from before. Then

Carson went back to the house and Tim sat with me until they came to tell me:

'She's had a cardiac arrest, Mr Woolf. There's no chance. If we operate, well, she won't be the same, she, er, well, she won't be . . .'

'He's not her husband,' Tim cut in. 'Someone has to contact her parents. I'll ring the local police,' he placed a restraining hand on my wrist before he got up and was led into an office to make the last call.

'I need to see her, doctor,' I pleaded.

'It's not a good idea, Mr Woolf; it's better to remember. . . .'

'You're a fucking shrink, already?' I grabbed his lapels. 'I know more about death than you'll ever know; I know about it, I've been there all my life.' I was shouting so loud the whole hospital was watching and Tim came back from the office to stop me: 'I'm going to see her.'

So they left me alone with her, just like in the movies with machines with lines and bleeps and tubes running out of every part of her and her eyes were shut and something was pumping up and down listlessly beside her and I kissed her on the lips hard like maybe she'd respond and then in anger in fury in next-to-hatred I was shrieking, thrashing out, breaking the connections, screaming:

'Don't, don't, don't dare fucking leave me, I'll never forgive you. Sandy, Sandy, please, please, I love you . . .'

Until they dragged me out and held me down and plunged a needle into my arm and thankfully I too could die.

It was a blast from the past that caught me just as I was going back to sleep again:

'Dave?'

'Ug.'

'Dave, this is Sandy . . .'

Sandy? Sandra? Sandra Nichol? My former partner? The woman who had personally, single-handedly, totally and utterly destroyed my career without hardly a helping hand from me? That Sandy?

'How are you, Sandy?'

'OK I guess. I'd like to see you. Are you free for lunch? I'll buy . . .'

She was there before me. She looked good. She was in a dark suit which meant she'd been to court. Her hair was permed which she didn't use to do. But she still didn't need any makeup. And hadn't put on a pound.

She was making me nervous. We'd been together five minutes, plus five on the 'phone made ten. She hadn't torn my head off once yet.

'How's Bernie?' I asked after the waiter'd gone. Bernie had been her bloke for six years when I met her; a decade of loving service by the time we broke up.

'We split up,' she said defiantly.

'And the other one?'

'That . . . that didn't work out either . . . I've missed you. Missed working with you, I mean.'

'What is this, Sandy?'

'Maybe I like you,' she said softly. 'What about giving it another try?'

'Jesus. You make it sound like we were married!'

After we'd ate, we went for a walk. We walked along to Kensington Palace Gardens, and through to Hyde Park. We sat and watched the ducks. They were cute. There were a lot of people in rowing boats. They weren't so cute.

We looked each other in the eyes. Something was stirring. It took me a while to recognise what it was. She didn't resist.

I'm not even that sure who it was finally took the plunge. Me or her. It was just happening.

'This is crazy,' I murmured after. 'I've known you ten years . . . We've had some of the worst times of my life together!'

She laughed:

'Such nice things you tell a girl.'

'Was it true? When you said that you weren't sleeping with him anymore?'

'Yes. That was true.'

All I wanted was the truth.

I got up to refill my glass.

She bit her lower lip nervously:

'Make me another drink, Dave.'

G-and-T, like the good English lady she wasn't. When I took it to her, she grabbed my wrist:

'He . . . he never suggested . . . what happened, in the park . . . that's the truth, Dave . . . I swear it . . .'

'That's supposed to be some big deal?'

'That's supposed to tell you . . . Oh, shit, I don't know . . . I wish . . . I wish I had got in touch with you before . . . It's a funny old world, isn't it, Dave? You can know someone so well, and not at all. Or, different sides of them. But,' she smiled wryly, 'it isn't news to me that I . . . liked you . . .' That wasn't news to me either. The news was . . . that I liked her too.

I was standing at the sideboard, doing what came most naturally within reach of a bottle. She got up and stood beside me, again placing her hand on my shoulder:

'Just let me say this, then.'

Her voice was choking. I glanced round. She had tears in her eyes. I turned away. I didn't need it.

'We haven't slept together for years . . . He's gone on coming to see me . . . turning up late . . . like he did the night he talked to me about you . . . a bit drunk . . . wanting . . . trying to . . . you know. I just want you to understand it's me that's said no . . .'

'So what, Sandy? So fucking what?'

'You're hurt, aren't you, Dave?'

'Who? Me? Forget it. I don't get close, and I don't get hurt.'

We were both more than a little pissed. Otherwise, she might have let it go then. Instead, she whispered: 'Are you sure?'

'What do you want from me, Sandy?'

She grinned:

'You know . . .'

I did know. What she wanted. Just then.

I glanced at my watch. It was nearly ten o'clock. She followed the movement of my eyes.

'What's that for?'

'I wanted to know what time to put down that I stopped work . . .'

'Bastard . . .'

'Do you still know what you want?'

She nodded. She was shivering.

I would have left. Only, I was too.

Kat had booked a table at the Cafe Pelican on St Martin's Lane. I wasn't complaining. Kat was paying.

'I know about you and Sandy,' she said.

It wasn't exactly a state secret, but we'd been out of touch for a long time and, so far as I knew, she and Sandy had never been close. I wasn't pleased she knew; I've never been able to think of an answer to female solidarity as an excuse not to hop into my bed.

'How?'

'I heard. I can't remember who from. It doesn't matter. It didn't surprise me. I always expected it.'

'You did?' I was truly shocked.

'Sure. Anyone could've guessed you'd end up together. You were made for each other, like a couple of old trees planted next to one another in a clearing in the forest.'

There were two calls on the answering machine when I got home. The second was from Sandy:

'Dave, it's me. I was wondering how you were feeling. I really am sorry about Katrina, Dave, I liked her too. Oh, shit, I hate these machines. I need to talk to you, Dave, it's time we talked. We can't keep carrying on like this, Dave. We're off more than we're on. Oh, I shouldn't have started. Look, just ring me, please.'

I didn't ring Sandy; it was too late, and I was too tired. Oh, shit, as she would say: I didn't ring Sandy because I couldn't face talking to her. I have a real problem with Sandy. A bit like the old Groucho Marx line, how can I stay with anyone who'd stay with me? I love Sandy, just about as much as Katrina had always assumed, long before I knew it; but it's easier to list the things that are wrong with our relationship than to remember what's right.

I was just about to leave for Companies House when the outside line rang:

'Dave Woolf.'

'Sandra Nichol,' she said dryly.

'Sandy. Hi. I was going to ring you. We ought to meet,' I said.

'What a good idea. I wish I'd thought of it.' Ouch.

'I'm ringing from the Law Society. What about lunch?' Double ouch. I couldn't lie my way out of it: my lies last in her presence like ice in a blast-furnace.

'I, uh, was figuring maybe you wouldn't want us to be seeing each other if I was working on it,' I said lamely, once we'd settled into a corner with our respective refreshments: white wine spritzer for her.

'And for the month before? Maybe you were waiting for the case to begin?' Sandy has a tongue you could circumcise with.

'Fine, you wanna row,' I downed my drink: 'Let's have a row already.' I got up to fetch another. I can't fight with Sandy when I'm sober: it's an unequal contest; I'm not saying I win when I'm drunk, but at least it don't hurt so much.

She looked at me curiously when I returned, like she was trying to figure out what she'd ever seen in me. I wondered if she'd tell me. I reached out and took her hand:

'I do love you, you know.'

'Yes, I do know. It's not about that, is it? I'm getting too old for all of this, Dave; I don't want to spend my fortieth birthday wondering whose bed I'll be sleeping in, or sleeping in my own alone.' It was hard to think of her as beginning the approach to forty: she looked ten years younger.

'What do you want to do, Sandy?' I didn't want her to say it, but I could neither say what it was she wanted to hear nor else could I bring it to an end myself.

'I don't want to give you an ultimatum, Dave, but I can't keep on like this. If you can't — oh, shit, I don't know — I want to say "grow up" but it seems such a trite thing to say. Just that, though: grow up; we're both getting older; we've both got to start settling down or we'll wear ourselves out. Think about it, Dave, think about what I'm saying. And remember, if you don't want me, someone else just might, y'know.'

Now that the case was coming to an end, the rest of my life started to come back into focus and a bit of it was missing. It was a long time since I'd seen or spoken to Sandy. I punched the number I knew as well as my own, as indeed once it had been.

'Hi,' she sounded brisk.

'Bad time?'

Pause.

'No.'

'Uh, well, you're obviously glad to hear from me.'

'Of course I'm glad to hear from you, Dave. I've been meaning to ring you. We ought to meet.'

'That was what I was thinking, kid.' She's four months older than I. 'I'm just about wrapped up here, at Mather's. 'Nother couple of days.'

'Yes.' Her enthusiasm and curiosity knew no bounds: they weren't even acquainted.

'Sandy, what's up?'

'What's up?' her voice raised. 'You let me walk out of a pub, on my own, in the middle of the day, without trying to stop me; you let me walk out of your life without even saying so long; you ignore me for weeks, then you ring up cheerful as a sand-boy, and you ask me — what's up already?'

I hadn't said 'already', had I?

'Look,' I said, calming and conciliatory, 'this hasn't been a lot of fun . . .'

'What's the matter? Weren't the high-class bimbos falling over themselves to hop into bed with you?'

Well, uh, yes, as a matter of fact.

'Oh, shit, we always argue on the 'phone. We'd better meet,' she conceded reluctantly: 'How about the twenty-third?'

If 'phones could see, I'd've boggled down the line: 'Sandy! That's nearly three weeks away!'

'Well,' she sulked, 'I'm pretty busy right now.'

You love someone in as many different ways and for as long as Sandy'n'I've loved each other, there's some things don't need spelling out:

'You're seeing someone, aren't you, Sandy?'

Silence. Then:

'I don't want to talk about it on the 'phone, Dave. Maybe I could make next Thursday, later on in the evening...'

'Tell me, Sandy.' Tell me Sandy: I love you; I know I'm a jerk; I know I've been fucking around with someone else, but I always thought, you know, you understood the way I was, am; I always thought you, you loved me anyhow, at any price. That was what I wanted, Sandy; that's what I needed; someone to love me more than life itself; someone to love me as much as Robin loves Mick.

She said flatly:

'I warned you, Dave.'

And so she had.

'You take care, Sandy. You take care, you hear? Doesn't matter how long; I'll still be here, well, there anyhow. Y'know, I'll still be around for you. You've only got to call; it'll always be true.'

I replaced the receiver gently before she could catch me start to cry.

The 'phone rang.

'It's me.' This is a universally accurate opening, but in this case it meant Sandy. 'Are you coming up this evening?'

'Am I allowed back in?' I asked dryly.

I could hear her smile down the line. In the case of anyone else, this would be a universally inaccurate proposition, but not when it's Sandy.

Every time I finish up with someone else, and go back to Sandy, I can't remember why I left. There's no one who's a patch on her, or with whom love-making comes as close to transcending isolation. If I say there's no one who's as good as her I don't mean that she's invariably kind, or sensitive, or moral, or unselfish. She has the sharpest tongue of anyone I know, can be intolerably demanding in the most irritating, petty ways, can cut someone down to size swifter than a Samurai's sword and when she wants something, heaven help anyone who stands in her way. What I mean is: no one else I know has got all their appealing and unappealing qualities in such perfect balance.

'Dave, I'll leave the office on time — get here early?'

'Can't, San. I've got an appointment at nine o'clock.'

'I want to talk to you, Dave,' she insisted. 'Can't you change it?'

'Would you believe — Russel Orbach wants to see me? At his new house?'

'Ah.' Sandy knew Orbach too. 'Try to keep it short, then. That shouldn't be difficult.'

'Sure. I won't be late.'

I was just about to hang up, when she said: 'Dave?'

'Yup.'

'Oh, nothing.' And she hung up.

I arrived at Sandy's considerably sobered. She, on the other hand, was a wee bit pissed: squiffy, she liked to call it. I didn't ring the bell: I had my own key to her house.

We kissed and hugged and wriggled against each other hornily. Someone I knew once referred to bad sex as like chewing someone else's stale gum. Sandy was rare fillet steak cooked at the Savoy Grill. I bore down on her and we tumbled onto the sofa. We both liked it that way: sudden, urgent, half-dressed, just the bits that counted.

After, while she went to wash, I poured us each another drink.

'Did you eat?'

I told her I'd eaten with Orbach:

'And, wait for this, his ward. He's got a child living with him.'

'Poor kid. How awful for her.' She meant living with Orbach, not her parents' death. 'What's she like?'

'Well, you know, she's a child. Isn't that enough? I mean, she's black, she's smart and she's incredibly beautiful, but she's a child all the same and you know how I feel about kids.'

'Oh, yes, I know,' she shut her eyes for a moment. 'But it's all a pose, isn't it, Dave? You don't really hate them, do you? I never thought you did?'

'Well, you know how it is. If I ain't got one, I don't see why anyone else should.'

'Did you never . . .' She hesitated, but plunged on: 'Didn't you ever, just once, think it might be nice if you did?'

'What? Me? Have a kid?' I laughed so hard I nearly fell off the sofa. 'What if it turned out like me?'

'I know,' she said gloomily. 'That's what's worryingme.'

'But, San, you're forty!'

'Gee, kid, you say the most romantic things. I know I'm forty. So are you. So what?'

'But I thought . . . well, you know. Shit.' I got up and went into the kitchen to fetch more ice. I turned the tray over and the cubes spilled out onto the floor. 'Shit,' I said again: 'Shit, shit, shit, shit,' I flung the tray after them.

I started to pick up the ice-cubes but I couldn't. Either they kept slithering about the floor, or else I couldn't see straight. I was kneeling on the floor, grabbing at ice-cubes, crying like someone had died. I didn't hear Sandy come in until she knelt down beside me and took my head in her hands, kissing my wet eyes until they were clear enough to see she was crying too. She said:

'I'm sorry, I'm sorry. I had no idea it'd upset you like this.'

I pushed her away.

'Don't be stupid, San, I'm not upset. I'm happy, you schmuk.'

'This's why you didn't want to see me last night? Why?'

She couldn't meet my gaze: she'd spent last night wondering whether to keep it. I got up and went and sat on the sofa with her, putting an arm around her shoulder. In the end, I just whispered:

'Thanks, San.'

We took the Passat because though I drive like a pig Sandy was now too big for comfort in her Peugeot GTL

In a moment of rare — perhaps unprecedented — honesty, I said:

'I still can't relate to the idea of being a father.'

I saw her smile out of the corner of my eye. She said:

'You think I feel like a mother?'

'Well, I suppose I thought, you know, carrying it around all the time . . .'

'I don't know, Dave. What I feel is a big, heavy weight, which could be a blob or a child but is somewhere between. It's a heartbeat, not a human yet. I think, well, I don't know what a mother's supposed to feel like, do I? Maybe this's how I'll feel when it's born, too.'

The party was in full swing when finally we arrived. I was getting drunk too fast and having thoughts that didn't work. Sandy whispered in my ear:

'They're on the edge, Dave, on the very edge. She told me, upstairs: she didn't want to get married so soon; it was the only way they could be together. He's just doing what he thinks he ought to do. Tell me, Dave,' she hissed, 'we're not doing it just because we ought to, are we? You're not, I mean, are you?'

I shook my head and put my arm around her waist:

'No, Sandy, I'm not, we're not.' I leaned down and kissed her cheek and felt unaccountably sad: 'We're doing it because probably we didn't ought to.' She turned her head and right in the middle of the party we did what no one is supposed to do at such an occasion: we kissed full on the lips, just as if we loved one another.

I got a little calm time with Sandy before it happened: in between spasms of labour-pain we still weren't prepared for notwithstanding the classes. She said:

'What I have to do to get you to pay me any attention.'

After I'd brought her up to date on the events of the last two days, she said:

'Is Carson alright? Are you alright?' She wasn't asking about either our physical or legal condition but about things we'd been forced to do.

'It's been heavy,' I admitted, my eyes searching hers to see what else she might be asking.

The intermittent outbursts of agony left her calmer than normal between.

'I'm glad. Glad she was with you, Dave. Glad I found her for you.'

I nodded.

'There's things you do that I know I'm not a part of I know I can't be; I don't want to be. But over the last few days, I've been thinking: maybe that's for the best; maybe that's part of why I've gone on loving you when you've given me a million reasons not to. I do love you, Dave, I do.'

I squeezed her hand in reply.

'And . . . And I know you love me too. So I'm glad you had her to share it with. It makes me a bit a part of it too.'

And then Sandy was screaming a meaningless noise and I was screaming with her and before I knew it a third voice had joined us. A tiny head, a tiny body, a squirming, squiggling, squawky little thing emerging half-afraid half-defiant from between Sandy's legs and somewhere back in the mists of time from between mine too. It sounded to my ears like it was crying: gimme a Southern Comfort, wanna stay up for Hill Street, gotta Camel?' Then I can't remember a couple of minutes maybe, including that one, until a nurse was showing me the child saying:

'It's a boy,' in case I couldn't tell the difference.

I leaned over him and kissed his tiny wrinkled head once for me and once for Lewis like he'd asked me to do; and to pacify all the available gods I baptised him with my tears.

It was alright. It was alright after all. She was not dead; she was still there. It was all a dream; just a bad dream.

The light woke me up.

Tim was standing in the doorway, watching, concerned, wondering if I was going to be alright, if I was going to be able to take it, able to withstand the shock, to withstand the pain.

I wasn't.

I opened my mouth to scream.

Not a sound came out.

Stupidly, all I could think was, we hadn't finished our fight. Sandy and me.

9 781911 124986